CURSED AT CONCEPTION
The Vampire's Henchman
J. K. Grueber

Mystic Ridge Publishing, LLC

Mysticridgepublishing.com

ISBN: 978-1-965796-04-7 (Hardcover)

ISBN: 978-1-965796-03-0 (Paperback)

ISBN: 978-1-965796-02-3 (Ebook)

Cover design by: J. K. Grueber, Bruce Sanderson, Anne Graff, Andrew Grueber, and William Grueber.

Contributing cover photo editor: Sanderson-Decello Design, LLC. reproduced with permission of Castle Inn Bed & Breakfast, 610 S Court St, Circleville, Ohio, 43113,

Printed in the United States of America.

Mystic Ridge Publishing, LLC

ALSO BY J. K. GRUEBER

The Envy Series:
COLORS OF ENVY: A Paranormal Romance Mystery
FACES OF ENVY: A Paranormal Romance Mystery
ECHOES OF ENVY: A Paranormal Romance Mystery

The MacDade Brothers Mysteries:
EXPOSED IN SHADOWS: He Who Plays.
A Paranormal Mystery Rekindling Lost Love
EXPOSED In The CROSSHAIRS: He Who Rides
A MacDade Brothers Paranormal Mystery
EXPOSED By The RIVERSIDE: He Who Lives
A MacDade Brothers Paranormal Mystery

The Vampire Tales:
Cursed At Conception: The Vampire's Henchman

PROLOGUE

A hammer slam echoed through the chamber, bouncing off the stone and reverberating through the blackness. In a corridor too-long sealed and hidden, a breath of fresh air pressed against the oppressive blackness.

"What the hell—?" Offensive, the gravelly voice, no more than a muffled whisper over the distance, resounded like a shout in the preternatural silence. "There's wood back here . . . Looks like a door—"

"Here! Let me have a look!"

"Grab that shovel . . . We gotta move more of those rocks—"

Scraping, slamming, crumbling debris filled the corridor, churning more than dust within the blackness. An awakening. Beneath the raucous of iron and stone, the tinkle of chain links remained masked, no more than an echo of an iron spade striking a hinge.

"Jesus! It really is a door! There's a lock—"

"Looks old! Gotta be at least a hundert years old!"

"Keep digging, man! We mighta hit the motherload!"

"You don't think—"

"Hell, yeah, I think! I bet this is what that old bastard meant to find!"

Excitement vibrated in the voices. The hammer blows pounded the wood and iron with renewed vigor. A pause then, "Get the sledge! This wood's gotta be rotted to hell and back with all this water—Feels like a fuckin' icebox—"

"Maybe we oughta get the boss down here—"

"Hell too!" the gravelly voice growled. "Gotta check it out first. Might just be another a them empty rooms."

"But you said you think—"

"We gotta find out first . . . We drag Clay down here, he'll have ta call Mr. von Hendricks. And if we drag them this far down for nothing, Clay'll have our fucking heads. Lest you ain't noticed, von Hendricks ain't too keen on getting his shiny shoes smudged."

"I'll get the sledge."

More scraping, thudding, crumbling, and cursing shuddered the darkness, and chain links clinked with the vibrations.

Come to meeee.

"What uh . . .? Did you say something, Ray?" the more fluid voice wondered.

"Yeah. Said hurry your ass up! Gimme that sledge . . ."

Hammer blows rained down, splintering wood, ricocheting off the damp walls, rippling the blackness. Tiny cracks of light spiked into the nebulous, barely enough to pierce the darkness. Still, in a place so long sealed even the sparks provided illumination.

"Jesus, it stinks—"

"You don't think there could be gas—? That's maybe why it's sealed—?"

"If there was gas, idiot, we'd already be dead," the other chided.

Come to meee.

"Ray . . .? I think we need uhm . . . We should probably go up. This . . . something ain't right."

Iron clattered. Wood shattered. A wave of dust shifted invisibly through the blackness and the sounds amplified between the close rough-hewn walls. "We're in! Grab that flashlight!"

Ahhh, come to meee

Illumination. A spear of fierce white light cut through the inky blackness, bobbing and jittering to and fro, up and down. Like a firefly flitting hither and yon, the slice of light drew near, still, barely a candle against the darkness as soles scraped the silt under hesitant footfalls.

"Jesus, that smell . . ." the gravelly voice roared in the silence despite the low volume. "Smells like something dead and rotting . . . Hold that fuckin light steady, Jer."

"Looks like another tunnel," the second man spoke in a hushed voice as if he feared to wake something within the cutting blackness. Nerves jangled in his voice: fear vibrated through the atmosphere, carried on the vapors like the aroma of fresh baked bread in distant memory.

Ahhh, clossser. Commme clossser.

Anticipation, an even blend of delight and distress, flowed through the drifting dust particles lifting and swirling for the first time in over a hundred years. The breaths became labored with the quickening heartbeats to resound like drumbeats in a symphony. Ah, and music filled the great halls so long ago. Memories awakened. Only in dreams, laughter and chatter rose above the din of an orchestra, and dancers waltzed in elegant gowns and tailored jackets. From the outside looking in, the couples flowed through the candlelight, the vivid silk and satin colors muted through the lacy drapes to adorn every window in the manor house.

Chain links jingled, clinking in the stygian darkness.

"Did you hear that, Ray?" the hushed voice echoed, closer, louder.

"Can't hear shit over your huffing and heaving."

"The airs colder—makin' it harder to breathe and . . . and that smell ain't helping. We need to go back—"

"What ta fuck you scared of? Think the boogeyman's gonna jump out and grab ya, Jer?" the growly voice chided, but an undercurrent of unease flowed beneath the whispery words. "Case yer forgetting, we're down here for a reason."

"Yeah, I know the reason, all right. I been hearin those same rumors my whole life, Ray, and I'm telling you, if there was a treasure down here, it's long gone. The only thing we're likes to find is the bones a all the ones who come down here hunting before us and n'er seen again."

"Well, we're getting paid good money to—There! Another room—and no door. We won't even need the sledge," the growler chided with nerves vibrating his machismo.

The beam of light cut through the darkness, offering a shallow glow to outline the black hole of a doorway. Hard soles shuffled in the silt, stirring more dust to fog the bobbing beam.

Closer. Commme closer.

"I don' feel so good, Ray . . . Think that smell. I gotta get some air—"

"Like hell! You ain't going nowhere till we check this out," the other commanded.

Shadows, only shadowy hulking images, hovered behind the circle of piercing light as it bobbed into the opening and froze.

"Jesus H.," the growler hissed.

The other huffed, "What the hell—?"

"We found it! We found the holy grail!" the low voice whispered as if fearing to be overheard.

Illuminated in the bright, jittery light, shelf after dusty shelf rose from the floor to the jagged stone ceiling Even coated by layers of dust, the jutting bottle tops looked like hundreds of dull eyeballs protruding from the circular slots. And the diffracted light spiked deeper into the abyss, illuminating row after row of identical shelves until disappearing into the darkness.

"There must be hunderts," the hushed voice heaved air; the stench and fear forgotten.

"Maybe thousands," the other awed, scraping his soles, lurching toward the nearest, brightest circle of bobbling light. A gloved hand reached into the light, destined for one of the dull eyes.

"Gees, Ray! Don't touch it—"

The mallet-sized glove wrapped about a dusty neck poking from the slot. "We gotta check—gotta be certain."

Commme to meee.

Disembodied, the voice seethed from the blackness, and the light froze, illuminating the dull eye protruding, as if squeezed and bulging from the filthy leather.

"Ray!" the weaker voice huffed, heaving in a breath. "Did you—do you hear that?"

Ahhh Ray.

"Ray! Damn it! What—? What is that—? Sounds like chains!"

Vibrating, the circle of brilliant light remained on the filthy cork as Ray uttered, "Huh?"

Heaving for air, boots scraped, and the slighter phantom image turned in place, pivoting and heaving. Muffling a cough, a gulped breath and choked sound, Jer huffed, "I'm outa here—"

Ssstop himmm.

Pivoting, colliding, the sounds of struggle ensued with grunts and huffs amplified. In a fleeting instant, the column of light spiked and stabbed at the darkness and with a single command, the heavy cylinder swung and connected, as effective as a hammer. With the thump and crunch, the struggle ceased, the smaller silhouette crumbled, thudding on the stone floor. A scent of blood, intoxicating, permeated the thick air, the chains rattled distinctly.

Heeerrre. Brinnng himmm heeere.

The hundred-year-old bottle dropped, shattered, spewing a new flavor, just as intoxicating, to collect on dust particles stirred into the dead air. The spoke of light jabbed fore and aft, illuminating a blood-red checkered cloth, filthy gray-black material. Labored, the breath whirled the heavy soot as the boot heels and thick cloth dragged deeper into the darkness. Chains clanged and clattered. A gnarled, skeletal hand swiped through the light, snatching the leather glove, ripping it away. Two growls merged, one snarling, the other yelping. As the long, curved spike sank into the thick, leatherlike palm, all motion ceased. A melding. A communion of minds. Terror flowed from one mind to the other, thrilling, and saturating as the blood of life flowed into the hollow incisors. The shaft of light, angled now, illuminated a scuff of beard on a narrow face, a mop of dirty brown hair dangling in the soot. And in the darkness behind the light, the phantom image descended, thudding on solid knees.

Mooore. Neeed. Mooore.

The sprawled body lay just out of reach of the skeletal phalanges. The tangy blood scent weighted the air, enhanced tenfold by the crimson trickle sliding from beneath the filthy ringlets, trickling at the temple to fill the closed eye socket. Amplified in the silence, both heartbeats had slowed to a thready thump-thump, a matching crescendo to become a symphony.

With a mere whisp of thought, the larger phantom image shifted on its knees, clasping a wad of red-checked flannel near the beard, jostling the light beam toward the ceiling before it rolled away. Only the sounds of buttons ripping, cloth tearing pierced the preternatural silence before the incisors plunged. In a split second the cry started and stopped, and elation seeped into the rancid atmosphere.

1

FRIDAY — DECEMBER 13, 1996

Someone would hang for this tableau. Resting behind the wheel of a rented Mercedes, Darius Brock panned his gaze over the incredible display of Christmas ornaments, as outraged as awed by the sight spread before him. For several delayed seconds, he wondered if he'd taken a wrong turn. In his rearview mirror, despite the spackling of snow already smearing the rear window, at least one of the black stone pillars remained visible . . . And in hindsight, he recalled the bright red ribbons floating from the ornate cast iron lamps embedded in the stone. A hallucination, perhaps. No man in his right mind would dare to deck the halls of the Chateau Suites Hotel, one of a half dozen hotels under the direct reign of the von Hendricks Corporation.

Shaking his head, Darius switched the wiper blades to high, rubbed his eyes, blinked, and looked again.

Nothing changed.

The Gothic arches glowed in a garland of tiny white lights. Candles stood in every visible window within the main office structure. The neon lights under the covered portico enhanced the brilliant red ribbons and pine sprays on every windowsill. Christmas. With the soft white flakes sprinkling through the electric coach lights, the ambiance enhanced tenfold and for a moment, he remained as awestruck as a child.

He hadn't thought about Christmas advancing. Couldn't even recall when he might have last considered the holiday. Surely, he'd glimpsed decorations in Los Angeles, but nothing to compare with this fantasia.

Heart hammering suddenly, Darius searched the high stone walls, squinting against the white haze. Windows and balconies stretched in either direction from the entry, emitting a more natural glow through curtains and blinds. Not entirely relieved by the absence of further ornaments, he scanned the slope, spotting the bright ribbons on every lamppost, following the sparkling lights laced along the hedges to either side of the lane. With the floating white flakes, the lights twinkled like candles from a different era, an era befitting the gothic style of the hotel.

Incredible . . . truly incredible.

With the Mercedes stopped at an angle, Darius lowered the driver's window and cleared his vision, drawing a chilly breath. Compared to the warm breeze off the California Coast, the wind whipping at his face was as cold as death, but doubtful the frigid air created the prickle down his spine.

Mason Gordon had lost his bloody mind. Only a madman would authorize this spectacle knowing the strict policy regarding holidays. And therein lay the travesty. Amad von Hendricks surely knew about this in advance.

Had the Baron sanctioned this madness ...? Or had he rerouted the Night Rider to correct this dereliction? Was this the reason for the change in his flight plan, landing Darius in Pittsburgh rather than Chicago?

As personal attaché to Baron Amad von Hendricks, head of the von Hendricks Corporation, Darius had handled more than his fair share of nasty situations, and scanning this scene only sent the first pangs of melancholy sailing through him. Doubtful Mason had authorized this travesty. The chap was little more than a puppet dangling on a string, dancing at the Baron's bid. More than likely, another von Hendricks heir had tampered with the natural order, but even that thought posed a contradiction. Of the dozens of heirs living in this eastern hemisphere, only one possessed the arrogance or audacity to order this atrocity, and doubtful Hubert von Hendricks, Amad's alleged younger brother and mirror reflection, had found religion.

Short hairs lifting and prickling under his collar, Darius scanned the wondrous scene more intently. Someone watched him, judging his reaction to this spectacle. No curtains shifted visibly, or shadows darted, but he'd lived under the looking glass for eight years, long enough not to be fooled by the absence of visual signs or the serenity abounding.

Peace on earth, he considered with a tight quirk quivering his mustache, and at the same moment, the irony collided with the ambiance sinking his mood by several degrees. Once, perhaps, he'd suffered the naivety and ignorance to believe in such foolishness, but those days had long ago passed. Hell on Earth might be far more accurate in his enlightenment. But just for a moment, he recalled the years before the Baron. Hard times, perhaps. But better times. And he remembered hoisting Dylan to his shoulders, laughing as he turned them both toward a lighted window display. A smile flickered on his lips and faded nearly as fast as the reality slamming him once more.

Some things were better left forgotten. He had a job to do, and whoever created this garish display would undoubtedly demand his attention. As much as Darius loathed the position, he'd held the post of Amad's henchman too long to deny the title.

Shifting his foot from the brake to the gas, he sped toward the entrance, recognizing the doorman who hurried through the glass doors. Tossing the shifter in park, Darius slipped from the front seat and pulled his long coat together against a quick gust of chilled wind. Another far more natural shiver sped over him as he rounded the front end, tossing the keys to the doorman. "See to my bags and the car, will you, Harris?"

"Of course, sir," the smart-dressed chap stated sharply.

Continuing through the doors, Darius faltered a step, only more dumbfounded and dismayed with the continuation of holiday decor from candles and holly, and bright gold and silver ribbons intertwined between the ancient design. In another place, at another time, he might be truly awed. Instead, he shivered internally. Someone truly would hang for this, and he suffered a wicked prickling at his nape, an almost overwhelming foreboding, that his own neck might find a noose.

In natural routine, he veered to the registration desk where a perky young woman, probably a college student, stood nearly at attention. If he'd ever met her, the memory eluded him. But she knew him. She wore the familiar spooked shine, a trademark reaction to a visiting dignitary from the parent company. "The keys to 606, miss?" he spoke smoothly.

"Yes, sir. Right here, sir," she said while presenting a key and a sheet of hotel stationery.

Darius accepted both, already unfolding the paper as he turned. He recognized Mason's tight little script. The message was brief. 'You're expected in the banquet hall.'

Christmas—the Chateau Suites. "Bloody hell," Darius muttered as he folded the page and pivoted back to the desk, removing his long coat. Catching the young woman's flustered eyes, he draped his coat on the varnished desk. "Be a luv, and send that up to my room with my bags, will you?"

How could he have become so blasted indifferent to the seasons and his destinations that he could forget the annual bash?

In perfect symmetry, the banquet hall of the Chateau Suites reflected the Christmas atmosphere of turn-of-the-century decor. Pine garland laced the chair rails on every wall; wreaths hung on the swirled raised wallpaper between gilt-framed oils depicting country landscapes. Delicate red ribbons trimmed in white Victorian lace bedecked the scalloped holders of a half dozen chandeliers. Recessed against a backdrop of French doors and windows where more wreaths and ribbons glowed against frosted glass, a ten-piece symphony stood on an elevated platform, and per instructions, had begun another holiday favorite with enough harpsichords and violins to carry an 18th-century tone. Nearly twelve-foot tall, an immense Blue Spruce occupied the entire corner of the outside wall, its bows draped in electric candles and laced ribbons, a perfect accent to the splendid stone hearth where poinsettias and holly wound a wondrous collage across the mantle.

The von Hendrick's Corporation knew how to throw a party and had spared no expense. Fine flowered china, seven-piece silver settings, crystal goblets, and lighted candles floating in oil above a ring of poinsettias or holly bedecked every round table. At the deep end of the room, centering two long tables of hors d'oeuvre from fruits to caviar, a three-foot ice sculpture of a candle and wreath stood emitting soft misty condensation.

At least it wasn't a life-sized depiction of jolly old St. Nick or a choir of angels.

No one danced on the black marbleized floor in front of the stage. Very few of the growing number of guests had ventured more than halfway into the room. Not a single body stood within fifteen feet of the fir tree as if they feared to be scorched.

Barely a moment passed before he heard his name called and the crowd descended en masse. But a moment more, his attention caught and snagged on the most stunning creature to grace the room, before the mob swallowed him.

The largest concentration of bodies clustered near the door, and although Jenna Windrow, creator of this masterpiece in historical accuracy, couldn't see him, she knew who stood at the center of that crowd.

The man of the hour.

When he'd first stepped through the open double doors, Jenna had glimpsed him, and even in retrospect, the effect was startling. Framed inside the pine garland arch, the hallway light mixing with the subdued light of the dining room chandeliers, he'd poised in perfect black contrast. The cut of his black Armani enhanced every micron of his solid physique. Six foot four if he stood over an inch, he might have posed for the cover of GQ . . . if not the centerfold of a woman's brown paper wrapper. Over forty feet separated them, yet his dark eyes had snared her, pinning her like a bird in a cat's hypnotic glare. From the curve of a manicured mustache to the mahogany shine of his waves . . . he was drop-dead gorgeous.

"Darius the Great," a deep voice idled at close range.

Drawn by the sarcastic tone and proximity, Jenna sized up the gentleman who leaned at the end of the bar, his gaze already watching her as if amused. Like Brock, he wore a dark formal suit and thin black tie, both designer label. Light-hair, brown beard cropped neatly about a firm jaw, the man's pale blue eyes enhanced a cocky smile that would wear well on a salesman. "Excuse me?"

"Pet name," the man said and eased off the bar, rising to an impressive height and stepping toward her, offering his hand. "Evan Trevane. Public Relations manager, Pittsburgh office," he said as if the title amused him.

"Jennifer Windrow," she said smoothly, accepting his hand and noting the firm grip, fingers only. He was tall, over six feet, and appeared young, early to mid-thirties. No ring graced his finger, but he might have ditched a wedding band when he stepped from his happy home. She'd met her share of those culprits.

"I probably should apologize," he said whimsically and winked. Leaning down a fraction, he confided, "I slipped the bartender a fin to learn that you're Mason's new assistant, and I'd like to be the first to congratulate you on a job well done."

"A bit early," she said lightly, appreciating the compliment despite an uneasy tingle at her nape.

"My dear, I've been attending these mandatory bashes for the past ten years. I can tell you, in all sincerity, I've never seen the hall look quite so festive. Since I know Mason's tastes, I can accurately assume we have your talent and handiwork to praise for this display." His gaze flashed toward the immense fir tree with a quick smile. "Especially that, dear. How did you convince Mason to retire that skeleton he generally plopped on a sideboard?"

"It wasn't easy, I'll admit."

"Truly a wonder," he said with a pleasant, almost wistful glance toward the tree. All too swiftly, his expression dimmed. "But I probably should tell you something else. Forewarned is forearmed, as the saying goes," he said carefully and flashed his gaze toward the collection around Brock. "You haven't met our esteemed visitor, have you?"

"I haven't had the pleasure," she said, noting his hesitation. "Forewarned?"

"How well do you and Mason get along, if you don't mind me asking?"

"Quite well," she admitted. "He's a very capable and fair man."

"He's a coward, dear," he said with a smirk and glance at the tree. His blue eyes sober, he continued, "Did he happen to mention that although we meet here under the pretense of a Christmas party, it's more of a timely year-end PR stunt to promote goodwill within our affiliates and customers? Or uhm . . . that the von Hendricks are rather devout atheists?"

Unfortunately, both revelations had come too late. Her days, if not her hours at the Chateau, were numbered. As much as she loved the Chateau Suites and the proximity to her family, she would probably return to Chicago right after the holidays. Never burn bridges, as her father had always said.

"I uh . . ." Evan interrupted with a curious smile, faintly worried. "I'd love to know what you're thinking," he said smoothly.

"About bridges, actually," she admitted with a smile. "Thank you for the warning, Mr. Trevane."

"Please, just Evan," he offered. "And if this isn't too forward, I wonder if I might ask you to join me for dinner, Miss Windrow?"

Judging by the distance her boss had maintained over the past hour, their original dinner arrangements had changed, and despite the circumstances, she wasn't about to slip away like a repentant child. Whatever the consequences, she'd loved every minute of the transformations. From its gothic arches and intricately carved crown moldings to the dark mahogany panels in Jacobean-style ceilings, the hotel had demanded her touch. Looking at Trevane, she decided, "I'd like that."

"Could I get you a drink before we sit down?"

"A gin and tonic would be nice," Jenna agreed.

As Trevane turned to the bar, Jenna fanned her gaze toward the French doors. The dusting of snow had transformed into a genuine snowfall, drifting past the frosted panes, and collecting on the sills. Already the lampposts at the edges of the veranda had become mere shadows, glowing softly behind the quickening white haze.

For a split second, Jenna's attention froze. A chill skittered down her spine. Déjà vu. As if she'd viewed this scene a thousand times, she watched the snowfall, believed she heard a gusty wind howling off a mountain peak, and suffered the draft from under an unsealed door. Nonsense of course. Not only was this the first winter storm, as well as her first winter employed in the Chateau Suites, the hotel rested on little more than a hillside in the foothills of the Alleghenies. The nearest mountain peak stood at least forty miles east, past the city of Pittsburgh, a junction of rivers, and a dozen hills. She'd never even visited a ski lodge in any mountain range to equate this scene with past experience.

Distracted, Jenna glanced toward a flash of red across the room, and a tremor of irritation sped through her system at the sight of her night shift assistant. The woman's conservative style of business suit and tight-bound hair had vanished.

In a flurry of red sequins and mounded dark hair, Lisa Blythe disappeared into the crowd at the door, undoubtedly drawn to the celebrity.

Twenty-twenty hindsight. For six months, Lisa had attempted all manners of deceit to hasten the dismissal of a certain new employee, and she'd become suspiciously enthusiastic over the hall's transformations. About now, Blythe stood, laying blame for this vast mistake at Jenna's feet.

Turning, Trevane delivered her drink, smiling reassurance as he commented, "For what it's worth . . . Do you mind if I call you Jennifer?"

"That's fine," she said lightly.

"I appreciate the effort you've put into these accommodations," he said sincerely, sending another wistful glance over the hall. "Truly," he said. "I've never seen the Chateau look so grand. I feel as if I've waltzed into a medieval castle and I'm paying court to a beautiful princess, and on that note, my dear, I hope you'll grant me the honor and pleasure of the first dance?"

Nothing slow or insecure about this fellow. If not public relations, he certainly mastered the art of social relations. "I'd imagine that can be arranged," she said lightly—unless the fellow across the room ordered her gone. Her gaze slid and her heart hammered a leaden beat as she caught the dark eyes lancing her. Lightening quick, those eyes shot away, but the curve remained on the mustached lips. How soon would the dismissal come? By now, he probably knew she'd masterminded this disaster, and a glimpse of the dark hair at his shoulder only confirmed Jenna's belief. Disgusted, angry suddenly, Jenna turned her gaze toward Evan. "We probably should sit down. Would you mind tremendously if we sit near the tree?"

His smile deepened as he glanced toward the pristine empty tables circling the tree, and he touched her arm in proper escort. "I would be delighted to sit near the tree."

Wading between the nearest tables, they strode across the dance floor, and Jenna chose the table nearest the veranda doors. Moving to a chair that put her back toward the guests, she accepted a panoramic view of the snow, the tree, and the fireplace flickering soft gas flames and crackling nicely.

In proper aplomb, Trevane held her chair then slid into the next, scanning the view before his attention returned, his eyes lighting with a misty shine of amusement. "Lovely. Truly, Jennifer. If I didn't know better, I'd feel as if we were sitting in a private dining room straight out of a sixteenth-century abode." His gaze misted, fleeting over her face, her hair, and into her eyes. "Have you any idea how stunning you are?"

She smiled appreciatively. "It's the light. It hides a world of sins, but I thank you for the compliment."

"The light hides nothing," he said soberly, his gaze intent, sincere. "If anything, the light only enhances your attributes."

"If you're attempting to make me blush, I should tell you, you'll probably succeed."

"I already have, and the effect is stunning."

He appeared entirely sincere, and the intensity in his eyes and wry smile sharpened his features into a striking handsomeness. Without a doubt, he could have invited a dozen women to this affair. Was he a man of variety? A genuine playboy? Or a married man with a roving eye? She'd met enough of the corporate executives over the past hour to realize the company trend leaned toward smooth operators, and the majority had come stag. Male and female alike.

A PR stunt . . . or a corporate meeting? Considering the presence of Darius Brock, a member of the hierarchy in the von Hendricks Corporation, a meeting might be called to order at any moment ... *With an orgy to follow?*

Maybe a dismissal would be a blessing. On a whim, Jenna had submitted her application to the Chateau when visiting her family last summer. She couldn't recall why she'd veered off course and sped between the stone pillars. As an assistant manager in one of the grander hotels in Chicago, she could have landed a job anywhere in the world if she'd truly sought a change of pace. Coming home. For the first time in nearly seven years, she lived close enough to share a holiday with her family rather than spend the day packing and racing to catch a plane. In retrospect, she considered the irony. She lived less than ten miles from the old homestead, but she hadn't seen her family since Thanksgiving. Planning and preparing this celebration had occupied more time than she cared to consider, and for what? Only to get fired? If not for the thought of Lisa gloating by the end of the evening, Jenna might find this situation amusing.

A tingle prickled her spine, drawing her attention as Evan glanced over her shoulder. The man of the hour had just arrived. The moment had come.

"Evan," the deep voice dropped like warm molasses.

"Darius," Evan said while rising sideways and offering his hand. "Good to see you again."

"Mutual, to be sure," the smooth deep voice responded, a touch of an English accent enhancing the rich timbre.

Too late to avoid and too close to ignore, Jenna lifted her gaze, and her attention focused on an immense diamond glittering within an intricate weave of gold where a dozen cut gems glinted. At her opposite side, the chair slid. Distracted, Jenna glanced to see her boss pulling out the next chair. Mason intended to maintain pretense and sit with her, after all. Noting his genuine discomfort and haunted eyes, Jenna nearly felt bad for him. A few words of advice or explanation might have spared them both a world of ills. Apparently, he wanted her out as badly as Blythe. Jenna flashed him a cutting dark glare that startled or disoriented him; his rheumy brown eyes darted away.

"Mason." Unbelievably deep, almost threatening, that single word halted Mason before he could sit. The clipped English accent became more apparent as Brock continued, "If you shouldn't mind, I'd prefer that view."

Uh-huh. Here it comes. An early evening, after all. As Mason shuffled aside, Jenna glimpsed the gems as the hand landed on the carved chair-back. Without pause or inhibition, she lifted her gaze. Despite a shag of thick black lashes, which should have softened the mahogany shine, Brock bore into her with an intensity to send another shiver down her spine. Rumor hadn't exaggerated. Darius Brock was the company henchman, and her neck hovered near the noose.

Head tilted, mustache quirked in a smile, he slid his hand from the chair and opened his palm. "I don't believe I've had the honor," he said and flashed his gaze over her head toward Trevane, expecting, demanding, or accusing by the sheer intensity of his gaze.

"Jennifer Windrow," Evan stated smoothly. "Jennifer," he said while touching her shoulder almost possessively. "Darius Brock."

"Mr. Brock," she said with a slight nod, her gaze direct. Her heart hammered a wicked beat as his hand clamped her fingertips, sending a flash of heat through her palm.

His gaze held fast as lifted her fingers and brushed a kiss on the back of her hand in regal elegance. "Darius, if you please," he said with a smile playing in the corner of his mustache. "Would you mind if I join you?"

Did she have a choice? Between his deep voice and dark eyes, a woman could get lost. Withdrawing her hand, Jenna nodded, "Please do."

Almost as an afterthought, he stepped aside and held the next chair for Lisa who sent Jenna a cutting glance, a thin smug smile.

Suddenly warm, rather than cold, Jenna returned Lisa's silent snipe while sizing up the outlandish red ensemble which would undoubtedly wear well in the Strip District in downtown Pittsburgh. The conservative Miss Blythe had truly vanished, and to Jenna's slight amusement, Blythe's current style appeared far more natural—a high-class hooker.

As Tony Ricotti, the head bartender, arrived personally, delivering a bottle of chilled wine for Brock's inspection, Jenna turned her attention to her drink and dinner date. With Mason's grim expression and thinning gray hair looming large against the backdrop of twinkling lights, Jenna suffered the first genuine throb at her temples. This could turn out to be the longest evening of her life, barring none. Lisa's generally curt voice bubbling and lilting with some reference to the wine, only amplified the pulse. The panoramic view had narrowed to the French doors where the thick flakes continued drifting past the glass in ignorant bliss. The warmth of the fire and festive cheer had vanished, overwhelmed by the neon red dress and black blur at the corner of Jenna's eye.

Leaning, as if in tune with her descending mood, Trevane drew her attention and spoke in a discreet whisper against her ear. "Pretend you're having fun, my dear. It'll drive him bonkers. Trust me."

Catching Evan's wink and smile, Jenna smiled, grateful for whatever had brought Trevane to her rescue. Leaning, she whispered, "You're terrible."

"We peons must have our fun," he mused. "Remember. The first dance is mine."

The only dance, she nearly said aloud but managed a smile and nod before the deep voice intruded at close range.

"Would you care for a glass of wine, luv?"

With the fluted glass already lifted in the ring-bedecked fingers, Jenna suffered an inkling of how the next hour would progress—she could end up feeling like a pinball. Far more uncomfortable, barely glimpsing his dark eyes, she declined smoothly, opting for coffee. If the signs were any indication, she'd be driving home soon and if the roads were slick under that snowfall, she'd need her full faculties to keep her Lincoln on the pavement.

2

More than eight years had passed since Darius had lingered this close to a Christmas tree or basked in the light of a glowing white star. He should be furious. Instead, he remained as wonderstruck and bewildered as a blasted child paying his first visit to St. Nick's original manse.

The source—the cause—the creator of this fantasia rested at his side, and he needed every ounce of his willpower not to turn and stare at her, half afraid of what he might say if she turned those deep blue lasers in his direction. Only half listening to the buzzing chatter on his right, Darius fanned his gaze past Mason and awed anew at the crystal ornaments, electric candle strings, and delicate red bows gracing the soft emerald branches. Despite all common sense, gazing at the glowing beacon of hope atop the fir tree, Darius fought an almost irresistible urge to trot out to the novelty shop off the lobby and buy a camera.

Raphael would love this, Darius considered, and a smile quivered on his lips as he imagined the devil-damned elf dancing around this spectacle, eyes wide as saucers and lips parted in unrestrained excitement. The lad would dart around this tree like a firefly, touching and sniffing, bouncing on his heels as if he stood on rubber balls. The little devil had probably never seen a Christmas tree, let alone one of this height or splendor . . . and barring all sense and sensibilities, Darius vowed to buy a camera and snap off a roll or two. He would decide later whether or not to develop the film . . . and almost in the same instant, he knew that he would. To bloody hell with the consequences. For Raphael . . . for Dylan . . . for himself, Darius would capture this tableau for posterity.

Unconsciously, his gaze listed, catching, fixing on the stunning young woman he would need to thank for this gift. She wore the same wistful smile that had captured him the instant he'd walked through the banquet hall doors. At close range—with the soft candle glow playing on her slender face—the effect was stunning. With little more than a dusting of cosmetics, she could spin heads and wrench necks, his own apparently not immune. Long, fawn-colored lashes, delicate full lips turned at the corner, she gazed toward the snowfall with such distance in her eyes that he restrained an uncanny urge to clasp her hand and anchor her in the room. Awesome. Truly awesome.

In Victorian elegance, she held her head high. Her long sleek neckline accommodated wisps of soft curls sprinkled from the mound of golden locks, golden hair dark enough to glisten bronze sparks in wild contrast to the shimmering black cloth at her shoulders. With the image of her poised against a backdrop of the French doors embedded in his mind, he needed no downward glance to remember how the gold-trimmed jacket hugged her slender arms and ribs. Gold filigree threads followed the rounded edges, falling no lower than her trim waist, covering and enhancing the outline of what he knew, now, to be impressively synonymous breasts, neither too large nor too slight for her frame. Conservative, almost simple in design, the dress rose in sheer black elegance riding over those mounds to form a V-neckline just low enough to send a healthy man's imagination into high gear—high enough to keep his wheels spinning no matter which way she turned or leaned.

What startled him more? His thoughts running rampant and his physical readiness straining below his belt, or her eyes turning, locking as if she read his mind? The latter thought stifled him, sobering him considerably. Stark deep blue, her eyes held him with an all too familiar directness. A von Hendricks. Another Goddamn von Hendricks, and suddenly, Darius understood the decor. For whatever reason, Amad had lent this young woman full rein. "I understand I have you to praise for this affair," he commented, careful to keep the edge from his voice.

"I do hope that means you're enjoying the cuisine," she said smoothly but her eyes crinkled at the outer edges, lighting a spark of amusement—that, too, familiar—though lacking the natural cynicism.

Oh, she was a von Hendricks. No doubt remained in his mind. Word games and cutting double-entendres were their stock in trade. He'd met enough of them over the past several years to know their wiles, and this young lady wasn't the exception, despite her soft smile and livid eyes.

"I'd like to congratulate you, Miss Windrow," he spoke carefully, candidly, gauging his words. Undoubtedly, at whim or whimsy, she could twist his words and slam them back at him with a cutting jibe. "I've never seen the Chateau appear either as splendid or as inviting. You have a fine talent for capturing aesthetic authenticity. Very fine indeed," he said and deliberately slid his gaze over the Victorian hairstyle, down the nape of her neck. A mistake, that. She was stunning, regardless of her heritage, and he was playing with fire.

A soft flush of color rose across her cheeks, doubt lifted within her direct eyes. "I'd like to apologize if I've offended you, Mr. Brock," she said lightly, holding his wandering gaze with a stunning power. "Had I been informed of unwritten policies in advance, I might have adhered. Though to be honest, it would have been difficult. And now I probably should apologize again." Her eyes flickered with genuine amusement. Her lips quivered in a slight smile as if straining against a laugh. "I loved transforming the Chateau."

His smile quivered, stifled, only more positive of a game or a punch line coming. "It must have taken you weeks," he said, and her smile tempered slightly. With a word, a phrase, or a glance, he could shift a mood but he hadn't meant to sound condescending or chiding. Cursing his talent, cursing the master who'd taught him those tricks, Darius held her gaze and forced himself to continue, "Jennifer's a lovely name. Would you mind if we dispense with formalities? I'd prefer, Darius." And now he'd made her more wary.

"Jenna," she offered lightly.

"Even more lovely," he said sincerely, but even to his own ears it sounded catty. His wine glass slipped into his hand, lifting to suggest she join him, only enhancing the implication. If the Baron had sent him here to meet her, he couldn't afford to offend her. Softening his gaze, he offered, "To aesthetics, Jenna."

"Merry Christmas," she fired back with a soft innocent note then rolled her eyes and flashed sparks of amusement, correcting, *"Dasvidaniya."*

Despite his effort, Darius lost his smirk and stifled a humph, clinking the crystal. "Cheers, Luv." Without losing her gaze, enjoying the light show in the blue depths, he sipped the wine, all too aware of her likewise steady gaze as she touched the crystal to her smiling lips. Oh, and to be that glass for just a few seconds. Blast! He was getting maudlin . . . or senile . . . or just weary.

Almost grateful for the interruption, he withdrew his gaze before the serving cart fully arrived at his back. Weary, he confirmed while acknowledging the chef's need for approval over the immense slice of prime rib dripping in juices . . . And hungry, he added, only to himself. By no small wonder, his appetite never waned, and dining was one of the few pleasures neither denied nor restrained. The same couldn't be said of the woman to his left. He turned his attention more fully, freely, to the tender meat, slicing and dicing, savoring the taste between ample bites of sautéed vegetables and sweet potato dripping in cinnamon and sugar. Not for a moment, could he forget or fully ignore the lovely woman to his left who ate with an enthusiasm to match his own, unlike the woman to his right who bemoaned the portions and feigned a light appetite, barely touching her plate.

Already tense, and far too weary, Darius ate quietly, halfheartedly listening to the subtle jibes that Blythe sent to imply Windrow was a glutton and would be as large as a barn before her thirtieth birthday. The Baron hadn't rerouted the Night Rider craft and landed Darius in this mix to either eavesdrop on female jealousy or enjoy this Christmas ambiance. If nothing else, Darius knew an ulterior motive existed.

Little more than six hours ago, he'd lifted off from the sunny California coast with every intention of landing in Chicago to finalize a business venture before the New Year. When his current pilot, Wayne Devoreaux had announced the third time zone, Darius had realized his destination had changed. In retrospect, he remembered his indifference. Had he become so complacent? So accustomed to his lack of control that even curiosity failed to register? He remembered simply looking at his watch, adjusting the time, and turning his attention to the printouts spread on the table in front of him.

If Devoreaux had simply overshot the last landing strip on the Atlantic coast and dumped them into the icy black ocean, would it have mattered any more or less?

In three months, he would turn thirty years old. Mentally, physically, he felt ancient. Landing in the black depths would be a relief, but unless the Baron found a means to prolong that descent, Darius doubted he would meet such a quick end.

Damnit. He was tired. Weeks of meetings, and midnight rendezvous had taken a serious toll on his reserves. The sooner he reached the bottom of whatever had landed him in Pittsburgh, the sooner he could finish his agenda in Chicago . . . and then what? Back to England for several days of uninterrupted sleep? Doubtful. Despite the holidays celebrated around the world, the Baron would inevitably find something to occupy his charge.

Catching a soft laugh to his left, Darius enjoyed the sound only until he remembered the young woman's lineage. Von Hendricks. He should be slightly relieved. At least he could stop worrying about the damned decorations and selfish beast that he was, simply enjoy the festive atmosphere. Unwittingly, his thoughts turned toward another time, a different life. Dylan. That first Christmas . . . dirt poor, Darius remembered absently. His gaze listed toward the twinkling candles on pine branches. With every pence he could scrape together, he'd managed to buy a scruffy tree and a few toys for his infant son . . .

Reflection was not good for the soul! And possibly that was a side benefit of this sojourn. If Amad had meant to torment him, landing him in this glittery celebration had certainly succeeded. Far too often of late, Darius caught himself thinking, worrying about Dylan. His son would be close to thirteen—

With a mental shake, Darius sent the thought aside and concentrated on the material world, listening, eavesdropping without regret as Evan Trevane entertained the young heiress. Slightly surprised, Darius listened, realizing Miss Windrow's ignorance. Unless she was lying to Trevane, which was possible, she'd grown up on a small farm just south of Pittsburgh, not too far from Trevane's childhood haunt.

A small world, Darius had decided long ago, not surprised that these two apparent strangers could relate to a shared experience, discussing some local amusement park. With a slightly keener interest, he listened, realizing the natural tempo of the young woman's voice. Perhaps, he was wrong. Perhaps, she truly was an innocent . . . and not a von Hendricks at all. Had he lived under the Baron's shadow so long that he would see a von Hendricks in every pair of deep blue eyes?

He was so damned tired, the kind of bone-weary tired that no amount of sleep could relieve or resolve. How he wished suddenly that he could just lie down, close his eyes, and call it a night. Such was not to be. Obligations, responsibilities. Even before Deke Whitman appeared over his shoulder, Darius knew the executive would ask him to perform one of the more mundane tasks of his occupation. Just another little twist of the screw.

As much as seven years ago, the Baron had learned how much one Darius Brock despised standing in front of an audience, and the bastard rarely missed an opportunity to stand him in the spotlight. It was a bloody wonder Darius never found himself in front of a blasted camera, and the mere thought threatened to lift sweat under his brow.

Maintaining his smile, which probably bordered a scowl for the glance and double take the livid blue eyes sent him, Darius offered a polite, "Do excuse me," and slid smoothly from his chair. As an afterthought, he paused, looking down into her eyes. Small pleasures. Stolen treasures. "Do promise you'll join me on the dance floor the minute this ordeal is past?"

Her eyes shadowed as if looking through him, but she smiled with a touch of dismay, "I've promised Evan the first dance."

Ah, if he were a less confident man, those words could shatter him. Smiling, Darius flashed Evan a wink and darted his gaze into the lovely blue depths. "If he stomps your toes, luv, do tell when I whisk you from his arms. I'd like nothing better than to return that gesture on your behalf."

She rose to the very brink of laughter and stifled a quaver in her voice. "I'm likely to be the one stomping on you after he limps away, honey. I do hope you're wearing steel-toed shoes."

Mercy, he enjoyed the livid shine in those eyes and the laughter in her voice. "I promise to grin and bear the pain without shame, Luv. If you'll excuse me . . .?"

Winking, she spoke smoothly, "Knock 'em dead."

Had his dismay been so obvious? Or was she truly gifted with the mentalism to look straight through his eyes into his blasted head? Alarm bells jangling, he very nearly withdrew then ducked impulsively and brushed a kiss on her cheek, touching her shoulder, winking as he rose. "A kiss for luck," he said smoothly, pivoted from her startled eyes, and maintained his smile until he spotted Whitman. Already across the dance floor, the chap stepped onto the stage, interrupting the musicians. Perhaps, he should have tasted her lips rather than her cheek. One-on-one, he enjoyed people, had no choice but to enjoy people, but standing at the head of a silent conclave, all eyes on him, quickened the beat of his heart to throb in his ears. To be singled out, stood on a pedestal, scorned or praised was far too reflective in his mind, but he doubted fainting behind the microphone would gain him any salvation.

"Ladies and gentlemen, if I could have your attention, please?" Whitman's voice echoed out of the speakers, charismatic, commanding, a voice to be heard and obeyed.

Bloody sheep! Darius seethed behind his sprinting gaze. Heads turned; voices faltered. People, damn it! Just normal people! . . . A hundred or so. Not many more than that.

"It comes as something of a surprise and unexpected pleasure to have a man with us this evening who may not need an introduction for most of you . . ." In a quiet cadence, the stocky executive continued spilling nonsensical accolades, sparing a moment to boast the branch office of Hendricks Distribution, a subsidiary of the von Hendrick's Corporation.

Standing aside, Darius panned his gaze over the faces, catching more than a few eyes already watching him rather than Whitman, prickling him as if they deliberately intended to make him squirm. He would rather they continued eating, drinking, chatting. Anything other than bursting into a round of applause to prod him toward the microphone that Whitman handed to him. Once. Once nearly eight years ago, he'd stood in a much smaller crowd, confident and determined, fairly bursting with as much fear as outrage. Had he a moment to change, that would have been the one . . . but in the next instant, he perished the thought and determined to survive the next two or three minutes of pure hell on earth.

Catching his breath, he drew from whatever innate determination had held him afoot eight years earlier and stood momentarily, panning his gaze over the enthralled audience, identifying as many sneers as leers. For another second or two, he was the same naive idiot who'd railed in bloody outrage, a randy child with no more common sense than a toddler in the face of adversity. He smiled slightly, refusing to hold the microphone close to his mouth. His voice generally carried well enough in a banquet hall.

Too bloody well at times.

Glancing at Whitman's beaming, rugged face, Darius thanked him for the introduction then turned his gaze to the crowd. "Most of you may know that I truly don't enjoy offering speeches or lectures, so you may rest assured, I'll be brief. As a representative and on behalf of the von Hendricks Corporation, I'd like to thank you all for coming and I hope you enjoyed the fine cuisine half as much as I have. To the staff of the Chateau Suites, and especially to the young woman responsible for coordinating and providing the atmosphere which I find especially exquisite, I extend my personal thanks and appreciation." Locking on the slightly startled blue eyes across the distance, he tipped his head and smiled. "A job well done, Miss Windrow . . .

"As I mentioned to her earlier," he spoke while sailing his gaze over the more stunned faces. "I especially enjoy the authenticity of the decor which bears striking resemblance to the era from which the Chateau drew its elegance. As you all know, the von Hendricks Corporation is an expansive organization that has survived through more years than I can fathom. Here in the United States alone, the corporation's roots predate the turn of the Nineteenth Century when the first Lord Amadeus von Hendricks traveled via sailing ship to the shores of Maine. Not quite with the early settlers or pilgrims perhaps, but long enough to appreciate the longevity and to reap a respectable position in the trends and posterity of the United States. That's not a claim unduly boasted or spoken out of hand. For more than a hundred and seventy-five years, the von Hendricks family has retained an intimate bond with the American people, sharing your trials and tribulations, your fears and concerns. Sharing, perhaps, the very heart of America since as most of you know, I'm sure, many of the family and extended family members remain on this continent as American citizens. In fact, I'm fairly certain, that at least a few extended members of the family may be in the audience, and if any of you would like to come forward and take this bloody microphone from me, I'd be more than delighted."

He waited, daring to hope but refusing to single out any man or woman in the conclave to take his place at the microphone. Sighing, he murmured, "Hmm, no takers." Shaking his head, his smile fading as if mocking sorrow, he commented, "It does hurt to hope, let no one fool you."

Several stifled laughs erupted around the room. No one lifted a fork or spoon. A few barely wavered their attention long enough to light a cigarette. In the subdued light across the room, several pairs of eyes glowed, feral, locked on him with an intensity to counter his earlier thought. They were not merely people. Therein lay the illusion. He might as well be speaking to a party of one, and Amad would not be happy if his spokesman bungled.

Damn it! A short speech . . .

"This year, as in years past, the von Hendricks Corporation has retained its nationwide prosperity, thanks to your hard work, dedication, and loyalty. I won't bore you with statistics. That information is made available to the public by way of the government regulations and Fair Trades Acts for anyone particularly interested. I will mention—at the end of this fiscal year, we were listed in the top one hundred on the Fortune 500. We received commendations in various divisions for quality of service and commodities. Several of the von Hendricks wines received honors in countless tests and competitions. We are diverse, but whether we're producing fine wine, pharmaceuticals or distributing those commodities internationally, you may rest assured, the quality you provide within your area reflects the integrity and quality the von Hendricks Corporation promotes globally . . ."

Automated, he continued speaking, running blather on the economic forecasts and company trends, and as a sidebar, he again mentioned the winery. As if he had stepped aside, he heard his voice enthusiastically suggesting a visit to the winery in upstate New York. Commemorating over a hundred years of producing fine wine, the original homestead had opened for public tours and continued to undergo extensive restorations. Even as he spoke, a prickle slid down his spine. Were the words his own? Could he have become so methodical?

"To our friends, customers, and associates who've joined us this evening to celebrate another year, I'd like to extend my thanks as well as my promise that you will continue to receive the quality, service, and support you've come to expect from the von Hendricks Corporation. I always feel like doing one of those silly rabbit impressions about now, but I will refrain and simply say again, thank you for coming, and do enjoy the evening."

Done! Finished! As the applause burst again, Darius tipped his head in appreciation, not hesitating more than a fraction to turn and toss the cord aside to keep from tripping. At the edge of the raised platform, the stout musician leaned to accept the microphone. Whistles, for blasted sake? If they anticipated an encore, they were destined for disappointment. He felt bad enough delivering that spiel. He'd certainly not compound the lies and risk damning his immortal soul further. Catching the musician's eye, Darius commented, "Do pick up the beat a tad, gentlemen. I believe we're ready to begin dancing. . . and make the first song lively, will you?"

Darius barely turned and glimpsed Windrow clapping, smiling, when Whitman stepped into his path again, extending his hand.

"Great job," Deke offered with an enthusiastic knuckle-bruising grip. "Sure you don't want to say just a few more words?"

Whitman was certifiable, Darius decided behind his smile. "A party, not a seminar, Deke. I'm certain everyone would rather be dancing. Why don't we—"

"I think most of them could sit here all night and listen to you," Whitman stated with a fanatical shine in his pale eyes, his hand still gripping, pumping.

"But I appreciate you taking a few moments. There are some people I'd like you to meet. If you wouldn't mind . . .?"

Why he even considered otherwise, Darius couldn't begin to fathom as he resigned to the inevitable. No rest for the wicked. Whether in the air or on the ground, his time—his life—was never his own. To believe otherwise was a fool's dream forfeited years ago. When one crawls into bed with the devil—damned near literally, he considered with a scathing note in his silent voice—the right to life is history.

3

"Hard to believe he grew up knocking about the back streets of London, isn't it?" Evan said with a wry smile as he caught Jenna watching Brock stride off the dance floor.

Uncertain of either a compliment or an intended sarcasm, Jenna studied the amused blue eyes. "Did he really?"

"Honest to the ever-loving," Trevane said lightly, and glanced toward the retreating celebrity. "Until about ten years ago, he didn't have a nickel to rub against another. As the story goes, the old man . . . and I do mean the old man," he said with emphasis. "Thaddeus, himself, discovered Darius and snatched him from one advertising company or another where the kid was trying to hustle a few bucks. The story's a bit mixed, but it didn't take long before Darius hit the jet set."

Maybe just a touch of jealousy, Jenna considered, but in the next instant, she noted the pale blue eyes flicking toward Brock. Evan appeared almost disgusted to have spoken by the time his gaze returned.

"I think they're playing our song," he said with a smooth recovery. "Shall we?"

Despite her earlier implication, Jenna was no klutz on the dance floor, and truth be told, she loved to dance.

Within seconds on the floor, Evan looked down at her and chuckled. "I wondered if you were referring strictly to dance when you mentioned stomping both of us," he confided and held her a little closer, still smiling. "I promise to be a gentleman. I'm not wearing toe guards, and I've seen your heels."

Joining his chuckle, Jenna relaxed entirely, feeling as if she'd received a second lease on life, and for that, she owed Mr. Darius Brock her gratitude. With a word or a glance, he could have snatched her future from her hands; instead, he'd landed it smoothly into her firm grip. Not entirely keen to gloating, Jenna wasn't above noticing and appreciating how Lisa had reacted to that smooth, deep voice offering public appreciation and personal praise. If the young woman's fake smiles and laughter were any indication, Jenna would need to watch her back closely for the next decade or two . . . or do the sensible thing and fire the young woman. Unfortunately, if this little witch was as vindictive as it seemed, firing her probably wouldn't eliminate the problem. Better to keep her close and stay ahead of her schemes. Eventually, Lisa would either wear out her hostility or find another target.

Dismissing her concern, Jenna turned her full attention to having fun, only amused when Mason cut in on the second dance and managed one of his naturally gloomy smiles. His expression never failed to amuse Jenna with her sense of the man's underlying patience and decency. Without mincing words, he extended his appreciation and admitted he'd taken the blame and responsibility. With a slightly scathing glance over Jenna's shoulder, he likewise admitted, he'd been apologizing for the possible offense when a certain party had intervened. "Darius is no idiot, Jenna," Mason said in quiet confidence, his dark eyes intent. "He probably took one look at this place and knew I had nothing to do with it. The thing is . . . hereafter, I'd appreciate it if you wouldn't put me on the spot like this, and not just for myself, Jenna," he said carefully and glanced off again without the temper; his gaze returned with a solemnity to match his grim smile. "I don't like putting him on the spot either."

No more needed said for her to realize the implication that Darius would take the heat for this exception to the family rules. Possibly for the second or third time, she truly regretted her breach of apparent protocol. Lovely or not, she would have stripped the hall bare if she'd known the extent of problems it would create. "Mase," she said smoothly, soberly. "Why didn't you just tell me they were atheists? Why did you lead me to believe this was a Christmas party rather than a simple business appreciation banquet?"

He appeared slightly uncomfortable as he studied her. "You may find this difficult to believe, Jenna, but I truly didn't think I needed to tell you. It just never occurred to me. I've been coordinating this affair for more than fifteen years." His eyes flickered a touch of mischief to betray his true nature. "And the decorations were here when I arrived."

Seeing, understanding, Jenna laughed softly and hugged his broad shoulders. The shit! He'd probably wanted to toss that pathetic excuse for a Christmas tree for the past fifteen years!

Returning a patriarchal squeeze, he verified her thought in spades. "Was a lucky day when you stepped through our front door," he said in a rare moment of emotion. "If I forget to tell you later, I agree with Darius. The hall . . . the whole Chateau looks beautiful."

Flying high again, she kept pace with Mason's gliding stride and barely considered returning to her chair when another lone male caught her in a half turn and offered his hand and a pleasant smile, "May I . . . ?"

Exchanging pleasantries, handshakes, pecks on the cheek, Darius moved through the crowd. At one point, he sidled close enough to the bar to switch from wine to bourbon, but not breaking away long enough to catch a breath much less consider dancing. International commodities, distributing . . .

Did he know if the rumor was true about von Hendricks buying into another pharmaceutical company? How was his flight? Where was he headed next? How was the Baron? How was the old man—Thaddeus von Hendricks? Had Darius visited the wineries lately? Was it true another of the grandsons was getting married? The conversations rolled from business to personal and back without a notable pause. The answer man, Darius considered, and barely thought to break away when the sound erupted from his inside jacket pocket. Excusing himself from another circle of employees, he sidled from the crowd, hating that sound, cursing the day not long ago when the handheld telly had arrived via courier. Finding the button to connect the call, Darius pressed the contraption to his ear, "Yes?"

"You are an accommodating lad," the dark voice slid into Darius's ear, slicing through the static of airwaves as clearly as symphony music. "I particularly liked that reference to the heart of America," the Baron mused. "Then you wonder why I extended your duties? A natural, so you are, lad. If I didn't already tax you so heavily, I'd be tempted to hire you out for stand-up comedy."

"Glad you approve," Darius said with a slightly twitching smile as his gaze panned the nearest faces watching him. No illusion. The Baron might as well be standing inside the hall.

"Darius, about this other," the voice changed, drawing Darius's attention inward. "Have you fired this young woman?"

"No," he said in a leaden tone, his gaze seeking and finding her swaying in another man's arms. A von Hendricks. Anger spiraled unbidden, rising. "I don't suppose you'd like me to correct that oversight—"

"Listen..."

His gaze listing over the nearest table, his brow furrowed. Whether seconds or minutes passed, he had no clear grasp. Tension coiled through his spine as he realized the weight of his oversight. He should have fired Miss Jenna Windrow . . . nothing held more clearly in his mind. He should have fired her the instant he strode into the hall. "She wasn't aware of her mistake," he said absently, refocusing swiftly. "Mason never—"

"Settle, lad," the deep voice sighed in mocked sympathy, sliding through the phone line with a paternal concern. "Your talent toward gallantry and chivalry is noted. I assume you're impressed with the woman along with her accomplishments, and I suppose I can afford to be magnanimous." In a darker tone, the Baron advised, "But do mind, lad."

Tense from head to heel, his attention riveted, Darius stated, "I'll handle it—her—"

"You'll drop it," the Baron stated shortly. "I said I'd be magnanimous. Enjoy my castle, lad. I'd imagine I'll see you before long."

"I should roll into O'Hare sometime tomorrow night unless you have other plans?"

"One never knows," the dark voice sighed. "So much to do, so little time."

Waiting, expecting a continuation, another order, Darius stood another thirty seconds before realizing the line had disengaged. Muttering a curse, he snapped the contraption off his ear and found the disconnect button. Two minutes or less. The grand master could still wind Darius into a million knots. Shoving the phone in his jacket, he stole another two seconds to find Jenna Windrow on the dance floor. A dance . . . at this moment, he wanted nothing more than to hold her against him.

Plotting a clear path, Darius reached the edge of the floor as a song ended, and without pause, he sidestepped between bodies, reaching Windrow as she declined the offer for another dance, turning. His hand already touching her silky sleeve, he looked into her startled eyes as he commented, "I seem to recall the mention of a dance?"

"Hmm, now that you mention it, the subject did come up once," she said with a touch of mocked reflection. "I can't seem to recall how it turned out, though."

"You promised to wound me, and I agreed to accept the consequence," he said smoothly and offered his other hand for her clasp as the next song began. "Shall we?"

"Let me ponder this and get back to you in five seconds or so," she said as her hand slid into his palm and her eyes brightened with mischief, "I guess that means we shall."

Silently, he agreed as he slipped his hand from her elbow to her wrist. Sliding her hand onto his shoulder he skimmed his palm down her rib cage to settle at the small of her back. Her eyes locked on him, he glimpsed a flicker of heat and sparks within those blue depths as his hand clasped her fingers more comfortably. Drawing her sleek black length against him, he suffered a distant thought of playing with fire. No fear in her eyes, no misty-eyed wonder or swooning bliss. She was at this moment, as aware of him as he was of her, his every electric pulse rising to swell at the ends of his raw nerves.

Dance! His feet moved, gliding. Her shoes brushed against his as the music carried them into a weird connection of motion and sound.

Dangerous, the thought flashed neon. Playing with fire. Beneath the soft glow of the chandeliers overhead, the bronze darts flared at the edges of soft wavy strands brushing at her high intelligent brow. Her eyelashes dipped lower with seduction, neither feigned nor plotted, a mere reaction to the intensity of her blue gaze peering into him. Internally, he shivered, wondering if she could truly read his thoughts or if she had any idea how much willpower he needed to stifle his hand from sliding under that short gold-tipped jacket. He wanted that jacket off, wanted to dip his head and brush his lips over the creamy white silk he would find beneath that cloth. Far too easily and far too readily, he could convince himself—

Not fully finishing that thought, Darius woke to his commiserating and scared the hell out of himself in a heartbeat flash. Subtly, he pulled away to wedge a half-inch space between them and noted her similar thought to add another half-inch. Still, the heat collected between them.

"I want to thank you for what you did, Darius," she said in a quiet, recovering breath and tone. "For your vote of confidence and extended appreciation and . . . I'd like to apologize if I've created any problems for you," she said quietly.

Far more aware of her hand on his shoulder, the delicate touch and soft weight only slightly more enthralling than her quiet sincerity, he read the concern in her eyes. "I'm fairly proficient at handling problems, Jenna," he said with a tighter rein on himself. "And I didn't extend my gratitude in self-sacrifice," he continued honestly. "What you've given me this evening, however innocent or misplaced, I've chosen to accept as a gift."

Unconsciously, he'd steered them toward the edge of the dance floor. His gaze turned listlessly, scanning the French doors and snowfall, the tree, the glowing star. Disoriented, he remembered sitting at the table . . . thinking about her. Looking down at her, he studied her lovely face, her warm eyes. "Someone told me most memories can be retained no matter the circumstances. I hope that's true. I'd like to hold onto this one—"

And you . . . forever.

She smiled almost sadly as if she shared his sorrow. With an unbridled innocence and sincerity, she hugged his shoulder and squeezed his hand leaning into him to rest her head against his chest and shoulder. "I'm glad then, and I hope you do," she said softly.

Looking down at her tilted face, Darius suffered a grip of pain he'd thought long since passed. A fantasy, a grand delusion, but what more was there to life? Nothing would he do. Nothing could he do about this physical attraction. For his sake, he could not—would not—let himself consider his present mood anything more than lust. What he was, what he'd become, he wouldn't wish on an enemy, let alone a woman who could be as pure and innocent as the snow outside that glass. On the block panes, he focused intently and saw their reflection. His reflection scattered and broken in sections as if dissected by a skilled hand—drawn and quartered.

With the song ending, fading, he held her swaying. His gaze dipped to find her watching him with a contentment he could neither fathom nor deny. He continued swaying, looking down at her with a slight smile, "Another?"

"Let me think about it," she said without moving from his grasp. A smile played at the corner of her lips as she inclined her head off him as if to contemplate. "Thought about," she said and relaxed against his shoulder. "Unless they switch to rock n' roll."

"I bet you'd do well in that mode as well," he mused.

"I'd have to take off my shoes," she said with a spark of mischief, her head tilted now to keep him in her sights. "And I'd drop at least two more inches."

"In which case, I'd need to bow out gracefully to avoid your toes," he mused. "And I'd return shortly after chatting with our fine musicians."

"You'd have a word or two with them, would you?"

"Just two," he mused.

"Let me guess . . . slow dance?" she ventured.

"Hmm, reading my mind."

"I doubt you'd waste words," she said with a smile. "Which reminds me . . . I enjoyed your speech. You did very well for a man who dreaded that ordeal."

"Ah, now I do feel transparent," he said with a wry smile. "Should I wonder how you reached that conclusion?"

"Elementary, my dear," she said with a lofty note. "You attempted to postpone it. Not once, but twice. If you'd been thrilled, I assumed you'd have dashed for the stage."

"You're an amazingly observant young woman, Jenna. An eye for more than aesthetic detail, as I've noticed." With a thought, he wondered, "Are you as oblivious to Miss Blythe as you seem to appear?" He needed little more than the sparks in her eyes to know she was neither oblivious nor ignorant. "Do forget I asked. I assume you can handle her without much trouble, but I may be able to—"

"Don't make the offer, Darius," she interrupted with a sober note. "I like where she is."

In plain sight, he realized and nodded, moving unconsciously into the rhythm of a new song. "As you wish, but should the need arise . . ." He left the offer open and implied, surprising himself that he should even suggest any blasted intervention. Personal interest . . . personal involvement. A shiver slid through his skin with a thought of consequences.

"Where did your thoughts just go?" Windrow asked, studying him intently.

"South, darling," he said before the sense of someone approaching distracted him. Over her shoulder, not pleased, he recognized Lawrence Fradden, head of the shipping department in the main distribution center in New York, striding toward them. Once or twice, Darius had spotted the fellow watching him from the sidelines. By the intensity of the dark eyes, Darius doubted Fradden intended to cut in for a dance.

Fradden came within arm's reach and halted, bouncing his dark gaze off Windrow who lifted, sensing the arrival as well.

Catching her eyes, Darius understood she'd reacted to him, not the intruder.

"Darius, I need to talk to you," Fradden stated in a low, slightly edgy tone.

His temper rising unbidden to the demand, nearly a command, Darius continued gliding while deciding, "I'll be through in a moment."

"I'm leaving shortly. I'm catching an early flight," Fradden stated unwisely.

"And I should give a bloody damn?" Darius asked in a lower pitch, his gaze locked and annoyed at the man's audacity.

Taken aback, Fradden's jaw clamped; his cheek twitched. His gaze darted off Windrow; his agitation tempered when he started to speak.

Reacting to the hand sliding off his shoulder, to the body easing away, Darius glanced off her tense eyes and realized his temper had just destroyed the mood. Fine. Good. Whatever her intentions toward him, she would gain perspective with a show of what belied his smiles. Too bloody well, he'd learned from the master. Letting her slip fully away, he decided, "If you'll excuse me . . . ?"

"Of course," she said smoothly and glanced off Fradden who appeared far more worried than agitated, now. Toward Darius, she offered, "Thank you for the dance."

"Thank you, Jenna," he said and held her gaze another instant, backing with a nod and turning to Fradden. If this chap's problem was anything other than an emergency, he would suffer a few more concerns to add to his burdens. For the first time in longer than Darius could remember, he'd almost begun to relax and enjoy the company of a female . . . and in the next instant, his thoughts spiraled toward business. He wasn't in Pittsburgh to enjoy a damned thing. Lawrence Fradden, New York distributor. Possibly, Fradden possessed the reason belying this visit.

Joining the stocky man against the wall near the fireplace, Darius stood, arms folded. "Do hope this is important, Larry."

"I wasn't even coming tonight until I heard you were flying in," Fradden said in a discreet low tone, confirming Darius's thought and gaining his undivided attention. The Baron had intended for them to meet.

Nervously, Fradden darted his gaze toward the nearest tables, judging the distance of eavesdroppers and lowering his volume accordingly. Wearing a three-piece suit, he stood, hands in his pants pockets, his jacket folded to either side in a mocked casual pose. He wasn't an exceptionally old man. His hair a premature gray and thinning at his pate, he wore the face of a middle-aged man with too many burdens. Lines carved around his lips and eyes, a visible sign of hard labor. "We have a problem."

"A phone call wouldn't suffice?"

"I've been making phone calls, Darius. I've been calling overseas distributors right and left and this isn't something I want to mention to uh . . ." He stepped closer, darting his gaze more warily toward the guests and looking up with an angry, faintly desperate shine. "I'm hoping we can keep this between you and me, all right? Hoping maybe we can work it out without getting anybody else involved."

"You know I won't promise that," Darius stated smoothly. "Wouldn't even if I thought it were possible."

"Look, you're closer to Mr. von Hendricks than I am to my old man," Fradden stated, his gaze heating. "I go to him with this, he'll probably fucking kill me," Larry stated, darting his gaze warily. "We lost some merchandise," he huffed.

"You . . ." No possible way. "Do tell me, I did not just hear you correctly," Darius said in a low voice.

"A whole fucking shipment."

Darius stared into the dark angry eyes, his anger on hold with the doubt. "All right," he said carefully. "Very slowly, convincingly, tell me that we're discussing something simple like cuticle cleaner or tongue depressors. Then tell me that you've tracked the shipment to its source and followed proper procedures to recover—"

"Darius," Fradden said with a weird light in his eyes. "We've been having some problems at the warehouses down on the docks. I mentioned that to Kevin Brock a couple weeks ago . . . I told him we had it under control, but the fucking truth is, we've had more. And the missing shit . . .? It's not tongue-depressors," he said warily, darting almost feral eyes to Darius. "It's his fucking wine—those fucking old bottles we've been shipping from the winery."

Darius drew back unconsciously as if distance would gain him perspective or a safety zone. "Bloody hell," he uttered as the words sank in. The 'old' bottles—the ancient bottles only recently recovered from the catacombs? "You cannot possibly—even remotely—be telling me that you're talking about the hundred-and-fifty-year-old bottles . . . ? You're not telling me this, Mr. Fradden. Because if that's what you were telling me, if you were even suggesting that some fifteen-year-old junky's sipping his bloody vintage wine in some bloody ally . . . you're a bloody dead man talking."

Fradden darted his focus over the nearest audience, lashing his gaze upward. "Keep your voice down, for Chrissake. You'll get me fucking killed."

"I'd kill you myself if I thought it would help," Darius hissed softly, his anger and anxiety rising as he realized the possible consequences of such a blunder. He shook his head, refusing to consider the possibility, needing to think and maintain control. "All right," he said in a controlled voice. "Tell me exactly how this happened. You mentioned phone calls. Is it possible the shipment went out, and it's sitting in a warehouse?"

Fradden shook his head; his entire posture reflected a whipped mutt betrayed only by the conflicts of anger and fear in his dark eyes. "That's what I hoped. The shipment was supposed to go out three weeks ago. It came into the warehouse on a Monday night. On Tuesday, we had another break-in, but it didn't look like anything was missing. Wednesday morning, we had three different shipments going out. The wine was supposed to be on the second one. A few days ago, I received a call from our branch office in London. They're asking me, where the fuck's the wine. So, I'm going nuts trying to track it. Then I remembered the fucking break-ins." He lifted a hand, smoothing his sweat-glistening scalp. Fear lighted higher in his eyes. "I don't know what the hell to do."

"Did you talk to the police?" *Please!*

"I can't fucking go to the police," Fradden hissed, angry again.

"If you've had break-ins—"

"Wise the fuck up," Fradden said with unnatural anger and audacity. "Not everything coming through the fucking house is straight up. I've got a few customs officials in my pocket, but we drag the fucking cops into this, the next thing we have the DEA crawling down our necks," he hissed in a low voice, his glare far more intense. "The old man keeps your ass clean because you're the fucking racehorse, Darius, but some of us work the trenches—"

His anger snapped like dry kindling. Darius advanced a step, never moving his hands from his pockets to back Fradden against the wall. Glaring down into the wide eyes, Darius growled, "Who the fuck do you think you're talking to, Larry?"

"I-I'm sorry, all right," Fradden stammered, seeming only now to realize what he'd said.

Only more annoyed, Darius glared into the more frightened eyes, holding the older man by the force of his anger. The words were not Fradden's, Darius knew at this moment. He might as well be looking into Amad's eyes. Still, Darius remained poised, exercising his will not to lift the man and slam him against the wall. "You do have a problem, Larry," he said in a low, volatile tone. "Several, in fact. Only beginning with the fact that the Baron probably knew two seconds after you did, that his wine's gone amiss. Ending with the fact that I really don't give a bloody damn what you do about your problems. Deal with them. We all have our crosses to bear, and this is one I won't even consider carrying unless I receive a direct order from on high. I'll give you a few words of advice," he continued angrily and dipped his head to hiss near the man's ear. "Find his fucking wine because, I can assure you, that's first and foremost on a priority list." Recoiling, Darius started to turn and halted before the hand clasped firmly on his jacket. At an angle, he looked into the desperate eyes with a warning high in his own.

"Darius, I'm sorry. I'm fucking sorry. I need your—"

"Back off, or I'll put you through that bloody wall," Darius said in a low voice and the chap shrank. The hand shot away and Darius continued his turn to find more than a dozen faces turned toward him, not excluding Whitman who stood two table-lengths away. Despite his words, Darius would call Kevin but not on an open traceable frequency. Checking his watch, Darius continued to Whitman.

"Is everything alright?" Whitman asked, darting his gaze off Darius to see Fradden hurrying toward the entrance.

"Of course," Darius commented, deciding he could use another drink before retiring for the night.

Not entirely relieved, Deke commented hesitantly, "Larry's not been acting quite right since he arrived. I hope it's nothing serious."

"I'm sure he'll handle whatever it is," Darius said smoothly and moved Whitman with body language alone. "Why don't I buy you a drink? You look a bit peaked. . ."

4

Not for all the tea in China would Jenna have wanted to stand in that man's shoes, and watching Darius back him into the corner hadn't relieved her thought. If Brock could become furious over an interrupted dance, she hated to see what he might do with a serious reason to be angry. As if his anger were a purely physical essence, the tension had spiked through him with a force to send her muscles recoiling. And to Jenna's dismay, she realized the accuracy of another of Lisa's benedictions. Darius Brock could be cruel, if not outright dangerous, despite how alluring and lulling those moments in his arms.

She wasn't alone too long with her thoughts before Evan returned carrying an extra drink and settling into the seat next to her, handing her the glass. "Gin and tonic," he mused. "Just as the lady likes it, according to our friend at the bar."

Relaxing, she thanked him and welcomed the clink of glass in a silent toast.

Faintly troubled, wearing a subdued smile, Evan commented, "Darius the Great strikes again."

"Excuse me?"

"Jenna," he said soberly, consolingly. "He's a dead end, and I'm not merely saying that because I find you extremely attractive. The man has a one-tracked mind, and it doesn't even roll in the same direction as the rest of the world. Granted, I've never seen him dance with the same woman twice in a row, but—" His gaze drifted toward where Darius had fallen into another large crowd, smiling and laughing. No less sober, almost pensive, Evan commented, "He looks pretty tired tonight."

Uncertain of what to make of Trevane's conflicting compassion toward Brock—one minute sounding slightly envious, the next genuinely concerned—Jenna decided against figuring it out. In fact, her own weariness was beginning to register. The party had spread out. Most of the tables had cleared, but the waiters and waitresses kept a running watch on empty glasses and filled ashtrays. The party was in full swing. Aside from the fellow who'd skulked out after an apparent dressing down, not another guest donned a coat. Most had loosened ties or jackets and let down their hair. Even Mason appeared content ensconced within an older crowd around a table across the room. Her gaze adrift, her attention halted on the French doors. Beyond the small rectangular panes, a white glow masked the coach lights, thick enough to mask the obvious.

Three to four inches, a weatherman had announced earlier, and Jenna wondered if that forecast could have changed. Her gaze fanning over the guests, the crowd at the bar, she considered the prearranged reservations that would spare about half of these fellows from a drive home on slick roads.

"Evan," she started before realizing he'd been watching her, studying her perhaps. "I've had a lovely evening," she said and rose smoothly, touching his shoulder before he could slide from his chair. "Don't get up on my account. If you'll excuse me?"

"You can't be leaving this early," he sounded aghast at the idea.

"With the way that snow's falling, we may have a rush on rooms," she said while remembering Trevane's reservation. "If nothing else, I need an update on the weather forecast and road conditions. I'd rather not have any of our staff stranded. I'm sure I'll see you again. The night is young."

"Are you working in the morning?" he asked.

"Not tomorrow."

He appeared disappointed until wondering, "Have you a room for this evening?"

"I don't live far," she said with a knowing smile and patted his shoulder. "See you later."

A stop at the bar assured her that the liquor supply would hold out, and she slipped into the kitchen where she chitchatted with Harry. According to the last radio broadcast, the snowfall should taper off after midnight with isolated pockets of accumulation up to six inches.

"We'll probably get the full six," Harry forecasted. "But Bob has the crew working overtime to clear the main entrance and lots."

"Something tells me you've been through this often," Jenna commented, and again, considered the probable flood of guests. "I think I better find out how many more rooms we have available."

At the front desk, as Rene took a call and Mark handled a check-in, Jenna pulled up the reservations on the computer, not entirely pleased to find they had twenty-seven rooms vacant, most singles, and if she included the open suites on the sixth floor, she still might come up short. The party had accommodated a hundred and fifty guests, and judging by the crowd, none had canceled. Checking the roster, she verified they could be about thirty rooms short. Muttering, she double-checked the numbers as Rene came alongside her, not quite looking over her shoulder.

When Jenna had begun working at the Chateau six months earlier, Rene had held a full-time position, but she, like Mark, had dropped to part-time when their fall college semesters started. No malice existed in the young woman. Rene was smart, no-nonsense, a pretty young woman in a teenage way despite her twenty-plus years, and generally, as pleasant-natured as Jenna. "Is there something I can help you with, Miss Windrow?"

"Unless you can build an extra wing in the next ten minutes or have an uncle with an R.V. dealership nearby, I don't think so."

Rene smiled, but she wasn't entirely amused. "I can't, and I don't. And that was my mom on the phone. She just heard on the 11: o'clock news—the airport's delaying and canceling flights, and the roads are already a disaster. If it gets too bad, we'll be booked solid before long."

"Lovely," Jenna mused. "I've been waiting for a full house for six months, and we're about to end up wall-to-wall, standing room only within the hour." Considering a half second, Jenna decided, "Find out how many cots we can provide and have one delivered to my office if you will. We may need to turn those singles into doubles. I'll phone you from the dining room." As Jenna started from the reception area, Rene spoke her name, halting her.

Rene appeared misty-eyed for a moment, smiling slightly. "I just wanted to tell you, you look fantastic. That dress is gorgeous on you."

"I agree," Mark said, and blushed as he returned his focus to the registration papers he'd been shuffling.

"Thank you both," Jenna said lightly despite her surprise and mild discomfort. Receiving compliments from men was certainly not unusual, even without spending a small fortune on a dress, but gaining the appreciation of the same gender usually delivered a false note . . . and that was Jenna's all-time low in cynical thoughts for this evening. Rene had neither feigned her appreciation nor belied the words with a motive toward brown-nosing.

Striding through the halls, Jenna steeled her nerve, wishing this evening was over, wishing the orchestra was already packed up and loaded into their van, wishing the kitchen was empty and the dining room dressed for breakfast. Her wishes collapsed to the sound of rowdy laughter and revelry, to the sight of a crowded dance floor and bar where serious drinkers and businessmen congregated. Without wasting a stride, Jenna found Mason and drew him aside, providing the update and watching his face turn grimmer despite his flushed cheeks and the liquid shine. She'd never seen him drunk, but this was probably as close as he came to that condition.

Patting her arm, he tried a smile, stating, "I'll handle it, dear. Just give me a moment."

Mason handled it by singling out Whitman, who waded into the bar crowd and emerged two minutes later with no other than Darius Brock in tow. Standing aside, Jenna caught the dark eyes only for a second before he smiled and turned, striding on a deliberate, steadfast course through the mishmash of tables. As he moved, he touched, brushing hands at men's shoulders, clasping fingers of women who reached toward him. Pensive, tense, Jenna watched him, deciding he would make a splendid politician. Her attention shifted to Whitman and Mason, both following Brock's course without near the accolades or tributes. She lost sight of Brock as he slipped into the dance crowd. He emerged, stepping onto the stage, and the orchestra sounds tapered, falling silent as Darius removed the microphone from its temporary base.

"Ladies and gentlemen," his rich, deep voice slid from the speakers with a baritone rhythm that could have accompanied the orchestra with no trouble at all. "It has reached my attention that we have a situation developing beyond these walls. The weather, so it appears, intends to dampen our festivities this evening . . ." He wasted few words, and within seconds, Jenna stood with her lips gaping slightly at his solution. Without hesitation, he informed the guests, employees, and friends of Hendricks Distributing, that the remainder of the hotel vacancies would be reserved by the von Hendricks Corporation for anyone who chose to spend the night.

"We may need to double up, but hopefully, we'll have cots rather than floors. Rooms will be secured on a first-come, first-serve basis, but do pull together. We'd like no one left stranded. At least two, preferably four to a room, would accommodate the bulk of us. Anyone intending to drive in this ghastly business should defer to the coffee stations very soon."

He paused as he lowered and covered the microphone, then engaged the head musician in private conversation. Smiling, nodding, he lifted the microphone. "Our immensely talented artists have agreed to extend their hours and will continue to enthrall us into the wee hours. A word to the wise, person to person, my friends, laugh in the face of adversity, and I believe the American saying is . . . party on?" To the sounds of cheers, hails, and laughter, he added, "Reservations first, though, if you please. Enjoy." With a nod to the musicians, he signaled them to continue as he returned the microphone to its stand. In a single smooth motion, he stepped off the stage and disappeared as if swallowed.

Obviously, he was not coming out. When next Jenna spotted his dark hair, it was mixed within a crown of wild black tangles, and she had no time to wonder if he would offer an encore. As if obeying a divine decree, dance partners scattered with the men heading toward the door. Obviously, headed for the front desk. As Jenna started to turn, Mason flagged her from the kitchen entrance, and she strode on a collision course through the tables, noting his smile.

"All taken care of, dear. Now, do relax," he advised. "I've spoken to Mark. I'm sure, he and Rene can handle the registrations. You're not planning to drive home, are you?"

"I've had a cot sent to my office," she admitted.

"Very good then," he said smoothly and patted her arm. "Relax, now, Jenna. That's an order. You've worked hard for this evening, and we don't get many opportunities like this."

Taking the order to heart, Jenna exercised her right to return to the kitchen and collected a cup of coffee, engaging Harry and his staff in light-hearted conversation. Returning to the merrymakers, she navigated a path to the abandoned table where the evening had begun. Her drink remained, but Trevane had turned his aspirations toward another. In genuine relief, she was alone for the moment. As much as she loved coordinating these events, she'd never combined pleasure with responsibility.

Enjoying the music, the view, the crackle of the fire, she was lost in her private world until she felt his presence—an almost tangible presence that prickled the hair at the nape of her neck.

Appearing at her side, Darius smiled, asking almost playfully, "Is there even a remote possibility that we might finish our dance?"

"I'm a little tired," she said honestly, although, under different circumstances, her weariness wouldn't have prevented her from another dance. As much as she might enjoy his company, however, as drawn by his smiles and charisma as all others in attendance, some people were better admired from a distance. Darius Brock was dangerous on too many levels, from his easy smiles to his intense dark eyes. Now he stood looking at her with a slightly tainted smile quivering his mustache, his thoughts cloaked behind a mahogany shine. "I think I'd rather pass. But I appreciate the offer."

"Would you mind terribly if I join you then?"

She did. But she shook her head slightly, gesturing to the next chair. "Please do."

He considered, and possibly something in her eyes or expression lent him pause before he slipped smoothly into the seat. "I'd like to apologize if I offended or . . . worried you in any way earlier, Jenna."

He sounded sincere, but as the subdued light played over his handsome features, she wondered if his sensuous smile might hide a world of sins. "You have a lot of responsibilities," she said lightly, remembering his position, and his function in the company. The Hatchet man, she'd heard, among other titles unrelated to market analysis. "And I doubt you've reached your position by being a pushover. There's no reason to apologize."

A soft wonder affected his eyes momentarily, his gaze slightly haunted as he commented, "You're an amazing young woman, Jenna."

She smiled faintly, a bit too weary to accept yet another dose of male flattery designed to secure a little female comfort at the end of the evening. As much as she knew she'd enjoy the experience, she had no intention of becoming another notch in a gunslinger's belt.

"Why do I have the feeling you've heard that line before?" he asked with a crinkle at the corner of his long lashes, a deeper kink at one end of his mustache.

With his English accent, his voice alone could offer new breath to any trite line, and with her thought, she reflected, "At least a dozen times this evening alone, but I never tire of flattery."

"Hmm, don't suppose you'd believe I was merely stating a fact, then, would you?"

"I appreciate the compliment, either way," she answered, slightly amused and enjoying the play of light on his dark, brooding eyes. He was a strange man, a conflict, and if she would encounter him bi-annually, she needed to set a precedent. "How long will you be staying with us?"

His thought shifted as if a dial turned. He reached for his drink while shrugging. "If the weather holds, I'm scheduled to fly out at dawn."

He pronounced the word 'sheduled,' she noticed as surely as the soft note of weariness in his tone. Evan's observation was accurate. Despite his constant motion and smiles, weariness underlaid his intensity. "It must be difficult keeping pace," she said, and his dark eyes flashed an odd heat. She had dealt with enough weary travelers to sense his misplaced anger, his volatile state under high pressure and hectic schedules. If this evening was any indication, he was a man forced to maintain pretenses, to keep smiling from the moment he entered a room, to mingle and address the woes of the world, and to solve problems with no regard for his own. "I've heard you spend a lot of time in the air," she said quietly. "Where do you call home?"

As if she'd slapped him, he held steady momentarily, then seemed to withdraw and study her from a greater distance without moving a single muscle. "A little flat in London," he answered without inflection. "Ironically," he donned a slightly bemused smile, which covered another world of sins as he glanced about the room. "It's a suite in a hotel much like this one, but it suits my needs," he said offhandedly, his gaze steady again. "I understand you live not far from here. You're from this area originally?"

He wanted the subject changed, apparently uncomfortable discussing himself. "Yes, I am," she said lightly and continued, "When you leave tomorrow, are you headed home?"

More curious, slightly wary, he commented, "I do so on rare occasions."

She trailed her gaze over his eyes and face, over the curve of his lips, then met his gaze. "If that was an affirmation, Darius, and if it's at all possible, I'd suggest taking a little time off. Even the little things become major when you push too long and too hard. I know I don't know you well enough to offer advice, but I've had a lot of experience with seasoned travelers. I don't know the English idiom, but the American term is fairly accurate. People tend to burn out under constant high pressure."

"Appears I've made an extremely bad impression," he said with a cute smile, his gaze unamused. "Assuming that's your observation, have I done something to justify your concern perhaps, in performance or reflection of the parent company?"

Feeling bad for him without a clear thought, she shook her head. "You've been the epitome of efficiency and showmanship, Darius, and I'd imagine you're well aware of it. You don't strike me as a man lacking confidence or one who needs constant praise to work well under pressure. I'm speaking from a personal perspective. I've always been something of an overachiever. Pushing is easy; slowing down is hard. I get caught up in my private races and forget the rest of the world has to tolerate me," she smiled honestly, flashing her gaze toward the tree, returning and seeing the strange light in his eyes. "I do get carried away on occasion. And to make matters worse, I'm a perfectionist. Granted, I don't have nearly the responsibilities you have, but I generally put more pressure on myself than others. And as the saying goes, it takes one to know one, honey. You need a break."

For a few seconds, the confirmation and acknowledgment hovered on his lips, but he masked his emotions as if dropping a curtain and studying her far more critically. "You truly are an amazing woman, Jenna. A rare and uniquely direct woman in the broader collection. Are you sure I couldn't convince you to share one more dance before I retire for the evening?"

When he looked at her with that dark shine and spoke in that deep tone, he was nearly irresistible, but with a thought of his plane leaving at dawn and the hour advancing toward midnight, she decided, "I'm sure, hon. It'll probably take you an hour to reach the door, and dawn isn't getting any further away." Before he could comment, she wondered, "Will you need a wake-up call?"

"I won't, but if I were staying until a reasonable hour, I'd be inclined to request a personal, verbal message off your lips," he said with a cagey, catty smile.

When he offered his hand, she reached automatically to bid him adieu and should have guessed he wouldn't settle for a handshake.

As he rose, he leaned and kissed her cheek rather than her lips, squeezing her fingertips as he ascended to his full height. "A unique and undefinable pleasure to meet you, Jenna. I do hope I'll see you again."

"I'm sure you will," she said lightly. Judging by this crowd, she might still be awake when he left for the airport. "Take care."

"You do the same, Luv," he said and winked, turning, leaving her to wonder if she'd misjudged him by a mile.

Watching him navigate a path toward Whitman, she countered her thoughts and smiled fondly. She hadn't misjudged the weariness, but the man hadn't reached his level of success by allowing personal issues to cloud his responsibilities. A market analyst, she'd heard, but she'd met enough to know—Darius Brock was slightly more valuable to the von Hendricks Corporation. His occupation was probably a collaboration of P.R. man and troubleshooter. The old man, Thaddeus von Hendricks, had known what he was doing when hiring this fellow. She wondered how many problems Darius had solved just by walking into this room and judging by the mob descending on him to say their farewells, she surmised quite a few.

5

Agitated, tense for no definite reason, Darius entered his suite on the sixth floor, scanning the serenity and grandeur with a scathing glance. He loathed the silence nearly as much as he'd despised the noise level ascending the hallways. Sleep was out of the question. Not even a slight possibility in fact. He moved to the fully stocked bar, stripping off his jacket and tossing it on a chair, hearing the thud of the mobile phone hitting the carved wood. For a split second, he worried about breaking the damn thing, then cursed his thought and concentrated on pouring a drink. Unconsciously, his gaze dropped to his watch. Only slightly past midnight.

The witching hour. He couldn't even remember when last he might have slept at this hour, and considering the time zones he crossed, the thought disturbed him. Not that it should. Twisting his days into nights and nights into days was only another of the games the grandmaster played. Not uncommon, Darius could leave at midnight and arrive at midnight or arrive at dawn and return to the blasted dawn without ever seeing a sunset. Warped. Time. Life. Reality. Whatever firm grasp Darius had once held on reality had snapped years ago.

Bourbon in hand, he moved from behind the bar and strode across the thick carpet into the bedroom. Ornately carved, the reproduction rendition of an eighteenth-century bed stood against the deep wall. The tall spiral columns rose nearly to the beamed ceiling overhead. Whether the room reflected the ambiance of an ancient pub or an actual bedroom, he couldn't decide. He'd seen similar rooms—original rooms—and knew damn well this hotel was designed with the integrity of another era, even without its roots in the turn of the century.

The master knew his game. He'd probably formed his strategy a few hundred years ago. The Chateau Suite, located less than twenty miles from the booming steel city, was only one more confirmation in the overall scheme. Wherever life throbbed, wherever the economy thrived, the von Hendricks name could be found, and this hotel chain was only one more connection in the network.

Darius barely stepped through the bathroom door, determined to soak the offensiv blend of colognes and perfumes from his pores, when he heard the hateful sound of that phone muffled through the open doors. Cursing, he pivoted and sped through the rooms, recovering his jacket and setting the glass down smoothly before fumbling the contraption to silence and snapping it to his ear. "Yes."

"Darius!"

His heart skipped a shocked beat at the shout, then settled as a smile slid into his lips, and relief swept through his system. "How many times need I tell you, lil chap? You don't need to shout in the telly."

Stifled, hushed, the soft voice slipped through the receiver. "I'm sorry. I think I'm getting senile. Where are you?"

Amused at the childish voice, the subtle attempt to sound mature, Darius commented, "Pittsburgh, USA."

"I doon't like this damn telly. Noot one damn bit. How am I supposed to know where ye are if ye could be anywhere? Pittsburgh. Are you in a car? On a roof? In the bloody air or doing what you do, eh?"

At the latter thought, Darius lost his slight amusement. "I'm in my suite at the Chateau."

"Good! I'll ring you there!" the young voice snapped.

Before Darius could breathe another word, the clatter of the dropped receiver erupted through the static. He shook his head, lowering the phone from his ear, sidling to the couch, and settling onto the cushion nearest the land phone on the end table. The little monster could call immediately or wait an hour just for the hell of it. Darius had forfeited any attempt to figure out Raphael long ago, but the sound of his thick Scottish brogue was a welcome relief on any phone line. As he settled back against the soft cushion to wait, Darius remembered his vow and made a mental note to ring the front desk. When the hubbub settled, he would jaunt downstairs.

The jangled ring interrupted his thought, and Darius reached, lifting the receiver nearly to his ear, anticipating another shout. "Yes."

"Helloo!"

Amused, again relieved, Darius brought the receiver closer. "Hello."

A giggle slid through the line. "I loove this telly."

"I'd never guess," Darius mused, considering how often this devil damned imp engaged the modern convenience. "How's everything?"

"Aye," the voice sobered abruptly. "There's what I'd call to learn from you, sir."

Despite the soft notes and the young voice, the intensity slid a shiver down Darius's spine. "What's wrong?"

"Aye, and there's the other question I have a mind to ask of you," Raphael said gravely. "Pappa's been in a fine rage. Ranting without e'er raising his voice and that's naw a fine state of affairs, I'll mention, sir," he sounded dreary now. His voice carried a desperate note. "Raging fierce, so he is. Was but a thought to have at a bit of fun, and he had at me. Quick as you blink, turned me heels to hither and walloped me to hell and back. Now, and do you know why—or who—we've to thank for this state of affairs?"

Darius might suffer an inkling, but not one he would share with a child, even if the child happened to be a boiling pot of contradictions and an anomaly to life itself. "Where's Kevin?"

"Keeping his distance if he's as smart as I'm giving him credit for being. Pappa's in no fair mood for practical advice."

Damn Lawrence Fradden! "Raphael, truth, my lad. Where's Kevin?"

"Aye, he's aboot, but nay pleased to be so, I can tell you."

Deciding he would phone Kevin directly rather than attempt pressing his luck with Raphael, Darius hesitated before another, more troubling thought crossed his mind. "Uh . . .? How's Dylan?"

Hesitation, naturally, then almost offhandedly, "You didnae ask aboot me, Darius. I'm ooffended. D' ye ask how I am after I've admitted to what's been done here?"

Uncomfortable, Daruis realized the accuracy as fierce as his regret. "Now, I am sorry, Raphael, but I'd rather hoped you were fabricating. Are you all right, pal?"

"Aye. Tis a fine thing to be back from hell," he admitted with a guarded note. "And I forgive you," he added drearily. "I wish you were here."

Heart aching, Darius slumped in the cushion, suddenly more tired as his gaze trailed about the empty room. No way out. Only that thought lingered in his mind as he sank on an even keel with the tempo of the voice from several thousand miles away. In one blinding flash of insanity . . . But that wasn't true either. Fate. Heredity. He'd been locked into this madness before he'd ever drawn his first breath. To believe otherwise was a fool's dream. "I wish I were there, too, m' lil lad," he said honestly, though what good it would do, he couldn't fathom. Whether he stood in the von Hendricks manse or across the globe, he wore the mark of the devil.

Unconsciously, his attention fell to his thumb in sharp contrast to the dark liquid in the glass. The scar was barely visible, now. Long ago healed to be little more than another hairline crack scored across the whirls of his personal stamp. Symbolism. Unique unto itself, a thumbprint symbolized the individuality of all men. His was sliced in half, severed. Whether he was half a man or merely severed from the mainstream, culled like a calf to be branded and slaughtered, he could never decide. He had no choice, had never had a bloody choice.

"Darius?" the soft voice intruded, a hint of irritation rising. "What's a dildo?"

Startled, abruptly amused, Darius wondered if Raphael had asked merely to throw him off his mood. "Ask Kevin," Darius advised.

"He said to ask you," Raphael said smugly.

The little shit probably knew the answer and merely found the entire ploy too good to resist. "We'll talk about it another time."

"Men!" Raphael huffed, sounding as disgusted and irritated as ever. "I dinnae see why we need put off sooch a simple question. Well, and there's the crux of it, then. You lads thrive on suspense. Loove to keep me guessing. Fine, then. That settles it."

"Settles what?"

"I won't tell you a thing, Darius. You'll need pay a visit to learn a single thing from me hereafter."

"You're being cruel."

"Aye, and I'm damn good at it," Raphael said in a low, angry tone.

"If the question's bothering you that bad—"

"It's not," he stated more angrily. "I know what the bloody hell a dildo is. Do ye think me an idiot? It's you I'll need worry about if ye cannae even answer a simple question. Maybe I should tell you, instead, if yee have some question in your mind to the function of sooch a device."

"Hey, pal?" Darius interrupted, a smile quivering on his lips despite the temper singeing the line. "Take it easy on me this evening, will you? I'm a wee bit weary, and it's well after midnight here. I'm assuming you haven't been up too long . . . Or are you getting ready for bed?" he asked, suddenly not entirely sure of which time zone he occupied. As instructed, he set his watch by the announcements from the cockpit, whether traveling via private jet or commercial flight. *Time. Damn [it.*

"Darius, are you alright?" the voice came with flawless English, the sound as concerned now as a parent.

"I did mention, I'm a little tired," Darius admitted, aware of how swiftly this night child could react to voice tones and subtle inflect. "Will you tell me, now . . .? How's Dylan?"

"I doon't want to talk aboot it," the voice changed again, edgy.

Tense abruptly, reacting just as swiftly, Darius controlled the mild panic threatening to swell through his system. "Come on, Raphael," he asked quietly, not quite pleading but sincerely concerned. He'd lost his rights. By no design of his own making or act of his free will, he'd forfeited his legal and parental rights to his only true son. Still, there were moments when he needed to know, needed to verify the boy's safety. Only twice . . . only twice in seven bloody long years had he set eyes upon his natural creation. Dylan would be thirteen . . . had turned twelve only a few months earlier. Three years? Had three bloody years passed since Darius had stood within arm's reach and looked upon the face of his child asleep on a satin pillow . . .?

Beautiful. The lad was beautiful when he slept. He possessed his mother's pale brown hair and soft brown eyes. The shape of his eyes and his face remained a reflection of his paternal heritage . . . and if ever Darius could regret a gift more, never more than when he realized what else he'd unwittingly gifted to his son.

"Raphael?" he asked, starkly aware of the silence stretching through the line. Not often would Darius ask or pursue an answer, half afraid of what he might hear, half afraid he would be stripped of even that single right to wonder. That Christmas tree. All the damned memories rising from the distant corners of his mind . . .

"You know he's getting older, Darius," the soft voice spoke with a careful note.

His heart slammed a mean beat, his stomach cramped, and his muscles knotted. Too damned well, he knew the child was getting older. Feared daily over that blasted natural progression. Darius needed only to look in a mirror, a dreading event he suffered daily, to know how much time had passed. He was not the same ignorant fool of twenty-two who'd accepted an alarming invitation in the bloody hopes of finding his missing son.

"He's getting older, Darius," Raphael said in a low, dreading tone. "And . . . And I willnae tell you a thing more," he decided in a firm, almost agitated voice. "I dinnae want to talk aboot this. I'll tell you when I see you."

Gripping the receiver, his palm suddenly damp, Darius realized there was something Raphael knew, some other reason for this call. "Raphael, you can't say something like that and leave me hanging—" Darius knew his mistake an instant too late to make amends.

"Can and will," Raphael snapped.

The force of the receiver slamming into its cradle jolted Darius. "No! God-damn it!" Slamming his own receiver down, he pushed off the couch in one motion. How could he have been so damned stupid yet again? A slip of the tongue. Just another slip of the tongue! As much as he'd come to love that devil-damned child, Darius knew better than to trust him. Might even hate him as often as he loved him. "How the bloody hell could it be any other way?" he muttered aloud, pacing, draining his bourbon, heading toward the bar for another.

Nothing. It had to be nothing. Just another of Raphael's wild, mean-spirited games. The boy had said he wanted to have a little fun and had gotten into trouble with his father for pulling one stunt or another. Between the two of them, it was a wonder the child even survived a single bloody day. His thought only sent a shudder sailing down his spine to shake the bourbon glass in his hand. His blood son was caught up in that madness! *Dylan could be . . . no! Goddamn it!* He would not even venture that thought! The Baron would . . . could . . . might.

Tears rose unbidden, burning his eyes with as much anger as fear. He'd promised himself, had vowed years ago to wipe this thought, this possibility from his mind.

"Bloody hell," Darius uttered and strode from behind the bar, moving to the phone, wanting, needing that phone to ring. Wiping his eyes, fighting an urge to lift the receiver, he stood trembling, waiting, hoping Raphael would change his mind. To call and press for details would be certain folly. A child . . . Raphael was a child. A cruel and sometimes malicious child but a child, nevertheless. If he'd wanted a human reaction, if he'd needed it, it was too damned possible the boy had satisfied his need at Darius's expense. The thought offered no relief or quick consolation. Trembling internally, Darius waited, glaring at the phone, willing it to ring. In retrospect, he could imagine Raphael reacting to his father's rage. This wouldn't be the first time the boy had chosen Darius to catch the heat rather than deliver the blow to Dylan.

"Let it be that simple," Darius hissed, restraining his panic. As much as he'd like to strangle Raphael for putting him through this, for using his wiles to create this turbulence . . . Darius couldn't help but recall the dread in those first notes, the anger in the second string of words . . . And the prickling sense of dread niggling at the edges of Darius's mind too often recently.

On the brink of an explosion, his throat tight with a knot, his muscles leaped at the erupting ring. In one motion, he grabbed the receiver and landed on the couch. "Yes!"

"I'm sorry, Darius," the soft voice lamented, worried. "I'm sorry. Are you mad at me?"

"N-n-no," Darius stammered, collecting his senses, his head sinking to catch on his palm. "No. I'm not mad."

"Darius," Raphael said in a soft strain. "A-are you crying?"

"C-close," he said with a genuine strain in his voice. "Very close, m'lad. D-don't . . . don't do this to me again."

"Darius, I . . . I willnae be able . . . I'm sorry," he whined.

Suddenly more worried, more alarmed, Darius uttered, "Ra-aphael?"

"Pa-appa took him," Raphael whined on the brink of a sob. "Pappa took him from me."

"Ah . . . ugh . . . n-no, Rafe . . . don't. Don't tell me this. Don't lie to me, now. Y-you won, pal. Don't—"

"I'm sorrry," Raphael whined. "I didnae want to tell you on the phone," he said while firming slowly, surely, and far more rapidly than Darius, who rested poised, staring at the carpet between his shoes through a wall of tears. "I didnae m-mean to make you cry either," he said solemnly and continued, "I joost didnae ken how to tell you, Darius. D-Dylan's gotten older. Taller . . . He's a fine lad, Darius. Pa-appa hasn't hurt him. Pappa won't hurt him, Darius. He . . . he just had to take him from me. He won't take him from you again. He can't. It's . . . it's joost my own self I'm worried for. I love Dylan. He's . . . we're still to be friends. I know Pappa's mad at me just now, but he won't take sooch out on Dylan. We'll play again. A-are yee mad at me, Darius?"

As if a vacuum had swept the air from his chest, Darius could neither answer nor breathe, felt nothing at the apex of pain . . . but the swell threatened to break inside of him.

"Darius?" Raphael whined softly, his voice a gentle cry through the vacuum.

Tears threatening, Darius trembled with the force of his will to restrain the anger and pain vying for space in his mind.

"I-I shouldnae have tooold you!" Raphael cried angrily.

"Ah . . . uh," Darius swallowed and lifted the trembling drink to his lips. He tasted as much salt as smooth bourbon as he gulped the smooth, dark liquid to clear the lumps and strain from his throat. Swallowing hurt. Everything hurt. His senses swam in a maelstrom of confusion and pain. Dylan . . . Dylan would be all right. Dylan had to be all right. Nothing had changed! Nothing! His son remained in the Baron's keep where he'd existed for the past eight years. Nothing had changed. If anything . . . if anything, the Baron had merely used Raphael to make one Darius Brock pay mentally for whatever pleasure he'd stolen this evening.

No pleasure went unrewarded. For every bloody smile, twice the tears must shed, and the Baron had gotten him again. Twice over, Darius knew at this moment. Taking Dylan from Raphael . . . terror and sorrow. Not just his pain. He felt it all. Terror for Dylan's safety, when the child's safety had existed beyond Darius's reach, out of his hands for years. Pain and sorrow for Raphael, who never understood the complexities of his devious mind. The boy had called with a sense of what seemed right; he'd phoned to share his pain.

The sobs broke against Darius's ear, soft hiccupping sobs over the possible loss of his friend, his only playmate, as surely as the child cried now for delivering such a mortal blow to his other friend. In soft heaves, Raphael lamented his evil for hurting Darius so badly, regretting his decision to call, pleading for forgiveness, for comfort.

If ever a child needed more comfort or forgiveness or wrenched more sorrow from a chilled heart, none more than Raphael. Heart breaking, Darius drew from whatever remained of his human compassion and spilled it through the line, comforting, assuring, collecting his equilibrium as he offered whatever Raphael needed.

Tangled and twisted, this relationship had forged on a night long ago.

Long after the line disengaged, Darius rested with his head caught between his hands, his elbows on his knees, remembering.

Moonlight . . . brilliant silver moonlight had spilled through the narrow windows, slicing across the room . . . slicing across the cherub face of a child hovering above him. A dream, a nightmare . . . no other thought had held firmer as Darius had jolted from a shallow sleep, but the nightmare hadn't ended. Stricken, thunderstruck, he'd stared into the feral eyes caught in the moonlight . . . red . . . wolf. But the face of a child, pale and round. A haunted smile had lingered on the soft, full lips, and the long black lashes had dipped down, shading the eyes that appeared more naturally blue as the tussled black ringlets tipped aside to escape the light.

Softly, sorrowfully, honestly . . . the child had spoken to him. 'I cannae give him back to you . . . Pappa gave him to me . . .' And the stunning little boy had made him a promise, '. . . to love him like me own brother . . . me friend . . . never be cruel to him . . . as long as I can . . .'

For him, for his friendship, for his understanding, Darius knew the child had kept his promise. Dylan had never known cruelty, only kindness at Raphael's hands. If nothing else, Darius knew that was true if only by the words Kevin slipped to him. Against every black thread of Raphael's nature, the boy had kept his promise, sharing only his innocence and decency, offering only friendship and protection.

As if punched in the stomach, Darius huffed a soft, pained breath, fearing for his son, fearing for himself if he ever learned the boy suffered a horror. And how could it be any other way? Trapped. Chained. Worse things than death. Only that thought offered a counterbalance to the rage that rocked through Darius's system. To live in ignorance had been bliss. To live at all had become hell . . . and there was no escape. Accept it. Whatever right or privilege had existed before his awakening had been forfeited.

The sound of hurried, natural footsteps passing outside his door rousted him from his thoughts, but none too quickly could he rally from the pit of despair. Even knowing, sensing the Baron's handiwork to have driven him this low, Darius couldn't rise to rage. Strength. Rage. Hot-blooded frustration. But he was so damned tired of the games, the motion, the rise and fall of panic at the bloody whim and whimsy of a monster. If he could transcend time, it wouldn't be a monster he would have slain with his bare hands. The Brocks. If he could go back in time, he'd strangle every last male among them and to bloody hell with the consequence of annihilating his own existence.

Anger helped, salving something of his battered spirit, but he wondered how much longer he could muster the strength to become angry. He wasn't twenty-two. Not a hotheaded idiot with a sense of self-righteousness . . . and at his thought, his breath slipped free in a humph. He was the same bloody idiot, and nothing would he have done differently. Not at twenty-two. Not at thirty.

Pushing heavily off his elbows, Darius swiped his sweated hair off his brow and reached for the phone. If this was the cost of that lost wine on him, he despaired to think what his cousin might be suffering. Their employer was a devout believer in equal opportunity damnation. Dialing the long series of numbers, Darius rested through the connections, neither anxious nor impatient as the long-distance ringing started against his ear.

Like him, Kevin answered the line with a single, monotone. "Yes?"

"How's your vision of hell?" Darius asked.

"I wondered if you'd ring any time soon," Kevin spoke with a touch of amusement that quelled a fraction of the dread in Darius's mind. "How are you?"

"On the upside of a downhill slide," Darius answered.

"That good, is it?" Kevin asked.

"Tell me I did something to deserve this, and I'll be happy as hell."

"You won't like what I have to say."

"I was afraid you'd say that."

"But I'll say it anyway."

"I assumed you'd say that."

"You're sitting on a powder keg, cousin, and I don't know how to help you."

"Fuck," Darius said heavily. "I desperately hoped you wouldn't say something like that."

"Then I'm sorry I doused your hope," Kevin said without sounding entirely sincere. "You're in Pittsburgh."

"I was rerouted this afternoon," Darius confirmed. "What is this about, Kev?"

"I'm not entirely sure, unfortunately," Kevin answered hesitantly, and Darius imagined him kicked back within the high-backed leather chair in his den. Day or night, Kevin could be reached within shouting distance of the Baron, but he wasn't fool enough to believe he knew anything more than the Baron intended to tell him. Eight years ago, Kevin Brock had been an extremely successful attorney with a thriving young practice in New York City. He'd made the adjustments, as brilliant now as ever, a corporate law genius and the wizard behind quite a few curtains . . . but he was no happier than Darius. His voice held steady as if negotiating a business contract, and Darius envied no man who needed to face off with Kevin Brock. "I do know the Baron personally routed your plane into Pittsburgh. As I understand, you were to attend the annual appreciation night. I trust all went well."

Considering, Darius wondered which would have outraged his employer more—the decorations or the missing wine? Distracted, he answered, "I have reason to doubt." Perhaps, if he'd strode into the hotel and raised holy hell over the harvest of lights, he would have fared better in this . . . but he'd offered to take matters in hand. Too little, too late? The Baron could sound reasonable while sticking a knife in a beating heart. "If he's annoyed with me, he refrained from hitting me over the head with a reason. Doubtful that's any indication, so if you have an explanation, lad, I'd love to hear it."

"Have you had any problems before today, Darius?"

"I've been adhering to my schedule. As far as I know, I've been following orders to the best of my ability."

"Which translates simply to—you're as unruly as ever, and all's right with your world."

"I don't think I appreciate your translation, cousin," Darius said honestly, warily.

Kevin's harrumph slid through the line. "Have no fear, cousin, our illustrious leader loves your unruly temperament. The more you annoy him, the better he likes you, and as far as I know, you haven't failed to annoy him at every turn."

"That's not fair, Kevin. I grovel as well as the next chap when I feel it's necessary."

Again, Kevin's humph. "Groveling is no more in your nature to do well than it is in my own, my friend. Which brings me to my point, Darius. I don't know why you've landed on the hot seat, but I doubt you've created the situation."

"Kevin, no word games this evening, all right? I ehm . . . I had a call from Raphael."

Silence, then a sigh. "I wondered," Kevin said quietly. "The elf's been miserable for the past few days. I assumed his resolve would have snapped before now. Perhaps, he's learning self-restraint, but I'm more tempted to believe, he loved his misery."

"Days?" Darius asked. "Dylan . . . They've been separated for days?"

Hesitation then, "What exactly did Raphael tell you, Darius?"

"That his father took Dylan from him and if he was lying—"

"He wasn't, as amazing as that sounds," Kevin interrupted.

"Where is Dylan now? How is he, Kevin?"

"A little confused, possibly, but he's fine, Darius. In fact, he's upstairs playing video games with Thomas."

Not sure whether to be furious or relieved, Darius stared at the phone, doubting the simplicity of the words. His son . . . his only son was at his cousin's house playing bloody video games? "What the bloody hell's going on here, Kevin?" Darius snapped in a low, slow boil. "I've been scraped through bloody hell and wrung inside out, and you're telling me that my son's in your house, safe and happy?"

"The Baron's made arrangements for him to attend a boarding school, Darius, and that's all I'm at liberty to say. You know the rules."

Now, it hurt again. The irony and cruelty of the situation was never far from his mind. The tears rose unbidden, burning and stinging despite the anger in his mind. His cousin knew Dylan. Dylan knew Kevin, knew Kevin's sons and daughter. They shared a relationship that was forbidden to Darius, and never was that detail easy to bear. Least of all when he knew, in those scant words, the Baron had forbidden any further communication. "If . . . if he ever needs—"

"Don't do this to yourself, Darius," Kevin said quietly.

With an angry humph, Darius hissed, "What the bloody hell do you expect me to do? Could you fucking live like this if you were me? He's my son!"

"He's not your son, Darius," Kevin stated in a firm tone. "He stopped being your son eight years ago, and you damn well know it. Persecute yourself if that's your desire, but don't delude yourself, cousin. The boy's no more yours than my sons and daughter are mine. We're living an illusion. Drive your Jag. Put on your diamonds. Indulge yourself within the parameters designed. Smile and live with it, cousin. Whatever choices we once enjoyed were stripped away at conception the same as our sons' lives were forfeit the instant we created them."

The silence lingered for seconds, possibly a full minute before Darius realized how badly he'd needed those words slammed into him, shared. "I fucking hate you, cousin."

"Back at you," Kevin snapped. "Now, is there anything you can think of to have our fearless leader in a snit?"

"A . . . snit," Darius said with a slight twitch of a smile. "I believe the words recited to me were more accurate. 'A fine rage,' as I understand. And if this began days ago, I haven't a bloody . . . Ahh, what have you heard from the New York distribution office?"

"Nothing of significance. There was a problem a month or so ago . . . What have you heard?"

Darius recapped the encounter with Lawrence Fradden, not entirely relieved by the ensuing silent commiseration on the line. Like no others, he and Kevin shared the knowledge of the Baron's pet peeves regarding personal possessions.

"Damn it," Kevin said with a firm rein on his concern. "That would explain a great deal; however, it doesn't entirely explain your position, Darius. Pardon the offense, cousin, but you're not generally counted upon to handle business disputes or concerns. If he's put you in the thick of this, he has a reason, but I fail to see what it might be. Have you heard from George?"

"Not since arriving," Darius said in an empty tone.

"Darius," Kevin said with quiet authority. "Steer clear of Fradden. You have more than your share of burdens. Your arrival there might be a coincidence, or more believably, you've just taken care of what you were sent there to accomplish. If Amad sensed a problem in New York, he might have arranged for you to be within Fradden's reach. Personal attaché and courier wear well on you, and you're worth your weight in gold, cousin. The Baron's aware of that."

"Did I mention I hate you?"

"At least once in the past ten minutes," Kevin mused. "Nearly a new record."

"If the boss doesn't know it before I do and you happen to see him, mention I may get snowed in, and I'll take off as soon as the runway clears. Bloody nasty snowstorm here."

"I'm sure if he's annoyed, he'll take it up with Mother Nature," Kevin commented.

"Kevin?" Awaiting the silence, Darius commented, "For what it's worth, I'm sorry to be the bearer of this news, and uh . . . I'll leave that ruddy phone on if you feel the need."

"Noted and appreciated, Darius," Kevin stated, and the edge in his voice reflected his understanding of the possible consequences of delivering this news to their employer. "This may be one of those cases where that old line about 'shit rolling downhill' applies, and you may rest assured, this one will be mashed under a steamroller."

"If there's anything I can do, let me know," Darius offered despite the futility.

"I hate you," Kevin said. "Pleasant dreams."

Darius sent a humph into the phone and signed off feeling slightly better than he had earlier. *Misery loves company,* he thought with a bitter edge and pushed off the couch. Debating between another drink and a hot bath, he strode to the bar, already loosening the buttons of his shirt. Life's small pleasures, self-indulgence. If George phoned—

He barely filled the tumbler, determined to make a dent in his consciousness, when the phone erupted, and his entire system bulked. Capping the bottle, he strolled around the end of the bar and returned to the couch, in no hurry to hear whatever voice would slam him. If he had a genuine nemesis, it was the sound and omnipresence of the telephone. "Yes?"

"Change in plans, m 'lad," the voice dripped with dark amusement.

Jolted, Darius glanced at the liquid sloshing over his hand and nearly muttered a curse aloud. *Twice. Twice in a single night!* This was the last voice he'd expected to hear again so soon, and doubtful his shock went unnoticed. "I'm listening," he said, recovering smoothly.

"Which would you like first, the good news or the bad?" the Baron played in a more natural voice.

"Dealer's choice," Darius stated.

The Baron chuckled, "So it is, m' lad. So, and I'll offer the good news first, You're a pappa again and within spitting distance of the grand event."

And the bad news?

"Unfortunately, it's a little girl," the Baron mused. "I don't fault your effort, m' lad, but you *really* need to do better than this if we're to meet with any success in this endeavor."

"I appreciate your advice," Darius said in a leaden tone. He should be accustomed to this game as well.

"The worst news is this, m' lad, I won't indulge your paternal instincts, nor are you coming home for the holidays," he said lightly. "And the truly grand news, I'm sure you'll agree, is that I'll see you in New York later this evening. I haven't spent the season in the city in some time, and I fully expect you to entertain me with your vast accumulated knowledge. Clear, am I?"

Fradden. "Perfectly, sir," Darius said temperately, wondering how soon he might need to phone Kevin again. New York was Kevin's territory. "Always happy to oblige."

"Liar," the Baron mused. "But you never know, m' lad, you might have a grand time despite yourself. You might even consider this something of a vacation and my gift to you for a job well done. So, and we'll see."

Only after he gripped the receiver for another thirty seconds, Darius realized the conversation had ended and cursed as he dropped the phone to its cradle. He had a theory about that dead air and the absence of a farewell or even an inflect of finale in the voice. No end. No 'good day.' No, 'so long.' Or 'see you again.' Never ending. Never ceasing. Infinity. This was it. The silence on the line offered a pause, an intermission between the next act in an ongoing tragedy. Shakespeare had nothing on the Baron von Hendricks.

Glancing at his watch en route to the bedroom, Darius stole a second glance. Nearly two. The witching hour was long gone . . . or just begun. And to bloody hell with the parameters! If for no other reason than to see the livid shine in Raphael's eyes, Darius confirmed his decision to buy a camera and fill a dozen rolls of film.

6

Passing once more around the kitchen, Jenna satisfied herself that the staff had restored order and prepared for the Saturday morning crowd. Snapping the lights off, she passed through the kitchen, glancing at the clock above the door. Not even four o'clock. She should be relieved with the evening finally ended. Finding accommodations for nearly sixty slightly or immensely intoxicated guests wasn't a job for two college kids. Glancing around the spotless kitchen, Jenna smiled in appreciation for Harry's efficiency and started toward the second door when a sound halted her. Turning, she froze, slightly startled and alarmed to see lights igniting in the main dining room.

The last she'd seen Mason, he was swaying and making his way to his office with as much dignity as he could muster. No one should be inside the dining room unless one of the guests had lost something and asked for Rene or Mark to assist in a search.

Striding to the swinging door, she barely started to push it open when her attention spun and riveted. No other than Darius Brock wove between the tables on a collision course with the glass doors . . . and fir tree. Dressed in dark jeans and a thick gray sweater, he looked as sleek as he appeared in a suit, and he moved with a natural grace, barely whispering a sound on the tile. Curious, she watched him stop at a center table and empty his hands of several bags. Only after he emptied the largest bag, she identified his cargo.

For a half second, she wondered if he'd snuck in here to collect evidence, and in the next, realized he wasn't taking any chances on his memory. He had enjoyed the transformations in this room. A smile slid onto her lips as she watched him rip open more packages, unloading batteries, and film, undoubtedly confiscated from the gift shop off the lobby. What kind of man travels the world and fails to carry a camera? A man with a one-tracked mind, she decided, debating whether to make her presence known or slip away and leave him to his task. Eventually, he'd either feel her watching or turn by accident and catch her in the doorway. Watching him was far too compelling, and if he caught her spying, she would simply tell him the truth and deal with his reaction.

Intent upon his apparent mission, he carried the camera toward the tree, granting her the opportunity to step fully into the dining room and sidle to lean at the wall. Without much effort, he found the switch to light the tree and backed away, merely gazing at it momentarily. He might not believe in Christmas, but he certainly seemed taken by the aesthetics. Almost casually, he lifted the camera, backing further, snapping off different angles, sidling, stooping, and twisting the camera to capture the floor-to-ceiling angle. Expanding his apparent interest, he filled the far corner with rapid clicks and flashes as he continued to step, focus, and snap. Almost in manic fluid motion, he snapped off shots of the fireplace, the doors, the chandeliers, turning—

Jenna saw only spots as the flash scattered through her vision, and she heard the low, deep chuckle with his almost amused, "Serves you right, you little snoop."

"I beg your pardon," she fired back while rising off the wall and wiping the quick blur from her eyes, vaguely aware of the second flash. "I thought you were a mouse," she mused. "Thought I should investigate."

"Hmm, then you've no concept of catching rodents," he fired back. "They don't generally turn on the lights before raiding a kitchen pantry."

"I'm glad you told me," she said, and her vision cleared as he returned to the cluttered table and ejected a roll of film from the camera. Obviously, he was neither offended nor embarrassed to be caught in his enterprise, nor was he easily sidetracked. Even as she strode toward him, he opened another roll of film with his teeth and began reloading. At least a dozen rolls of film—of various shutter speeds—rested in neat stacks within the clutter of empty packages. "A closet photographer, by any chance?" she asked and caught his smirk.

"A hobby once upon a time," he said smoothly and studied her momentarily, running his gaze down and up. "However did you manage that?"

"Pardon me?"

A smile crept more fully into his lips. "You're as beautiful now as you were when I first saw you, and I know you haven't caught a wink of sleep. Most women would bear the look of a wet dishrag after seven or eight hours of hosting a grand ball."

"Either looks are deceiving, or you need glasses, sir. I feel like a dishrag."

He chuckled, shook his head, and snapped the camera shut, clicking off a dozen black shots. "Twenty-twenty eyesight, Luv," he commented and whipped the camera up, snapping a close-up that left her startled and blinded.

"Good grief!" she huffed and covered her stung eyes. "You are a mean man!"

"I'm a self-indulgent creature who absolutely could not resist," he mused. "I'd apologize. But I'm not sorry for that."

"Oh, that makes me feel better," she said and squeezed unemotional tears from her eyes, warily seeking and finding him standing directly in front of her. Without the overwhelming scents from others and the kitchen smells, a soft scent of undoubtedly expensive cologne touched her breath, and his sweater hadn't slid off a department store rack.

He tilted his head, looking down with a faintly troubled smile. "Now, I probably should apologize, but I'll promise—no more snapshots without forewarning. Are you alright? Can you see yet?" he asked, sounding almost genuinely concerned as he touched her elbow.

"I'm sure I'll regain that ability in the next week or so," she played and smiled, shaking her head and glancing at the camera at his side. Looking into his dark eyes, she stated, "I'll hold you to that promise and let you off the hook to admit . . . aside from a few white freckles on your nose, I'm seeing quite well."

"I don't have freckles, darling, white or otherwise. Possibly you should sit down?"

"I think I'll leave you to your endeavors, sir," she said and winked. "Be sure and catch one long shot of the entire hall and promise to send me a copy?"

"Could I convince you to stay a moment or two?" he asked lightly.

"A purpose?"

"I enjoy your company," he mused. "And I'd like you to sit by the fireplace once I determine how to ignite it."

"Really, Darius," she said, slightly dismayed. "If I look even half as bad as I feel, I'm not in any condition to pose for a camera."

"You don't, and I'm afraid I cannot accept rejection," he said and flashed a smile, the first one to offer a glimpse of pearly whites. "I admitted I'm self-indulgent, and I'm ruthless enough to demand your cooperation, though I will say . . . please?"

"That was in extremely poor taste," she said in mocked offense. "And underhanded, Mr. Brock. A truly childish, despicable exploitation of your obvious position, but since you said please . . . I'll do it," she agreed, and his subtle transition wasn't lost on her. "And I won't apologize for putting you in your place either," she said smugly, and his smile returned in a flash.

"Is that what it was then, a proper dressing down for a deserving common thug?"

"Hmm, couldn't have said it better myself," she said and laughed at his slight surprise. "If you want, I'll help you light the fire."

"Humph," he said. "First shred my ego—now threaten my manly duties? Have you thought to leave me with nothing?"

She laughed and shook her head. "All right, dear. You light the fire, and I'll play the helpless female to repair your wounds."

"I'm tempted to believe you could do just that," he said with an oddly sober shine and motioned with his hand to start her striding ahead of him. "I wouldn't mind if you'd like to talk me through this fire business though. You look tired, and I'm not exactly mechanically inclined."

Doubting there was anything to which he would not excel, Jenna huffed her laugh and continued to the fireplace. Settling sidesaddle on the raised hearth, she leaned against the chilled stone as he stopped before the mantel.

Appearing to ponder the cold hearth, he tipped his head pensively and looked down at her. "Step one?"

Smiling, she tipped her head and glanced toward the mantel overhead then into his eyes, "Step one, reach behind the oil lamp, turn the brass handle, and push button."

Stepping closer, near enough to brush against her skirt, he found the appropriate handle and button, then stood watching as the flames slid along the rod beneath the logs. His eyes caught the flames, his hand resting on the mantel, he tilted his focus to her with a quick smile, "Touch of the devil in you, isn't there?"

Struggling to stifle a laugh at his purely wicked tone, she lost the battle and a laugh vibrated her voice. "I didn't say it was complicated."

"Humph," he said and stepped back, shaking his head, sending his fiery gaze off the flames to her. "Determined to land me on my knees at your confounded mercy, I can see it clearly."

In a half second or less, the intensity she'd experienced more than once in his presence loomed large between them. Whatever Jenna had been about to say slid away. An awareness too powerful to be derailed by amusement sped into her mind, and she sensed his thoughts taking a similar turn. If ever she'd suffered a more intense desire to reach and touch, to be held and touched, never more than at this moment. The wine, the hour of the night, and the crackle of the fire which enhanced rather than hid the sheer magnetism of his overwhelming masculinity...?

Whatever the cause, her heart hammered a quickened beat, her thoughts raced, and he felt it too. She could almost feel his heat ascending, could see his posture firming. Momentarily, her senses swam, and her temperature rose as if drawn into the flames reflecting in his eyes. Abruptly, he blinked and recoiled, and Jenna wasn't sure whether to be relieved or dismayed by his withdrawal.

For a split second, he appeared visibly shaken, drawing his hand off the mantel, recovering, fumbling with the camera. "It's late," he said in a slightly deeper voice, his eyes catching hers as he backed away. "And you look tired."

"Did you get any rest?" she asked, far more breathlessly than intended, but if he noticed, nothing showed in his eyes or his twitching smile.

"Enough to get by," he said offhandedly and backed further away, darting his gaze over her, the mantel, the fire, judging the angles and light. Even through the camera lens, the intensity of his gaze transcended as he sized her up through the camera eye. His voice low, affected with a dark note, he coaxed quietly, "Smile pretty, Luv. This one's for me."

In natural defense, if only to recover more fully, Jenna asked, "Have a fascination with dishrags, sir?" At his stifled humph, she smiled, and the light flashed. Blinking, she recovered enough to find him watching her over the top of the camera. "Done," she said and barely started to collect her skirt to rise.

"We'll need to take another, you do realize," he said haltingly.

Stopped, she commented, "I hadn't realized."

"It's a fact, Jenna," he said as if dismayed. "We may even need another after that. I'm a perfectionist. Dreadfully bad trait, I know, but I can't help myself. Besides which," he smiled more warily. "The light in here, the background . . .? It's too compelling to ignore when I find myself with such a stunning model."

"Darius, it's late," she said quietly. "And I'm lucky to be awake, much less stunning at this hour."

"Jenna," he interrupted quietly, his tone sober and gaze intent. "Humor me," he continued in a low silky tone. "I'll ask for no more than your photographs. Just a few, perhaps by the tree and the doors."

Whether the note of abandon in his voice or the haunting shine of sadness that not even the reflection of fire could conceal compelled her, Jenna knew she would humor him, at least to a degree. "One in each location," she agreed quietly.

"Will you . . . let your hair down?" he asked almost sheepishly. "And um . . . slip out of that lovely jacket which has been driving me crazy since I first saw you?"

Considering where that request might lead, she studied his nearly reluctant expression. For a man with the brass and confidence to make such a suggestion, he appeared as tense and uncomfortable as a schoolboy, and she realized, abruptly, she had no idea just who this fellow was. One minute oozing charm and confidence, the next detached and unreadable. Was this a game? A game she'd unwittingly fallen into when indulging her whim to watch him? She was a new employee, single, attractive enough to get by in a pinch. After all his praise and flattery, did he think she'd climbed the management ladder by smiling and jumping into executives' beds? Another Lisa? Was he setting her up for a change in pace, possibly to replace Blythe? In split seconds, Jenna's thoughts turned. There was something . . . not quite right about this high-energy, contradictory corporate executive, and she remembered her earlier decision to maintain a strictly professional relationship.

"I've offended you," he realized. "I do apologize. I—"

She lifted her hands in unison, ducking her head, collecting pins, removing the combs, and tumbling her hair from the folds. Leaning, she dumped the mass of natural waves forward in a curtain and combed her fingers through the tangles. Satisfied, she swept her hair back and sat up. She wasn't entirely oblivious to how her hair could catch the light and draw more than a passing glance when she fussed with it just a bit. When she tamed the natural curls to reasonable order, she found him staring again with an unmistakable intensity. Steeling her nerve, she refused to be drawn into that heat. "The jacket stays, Darius," she said lightly. "If this will do, I suggest you take aim and shoot."

Silently, without ever taking his eyes off her, he stooped several paces away and obeyed her command, spying on her through the camera and snapping off the shot. In one motion, he rose and stepped toward her, offering his hand.

Rising smoothly, Jenna rejected his hand, avoiding his eyes as she started toward the tree. She'd held that hand and met those eyes too often already, and he was far too smooth, too attractive for her safety. Without a doubt, he was her type. High powered, high intensity with a cutting-edge intelligence . . . and she had no intention of offering any further indication that they might share something more than a working relationship. If she'd considered how he might regard her arrival, had she even thought about sending the wrong signals by watching him in action, she would have denied herself that pleasure and backed into the kitchen. The last thing she intended was to have this handsome powerhouse turn up the heat on his natural charm. Blast the hour! Blast the snowstorm to keep her here! Blast the wine and the damned hour of the night!

Choosing a position and pose that should satisfy his request sufficiently, she half-turned and put her best side forward, smiling without a need for verbal direction. She'd posed for enough snapshots with celebrity guests and landed in enough promotional brochures to grasp the concept of a photo shoot without losing her professional edge. She wasn't a model. Not a sex symbol to offer him some raunchy thrill or bawdy laughs over drinks when he shared these pictures with his friends. Her dignity and confidence restored, she held his hidden gaze directly, firmly, as he took aim.

"Lovely," he said and snapped the shot from a reasonable distance.

"Do you still want another?" she asked smoothly.

"Yes," he answered while lowering the camera and forcing his gaze toward the door.

Oh, he was powerful, no doubt of that. If she hadn't agreed to the third shot, the force of his gaze would have nudged her toward the door. Turning, she started around the tree. "One more," she confirmed and agreed, assuring him it was the last. Without fanfare, she strode to the doors, scanning the frosted glass, the antique-style curtains, ribbons, and garland. Keenly aware of aesthetics and her eye for detail, she moved to a spot where the soft glow of the chandeliers and the murky light outside converged, affording him ample space to capture the glass and the decor. Frosted, the fresh snow still clinging to the panes, Jenna caught a slight chill, and her attention riveted momentarily. The snap and flash startled her from her reflection, and she pivoted to see him lowering the camera. His face, a mask of conflicts, wore a stunning sadness in his tainted smile.

"Thank you," he said in a troubling dark tone.

Such simple words and yet as powerful as all else about him, as if he meant to touch her heart at the deepest level . . . and it worked too well. As intense as his smile, his sadness and loneliness reached her. She could fall for him, could fall extremely hard, wanting nothing more than to lift that cloak of despair that seemed as palpable as the beat of her heart. With an iron resolve, she drew herself from the thought, seeking safety in her innate strength and determination. "You're welcome," she said quietly and broke from her pose, walking toward him, refusing to be drawn by the abandon in his eyes. He would catch his flight, continue his occupation, driven by the intensity inside of him, and she would see him again when next he passed through the hotel, providing she remained on staff. Pausing just shy of arm's reach, she looked into his haunted eyes, read his jaded smile, and offered her hand. "It's been a pleasure meeting you, Darius," she said sincerely.

"Likewise," he said in a soft, low voice and touched her fingers gently.

Before she could be trapped, caught, she slipped her hand free. "I assume you have the keys," she said with an iron will, keeping her dignity, her head. "If you'd turn that brass handle and shut off the lights when you're finished, I'd appreciate it immensely."

"I will," he agreed.

"Have fun and good night then," she said and started around him. At his hand touching her arm, her system froze, electrified, and her attention swiveled to see something far more intense, more conflicted between pain and sorrow. "Darius—"

"Jenna," he said quietly, his voice strained low, careful. Tension spiraled through his expression and his touch. "Please don't take this for anything more than practical advice," he said in quiet determination. "You're too good to be working in this hotel. Resign from here and find a position where your skills can be appreciated, somewhere with promise and opportunity for advancement. Your . . . options will always be limited here."

"Are you asking for my resignation?" she asked directly, uncertain of his intentions with the hesitation in that last line. That wasn't what he'd meant to say.

"Practical advice, Jenna," he repeated soberly, his dark eyes hooded. "Strictly between you and me. You will burn out attempting to make a difference here. Leave the Chateau to Mason and others like Lisa Blythe. This is not a life that will grant you the happiness you deserve."

'Get out while you still can,' he might have spoken aloud for as powerfully as his words reached her. A warning hinged on every soft syllable. Internally, she shivered with an unnatural alarm. "I may do that, Darius," she said quietly, wondering if she would receive an option.

Momentarily, he looked at her as if he meant to say more, then nodded, leaned, and brushed a kiss on her cheek, withdrawing slowly and smiling sadly. "Good night, Jenna. Only pleasant dreams."

7

If only to unwind, Jenna engaged the shower in the pool area, standing under the hot spray for several moments, then dried and slipped into the sweatsuit she kept in her office. Managing a hotel offered a few perks, including unlimited access to the heated pool, where she generally spent at least a half hour after a hectic workday. Too tired for a swim, too wound for sleep, the shower had helped. In a comfortably drowsy haze, she strode through the halls.

Whether Darius was still in the dining room, she neither knew nor cared to investigate. With little more than a half-hour remaining before the first guests would begin to rise, she determined to lie down at least for a few minutes. With her office so close to the front desk, doubtful she'd remain asleep through the hubbub of early departures . . . and with her thought, she was tempted to continue to and through the main doors, to slide behind the wheel of her Lincoln, and brave the slick roads.

Mark was nowhere in sight when Jenna rounded the arch and entered the lobby. Rene stood behind the desk, checking something on the computer. She looked up and over, wearing a puzzled frown that nearly aged her round face to its proper years.

"A problem?"

"Not exactly a problem," she said lightly and glanced at the computer, reading whatever information existed on the glowing screen.

Across the lobby, the industrial coffeemaker emitted the first aromas of the promised continental breakfast. The kitchen staff and hostess should be arriving soon to deliver the trays and arrange the complimentary table. Jenna reconsidered sleep, torn by the rich brew that promised to shake the comfortable daze from her mind. Rene's troubled expression started the process before Jenna quite reached the desk. "What's wrong?" Jenna asked as she rounded the desk.

"Quite a few of our guests requested a wake-up call," she said offhandedly and looked over, no less relieved. "Just about all of them responded . . . but," she glanced to the screen. "I've been trying to reach Mr. Fradden, the gentleman from New York, for the past hour," she said worriedly. "He's booked in 610."

One of the executive suites, Jenna understood.

"He stopped by here last night and made a point of telling me he needed to catch an early flight. I'm pretty sure he said his flight leaves around five thirty, and I know he hasn't checked out," she appeared slightly more concerned as she smiled nervously. "If he misses that flight, I hope I'm already off duty. I don't think he'll be too happy with us."

"Did you try turning off the phone and restarting the call?" Jenna asked.

She nodded. "At least a half dozen times."

"Where's Mark?"

"I sent him up to try knocking," Rene admitted with a wry smile. "Actually, he volunteered," she started, then frowned, glancing at her watch. "He's been up there almost ten minutes," she realized and appeared more worried. "You don't think something could be wrong, do you?"

Uncomfortably, Jenna recalled at least two incidents in Chicago when something had been terribly wrong. On both occasions, a maid had found the guest sprawled on the floor. "I'll get my keys," Jenna decided, steeling her nerves.

With any luck, Mr. Fradden was a sound sleeper and would need a good, hardy shake. A job she would assign to Mark, she considered with a wiry smile while dumping her crumpled clothes on her office chair. Ignoring the cot resting invitingly in front of her desk, she collected her keys from the top drawer and returned to the registration area. "If I miss Mark on the elevator, send him up to the sixth floor, if you please," she threw over her shoulder while crossing the lobby.

Within an arched alcove, the elevators reflected the Chateau's original era. A dual set of black cast iron doors covered the shaft. Not until the elevator reached the designated floor would the doors open. Jenna stood impatiently, waiting less than a minute before the car descended to cover the dark, swirled wallpaper that enclosed the shaft on each floor. On the inside, the elevator maintained its integrity of mahogany wood shined to an aged patina with carved crown molding to enhance the elegance.

Not for a moment had Jenna forgotten Darius Brock's 'practical advice', and as she rode to the sixth floor, she suffered a greater dismay. She loved working here. From the moment she'd entered the blasted front doors and submitted her application, she'd experienced an odd sense of coming home. The rich woods, the detail and quality which was so lacking in other hotels . . .? How could she just walk away? Would she have a choice? Darius hadn't implied that he'd demand her resignation or her severance, but the sincerity and intensity in his eyes . . . Mark stood outside the elevator doors, appearing slightly surprised and undoubtedly uncomfortable as he slid the scrolled doors aside for her to step out. "Rene told you?"

"You didn't have any luck?"

"Short of shouting and banging," he said as they started up the oriental-style carpet. "I've tried everything I can think of, and I don't want to think of how many people I might have already disturbed up here."

"Maybe his phone's disconnected," she said hopefully. "We'll try banging on his bedroom door."

Unlocking the main door, Jenna prepared to encounter an extremely irate man railing a million choice words at her. Only a soft strip of fluorescent light from the parking lot below sliced across the ceiling barely illuminated the parlor chairs. What struck first—the strange smell or the unnatural silence—Jenna knew only the hair follicles lifting at the nape or her neck. Reaching automatically, she flipped the switch to light the half dozen lamps around the sitting room and her attention froze, her heart skipped a beat.

Across the room, in one of the four wing-backed armchairs, the suited man slumped with his head angled against the upholstered wing . . . and it was a face she'd seen before. She'd glimpsed the fellow in passing last evening and she'd seen him up close when he'd interrupted her and Darius Brock on the dance floor. Wide open, his black eyes stared at her as if startled awake and accusing, but his twisted posture—shoulders sagging one way, his head the other—enlightened her in a split second. Unconsciously, Jenna started a step forward but froze.

Clearly, she identified the vacancy under the dull black sheen of unblinking eyes. One oddly shriveled hand dangled motionless off the edge of the cushion near his knee; the other collapsed crookedly on his thigh. He appeared staged as if he were a marionette propped in place. His lips formed a dark gap hanging at an unhinged angle . . . and a thin black line followed a deep crevice from the corner of his lips, enhancing the crag along his sagging jowl. Distorted, his features twisted in a ghastly expression . . . freakishly so.

"Uh-uh-uh-is-is-is—"

Without a thought, Jenna backed and clasped Mark's sleeve as she turned, glimpsing his wide stricken eyes as she propelled them into the hall. Clumsily, she tugged the door shut and stood staring at Mark, who stared back at her, his lips parted and face drained.

Dead. Mr. Fradden was dead. And without ever glimpsing someone dead by an unnatural cause, she knew he hadn't merely slipped away. As if ice water poured through her hair follicles, her muscles gripped, a sense of danger quickened. This was not a natural death. *Twisted. His face . . . no!* She refused to consider the possibility of foul play! *Not unnatural! Not dead by unnatural causes! Probably, a heart attack!*

Heaving a breath, she pulled herself together and turned to the door. "We . . . we'll use this phone," she huffed, and her hands shook, missing the keyhole on her first attempt to enlist her master key. *An ambulance!* An ambulance wouldn't help. *The police!* Without a doubt, they needed to phone the police and report this. Mason was downstairs! Passed out, but here. He could call the authorities. Heaving breaths, steeling her nerves, she forced herself through the door, sidling to the nearest phone just inside the door and pushing the appropriate buttons. Surprisingly, when the groggy voice answered, Jenna's voice quavered only slightly. "Mason, we have a . . . a situation."

"Wha-huh?"

"I'm in room 610," she said in a hushed voice as if fearing to wake the man staring at her through dull glazed black marbles. "It's Mr. Fradden . . . room 610. We need . . . He's dead, Mason. We need to phone the police."

Mason blurted and sputtered his waking words, his voice clearing to ask, "How?"

"I don't know," she managed, trying to stop the quaver in her vision, the sense of vertigo threatening to knock her off balance. "It . . . I just don't know. He's sitting . . . His neck's crooked. Geesus, Mason, get the police here. The man's dead," she huffed, withdrawing any mention of an ambulance—an ambulance wouldn't help Lawrence Fradden. "I'm—Mark's with me. We'll wait outside the door. Get someone here." Without another thought, she lowered the receiver and backed toward the door, turning clumsily and passing into the hallway where Mark clasped her arm, lending his shallow support as she pulled the door closed.

"He . . . I . . . He's really . . .?" Mark stammered.

She couldn't afford to panic or buckle to whatever threatened her quaking knees. Firming, she found the young man's stricken gaze spiraling off the door, and she clasped his arm in a tight grip. Keeping her voice soft with a thought of the guests who could be stirring in the surrounding suites, she stated, "Take a deep breath and calm down. The man's dead, but we don't know what happened to him. There's no reason to panic." In her words, she found comfort. "We'll just stand here and wait for the police."

Never a deep sleeper, the sound of footsteps and voices outside the door rousted Darius from the first genuine doze since landing in this godforsaken hotel. Bad enough he was held hostage by the bloody snow, his flight delayed indefinitely according to the latest update from his pilot, at least he should be allowed an hour's peace. Sleep, after all, was an elusive pleasure to be stolen only in short spurts depending upon the distance between flights . . . and Darius wouldn't be a bit surprised to learn this raucous was designed with the explicit purpose of keeping him awake and on edge. Nothing would he put past the Baron von Hendricks. No trick was too grand, no plot too dark. If nothing else, Darius knew that much, and he'd forfeited any attempt to decipher between coincidence and design.

Annoyed, Darius dropped his feet off the couch and sat up, abandoning even the idea of stealing the forbidden fruit. Whether he recognized the soft voice or merely sensed the woman's presence, he knew the object of his latest torment stood just down the hall. By coincidence or design, he could neither decide nor guess. She was a torment that he could ill afford and one that might already cost him dearly. Far too easy to look into those blue depths, far too hard to maintain the distance required. Just thinking about those blasted photographs, those moments in the dining room, awakened him more completely. Too blasted awake. Taking the pictures for Raphael had been risky enough, taking the bloody shots for himself . . .?

His muscles gripped with as much frustration as anger over his foolish indulgence. If he retained any good sense, he would toss that film in the nearest fire and save himself a bit of grief. And damned his cousin for being so bloody accurate. By his own blasted nature, he could land himself from the pan to the fire, and no blasted wonder Kevin assumed Darius was the cause of this latest rage. To the best of his blasted ability, he followed the rules. He was a self-indulgent creature with a will of his own . . . sometimes.

More footsteps, more low voices. His interest rising, another damned nature ascending, Darius followed the steps passing outside his door, his curiosity enhancing. If these were guests, they were headed in the wrong direction; the elevator, hence, the lobby, resided in the opposite direction. Habitually, he glanced at his watch. Most, if not all guests on the sixth floor were employed by von Hendricks, and most hadn't even reached the rooms until well after three a.m. He'd been awake then, too, and heard enough of the hushed, slurred laughs and giggles to know very few patrons should be in a condition to rise and cavort at this hour.

Muttering a curse, he stepped into his shoes and pushed off the couch. He should have known better than to attempt sleeping. Between heated thoughts and images of Miss Windrow and thoughts of what his employer might have in store for him, he was surprised he'd even closed his eyes. Sleep deprivation was as much a blessing as a curse.

He hesitated at the door, half convinced he truly wanted no part of whatever awaited in the hall then realized the futility. If, as he was beginning to suspect, a problem existed, he would land in the middle regardless, if only by his position in the von Hendricks Corporation. Muttering another curse, Darius tugged the door and stepped into the corridor just as Mason stepped backward, emerging from a room at the end of the hall. Jenna stood aside, her arms folded as if hugging herself, her attention turned toward Mason.

How could the woman look so damned sexy wearing navy-blue sweat pants and a yellow T-shirt? Her hair had transformed again, pulled into a thick ponytail that fell halfway down her back, a mere brush of bangs swept aside on her lovely brow.

Shaking himself with a mental curse, Darius forced his attention on the furrowed planes of Mason's pale face. If ever a man wore his burdens on the surface, none more than Mason Gordon, but currently, he appeared on the verge of buckling under his load. More deeply curious, Darius caught the chap's stricken, bloodshot eyes turning toward him, and the face paled another degree to appear cadaverous. At the opposite wall, the young registration clerk leaned wearing a likewise spooked shine in his wide eyes. To either side of Mason, the night security guards stood, silent and wary.

"What is it, Mason?" Darius asked, his stride lengthening.

"Darius, it's . . ." Mason withdrew his hand from the doorknob and shuddered visibly. "It's Mr. Fradden. Something's happened to him," he said heavily.

Controlling his immediate dread and fear with a natural talent, Darius allowed only his curiosity to deepen as he joined the trio, but as the blue eyes lifted to him, something of his concern became genuine. Slightly too wide, and too bright with shock, Jenna stared at him, seeing him, not seeing him. Unconsciously, he touched her elbow as he pivoted his attention to Mason. "What exactly has happened to him?"

"I'm . . . We're . . . not sure," Mason struggled to regain his natural authority. "It doesn't look like a heart attack, but . . ."

Obviously, the man was dead, and Darius's mood darkened rapidly. Apparently, he would need to see for himself if he intended to learn any details. Glancing off the door, he nudged Jenna aside and flagged his hand for Mason to open the door.

Oh, the fellow was dead. No doubt about it. Striding into the room, Darius crossed the oriental carpet, while introverting the details at light speed. Fradden still wore his pinstriped suit. His tie—loosened—sagged on his deflated, wide chest. A trickle of blood ran off the crook of his drooping jowl and dotted a stain on his pale blue shirt. His head kinked at an unnatural angle, and his body appeared to puddle between the ornate tapestry arms. No need to touch him. The pasty gray flesh and dead haze in the eyes suggested the chap had been gone for quite a while. The scent of death touched Darius's lips and nostrils, a tangy bitter blend threatening to choke him. Stopped, Darius studied the posture and tipped his head to judge the angle of the neck. No expert on the cause of death, he took a wild guess to assume the man's neck was broken and the color of the skin . . . the near shriveled texture of waxy flesh? The lad had died badly.

Internally, Darius shivered.

"We ehm . . . I have the police coming," Mason said from behind Darius. "And an ambulance. Discreetly, of course."

Looking into the uncomfortable living eyes, Darius commented, "Obviously the latter's rather unnecessary, but I suggest you trot down to your office and ring the hotel's legal consultants. I don't know the local laws governing crime, but I assume homicide can be complicated in any country."

Mason's face paled; his eyes widened, "You think . . ."

"I could be wrong, but I doubt that's a chance you should take," Darius said and turned as he spoke, touching Mason's arm and guiding him to the door. Neither shaken nor entirely shocked, Darius stepped through, and Mason drew the door closed behind them. Far more intent, Darius looked into the stunned, deep blue eyes, recognizing her lingering shock. "You found him," he said.

She nodded and glanced at the door. "He requested a wake-up call," she said in a surprisingly firm voice. "When he didn't answer, Rene was concerned . . . Mark tried knocking."

He touched her shoulder in reflex to her shiver, which she seemed not to notice. His gaze slid toward Mason as the man ordered one of the security guards to remain at the door. The young clerk appeared on the verge of collapse, slumped against the wall, his face chalky. "Mason, take the lad with you and let him calm down," Darius advised and looked to Jenna. She held herself steady with impressive strength, but this was no place for her. "Go with them," Darius said smoothly. "Mr. Eigler can remain and wait for the police."

She shook her head, deciding, "I'm fine. It's just . . . it was just a shock. I can stay."

Darius locked his gaze more firmly, his hand still riding her quivering shoulder. "There's no need for you to remain outside this door, Miss Windrow," he stated with quiet emphasis. "I'm sure the police will need your statement, but they can certainly wait until you've calmed down." His gaze shot to Mason as he nudged Jenna toward him. "Take her with you, Mason, and see that she has somewhere to lie down. Ring me up when the police arrive."

"Will do," Mason said grimly and took Jenna's arm, his grim face caught between recovering poise and concern as he started the collection down the hall, muttering a few words to the visibly confused young woman.

As an afterthought, Darius caught up to them, catching Mason's eye over Jenna's head. "Delay any early departures and ring me before completing the paperwork, Mason."

With Mason's nod, Darius veered to his door, entering and letting it close in his wake as he strode to the phone. This was one complication he could do without.

Dialing the long series of numbers, Darius settled onto the single chair, absently reaching for the tumbler of bourbon under the lamp. His thoughts spiraling, he recalled those moments with Fradden, the conversation with Kevin, the Baron's second call . . . and the unnatural position of the corpse down the hall.

Despite himself, he shivered again as Kevin's voice erupted on the line with a single, "Yes?"

"We have a problem," Darius commented without preamble.

"I thought we'd already established that."

"Yes, well, it's just become more of a problem. I just came from Fradden's suite down the hall. The man's dead, and . . . I'm no expert, cousin, but I fear the man's been exsanguinated—entirely drained. Not another drop of blood left to him. Please, do tell me there's no way that could be possible." His words hung on the line in the dead silence, no relief forthcoming as the possibilities and incredibility snapped like an electric current between himself and his cousin. Kevin was one of the few men Darius truly trusted.

"It shouldn't be possible," Kevin said by way of collecting his thoughts. "How positive are you of the means?"

"I'd not bloody swear to it under oath, cousin, but I'm fairly certain of my accuracy. The man's neck's broken. That, I can safely judge."

"Have appropriate measures been taken?"

"Mason, the manager here, contacted the authorities. Discreetly, of course," Darius repeated with an edge. "I'd imagine we'll have the inspectors knocking about soon, but we should be able to control at least part of the chaos."

"Has your flight been delayed?"

"Indefinitely, as of a half hour ago. A few commercial flights may depart, but small crafts are grounded until further notice. It could be a few hours."

"I don't like this," Kevin said as if distracted.

"My blasted sentiments exactly, and you do realize those are not the words I'd hoped to hear from you, cousin. Advice, I'll accept, gladly, if you're so inclined."

"You are in a world of shit," Kevin commented.

"If that's your idea of comfort or constructive advice, Kevin, it's sorely lacking," Darius said in disgust.

"Calling it as I see it," Kevin continued and outlined an extremely bleak set of circumstances to enhance rather than relieve Darius's tension by the time his cousin concluded. "On the bright side," Kevin said after a heavy pause. "Our fearless leader will have a blast and he might even be inclined to let you off the hook."

"I have the distinct impression that he put me on the bloody hook, Kevin, and I fail to see that particular outlook as bright."

"We have a problem," Kevin said then.

"Oh, and here I believed we were sailing in clear skies."

"You do know the Baron's on his way to New York."

"Now, you fully realize the state of my distress."

"Do you really think he'd have left our associate off the hook?"

The question hung in the dead air between the continents. That thought had been niggling at Darius's mind, a mere whisper of doubt which posed too many other questions to be fully realized. With Kevin's voiced thought, Darius commented, "Nothing about this rings true to form, Kevin. Unless he's decided to terminate my service, I don't see him holding me to account here. You uh . . . you're in a position to know, cousin," he said with a mild chill threatening the edges of his mind. "Have I . . .? Am I finished?"

"You haven't told me you hate me, yet. Do you need me to offer a reason?"

"By all means," Darius said in a low controlled voice.

"Then, here it is. You're too Goddamn much fun for him to toss you to the wolves, cousin, and he's a man of his word."

"Well, that certainly makes me hate you," Darius said with a twitch of a smile returning. "Great life if we don't weaken, isn't that the way of it?"

"Let's look at this from a rational perspective," Kevin said with a change in tempo. "Over and above any affiliation with his occupation, Fradden undoubtedly made enemies. It's a given. Now, let's suppose someone knew he was coming to Pittsburgh to speak to you—which he did. If said someone feared what might have been conveyed, ergo—as you say—a genuine motive."

"Good Goddamn," Darius uttered. "You're telling me this could truly be an external threat?" At his own words, the image of Fradden's ghastly face, the expression of horror frozen in the pasty flesh, Darius shuddered yet again. "And you're not about to tell me I have a bloody New York drug lord in my midst, are you?"

"This might be a good time to demure to the Baron, my friend. I shouldn't need to tell you there are other threats in this world."

At times, that was the most difficult to believe, Darius might have admitted, his gaze listing to the window, his thoughts distracted. "Do you ever wonder . . . how long you can live like this?" Darius asked quietly.

"I try not to think about it, and I suggest you do the same."

"I'm so damned tired," Darius uttered. "Just so damned tired, and maybe he knows that. Maybe he fucking knows I'm at the end of my rope. I don't know what's right or wrong. I've lost my humanity. If I landed in an electric chair, it might be a bloody relief."

"Goddamn you," Kevin snapped. "Pull yourself together."

"That's the problem, cousin," Darius said quietly. "I don't know if I can. I was once able to convince myself there would be an end, a reward, a life after. It doesn't work that way, does it? You, me, the others—we've lost whatever life we ever had, and there's nothing left for us but to be sheep in a bloody pasture."

"Darius," Kevin's voice rose carefully, forcefully. "This isn't what we'd have chosen—"

Darius sent a humph through the line. "Save the lecture or pep talk, Kevin. I'll do whatever's expected, but it's occurred to me, I really don't give a bloody damn what comes next." And his brow furrowed with the revelation. "I didn't give a bloody damn. The man was dead before my eyes, and I didn't feel a bloody thing for him. He has a wife and children who will weep over him . . . but it means nothing to me. What kind of monster does that make of me?"

"A living one, you bloomin' idiot," Kevin said in a mocked cockney accent.

With another humph, Darius pulled from his maudlin tone if only for Kevin's benefit. "Thank you for listening, Kev. I needed the ear. As for my travel plans, you might want to extend my apologies."

"About the legal issues, Darius . . .? You're not a US citizen. If the need arises, we'll pull some strings and slide you out of there."

"I do believe I'll handle this from a different perspective," Darius decided. "Ignorance is bliss. To err, divine. Complacency, a waste of precious little time."

"There's the Darius I know and despise."

"Back at you," Darius mused and dropped the receiver into its cradle. His smile ebbed as he settled back in the chair and lifted the tumbler, sipping the warm, dark liquid. To believe that the Baron had needed Fradden's voiced guilt to know the extent of his loss was, perhaps, the greatest curiosity. Despite the von Hendricks' heirs, who held dominion in various states and locations around the globe, Darius had gleaned the illusion years ago. Only one von Hendricks held the strings on the empire. The others were more like pawns, not unlike him, taking orders from the top with far less conscious knowledge. He, Kevin, and a handful of others truly knew the extent of the Baron's holdings, and no comfort surfaced with that knowledge. He and Kevin alone fully realized the nature of the beast, and there were times . . . far too many times

when Darius needed to wonder how much of his consciousness he retained. How much of his day-to-day affairs were of his own making, his
own free will?

Oh, and there was a string of words that Darius had come to despise.
'His own free will.' If ever he'd held such a thing in his grasp, that, too,
had been forfeit. Unconsciously, rubbing the pad of his thumb against his
crooked index finger, he studied the action, his thoughts turning.

What if . . .? What if Kevin's implication held a degree of truth? To
believe the Baron had allowed Fradden to die was nearly inconceivable.
Too well, Darius knew the devil's nature. Allowing Fradden to return to
New York, inviting the man for tea, and then ripping the bugger to shreds
mentally would have been more to the Baron's liking . . . on the outside
chance that the Baron hadn't already known about the chap's negligence.
One does not lose several cases of finely aged wine slated for the Baron's
table. That alone could have cost Fradden his life. But not before the chap
had paid fully, coherently. What the bloody hell good was a dead man when
the living could be so much more entertaining?

The Baron had neither sanctioned nor arranged for Lawrence Fradden's
demise.

Darius knew his accuracy at a base level, and the shudder to launch him
off the couch was no more within his control than a purely human reaction
to panic. The latter, however, could be controlled despite the need. In fact,
it damn sure better be controlled if he had any aspirations to survive.

Indulging his desire, he sidled behind the bar, poured another drab of
brandy, and knocked it down in three swallows. Why he bothered, he
couldn't imagine. He had as much hope of finding oblivion in a bottle as
he had confidence in his ability to find Fradden's killer, but neither futility
would prohibit him from trying. Human weakness. To err truly was divine.

By the time Mason knocked, Darius had recovered enough of his equilibrium to join the manager and two plainclothes officials converging on
the door to room 610.

The elder of the two wore a knee-length dark coat hanging open over a
leisure ensemble of boots, casual slacks, and a thick sweater. Mid-aged but
physically fit, he scanned Darius from head to heel, his pale blue eyes intent
and calculating despite the early hour. "Who are you?"

Mason offered the introduction, including Darius' position in the parent
company, and Darius offered his hand. Det. Jackson merely looked at him,
ignoring the amenity. Whatever this chap's affiliation to the hotel—or Mason—he wasn't pleased to be standing in this hall at the crack of dawn, and
obviously, he intended to express that detail. The younger lad wore a suit under

a black parka and accepted the handshake, offering a pleasant amenity despite the grim circumstances.

"Let's have a look," Jackson growled and turned to the door as Mason fumbled with his keys at the brass knob.

8

Nothing had changed within the room. The stillness and scent of death were as overwhelming as the moments when Darius had first entered. On the single, high-backed armchair near the window, Fradden slumped in a twisted heap, and Darius didn't need a close-up view to recall the waxy texture, the pasty gray hue. Between the lamplight and the first hazy light of dawn creeping through the frosted glass on the balcony doors, Fradden appeared even more lifeless, as if he were a man-made construct placed for grizzly effect in a haunted house.

Standing aside, in a position to watch the senior detective inspecting the corpse, Darius glimpsed the dark eyes scanning the surrounding scenery, collecting details while orienting himself to the overall picture. The fellow had a sturdy face, a firm countenance which the younger man mirrored while likewise studying the remains. All too soon, Jackson turned and met Mason's gaze with a compelling sobriety. "You definitely have a problem here, Mr. Gordon. We might be able to keep it out of the morning news, but that's as far as I'll accommodate you."

"I don't understand," Mason said tensely.

"We'll have to call in our lab techs and the coroner," Jackson stated, and his gaze shifted to Darius, back to Mason. "I'm judging the man's been dead for several hours, and unless he found a way to break his own neck while sitting down, I'll wager he wasn't alone when he died. Frankly, we have a homicide on our hands, and since I received the call, I'm sure you knew that before calling. We can try to be discreet. We can bring the crime scene techs through a back entrance, but I'm not promising anything." He looked to his partner, a man close to Darius's age and height. "Find a phone and get the coroner over here. I want to know why this guy looks like a dried apricot." His gaze shifted to Darius. "You want to be useful—you could show him where to find a phone outside this room."

Controlling his reaction, accepting the detective's sarcasm, Darius nodded and glanced at the younger man, who wore a thin, snarky smile. For the moment, Darius had no choice other than to maintain his role as company executive. In his suite, he motioned the detective to the phone and listened halfheartedly as Det. Magowski called the coroner with easy familiarity to suggest they shared a working rapport.

By no surprise, when Magowski hung up, he started toward the door, then paused. "It's probably a good idea for you to stay over here, Mr. Brock. Let me and my partner take care of this. I'm sure we'll be over to talk with you before too long."

"Yes, of course," Darius said as if he were grateful for the excuse to be held at arm's reach from this obvious disaster. As he let the detective out and closed the door, his troubled expression ebbed into a far more honest annoyance. Undoubtedly, these detectives preferred to deal with Mason, a known ally or adversary, rather than risk the weight of the von Hendricks Corporation pitched against them. Mason might enlighten Darius, but doubtfully, the manager would confide in a man who could terminate his employment. That attitude could reap reward. At least Darius wouldn't become directly involved in this investigation, and Mason could be relied upon to consider the von Hendricks' best interests.

At the same time, however, could Darius afford to leave this situation in another's hands? Regardless of how much he despised his position in the Baron's dynasty, Darius had learned long ago to accept the damned responsibility. He was one of the corporation's hierarchy. An illusion, a grand hoax, a bloody jest, perhaps, but a fact for anyone who cared to investigate the pecking order. At any hour, day or night, Darius could lift a telly and chat with the second in command, who in turn, could gain the patriarch's attention in seconds. His was a position of exorbitance which other men undoubtedly dreamed of achieving, a measure of material wealth which would seem inconceivable . . . had seemed inconceivable upon a time. Where other men might hock their damned soul to stand in his shoes, he'd hock his own to stand in a pair of worn-out tennies. None of which consoled his present frame of mind. He was third in the pecking order of a dynasty that could bloody well shift the economic conditions of several small countries—and he was presently resting down the hall from a room where one of his corporate underlings crumbled in a heap of ruined flesh—an understatement of unnatural death.

'. . . a dried apricot.'

"Bloody hell," Darius uttered as he moved to the French doors, scanning the platinum sky. Sunrise remained at least an hour away, not that it mattered. Fradden's murder would create problems, only beginning with a longer delay. And no matter the Baron's direct involvement, the next several hours could be pure hell. Was this murder by design? A product of the Baron's manipulations? Or the work of an outside enemy? Either way, landing in the crossfire would not bode well on his health, and one thought remained tantamount—Darius had never arrived anywhere by accident.

Muttering another curse, he pivoted to the soft rap of knuckles on his door. It was far too late to start worrying about his future. To what extent the Baron manipulated the bloody situation remained the only question, and at times, Darius doubted any detail could be left to chance. No choice. He would play his damned role to the best of his ability and hope his employer turned down the flames before too many others got burnt.

For an instant, Darius Brock appeared to look through her as blind as a manikin before his dark eyes focused, relieving Jenna's quick dread. She'd tried lying down, had contemplated going home, and had considered jogging the mile if only to relax the tension coiled through her system. With a glance down the hall to Jes Eigler who stood guard outside room 610, Jenna returned her gaze to find Darius studying her with a more natural concern and curiosity. "Can I come in?"

"Yes, of course," he said smoothly and stepped aside, searching her more intently as she sidestepped. "Are you all right, Jenna?"

Hugging her arms to herself, she offset the internal chill, understanding the effect of her nerves. "I'm fine. I just . . ."

How to explain her concerns? Even though he probably had a great deal on his mind, she needed to try, if only to make sense of this. Too quiet, too deceptively quiet. She knew how this situation should be handled. Uniformed officers should have arrived, an ambulance should have rolled to the front doors . . . despite how futile. Fradden should either be en route to a hospital to be pronounced dead by a licensed physician or the county coroner should be here to record his official assessment. She knew the routine, the protocol. Instead, two plainclothes men had arrived, and Mason had ridden with them in the elevator. No ambulance. No uniformed officers. No coroner. At the front desk, Rene remained worried but oblivious. Only Jenna and Mark had been escorted to the security station and asked to keep this situation quiet.

At the hand touching her arm, she responded without a thought, traveling as far as the nearest armchair. On a separate plane, she became starkly aware of the deep voice offering words of reassurance and comfort. Collecting her thoughts, she spied Darius at the bar, collecting two crystal glasses and a fifth of bourbon. She'd wondered about that fully stocked bar in room 606. And she'd assumed correctly by the sheer elegance of the furnishings, the room was reserved for the hierarchy of the corporation. And here was the benefactor—tall and elegant, as aesthetically pleasing as the lush accommodations. Lord almighty, he was something—as sleek in his black jeans and gray cashmere as he was when wearing his Armani.

With a mental shake, Jenna drew a soft breath, deciding, "It's either too late or too early for a drink, Darius. Why don't I ring the kitchen and have a pot of coffee delivered?"

He paused and looked toward her. "If that's what you'd prefer," he said and replaced only one glass, reaching for the phone on the counter. As she started from the chair, he gestured, "Do sit down, Jenna. Regardless of how well you're handling this, it is a shock."

"This isn't the first time I've dealt with something like this, Darius," she said honestly. "It's a shock, but I faced a similar situation in Chicago when one of our guests suffered a heart attack."

"Hmm," was his only response before he engaged the telephone. Watching him, listening to him place the order for coffee in his deep lyrical accent, she studied his pensive features, his impressive control. He was a man accustomed to holding the reins and lending commands . . . and was he responsible for the quiet around them?

Replacing the receiver, he reached again for the bottle and filled one of the tumblers. Bringing it with him, he joined her in the small circle of comfortable antique chairs. Only the furniture design and parlor ambiance remained the same as all other suites on the sixth floor. Here, the settees and delicate end tables were original, the crystal genuine Waterford and the mahogany wood wore an authentic patina. . . nearly the same vivid color and depth as the brown eyes watching her.

"Would you mind if I ask you something?" Jenna asked carefully, sensing his instant wariness as clearly as his weariness.

"Not at all."

"What's going on here?"

"Pardon?"

The wrong question, the wrong approach. This was the same man who'd offered her practical advice, strongly suggesting that she should resign. But the circumstances had changed. She wasn't naive to the working mechanics of the upper echelon. He held an obligation to his employers to protect the integrity of this establishment, to maintain order, and to control whatever damaging publicity resulted.

"I uhm . . . it just seems strange," she said, uncomfortably aware of his searching gaze. A fleeting image of the gnarled face and that thin black vein from the man's gaping lips sent a shiver down her spine. Her eyes reflecting something of her lingering panic, she realized, "He was murdered, wasn't he?"

If he knew, the answer remained hidden behind his dark eyes. He appeared only troubled. "I believe that's what the police are attempting to determine," he said quietly. "I'd like to think not."

"It wouldn't be good for business."

"No, it wouldn't," he said with a shadow of a smile.

Discretion. Loyalty to the company. How loyal could she afford to be? How far would the facts be distorted under the auspices of discretion? If Fradden was murdered, the murderer could be in this hotel at this very moment. Truly not naive to the politics of upper management, to the protocols expected of her for the good of the company and guests, Jenna wore a troubled frown as she searched his calm gaze. "Will you cooperate with the authorities regardless?"

Surprise touched his eyes with his more tainted smile. "Jenna, if the man's been murdered, I could ill afford to neglect demanding a full investigation, and that would include assisting however I can."

Relieved, immensely relieved, she relaxed slightly with a silent apology. How could she explain what she had yet to work out in her mind, though? Something about Mason's quick, firm control had disturbed her. And this Englishman's quiet resolve, his unshakeable demeanor when he'd returned from that room, had enhanced her discomfort. At least Mason had appeared shocked after stepping into that room; Darius Brock had appeared annoyed as if Lawrence Fradden's death was an inconvenience. She had no idea who Darius Brock was or how he might react in any given situation. Her intuition and his arrogance would suggest he was not easily disturbed and likely a powerhouse under fire. "I'm sorry for implying otherwise."

"It's been a long, trying evening without this macabre event," he said with a hint of weariness affecting his tone. He lifted his drink, glancing at her. "You sure you won't indulge, Luv? It doesn't help, but it offers an illusion of doing something constructive. In your case, it might help you relax long enough to indulge in a long overdue sleep."

"I tried that for a few moments," she said absently. "Sleep, I mean. Afraid until we know something, it's doubtful I'll succeed."

"I know precisely what you mean," he said lightly and held her gaze momentarily. The male voices passing in the hall countered whatever he might have added. His gaze listed toward the door as if following the arrivals through the corridor.

Hopefully, a coroner and the crime scene techs were arriving, but they were not talking shop. Not quite muffled, a male voice commented on the cost of staying in one of these suites.

When Darius returned his gaze, he appeared only more weary.

"Did you know Mr. Fradden well?" she asked quietly.

"In a professional capacity, I'd imagine I knew him well enough."

"You don't seem surprised, Darius."

"Very few things in life surprise me," he answered in a disgusted tone.

"It just seems hard to believe," she said absently and looked at him with a livid concern. "Do you know if he has family? A wife and children?"

"Both, I'd imagine," he answered quietly.

Before she could react with more than a rise of moisture, the knock interrupted, announcing the arrival of room service. Even as she rose to answer the door, the thought of the Fradden family receiving this news sent an ache deeper into her chest. Natural death, even expected death after a long life or a long illness, could be painful, but to hear about a violent death could be devastating. With an effort, she forced a faint smile to the waiter, not particularly caring when the fellow appeared surprised to find her in Mr. Brock's room. She would deal with the rumors if it became necessary. At the table, Darius slipped a sizeable tip into Bobby's hand and landed a gaze that sent the waiter scurrying through the door. Joining Darius at the table, reaching for the silver server, she read his slightly apologetic expression.

"That won't be good for your reputation," he said lightly.

She smiled faintly, too weary to care. "I'm sure it's no worse than I'd face eventually. Hotels are ripe for juicy gossip." She'd been there, too, unfortunately. Seeing his increased dismay, she forced a reassuring smile. "Seriously, Darius, it's not a problem."

Not for her, obviously, Darius considered uncomfortably, his thoughts turning toward that memory flash of moisture in her eyes. For a moment, she'd appeared wounded, as if she would weep in sorrow for the surviving Fraddens whom she'd never known. And something of her sympathy touched Darius even now. His words to Kevin hit harder as he accepted a cup of coffee from her lovely hands. Lawrence Fradden had a family—a wife, two daughters, and a son. The youngest had just recently graduated from high school if Darius remembered correctly. Had he become such a monster that he could feel nothing for these survivors? Had he lost so much of his humanity that he retained no capacity for sorrow or grief or even remorse? Fradden was a man. Doubtful a good man, but a living, breathing man with a life outside of von Hendricks Distribution.

Before his thoughts could dip too low, the knock interrupted.

Barely awaiting the door to open, Det. Jackson entered, his gaze speeding over the room, spying Jenna. As Jenna started to rise, Jackson flagged her down with an offhanded, "Don't get up on our account, Ma'am."

In a fleeting instant, Darius realized the man's misconception and was sorely tempted to allow the chap the delusion. Darius couldn't even recall when last he might have entertained a female in his room, much less been caught red-handed, so to speak. Even Mason eyed them curiously, deeply, as if he suspected Jenna had been inside this room—possibly before finding Fradden. For a full thirty seconds, Darius enjoyed the purely natural reactions between suspicion and envy, considering the extremely beautiful woman seated comfortably at his table. He even allowed himself a moment of self-indulgence, to feel as if he'd spent the night as these gentlemen believed.

Not to be. In a few words, Darius cleared the misconception and introduced the hotel's assistant manager, not entirely surprised when Jackson and his partner continued to believe the delusion. Murder, sex scandal between the upper echelon . . . a ready-made drama for a man who obviously held the wealthy and over-privileged in contempt. Jackson only changed his tone after enlisting Jenna to tell her story. She was incredible and credible and clearly shaken despite her quiet control as she described the details of walking unexpectedly into Fradden's room. By the time she finished and answered Jackson's questions, the detective had fallen under her spell, and by no surprise, offered her a few words of consolation.

Almost as an afterthought, Jackson turned his gaze to Darius. His dark eyes conveyed the same controlled contempt that he'd displayed outside and inside Fradden's room. "I noticed your accent," Jackson said smoothly. "For our records, we'll need your address."

Darius obliged, offering the address of his flat in London and pausing as the man jotted the words on a notepad he held on his raised knee.

"You're English. Born or are you originally from somewhere else?"

"Born," Darius answered. "I'm a citizen of England."

Jackson studied him momentarily as if impressed. "Have you been in the US long?"

"Nearly a month," he answered.

"Mr. Mason mentioned you were here for the party last night. You represent the von Hendricks Corporation. Where were you before coming here—if you don't mind me asking?"

"I fail to see any relevance, but I don't mind answering, detective. I flew in from California early last evening."

"Commercial flight?"

"Private plane."

"What's your official title or occupation?" Jackson asked.

"Executive attaché," Darius answered.

Jackson jotted the words, feigning to appear curious rather than contemptuous. "That's rather vague, Mr. Brock. What exactly does your job entail?"

"More often than not, attending social functions as I did last evening, Det. Jackson."

Jackson cracked a tiny smile. "You get paid to run around in a private jet and attend parties?"

Darius likewise smiled a fraction. "Trivial as you make that sound, I'm nearly afraid to admit the accuracy."

"I didn't mean to offend you, Mr. Brock," Jackson said with a musing tone. "Just seems like a hell of an occupation. I sure wouldn't mind landing a job like that."

Darius let the comment ride, merely donning one of his loftier smirks with an acknowledging nod.

"Seriously, now," Jackson said, mocking his sobriety. "What's involved in your uh . . . occupation?"

"When I'm not attending parties, do you mean?" Darius mused.

"Right," Jackson coaxed.

"Basically, I'm a P.R. man, Det. Jackson," Darius said smoothly. "Rather a personal liaison between the corporate heads and the divisions. I've been known to conduct seminars on sales and offer advice on market analysis."

"Sort of a jack of all trades and a master of none?"

Darius studied the man's sheepish expression despite his tempered amusement. "You have an odd technique if you don't mind me noticing, Detective. Is there any particular reason why you're determined to reduce my skills to the mundane? Or is it simply that you are uh . . . I believe the American saying is—trying to get my goat?"

"Just trying to find out where you fit in this picture," Jackson said offhandedly and glanced around the room. His gaze returned, amused only on the surface. "The von Hendricks Corporation—just judging by our present circumstances—is fairly diverse. If I understood Mr. Gordon correctly, you're one of the uh . . . big wigs? But you're telling me, you're no more than a glorified messenger boy and bearer of goodwill? I'm not getting it, Mr. Brock, and I like to know who I'm talking to if you get my meaning."

"I'm a spokesman for the company, Detective, whether conducting seminars or just paying a goodwill visit to a branch office. That's as simply as I can describe my occupation, and frankly, though it's oversimplified, you may make of that what you will. As I'm far more interested in what's happened to Mr.

Fradden, perhaps, you'd be kind enough to ask whatever relevant questions you feel are necessary. After which, you can tell me if you've determined the cause of death."

"That's where this could get sticky," Jackson said and reached for his coffee, not entirely taking his gaze from Darius. "Did Mr. Gordon inform you directly as to Mr. Fradden's circumstance?"

"Pardon?"

"Did he buzz your room or knock on your door to have your involvement?"

"No."

"What brought you out into the hall?"

"At five in the a.m., voices and footsteps have a tendency to arouse curiosity, especially when one happens to know the location of the elevator and doubts anyone would be checking in rather than departing."

"Excuse me?"

"My flight was delayed," Darius stated, deciding to be candid and not just a little condescending with his arrogance ascending. In a tone befitting a moron, Darius held the man's fixed gaze while continuing, "I was dozing when I heard the voices. Doubting anyone should be arriving, I satisfied my curiosity. Ergo, I joined the ensemble outside Mr. Fradden's room."

"Why did you insist on entering the room?" Jackson asked directly.

"If you walked into a hall and found three of your associates pale-faced and shaken outside another associate's room and your questions were not answered swiftly enough, what would be your reaction?"

"Apples and oranges, by your own admission, Mr. Brock," Jackson said smoothly. "I'm an investigator by trade." *You're an overpaid moron pretending to appear important.* "I'd think you'd be a little reluctant, assuming you knew Mr. Fradden was dead before you entered the room."

Darius refrained from comment, merely awaited another question, his gaze direct.

"Were you reluctant?" Jackson refrained.

"Without boasting, detective, I will admit I tend to take charge when I enter a situation. Reluctance never factors into that responsibility."

"Did you touch anything inside the room?" Jackson asked.

"Nothing," Darius answered.

"You just went in, took a look at Fradden, and walked back out. Never touched the door or Fradden? Didn't check for a pulse? Didn't run to the can and throw up?"

His gaze darkening, Darius held Jackson's gaze. "As I said, I touched nothing, and I'd think, with your investigative skills, you'd have determined a splatter of vomit if such existed."

Jackson's cheek muscle twitched. "You didn't think to check and make sure your associate was dead? Never thought about trying CPR."

"No."

"Why is that, Mr. Brock?"

"Seemed rather pointless and extremely belated."

"Want to explain?"

"The man was obviously deceased."

"Have you ever seen a dead body before today?"

"Imagine so," Darius answered.

"I'm not talking about maybe attending a funeral," Jackson persisted. "Let's say, have you ever seen a body without a mortician's handiwork."

"Detective, I find this line of questioning absurd and in fine poor taste, considering that several of us in this room have just undergone a dreadful experience," Darius said honestly and turned his genuinely concerned gaze to find Jenna slightly shaken. Annoyed, he looked toward Jackson. "And I do believe we've cooperated to the best of our ability. As Mr. Fradden does have a wife and family who will expect to hear from him soon, if not by now, and we likewise have a hotel filled with guests, many of whom are personally acquainted with Mr. Fradden, I suggest we conclude this interview. If you can offer a cause of death that we might extend to his loved ones, I would appreciate it."

"What was your take when you entered the room?" Jackson asked.

"Pardon?"

"What do you think happened to him?"

"I have neither the expertise nor experience to make an assessment, detective. If I did, doubtful I would be awaiting your consensus and educated take on this situation. If you know what's happened or have a reasonable assumption, I'd love to hear it."

Jackson maintained his gaze, his cheek twitching. "You pal was murdered, Mr. Brock, and I don't know how they handle that situation in England, but here, in the US of A, that has a tendency to stir things up. In fact, I'm pretty sure I'm going to complicate your personal life just a little bit. How about—just for the hell of it—you show me your identification and passport?"

Unfortunately, Darius wasn't surprised. Silently, he rose and strode to the leather garment bag resting on a side chair. With Jackson's announcement and request, the tension had hiked a notch inside the room, and Darius felt the woman watching him worriedly even before he turned and found her gaze. She was worried—for him?

Muffled voices breached the door, and Darius distracted with a glance at his watch. Surprised and dismayed, he spied the daylight glow on the frosted glass of the balcony. He should be on route to New York and might have preferred that flight to the advancing moments of confusion and chaos. Returning to the table, he handed his passport to Jackson, his thoughts clicking over the immediate details even as he watched Jackson begin flipping through the stamped pages.

Far more critically, Jackson glanced off Darius while handing the booklet to his silent plainclothes companion. To Darius he commented, "You understand, under the circumstances, we'll need to run a routine check on your credentials, and I'll have to ask you to change any plans about leaving in the immediate future."

"Do you intend to detain every guest in this hotel?" Darius asked.

Jackson twitched a smile, his gaze intent. "Only the ones with a passport that reads like a world atlas, Mr. Brock."

"I see," Darius pondered, his gaze unwavering. "And what will be your chosen course of action toward the other two hundred-plus possible suspects?"

"We'll be making discreet inquiries and checking the guest and registration lists," he said as he pushed from his chair. Attempting to appear dismayed, he added, "I don't have to tell you not to leave town, right? You're planning on sticking around."

With a dark glance toward Mason, who turned a ghostly white, Darius connected with Jackson. "I'll expect my credentials returned within the hour, Det. Jackson, and if I learn that you are incapable of conducting this investigation effectively, I will have you usurped."

Jackson's eyes fired. "Oh, there's no fear, Mr. Brock. I'll give this case my full attention and capability." His gaze slid toward Jenna who'd risen and stood with an expression of dumbfound. "I suggest you come with us, Miss Windrow. I have a few more questions I'd like to ask you."

When her worried gaze touched him, Darius offered a faintly reassuring smile and nodded, gesturing toward the door with his gaze. "Go on then, Jenna, but if you find his interrogation offensive, do ring me up, and I'll enlist our solicitors." Sending the warning to Jackson with a glance, he returned his gaze to the weary young woman. "When he's through, I suggest you go home and try to get some rest."

She hesitated, seemed to search him before agreeing by action, starting toward the door. "If you need anything, I'll be downstairs for a little while," she offered quietly.

"Noted and appreciated," he said lightly and walked her to the door, touching her elbow and receiving a faint flicker of her smile. What could he say? From the moment he'd seen Fradden, he'd known it was murder, and he was the most likely suspect. "It'll work out, Jenna," he said confidently, only wishing he felt as sure as he sounded. Where the Baron was concerned, things had a way of turning bad before a glimmer of good appeared.

Closing the door behind them, Darius stood momentarily, considering his options, cursing his short temper. If Jackson wasn't to be trusted or highly regarded for his skills, doubtful, he would have arrived first on this scene. Making an enemy of the chap had served no purpose whatsoever, but the lad had given Darius no choice. He might be chained to a bloody vampire, but he'd damned sure not gained that unholy position by being a pushover. If this arrogant, cynical detective wanted a bloody war, then so be it.

Rather than a war, he should have requested Jackson's termination, but in an odd moment, Darius caught himself smiling. Blast it anyway, he liked this surly chap . . . or at least liked sparring with the chap. So few challenges truly existed. To match wits with an able opponent was more than any man could hope for in a day. More often, he walked through life smiling and shaking hands with fellows who'd kiss his blasted feet and women who'd climb his trunk with a wink. To have met Jenna Windrow and felt . . . alive. He'd felt alive. Conscious. Fully aware of sensations he'd thought long forgotten.

Could he have even cried . . .? Would he have cried a week ago, a month ago, if Raphael had told him about Dylan? Could he have found the heart to be affected by the virtual loss of his only natural son?

For Dylan . . . Because of Dylan, Darius remembered absently, drawn to the window to watch the dawn unfolding beyond the frosted glass. Because of Dylan, Darius had answered that letter, and accepted the invitation cum demand to travel across Europe . . .

He'd taken the bloody midnight express and arrived in the wee hours of the morning . . . and by the stroke of midnight, he'd been a dead man.

As cold and chilled as the glass, Darius watched the salmon and yellow hues suffusing across the sky. He'd seen this view dozens of times, in the winter, in the summer. An immense hillside of barren trees and black gnarled branches faded toward gray and brown as the sun crept across the hillside. To either side of the doors, the heavy curtains draped and tucked within gold braided chords, and without more than an impulsive thought, Darius sidled and yanked the chords to send the drapes sweeping and falling, blinds dropping against the frosted glass. For a moment, turning, he was nearly blinded by the light, and a rush of mild panic raged through his mind. Manic, he wiped at his spotted vision, clearing his sight and breathing a heavy sigh. If ever . . . if ever he knew for certain—if ever he became positive of what he half believed—he would find a means to end this wretched existence.

The thought barely crossed his mind when the telephone bell erupted on the stand, and he suffered a slight edge of renewed panic. More than a dozen calls could come on that line, but Darius knew before he ever lifted the receiver . . . another turn of the screw. "Yes?"

"I booked you on a late afternoon flight to New York," Kevin said without preamble. "Be on it, m' lad, and if you have half the sense I accredit you, keep your head and keep your tongue rooted to your pallet."

"I've had a slight turn," Darius commented smoothly. "Seems my passport just departed in the pocket of a police inspector. I should have it back soon, but there's no guarantee."

"You won't need a passport to get to New York. Take a taxi to the Grand."

"Now, I do hate you," Darius decided.

"Back at you."

9

Within seconds after the second interview began, Jenna realized exactly where the investigation was headed, and no relief came with her revelation. Her words could—or already had amplified the suspicion cast toward Darius. Sitting in her office chair, with Att. Mendel at her left hand and Det. Jackson sitting directly across from her, Jenna poised for another round of questions relating to the details of last evening.

Under cross-examination, or so it seemed, Jackson had reworded the same questions several times with the apparent sole purpose of implicating her employer. Why the fellow had honed in on Darius was yet to be determined, although Jenna had her suspicions only beginning with Brock's smooth countenance and stark physical attributes. Jackson had taken offense—to the cashmere sweater, designer jeans, hand-tooled Italian loafers, jeweled rings, and diamond studded watch. Clearly, in Jackson's opinion, those were the sure sign of a homicidal maniac.

Already slap-happy, Jenna stifled a smile at her internal kibitzing and silently added a thought of an almost primal charisma. If ever there was a man who could justify a one-night stand, Darius Brock qualified. Unfortunately, Jenna had always held herself to a higher moral code. She was not a Lisa Blythe to climb the corporate ladder one bed at a time . . . but if she was already on her way out?

"All right, Miss, you said Mr. Fradden pulled Mr. Brock from the dance floor. Is that right?"

Sighing, Jenna drew on her unerring patience and admitted yet again. "They stepped aside, detective. And as I've already mentioned—several times, in fact—Mr. Brock spoke with dozens of men last evening. He was very much in demand which is dictated by his position in the company." A fact that Att. Mendel—short, plump, and half-asleep by the murky gaze over his pale eyes—should be reiterating.', Instead, the fellow merely bobbed his rounded, flushed face in agreement for the dozenth time in the past hour.

"Did you see Mr. Fradden speaking to anyone else?"

"I would imagine he spoke to several others, but don't ask me to remember each and every one," she said in mild exasperation. ."As I've already mentioned, we had nearly a hundred and fifty guests last evening."

"Well, let me ask you then—did you happen to see when either of them left the party?"

"I know Mr. Fradden left shortly after he and Darius spoke. He had an early flight to catch."

"How well do you know Darius Brock, Miss Windrow?"

"I only met him last evening," she admitted.

"How much do you know about him?"

"I know he's upper echelon in the von Hendricks Corporation." And she wasn't about to mention the nickname she'd heard long before his arrival. The Henchman would not go over well with Jackson.

"How well do you know him personally?" Jackson pushed.

Was he asking if she'd slept with him? Jenna studied the plain-faced man, withholding her initial reaction to be offended. Glancing at Mendel, expecting him to object or intervene, Jenna decided she was on her own, and the question qualified as insulting. "Det. Jackson, as I'm sure I mentioned at least once already, I only met Mr. Brock last evening. We danced and chatted a time or two but I can't claim to know him personally—or intimately if that's what you're implying."

The pictures . . . the private photo shoot in the dining hall. Jenna controlled a fleeting panic and realized the futility. Undoubtedly, Jackson had interviewed the night-shift staff before dismissing them.

"Did you know that Mr. Brock had one of the desk clerks open the novelty shop last night?"

Honestly, she could admit, "I didn't, but I'd imagine it was within his power to do so."

"Do you know why Mr. Brock might have wanted a camera in the middle of the night?"

If it was meant as a trick question to trip her up, it failed miserably. By natural order, Jackson would have already scanned the lobby security footage; hence, he'd likely seen her emerge from the dining room in the designated time frame.

"Yes, I do, detective," she answered honestly and seized the opportunity to cast Darius in a softer light. "Mr. Brock was quite taken with the Christmas decorations in the banquet hall. As I was responsible, he made a point of congratulating me and complimenting me several times, including during his opening address to our guests. Considering he was scheduled to fly out early, it's no surprise he was taking pictures after the party broke up. I was under the impression, he intended to show them off—possibly at a corporate meeting.

And to be honest, I was flattered when he asked me to assist in his endeavor in the dining room. . ."

Whether Jackson believed her or not, she neither knew nor cared. To the best of her ability, she'd offered a side of Darius Brock that defied the image of a corporate henchman. Becoming more disgusted by the minute, Jenna half-heartedly listened as Jackson continued to bend his questions in a direction to implicate Brock while Mendel, squat and balding, sat as silent as a mouse in a corner, wearing an expression of doom.

"I have no idea what Mr. Brock and Mr. Fradden discussed, detective, and truthfully, I find your questions and your attitude toward Mr. Brock as offensive as he did. For God's sake, detective, you couldn't have been more rude and blatantly insulting to any of us upstairs if you'd deliberately set out to achieve that goal. Was it his diamond ring and or his Rolex to offend you? Or even more basic? The fact that he didn't quake at your presence?"

"Miss, I'm investigating a—"

"You're not investigating a damn thing," she snapped, flashing fire in her dark blue eyes. "You've already tried and convicted Mr. Brock by convenience. Meanwhile, Mr. Fradden's killer could be halfway to Timbuktu. We had over three hundred people in this hotel last evening, between registered guests, those here for the party, and staff, and you've chosen the one man who is probably the least likely suspect . . .

"Do you honestly believe he's fool enough to kill his own employee and leave himself wide open for just this sort of assault? If I were you, sir, I think I'd be paying closer attention to those who came with Mr. Fradden from New York, and you probably should speak to Darius and find out what they discussed last evening. At least, by God, you might find a serious suspect or a Goddamn motive to pursue. And I do think that concludes this interview. I've now been awake for over twenty-four hours, and I'm going home. If you have other, more productive questions, you have my number and my address."

"Miss—"

"I'm serious," she stated, her angry gaze level on Jackson's tense brown eyes. "Unless you intend to hold me as a suspect alongside Mr. Brock, I'm not answering any further questions right now." Her gaze pivoted to Mendel. "And if you don't intend to defend my rights, Mr. Mendel, I will most assuredly have my own attorney here within the hour."

Mendel pulled himself up and looked at Jackson. "I do believe Miss Windrow's cooperated, detective."

Jackson collected his notebook and dropped his foot to the floor, pushing smoothly to his feet, turning toward the door and his associate. As an afterthought, he paused. "Just one more question, Miss. Did you sleep with him?"

Without missing a beat, Jenna asked as if dumbstruck, "Mr. Fradden . . .?"

Jackson's cheek muscle twitched in agitation. "Brock," he stated.

Dropping the pretense of surprise, she spoke calmly, "That would certainly put a crimp in your theory, wouldn't it, detective? At least your murder theory. While confirming your conviction that we're all morally corrupt and capable of all manner of wicked crime."

"You didn't answer the question," Jackson stated.

"I'm glad you noticed, detective," she said in a chilly tone. "As I stated, this interview was over a moment ago." Pushing from her chair, she slid it aside and moved to the coat rack in the corner, lifting her coat. By the time she turned, Jackson had passed through the door, and his partner had followed. Glancing at Mendel, who appeared only sorrowful, she stated, "I suggest you offer Mr. Brock more of your expertise than you've offered me, sir."

"Miss, he was within the lines of his jurisdiction—"

"He's a pompous ass, sir," she stated and reached, lifting her phone and punching the line to room 606. The line was busy. Muttering a curse, she replaced the receiver and debated for thirty seconds while lifting her garment bag. Darius needed fair warning.

"Hello, Darius."

Dropping into the corner of the couch, Darius winced with the sudden knot in his stomach. If ever he despised answering a telephone, never more than when this stout elder statesman's voice slid through the line. "Hello, George."

"I've heard you've been detained," the sorrowful voice spoke with the usual woe that only darkened Darius's mood. "I've been advised to phone you, lad. How are you?"

"Never better, ole chap," Darius said sarcastically. "A little bored. So little to do. So much fucking time. What's on your mind?"

"Well, there is something, lad. Just came to my attention, mind you. I can't imagine how it nearly slipped by me."

The paradox created by those words tamped the building hostility. Perhaps something of his humanity had survived after all. As much as he despised George Halbrook, he could never entirely blame the man for these wretched calls; they were as much a curse on him as on Darius. "What is it, George?"

"Well, it's the most amazing thing. I'm so sorry. I know how you . . . Well, lad, it seems there's a wedding you should attend."

Naturally, Darius nearly spoke aloud, his thoughts listing. He'd assumed as much when Franky Millstone, his pilot, had announced their layover in Pittsburgh. Not once in these past seven years had the Baron sent him to a destination without a dual purpose. "Go on, George."

In a leaden tone, George conveyed the details, assuring Darius the invitation would arrive posthaste and . . ."Oh, by the way . . .

Well, and this is incredible. Did I mention your cousin Lydia had her baby?"

"Must have slipped your mind, old man," Darius said lightly and suffered a mild tremor, realizing he'd forced that announcement from his mind nearly as swiftly as the Baron had confided it. "What was the date, George?"

"Just yesterday, Darius. It's rather amazing that you should be so close. Perhaps, you should pay a short visit and extend your congratulations. The young lady's in Allegheny General. If you give me a moment, I should have the address."

"I have it," Darius said absently. This was not his first layover in Pittsburgh.

"Yes of course, so sorry, lad," George chortled. "Do make a good show of it then, will you? There are too few causes for celebration. We really must take advantage of every opportunity, don't you agree?"

"Wholeheartedly," Darius said dryly, loathing the old man nearly as much as he felt sorry for him. "Is there anything else I should know?"

"No, I don't believe . . . Oh, how thoughtless. Did you hear about Dylan?"

"What about him, George?"

"Well, he's to attend a fine school, and what a joy that is for me. I will miss him tremendously, though. He was always such a fine lad. Truly, Darius, an exemplary student and a loving child. You should be only proud of him. I just don't know what we'll do without him underfoot and Raphael . . . he's heartbroken. I feel so sorry for him, but there's nothing we can do, is there? It's out of our hands—"

The knock at the door offered a welcome relief. "George, I have to go. Is there anything else?"

"Oh, I'm sorry. I'm keeping you from something. I'll ring off then. Tally ho."

Restraining the need to slam the phone, Darius set it down carefully and pushed from the chair as the second light rap of knuckles beckoned. Now, after all these bloody years. Now, they could discuss his son? seemed to insist on it, in fact. Should it surprise him? For years, he would have given his bloody right arm to know his son was safe, or happy, to hear he was an 'exemplary student' and 'a loving child.' Now . . . now he could hear that his son could play video games and associate with other children. Now . . . he could be led to believe that his son had lived a normal, happy childhood. Angry, hurt, and tense, Darius opened the door to find Jenna Windrow poised as if to take flight.

"May I come in, Mr. Brock?"

"By all means," he said without effect and sidestepped, holding the door, half wondering if this was yet another turn of the damned screw. He would like nothing better than to take this stunning woman in his arms and engage in every sort of carnal fantasy—and the blasted thought shook him nearly to his toes.

Relief swept through her eyes as she passed him and ventured only a few steps as he closed the door in her wake. In a graceful turn for a woman in tennis shoes, she stood and looked at him with a glimmer of anger that vanished and switched to concern in her deep blue eyes. "Is everything all right?"

He looked like a man who'd just lost his dearest friend—or his only friend. The sadness in his eyes compelled her to step toward him, but he swept the emotions away as if blowing dust off a mahogany tabletop. His eyes darkened with a sharp focus, an intensity as fierce as the words he'd sent at Jackson hours ago.

"I wonder if I shouldn't be asking you the same, Jenna. Please don't tell me they've detained you for this duration or that you've been downstairs handling administrative affairs in Mason's stead."

With a pensive smile, she commented, "Things have been rather hectic. I just finished an interview with Det. Jackson." Of all the reactions, a glint of amusement in his dark eyes and a twitch in his mustached lips would have been the last expected. "Darius," she said gravely, and he attempted to wipe the smirk from his lips. "I came to warn you. I have the distinct impression from his line of questioning that Det. Jackson—"

"Wait, do let me guess," he said with a deeper smirk and motioned her toward the table. "He's convinced I'm an international assassin."

Her heart leaped at the whimsy and amusement in his deep voice. "Darius, he is seriously attempting to find evidence that you are somehow involved in this incident."

"My dearest, I may not know the American justice system as well as I should under the circumstances, but it is my understanding that one must have evidence to be found before accusing another of a crime. Now, were I standing on the soil of a Third World country, I'd be a trifle concerned. America doesn't sanction torture or firing squads, does it?"

His attitude could be as confounding as the heat of his eyes. Bewildered, Jenna followed him to the table, watching him as he refilled his coffee cup and filled a second fresh cup from the tray centering the table. "You don't find this just a trifle alarming?" she asked and watched his eyes light with a flash of humor or anger, a combination and conflict.

"This certainly isn't the first time I've faced a slightly inconvenient situation, Jenna. I do travel a great deal. Have you just come up from the lobby?"

"Yes."

"Did you happen to notice if Mr. Trevane's about?"

"He was with . . . Mason," she said and realized why Trevane had stood alongside Mason. In retrospect, she recalled seeing the security guards stationed at the door intimidating Charlie and Mac, the bellhops, as well as the crowd bundled against the cold and awaiting transportation outside the door. Her thoughts spinning, she studied the slightly innocent smile on the handsome face and shook her head slowly, not even sure why she should be amazed. Simply because the man had remained in this room, didn't mean he was either oblivious or idle. He was pulling the strings, she realized. "You already knew about Jackson's line of investigation."

"I'd be suspicious of me if I were him," Darius mused. "It seems only natural."

Not entirely relieved, she studied him momentarily and noticed the shadows playing across his face. Belatedly, she realized the darkness in the room and glanced at the drawn curtains through which nothing of the morning sunlight penetrated. From her walk through the lobby, she knew daylight had arrived, with sunlight sparkling on the fresh snow and glistening with an intensity to create sunspots on unshaded eyes. For a half second, she wondered if he'd meant to sleep but considered the bedroom where he would have been far more comfortable. He was awake . . . wide awake despite the long hours and his apparent weariness before the midnight madness. Searching his deeply curious eyes, she felt that tug of shared awareness and thought of Jackson's final question. Yanking herself from that shallow thought, she looked again to the curtains and back. "The sun's out."

"I'm sure it is."

Annoyed with her blurted, senseless statement, she studied him more critically. He was comfortable in the darkness, well suited to this weird dull light. "Would you mind if I open the drapes?"

"Yes, I would," he said quietly. "I found the glare a tad offensive. Was there anything else you've come to impart?"

"No," she decided and sipped a swallow of coffee, lowering the cup to the table.

"I'm sorry," he said quietly, sounding sincere and genuinely dismayed. "That was rude and thoughtless, and you're deserving neither, Luv."

"There's no need to apologize, Darius. It's been a very long night," she said. "I did want you to be forewarned and forearmed. I'm sure Det. Jackson will be back to speak with you before long, and I wanted you to be prepared. Obviously, that wasn't necessary, and I'm sorry for bothering you," she said and started to turn. In two steps, he caught her arm, and she halted, looking into his eyes, seeing the conflicts again, the sadness.

"I truly do apologize, Jenna. I . . . It's been so bloody long since I've had someone genuinely concerned for my welfare . . . It's no excuse. You've been more than kind and honest with me, and I've thrown it in your face. Will you forgive me?"

Unconsciously, she found his hand and clasped his fingers, not losing his eyes and seeing the startled flash, the confusion. "You have a lot on your mind, Darius, and I know you were tired before this situation developed. There's nothing to forgive. Why don't you lie down and try to get some sleep? I'm taking your advice and going home. I've asked Julia to call me if there's anything I should know. I'll ask you to call me if there's anything I can do. I don't live too far away, but I need to go home and get some sleep. I don't work well when I'm tired, either."

"Will you be all right to drive home?"

"I'll be fine."

"If there's anything you need, you have the private number to reach me here. Don't hesitate to ring me."

"Thank you."

"That extends to any further harassment from our industrious investigator, Jenna. If he contacts you at home, ring me up. I do believe we've cooperated as far as the situation warrants."

"I agree and said as much," she said lightly, half smiling. "I don't think he'll bother me at home."

"I keep forgetting your fortitude," he said with a slight smirk. "You're a formidable woman, Miss Windrow, and more than capable of handling a chap like Jackson." He winked and nudged her toward the door. "If my orders mean a thing to you, darling, go home, soak in a heated, scented bath, drink a glass of wine, and settle under a warm blanket. The combination will assure you of a good night's rest despite the daylight."

"You left out drawing the drapes," she mused.

"I trust you to work out the remaining details," he said smoothly and opened the door. He might have timed that action for dramatic effect as quickly as Jackson recoiled his fist from the start of a knock. "Hmm, back so soon, detective?"

Jackson's cheek muscle twitched as he bounced his glance off Darius to Jenna. "Miss," he said with quiet anger, acknowledging and accusing her in that single word.

The 'chap' was in for an extremely rude awakening if he intended to match wits with the Englishman who leaned and brushed a chaste kiss on Jenna's lips, tossing her a discreet wink. Toward Jackson, Darius commented, "Do be a good sport and let the young lady pass."

For just an instant, Jenna thought to be amused, but as she stepped through the parted opening, she landed a clear gaze on the two gentlemen who had accompanied Jackson. The dark, crisp suits gave them away without the sober set on their faces. In the shadow of the two FBI agents, Att. Mendel appeared as insignificant as a child. Tempted to back-step into the room, Jenna forced herself forward and stepped between the men who eyed her critically. She would be no help to Darius in her present mental decline, and she had no doubt of his ability to handle these staid gentlemen.

Gathering her wits, she barely glanced to see the foursome filing into the suite and sent a silent vote of confidence to Darius as she headed for the elevator.

"Mind if we ask you a few questions, Mr. Brock?"

The request came in delay, Darius noted while bouncing his glance between the three somber faces. Jackson appeared smug behind his steady gaze. Mirroring the grim expression, Darius motioned his guests to the table, his gaze listing to Jackson, who remained the senior in this group, closely followed by the stockier of his dark-suited comrades. "Have you learned anything of significance?" he asked soberly.

"Little too early to get our hopes up," Jackson said with an undertow of sarcasm.

"I'm a little low on coffee, but if you like, I'll send for another pot," he offered toward the oldest government agent.

"We're fine," the man stated, lifted his jacket, and extracted a wallet, offering Darius a glimpse of the Beretta tucked into a fine leather holster. Flipping the wallet, the man displayed his credentials. "Federal Agents, Warton and Kendel," Warton offered. "Why don't we sit down?"

"By all means," Darius agreed. Pulling his chair from under the table, he motioned to the agent to join him, donning a more natural curiosity and concern. "I'm at a serious loss here, gentlemen," he admitted. "I wasn't aware of this investigation falling under federal jurisdiction. Is that common practice?"

"We've been asked to assist in the investigation," Warton said smoothly.

"By whom, if you don't mind me asking?"

"I brought them into it," Jackson answered, feigning to sound important.

Darius looked at him with a blank gaze, his tone indifferent, "If I somehow inspired your lack of confidence in your abilities, inspector, I do apologize." Jackson restrained his anger with impressive control, and Darius looked to the senior agent. "How may I assist, Agent Warton?"

"What exactly is your affiliation to Hendricks Distribution?" Wharton asked.

"As I mentioned to Insp. Jackson earlier, I'm an executive attaché to the von Hendricks Corporation. Hendricks Distributing is one of the subsidiaries."

"I understand you're from the head office, Mr. Brock. I know von Hendricks is an international conglomerate. Where exactly is your headquarters located?"

"We have several headquarters, Agent Warton. Two within the United States, which I assume you know. One in New York, another in Chicago."

"Which office do you work out of?"

"I travel a great deal between the headquarters, but I'm based most often out of the London Branch Office."

"That's not exactly what I asked," Wharton commented. "Where's your main headquarters?"

"Pardon me for saying, Agent Wharton, I'm not sure what bearing the location of my company has upon this investigation."

"Who do you answer to, Mr. Brock? Who is your direct superior?"

"I answer to any number of executives on the Corporation's Board of Directors, several of whom are United States citizens. I'll be glad to offer you the numbers to reach them if you don't have that information. I should warn you in advance, however, they would probably reroute your inquiries back to me, and I'd, in turn, route any inquiries of a corporate nature to our legal department. Now, sir, we are at an impasse. If you have relative questions about the investigation of Mr. Fradden's demise, I'd be happy to answer them. If not, I'd like to know if your investigation thus far is bearing fruit."

"About what time did you leave the party last evening?"

"Shortly after midnight," Darius answered. "I don't know the exact time."

"Did you come directly to your room?"

"Yes, I did."

"Were you alone?"

"Yes."

"Do you know about what time Mr. Fradden left the ballroom?"

"As I recall, he departed before I did," Darius answered, aware of both other men studying him.

"How well did you know Mr. Fradden?" Wharton asked.

"Personally, not well, but I've known him for several years in a business capacity."

"You ever visit his house when you were in New York?"

"Not that I can recall," Darius said honestly.

"What was his position in the company?"

Darius studied the man critically for a moment, "I'd think that question's rather late in coming, and I do hope I'm not the first person with whom you've spoken."

"Excuse me?"

"All due respect, if you don't even know the man's bloomin' occupation, you can't have spent much of the past several hours searching for his killer," Darius stated while turning his heated gaze toward Jackson. "What the bloody hell have you been doing?"

Wharton stated, "Answer the question, Mr. Brock."

Darius turned his gaze to Wharton. "The bloody hell if I will, Agent Wharton," he stated in a chilly tone. "I have an associate whose family will demand answers from me very shortly. I'll have to face this man's wife and children and explain my ignorance. If you can't even learn his occupation without asking the head of the Goddamn company, your chance of finding his killer—"

"We know his Goddamn occupation," Jackson snapped.

"Then why the bloody 'ell are you wasting time asking me?" Darius fired back with an angry glance. "Do you believe I don't know it?" When his temper riled, his cockney accent erupted, and it nearly stifled his anger to hear it echoing back to him. "By rote, I'm not a pleasant bloke when faced with incompetence," he stated crisply, his gaze returned to the senior agent. "Unless, by damned, you've questions that will ultimately assist in solving this crime, I suggest you waste someone else's time."

"Were you in your room all evening?" Wharton asked with a firm resolve.

"No, as a matter of fact, I wasn't. I went downstairs around three, and I'm sure if you haven't, you may verify that detail with the night crew employees."

"Why did you go downstairs?"

"I haven't seen the hotel appear quite so grand in holiday trim. I took advantage of the few hours before my flight to capture the elegance on film."

"Did you see anyone or speak with anyone during your photography session?"

"Yes," he said smoothly. "Registration clerks, both of them. Miss Windrow, the assistant manager here, and at least one of the night guards when I stepped out to capture the front entrance." His thoughts clicking, Darius ran the time sequence in his head, recalling his departure from the dining room around midnight. Fradden had departed nearly a half hour earlier . . . and in a fleeting instant, Darius recalled the footsteps passing outside his door. Hurried footsteps. He'd been talking on the phone . . . to Raphael. Unless the coroner could cite the time of death to the moment, a telephone call would not offer an alibi, but it might offer a lead for these blokes to follow.

Focusing on Wharton's staid gaze, Darius commented, "I'll assume you're attempting to find a time frame or a possible witness rather than a killer at this moment, and thus, I'll mention something which struck me slightly odd last evening." Not one of the three flinched, but Darius sensed his latter assumption was far more accurate. "As I said, I returned to my room shortly after midnight. It's not unheard of for me to spend most of the night on the telephone, especially on an overnight stop. I was on the telly last evening, sitting on the couch there," he said with a glance toward the couch, back to Wharton. "It would have been between 12:30 and 1:00. I hadn't been on the line long. It struck me odd to hear someone hurrying past the door at that hour. Honestly, I didn't even know Fradden was on this floor, and I assumed most of the executives would be found at the party."

"You assume that was the killer passing?"

"The footsteps were headed toward the elevator, and I hadn't heard anyone come onto the floor," he shrugged. "You tell me, Agent Wharton. Is it even possible? Have you checked with other of my associates in the surrounding rooms? Have any mentioned coming upstairs, possibly to collect a wife's compact or his wallet? The footsteps seemed too heavy for a woman and, like I said, hurried."

As if to verify his words, which Darius would not consider a coincidence, not for all the world, a dual set of footsteps passed, creaking the floorboards outside the door. Murmured voices accompanied the footsteps, breaching the walls without concise words. His gaze following the sounds across the wall, he donned a faintly curious smile and brought his attention to see Wharton's gaze returning. "There it is then," Darius said lightly. "One of my life's more annoying inconveniences. Regardless of the depth of the walls, the floors in some of these older buildings creak and thud like tinderbox constructs."

"You say you heard that around 12:30?"

"Unfortunately, it was an incoming call on a direct line to this suite. There won't be a phone record of the call to accurately pinpoint the time, and I didn't think to look at my watch."

"Who were you talking to?"

"A friend overseas," Darius answered and knew they assumed a female friend, which was just as well. "It was a personal call, and it will remain so," Darius commented.

"They might be able to give us a time frame."

"I would assume a coroner would be swifter and more accurate. If Mr. Fradden died during that span, I suggest you make discreet inquiries and find out who might have been missing from the party. Or you might check with the registration clerks to learn if they noticed anyone come from the elevator and head for the door. If I remember accurately, the snowfall was supposed to end near midnight. Surely you have leads you might follow."

"Did you speak with Mr. Fradden any time last evening?"

"Yes, I did," Darius admitted smoothly.

"What did you talk about?"

"Business," Darius answered.

"What was his mood when you talked?" Kendel asked.

"Pompous," Darius answered.

"In what way?" Kendel asked.

"He seemed to believe he was entitled to capitalize on my time," Darius said without emphasis. "As I didn't have a great deal of time to waste and had no desire to spend it consumed in a business discussion, I suppose I was rather short with him. He stomped out directly after that as I recall."

"What did he want to talk about?" Wharton asked.

"Regrettably, I have no clue," Darius said quietly. "The conversation didn't progress much past his initial demands. The poor bloke chose to interrupt me on the dance floor and compounded the affront by demanding my immediate—undivided—attention. I'm truly not as accommodating as I should be when faced with over a hundred people vying for my attention. Had I even suspected he could have had a serious problem . . .? Twenty-twenty hindsight," he said in self-disgust.

"We have a few people who seemed to think you were quarreling," Wharton commented.

"I have a bit of a temper, but I certainly wouldn't go to blows over an interrupted dance, Agent Wharton, nor would I murder an employee for any reason. Rather be like cutting off my nose to spite my face, and I rather enjoy my occupation when I'm not in the crux of a murder investigation."

"As far as you know, were there any problems with the New York Distribution office?"

"I hadn't heard of anything, but I assure you, I have people looking into it as we speak."

"I suggest you leave the investigation to us, Mr. Brock."

"You truly don't expect me to do that, do you, Agent Wharton?" Darius asked quietly.

"If we find out you're interfering with this investigation, Mr. Brock, we won't hesitate to take action."

10

The Grand, or Baby Grand, as Darius had heard it called in the past, stood on a stretch of beachfront on the Sound. The property had probably cost a fortune even in the latter half of the past century when it had fallen into Baron von Hendricks' hands. Pre-dating the Chateau by nearly fifty years, the Grand stood as firmly rooted as the wide-trunk oaks and pines that crowded its black walls and braced against the coastal winds. Like all other of the Baron's lodgings, the hotel adhered to ancient tradition, sporting a magnificent entryway alight under two immense teardrop chandeliers. Brass balustrades accented the mezzanine and balcony, overlooking the lobby, gold leaf ceilings, and ornate archways.

At dusk, the Grand was magnificent, already aglow against the backdrop of black water, but day or night, the ambiance never failed to impress. Close enough to the city to host some of the most prestigious clientele and far enough to keep out the riffraff, the Grand employed a year-round staff, rarely suffering an off-season. Guests arrived for the elegance, the quiet, and the quality of service, whether to enjoy the immense beds and fine cuisine or to be treated with the reverence and pampered care they received from the impeccable waitstaff.

Before Darius fully stepped from the cab, a young bellhop sporting a red wool jacket and cap arrived at his heels and collected his single garment bag, bidding an anxious welcome. Darius was expected. Apparently, Kevin had phoned ahead. The manager, Quisten, a portly chap who'd probably begun his career as a bellhop in this lobby, hustled from his office carrying the appropriate key and a sealed envelope, smiling and bidding a welcome as he thrust both items into Darius's hands. In the elevator that rose only to the fourth floor, Darius broke the seal and read the single message, unconsciously checking his watch.

He'd reached the hotel less than a half hour ahead of the Baron's scheduled arrival. Stepping onto the fourth floor, the bellhop hurrying at his heels, Darius strode the length of the carpeted hall through a half-light of brass wall sconces twinkling electric flames. The single door at the end of the tunnel opened into a small entry and spiral staircase, where Darius tipped his escort and sent him away.

With no trouble at all, Darius imagined the Baron residing indefinitely within the private west wing. A tower unto itself, protected from the rising sun by the bulk of stone walls, it was positioned carefully to prohibit any portal windows from facing west. In effect, the stairwell and collection of rooms carried a perpetual twilight, enhanced by dark woods and thick velvet drapes. Only the shade of curtains and swirled, velveteen wallpaper changed between the rounded sitting room and connecting bed and dining area. Unlike the Chateau, no paying guest had ever shared the splendor of this private suite. The Baron's home away from home, a permanent residence from which he could venture north, south, or west as the spirit moved him.

Fine wines stocked the etched glass liquor closets within the sitting room, and Darius moved to the doors immediately, checking, assuring himself the selection remained intact. Books, from first editions pre-dating America to modern texts, filled the shelves, forming an octagonal shape within the inside walls. Dusted recently, if not just today, Darius assured himself. If only by routine, he climbed the short flight of steps to the master bedroom, an elegant windowless room to accommodate a king. Thick black velvet curtains slid smoothly on tracks that extended between the spiral columns. Electric, candle-shaped bulbs flickered soft light, illuminating freshly laundered bedding and spit-shined armoires, likely aired to await the arsenal of clothes to arrive soon.

After he assured himself all was in order, cursing himself throughout the ordeal, Darius retreated to the main floor of the suite and carried his garment bag into the privy. Hurrying, he shed his leisure ensemble, indulged in a quick hot bath if only to settle his jangled nerves, and donned a black camel hair suit, charcoal chambray shirt, and black tie. Depending on his employer's mood, the tailored suit would undoubtedly gain him a snide comment masked in praise or vice versa.

Dressed, Darius fumbled with the tie in a small vanity mirror, cursing his anxiety. Even after all this bloody time, coming face to face with the Baron could set his teeth on edge. Fear never factored into his anxiety. Not for his life, in any event. Inevitably, by his damned nature, he would say the wrong thing, snap at the wrong moment, flash his hatred on the surface, and see it mashed under a cutting blow. Worse, by far, was the simple, undeniable futility of his hatred. The Baron loved it. And by extension, loved Darius, which only outraged him more, compounded tenfold when the Baron reduced him to a damned obstinate child.

With a glance at his watch, Darius uttered a curse, pulled himself together, and trotted down the spiral steps, letting himself onto the fourth floor. At the elevators, he joined an elegant couple of considerable vintage; both dressed with the careless grace of old wealth that Darius had come to appreciate. They were the Grand's typical clientele, class-conscious without a need to flaunt diamonds or designer labels. The cut of the man's suit and string of pearls resting on exquisite pale blue wool spoke volumes.

Darius wore that same appearance, he knew if only by the quick acceptance on both faces and their subtle acknowledging nods and smiles. Not that long ago, these elder sophisticates would have cringed to see him stepping into the elevator alongside them. Time and again at the onset, the Baron had told him he looked like a mule dressed to trot in a minstrel's rendition of a king's parade.

'Wealth is not the size of a bank account,' the Baron had dripped sarcasm. 'It's an attitude, a presence, a manner of thinking and looking at the world as if it's your own . . .'

Barely stepping from the elevator, Darius caught the hustle behind the registration desk, two classy blonds wearing gold-buttoned jackets, both vying for the opportunity to run toward him and offer assistance. The bellhop, stationed at a podium near the door, likewise paid heed, and by no surprise, Quisten stepped lively from his office, heading on a collision course. Without a thought to his actions, Darius gestured the man away, his interest and attention riveted on the glass doors. Unconsciously, he lifted a pack of thin cigars from his jacket, lighting one as he stopped within arm's reach of the etched glass and brass doors.

Either it had begun to snow again, or sea mist had turned to fine ice flakes to swirl within the covered breezeway over the entrance. Not much of the drive to the Grand could he recall. The bustle at the airport, the crowds and voices, and the rush of motion and faces had offered relief and an odd comfort that abandoned him when he offered the cab driver his destination. Life existed beyond his tunnel-vision world. People, common people, conducted their daily lives in sweet oblivion, anxious to catch planes or hug loved ones, pushing strollers and pulling children, raising families, working, laughing . . .

He caught himself thinking of Jenna Windrow, seeing her smile to suggest she held an amusing secret, hearing her soft laugh that conveyed a contagious infection of delight. As if even such a memory and thought were forbidden, Darius's attention riveted on the sleek black fenders gliding, lengthening, stretching into his line of sight. Instantly, he started forward, not surprised when the doorman lurched ahead and the porter bumped into him in his haste. The second doorman was faster, clearing the path and letting the chilly blast slam Darius full force.

Night had descended fully, as black as the limousine from its wheels to its roof, the windows as dark as the paint. When the limo halted, a suited man stepped from the front passenger seat; his partner, the driver, emerged across the hood. Darius paused before reaching the car, his focus fixed on the rear doors, his senses keening to a prickle of the gaze through the glass. Presence. Even if Darius had never met him, had glimpsed him only in passing, Darius would have recognized the presence and power in the man who slid smoothly from the rear compartment.

By physical stature alone, Amadeus von Hendricks would demand more than a passing glance. Six foot seven, proportionately built across the shoulders and hips, he carried himself with a grace to defy his size. 'A Greek god,' one paparazzi had written not long ago, and the Baron had raged his amusement, correcting, 'A Romanian Lord.' The Baron's rendition was more accurate, Darius agreed. With a scatter of long black waves catching the wind and his piercing blue eyes, the Baron appeared far more gypsy lord than Greek god, far more otherworldly than human despite his thick black mustache curved immaculately over full, musing lips. Physically, in his human form, he remained, without exception, the most beautiful being Darius had ever had the displeasure to encounter.

Ebony cashmere, his long overcoat flagged in the wind, whipping at his shins as he closed the distance without seeming to walk. With a flicker of sparks in his cobalt eyes and a musing smirk in his mustache, the Baron tsked, and his silky voice dripped like oil off his sensuous lips. "Where are your manners, m' lad? Not a hug or even a handshake for your beloved master?"

The words carried the intended effect. Darius snapped from his start and woke to the jewel-bedecked hands opening to either side, demanding. Every muscle taut, he obliged, offering his hand, knowing the futility as the immense palm captured his. Encompassing, the cashmere sleeves landed over Darius's shoulders and dragged him into a suffocating embrace.

Overhead, the Baron rumbled a deep laugh. "Never a dull moment with you, eh? Always a pleasure to see you."

If the force of the hold were any indication, the pleasure would be the Baron's exclusively. Catching his breath, barely, Darius stepped from the embrace and caught sight of yet another man standing outside the car.

In a doubletake, Darius recognized his younger cousin Ted, who appeared nearly as dazzled as he was dazed, likewise dressed to the nines in a long cashmere coat and suit. His cousin, at twenty-six, was far more naturally pretty than beautiful in masculine proportions. His face was smooth, his cheeks and jaw softly curved rather than cut, his hair a sandy blond and slightly longer than Darius remembered. By far, the long lashes swamping his pale eyes were his most stunning attribute, accented by soft, lush lips, forever pouting despite the worried frowns and smiles fleeting randomly across his features. Just the sight of Teddy Brock ripped Darius's thoughts between disgust and sorrow, a paradox to grip his chest and spin his senses between his good fortune and possible fates worse than death. Nothing could Darius hide from the man who stood watching him, and by no surprise, the nudge came at his shoulder.

"Well, go on, then. Give your cousin a hug. It's been a while since you've seen him as I seem to recall," the Baron said with a lofty note, a dark amusement.

What bothered him more, coming face to face with the Baron or his cousin, Darius couldn't decide, but he suspended his thoughts and donned a smile, offering a handshake. "Teddy, good to see you."

Nearly manic, a smile exploded on his soft lips and he ignored the handshake, tossing his arms about Darius's shoulders, demanding an embrace as needy as any child. In French, Teddy huffed a greeting, sounding both desperate and breathless, lending Darius a hint about what kind of trip the boy had endured.

In his mind, Darius barely started to correct his thoughts and realized the futility. Forever, he would think of Teddy as a boy, an innocent child caught in wicked circumstances that he'd been ill-equipped to grasp. Aware of the Baron watching, Darius eased from his cousin's embrace and directed the boy with a gesture while likewise directing the porter to hurry ahead with the bags.

Naturally, the Baron clasped Darius around the shoulders in an embrace to pass for fondness, ushering him through the held doors. Several heads turned, from the receptionist manning the desk to several guests checking. Mouths parted, eyes widened, likely alarmed and alert at a primal level—although they might be reacting to the presence of royalty or struggling to identify a celebrity.

Enjoying himself, the attention and shock he created as they entered the lobby, the Baron ducked his head to whisper in Darius's captive ear. "Kept our secret, so I see. I wasn't expected."

If the Baron wanted his presence known, he would have announced his arrival.

"Hmm," the Baron murmured, then turned his attention to Quisten who approached hastily, stammering a greeting in his excitement. Offhandedly, the Baron commented, "Find lodging for my drivers, will you, m' lad, and see that I'm not disturbed."

In the elevator, the Baron overwhelmed the car, clasping Teddy to his other side and hugging them both like wayward sons. Against Darius's ear again, he mused, "I'd have brought the matched set to this bookend, but I'd rather not suffer the distraction of a third wheel. You understand, I'm sure. A pity, though. I know Brian would have loved to see you."

The tempo was set, Darius realized and maintained his smile, his eyes darkening considerably. He held his tongue, refusing to take the bait, halting even a thought to what the Baron might have implied in those few words.

At the entrance to the stairwell, Darius produced the key and stood aside. In the sitting room, the Baron dismissed the porter, then tipped his gaze to Teddy. "Take the bags upstairs, m' lad, and do spend a few moments to acclimate and unpack."

"Yes, sir," Teddy said, gathering the leather cases and hurrying to the steps.

The Baron watched him depart with a smile easily mistaken for fondness. Sighing, he sped his gaze about the room, acclimating rapidly and moving to one of the couches, his gaze falling on Darius. "Do believe a glass of wine would be appropriate, m' lad. You won't mind pouring, will you?"

"Not at all, sir," Darius said and moved to the liquor closet, selecting a vintage and brand to the Baron's liking. As he brought a single glass from the shelf, the Baron commented, "You will join me, I trust, Darius."

Darius brought another glass from the shelf, his actions animated. With both filled crystal flutes in hand, he turned smoothly and strode to the couch, more uncomfortably aware of the dark blue eyes studying him. Never had Darius met a man whose expressions could betray so little of his thoughts, but then, Baron Amadeus von Hendricks was as far from a man as the sun from the moon.

On the surface, the Baron appeared only amused, his blue eyes glittering with a comfortable shine, as much approval as delight as he accepted the glass and motioned Darius into a side chair. Maintaining his fond smile, Amad leaned and lifted his glass toward Darius, demanding a toast. "To what shall we toast, m' lad?"

"Whatever you like, sir," Darius said smoothly, noting the darker shine.

"To fond reunions, then," the Baron mused and touched Darius's glass to emit a soft, resonant ping. "And loyal relationships."

"Das vi donia," Darius said without conscious thought, and his mind jack-knifed with a glimpse of another pair of blue eyes brightened with honest amusement. Snapping his mind shut at the sound of a lyrical soft voice, he held his council despite the lifted black brow and twitching smile.

"Quite a predicament you've gotten yourself into this time, isn't it, my boy?"

A murder investigation. A confiscated passport. Darius studied the suddenly indifferent gaze, his own near mirror reflection. "As I didn't get myself in, I doubt I'll get myself out," he said smoothly. "I'd imagine you have the situation in hand."

Without losing his smile, the Baron commented, "Don't test your arrogance, m' lad."

"I wasn't," Darius said honestly.

The Baron studied him, then emitted a soft humph. "You are a fickle lad, Darius," he mused. "It's not a wonder that you and Raphael get along so well. The lad sends his love, by the way."

"I spoke to him last night," Darius admitted, refusing to consider the discussion or the details the boy had imparted. With an iron resolve, he held his gaze steady and concentrated on the moment at hand.

"Sounds as if you're resigned to the loss, m'lad."

Uncontrollably, Darius tipped his gaze toward his wine glass, remembering the hurt not that many hours passed. "As a wise man pointed out," he said quietly, looking at the Baron's more intrigued gaze. "Whatever I beheld was lost at conception."

"And you accept thus?" the Baron asked gravely.

"Do I have a choice?"

Split second, the Baron emitted surprise and mocked astound, "Well, Blimey! It sounds as if you're finally growing up, lad."

"Imagine that happens on occasion."

The Baron lost his astound toward dark amusement. "You've lied, m' lad. I happen to know you took the announcement extremely hard." He feigned sorrow, leaning and offering his hand, demanding Darius lean and clasp the hand despite his dread. With a firm, chilled grip, the Baron spoke grimly, "I'd just like you to know . . . I feel your pain. I should also like to point out—I haven't killed the lad or sent him to work in a bloody sweathouse. Despite the ages, Darius, such places do exist, and I should further mention, that I expected slightly more gratitude. If such is beyond you, I can certainly make changes in the present plans."

His attention hinged on every word, on the warning, Darius held the blank gaze as firmly as the hand. "What the bloody hell do you expect from me? To be grateful? Aye, I'm grateful that you've kept my only son alive. For eight fucking years, you've divined to be bloody merciful and let me know he was such when you knew I'd go bloody bats from fear for him. And now, I'll pay for my honesty, for my temper when you know damned well, I have no choice but to rage. You even expect it. Prefer it to fucking complacency. But I'll pay for it just the same. So, to bloody hell with you. Aye, you can punish me with untold horrors and to bloody hell with that, too," he said bluntly, his dark eyes livid with anger. "Chain me to a fucking wall, and drink my fucking blood. What the bloody hell can I do to stop you? Nothing. Not a damned thing. I'm avowed and honor-fucking-bound to bow at your command—"

Amusement blasted into the blue eyes, the smile sliding more fully into the lips as the Baron idled a low chuckle. "Oh, Darius, I knew I could count on you to raise my mood. Nearly worth the trip alone to see a bit of that hot English blood in your eyes. A noble lot, you lads."

"Damn you," Darius uttered and pivoted his angry gaze away, torn between a thought of his words and the consequences of the same. Where was Kevin when he was needed? Where was the kick under the table, a fierce reminder to hold his tongue? He might well have consigned Dylan to a fate worse than hell! His thoughts shattered, his anger ebbing toward sorrow and genuine regret, he lowered his gaze deeper. "Now, I am sorry."

"Of course you are," the Baron consoled. "You're a bright lad when you stop to think for a split second."

He hated this. Truly hated the roller coaster of his emotions to be stoked with a word or a glance. As impotent now as when he had first matched wits against this monster, he had little choice but to resign. With a shallow hold on his desperation, knowing the futility of even attempting to hide it, he looked into the dark, brooding eyes. "I have tried to accept my losses. I've resigned to never seeing Dylan again in this life. As much as I once wanted to be a part of his life, to see him grow, to even hold his hand for a few seconds or touch his hair as he slept—I've resigned to the futility and vowed to honor the oath I took. You knew I was a self-indulgent bastard when you first looked at me. I'd ask you not to punish him for that, but even that I've lost the right and privilege to plead. He's in your hands, and I'll need to accept whatever you deem for his fate."

"The lad looks a bit like you," the Baron said, sliding his hand away and leaning back, his gaze pensive, almost appraising. "Fine looking lad, in fact. Plenty of thick dark waves. His eyes are a shade lighter, more like the bitch who whelped him, I trust," he said with a hint of disgust, his eyes still intent. "I probably did you a favor, though, Darius. He doesn't have your spirit or your zest for life. He certainly doesn't have your arrogance or quick wit. You probably shouldn't have locked my lad into that promise. A few good bruises might have given the boy character. As it is, he's something of a dolt."

Hinged on every word, Darius refused to be offended, genuinely grateful, and mildly surprised to hear even this much. At a gut level, his tension rose, anticipating the worst, feeling as if the Baron were leading to another harsh blow. Calling Dylan a 'dolt,' criticizing the lad was more of a jest than a serious attempt to hurt. Waiting for the shoe to drop, Darius gazed into the bemused blue eyes.

"Worried you, have I?"

"Yes, sir," he said honestly.

"Were I to give you a choice to determine your son's fate, Darius, what would you desire for him?"

His heart hammered a leaden blow, knowing this game too well, refusing to play. "Whatever you desire for him."

"Liar," the Baron mused and intensified his gaze. "Answer the question."

"I-I'd want him to live as I hope you've let him live this long."

"Meaning?"

"Oblivious and ignorant. Happy and unharmed. Burdened less by what could be than what is. I'd want him to be decent and live a normal life with people to love him and be loved by him. No more or less."

The Baron snickered, "You'd prefer him to be a dolt."

"A happy dolt."

"I could dress him in fine clothes, put him up in a mansion on a grand countryside, see that he marries well and has at least two to call his own, and you would prefer that I leave him to his own devices, is that so?"

"I can't control how I feel," Darius conceded. "You asked. I answered honestly."

"Have you thought of what the consequences would be, Darius, if as time progresses, your son learned that you, Darius the Great, hold such a position in my company? That you abandoned him, as much as traded him for the lifestyle I've given you? I wonder what his thoughts would be if he learned his father preferred wealth over raising him. Ah, and enhance that issue when he learns that you've asked me to give him no more than a pauper's pittance. You are a horrid father, Darius. Truly, lad, I spared you a great deal of pain by relieving you of that responsibility. Any man who would want his lad to struggle as he so struggled . . . Truly, you're a man lacking compassion."

"You . . . intend to tell him that," Darius realized.

The Baron smiled. "Have I mentioned I've been something of a father to the lad? Did a much better job of it than you, to be sure. The lil fellow's never wanted for a thing. If, Darius, tis pain you want and need, then know that I've stolen not your son but the love he might have given you. He calls me Pappa, by the way."

"Damn you."

The Baron chuckled. "Damn me, indeed. The lad does know you, by the way. He's heard a great deal about his natural father. I do believe he hates you just a smidgeon for your indifference to him, but I have tried to explain man's ambitions. I might have also mentioned that you're incapable of committing to intimate relationships, and the lad's bright enough to have heard and grasped the more lucrative rumors concerning your romantic endeavors. As I heard recently, he's just a tad ashamed of you. If not for Kevin, I shouldn't wonder if the lad would have begged me long ago to make him my adopted son and give him my name. Truth be known, I've even considered obliging him. He certainly wouldn't be the first bastard to receive that prestigious name to call his own."

Darius had heard enough, but in the way of most encounters, he could no more run from the words than fight them. Pushing off the chair, he tugged his angry gaze from the cobalt blue orbs and turned, striding a few paces away. Lies. Every word could be a lie, or it could be the truth told in such a way as to deliver maximum pain. Either way, his stomach knotted with the tension, and his chest tightened in anger. His Achilles heel, his son. Even now, his son could spiral him to the brink of emotions. A weakness to be used against him, to manipulate him toward the fiercest dread or most futile rage. To think of Dylan loving this monster . . . running to him, hugging him, adoring him, and idolizing him . . .

Nothing could be done to alter those details if they held a grain of truth. He couldn't even verify the words one way or another. Raphael might confide a few words, but no more or less than the Baron would allow. No others would bridge the gulf between him and his son. The child's mother, Sherry . . .

As much as Darius hated to admit it, the woman had meant very little to him even before eight years ago. Whatever torch he'd carried for her had burned away long before Darius had met the Baron. Affairs . . . seven lighthearted affairs had evidenced the dissatisfaction he'd suffered in his marriage and pre-empted what was to become of his life. Dylan was the only good thing to come of that marriage, the only living connection to the world even then. With no others had Darius ever shared a common bond, a natural tie. His own father had left him. His mother had slid toward the bottle before he was of age to understand her decline. Perhaps they'd both suffered something they had neither understood . . . both suffered the sickness that had reached epic proportions eight years ago.

On the surface of his eyes, the moisture lingered. But no tears fell. He'd understood the loss, the severance. If nothing else, Darius remembered the isolation he'd experienced when standing in that conclave of cousins years ago. He'd known his son was lost to him; he'd grasped the complexity of that separation at a primal level. For himself, perhaps, he would weep later as he had in the past. At the moment, he could only stand and await the next cutting blow, the next wave of the roller coaster, before the Baron satisfied his apparent need and moved in a more productive direction.

"Darius, come here, lad."

Every muscle gripped, Darius stood, his back to the Baron. He hated that too. How that voice drove him to the brink, then lowered to this deep pitch to drip like honey through his ears into his veins. To soothe and cajole. To drag him from the edge of an abyss.

"Darius."

Railing a silent curse only in his mind, he tossed the last swallows of wine down his throat and turned, walking woodenly to the chair. Avoiding the eyes looking into him, through him, he settled onto the cushion, setting the empty wine glass aside. How much more of this could he stand? When would it be enough? Would it ever?

"Tell me about this other, now," the Baron said in a far more natural tone. "When did you first encounter Fradden? What exactly did he say to you?"

Collecting his scattered thoughts, no easy feat, Darius began hesitantly, admitting that he'd noticed Fradden hovering on the edge of the crowd to swarm around him. Without placing undue significance on his dance partner, Darius admitted to dancing when Fradden approached and demanded his attention. He disguised nothing of his arrogance or annoyance with Fradden. In detail, omitting nothing, Darius recited the conversation, imparting the warning he'd given, the advice he'd offered. In replaying the words, he found himself no more or less affected than the evening past. He knew how the Baron would react to losing a treasured possession. Not entirely, even now, could Darius eliminate the possibility that the Baron had devised that fateful strike. Only the condition of the body—drained—countered his belief, and that thought disturbed him, prickling him even now. Too well, he knew the Baron was capable of delivering that end to any man who crossed him but alive . . . It was so much more fun to feed on the living.

"I expect you to continue, Darius," the Baron interrupted the silence, his tone indifferent.

Curious, and mildly uncomfortable, Darius found the blue eyes studying him. Easily, he could believe his every thought remained open and as legible as written script. "I don't know a great deal more, sir. When next I saw the chap, he was sitting crumpled like an empty sack in a chair several rooms from my own. I believe I may have heard his killer depart, but I never thought to investigate. Had no reason to."

"How was he murdered?" the Baron asked, his gaze unwavering.

"He ehm . . . his neck appeared broken and his . . . He looked like a piece of dried fruit even to the police officer who viewed him."

"You assumed I killed him or had him killed. Is that so?" the Baron asked.

"The thought crossed my mind briefly, but I had cause to wonder."

"Explain yourself."

If ever Darius had felt uncomfortable with that command, the time had passed. The Baron knew him. He explained himself without a second or first thought, admitting he believed—"The first interview this evening would have been with Fradden. I wasn't looking forward to it, but I assumed you'd take your due from the chap, and he'd still breathe at its conclusion."

"Bright lad, you are," the Baron said and distracted. His head tipped; a smile slipped onto his lips as he looked toward the stairwell.

Darius heard the footsteps, understanding his cousin's reluctance at a base level, knowing, too, the boy had no choice but to answer his calling. Already frowning, Darius watched Teddy emerge hesitantly and pause, looking at the Baron with as much intimidation as hope.

"Come ahead, then, lad. Collect another glass and that wine, if you will. Your cousin and I could both use a refill."

The innocence that had slated Teddy's demise had not abandoned him. He moved with slightly more grace, as timid as ever, a flush of color to his cheeks as he obeyed the command, appearing thrilled with the directive. Before filling his own glass, he came to the Baron and filled the glass, flashing a smile to melt butter.

Darius failed to understand Theodore Brock. Would like nothing better than to slam the pretty jaw and give the youngster a wake-up call. From the first time Darius had met this cousin in that damned collection, he'd suffered as much disgust as sorrow for the boy. Every man to his own, Darius considered silently and caught the fleeting pale blue eyes as the boy collected his glass off the stand. "How've you been, Ted?"

"Good," he answered a little nervously and fleeted a smile. "And you, Darius?"

"Can't complain," Darius answered offhandedly, literally.

The boy frowned his disapproval, apparently not agreeing that they might suffer a great deal to complain about.

Amused, the Baron patted the seat cushion next to him and might have given Teddy the stars as swiftly as the lad sailed onto the tapestry and smiled his gratitude.

Damned fool, Darius nearly uttered aloud and tipped his glass, preferring the distraction as his cousin clinked his goblet against the Baron's in a silent toast.

The Baron dripped a low laugh, his voice dropped to confide in Teddy, "I don't think your cousin approves of our relationship even now, my love."

"*Oui je sais,*" Teddy confided in his native tongue, sounding slightly miserable with the acknowledgment despite the melodious language.

"He's really a rather cold-hearted lad," the Baron continued in his playful tone. "Fails to realize some men have fewer needs and less aspirations than himself."

"C'est probablement vrai," Teddy agreed, attempting to sound all grown up. His soft voice betrayed the illusion.

Shaking his head, forcing a half smile, Darius glanced at the twosome at precisely the wrong moment to see his cousin's wistful gaze as the Baron brushed a finger on his jaw. Nothing had bloody changed. Not for any of them. Barely, Darius started to move, deciding he could avoid this bit of torture with a walk around the room.

"Remain seated, Darius."

Obviously, the Baron was not through torturing him either, and this was one of those torments that could twist him in knots. And probably the only blasted reason Teddy was along for this ride. As much as Darius despised the Baron at a gut level, his cousin loved the bastard. The boy was no more than a bloody toy to be played with, and that knowledge only darkened Darius's mood.

Why bother? Why bother obeying commands and adhering to the bloody covenant? Why not let the whole bloody clan take their due and fall? Why the devil was he forced to play his role in the fucking resurgence when every bloomin' thought in his head cried out to end this torment—for him, for his son, for his cousin whose face flamed with shame and confusion under the Baron's taunting seduction. From the first blasted moments in that great hall in Romania, the Baron had worked his wiles, forcing Teddy to humiliate himself, and nothing had changed. The poor bugger had no idea what he wanted, gleaned only the faintest idea of where his desire could lead. Should Darius be relieved that the idiot remained innocent and obviously clean-blooded? A bloody curse, if ever there was one. The boy would never experience the satisfaction the Baron promised with his silky voice and touches. The lad was doomed for unrequited love, and if ever that changed, the poor bloke would be too blasted lost to appreciate his triumph. Teddy was safe. Aye, safe to be humiliated and tormented until he fairly squirmed with desire.

Disgusted, Darius nursed his wine, refusing to acknowledge the torment and knowing the futility. They were connected. Whether or not he felt shame or sorrow, disgust or sympathy for his cousin, his reaction would be the same. Knowing the boy was as helpless as himself remained his only salvation, and he could be only bloody glad for his own tormented fate. Without a doubt, Teddy would be too ashamed to look at him, and no amount of understanding could wash away the boy's confusion and humiliation once the Baron finished with him.

Raphael had told Darius once—'Emotions have a scent I cannae resist. To feel alive, I need those scents . . . Cannae you understand? 'Tis like looking at a feast through a window when I'm half starved . . . I can remember the smells. Aye, and I've echoes to remember . . . What you feel, I can oonly taste . . .'

Understanding offered no relief, but even as he remembered the words, Darius thought of Raphael, hearing the soft, desperate sorrow in the voice. As much as he loathed that child, he loved him. What did that make him? Any better or worse than Teddy? Any more or less vulnerable to the torment? To lose Dylan was painful. To lose Raphael would be devastating. And even that revelation was a torment. At the heart of his ruin, therein rested Raphael, and yet he could never look upon that damned lad without feeling his heart wrench, could never suffer one of the lad's blasted phone calls without feeling his emotions hike or plummet. Raphael might need emotions, but in one blinding flash, Darius realized, he needed Raphael if only to survive these moments and cling to his sanity, however tenuous his grasp.

When Teddy had been reduced to near sobs, the Baron turned the same silky low tone to Darius to comment, "You refrained from mentioning a few small details, Darius. I would like to hear those now."

Far more tense and miserable in his own right, Darius glanced toward the Baron and glimpsed his cousin huddled like a small child under the arm, blond head bowed to shade his flushed cheeks. Dismay vied for disgust as Darius asked, "I wasn't aware of overlooking anything, sir."

Amad smiled even as he clasped Teddy's shoulder to fold the boy deeper under his wing. "Come now, m' lad. Would you prefer taking your cousin's place to have your confession heard?"

"I didn't bloody kill the bugger," Darius said hesitantly. "Thought about putting him through a wall, but that's the extent of my decline. If I've done something to confess, I'll be more than happy to oblige, without further torment."

The Baron emitted a humph and lifted his hand off the shoulder, scuffing the blond waves under his immense palm, his gaze dipped to confide, "Your cousin's a grand liar as well as heartless."

"The hell you say," Darius stated. "I haven't lied about a bloody thing. You've asked. I've stated in full, what I know."

"Tell me thus," The Baron interrupted smoothly, his cobalt gaze heated. "With whom were you dancing when Fradden rudely intruded?"

In a heartbeat second, Darius understood and held his mind in check. "With Jennifer Windrow, the hotel's assistant manager, as I recall."

A smile dipped the black mustache deeper at one corner. "You are good, lad," the Baron mused. "Learned well the tricks I've taught you, but I should mention, where you may deceive yourself, it's doubtful you could hide the truth from me."

"There's nothing to hide," Darius said carefully. "I won't deny I enjoyed the dance or her company. If you expect anything less, then you've chosen the wrong man for the service you've enlisted me to render."

"Ah, better. You're improving on your honesty. Feel a bit of a twinge for this lass, have you?"

"I haven't acted on it, nor will I," Darius said in a far chillier tone, his conviction as dark as his direct gaze. "I bloody well know the costs."

"You have something in your bag," the Baron commented, smirking. "Something I've a desire to see, m' lad. Be a good chap, and while you're downstairs delivering those to the gift shop to be developed, order a bit of room service. Wink to one of those blonds at the desk and have her agree to deliver the meal personally, will you? I fancy the taller one."

11

In her first waking moments, Jenna thought about Darius Brock and remembered how his dark eyes penetrated, seeing more than any man had a right to see. She remembered the tone of his voice as he spoke her name ... and the sadness to enshroud him in those seconds when he'd opened the door to his room. Annoyed with her infatuation, Jenna rolled and fumbled in the shadows, finding the lighted digital on her nightstand, waking more with her surprise. How could she have slept an entire afternoon away? Unless the clock had stopped, it was almost six o'clock. She remembered arriving at her apartment around ten and spending a few moments reassuring her mother of her safety.

The incident at the hotel had made the news. Someone on staff, a guest, or the police had tipped off the media, and the Chateau Suites had become famous overnight. Without full detail, the announcers had offered the main point—a businessman from New York had been found dead in one of the luxury suites. The police hadn't released the victim's identity but linked the male executive to Hendricks Distributing, a national company with a base in Pittsburgh. Pending an autopsy, the cause of death remained unconfirmed.

With her waking thoughts gaining momentum, Jenna realized the futility of returning to sleep and pushed off the bed. Falling into her morning routine despite the hour, she padded to the kitchen to start coffee brewing, twisted the knob on the wall-imbedded radio. Rock n' roll erupted through the apartment at a comfortable decibel in every room as she returned to her bedroom and connecting bath. Rather than a business suit, she collected jeans and a thick sweater while glancing through the terrace window. A light snow had begun to fall again—if it had ever stopped. A white haze glowed in the parking lot's vapor lights and filled the space beyond her balcony like thick white gauze. Not even a hint of the forest surrounding her apartment complex remained evident.

Routinely, Jenna paused at the glass doors to ignite the string of Christmas lights affixed to her balcony railing, and on return from her bath, she veered to the second set of glass doors. She'd positioned the small artificial tree in front of the sliding doors and left the drapes parted Against the glowing white background, the colored lights enhanced and illuminated in a stunning display. For a moment, she stood appreciating the tinsel and bulbs, the pulsating lights ... and again, she thought about Darius, about those moments on the dance floor when he'd mentioned the gift she'd given him.

With the soft light playing on his eyes, his deep accented voice inflected with quiet sincerity, she'd believed him. Nothing of his arrogance had belied his decision to consider the decor a gift explicitly for him, and he'd not meant to imply as much. Whatever his religious inclinations, he'd not forfeited the grandeur of Christmas by choice. She could imagine him as a happier man, a man whose laugh could come easy and often, whose eyes could spark with genuine amusement, but that wasn't the man who'd entered the dining room last evening or ushered her from his suite this morning.

Clearly, he carried the burdens of his profession and he didn't take his responsibilities lightly despite how often he smiled.

He was a paradox. Or conflicted. As quick to smile as to rile, he was a fellow who would likely drop into the Chateau occasionally and create a stir, whether to attend a party or crack the whip. By his manner, he enjoyed people—touching arms as he spoke, affording his full attention to everyone who approached him—but he maintained distance, no part of the crowd. Over and above it. Isolated and aloof.

He was also a man caught in the middle of a murder investigation, and he would probably remain at the hotel for a time if the powers that be had any say in his decision.

At her kitchen counter, she poured a cup of coffee, her thoughts listing along with her gaze to pass through the window toward the hazy white glow and darkness beyond. She should phone the Chateau and at least speak to Mason. A hundred good reasons for that decision passed through her mind, only beginning with a desire to learn that Mr. Fradden's killer had been apprehended. Doubtful anything would happen that quickly, but hope was free. With any luck, between the joint endeavors of the local authorities and the FBI, which she chose to consider a good thing, the list of suspects had narrowed ... and shifted toward someone other than the least likely candidate.

How that idiot Jackson could even consider Darius Brock a killer was beyond her understanding.

'. . . International assassin,' Darius had said, tongue-in-cheek, appearing sincerely amused. 'If I was him, I'd suspect me.'

Doubtful, Jenna nearly said aloud, a smile playing at the corner of her lips. More than likely, if Darius conducted the investigation, the killer would already be behind bars. Even an amateur sleuth could determine the absurdity of suspecting a man who made his living in a visible capacity . . . and Jenna caught herself frowning again. Darius held a prominent position and with good reason. As calculating as any man she'd ever met. Shrewd and powerful. Smart enough to walk down a hall, snap a man's neck, and return to his room without leaving a trace—business as usual.

"Goddamn it," she uttered and pulled herself up short.

The top executive of a company as vast as von Hendricks Corporation does not literally wear the title troubleshooter, as in—shooting any man who could be trouble. The concept defied serious consideration, and yet, she remembered her chill when Fradden interrupted their dance.

Clearly, she recalled the quick heat in Darius's mahogany eyes, the split-second transition in his manner. On the surface, she could nearly—just nearly—justify Jackson's belief. At a deeper level, she rejected the thought entirely, instinctively. If the company needed Fradden killed, they could have handled it in New York without threatening bad publicity in two separate divisions.

Cursing her callousness, Jenna turned from the window and strode into her living room to check her answering machine. By no surprise, the red indicator light blinked. Vaguely, she recalled turning off the ringer after speaking with her mother.

Hitting the play button, she stood contemplating the chilling thought to linger in her mind. Hired guns could exist, and she wasn't naive enough to doubt that some large corporations might enlist such a service. Big business. Big guns. Politics could fall into the same blasted category, and she could cite history to know not even presidents could be immune if they stepped on the wrong toes. Whether the assailant was a madman with a cause or a hired assassin, the target could be just as dead.

She hoped Fradden fell into the latter category, as cold as that thought sounded even in her mind. If the hotel had attracted some lunatic with the strength to snap the neck of a man Fradden's size, Jenna would rather not know about it. Too many evenings, she strode alone through the halls, visited the pool, or occupied her office just off the lobby. Would the staff be immune to such a maniac? Could one of her staff *be* the blasted lunatic? Had Fradden merely become the target by convenience? Or had the man done something to initiate a personal assault?

A doggone bullet would have nearly been a relief. At least if she'd found Fradden with a hole in his head, she could accept the idea of a hired assassin and feel slightly safer.

Again, she thought of Darius—his 'practical advice' to get out—when the first voice from the machine interrupted. Her sister, Lonnie wanted her to call, "ASAP, Jen. I'm going nuts here. Mom said you sounded wiped out." The next call was from Matt Cord, who lived downstairs. She'd met him in passing a million times, not entirely ignorant of his subtle infatuation with the girl next door. He seemed to make a habit of collecting his mail or stepping outside for a walk to coincide with her arrival in the parking lot. In his mid-thirties, he wore a slightly receding hairline and the start of a mid-aged spread despite his designer clothes contoured to conceal that detail.

"I heard about that trouble at your hotel," his voice came hesitantly through the speaker. "Just called to make sure you're alright, Jen. Call me soon. If uhm . . . If you don't have other plans, I have a couple huge steaks unthawing." His confidence wavered, and he rushed an invitation, assuring her of his cooking skills. Matt was cute. Shy. Not her type, but cute and sweet. Maybe she should make him her type and join him for dinner. Being attracted to powerful men—like Darius Brock—was seriously hazardous.

"Jenna?"

For a split second, her attention riveted with a thought of Darius, but the voice continued.

"This is Evan. Evan Trevane. We met last night. I hope you haven't forgotten me already." He even spoke with a wry smile. "Hope you don't mind, I weasled your phone number from Mason. Your voice is as lovely on tape as in person. Give me a call if you will, Jenna. I'm staying at the hotel for another night. Room 211. I'd really like to speak with you. A little business, a lot of personal interest. First and foremost, I need to know you're alright. Do call, dearest."

She caught herself smiling, remembering his left-handed comments over dinner, most of which had been playfully directed toward Darius Brock. Antagonism, possibly, but in a way to suggest they'd both been playing the game a while. Darius was far more subtle and sleek in his retaliation.

"Miss Windrow," the distinctly unfamiliar voice snapped her from reverie. "This is Agent Wharton with the Federal Bureau of Investigation. You must return my call. You can reach me—"

Her attention shattered at the sound of knuckles rapping on her apartment door. Apparently, Matt had garnered the courage to extend his dinner invitation in person. Any other callers would need to ring her apartment from the entry and receive a buzz to unlock the security door. Halfheartedly listening to the agent offering a number she recognized as a direct line into the hotel suites, she strode to the door as the answering machine beeped to reset. Without bothering to glance through the spyglass, she unbolted the door latch and cursed her negligence as her focus slid up the dark suits and bounced, startled between the two vaguely familiar faces.

"Miss Windrow, may we come in?" the same voice from the machine spoke as a badge flipped open in front of her. "I left a message—"

"I just heard it," she said and sidestepped, doubting she had a choice about inviting them in. "Your timing's rather amazing."

"I'm Agent Wharton," the same man, broader, slightly older with keen darting eyes, spoke while stuffing his badge into his coat pocket. "This is Agent Kendel. We'd appreciate a few moments of your time, miss."

"Apparently, the request isn't negotiable," she said flippantly, deciding she needed more than one cup of coffee to deal with two incredibly arrogant, deliberately intimidating men. "Can I get either of you a cup of coffee?"

"None for me," Wharton said, and his partner followed suit.

"I'm sure you won't mind if I pour myself another cup. I haven't been awake that long. Please, make yourselves at home," she added with just a touch of sarcasm since they happened to be sizing up her leather chairs and glass-topped stands as if appraising her wares for resale value. Leaving them to snoop and investigate, she walked across the beige carpet, refraining from an urge to mention the apartment had come furnished and they'd need to speak to the super if they wanted to make an offer. Either by sense or sound, she knew they followed her into the kitchen. Bringing the milk from her refrigerator, she glanced between them, again noting them sizing up her quarters. "Are you sure I can't offer you a cup?" Preferable to the collection of porcelain teapots and candlesticks decorating the buffet, which seemed to hold at least Kendel's attention.

"No, we're fine," Wharton assured her, holding her gaze. "I apologize if our visit's disturbing you."

"You're doing your job," she said smoothly, adding a touch of cream to her cup as her words sunk in. With a slightly apologetic smile, she glanced at the agent. "I should probably apologize. I truly haven't been awake long, and I'm a two-cup person. If you'll bear with me, I'll try to be civil."

The man flickered a twitch that almost passed for a smile, his eyes less intimidating with the effect. "We'd just like to ask you a few questions."

"I assume as much, sir," she said and collected her cup while motioning toward the dining room table. White lace doilies contrasted beautifully with the bright red tablecloth, and the colored lights danced on the crystal vase holding a bouquet of silk poinsettias. "Why don't we sit down?"

When they were all seated, Jenna moved the vase aside to clear the obstruction, then focused on the man directly across from her. "Now, how can I help?"

"We understand you've only been employed at the hotel for the last six months," Wharton began smoothly. "For the past five years, you've lived and worked in Chicago. Would you mind if I ask why you made the move?"

"My family's around here, as I'm sure you already know," she said honestly. "I applied at the Chateau when I came home last summer. The pay was commensurate, and the position comparable."

"You have a nice apartment," Kendel said almost offhandedly, his gaze listing, returning. "It must run pretty high a month."

"I earn a decent salary, Agent Kendel," Jenna said candidly, not appreciating the half note of innuendo in his tone and eyes. Did he think, like others in the past had believed, that she accepted side jobs with some of the more prestigious hotel clients? "If you have questions concerning my bank account, I'm sure you can have those answered by either my employer or your associates in the IRS, who could certainly provide you with my W-2s."

Wharton flashed his partner an annoyed glance before wiping the expression and continuing, "I know this might be a little uncomfortable, Miss Windrow, but would you mind telling us about last night or rather . . . early this morning?"

"I gave Det. Jackson my statement. I also wrote it down and applied my signature as his partner requested—or demanded—before allowing me to leave this morning. Frankly, I think I've recited it often enough to know, I'd rather not remember it any more vividly than I've already detailed."

"Miss, we read your statement," Wharton said carefully.

"Then don't ask me to repeat the obvious," she said firmly. "If you have some questions relating to that statement, I'll answer them."

Wharton considered while studying her gaze and apparently reached a conclusion. "Do you remember exactly when Mr. Brock joined you in the hallway outside room 610?"

"He came from his room about the same time that Mr. Mason was coming out of 610," she answered, her interest peaking to wonder if the FBI would likewise suspect Darius.

"Last night was the first time you met Mr. Brock. Is that right?"

"Yes, it was."

"Your manager tells us that you coordinated the party last evening, that you handled most of the arrangements and the guestlist."

"Yes, I did."

"Was Mr. Brock on the initial list?"

"I wasn't responsible for writing or sending the invitations," she said honestly. "I worked with whatever information Mr. Whitman provided. I really don't know who all was invited."

"When did you find out that Mr. Brock would be attending?"

"Shortly after noon, yesterday," she said honestly. "As I understand, it's not unusual for him to arrive unexpectedly and he certainly doesn't need an invitation."

"Is it true, suite 606 is generally reserved for his visits? Or uh . . . remains fully stocked, exclusively for his use?"

"In a pinch, the room's rented, but I'd imagine, it's generally available for his use. I wouldn't exactly say that it's exclusive. As I've heard, the room's also held for the von Hendricks heirs and their families, many of whom venture this way now and again.

"Have you ever met any of the von Hendricks, miss?"

"Not at the Chateau," she said honestly and noted Wharton's attention rivet.

"You have met them?"

"When I worked in Chicago, we had several of them stay with us. They rented several rooms on the top floor," she added with a slight smile. "Personally, I never met them, but I sent extra towels to their rooms at least once."

"You never spoke to them?"

"No, I didn't."

"Did you ever see or meet Mr. Brock before last evening?"

"No, I didn't."

"As I've heard, and please don't take this as an offense, Miss Windrow, Mr. Brock seemed quite taken with you last evening. I understand, you dined with him and had several opportunities to speak with him throughout the evening."

"Actually, I dined with Mr. Trevane, but Mr. Brock occupied the seat next to me, and I'll take into consideration that you have some direction with these questions. Yes, I spoke with him a few times. I also danced with him and learned that he's a marvelous dancer. I'm sure you also know that I ran into him after the party and had my picture taken a few times in front of the decorations. No, I didn't spend the night with him or perjure myself on that statement in any way. If you'd prefer that, however, I'll be glad to lie and give the man an alibi to counter this obvious witch hunt."

"Miss, I wasn't implying—"

"Bullshit," she snapped, her temper flaring and flashing between the two tense men. On Wharton, she glared. "If you've spent more than ten minutes with Det. Jackson, I'm more than certain that you came here convinced that I'm the man's latest mistress—if not his whore. And I'm damned tired of the innuendos," she continued without prompting. "Mr. Brock was nothing but a perfect gentleman in my presence, possibly to my chagrin, as I might not have minded breaking my own golden rule to spend slightly more time with him. If you'd like a sordid story, there you have it. I find the man extremely attractive, and I thoroughly enjoyed the few moments I spent with him. Despite what you believe, however, I do have scruples, and I do not generally fraternize with my associates, hotel guests, or the company executives of my employers."

"Mr. Brock doesn't seem to share your high moral standards," Kendel commented quietly.

"I can't speak for others, Agent Kendel," she said in a chilly tone. "I can only vouch for the way I was treated." And she chose not to dwell too deeply on letting her hair down or the request to remove her jacket. If he was testing her, she'd passed, and he'd backed off accordingly. In twenty-twenty hindsight, she might suffer regrets. At least, by God, there would be some justification for these repeated insinuations.

"Miss," Wharton began again carefully. "How much do you know about the von Hendricks Corporation?"

"I know it's an extremely diverse, family-controlled company," she answered.

"Do you know who controls that family at the moment?"

"As I've heard, up until a few years ago, Thaddeus von Hendricks held the controlling vote. I believe with his advancing years, he passed the mantel to his grandson . . . Amadeus," she remembered. "I believe the eldest son died in a boating accident seven or eight years ago off the coast of Maine."

"Are you aware that Darius Brock went to work for the von Hendricks shortly after that accident?"

"No, I wasn't aware."

"Did you know that Mr. Brock was married at one time?"

"I've heard he was divorced. The subject of his marriage or personal life never came up."

"About eight years ago, Mr. Brock was married, living in a little apartment in London, working for an advertising firm. He drove around in a battered Peugeot—comparable to our mid-range Chevrolet. He had two children, a son, and a daughter, and had trouble meeting the rent from month to month. Eight years ago, he took his son and left the daughter with his wife. Shortly after, he divorced his wife with a sizeable settlement. From what we've pieced together, he turned over custody of his son to Amadeus von Hendricks, then took a suite in the London equivalent of the Chateau. If he traveled via commercial flights, he'd have enough frequent flyer miles to stay off the ground for about three years without paying a cent. When he touches ground, he favors Jaguars, one of which he owns and keeps garaged in London; others, he rents when he lands in decent weather. A sporty Mercedes Benz rented in his name is parked at the Chateau Suites, Miss Windrow, but Mr. Brock's no longer present."

Far too much information. Far more than she cared to consider, and those last words, added like icing on a cake, took a moment to sink in. "Excuse me?"

she asked with quiet curiosity and rising alarm. *Darius missing?* "Dear God, you don't think anything's happened to him—"

Wharton's sculpted features transformed from stone to dismay. "No, I don't think anything's happened to him, Miss Windrow," he stated quickly. "Not that he hasn't planned, in any event. More to the point, we know he took a taxi to the airport and boarded a flight to Kennedy Airport in New York. That's unfortunately, as far as we've tracked him so far."

Relieved, Jenna twitched a smile. She knew where he was.

"Miss," Wharton stated. "I don't think you understand the gravity of this situation."

"By all means, Agent Wharton. Enlighten me."

"We've been investigating Mr. Brock for quite some time, Miss Windrow. From what we've discovered, we believe his position with von Hendricks is no more than a front."

"A front . . .? For what, if you don't mind me asking," she said carefully.

Wharton never blinked, never hesitated, "We think he's the front runner for an extensive drug cartel, Miss Windrow. We're about ninety-nine percent sure Mr. Fradden was involved in that operation. The DEA's been tracking him for quite some time, and there are undercover agents in key locations—"

"Why the hell are you telling me this?" she asked shortly, her attention riveted.

"Frankly, miss, because last night, he broke a pattern," Wharton said carefully. "And you might be our one chance of catching him."

Either the rapid-fire information had overloaded her circuits or her hearing had been disabled. "Excuse me?" she said again.

"We've looked into your background, Miss Windrow," Wharton continued quietly. "We know that you could have written your own ticket in any number of occupations. You graduated at the top of your high school class. You entered Duquesne University on a partial academic scholarship and supplemented your income by working part-time in hotels. After receiving your bachelor's, you went into travel and tourism and used your business degree to enter management. You've worked your way through the chain of command. You work hard. You are, as I've noted for myself, independent and extremely cool under pressure. You're also, like I said, the one chance we have of getting close enough to Darius Brock to figure out just what he's up to and stop him before anyone else gets hurt."

"Even if I thought that was possible, which I don't particularly," she said candidly. "Why would I help you?"

"Because we're talking about a multi-million-dollar operation and probably enough drugs in the long haul to OD half the state of New York," Wharton said gravely. "And this might be the one chance to stop him before anyone else gets killed . . . and make no mistake, Miss Windrow. Mr. Fradden's not the first man to meet his end with Mr. Brock in the vicinity. Brock is not what he appears to be."

"And you want me . . . to what? Help you? After telling me, he's a killer?"

"We'll see that you're protected, miss," Wharton said.

"Oh, that's such a relief," she said in quiet sarcasm. "Did you, by any chance, offer Mr. Fradden the same reassurance?"

"Fradden wasn't working for us," Wharton said.

"That makes me feel better. I'm happy to know you just had a few undercover agents hanging around when Mr. Fradden had his neck snapped . . . Are you nuts?" she asked with a sharp, annoyed edge. "Seriously, gentlemen? Bearing in mind that I'm not an idiot, even if I thought helping you was the right thing to do, do you really think I'd risk my life after what you just so kindly told me?"

"Miss, last night was the first time Darius Brock even alluded to being human," Wharton said carefully. "As much as I know he's probably been with more women than I can readily count, he's never openly taken an interest in any others. We have been watching him. Enough to know, he doesn't generally sit and chat with any women or offer any sign of appreciation or approval. That might seem slim, miss, but stacked against his general routine and indifference, last night was a record. He apparently likes you."

"Great," Jenna huffed, only more annoyed. "So, what you're saying is . . .? Since he likes me, I should be the one to betray his trust and throw it in his face."

"The man's a murderer and a drug smuggler," Kendel stated.

"The man could be from Mars, Agent Kendel. That's as believable and firmly evidenced by this load of tripe as anything else. You're telling me that because he jet-sets, smiles a lot, and is probably the most dynamic man I've ever met without half trying . . .? He's automatically a drug smuggler, and I should agree to some asinine plot to have him tried and convicted?"

"What would it take to convince you? Or to gain your cooperation?" Wharton asked.

"I'm not entirely sure, but you apparently haven't offered either yet," she said honestly. "You're asking me to stake my life, my career, my reputation, and my integrity on nothing more than innuendos and accusations."

"Miss," Wharton said quietly. "If we've made a mistake speaking with you, there's a good possibility that it's one you could ultimately pay for."

"What the hell is that supposed to mean?"

"Judging by how he operates, Miss Windrow, it's a very remote possibility that his change in pace last evening wasn't merely infatuation. He might, in fact, already believe that you're working with us."

"You truly are insane," she decided.

"Think about it, miss. You're a bright young woman with the intelligence and potential to go anywhere and do anything, and you chose to take an assistant manager's position in one of his hotels. Within six months you gain enough trust of the manager to handle the big company party . . . And maybe he figured it was time to figure out who you are and what you're made of."

She was thinking about it, recalling those last moments in the dining room, the subtle warning, the 'practical advice' to get out while she could. Brock had even said something along the lines of her potential.

"Just give it some thought," Wharton said and pushed from his chair.

She was thinking about it and not liking her thoughts.

"You know where to reach me," Wharton commented and motioned to his tense partner even as he looked down at Jenna. "Chances are, he'll be back, miss. I don't think he'll wait too long without attempting to reclaim his ride. He likes riding in class, and his Lear jet's decked to the max. If you get the chance, ride out to the airport and take a look at it. You can't miss it. It's pet-named the 'Nightrider,' and it wears one hell of a mural of a black-winged stallion from nose to tail. I've heard the artwork alone cost a fortune. It's well worth a look if you appreciate art."

12

Waiting for the hammer to drop, Darius assaulted the spareribs with the appetite of a starving mutt, the gusto of an ill-trained idiot. Any pretense of class or dignity evaporated. Using his fingers, he paused long enough to lick away barbecue sauce when the baby bones started to slide from his grip. Consequences were what other men dared to consider and fret about.

Darkly amused, Darius noted his cousin's slightly stunned, extremely disapproving expression across the small table. Almost daintily, the fellow picked at his identical plate the size of a serving platter, which still held more than a half-rack. To one side of the flowered, porcelain platter, a small collection of thin bones stacked like cordwood in a neat row. The baked potato and side orders of garden salad, fruit wedges, and broccoli soup stood around the collection, barely touched as far as Darius could tell. His side of the table looked more like an archeological dig by comparison.

Shaking his head, confounded, Darius reached and collected the linen napkin that he'd retained the foresight to unfold and lie within reach. Using the finger bowl, he studied Ted's dismal downcast gaze. If his mood was less reckless and tension lower, Darius might enlist his natural compassion to consider the boy's flushed face and pouting lips as a sign of genuine distress, rather than sulking. He might even be less inclined toward hostility, but his anger ascended. "What the bloody hell's wrong with you, Ted?"

"Pardon moi?" the worried voice accompanied a quick, anxious flash.

Heated, not quite sated, Darius glared at his cousin across the table. A half floor overhead, the Baron was undoubtedly preoccupied with the busty blond who'd nearly leaped into Darius's arms after his wink and smile. If not for the tall reception counter, the woman would have flounced her entire upper half into him while leaning to receive his whispered suggestion. Turning over the incriminating mound of film to be developed—in a bloody one-hour process—and enlisting the blond had certainly brought out the monster in him.

Was his cousin mad at him for following the damned orders? Jealous of the blond currently climbing the Baron's trunk and, undoubtedly, relieving his genuine manly urges? Or was the boy so bloody naive that he believed those giggles and howls were as fake as all else in their life?

Annoyed, tense, loathing himself more than Ted ever could, Darius snapped, "If you want my pardon, then by damned, ask for it in English! You're as fluent in my language as I am in yours, and I've no intention of indulging you beyond this fit of sulking."

"I am sorry, Darius," Ted said with a heavy French accent.

Muttering a curse, feeling worse, Darius wiped his mouth, bouncing a scathing glance off the third, untouched platter of ribs. On a good day, he could probably clear that platter as well. This was not a good day. It hadn't been good even before it had become a day. To make things worse, he suspected the Baron was just killing time upstairs, letting Darius simmer before coming in for the kill.

Well, to bloody hell with that too. Darius pushed from his chair and strode three paces toward the stairwell before realizing the futility. Nowhere to go. Even if he thought about going somewhere, there was nowhere to go.

If he were alone, he might venture to the bar for a decent bourbon. He wasn't alone. And he was in enough trouble without lending the master further cause for annoyance. Doubtful the Baron would appreciate him taking leave.

Consequences. For every action, a reaction. And Darius had resigned to paying the consequences the moment he'd enlisted Rene to open the gift shop. Even if he'd decided to capture the Chateau's ambiance exclusively for Raphael, he'd likely pay the piper. But he'd taken at least two of those shots for himself, and for those, he would suffer. But what the hell. Life was dull. Life was futile. At least while he awaited the hammer to drop, he felt something other than futility. Was it his thought or one divined by the Baron that he should feel like an obstinate child seeking attention—even punishment—from an indifferent parent?

"Bloody hell," he muttered as another knot of self-loathing twisted through his system.

"Darius?" Ted asked quietly. "What's wrong?"

Turning, looking into the soft, worried eyes, Darius felt the weariness creeping over him, through him. "What's bloody right would be more the question, Ted. Do you ever tire of what's become of you?"

"I . . . I try not to think about it," Ted said grimly. Primly, lowering his gaze to his plate, he picked and pried another sliver of meat from a tiny bone.

"Well, there's advice worth taking," Darius uttered in disgust and returned to the table. "I'm tired, Ted," he said absently and settled into the chair, his gaze listing over the ravaged bones and smeared red sauce. His gaze drifted and lifted, rising to find his cousin studying him, and suddenly, he felt as vulnerable as this reflected image. "I think I'm getting old. Or just too fucking used up. I keep thinking . . . I just don't give a bloody damn what happens next. If the Baron ripped out my throat, I think I'd pray for a last breath only to thank him. That's dangerous for us. For me. For you. It's self-indulgent, self-defeating. Why the bloody hell don't you say something to shut me up?"

"You need to vent, mon ami," Ted said quietly.

"Fuck you," Darius stated. "Vent that."

The boy smiled slowly, his pale eyes glimmering with something other than tears. "You do have sush a way with words, cousin."

Darius lost his anger as his faint smile emerged. Shaking his head, he glanced to the steps, aware of the silence now, knowing what could be happening. His heart thudded a dull, painful beat, but the outrage failed to surface.

Burn out. The soft words echoed in his inner ear. Jenna had called it without ever knowing him. He was burned out. Barren. Like a wasteland after a raging fire. Whatever passion had once driven him seemed long gone if it had ever existed. He felt nothing for that tart on the upper floor. Like a ghostly reflection of his former self, he knew he should feel something in the young woman's regard. Still, he suffered only an echo of regret and remorse . . . of horror.

"Darius, he won't let you go," Ted said quietly.

Looking at the pale blue eyes, Darius realized the words were meant more as reassurance than warning. "I feel bad for you, Ted. I can't help you. But I do feel some touch of sorrow for you."

"Don't," Ted said quietly, his gaze reflecting the intelligence belying his pale eyes. "But if you need sush, mon ami, you have my sympathy. What you do, no other of us could. He shose well, Darius. No matter your weariness, you won't quit because you know others depend on you, count on you. On your honor and nobility, you will stand no matter how much of your humanity suf'fairs."

Darius studied the genuine sympathy, seeing the innocence in the boy's eyes, the sincerity and decency. Feeling worse for his earlier words, Darius smiled grimly. "You've made me feel worse, Ted. Thank you so much."

Ted frowned. "I'm a poor shoice to offer comfort, Darius, but I do try."

"He offered you as a whipping post, and alas, Darius the Scourge accepts his offering with zeal. I am sorry, Ted. For whatever it's worth, you don't deserve what I've given you to add to your burdens. Isn't that his favorite line, after all? His favorite promise, not to give us—any of us—more than our fair share of burdens? You carry yours well, cousin. Perhaps, I need take lessons. If I loved him, do you think he'd kill me?"

Ted smiled, the concept beyond his immediate grasp. "He loves you regardless."

"Oh, there's a bloody relief. I'd rather not see what he does to those he hates."

"No, I don't think you would," Ted said with a suddenly haunted shine, his soft features masked in solemn dread.

Whatever lingered in Ted's mind, Darius preferred not to know. The soft tap of knuckles on the lower door offered a welcome relief only until he remembered the expected delivery. Before Ted could slide from his chair, Darius rose and gestured him to remain at the table, to finish his dinner. All too soon, Darius collected the dozen packets and tipped the misty-eyed salesclerk without a second thought. Closing the door with his heel, he stood looking down at the evidence which would surely burn him . . . and to hell with it. He'd stolen the liberty and pleasure of taking the shots and thoroughly enjoyed those moments. Once glimpsed, never forgotten. If the Baron confiscated every film and photo, the images in his mind couldn't be stripped away without removing the importance of those images. In which case, Darius would feel nothing over the bloomin' loss.

That he might prefer to have the images removed and forgotten occurred to him as he rested on the couch holding the most fascinating photograph he'd ever seen. Poised at the French doors, caught in a matrix of soft white light against frosted glass, she was as mysterious and enchanting as when he'd first seen her. The light had captured the essence of the wild waves of bronze and gold-toned locks. Her face, as if sculpted in alabaster by a master, caught the shadows, even more enthralling with the soft wistful curve in her lips. Not a word could he speak, not a breath could he draw as he'd snapped that shot, and looking at the magnificence captured exquisitely, hot tears lifted. She was incredible. Fascinating. Magnificent. And his ultimate ruin, he knew before the Baron ever settled onto the cushion alongside him.

Doomed. Damned. Darius knew at this moment, he would pay for every ounce of emotion she'd wrenched from the depths of his battered soul. As the picture slipped from his fingertips, he leaned and dropped his elbows on his knees, catching his head between his hands.

He'd done it. The one thing he'd promised never to do again. The vow he'd made to himself. Snapped and broken. This woman he barely knew had ripped down the wall around his heart as if shredding paper. Even if he never saw her again, he'd never wipe her from his head or heart, and she could be used against him, would be used against him. Another turn on the rack.

"Ohhh, lad," the Baron spoke in a low, faintly disappointed tone. "This isn't good."

Darius shook his head, agreeing with a negative.

"Hmm, but how can I fault you?" the Baron spoke in a quiet, consoling tone. "If ever a woman could work her wiles on a man, I'd venture this one more than capable. Has your head in your hands and your heart in your throat, so I'm noticing."

Darius rejected the words, collecting himself, firming. With an angry shine, he looked up and ran into the penetrating cobalt eyes. "I won't. Haven't. Absolutely will not . . ."

"You're stammering, m' lad."

He nodded absently, deciding. "Give me a bloody minute, I'll think of something."

A humph slid off the curved lips. "Will you, now?"

"No. Probably not," Darius admitted in disgust and self-loathing.

Again, the Baron laughed in a humph, his eyes glittering. "What am I to do with you, lad?"

"I'm sure you'll think of something."

"You don't trust me for a second, do you, Darius?" the Baron said in mocked dismay.

"Should I?"

The smile returned. "You're too bright to believe that. It's one of your traits that I find most intriguing. You don't trust anyone. Not me, not your cousins, probably not your own mother, and least of all, lad, yourself. The latter, I'll mention, with good cause. You deceive yourself as often as you deceive others. By no fault of mine, mind, lad." As if distracted, he dropped his gaze to the picture hovering in his hand. "For this, I don't blame you," he mused and glanced over with a wink. "If it had to be, lad, I can't fault your choice. Can't condone it, mind. Can't allow it, naturally. But fault you for being young, virile, and healthy . . .? Never, my lad."

At odd moments, Darius found sense to hold his tongue. He chose wisdom and silence. His heart hammered a leaden beat as the Baron leaned forward, forearms on his knees, and lifted a stack of photos from the coffee table in front of them.

Across the room, the blond desk clerk rested at the dining table, her long blond hair askew, her eyes murky. She picked at the Baron's meal no differently than Ted, who continued eating silently, his lowered eyes shaded behind thick black lashes.

Watching the pictures turning one under another, Darius suffered a touch of vertigo, the rhythm mesmerizing. With an effort, he lifted his gaze to see the Baron's mustache turned down in a frown, to see the eyes sprinting over the details in every frame. Only once had Darius seen the man whom the Baron had been. Only once had Darius seen the monster that the Baron had become. At the moment, Darius could imagine only the man—a nobleman with a great deal of responsibility and innumerable burdens. A lord to be admired—

His thought startled him, drawing him up short. By no surprise, the cobalt eyes looked over, leveling on him. Whether outraged or pained, Darius could neither decide nor ponder. A chill slid down his spine; he dropped his gaze to the halted photo—a picture of the fur tree standing in full livid glory. The candles appeared realistic against the livid red bows and pine garland decorating the elegant stone and wood mantel.

"You didn't take all of these for yourself, did you?" the deep voice asked.

Darius shook his head slightly, admitting, "No. I didn't."

"For whom then?"

"For Raphael," Darius admitted and as an afterthought, added, "And Dylan."

"You do work overtime—in the true sense of the word—to annoy the hell out of me."

"I won't apologize or deny it, but this isn't one of those moments," Darius said without sarcasm. The weariness tugged at his mind and voice. He couldn't even recall when he'd last slept. Possibly an hour or so on the flight to Pittsburgh, not much more . . . and the past few weeks had been hell. Chicago should have been his last stop. A short stop, then back to London and his own bed for a few days. No rest for the wicked. No respite for the damned.

"This woman—Jenna Windrow? She did all of this?" the Baron's low voice seethed.

Darius cringed by reflex and nodded. "Her design. The staff helped, I'm sure."

"What a witch," the Baron hissed softly. "Transforms an entire castle and captures the heart of my own damned stallion—all in one fucking night."

The words stirred a flicker of anger and Darius shifted his dark gaze to the livid blue shine. In the cobalt depths, tiny red darts sparked.

The Baron smiled then, a particularly amused smile in perfect contrast with his eyes. "So, and there's still life in you, after all. I was beginning to wonder," he said conversationally. "I was tempted to send you to a physician in Chicago, have him check your pulse, possibly give you a shot of Bute to keep you afoot. I'm almost glad I sent you to Pittsburgh instead." Conversationally, he continued, "Didn't get around to visiting your new daughter, did you? What with all that other nasty business."

Not taking the bait, Darius held his council.

"I *asked* you a question, lad."

"No, I never got around to it."

"Your visit to Pittsburgh, though, it wasn't a total waste," he glanced at the pictures and back. "Hasn't worked out exactly as planned either. Fradden—the ass—had the poor taste to get himself killed."

"Thoughtless of him," Darius agreed, cursing his subtle sarcasm.

"Wasn't it though," the voice darkened; the exotic cobalt eyes held steady. "Inconvenient as well, lad. I'd so hoped we might enjoy this visit together."

"I was looking forward to it."

"Lad, don't annoy me any further," the Baron said with a twitch in his mustache and slid his arm over Darius's back, clasping him at the shoulder and tugging him close. At close range, the eyes glittered like blue glass reflecting a flame, and the scent of expensive cologne couldn't quite mask the deeper musk scents. "We have a bit of a situation here, Darius. One—I loath to admit—I've seen developing for some little time. Annoys me immensely." He admitted with a conflicting, wry note. "How do you suppose someone might slip into our warehouses here and make off with the goods? Bearing in mind, you have some base knowledge of how I operate."

He felt like a child facing a pivotal quiz, and that revelation disturbed him nearly as much as the question. He knew how the Baron operated, knew enough to wonder at the incredible announcement the moment Fradden had admitted it. No one in the warehouse could have participated in that theft without the Baron's knowledge, and the warehouse should have been guarded by at least two or three men. Any of whom, all of whom, should have been capable of handling thieves. His brow furrowed, his gaze troubled, he admitted, "As much as I know it's neither my place nor my burden to carry, I've wondered about the impossibility nearly from the onset." His gaze intent, more curious, Darius commented, "It shouldn't have been possible, and truthfully, I assumed it was some kind of hoax."

"Do explain."

"I assumed you were having ah . . . some fun with all of us. Possibly to place the blame on the winery and provide an excuse to chat with your . . . family?" Too well, Darius knew, the Baron wasn't very fond of his descendants. Had likely altered the fates of some of them over the years.

"I see," the Baron idled. "You assume then, I'm controlling this endeavor."

Far easier to believe than the alternative. Darius nodded slightly. "Possibly, a bit of faulty thinking on my part," he admitted. "I found it damn hard to believe that anything could have departed your warehouse without your knowledge. More true, I imagined Fradden was an unwitting pawn or his time had come, and you handed him the rope to hang himself. If I'm wrong, I'd really rather not know."

"Liar," the Baron mused and studied him. "Bothers you immensely, so I see, Darius, and with good cause. I've given you an extremely high stake in my enterprise. On the one hand, you question my capabilities if a common idiot can slip something from my grasp. On the other, you need to wonder why I may be playing this game and letting the situation escalate. Ah, and you ask, then, who am I? Not the almighty you've come to consider? A fraud and incompetent, no different than any common bloke with too much money and too little brains. I see your dilemma, my lad. Rather opens the gates inside your brilliant mind and makes you wonder if such a plot could be to your benefit."

"That, I will mention, *didn't* cross my mind," Darius said honestly, his gaze intent. "What you do with your wine and others in your keep isn't my concern. If you want to line them all up and cut them down like kindling, it's not my business. I've drawn my lot, and I'll abide by my oath for however long you let me."

"Oh, and I do like you, Darius. You have a talent for words. And no slip was that—however long I let you. " The Baron wore a faint smile, no more than a twitch. "What if I were to tell you, you're caught up in this situation slightly deeper than it would appear?"

"What could I say?"

"Such was my question, lad? What would you?"

Considering momentarily, Darius realized, he could say very little. He'd stopped plotting his destiny years ago. "Then I hope you have fun."

"Doesn't worry you, just a tad?" the Baron mused.

He hated the games, the prodding, the taunting. His temper threatened as he asked, "What the bloody hell do you want from me? Terror . . .? You've had that a few times over. Submission . . .? You've had that. Resignation . . .? I've been there more often than I care to consider. What's left then . . .? To live in fear for my damned life? To worry that today or tomorrow will be my last? Or worse, to wonder if I'll still be around the day after? You'll drive me to the bloody edge and back whether I worry or not. If you want to line me up with the others and cut me down, then so be it. I'll live as long as you let me, and die when you feel it's my due. That's what's left to me. I don't dream of dying quietly or lying down at the end of a long, fulfilling life and drifting off in my sleep. Why the bloody hell would I worry about what comes next?"

Sparks glittered on the surface of the cobalt eyes. The mustache quivered on the brink of laughter. "You are an extremely morbid child, Darius. And a liar."

"Human," Darius stated, his eyes angry as the silent words sped across his mind—*that's more than you can say!*

All too smoothly, the Baron's free hand lifted, catching Darius's jaw in a firm chilly grip. His eyes still glittering, he moved his thumb over Darius's mustache, applying only enough pressure to make his touch known. "You are that," the Baron said in a deep rhythm. "But I wonder, lad. Have you considered how badly you need to believe your own lies? To believe that you await death, welcome it with open arms, embrace that end that plays so heavily in your weary mind? Fear . . .? You do live in fear, knowing at any moment, your service could be fulfilled and your life forfeit. So it is, you prepare as your nature dictates. Hot-blooded and fearless, high-strung, you ply your lies to keep your feet on the ground.

"You are courageous, Darius. Such, I've known since you stood your ground some little time ago. Terrified, yet determined, you stood before me, facing what you knew to be the end and a beginning to a horror you could not have fathomed hence. Had you lived four hundred years ago, I might have loved you like a brother, if not a son. A pity time toys with us. A master in itself. Were I kind, Darius, I'd continue to keep my knowledge to myself, but I fear, the time's come to enlighten you, lad."

Whatever this enlightenment, Darius preferred not to hear it, and that alone sealed his fate.

"You remember the scroll I disbursed among you years ago, the legend I divulged. A farce, a fabrication, a grand tale, most of you believed, and it amused me to watch as you were enlightened and woke swiftly to the reality." His mustache crooked in a thin smile, his eyes more human with the black dots spiraling within the dark blue hues. "You didn't laugh or believe it a hoax, my own. And later, when more of the story was revealed to you, you suffered remorse and regret for things long since beyond your control. Compassion. Such is a strong word, lad, and like all men of honor, you had thus in abundance despite your youth and the anger that drove you even then. You have it still, lad.

"By no fault of your own, you have a vast propensity to feel compassion regardless of how you battle against such an affliction." His smile quivered, his eyes livid, enthralling by the purely human essence and the tempo of his voice. "Few men, perhaps, no others, could endure the life I've forced upon you, much less carry the burden with such grace and dignity. At times, I almost regret putting you through this endless hell."

A fine time to remain silent! But the words reached him at a deeper level, and he sought the lie, felt the words leading to a revelation that would surely not bode well on him.

"You are brilliant, Darius, so let me ask you thus," the Baron's eyes haunted with a darker light, a fierce shine. "Has it ever crossed your mind that I was not the first, might not have been the last man condemned to live as I do? Torn between a will to live and a desire to die?"

It had. Just such a thought had crossed his mind in the wee hours when he'd looked upon that shriveled corpse, knowing damned full well the Baron should be a half continent away. Lightning quick, his concern notched a degree higher.

"I see that you have," the Baron continued gravely. "The problem is this, Darius. You are my own. Where the von Hendricks name has been, so are you. The second problem is this, my lad—anyone with a certain talent would recognize what's inside of you, what's been inside of you since your conception. That I might have put it there long before you were a twitch in your great grandfather's loins makes little difference. Where others of your lineage carry traces and echoes, lad, in you and certain others, I needn't mention, the seeds found fertile ground. I've never needed to enhance our union, lad. You are as familiar to me as my own black nature. Fine for me, not so fine for you," he said almost lightheartedly, his smile more naturally amused as Darius's mood declined.

"Therein lies the crux of our current situation, the problem which spirals from those two bases. You are my familiar. A living, breathing entity with an unruly will and temperament. As alive as you are one instant and dead the next. But all men have their flaws. That you don't wear the von Hendricks name makes no difference. Anyone with a desire to know knows you for what you are, my own, and the fact is, I haven't lived so long without making an impression. Apparently, as the situation appears, one of those impressed has deemed to work his wiles, and sad to say, you're presently caught directly in the center of this mischief by no fault of your own."

"I . . . don't think I'm following this," Darius admitted carefully. Hopefully, he misunderstood even the words he thought he followed.

"Lad," the Baron spoke with a consoling, sighing note. "I have enemies. Obviously, one with a devious mind and a penchant for retaliation. Damned if I know what I've done to create such a fix. Might have nipped a fellow by mistake and left him lying in a dark alley somewhere. For a time, I had little control and an insatiable appetite. Whether my enemy evolves from the distant past or a hundred years hence, I haven't decided, but he's certainly of a nature to be clever, which leads me to believe he's lived and learned for a time."

"Damn," Darius uttered, grasping the words and the import, hoping to see the lie behind the blue eyes studying him with a bemused shine.

"Aye, lad, damn. Or damned. The bugger has a design in mind to complicate my life and annoy me to be sure, that he'd desire to drink my wine. Unfortunately, what could be a complication and inconvenience for me, could be pure, undefined hell for you."

"Me."

The Baron nodded, his thumb moving again over Darius's mustache. "Now, I have worried you, and probably with good cause. Though my options are many, my nature defines the rules I live by. One of those, thus defined—I can't simply pull you from the fire. First and foremost, the bastard might see such as a victory. Second, as long as you are visible, the chance of finding the devil behind these raids is vastly improved. I'm an opportunist, as you well know. On a side note, lad, I'm anxious to see how you'll handle this. The fact is, you've had this threat on your tail for the better part of two years. I try not to give you more than your due; thus, I never mentioned the corpses you've left in your wake."

"No," Darius decided and shook his head. "I'm not listening to this. Not falling for it. Whatever damned game you're working—"

"Darius, this is not a good time to be obstinate," the Baron mused. "I've protected you thus far and intend to continue, if only because you are in my keep. Like my wine, lad, you are mine. If this enemy puts his designs on snatching you, I'll be more than slightly annoyed. My wine, I certainly couldn't warn, but you, lad, have sense enough to avoid seizure. Thus, I'm enlightening you and giving you fair warning . . . if you let him catch you, you need hope he kills you." The cobalt eyes colored nearly the shade of a midnight sky; the voice lowered as if reaching from the depths of hell and held Darius in a quick state of awareness. "Whether I drink my wine from its bottle or from his veins, I will recover what belongs to me and have my fill. Do you understand?"

Darius nodded slowly, understanding far too clearly. If he ended up in the service of another damned monster, this one would finish him off. "Don't uhm . . .? Don't suppose this would be a good time to ask for some time off, would it?" he asked quietly, a little hopefully.

The Baron studied him for another ten seconds then drew back releasing Darius's jaw and shoulder in one smooth move. Darting his livid eyes over Darius's face, the Baron cracked a smile to have his white—purely hu-man—ivories flashing and let out a laugh. "No, I don't suppose it would."

"You do realize if your enemy is uhm . . . anything like you, and he puts his designs on me, the chance of me avoiding him solo are about zero to none. You realize that, don't you?" Darius asked, his weariness only compounding his rising temper that bordered hysteria. "How the bloody hell do you expect me to fight him? Run about with a wooden stake in my pocket?"

"Wouldn't help, lad," the Baron idled with a chuckle. "Honestly, the only sure bet with a fellow such as this is to take him out to a clearing and stake him for the morning sun. For me, child's play. For you, a tad more difficult."

Slumping into the corner of the couch, Darius looked at the man, the monster, seated next to him, not appreciating the livid black humor in the eyes or the smile quick on the lips. "So, I'm to understand this . . . there's not a damned thing I can do to stop him from coming at me directly, but at the same time, if he does and I'm still breathing, I won't be breathing when you're through with me? Where the bloody hell is the fair play you're always boasting, sir?"

"Only you, Darius," the Baron chuckled. "Think it's the English blood in you. Would be a pity if I had to take it from you."

"I'm not better or worse off than I was before this news," Darius decided abruptly. With the revelation, his muscles drained of tension. "I'm a dead man talking, and you bloody well know it. Whether it's you or him or a plane crash—as the laws of average are stacking against me in that area as well—my days have been numbered from the start. Fine, then. Have your fun. Let him catch me. Toss me to him if you have that in mind next. I don't give a bloody damn."

Rather than comment, the Baron leaned forward and lifted the nearest stack of photos, sifting through them momentarily. On the top, remained the picture of Jenna standing at the doors, and Darius watched as the Baron lifted it from the stack and studied it momentarily. Looking over with a smirk, he slipped the photo under his black jacket and into an inside pocket. Almost casually, he dropped his gaze and lifted a second picture—the picture of Jenna seated on the hearthstone, her hair catching the flames, her expression pensive, and her pose somewhat arrogant. Smiling, the Baron handed the photo to Darius and winked, "You can keep that one."

Nearly positive he should hand it back, Darius knew the futility as the Baron turned and began collecting the others, sliding them into their packets.

"These, I'll hang onto for a time," he commented and favored Darius with a natural smile. "I really shouldn't be surprised at your talent with a camera. Rather disappointed that it's taken you so long to divulge that tidbit, though. We might have handled things altogether differently had I realized you could impersonate a world-class photographer. Such is life," he sighed and leaned back again, his gaze sobered entirely. "You've left a mess in your wake, Darius. I won't fault you for coming at my command, I'd expect nothing less. But you will return and handle that affair however you see fit."

Somehow, Darius expected nothing less.

"I'll have my driver take you to the Amtrack station. It's little more than six hours or so, and the change in pace may do you some good. I suggest you take time to indulge your fantasies and pay that honorary visit you deem necessary. Until further notice, you will remain in Pittsburgh."

13

Under the surrealistic glow of spotlights, the small plane stood off to one end, poised as if for takeoff in front of a long line of hangar doors. Even with Jenna's limited knowledge, she knew this was no twin-engine crop duster. From where she rested, chilled despite the warm air blowing from the heater vents of her Lincoln, she clearly identified the mural and verified Agent Wharton's words. Across the streamlined haul, the distinctive sleek silhouette of a black Pegasus galloped toward the nose, spreading its massive wings with its flowing tail fading into roiling gray clouds. If words existed, none remained visible from her position behind the mesh fence, but she imagined the name Wharton had mentioned scrolled across the base of those hooves. Night Rider. The implication in those words slid another tingle down her spine.

Why she'd buckled to Wharton's suggestion and made this trip, she couldn't decide. She hadn't consciously planned to oblige him.

Muttering a curse, Jenna slammed the console shifter into reverse and twisted enough to verify—no oncoming cars. Without a doubt, a federal agent or some rendition thereof lurked within the main buildings, keeping vigil in case Darius or his pilot returned. If they recorded her license, she couldn't care less. For her peace of mind, she'd needed to see that blasted plane and confirm that Darius Brock had flown rather than glided on phantom wings, here and gone without a trace.

Splashing over the wet pavement with mounds of dirty snow forming a border at the entrance, Jenna returned to the red light and waited for the light to turn. Murder. Drugs. The FBI attempting to enlist her help . . .? Her thoughts ran rampant despite the past several hours of natural chaos that she'd tried using as a distraction.

Christmas shopping had proved to be a waste of time. Not even the fight to find a checkout line had offered any reprieve from her distress, and that detail only annoyed her more. With less than two weeks to finish shopping—one weekend remaining—she'd intended to capitalize on the free evening and her excess energy. With the company party past, she might have concentrated on completing her Christmas list and shifted her full attention to the holiday.

For the first time in several years, she would be close enough to home to spend quality time with her family and maybe visit some old friends.

A genuine holiday . . . and a joke. A grand joke. If anything, she was less inclined toward celebrating than ever in the past. If even one more shopper had tramped on her toes, she might have resorted to fisticuffs.

How dare the FBI come to her apartment, fill her head with far too much information—more than she either wanted or needed to know—then dare to imply it was her civic duty to help them? To betray a man she hardly knew but already liked. To break an unwritten trust and loyalty that she'd agreed to abide by when accepting the position at the Chateau Suites. An unwritten loyalty. A vow to maintain the hotel's reputation and integrity.

God knows, in her line of work, details were often held in trust, and guests paid a tidy sum for that trust. Granted, she would never conceal a murder for a guest and wouldn't condone a drug deal in a hotel corridor; however, she would never approach a senator's wife or a reporter and mention a questionable guest arriving after hours in a senator's suite. Nor would she slander Mason or any other employee, burning up the phone lines with tidbits of gossip or whispering behind anyone's back. If Mason wanted to keep a bottle of whiskey in his desk drawer, that was his business, so long as it never interfered with his judgment. If Lisa had a crush on Tony, the bartender, and flirted shamelessly, so what? If Lyle, the doorman, ever staggered into work drunk and she caught him, he'd either land in rehab or on the street, but regardless, the details would remain between Lyle, herself, and Mason. Job security. Job integrity. *Personal* integrity.

The FBI was asking her to toss her standards like so much trash and throw in with them, join their crusade in the fight against crime. So what if Darius Brock could be innocent? So what if they had little more than supposition and circumstance? Hang the fellow. Tie him to a stake and light a match, if only as a warning to other successful businessmen . . . and that's how this felt. Regardless of what Wharton and his obnoxious companion had imparted, the whole damned thing stunk like a witch hunt. They had nothing on Brock. If they did, he wouldn't be running loose, and if he was under investigation for as long as they proposed, he was either the cleverest maniac around or innocent. As much as she might consider him clever, the maniac part didn't track. Calculated. Chilly, possibly. But a cold-blooded killer and drug lord? Well, maybe the drug lord persona fit. He carried himself with an air of confidence and arrogance.

Without ever considering a destination, Jenna turned south on Rt. 60, the expressway that traveled from the city of Pittsburgh to Pittsburgh International and north toward the Valley, which referred to the steel towns along the banks of the Ohio River. On autopilot, she passed through the string of entrances designating the main terminal and cargo areas, remaining in the steady flow of headlights. After bypassing the highway exit for her apartment, she realized her new destination.

When all else fails—go home.

A grand plan, except for one tiny detail that occurred to her as she skidded onto the first secondary road. Where the main roads might be clear of last night's blast, the tributaries remained covered in slush, and the night chill had taken a toll on the salt and ash. With ice crunching under her tires and a glaze reflecting in her headlight beams, the thought of traveling another ten miles through farm country lacked appeal. If the highway was this bad, the country roads leading to her parents' door would be far more treacherous.

Muttering curses, Jenna reconsidered her decision before reaching the first bend. The old familiar gas station stood like a lighthouse beacon, with its neon signs glowing and the parking lot glistening wet rather than icy. At the last moment, she engaged her turning signal, although the headlights in her rearview mirror were too far away to need a warning. Pumping the brakes as her father had taught her years ago, she rolled into the lot and checked her gas gauge. She didn't need fuel and, with a pickup truck at the pumps and the attendant busy, Jenna navigated a three-point turn on the cleared pavement and waited for the sedan to pass through her headlight beams. Unconsciously, she watched the car pass and saw its taillights brighten for a split second.

She knew abruptly . . . Whoever those two—men—were inside that car, they were following her.

FBI . . .? Or drug dealer thugs?

How long had they been following her? Since she'd left her apartment? Had they followed her through the crowds or merely stood guard at her car in the parking lot? She hadn't noticed anyone pull into the delivery entrances for noncommercial flights at the airport, but then, she hadn't been looking for anyone.

Pulling out in the direction from which she had come, she watched the rearview mirror, not surprised when the headlights winked at the bend in her wake. Maintaining her speed and course, she weighed her options. By logical deduction, she decided these fellows were FBI. Somehow, she couldn't fit Darius Brock as the kingpin of a drug operation. If this sedan ran her off the road, she might learn differently . . . and it was somewhat of a relief to roll onto the wet pavement of Rt 60.

Accelerating, she added more distance between her and her followers, re-peatedly glancing in her rearview mirror to judge their tenacity. Halfheartedly, she considered exiting the highway on another busy exit to judge their determination, but she was already pushing her luck with the speed limit and road conditions. Under different circumstances, she might give them a run for their money.

Decidedly, Jenna pushed the speed limit, settling on reaching her apartment ahead of them, and if luck rode on her side, Matt would be standing vigil.

Her course set, she kept watch on the headlights, not losing sight of them despite the traffic heading out of Pittsburgh fore and aft. By the time Jenna sped to the end of the exit ramp, her followers had reached the entrance to the exit. She wasted no time at the stop sign, sped into oncoming traffic, and thanked God her luck held. In her wake, the dark sedan remained gridlocked at the exit, and even on a slow day, that intersection was a challenge. With holiday traffic, she gained at least two minutes and wasted not a second, keeping pace, pushing the Lincoln just a little. Without looking back, she sped through the entrance to the Terrace Apartments, rolled into her private space, already grabbing shopping bags and her purse as she yanked the door handle . . . and Matt was there.

Even before Jenna passed through the first security door and reached the second glass, he held it open, wearing his usual smile and sweat jacket as if returning from the gym. Jenna returned the amenity with more genuine gratitude than ever before.

"Looks like you've been busy," Matt said while darting his gaze, already reaching for a slipping bag. "And it looks like you could use a hand."

"You're a lifesaver," she said smoothly, glancing through the glass in time to see the headlights at the main entrance. A phone call, she decided abruptly and flashed Matt a smile. "I could probably manage these, though," she said while repositioning the bags. "I didn't get too carried away."

He appeared disappointed. "I'd be glad to help."

"Really, Matt, I don't want to put you out, and it looks like you were just leaving."

"Just heading to the gym. It could wait."

"No, really. I have these. Why don't you give me a call when you get back?"

Matt settled for the escape she offered with a promise to call soon.

If anything, his infatuation with her might do him a world of physical good for as often as he visited the Terrace's gym or jogged around the parking lot. Even if he merely jogged around the building, it would be healthier than spending time in front of a television.

Juggling packages to find her keys as she rode to the fourth floor, Jenna stepped off the elevator and into the quiet, carpeted hallway, never more conscious of the empty corridor that seemed twice as long as usual. On hy-per-awareness, she managed to avoid dropping anything while she opened her door and flipped the light switch on the panel on the inside wall. Several lamps ignited to bask her living room in a soft glow, but she wasn't relieved until slamming the deadbolt closed.

She still suffered the crawlies. Whether from the previous night's tragedy or from being followed, she couldn't shake the haunting essence of doom.

Dropping her packages on the nearest armchair, she slid out of her ski coat en route to the end table and telephone. The message indicator light was blinking again. Surprise. Surprise.

"Hi, Jenna," Evan Trevane's smooth deep voice slid through the speaker. "Hope all is well. Please, give me a call when you get this."

Muttering a curse, she slightly regretted her failure to return Evan's first call before her shopping expedition. In retrospect, she remembered raiding her refrigerator after the agents' visit and coming away with slim pickings. So had begun the past several hours of madness between stopping at the Mall's food court for a sandwich to running with the pack between stores with extended hours and holiday sales. She couldn't even recall what she'd bought—which meant, she'd likely return the whole mess and start over.

Just one more irritation, she considered as she jabbed the numbers to reach the agents at the Chateau. Before the call connected, she pressed the disconnect button and held her finger down. If she phoned and asked, would they admit putting a tail on her . . .? Or would they attempt to use this ordeal to convince her that her life was in danger?

With her thoughts, she suffered an odd epiphany. She didn't trust this fellow, Wharton, or his cohort, any more than she trusted Det. Jackson. The only one she truly trusted was Darius Brock. And what an odd thought, that. Three credible—even slightly impressive officials vs one extremely handsome, slightly disturbing man she'd just met?

The fact remained, however. She trusted Darius Brock regardless of how cool and collected he appeared when stepping from Fradden's room—or perhaps, because of it. Or how his eyes could darken and mask his thoughts while pinning her in a fierce heat and sending her blood racing. He was dangerous. Everything about him transmitted a vibration of danger at a primal level . . . but she couldn't picture him as a cold-blooded killer or a man responsible for killing half the population of New York.

Deciding, she dialed the number to room 211 and waited through two rings before Trevane answered. "Hi, Evan. This is Jen Windrow. You called?"

"Hi. How are you?" he asked with an odd lighthearted tone.

"Fine, you?" she answered hesitantly, instantly curious.

"A little busy at the moment," he said, sounding apologetic. "Would you mind if I give you a ring back shortly?"

He wasn't alone. "Not at all, I'm here."

"Good, then. Talk to you soon."

Public relations, she remembered as she replaced the receiver, hoping he returned her call before Matt lapped the building. Taking her coat to hang in the closet, she started into the routine to ignite her Christmas lights, then paused. Wharton's voice on the machine? She'd moved through her routine, igniting the bedroom lights, dining room lights . . . less than fifteen minutes after waking, they were knocking, and it was a two-minute drive from the Chateau. The sons-a-bitches were watching her apartment! Annoyed, she moved into her dining room, catching the strings to send the long drapes sweeping between the fir branches and glass. Her bedroom curtains were closed and would remain closed. No windows opened into her living room. The kitchen window might soon grace a thicker curtain or a dark towel. The idea of someone spying through her windows was more irritating than disturbing.

And that cemented it. On slow boil, she moved to her coffee pot, dumping the grounds and blackened remnants from the pot. Her answer would remain, incontestably, unquestionably, immovably—no way. If they wanted to incriminate Mr. Darius Brock, they would need to find another patsy. If Darius returned, she would keep her professional distance and maintain her integrity.

The phone rang in the next room, and when she lifted the receiver, a far more natural, relieved tone, huffed, "Jenna, sorry about that. Truly. You wouldn't believe the hassles I've had today."

"I bet I can guess," she said with a thought of Jackson and Wharton.

"To add to the obvious," he said with a musing ring. "Did you know that our illustrious leader has taken a powder?"

"Uh, if you mean, do I know Mr. Brock's taken off, I'd say, yes."

"Exactly. Taken off is a good term for it. Flew the coop. Vanished. Abracadabra. The ever-loving son of a . . . left us amid a crisis."

"Apparently, he believed we could handle the situation," Jenna said with a smile, considering her similar exodus from the hotel. She hadn't even phoned Mason. She should feel guilty, but if Mason needed her, he would call. Besides, other assistant managers existed no matter how swiftly Mason had shifted the bulk of duties in Jenna's direction. About danged time Dan Sandel or Karen Flinn pulled their weight instead of pushing it.

"It's just no use, is it?" Evan said with a mocked dismay.

"Excuse me?"

"It's just no use. No matter how I try, I can't seem to undermine your opinion of Darius the Great," he sighed, then chuckled. "Actually, I probably shouldn't try because I don't blame you a bit." Mocking an English accent, he commented, "The bloke makes me bloody nuts." He dropped the accent. "But I like him anyway. And I really don't blame him for sliding out from under this. People tend to believe that since he maintains carte blanche in the company, he should handle everything to come down the pike. That he usually does, doesn't help him one lousy bit. And in case you're wondering, dear, I'm trying to apologize and convey a slightly important message on our illustrious leader's behalf."

"Interesting approach," she mused.

He chuckled, "If by any chance, the FBI come tromping about and attempt to feed you any particular line about Darius running from a murder rap, tell them to cram it. Darius doesn't run, and the chances are good that he's gone in search of answers. Now, on that note, have they been to see you?"

"I take it—they've been to see you?"

"We're practically dating," he mused. "That younger chap's just the cat's meow and personality? . . . My God, the man's fairly dripping in it."

Uncontrollably, Jenna laughed, remembering how much she'd enjoyed Evan's company and wishing she'd called him hours ago. "They were here," she admitted. "And that's basically what I did tell them—in kinder words of course."

"Afraid of that," he said with a tempered amusement. "Which leads to the other reason I called. We're trying—a bit desperately—to keep a lid on this situation. So far, we've managed to keep any names out of the news, but we'll probably lose that edge soon. I've talked to most of the staff and guests. Most were detained and questioned briefly before departing without a hassle. If, by some chance, the press learns your name, I won't tell you not to speak to them, but I will ask, as a favor to me and in the interest of the hotel, to talk to me before you agree to any interviews. If possible, I'd like to be with you—if or when that comes to pass. I'm in a position where that old adage rings true—it's a crappy job, but someone has to do it—which is a lousy way of saying, I've been handed the privilege of writing press releases and making regular statements until we figure out what the hell happened here last night."

"Have they made any progress in that regard?" Jenna asked.

Evan harrumphed before admitting, "I'm sure they think so, if 'they' means the local police and our charming Federal Agents."

"Meaning?"

"They—the Feds in particular—have been trying to nail Darius for one thing or another for the past several years. They're convinced they've hit the jackpot. Finding out he was in the same building, on the same floor, and had a motive is all they needed to hear. Bluntly, dear, they don't know shit. That

Mr. Fradden is deceased by unnatural causes, and he worked for a subsidiary of the von Hendricks Corporation . . . that about sums it up."

"Does . . . Mr. Brock know?"

"Meaning?"

"About the Federal Bureau?"

"I'm sure he does, dear," he sounded amused again. "The chap's nothing if not smart." He paused a half second. "I'd like to get out of here for a while. What are the chances you could meet me, possibly somewhere we might find anonymity, if not peace and quiet, to share a drink—dinner if you're interested?"

She barely considered accepting before remembering the agents outside the building, and she wasn't altogether sure she wanted to deal with either more crowds or company. "I'm afraid I'll have to pass, Evan. I'll be in early tomorrow morning though. Possibly, I'll see you before you check out and we could grab a cup of coffee."

She needed to think, needed to breathe, needed to figure out exactly what she thought about Mr. Brock, who seemed to garner as many emissaries as adversaries. Hopefully, by the time he passed through Pittsburgh again, she would find some perspective. The man was far too easy to like and far too difficult to understand.

Even before reaching the train station, the plans had changed, and Darius had trotted through the crowds in La Guardia to catch his return flight to Pittsburgh. A game. A damned game to keep him guessing, keep him jumping. With little more than an hour, compared to six or seven hours of uninterrupted vibrations, he might as well have run the distance. Awake, irritated, and more tense than on the initial flight, Darius spent the hour watching the night sky and attempting not to make sense of the Baron's words and warnings.

Useless. He understood. The stakes, never low, had risen several notches on the danger scale.

Bad enough, he was chained to a vampire, probably for the duration of his useless life, he might now have become the target of another.

For a time, Darius rested, numb, listening to the quiet chatter aboard the plane. Somewhere in the rear compartment, an infant wailed incessantly, only enhancing his tension. While across the aisle, an elderly gentleman—who faintly resembled Orson Wells—sat in all his collected, grim sophistication, leafing through a business journal, pausing occasionally to read the first lines of an article before moving to the next.

How would it feel to be comfortably rounded? To worry about the world economy or the next Prime Minister? . . . To fret about the next business meeting or lecture? . . . To have time to write a business plan or proposal and outline an agenda for a coming event?

Spontaneity was not the spice of life. If it was, Darius would have preferred his serving bland. Believing himself about to board a train and finding himself racing for an airplane . . . no spice. It was just another bit of hellish torment designed to wear him thin.

Half expecting to be stopped and hauled to the local slammer, Darius strode off the plane behind the Orson Wells impersonator and slipped into the pedestrian traffic without attracting attention. Rather than another rental, he opted for a taxi. Slipping into and out of crowds, tempted to believe he'd become invisible, he slid into a waiting cab.

Not invisible, after all. The cab driver, a younger black man wearing an earring in his left ear, flipped the time clock under his dashboard and looked over the seat. "Where too, bro?"

"Downtown . . . Allegheny General," Darius decided.

The fellow eyed him a half second as if judging his health then decided, "You got it, dude."

Running through the possible reasons for a visibly frayed man to rush from an airport directly to a hospital, Darius understood why the driver stomped the gas and sped out as if to avoid a police raid. Doctor . . . about to conduct emergency surgery? Relative . . . about to lose a loved one? Doubtful the fellow would guess, father . . . about to see a daughter. *Once. Just once.*

How exactly this routine had even begun, Darius couldn't readily remember. Doubtful, an accident. Likely, something he'd said to the Baron. Another of his wild flights of fancy where he opened his mouth and jammed his shoe down his throat . . . or at the least, should have. At whim and whimsy, the Baron indulged his need . . . and Darius wondered about that. His need. Was he as masochistic as he believed? Or did this torment fall under some unwritten code of dignity and honor that he failed to realize in himself? Duty, perhaps? Or was it even more basic? He simply needed to find the reality, needed to reaffirm his convictions to continue. Life. His own wasn't worth a tinker's damn, but these infants . . . would theirs be any different? Was he condemning them as he, himself, had been cursed at conception?

Shaking off the thought, refusing to accept the answer hinged inside his mind, he lifted a cigar from under his suit coat. His vacant gaze listed through the window, his attention distracted to the spurting flame reflected on the glass.

More distracted, he recorded the steady stream of headlights flowing fore and aft. He had landed in the same time zone . . . and it wasn't too late. Not even the devil's hour, he verified with a glance at his Rolex. He had some time to kill, and if the heavy traffic was any indication, stores were open despite it being a Sunday night. The holidays . . .

"Would you know of a gift boutique on our route, lad?" Darius asked and caught the eyes in the mirror.

"Ah . . . like a giftshop?"

"Yes."

"Sure. No problem," the driver said offhandedly. "There's a couple malls and shopping centers. We're probably cutting it close to catch one open, but hey . . . the meter's running. Where you wanna stop?"

"Preferably, a . . . novelty or card shop by chance? Open, would be nice."

The man laughed and touched the gas deeper, sprinting past several cars cruising in the slow lane. "Top a the hill here. We oughta just make it."

Darius glimpsed the road signs, orienting himself to realize they had already passed the exit for the Chateau. Soon enough, he would return to that mess, and he could imagine the chaos to erupt with his arrival.

True to his word, the cabby rolled into a busy strip mall and pulled to the curb in front of an elaborate Christmas display window. Handing a few bills over the seat to keep the meter running, Darius carried his overnight bag with him. Even on a good day, he wasn't the most trusting soul.

Typical gift shop, the store offered three aisles of greeting cards and an abundance of glass shelves of novelty items. Darius wasted little time, finding what he sought, and despite his weariness, managed a smile to coerce the young clerk into gift-wrapping his purchase. Some things were far too easy. With a wink and a smile, he could generally get whatever he wanted, and seducing this lovely young woman was child's play. A gift and a curse—he'd always been an avid flirt.

The cab waited at the curb. The driver was either intrigued or comfortable enough to be patient, more than likely catching the scent of an expensive fare. That it might be the chap's lucky night, Darius refrained from mentioning.

Less than a half hour later, Darius handed over another small stack of twenties to keep the meter ticking, then strode through the emergency entrance doors of Allegheny General Hospital. Without missing a step, he passed through the mayhem as if he owned stock in the building and didn't need to ask directions to navigate through the matrix of corridors. He'd been here before at least once. Passing the maternity ward without a glance or pause, he acknowledged a few nurses with a smile and nod. No one questioned him as he continued to the pediatrics ward. In front of a wide viewing window, he stopped and scanned the half dozen clear plastic bassinets. He found her in the fourth bin toward the deep end. A pink bundle with a shock of dark ringlets stark against the white sheets—the newest addition to the Brock clan, sleeping soundly despite the raucous of a blue bundle in the arms of a nearby nurse. Several other infants stirred and squeaked, their tiny voices muffled as if through a tunnel. Not long could he stand staring. No words of wisdom could he impart. It was already past visiting hours. In the dim light of the corridor, he felt more like a villain, a dark cloud to hover over this child's head until her last breath.

The bloody grim reaper in person, Darius considered with an internal edge. At the beginning to herald the end. He should not have come. His mood was already too bleak. He needed little else to rise him to the brink of destruction and yet, he couldn't pull himself away. One hand dipped in his pocket, holding himself together, the other holding the small bag with the silver spoon . . . and what an incredibly fine thing to offer this lass who—with hope reigning eternal—might never learn about her roots. If he could wipe the slate of history clean and lay it blank before this innocent, he surely would. And like all else, he knew the futility of desire. What became of her from this moment forward was neither his right to wonder nor worry.

Too long he'd stood. He knew the instant the door cracked open—a nurse looking out at him—he had stood too long in one place. Wearily, he smiled and shrugged, starting toward her and noting her eyes soften. "Sorry to have disturbed you, miss. If you—"

"Which little one's yours?" she asked quietly.

"None," he answered smoothly. "My cousin's," he added and handed her the novelty gift bag. "If you'd put that with the Brock lass and see that it reaches her mother, I'd appreciate it, miss."

The nurse smiled and accepted the gift with a hint of curiosity. "You might be able to visit her mother if she's not asleep. I think she's getting discharged tomorrow."

"Hmm, then I won't disturb her this evening. Thank you," he said smoothly despite his stomach clenching. He had no desire to see Amy Brock. Too often wives experienced that sense of familiarity at a primal level.

Glancing once more at the bassinet, he reconsidered his apprehension. He might see this little one again, after all. If Robert Brock heard about the incident at the Chateau, the lad might have contacted the hotel to extend his support. A clannish lot, the Brocks. Even the oblivious seemed to sense a connection, and that thought only verified the Baron's enlightenment.

The cab driver had stationed himself on a yellow line, not moving a tire length in either direction, merely waiting, smoking a cigarette that he pitched through his cracked window as Darius rounded the corner. Over the seat, he spoke as Darius slid inside, "Where to next, bro?"

"Greentree," Darius answered, and his thoughts snagged, hearing that word spoken in his inner ear in a soft, lulling voice, a voice that he wouldn't mind hearing again. As if the picture pulsed, he felt it in his jacket pocket . . . and he reached a decision before the driver sped across the bridges and into the Squirrel Hill Tunnel.

Far more alert than any man had a right to be at midnight, Darius watched the flashing lights of the tunnel, mesmerized momentarily before focusing on passing road signs. Waiting until he recognized the exit for the Chateau advancing, Darius asked the driver if he knew how to reach the Hazel Terrace Apartments.

"Sure do," the driver assured him and fell into a litany of gossip as the sign for the Chateau passed. "Some dude from New York bought it there last night, but they're not saying much about it . . .. I figure, by the way they're keeping it under wraps, it was probably murder or some shit . . .. Wouldn't be surprised if it was a hit. They're saying the New York guy was at some big bash for that Hendricks Distributing. You ever hear of that company?"

"Believe I have," Darius answered soberly, half amused.

"Hell, I had a brother worked for them for a while. Decent pay and good hours. Lotta shit coming and going, though. . . . He worked in the warehouse, but they have offices downtown. He knew a couple of the big shots. Figure they're mafia, you ask me. Anybody with that kind of bread . . ."

Halfheartedly listening to the cabby's diatribe, Darius commented, "Drive through that complex, will you, lad?"

"Sure. No problem," the fellow agreed and drove between the dirty mounds of snow at the entrance.

The Hazel Terrace Apartment Complex wasn't a gated community nor adhered to the modern trend of condos tucked one against the other like fancy rowhouses. Red brick buildings sporting cast-iron rail balconies, six deep and five rows high, towered over islands of decorative trees and bushes, creating shadows throughout the central parking lot. Vapor lights illuminated the shoveled sidewalks and created a surrealistic glow over the hoods of frosted cars. Decorative lantern posts decked in bright ribbon and garland scattered throughout the lot.

Halfheartedly, Darius wondered if Jenna had lent her handiwork to this decor, as well, and a smirk quivered his mustache. He might never see another red ribbon without thinking about her.

Judging the numbers on the first buildings to either side, he barely considered asking the cabby to stop at the fourth building when his senses keened.

He wasn't the only person wide awake at midnight.

Short hairs lifting under his collar, he scanned the shadowy parking lot, unconsciously searching for discrepancies. And his attention rose, panning the upper floors and terraces through spiderwebs of barren tree branches. Convenient. Convenient as bloody hell to sit behind one of those curtained windows and watch the canyon-style parking lot below.

With an inherent enhanced night vision, he spotted the twist of a long louver blind on a glass sliding door, along with the circle reflection of a telephoto lens directed toward the main entrance of Jenna's building. Federal agents seemed the most likely culprits, but why were they watching Jenna Windrow's apartment . . .? And wasn't that just a foolish question? Either the Baron had pulled strings, or the agents were seriously irritated with a certain disappearing Englishman, rightly assuming the chap would visit his latest lover—for all the wrong reasons. *Only beginning with Miss Windrow not being his lover.*

Annoyed on every level with his senses still too keen, Darius judged the shadows at the end of building four, estimating the sightline of the surveillance of apartment 447. In a split second, he decided to tempt fate. What was one more turn of the bloody screw?

"Stop up at this next corner, lad."

A gamble. Either he would succeed and gain a quiet haven for a time, or all hell would break loose when the FBI learned of his return. Another of life's small pleasures -to toss a coin.

Paying the driver, Darius thanked him properly and slipped from the cab, catching his overnight bag strap over his shoulder. Without ever passing into the light, he strode around the corner of the building, grateful for the cleared sidewalk to reach the side entrance. A glass vestibule offered the residents respite from the cold to collect their keys or whatnot. In a panel alongside the second glass door, a row of numbered buttons and corresponding names designated the apartments within. Without the need for a coin toss, Darius identified the nearest apartment and pressed the button.

On the third prolonged press on the button, a cranky voice crackled through the faulty speaker. "Yea? What?"

With a smile conflicting with his sorrowful tone, Darius spoke simply, "So sorry to bother you, Mr. Hammil. I just moved in on the fifth floor—lost my door key. My spare's in my apartment. Would you mind buzzing me in, sir?"

Grumbling, the man pushed the button, and Darius clasped the second door handle, pushing through without a hitch.

Some things were just too damned easy, while others were damned near impossible. Such was the true curse of life. He'd been a bloody con man before he'd ever become much—or less—of anything else, and at times, those early lessons were a blessing.

14

B efore the second light rap of knuckles at her apartment door, Jenna was awake and already furious when her bare feet sank into her thick bedroom carpet. If this was Wharton and his cohort, she might just pick up a lamp and threaten assault on two federal agents! If it was Matt, here to share some insight over the movie she'd declined to watch with him, he might suffer a similar fate! Glancing at the clock above her stove, fuming over the midnight hour, she belted her long robe, muttering curses as she passed through the kitchen. Dead men. Or woman—if this happened to be Sally Albertson, the neighborhood gossip down the hall. One certainty, Jenna would not just unlock the door—not with the flashing image of Lawrence Fradden—

Her thoughts halted as she identified the dark image magnified within the spyhole. Unconsciously, she drew back, her hand already fumbling with the locks, her thoughts on hold. Impossible, really. She might be asleep, just dreaming that she found this visitor outside her door. Would she fall into his arms next and shower him with kisses like some ditz in a romance novel? Tugging the door inward, she slid her gaze from his shiny black shoes to his canted tussled hair and dark eyes, took in the faintly amused, slightly jaded tip of his mustache, and decided—a dream. Darius Brock could not be at her door.

"Could I come in?" he asked.

It sounded more like a threat than a request, but she inclined her head and pulled the door open more, blinking to clear whatever remained of heavy sleep from her eyes. Not the onset of an erotic dream. He moved inside, a leather strap slung over his shoulder, his long black coat adding to the shadows and lending him a haunting essence. She hadn't turned on a lamp. The neon light above the stove cast a soft glow across the living room and her phantom visitor. Shutting, locking the door by habit, she watched him slide his leather bag to the floor and caught his dark eyes looking down at her still.

"I'm truly sorry if I woke you," he said in a low, silky voice.

"It's nearly midnight."

"I know," he said. "Truly sorry to barge in at such an hour."

"Uh . . . no. It's alright." No lamp threat for this character.

"I do hate to impose . . . Actually, I don't hate to impose. I do so despise needing to impose at this hour. Do hope you'll forgive me."

"Is uhm . . . would you mind . . .." *What the hell are you doing here?* "I need a cup of coffee," she decided. This could be another extremely long night. "Would you like a cup?"

"I'd love a cup," he said smoothly.

Jenna nodded, deciding she better collect her bearings. All too easily, she sensed him moving behind her, following. The soft, masculine scent of cologne overwhelmed the aroma of pine-scented candles and potpourri. Awake, barely, she pushed the button on her coffeemaker, wishing this once, she'd neglected to prepare it for the morning. She could have used a few more seconds. Turning, she found him leaning in the arch that connected her living room, dining room, and kitchen. His gaze fixed on her slight tree against the drawn drapes. Within the weird soft neon against a backdrop of hazy images of her living room, he appeared not to breathe . . . and far more distant. The familiar sadness lingered in his jaded smile and shuttered lashes. In shadow or brilliant light, the man would be handsome, but this soft ambiance . . .? It touched him, embraced him. He was built for the night.

His gaze shifted to her, the weariness more apparent. "I am sorry to have awoken you."

"You look tired," she said quietly. "Why don't you take off your coat and try to relax?"

For a moment, he seemed either too tired to recover his balance or undecided whether to accept the offer. Smoothly, he rose and slid the coat off, walking into the dining room rather than the living room. Folding the coat over the back of a chair, he settled onto the end chair, in a position to watch her and the tree with equal fascination.

Pulling cups from a wooden rack, Jenna brought the milk from the refrigerator and poured more than necessary into her cup. He took his coffee black, she remembered. What to do, she wondered while replacing the cream. Unconsciously, she spotted the cheeseball and remembered the snack crackers she'd picked up in her shopping spree. It was the best she could offer on short notice, and she needed to do something. Collecting a Christmas plate from her cupboard, she'd already begun arranging the crackers, her thoughts clicking, when his deep voice suggested.

"Please, don't go to any trouble, Jenna."

Her gaze bounced toward him and back in time to avoid spilling the crackers off the counter. Carrying the plate, she passed around the raised bar counter and caught him watching her slide the plate toward the center of the shadowed table. Halted, she studied him for a half second before deciding on the direct approach. "Why are you here?"

"I'm half afraid to admit this," he said with a weary smile. "I'm avoiding the authorities."

Honest and direct. Should she expect anything less? "Any particular reason?"

"Only one, really," he said smoothly. "I don't feel like speaking to them yet."

All too cute, that quick flicker of a smile. "You do intend to speak to them, though?"

"Of course," he answered. "Not that I have much faith in their progress. These chaps, I've noted are rude and irascible. Damned stubborn, too," he added with a sigh. "I'm assuming, I've annoyed them tremendously, and I don't foresee my return offering any consolation."

"Where did you go?" she asked, ignoring the burping and bubbling from the kitchen.

"I had business to attend," he answered.

"Did you . . . ?" Damn it, this was really none of her business. She couldn't very well ask him what he'd learned about Mr. Fradden's murder. Avoiding authorities. Avoiding conversation. Deciding abruptly, she said, "Never mind. It's not my business." He'd come here for refuge, undoubtedly, aware of what would happen when he reached the hotel. She barely started to turn when the revelation struck. "They're watching my apartment," she stated.

His smile flickered again, "I know."

"You . . . know?"

"I assume they're looking for me."

"So, they already know you're here."

"We'll know in a few moments," he commented indifferently. "But I doubt it."

For a man hiding from the law, he certainly appeared calm and cool . . . and that seemed in perfect harmony with his nature. Shaking her head, she turned and strode around the corner, deciding—a cup of coffee might do her a world of good just to catch up with this conversation. He, however, could use something slightly less invigorating. For a half second, she considered offering wine and in the next, lifted a mug from the wooden tree on the countertop. Without more than a second thought, she filled the cup with water, set it in the microwave, and set the timer for three minutes. Automated, she continued her mission, collecting a box of instant cocoa from an overhead cupboard, a half-gallon milk container, and spray-on whipped cream from the refrigerator. He might think she was nuts, but it was the most harmless, least lurid, most sensible drink she thought to offer a man who looked like he could benefit from a solid eight hours of uninterrupted sleep.

By the time she finished doctoring the concoction of hot cocoa and mounding the whipped cream, the coffee had finished its cycle. Filling her mug, she carried both around the counter, catching a faintly curious glance and that same flicker of a smile; both enhanced tenfold when she set the heaped mug in front of him. With a shrug and quivering smile, she moved into the next chair and caught him looking at the mug as if it might bite. "Hope you like hot chocolate."

His gaze lifted, more curious and intent. "I . . . ehm," he glanced at the white mountain again, apparently not entirely positive what to say. His gaze darted off her steaming cup to her eyes.

Trying not to smile, she bit her lip then wondered, "You uh . . . you do like hot chocolate, right?"

"I'm . . . I generally pass on sweet liquors, Jenna. A shot of bourbon—"

"I've seen you handle bourbon, honey," she said as she caught on. Winking, she smiled. "Try it before you knock it, Darius. It's an old family remedy for insomnia, and I assure you, the only spice is a touch of vanilla to give it a kick."

Appearing only curious, he considered a moment, then apparently decided to humor her. He lifted the mug and managed to tip his mustache in white as he sipped from the rim.

The whipped cream might have been an extremely bad idea. With his brow arched under a tussle of wind-blown dark waves and his lips quirked in curiosity, he somehow managed to add an entirely new dimension to the word 'sexy.' With his gaze bouncing off the drink, to her eyes, to the drink, he appeared to struggle with assimilating details or reaching conclusions. On him, confusion was cute. Different. Cute. Sexy. And she couldn't help but smile when he settled on a bemused smirk and lanced her with his dark eyes.

"Hot chocolate," he said deftly.

She shrugged innocently. "I'm fairly sure that's what I said it was."

"I'd wager you knew I didn't believe you."

"You're half asleep on your feet, honey," she said sobering. "Coffee might keep you there . . . and hot cocoa on a winter's night is truly an old family recipe for a good night's sleep. I assume you'd rather not check into the hotel and get bombarded by the authorities or the press. You're welcome to stay and use my couch." Which would be pure misery for her if she drank too much coffee.

"I uh . . . I'd just managed to talk myself out of asking for that imposition. Decided I'd finish a cup of coffee and face the music at the hotel so to speak." His gaze ventured toward the cup as he lifted it, taking a slightly larger gulp, licking his lips, and smirking. "I'd imagine I'd better stick to my decision. Too many of these, and I might sleep through the new year."

"Na, just 'til morning . . . early afternoon at most," she helped and held his gaze. "You were tired last night, and somehow, I don't think you've slept any time since. If we're going to figure out what happened to Mr. Fradden, it would probably be a good idea if you were awake."

"I . . . seem to have missed something," he said lightly. "I don't recall saying anything about investigating Fradden's demise."

"I don't believe in leaving anything to chance," she said honestly. She'd reached the only possible solution hours ago. "I'm not asking for your approval or even your trust. I assume you're already attempting to find out what happened. I intend to do a little investigating on my own. We have a list of anyone who stayed at the hotel," she halted her thoughts and studied him. "No," she decided. "We're not getting into this tonight. Suffice it to say, I intend to take matters into my own hands if only for my peace of mind. Right now, it's late. I'm tired, and you're exhausted." She slid off her chair. "I'll get you a pillow and blankets."

He caught her wrist in a light grip without seeming to move, his gaze lifted, searching and sober, intent. "We will discuss this tomorrow, Jenna, but my decision will be the same. And that's simply—no. I won't have you involved in this situation any deeper than you already are. You are not investigating this murder. I may ask for that list, but that's as far as I'll allow you to participate."

Despite the gentle grip, she felt the power of his hold, the strength underlying his words. Exhausted, no doubt, but not to the point of either maudlin or vulnerable. She held his gaze, as conscious of his conviction as she was of his presence. How easy it would be to get lost in those dark, intense eyes and muscled arms—too easy. "We'll talk tomorrow," she said smoothly and slipped her wrist free, pulling her gaze away with far more difficulty.

From a hall closet, she collected extra linens, blankets, and pillows, returning to the living room and making up the couch without bothering to ignite a lamp. In the kitchen, he moved, rinsing his cup and her own, overturning both on the counter. By the time she finished, he'd moved to the entryway and leaned, watching her. Striding toward him, refusing to acknowledge the overwhelming force of his presence, she glanced up as she started around him. "Good—"

"Thank you," he said quietly, and she stopped, looking into his calm gaze. "I haven't had hot cocoa in so long, I'd forgotten how it tasted. For that, for the couch, for not making me feel like a damn fool for coming here . . . thank you. Sincerely."

"You're welcome, Darius," she said quietly. "Only good dreams."

"I'm tempted to believe even that's possible," he said with a faintly wry smile and dipped his head too fast for her to move even if she wanted to. The whisper of a kiss brushed her cheek. "Good night, Luv."

Halfway across her kitchen, lost in the resonance of that soft endearment, she pulled herself up with a thought and glanced back, finding him still watching her. Refraining from a stammer, she mentioned the bath and fresh towels, and offered, "Make yourself at home."

Long after he heard the sounds fade at the end of the hall, Darius rested atop the carefully made linens, breathing in the fragrances of Jenna Windrow. His thoughts spun too quick to consider sleep. Even drowsy, with the taste of cocoa and cream lingering on his tongue, the power of the night held him at the brink of awareness. Physically, mentally agitated, he forfeited the effort and found himself buckling to his need, rising, and prowling.

With a restraint born of desperation, he lingered outside Jenna's door, picking up the faint rhythm of her breath. His imagination ran rampant. Clearly, he visualized her wild, long hair askew on a pillow, her lips turned in a half smile, conveying her hidden secrets even in sleep. Awake or asleep, a state or a country apart, she would touch him. No others in the past had affected him so swiftly, reached him so deeply. From the moment he'd seen her standing so still within that enchanted backdrop of ancient decor, he'd been drawn to her. And not for an instant—despite how many others had approached and touched and talked—had he lost track of her within that ensemble.

The Baron was right, damn him. Darius deceived only himself when trying to deny his desire or attraction to this enchanting woman. No others had ever smiled at him from the heart rather than that darker place where motive and lust could dwell. None had ever made him want to smile or join her in laughter. And it was no blasted wonder the Baron had sent him back. Separated by physical distance, Darius could hold onto this fantasy without testing his willpower. At arm's reach, separated by a single, flimsy door, the desire to taste and touch, to wake her the way a beautiful woman should be awakened—

If he had come to her door to torment himself or to discover the depth of his desire, he'd succeeded too blasted well.

In her kitchen, he found a notepad tacked to a corkboard alongside her wall-mounted telly. Jotting a note, he smiled faintly at the whimsical yellow flowers bordering the to-do list pad. He imagined roses with delicate velvet petals to be closer to her style, but the daisies reflected her earthy charm.

With a thought of her pushing the button on her coffee pot, Darius drew a cup of coffee, readied the pot for the morning, and leaned the note against the coffeemaker. In the living room, he collected his suit jacket, recovered his coat from the dining room, and let himself out without a backward glance. For her sake, if not his own, he would keep his distance.

Slipping out of the building was even easier than entering. Clinging to shadows and walking on clear strips of sidewalk wherever possible, Darius followed the backs of buildings to reach the highway. Avoiding headlights and streetlights, he jogged wherever possible. Whether he'd grown accustomed to the night or had always held an affinity toward darkness, he rarely wondered. But even in his earliest memories, awoken now through Jenna's ministrations, he remembered growing restless and pacing within the shoddy apartments he'd shared with his mother. The moonlight had attracted him even then, holding some strange power and mystery to entice him. Silver, the light danced on swells of unbroken snow, more like daylight despite a mere half-crescent hovering against the blackness overhead. Enhanced, he heard his own footfalls and breaths, the soft whisper of wind through barren branches as he swept past wooded lots and tall shrubs marking private residences. Rather than adding to his weariness, the sprints combined with the bracing chill to pump his blood faster and clear his foggy mind . . . and he felt it then, sensed it on every level.

He was not alone in this darkness. Something, someone hovered in his wake, advancing on him, following at a distance but close enough to lift short hairs under his collar.

Always and forever, he'd known this difference in himself, an awareness of the world around him. Even before eight years ago, he'd known when danger lurked and had the forewarning of sound and scent to avoid trouble, whether a pub brawl or an angry drunk lurking behind a corner. Many a damned night, he'd snuck out of bed and through his window, fading into the night before his mother and her drunken companion could reach the apartment door.

He felt that now, something dangerous in his wake. A whisper of sound, no more than a scrape against an icy mound, a displacement of wind shifting the branches that stilled in his wake. If he turned, he knew better than to believe he would see anything more than his shadow, black against the white blanket. He knew too much—and probably too little, even now. With a speed he couldn't hope to match, this beast would catch him. At the corner of his eye, he might glimpse movement. But if this phantom was another of the baron's ilk, even its shadow would be lost.

Darius need only recall the games Raphael played on him through the gardens . . . a step and gone. No more than an optical impression, a retina stain like the negative spot of a camera flash.

'Fading,' the devil's elf called that trick, and the lad was a master of that game. For Raphael, it was a trick, a wicked prank to startle and impress the unsuspecting. The damned elf loved to scare the devil from a less-than-hardy heart. Whether the waif vanished, imposed his will to remain invisible, or moved too swiftly, the effect remained the same. There and gone in an instant. And no force of human dominion could capture him again until he chose to be caught. If this phantom stalker possessed even half of that child's talent, Darius had little hope of avoiding his fate.

Still, he hastened his pace, his senses keening, neck prickling, and his attention riveted ahead toward the glow of the Chateau in the distance. Thoughts spiraling, he remembered those heavy footfalls outside his suite door on the fifth floor and made a mental note to investigate those himself. No fully human beast had taken Fradden's life. But was it a game to this devil, like it was to the Baron over these past several years? Were those footsteps intended to be heard? Or was it a coincidence? An innocent as Darius had first imagined? A guest hurrying to return to the party with a fresh pack of cigarettes or a companion's compact? Questions he would need answered if he intended to stay alive in this wretched game.

Far more uncomfortably, he realized his mistake and wondered when this beast might have caught his scent. Had it followed him from the airport? To the hospital? Or had it hovered outside Jenna's apartment? Was this ghoul behind that prickling awareness when he'd entered that parking lot? He feared the answer but knew his talent too well to deceive himself. Jenna had entered this game. Somehow, he'd brought her into it, however, unwittingly.

Her life could be in as much, if not more danger, than his own. The Baron needed him. If for no other reason, Amadeus would honor his oath and offer a degree of safety—at whim and whimsy, naturally—but Jenna Windrow had become a pawn on both damned sides of this bloody war. No fool and not naive of the Baron's wiles, Darius clearly understood the significance of the photograph and subsequent command to return.

Angry, tense, and not slightly alarmed, Darius sprinted through the grand pillars, clinging to the shadows of hedges and grateful that Mason had ordered the white twinkly lights turned off, if not removed. Hulking in shadows behind tall, barren trees and camouflaged behind islands of parked cars, the black stone walls circled the parking lot in a crescent-moon shape. Only pockets of yellow light offered guests a modicum of safety to reach their vehicles. The moonlight sprinkled over shiny roofs and hoods and lanced the glazed gray tarmac with a daylight glow. With a glance toward the lighted entrance, Darius sensed the purely human threat awaiting him inside and stayed low, gliding between cars and shrubs. As he leaped and caught the scrolled cast iron beneath the first balcony, he considered the ramifications and dropped lightly on a mound of ice-encrusted snow.

Far too blasted programmed, he considered wryly. He'd been slipping in and out of hotel rooms for years, arriving and departing like a thief in the night. Merely showing up undetected inside his suite on the sixth floor, however, would not bode well on his claim of innocence, not in the eyes of the authorities who meant to accuse him of murder. Muttering a curse, Darius glanced through the shadows and set a course toward the front entrance. If anything moved, it moved too fast for his eye to perceive, but he had no doubts, the shadows were full. Someone, something, watched him, and he possessed the wherewithal to feel that oily touch brushing against his mind and heightening the prickle at his nape. If he doubted Amad's enlightenment, those doubts vanished and lent him pause. He might truly have felt this phantom before this evening, might recognize that slimy touch, the mental probe.

"Get the bloody hell out of here," he growled at a low decibel, knowing the wraith would hear him even if he'd merely breathed the words. For a time, at least, he might hold that probe outside his head. By sense, this beast might know him, might judge him, but if the demon had touched too deeply, the Baron would have recognized a taint the instant they met. Would Amadeus tell him, though? Or use him blindly to foul this enemy's plans?

Oh, and that was not a pleasant thought to ponder. Far too easily, Darius could imagine the Baron playing with him, letting him believe he still might survive when he might already be lost to this other. A man's will could be taken, his mind manipulated, his actions altered without conscious thought . . . but would Darius have felt this pulse, this pressure, and alien presence if it was already a part of him?

Grasping that slight relief, grateful for whatever lingered inside of him to break that mode of dark reflections, Darius strode into the hazy light of the entrance. Without hesitation, he walked through the parting glass doors, startling one of the security men who leaned at the high counter, stunning the young woman whose lips parted and sentence halted. Faintly amused, Darius continued toward the desk as the security man rose onto his feet. Appearing far more worried, his gaze darted to the doors, back, a warning in his eyes.

"My room's not been rented in my absence, has it?" Darius asked the receptionist.

Snapping her lips closed, Rene jerked her bouncy brown bob in a negative and managed a stammer. "Uhm, no. It's . . ."

"Sir," the guard stated as if to rescue her and moved closer, his voice tempered, lowered. "We have . . . the hotels crawling with cops and FBI."

"Good," Darius said simply, apparently startling the fellow. "That chap, Agent Wharton? Is he lurking about by chance?"

"I—yes, I think so, sir."

Doubting the necessity, Darius looked to the clerk. "Ring his room, will you? Have him meet me down here in a few moments." His gaze fleeted toward the administration room entrance and back to the receptionist. "Mr. Mason's not occupying his office, is he?"

"Uh—no, sir."

"Good then. Do make a fresh pot of coffee, dear. It may be a long night."

15

Covering no more distance than half the lobby, Darius stopped as agents poured out of the woodwork, moving like dancers in a choreographed musical. Blocking off the main doors and the side corridors, they closed in from every angle. Donning one of his more curious smiles, Darius turned toward the nearest dark-clad pair and darted his gaze over the others around the lobby. "Well, now. Here's the fastest response I've ever received to a request," he commented as he caught the young agent's eye. "I specifically asked for Agent Wharton, however. Do be a good sport and ring him up, will you?"

Belatedly, the man pulled his badge from his jacket and flipped it open as the half dozen others poised to draw weapons from under loose parted lapels. "FBI."

"Lad, I didn't doubt that for a second," Darius interrupted and glanced off the equally young man, a man not much older than himself. "Are you swifter on the uptake, lad?"

"Put the bag down slowly, Mr. Brock," the man ordered. "And keep your hands where we can see them."

Darius considered momentarily, then eased his hand upward and started the leather strap off his shoulder, his gaze locked on the spokesman. In a chilly, low voice, he commented, "Unless you have every intention of creating an international incident in this lobby, lad, I suggest you refrain from any further insult and contact your superior."

"We have orders to—"

"Fuck your bloody orders," Darius stated indifferently. "I just gave you new orders, and I damn well expect them to be followed. If you'd like to hold a bloody gun on me, I've no objection, but if you've aspirations toward using it or assaulting my person in any way, I will likely take exception." His gaze flashed toward the desk where the woman held the phone at her ear but stared wide-eyed. The Chateau security guard stood near the desk with his hand on his holstered gun, eyes darting as if choosing a target in a skeet gallery. "Miss, ring Wharton's room if you haven't already," he stated, jolting her from her shock. As she sputtered into the phone, his gaze leveled on the quicker of the pair. "I've relieved you of one order. Now, I suggest you follow the other and stand down."

"I don't know who you think you are, mister, but you're not—"

"Darius Adian Brock. And unless you have a bloody warrant for my arrest, I am most certainly giving the orders on these premises." Unwavering, he held the man's angry blue eyes and knew a warrant did not yet exist. "Now, I suggest you take my orders, or I'll have you removed from this building under the hotel's legal policy to remove troublesome guests."

"In case you haven't noticed, we're not guests," the man started.

"All the more reason to have you evicted unconditionally. Falls under unlawful trespass and loitering. I do believe there are proper procedures and regulations governing how you conduct an apparent stakeout, and believe me, whatever procedures were followed were null and void the instant I walked through that door. You and your comrades may not realize it, but Mr. Mason certainly would enlighten you on the matter of protocol. Now, do not fucking push me further, or I will have this building evacuated under the safety regulations which I have the authority and power to uphold."

The words created the anticipated pause, and for several tense moments, not a man moved within the lobby. Wharton came from the elevator alcove, a tie askew and wrinkled jacket falling into place on his shoulders, covering his leather holster and gun. He was not a happy man by the time he joined the ensemble, his face dented with a pillow mark from his brow to his ear. Less happy, he stood through a recap of the past few seconds, most of which Darius offered, while watching the agent's anger rise. "Now, Agent Wharton," Darius stated in conclusion. "Why don't you join me in Mr. Mason's office which I have commandeered for my own use, and we'll have a little chat . . ."

Inside the office, sitting behind Mason's immaculately clutter-free desk, Darius offered Wharton his due, allowing the man to begin the interrogation. Willingly, Darius admitted he'd flown to New York in search of answers, waving off the man's subtle accusations and insults intended to either incite anger or arouse an incriminating word. At the end of a half hour, leaned back in the comfortable leather chair, his ankle across his knee, Darius paused to light a cigar and held the man's outraged gaze over the flame.

With the exhale, he spoke simply, "You and I can either work together to solve this murder, Agent Wharton, or you can go to bloody hell. That's your choice. The fact is, I don't give a good damn either way. I do have the faculties and resources to investigate this incident, and truthfully, I have a responsibility to solve it. You have an apparently one-tracked mind and it's not seemed to occur to you, even remotely, that I didn't kill Mr. Lawrence Fradden. Fortunately, that gives me a serious advantage since I'm reasonably assured of my own innocence and therefore privy to the further fact that a killer remains at large and may strike again. Leaves me in a bit of a sticky wicket, as you can certainly see. Do I trust the American intelligence agency to devote its resources to this case, or do I pull strings and have you removed?"

"You don't have that kind of clout," Wharton said. "We are—"

"Don't I, now?" Darius said in a far lower tone, his gaze unwavering.

Wharton's jaw gripped, his gaze pointedly more tense.

In the same low, unwavering tone, Darius asked, "What would you like to wager that I can reach your direct superior in thirty seconds or less and your current president in under a minute?"

Wharton hesitated, holding steady, but his thoughts were turning rapidly behind his angry gaze.

Unruffled, unmoving, Darius waited him out, merely watching him. The stakes were on the table. Either Wharton would fold and go home to sulk and lick his wounds, or he would cling to his single-minded purpose and attempt to play both sides of the fence. Darius had no doubt the man would continue to suspect him and likewise continue to seek incriminating evidence with one suspect in mind. Still, the chap might provide a facsimile of cooperation that might uncover credible tidbits of information. Even having the token faculties of the FBI at his disposal offered a self-indulgence Darius found particularly satisfying and intriguing. That he wasn't bluffing only made the negotiation that much more rewarding. If the need arose, he could pull the aforementioned strings. The Baron was nothing, if not diverse, and a highly sociable creature who dwelt in the house of Kings. Men like Wharton, dedicated to a single purpose, could not begin to fathom the power of international relations any more than he understood the first rules of any negotiation.

Wharton broke the silence. "If you think for one moment, I'm going to divulge any aspect of this case to you, you have another thought coming."

"Damned inconsiderate of you," Darius said smoothly. "Suppose I'll need to make a call, then." He slid his foot to the floor and reached for the phone, already dialing when he looked at Wharton. "About that other—the investigation you've been conducting—regarding drug smuggling, I believe? The phone taps. Stakeouts. Surveillance—"

Wharton's face betrayed him, his shock a flash of heated light.

Darius paused his hand hovering over another button, and looked at him. "Seriously, Agent Wharton, you suspected I knew long before now, didn't you?"

"I don't know what you're talking about," Wharton growled.

Darius smiled slowly, lowered the receiver to the base, and met the man's gaze while settling back in the chair. "I think you and I truly need to reach an understanding, Agent Wharton. I'm neither a drug smuggler nor an international assassin. I'm a reputable businessman. I make my living talking, meeting people, promoting a sense of goodwill, and handling negotiations. I dabble in market analysis and looking into business ventures which I then pass on to corporate heads around the globe. On occasion, I handle negotiations for new companies. I make an extremely good living conducting those affairs, and truthfully, if I chose such a life, I could probably do well in the drug trade. Fortunately, I value my life and tend to steer clear of ventures detrimental to my health. Having said as much," Darius paused for effect, his gaze lighting with a touch of anger. "Can you even remotely consider how I might feel knowing that a man was murdered a few doors from my own? Honestly, do you have any fucking clue how angry I might be that you'd consider me the killer when I know how close I was to a maniac? For all the bloody hell I know, it could have been a deliberate hit, and the bastard assassin ended up in the wrong bloody room. Put yourself in my shoes, you bloomin' idiot. I do move in international circles and I'm one of the fucking key men in von Hendricks Corporation . . . and you, you dumb fuck, you're too busy trying to hang me to help me save my own bloody life."

"You believe you were the target?"

"How the bloody hell should I know?" Darius asked without losing a beat. "As I said, I am a legitimate businessman. I don't make a point of associating with maniacs, drug smugglers, or assassins. I am not naive, however. Anyone who travels as much as I do and carries as many responsibilities could become a target for countless reasons. I might not have personally triggered this ordeal. It could be as bloody simple as someone with a grudge against the distributing company, or this hotel. As an extremely visible spokesman for the company, I'd be one bloody good feather in someone's cap."

Wharton studied him for a moment before asking, "What did you find out in New York?"

"Not enough to rule out that bloody scenario," Darius answered honestly. "A few extremely troubling tidbits, however," he said and weighed the odds in his head as he continued to study Wharton, letting a bit of his wariness rise into his gaze.

"Like what?"

"If I were to answer that, you'd be left with yet another decision," Darius said grimly. "And depending on that decision, I would be either in far greater jeopardy or slightly safer than I am at this moment."

"If you want my help as much as it sounds, I don't think you have much choice, Mr. Brock," Wharton stated. "Frankly, we could pull out of this and leave it to the locals and if someone does have you in their sights, you might not fair too well."

"If I were open to intimidation, do you think I'd be sitting behind this desk?"

Wharton considered him for another moment then eased back in his chair, changing his tone, "So, what did you find out? Assuming you want my help?"

Darius feigned contemplation in a brief pause, then met Wharton's gaze. "Two things. First, not foremost, I might have learned what Mr. Fradden intended to tell me."

Interest rose in Wharton's eyes. "Are you going to tell me?"

"Suppose having said that much, it would seem appropriate," Darius said grimly and shifted his gaze to flick a cigar ash into a crystal ashtray on the desk. Looking again to Wharton, he continued, "About a month or so ago, there was a series of break-ins in the New York branch warehouse. Apparently, nothing was taken or destroyed. The crimes were never reported to the police. I have yet to determine if Fradden spoke to the head office or acted on his own decision. If, as I suspect, he simply ignored those break-ins, it could explain his agitation when approaching me. Considering the latter half of this, it's more than feasible," Darius spoke as if weighing his words.

"About three weeks ago as near as I've ascertained, the warehouse was again breached. I'm supposing those early invasions were merely a clever means of casing the warehouse. Whoever the culprits were, they managed to slip in undetected and slip out the same way. Through negligence, the theft wasn't even discovered until a few days ago. I'm assuming, Mr. Fradden was desperate and when he learned I'd be here, he decided he better come speak to me directly."

"You're saying something of considerable value was stolen?"

"Valuable, financially and intrinsically," Darius admitted. "You do know the affiliation between the wineries in upper New York and the distribution companies. Is that correct?"

"The wineries are held in part by the von Hendricks who live there if I understand it."

Darius nodded. "Hubert von Hendricks lives there and manages the wineries on a full-time basis, but the full control and personal vested interest remains with Amadeus—Baron Amadeus von Hendricks, the current chairman of the Corporation. How much do you know about him?"

"Not much more than what you've just said," Wharton said, lying badly.

Darius studied him momentarily, then nodded and continued, letting the lie pass. "As you may or may not know, Amad spent a great deal of time at the wineries in his youth. It's rather well known that he's an acclaimed wine connoisseur and only recently, our wines have been recognized in several prestigious circles."

"You're telling me someone heisted some wine?"

"Oversimplified by kilos," Darius said with a conflict of amusement and dismay. "Three cases of extremely old, extremely expensive cases of von Hendricks wine, disappeared, and I suspect, they didn't just get up and walk away, nor find passage on another ship. Fradden himself, after becoming aware of the missed connection in London, made several calls to other destinations in the hopes of an oversight. We're referring to over a million dollars worth of wine slated for Amad's private archives."

Wharton's eyes snapped, his lips parted then clamped with a tight knot, apparently searching for the lie or joke. "You're not kidding."

Darius shook his head. "I wish the devil I was," he said honestly. "Unfortunately, it's a fact, but whether it has anything to do with Mr. Fradden's demise, I have reason to doubt."

"Seems like a fairly good reason," Wharton said without rancor.

"Unless he actually knew who could have stolen that cargo, I fail to agree," Darius said. "And thus far, I haven't confirmed that detail. What I suspect is simply that he intended to speak with me in the hope of keeping his job. Frankly, I would have fired him on the spot, but that's neither here nor there. The fact remains, the wine's missing without a trace and the New York office is in turmoil."

"I take it the theft has been reported?"

"Amad's handling that personally, Agent Wharton," Darius said honestly. "I'd imagine he has reported it, but to whom or how publicly, I'd have to wonder. If this were to reach certain circles, it's not beyond the realm of possibility that we'd have a few other factions involved in attempting to sideline that search. To be clear, the information I just imparted should remain between you and me, as I, personally, don't want the responsibility of adding a few marketeers to that hunt, and believe me, that is within the realm of probability. With the current recognition, it's a fair bet that wine could bring a great deal more than market value."

"You're saying it could be worth a hell of a lot more on the black market."

"A single bottle would be worth a small fortune today. Imagine the value of a case tomorrow."

"Bearing that in mind, I'd wager Mr. Fradden was in serious danger if he knew the thieves," Wharton commented.

"On the surface, I'd agree," Darius said with a touch of concern lifting in his eyes.

"Let's say it was an inside job, and Fradden decided to bail out to save his gonads," Wharton speculated, his thoughts turned toward more productive circles. "It's more than possible someone decided to shut him up."

"On that theory alone, you may grasp something of my own precarious position, Agent Wharton. I may not have known what he wanted to tell me, but whether Mr. Fradden was able to pass on that detail remains a mystery."

Wharton looked at him slightly differently. "Has there been an assault on your life?"

"I've certainly not availed myself to the possibility."

With a nod, the agent continued to consider. "You said there was something else. Two things. What was the second?"

"This could become another sticky wicket," Darius commented with his thoughts and expression shifting accordingly. Far more gravely, he studied Wharton. "The problem is this, Agent Wharton, I've come across certain information which I'm certain you already possess. Information which explains why you have every intention of accusing and convicting me of this crime. Information, I bloody well should have learned long before now."

"Maybe you better tell me what it is," Wharton said, but he already knew. His eyes conveyed his tension.

"Let me ask you this first," Darius said carefully. "Was there anything particularly strange or . . . different about Mr. Fradden's cause of death?"

"A broken neck isn't all that common for a man his size."

"Don't humor me, Agent Wharton. If we're to be associated beyond this moment, I'd like an answer. You don't necessarily need to tell me details but was there something . . . a recognizable, possibly notable, signature to this man's death?"

"I assume you mean, have I seen something like this before, and the answer's, yes," Wharton said carefully, his gaze intent.

"Then what I've heard is true," Darius said with mirror speculation, a touch of concern added in fair measure. "How many have there been? How many have you seen?"

"A few," Wharton answered, still carefully.

Darius studied the man's blank gaze, his poker face, and decided, "I really don't have a choice, Agent Wharton. I do know you've been investigating me. Off and on for several years, more avidly for the past two. I don't particularly like it, but I've gotten accustomed to it as America is not the only place where I run into that sort of thing. On occasion, I almost feel a sense of comfort in having the authorities near at hand. There are places in this world where an Englishman is regarded with the same scorn and hatred as an American. I cross too many borders not to have encountered social ignorance and bigotry, as well as hostility. The problem is this, Agent Wharton, I didn't take your interest seriously. I know I'm no bloody smuggler or dope dealer, and even if you watched me for the next decade, you'd not find evidence that doesn't exist. When you arrived yesterday morning, I assumed you were using this incident to your own ends. It never occurred to me that you might have an extremely good reason for being here, or that your investigation had shifted. I am aware of it, now, however."

"What exactly are you aware of?" Wharton asked.

"That you wholeheartedly believe I killed Lawrence Fradden, and that you're basing your conclusion on . . . questionable circumstances from the past two years."

"For the hell of it, why don't you tell me what those questionable circumstances are."

"I'd rather you tell me. How exactly can you honestly suspect me of these circumstances when you've had me under surveillance around the bloody clock every time I've entered the country? While you're at it, please convince me that you've considered the possibility of my innocence and ignorance. I'd rather believe you were protecting me from this bloody stalker than to think you've automatically accused and convicted me in a land where something like the 'Constitution of the United States' is a practice and belief."

Wharton offered nothing in his expression, but his eyes held the intensity on high. "What exactly do you know about this stalker?"

"What I know is that a man's dead, and much to my surprise, he's not the first. What I'd love to know is how the bloody hell you could believe I'm responsible when you do watch me?"

"That's simple, Mr. Brock," Wharton stated as if coming in for the kill. "We do know for a fact that today isn't the first time you've slid out from under our surveillance."

"You can bloody well blame yourself for that as well, Agent Wharton," Darius stated without missing a beat. "If you think I'm about to give you an itemized list of the women I've been with, you can go to blazes."

For a long moment, Wharton stared at him then stated, "You expect me to believe you slip out to what . . . have an occasional affair?"

"I don't particularly give a damn what you believe. I'm simply stating a fact of life, lad," Darius answered. "Though I'll mention, I neither consider my affairs occasional nor casual. My decision will remain the same, regardless of how you choose to accept my words. For my safety, I'd prefer your belief, naturally, but I won't destroy another's reputation or allow you to harass the women I've known toward your own end."

"I don't see that you have a choice."

"Oh, but I do, Agent Wharton," Darius said quietly. "I can open my affairs to the public and have my female acquaintances hate me, or I can accept your antagonism and distrust. By my calculations, you are the lesser of the two evils. The choice is made, and I won't apologize for it. How you choose to continue this accord remains your decision."

"Give me some names to verify—"

"No."

"One."

"Go to blazes."

"I don't think you understand the gravity of this situation, Mr. Brock."

"Ah, wait, there is a name I might give you. I've not slept with her, but I did pay a short visit earlier this evening if that would help. As she's already aware of this situation, she probably wouldn't mind verifying my whereabouts."

"Who?"

"Jenna Windrow, the assistant manager here," he answered. "I stopped by her flat before returning here. As much as I would have loved to stay, I didn't feel it was appropriate."

Wharton wore a visibly smug expression as he nodded, "I'm sure we can have a talk with her."

"Sticky wicket," Darius said with a faint smile. "You assume I'm lying because you have your men watching her apartment. Discreetly, of course. You might just phone the lads and ask if they noticed a taxi arrive a while ago. As I said, I do tend to keep my private affairs, private. Had I slept with her, I wouldn't be enlightening you of this and you wouldn't know about it," he said honestly. "As it stands, if you even allude to the possibility or make her uncomfortable when you speak to her, you and I will have a serious breakdown in our relationship, Agent Wharton."

"Why did you go to her apartment?" Wharton asked with an edge.

"Are you daft, lad? You need to ask?"

Wharton might not approve, but he was beginning to believe. "She turned you down, huh?" he asked as if the thought pleased him immensely.

"She offered me the couch," Darius mused as if he'd expected nothing less. "She's a woman of rare high standards and principles, which is precisely why I won't stand idle and have you battering about her honor. Understand, if you're less than respectful of her dignity, we'll have a bloody roe in the winds." By expression and gaze alone, he confirmed the warning.

Wharton's belief remained in doubt, but, at least, he'd begun to weigh the details more carefully.

"Now that we've reached at least a base understanding, Agent Wharton, possibly you could tell me . . .? Is there any truth to the rumor that these others have uhm . . . been drained?"

Riveted, Wharton's attention and gaze held steady. "Drained of what?"

"Come now," Darius said quietly, uncomfortably. "I did glimpse Lawrence Fradden and there was something . . . particularly confounding about that chap's appearance. I couldn't pinpoint the oddity, but I've since heard the rumor. Was he—were the others—drained of their blasted blood?"

Wharton wondered, "Where did you hear that?"

Obviously, it wasn't a detail bandied about. Darius studied the hard gaze and asked, "Do you really want me to phone your president at—" He moved his sleeve to read his watch then looked to Wharton. "—4:30 am?"

"It just might come to that, Brock," he stated.

"Mr. Brock, or Darius if you prefer, Agent Wharton. A surname standing alone is in fine poor form and a tad insulting." He hesitated a half second before commenting, "By your reaction, I'd imagine the information's accurate. Now, since I don't happen to believe in vampires, possibly, you'll share your theory as to how this could happen?"

"Why don't you tell me," Wharton said pointedly.

"Were there marks? Point of entry indicators possibly?"

"You tell me."

Annoyed, Darius held the man's gaze. "Perhaps, I will, Agent Wharton," he said and leaned forward, lifting the receiver, dialing a number from memory. With the telephone ringing at his ear, he leaned back and held Wharton's gaze as he waited. The line engaged and a groggy, familiar voice erupted in his ear. "Do hate to bother you at such an unearthly hour, Michael, but I've run into a bit of trouble as I'm sure you're aware."

"Darius?" the waking husky voice of a member of the President's cabinet asked.

"Right-o, lad. As I prefer not to wake your employer, I wonder if you might handle this for me?"

By Wharton's smug expression, he considered it a hoax.

"I did hear your name mentioned recently. What's the problem?"

"At the moment, an extremely rude brick wall sitting across from me. I've spent the last bloody hour or more attempting to convince him that I'm neither a smuggler, drug dealer, nor a homicidal maniac, but the chap's prepared to haul me to the nearest lockup. Frankly, Michael, if that happens, you may rest assured—international relations will suffer."

"Where are you, Darius?"

"Presently, I'm at the Chateau Suites in Pittsburgh, Pennsylvania, and while I have you on the line, I will mention—I've not been entirely pleased with this asinine investigation from the start. If this is the reception and treatment businessmen should expect on your soil, sir, you may find your import and export trade sorely declining soon."

"Slow down, Darius, tell me what's going on, and I can assure you, I'll take care of it."

"I suggest you wake the director of your FBI and learn the details firsthand. I've come into this a tad late. The sons of bitches have been following me about and playing cold war bloody spy games while my life's been threatened and endangered. Apparently, several times. Though I've yet to learn how many times, or how close this maniac's come. Now, your officials have the bloody nerve to accuse me of the fucking crimes? I'm angry, growing impatient, and damned irritated by this fellow pompous attitude. You have ten minutes to deal with this chap, Michael, or this phone will be very busy when you attempt to get through. If I must import a few chaps from the Queen Mother's cabinet, I'll damn sure get this situation resolved. Ten minutes, Michael." Leaning slightly, he dropped the phone in the receiver.

"Who was that supposed to be? The Secretary of State?"

"Very close," Darius said and lifted the receiver, buzzing the front desk. "Lori, dear. We could use another carafe of coffee and a few fresh pastries if the delivery arrived. Have one of the lads out there trot over to the kitchen and take care of it, will you?"

"Yes, sir!" the girl said sharply.

Leaning back more comfortably, Darius caught Wharton's angry gaze. "We have a few moments to kill, Agent Wharton. Are you married?"

"I don't know what your game is, Mister . . . Brock—"

"Making small talk, ole' man. I assumed that was a safe subject. Perhaps, I was wrong. Are you a golfer? Fisherman, perhaps?"

"If I recall, you were about to tell me a little about those murders."

"Be glad to, shortly," Darius answered. "I have a feeling we'll discuss a great deal after you have had a chat with your director." His gaze level, he stated, "I don't play games, and I don't bluff, Mr. Wharton. If I were you, I'd hope that call comes within ten minutes. If it doesn't, you may need to find a hobby to spend all the free time you'll have."

"You expect me to believe you just spoke to someone in Washington, and based on that ploy, you expect me to discuss the details of this case."

"I don't recall mentioning the case since hanging up, Mr. Wharton, and frankly, I'm not about to discuss the case with you again unless that phone rings. I will enlist able, more efficient, and amicable investigators if such becomes necessary. I am not an American citizen, and my personal safety has been jeopardized by your incompetency. I gave you the benefit of my doubt, but you've chosen your position."

The knock at the door intruded, and Darius bid the intruder to enter. Nearly trotting, the same young clerk to man the front desk hurried across the short distance and bounced her worried gaze off Darius to Wharton and back. "I've sent for the pastries. They should be here any second, Mr. Brock," she spoke breathlessly, clattering the carafe on the desk.

"You needn't have flown, lass. We may be thirsty but not near dehydrated. Do catch your breath on your way out."

"Yes, sir," she said with the vaporous gaze and smile that he'd seen often enough to recognize as awe. "If there's anything else, I'll be right outside."

"Thank you, lass," he said offhandedly and watched her hurry out, pulling the door closed as if exiting a king's chamber, barely making a sound. The girl was not new. He'd seen her several times in passing. Shaking his head, he sat forward and lifted the pot, refilling his cup. Sliding the pot across the desk, he motioned to Wharton and started to lean back when the phone erupted. Lifting the receiver, he spoke simply, "Yes?"

"Sir, there's a call for Mr. Wharton on line two."

Darius leaned further handing the receiver across the desk. "For you," he said and engaged the lighted button, leaning back and watching Wharton who barked his surname into the receiver. Within seconds, the man's eyes misted; his tense expression faded to mild shock and dumbfound. Darius merely waited. Gloating had never been his style. Why bother? He detested the power granted him, and never reveled in humbling any man. Far too well, he knew the depth of pain such a blow could deliver to an ego. Wharton's jaw clenched; his focus quickened as he sat through an apparently heated discourse. At the end of two minutes, he offered a short affirmation, then leaned across the desk, handing the receiver to Darius, his gaze fixed. "My director would like a word with you."

Accepting the phone, Darius said, "Yes."

"Mr. Brock, I'd like to apologize for how this has been handled," the husky voice began, no happier than Wharton to have been put on a hot seat in the middle of the night. "I've instructed Agent Wharton to remain on the scene and conduct the investigation; however, I'm sending a senior agent to oversee the operation. If there's anything—"

"That won't be necessary," Darius interrupted smoothly, his gaze holding Wharton's. "I believe Agent Wharton and I have reached an understanding. I'd appreciate it though, if you'd authorize Agent Wharton to provide me with a copy of the autopsy report on my associate as soon as it becomes available.

I'd further appreciate it if you'd authorize Agent Wharton to bring me up to speed on these prior incidents. If, as my associate's demise seems to indicate, I've picked up some sort of ghoul in my travels . . . I'd damn sure like to know when, where and to what extent this lunatic's already gone. I feel like a bloody hare with a hawk circling while the fox gives chase. Now, can I expect your cooperation, sir . . .?"

16

In slow stages, his genuine surprise and discomfort growing by leaps, Darius collected the details from a gentleman who didn't appreciate the orders to share his collected data. Slowly, if only by the brief glimpses of shock as well as the questions asked, Wharton seemed to realize Darius was as innocent as he professed, at least regarding the homicides. No coincidences. Darius fully understood the FBI's attempt to conceal this secondary investigation.

On each of his trips into the United States, as well as one in New Mexico, another body had been discovered, a total of eight in the past two years. The first two had been females, hookers who worked the streets not far from where Darius had stayed, one in Chicago, another in LA. Neither corpse had revealed physical evidence. The third victim, a businessman, had patronized the same hotel as Darius; his body had been found in a parked car several miles from the hotel.

Darius had never heard the name before, but according to Wharton, that fellow's demise initiated the first connection to him. And so the investigation had begun.

A teenager had come next, a courier in New York who'd often handled deliveries at the hotel where Darius had stayed. A baked goods delivery man, a woman salesclerk from a department store, a panhandler who'd worked the area around another hotel, and a waiter at a restaurant where Darius had dined. The hawk had been circling the hare, and after Wharton's rather blatant grizzly recital—told for dramatic effect—Darius suffered a genuine shudder that he deemed not to hide.

"Eight," Darius uttered, letting the word sink in, his gaze listing with the incredibility, his distraction genuine. "I've had this ghoul on my tail for two years . . ." His gaze returned to Wharton with his distress rising on a dozen planes behind his blank dark eyes. "This bastard's killed eight times? And I'm the only bloody suspect you have?"

"Put yourself in our place—"

"I'd be damned glad to," Darius stated sincerely. "My own place seems a tad more bleak and precarious at the moment."

"You fly into the country several times a year," Wharton continued, ignoring the comment, his gaze direct. "You make a habit of arriving and checking in early or late morning. We know you don't remain in your hotel rooms every night and you check out at odd hours. If not directly associated with the victims, you've met or crossed paths with each one. Within twelve hours after your departure, we find another corpse, and we can place you in the immediate area of every murder."

Darius studied the agent momentarily, then stated, "Considering the international scope of my affairs, I'd imagine you've contacted various other authorities. Have you contacted Interpol? Is this lunatic following me around the globe?"

"Not that we've discovered," Wharton answered reluctantly.

Darius nodded, his thoughts turning. "For the record, I will mention—I don't harbor any ill-will or poor regard for the United States or Americans. Since, as at least I know I'm not this miscreant, we can assume my ghoul has never applied for a passport, nor I assume, does he travel via private craft . . ."

And therein remained the mystery that started Darius pacing within the office after nearly two hours of verbal briefing.

How the blazes was this lunatic finding him, following him? To successfully follow him and arrive in his wake, this creature needed access to a schedule, a detail that remained the most alarming aspect of this situation. There was no schedule to lend forewarning and advance notice. Not unless this beast lurked within the upper ranks of the von Hendricks Corporation and could access whatever credible records dictated the schedule. Without notice, a destination could change, not unlike Friday afternoon, and still, this monster had arrived by nightfall.

With a glance at the louver blinds, Darius uttered a curse. He needed that answer, needed to know how this beast followed him, and he knew who held that answer.

Not much of the night remained. He was running out of time, procrastinating. And unless he intended to battle his wits, throughout what could prove to be an extremely difficult day, he couldn't afford to avoid placing this call.

Moving behind the desk, he settled into the chair, lifting the phone receiver and punching numbers for the New York area code. Not often, and only under extreme circumstances, would he subject himself to this added torment, but he needed to know. If he had any chance of staying ahead and out of this monster's grip, he damn well needed some answers. Hopefully, the Baron would understand and offer assistance.

More than likely, Darius knew he was falling into a trap, playing directly into a game that he had scant chance of winning. Already half-sick with tension, he rested in the chair, collecting his bearings as the phone rang once, twice . . .

Four times, the ring resounded before the deep baritone voice commented, "This is a surprise. I didn't expect to hear from you so soon, lad. What's troubling you?"

Oh, hell, that voice rang of concern, which didn't bode well for the coming moments. "I ehm. . . I do hate to bother you, but I've learned enough details about this situation to have several questions. If I've made a mistake, calling to ask, I'll apologize in advance, but I don't see how I'll ehm . . . help to resolve this situation without the answers."

"A tad out of character, lad, this careful wording," the Baron said with a touch of warning. "I've come to appreciate your straightforward, often brazen nature."

"I don't know what to make of this," Darius said honestly. "How is it . . . possible for this miscreant to be in my shadow within hours when I've no bloody idea where I'll be from one moment to the next? Has he . . . is it even possible that he's found a line into our upper ranks? Or is there something . . . otherworldly about his endeavors?"

"Explain yourself," the Baron stated.

Considering the experience on his way from the Terrace Apartments, Darius admitted, "I have a sense of his presence. I uhm . . . I'm certain he's here. And in retrospect, I might have felt him on other occasions, sir. I didn't lend it a great deal of thought. I ehm . . . I've become accustomed to the watchers. I assumed they were all yours. Now, I wonder, and tonight, I sensed him following. How does he follow me? How is that possible?"

"Felt him, have you?"

Uncomfortably, Darius answered, "Yes."

"Tell me about this, my lad. What did you feel?"

"I uh . . . I'm not entirely sure how to describe this," Darius admitted, suffering a great many second thoughts and knowing it was too damn late to retract. "I uh . . . I've never been able to tell exactly when you're reading my thoughts, but I know you do," he stated bluntly. "This . . . this was a pressure. I felt an alien sense . . . an extremely uncomfortable touch as if . . .? Well . . . as if I'd touched or been touched by something hot and slimy. I don't know how else to describe it. I felt something pushing at my mind, trying to intrude."

"And did it succeed?"

"No, I'm fairly certain it didn't and it didn't attack directly. It just . . . kept a reasonable distance and watched me from the shadows. It uhm . . . it knows I'm aware of it now, though." Collecting his thoughts, firming, he asked again,

"How is it finding me? Do you know? Or should I simply ask, will you tell me and give me some slight advantage?"

A low, silky laugh slid through the phone. "Lad, I've no intention of letting him have at you if it's within my power to prevent. Unfortunately, the answer I will impart is not likely to offer you either comfort or an edge. Fact, my lad, it might make you a tad more distressed."

"I'd doubt that were possible if any other had told me so," Darius said warily.

"Let me tell you a story, Darius, a little incident that happened in my own life several years ago," the Baron paused, apparently becoming comfortable, finding his rhythm. "I had a lad in my tow, a boy not much younger than my present valet, with similar proclivities, I'll admit. That fellow, however, was neither of a decent nature nor purity. No comparison, really. The lad was a self-centered, vile sort and quite the villain before I ever met him. For a time, he amused me. You have a sense of how I make use of certain resources. The semantics, if you will. So, and he was no different. He had his duties, and I allowed him the freedom to conduct them sufficiently." He barely paused, only to build suspense as he never need take a breath. "Upon a time, he managed to offend me as most such creatures do in their time. The fellow did have a wicked streak and an impressive will. I won't offer you the details, lad, but suffice it to say, I made of him something more and less than he was, and for a time, I held him in such a state . . ."

Whether the story had ended and should make sense, or if the Baron had merely paused for effect, Darius couldn't decide. In silence he waited, hoping for a continuance while dreading that very thing.

"Perhaps, I'll need be more direct with you, eh, lad?"

"I understand the basics," Darius admitted. Firsthand, he knew how the Baron managed and maintained a houseful of loyal servants, as well as a thriving empire.

"I don't think you do, Darius. Meaning not to offend your intelligence," the Baron said in a musing tone. "The fact is simply this, this chap doesn't need to travel to your locations to make his presence known. It's what I've suspected since the beginning," he said lightly.

Not grasping the facts, simple or otherwise, Darius considered the condition of Lawrence Fradden. The chap couldn't have reached and snapped his own neck or emptied his own veins. The holes Wharton had finally mentioned. Two circular incisions on the carotid artery would suggest the presence of another of the Baron's ilk. If Darius stood in a less dangerous position, he might find some humor in the FBI's explanation. Doubtful, very doubtful, the villain carried a bastardized compact dialysis machine capable of siphoning rather than sifting blood.

"I'm still at a loss," Darius admitted. "If not in person, how is he doing this?"

"The simple and most direct answer, Darius, is the most obvious, and I'm disappointed in your grasp. Simply, the lad has help. Very loyal—probably very dark—minions. Sadly, lad, those in his thrall are probably confined to the darkness but still very much in his keep. Were I him, and from my vast collected knowledge, I'd allow them a steady ration of rats and the like. I'd wager that the bodies littering your wake are their rewards for keeping tabs on you. What they see, he sees. Are you beginning to grasp this situation now?"

Only too damn clear! In those short sentences, the Baron had multiplied the threat by at least eight. If Darius understood, then each murder could be attributed to a separate entity. "You're telling me that I'm not dealing with this chap directly. That it's not one, but possibly more than a half dozen of these bastards merely waiting for me to fly into port? And what then? Does he intend to have me viewed as a serial killer? Intend to see me imprisoned in a ward for the criminally insane? What is the sense of this? What does he want from me?"

"He's playing with you, my lad. Having a bit of fun at your expense. I'd imagine, he'll decide to take you soon if he suspects the game's over. You, lad, are a temptation he can't resist."

And the Baron intended to keep the bait dangling a bit longer. "You were right, you know. This isn't a relief . . . Especially if the bastard's now here in person."

"Doubtful, lad. No need to panic yet," the Baron said in a faintly bemused tone. "More than likely, you have only one of his spies on your heels. Were he anything else, I'm sad to say, it's doubtful you could have withstood his mentalism. You're impressively strong-willed, Darius. No shame in your strength. If you were otherwise, you'd not be what you are. I have no doubt you can withstand and outsmart these lesser lads."

"Your confidence is appreciated," Darius said dryly, not relieved one damn bit.

The Baron idled a laugh. "Take heart, m' lad. These ones won't come after you with serious intent. Were they mine and stole the coup from under me, I'd have to kill them. As much as they might want to nip you, they won't without his order, and he won't give that order."

And the Baron's arrival in New York suddenly made sense! The Baron was within a one-hour flight with his private jet on standby. A trap . . . some bloody trap had already been laid, and Darius knew at this moment, he was the cheese stuck to the spring. The other possibility, one which offered a degree of comfort, was simply that the Baron had just led Darius through a carefully plotted story to make him slightly more nervous. "Is uhm . . . is there any point in attempting to learn the details of this situation? Or should I just idle about and wait for the strike?"

"You need to keep busy, m' lad," the Baron mused. "I'm sure you'll make yourself useful there, and as I recall, you have a duty you must perform later this evening."

Darius could have survived without the reminder. "I'd thought that order might change," he said honestly.

"On the contrary, my lad," the Baron said as if Darius should perish the thought. "You've a service to offer, and I'm honor-bound to see that you carry through. I wouldn't suggest taking that trip alone, though, lad."

"Pardon me?"

A deep sigh slid through the receiver. "Suppose I can't blame you for doubting my honesty," the baritone voice inflected a degree of deep concern. "Nor can I blame you for bulking. Free-spirited or not, you do tend to follow the basic rules. Here then—a literal command, lad. Invite and enlist your natural charm to have that lovely thorn in your heart accompany you to the reception."

For a half second, Darius considered the idea a hoax, a grand jest, and in the next, he knew the integrity of the command. Another nail in his side, or spike in his heart. And this was just the beginning of the price he would pay for his interest and attraction to Jenna Windrow.

"I notice you're not thanking me for such a magnanimous order, Darius. Where are those crisp English manners I've so come to enjoy?"

"Thank you," he said tonelessly.

The Baron chuckled. "One more suggestion, lad. You'd be much better off sleeping while the sun's high. These soldiers won't possess the talent to move through those hours with either grace or speed. Take advantage of the reprieve and stay vigilant whence the sun sets. If you can stay in a crowd, you'd fare better, though you need watch your back and call on those natural instincts you embrace. These li'l devils might have more tricks up their sleeves, and you wouldn't fare well in prison for murder no matter how you attempt to fool yourself. The glitter and glitz, the gold and the prestige—you may despise those luxuries, but they've become your way of life. You wouldn't be happy stripped of those."

Expecting more digs, possibly another command, Darius held the phone for nearly a full minute before he realized the dead silence. Muttering a curse, he leaned and dropped the receiver into its cradle. No rest, no hope, no mercy for the wicked. And no damn relief. He'd known better than to expect any genuine relief. Calling the Baron, asking anything, was asking for trouble, and as he considered the words, the new threat, the sinking sensation crept through him.

When it amused the Baron, he offered the truth. Especially when the truth was slightly more incredible and damning than a lie . . . and with every spoken word, the Baron had confirmed the threat. Darius need only remember those moments outside the hotel to know his accuracy. He'd been wide open, easy pickings. If he'd truly become the target of another of the Baron's ilk, the chance of him sending the chap packing with a few words, an idle threat, was a joke.

"I'm finished," he muttered in a lame moment of crystal clarity. Chained to one, the target of another. It was just a matter of time before the game ended, and he became a monster's meal. His days . . . more probably, his hours were numbered, and strangely, he felt nothing. Not shock or horror. Not even a mild surprise. Time. He'd been living on borrowed time for the past eight years, knowing the futility of escape, bound by his word, his honor, and his blood.

Wallowing in self-pity wouldn't solve a damn thing, and by damn, if this was his last hoorah, then there were certain steps he would take, could take. A single safety measure that he'd contemplated for the past several years, keeping it in the back of his mind to implement if he ever received forewarning toward this very situation.

Lifting the receiver, he started punching buttons for the long series of numbers. As the distant ring started in his ear, he leaned back and waited. Tabulating the hours, estimating the time zone, he wondered if the phone would be answered and dared to hope, nearly thought to pray.

"Hello, Darius!" the young voice shouted in delight.

"Hello, to you, li'l lad."

A wild giggle echoed through the phone line. "I knew I'd hear froom you! I wanted to call you! Aunt Rebecca said I wasnae to boother you! Aye, and I hate that ole' lass! She struts aboot like a peahen, giving me oorders like she's the Queen M'athair a Scots! Well, I woon't stand for that, I can tell ye!" His voice changed as he spoke, adopting the weird combination of childish anger and ancient wisdom that Darius had found fascinating at the onset. "Aye, and here I'm ranting and raving like ye've all night. Do ye, Darius? Is it night there where you are? Where are you, me lad?"

"Still in Pittsburgh," Darius said, smiling faintly. "The Chateau Suites, but not in my room at the moment."

"You've spoken to father." It was neither guess nor question. In his way, Raphael practiced mentalism to reach his conclusions. "And it went badly."

"Well, not too, actually," Darius said honestly. All things considered, the visit and subsequent conversation could have gone worse. "Raphael, I need a bit of help. Could I trouble you with a few questions and receive a few honest answers?"

"I'm seeing no reason you cannae ask, Darius."

That was as close to an affirmation as Raphael would offer. "Have you ever known—or met—any others like your father, li'l chap?"

The silence dropped. An unnaturally long silence before the low, grave voice slid quietly through the line. "Aye, Darius. There was one upon a time, but he's gone on to hell before us. Why do you ask sooch?"

"As I mentioned, I have some problems here, and that question's been bothering me. It's probably nothing to worry about or too serious," Darius lied smoothly, hoping this was not one of those moments when Raphael would look through him. "There's—"

"I dinnae like it when you try to fool me, Darius. I dinnae like it one bit."

"I'm sorry," he answered quietly. "I'd not wanted to worry you needlessly. Please, don't hang up, lad. I need you, and I need to ask something of you. A favor," Darius continued. "You've proven to me, you can make and keep a promise, Raphael, and I need you to enter into another with me. First, though, I need to ask another question. One I believe only you could answer for me."

"A'right then," the young voice grumbled, his natural curiosity and wariness apparent. "Ask, m' lad."

"It's a rather technical question, Rafe, within your realm of expertise. I ehm . . . let's say, hypothetically, if I was tainted, would you know it? Would you be able to tell even if I didn't know it?"

Raphael huffed a breath, sounding amused and relieved. "Aye, I think so, Darius, but I'm nae sensing sooch a thing. Clean as new-fallen snow, so you are. Aye, and you've your full faculties. Father would never—" Whether he halted his words knowing his father could or because he remembered the question of another, he began again in a far more grave and troubled tone, "I'd know, Darius. It's a change you could nae hide froom me. Boot . . . boot I widnae tell you if you didnae know. I'd not be so cruel to you, my friend."

Darius considered the words and understood the integrity and the reasoning. For all the child's mischief and dark wiles, he was not a devil to be cruel without provocation. "What if I asked you to tell me, lad? If I asked you, now, to tell me if you ever sense a change in me—would you tell me then?"

"I would not be so cruel to you," Raphael stated almost angrily, offended. "And if you didnae know, it wid be cruel and troobling for you! I'd not burden you with such a thing! Dinnae ask it of me! If yer changed, I'll accept you as you are, as you've taught me, yourself, Darius. As you've accepted me."

The profound truth touched Darius. The child's pain and anxiety echoed in every syllable, and for the first time, Darius knew. He knew without a doubt what he'd suspected for the past eight years, knew incontestably, he had lost his son. Dylan had suffered the change. The sadness touched Darius more deeply, the futility of his existence never more certain. "That's not the favor I wanted to ask of you, pal," he forced himself to continue. "This one, I'm afraid is far more selfish on my part and may be far more difficult for you. But I need to ask, and I will beg of you to be as kind to me as you were to my son. I need your promise, lad. The favor is this . . . If ever I am changed, I won't ask you to tell me. I will ask only this, lad, that you finish me. Only you could make me this promise and do as I ask, Raphael, and I'd consider it an honor, a kindness."

"Ohhh, Darius," the voice slid morosely through the receiver. "You dinnae know what you ask."

"I do, Raphael. I know it won't be easy for you but—"

"The change willnae kill you—"

"It will, lad. As a man of free will, knowing what I know, I don't want to live a life wearing invisible chains. Promise you won't let that happen to me. Promise me, you'll find a way to set me free and let me take my due in limbo. I wouldn't be alive with that change, lad. I might walk and talk, but somewhere in my mind, I'd know the actions and words were not my own. As my only friend—as the only child I've ever known as my own—promise me, you will be the one to end that misery for me when it comes."

A strained silence lasted only a second. A sob broke, and the soft, hiccupped words reached through the line. "I proomise." The line clattered. The silence dropped within the receiver at Darius's ear.

For Raphael, Darius suffered a quick pain and regret, but in the child's words, Darius knew his relief as if a burden had lifted, as it surely had. If only to keep his mind free of that burden, he needed to believe the child would keep his promise. Therein, Darius found heart to be liberated from the crippling fear and hopelessness, from the desperation that threatened to buckle him. He could play the game now, the stakes no different than any time past. Without remorse or regret, without a burden of consequence. Come what may, he would not become another George Halbrook, or Mason or Whitman, destined to live his life in dim-witted submission to something which he would have neither will nor sense to grasp. He wouldn't become another blind minion to be moved about like a pawn on a chessboard.

To live without freedom of will, or spirit to survive, would be worse than death.

In a flowing elegant script reflective of the man himself, the note was simple and direct, to the point, but still Jenna stood holding it, rereading it, hearing the words in his deep resonant pitch. "Good morning, Luv. Thank you for your hospitality and again, for the hot chocolate. I'll see you at the hotel. Please, don't hurry on my account. See you soon . . ."

Why she'd even believed that he'd sleep on her couch, she couldn't fathom in the light of day. With a glance at the living room, she verified her thought. He hadn't even laid down, much less slept on the linens. Shaking her head, she pushed the button on the coffeemaker, not sure whether to be relieved or disappointed as she returned to her bedroom. If she'd invited him into her bed, she wondered if he would have stayed, then cursed the thought.

Too many reasons existed, only beginning with his position in the company that would break her golden rule. First and foremost was the most obvious. She had no idea who he was, and too many questions remained regarding what she knew about him. For her sake, she needed to cling to her morals and principles, even if it cost her an extremely restless night.

Automated, her thoughts turning in rampant circles, Jenna moved through her morning routine, showering, blow drying her hair, and dressing in a casual ensemble of dress slacks, silk blouse, and jacket. Under the circumstances, no one should question her arrival at the hotel. The decision was made, confirmed, and apparently accepted by Darius Brock.

Halfway through her second cup of coffee, with the Sunday paper scattered over the table, she found the article highlighting the tragedy at the Chateau Suites. The paper announced simply—Lawrence Fradden, 52, had been found dead in a room within the Chateau Suites Hotel. The cause of death remained unknown, but the circumstances remained suspicious. Local police and the Federal Bureau of Investigation were conducting a joint investigation. Unconfirmed, the reporter had merely alluded to the possibility of homicide, but the nature of the article provided confirmation in itself.

Evan Trevane's talent in action, Jenna surmised. The article contained a hint of New York connections to explain the FBI's interest in Mr. Fradden's demise. How much was true, Jenna couldn't decide. The fact remained; the murder had occurred inside the hotel. Undoubtedly, with Trevane's full consent and guidance, Mason had offered a brief statement, assuring the public that the incident was well in hand and the Chateau was cooperating fully with the investigation.

"The Chateau Suites," Mason assured the reporter and public, "will continue to conduct its business and offer the exemplary service for which it's reputed without either inconvenience or danger to its customers. Unfortunate, though it is," Mason added, "I don't believe this incident will affect business at the Chateau Suites. . ."

A line of bunk, Jenna knew, or possibly not. For the pure bizarre thrill, people would call and make reservations to satisfy some penchant for danger. She wouldn't be surprised to learn that room 610 was already booked solid for the next six months. Inevitably, a dozen crackpots would rent the room to conduct a seance and communicate with the dead man. People were sick. Their inclination for the macabre was at a record high, or so it seemed. She supposed if she scored history books, she would find plenty of other eras where an attraction to the unknown had become tantamount. The Salem Witch Trials . . . the Crusades . . . heck, the Crucifixion of Christ. All could be attributed to a thirst for blood or fear of unexplained phenomena. Doubtful the present was any different, just more blasted informed, thanks to the media—and more mobile, thanks to whoever the hell had invented the steam engine. If the Crusades transpired in this era, they certainly wouldn't have taken centuries to begin and end. More like twenty-four hours before the nukes started sailing and half the population evaporated in an eye-blink.

Shaking her head, disgusted to have fallen so readily into the bleak, doomsday mood, especially on a blasted Sunday morning this close to Christmas, Jenna folded the paper and pushed from her chair. If she did nothing else to aid this investigation, she could at least score through the names on the combined lists and try to find another blasted suspect for the FBI to investigate. Darius Brock might be the most arrogant, confounding man she'd ever met—might even suffer a few dark blemishes in his past—but she couldn't think of him as a blasted killer.

Gathering her purse and coat, she passed through the apartment, shutting off lights in her wake. With the drapes closed, the apartment lingered in a half-light, a dusk light that reminded her of her unwanted spectators. Considering her night visitor, a smile slid into her lips. The man certainly had a few tricks. Either that, or he had little regard for the Federal Agents who might have hammered at her door. Probably the latter, she considered as she rode the elevator to the first floor. And it was no surprise he hadn't stayed long or spent the night. All too readily, she recalled his mention of her reputation.

From her kitchen window, she'd seen the bright promise of morning, and before reaching the first glass doors, she fumbled in her purse and donned her sunglasses to cut the glare. At a hundred bucks a pop, the filtered lenses sufficiently muted the sunspots on frosted windshield and chrome. Her car wasn't as heavily frosted as most others in the row. Parked at the end of the building, beneath one of the mulberry trees, her Lincoln rested under a soft white sheen . . . with a mound of snow splattered over the driver's side window, apparently compliments of the mulberry branches overhead.

Apparently, she'd need another chat with the super about this designated slot. Bad enough she was forever cleaning bird droppings and had nearly needed a new paint job after the berries assaulted her blasted car last fall—to remove mounds of blasted snow with the chill factor below freezing was the final straw.

Unlocking the car, she slid behind the wheel and ignited the engine before pulling her gloves from her purse and finding the snow scraper behind the bucket seat. At least in Chicago, she'd parked indoors. Here, she either needed to find another apartment or buy a blasted house with a garage . . . or simply return to the Windy City and be done with this mess.

She was still mulling over that thought when her attention and scraper snagged on a folded paper tucked under her windshield wiper blade. Terrific! Either a message from the local Christian Society who stood on street corners waving bibles and trotted through parking lots dispensing fliers, another political campaign brochure, or another Grand Opening announcement. Not bothering to look, she cleaned the windshield, turned the rubber scraper, and dispatched the last dusting of snow. The sun had already touched the back window; the ice slid away in thick mats. Slipping into the driver's seat, already chilled, Jenna tugged off her gloves and turned on the heat despite the unmoved thermostat gauge.

Debating between awaiting the heat or burdening the engine, she barely decided to pull out when her attention landed and locked on the wet folded paper. Bled through, the faint image of the crown logo of the Chateau appeared on the white exterior. Curious, she lifted it off the console and peeled it open. Instantly, a chill skittered down her spine.

Bold black ink, the lines sliced like daggers, the note read simply, "Enjoy your freedom, Bitch. Your time's coming."

For a half second longer, Jenna gripped with the cold chill. Swiftly, smoothly, her apprehension transformed into anger. Lisa Blythe. That sneaky little tramp had written this note, apparently attempting to disguise her scrawl. The handwriting was unmistakable. Even under normal circumstances, Blythe slashed her words in dagger-like strokes, stabbing the end lines like exclamation points.

If this little bitch thought for one blasted moment that she could scare Jenna Windrow with this shitty stunt, that young lady had another thought coming!

Hot enough to raise the engine temperature, Jenna folded the note and tucked it in her purse. Shoving the shifter into reverse, she twisted in the seat and backed smoothly from the space. Apparently, this situation would need to be addressed. And for the next mile, Jenna contemplated ripping the neon blond hair from the scalp, strand by strand. By the time she pulled through the gates of the Chateau, she'd satisfied her need for blood and turned her thoughts toward a more practical solution. Miss Blythe was in for an extremely rude awakening, and silently, Jenna justified her decision, vowing to give herself this Christmas present . . . and it just might be a merry Christmas after all.

In the true spirit of the season, Jenna smiled as she pulled into her designated spot toward the side of the administration wing. As much as Jenna tried to restrain the hot German temper that her mother had gifted to her, there were times when her father's English diplomacy couldn't hold a blasted candle to the heat. This was one of those times. This spiteful little tramp had just tread upon Jenna's last nerve. She would slam dunk this bitch with holiday cheer and just for the fun of it, hold her head under hot water for a little while.

Jenna maintained her internal amusement only until she passed through the front doors. The doorman's grim expression offered a quick reminder of the situation, compounded by the glance at the dark-suited gentlemen loitering within the area of the continental breakfast bar. The morning shift had already changed. The young, smiling hostess at the bar, chitchatted avidly with the paying guests who were taking advantage of toasters and coffee dispensers. From the main dining room, a din of voices echoed with the waitstaff in full swing, tending to the guests who preferred omelets and Belgian waffles over pastries.

Jenna barely started toward the registration desk when she spotted Wharton stepping from a door past the desk, one of the rooms explicitly designed for conferences, lectures, and business meetings. If she remembered correctly, the room was booked for the rest of the week. Today was not the exception. A woman's auxiliary had scheduled this evening for a small holiday party to be catered by the dining room. Jenna hoped Wharton hadn't made himself too comfortable in that room. He would need to clear out by four to allow the auxiliary's decorating committee to arrange and dress the tables to their own tastes. Without missing a step, sensing by his attention he wanted to speak to her, she veered and started toward him.

"Miss, could I have a word with you?"

"I'd imagine you'll have more than one," she said with an edge before noting a genuine weariness in the man's eyes, in his expression. He was not the same righteous zealot who'd visited her apartment with every intention of either blackmailing or intimidating her into public service. She read the change in his manner even before stepping into the room where he and four other gentlemen had sequestered two tables for their personal use. At least three telephones, two computers, and several display boards detracted from the general decor of long, shiny tables and padded, collapsible chairs. To an empty table, visibly distanced from the others, Wharton gestured and seemed to remember her need for coffee, offering to have one brought.

"I'll get one soon, Agent Wharton," she said bluntly and slid off her coat, lying it on the table and meeting his gaze directly. "I don't believe this will take long." About two seconds to tell him 'no deal.'

"Please, let's sit down. I just want to ask you a few questions."

"I'm comfortable on my feet," she said simply. "What would you like to ask?"

He appeared uncomfortable and far more reserved than the evening past. "Are you aware of the fact that Mr. Brock's returned?"

"Should I be?" she asked, wondering if Darius had postponed his return. Nothing of her thoughts appeared in her gaze.

Wharton hesitated, then nodded, his gaze intent. "I think you should. He came to see you last evening, is that right?"

"You tell me," she said bluntly, refusing to budge and only annoyed with the thought of surveillance on her apartment.

"We're not on opposing sides, Miss Windrow," he said with a weary note, his expression more human and resigned. "The truth is, he suggested I speak with you, and to satisfy my own curiosity, I am."

"Then you've spoken with him?"

"I've been chatting with him most of the night," Wharton admitted. "And before you get the wrong idea, he's not in danger of either arrest or prosecution. In fact, we've removed him from the suspect list. Did he stop by for a chat last night?"

This fellow had changed his tone too drastically in less than twelve hours. Either he'd discovered something of significance or he was employing a new tactic. "If he's told you, then you apparently already know."

"Would you tell me what you discussed?" he asked.

"I'd imagine if we chatted, the content would be our business, Agent Wharton," she said in a chilly tone, her gaze direct and firm. "My decision hasn't changed overnight, regardless of how your position . . . or uh, tactics, have. Now, if there's nothing else, I do need a cup of coffee. If you need anything else, you'll find me in my office."

Wharton considered asking something more, then shook his head and gestured toward the door. As she gathered her coat, he commented, "You'll find him in the manager's office."

The curiosity of that comment lingered as she strode from the room. Had something, as it appeared, happened during the night? Something to demand Mason's presence in his office at this hour on a Sunday morning?

Regardless, she had no intention of barging in on either of them just to say hello. From her office, she could ring Mason's desk.

By face and first name, Jenna knew most of the staff, and she offered the appropriate greetings while passing through the registration office, grateful for the early departures that held the clerk's attention and spared her from any idle conversation. Returning to her office was rather like returning to the scene of a crime. The foldaway bed stood, collapsed against the interior wall, a testament to how many times she'd attempted to use it and failed. Her desk remained in order, apparently dusted by the maintenance crew.

Settling behind the desk, Jenna rested, scanning the small compact space and considering Lisa's hostility. In retrospect, Jenna understood Blythe's anger, although neither of the other two part-time assistants had shared Lisa's jealousy. Out of the three, Lisa had worked in the Chateau the longest—more than five years, according to the hotel records. She'd allegedly worked her way through a tech school, achieving a degree in business . . . rather like a secretary.

From an educational standpoint, Jenna knew her own personal qualifications had landed her the second in command post within the Chateau. Compounded by her experience, she'd gained the privilege of a private office through hard work and ambition, whereas Blythe had probably coerced her way through the ranks on smiles and after-hour perks. God knows her college transcripts were nothing to brag about, a detail Jenna had confirmed shortly after arriving at the Chateau. Knowing one's adversaries always proved beneficial in the past.

The buzz of the intercom interrupted, and somehow, she knew whose voice she would hear even before reaching and pressing the button, "Yes?"

"Are you determined to shred my ego at every turn., Jenna?"

"Not that I'm aware of," she answered smoothly and donned a slight smile.

"I happen to know you've been in the building more than ten minutes, dear. As much as it grieves me to admit, I thought you'd at least attempt to locate me. Do you, though . . . ? No. Pass me by without so much as a jolly good day. If it's not too much trouble, do you think you might venture toward Mason's office sometime soon?"

"Would a . . . five minutes be too long?"

"Blast, woman! You'd keep me waiting that long?"

"I'd like to uh…" Mason could be in the office. "Take care of those things we discussed last evening."

"Ah, I see then. I should be relieved you have a bloody good excuse, and I'll admit, I thought I better catch you beforehand. Do postpone your affairs and come immediately, will you? I have a pot of coffee on hand and an extra cup on standby if you need it."

"I'll be right over," she decided, disengaging the intercom while sliding from her chair. She probably should have spoken with him before coming to her office. The investigation had apparently taken a turn, and he'd likely collected the appropriate lists. At the closed door, she knocked and heard the called, muffled greeting. Slightly surprised, she entered, glancing between Darius, who rose from Mason's chair, and Evan Trevane likewise lifting from a chair alongside the desk. Both appeared slightly amused, although, with Darius's dark eyes, the mischief held far more power. To crush his ego, she would need something akin to a twenty-pound sledgehammer. He motioned to the empty chair to his right, offering, "So good of you to join us, Luv."

"Sounded distinctly like an order," she commented and moved to the chair, smiling at Evan, who appeared only more amused.

"G'morning, Jen," he said lightly and reached for the thermal pot on the edge of the desk. "Coffee, I trust?"

She nodded, aware of Darius studying her with one of his more pensive expressions. Doubtful he'd slept, but he appeared no different now than two nights ago. If not for the clear, dark shine in his eyes, she might believe he lived on amphetamines.

"Do you ever sleep?" she asked while slipping into the chair, barely breezing a glance at the clutter on the desk.

"Enough to get by," he answered offhandedly and settled into Mason's chair, still studying her. "Agent Wharton spoke to you?"

"For a moment," she said and her gaze distracted to accept the coffee cup Evan handed to her. Her attention returned to Darius as he leaned back in the chair, reaching, lifting a thin smoldering cigar from an ashtray. "He mentioned you'd spoken for quite a while."

"We reached an understanding," he said smoothly. "Did you get my note?"

She smiled slightly, "Yes."

His gaze softened momentarily, a more natural smile slipping into the corner of his mustache. "I do apologize, Luv. As much as it pained me, I needed to return here and put things in order."

Fanning her gaze over the clutter, she recognized the computer printouts of registration, noting quite a few yellow highlights. "You've been busy."

Indifference slid across his eyes as he glanced over the spread of pages. "Not that we're making much headway," he said offhandedly and again, met her gaze. "I'm rather hoping you'll lend a hand for a little while."

"Of course," she said and included Evan in a glance. The man wore one of his more bemused smiles, a faint echo of amusement within his pale blue eyes. Like Darius, he wore a cotton shirt, no tie, and rested, leaning back in the wingback leather chair. A suit jacket rested over the back of another chair against the outside wall. With the blinds drawn over the windows at this back and the desk lamp shedding a glow to shadow his features, he appeared as handsome as Darius and slightly more haggard as if still trying to shake the morning haze. "I'd imagine he woke you at the crack of dawn."

"Don't believe his comment, dear," Evan said with a flashing smile. "The man never sleeps, and he's relentless."

Darius cleared his throat politely, drawing Jenna's amused gaze. "I do sleep, I'll have you know," he said soberly. "As a matter of fact, I'm already rather looking forward to several uninterrupted hours, and the sooner we get busy, the sooner I might manage that. Do hate to be rude," he tossed toward Evan. "But there are rather pressing matters at hand."

Evan sobered immediately; his attention turned toward business as swiftly as Darius. "I'm not sure how much more help I can offer. Honestly, Darius. We've covered just about everyone on the roster, including the guests," he said. "If I knew exactly what you're looking for, I could have someone—"

"If I knew exactly what the bloody hell I was looking for, lad, chances are I wouldn't require your help to find it."

The low voice and temper in the dark eyes drew and held Jenna momentarily.

Across the desk, Evan held a spark of started anger, then recoiled under the dark gaze, wisely. His attention shifted to Jenna and returned to Darius with slightly more reluctance. "I just thought if we enlisted someone from personnel, it might help."

Darius let it drop, turning his focus on Jenna. "What did you intend to accomplish by perusing the guestlists and such, Jenna?"

"Honestly, I'm not entirely sure," she answered lightly. "It seems to me, that whoever did this has to be on one of those lists. I'm assuming the police already questioned our doorman, security guards, and desk clerks. If some stranger had walked in and back out, one of our staff would have noticed. I thought we might check any outside registrations near or after Mr. Fradden's arrival. With the snow and airport cancellations, it was hectic, but if we cross-reference any names from our list with the airport, we might narrow the list considerably. As far as the guestlist . . . I don't believe we had many guests from New York."

Whether he was impressed or merely thoughtful, he nodded and leaned, shuffling papers and finding what he apparently sought. Leaning back, he collected a yellow pen and looked at her. "A lot of that's already been done," he admitted. "I know you haven't held your position long, but with your people skills, I'd imagine you know most of the employees. This may be a long shot, but I'd like to ask you about them. Mainly, those who were working Friday evening and night." Barely pausing, he looked at Evan and continued, "If I think of anything else, I'll ring your room. Thank you for your help."

With a conflict of visible relief and subtle discomfort, Evan slid off his chair, lifted his jacket, and flashed Jenna a half-smile and reassuring nod with his parting amenity.

Jenna had seen Darius dance, had seen him play, had listened to him give a speech and work a crowd. She'd seen him at rest and tense, but none were as impressive as seeing and watching him at work. In a quiet rhythm, he began with the first questions, referring and reverting to the personnel files, which he'd apparently pulled from a file cabinet and arranged on the corner of the desk. From questions about work habits to general skills, he asked more in-depth questions concerning personal habits, attitudes, and efficiency. The man missed nothing. He asked about Tom Eigler, the night-shift guard. About Earl Benning. About Rene, Mark, and others who manned the desk. He covered the maids on duty and the maintenance crews' habits. Did those lads come into the lobby to get warm? Did they stop for coffee in the security booth or at vending machines in the delivery areas? How many people held keys to the maintenance rooms or linen closets? He asked about Lisa Blythe, pulling her file to ask about her habit of showing up late and leaving early. In detail, he managed to coerce Jenna into a heated discourse, which started her fuming anew, twice over, because she'd meant to deal with Blythe on her own ground, in her own sweet time. The man was relentless when he wanted answers, seeming to possess some innate talent to swivel words and moods in mid-stream to leave little space for thought.

Two hours with him and Jenna felt as though she'd run a marathon while he sat back, ankle hooked over his knee, seeming as cool, calm, and collected as ever. As blasted handsome as ever as well which irritated her slightly more. He had a lot of danged nerve, sitting back, toking on his cigar, studying her with those dark, fathomless eyes.

"You ought to be passed out on your feet!" she snapped at him and gained slight satisfaction to note his eyes sparked surprise. He'd probably been sleeping!

A smile flickered on his lips. The first natural smile since she'd entered. "You're even more beautiful with a touch of fire in your eyes, Luv."

Two hours, she considered. That was the maximum time limit for standing—or sitting—in the same room with this gentleman without feeling as if her blood would boil over. If she had any sense, she'd pass around the corner of this desk and kiss those smirking lips until one of them incinerated. God knows he generated enough heat without moving to start her wishing for a glass of ice water. Whether she would douse him or herself, she couldn't decide.

"Do you have any plans for this evening?" he interrupted smoothly, his gaze intent.

She should have, but not one blasted thing came to mind. "No."

"I've been invited to a cousin's wedding," he said simply. "It's about a two-hour drive from here. Canton, Ohio, I believe. Would you join me?"

Two hours, maximum limit. "I uh. . ." Every practical thought warned her to decline. But the look in his eyes, the soft smile—

"I'll promise to be a perfect gentleman. Won't guarantee we'll get home early. In fact, you might want to bring an overnight bag, but I'll see that you have your own room."

"I have to work in the morning," she said lamely.

His smile quivered slightly with honest amusement. "I have an in with your boss, dear. I don't think that will be a problem. And if you'd rather not spend the night, we'll simply return late this evening. Say you'll come?"

"What uh . . . what time would you want to leave?"

"I'll pick you up at five."

Just like that, the decision was made. "All right."

"I probably should mention, we'll have chaperones," he said as if the thought amused him.

The FBI, she realized in a lame moment and thought again of Wharton, the surveillance, and the change in dispositions. "What's really going on here, Darius? Are they still trying to blame you for this?"

"Not likely."

17

Temptation could create its own wicked twist of misery. From the moment Darius stood outside her door appraising the long, sleek length of Jenna Windrow, he'd dropped into an inferno of living hell. Dressed in a shimmery black cloth, she'd donned that tiny smile and offered some quiet words to cool the heat leaping into his eyes. Not that it worked. On dual planes, he answered her, his attention fanning over her with the appreciation and awe one awards any masterpiece.

Tuxedo-cut, the dress enhanced every distinctive curve while concealing the same, offering just enough evidence of the body within to send a healthy man's imagination flying. Add the long chiffon sleeves turning her slender arms to shadows, the satin cuffs and collar to dip into a modest V where a small diamond pendant glittered to draw his eye, and the flames threatened to engulf him. The hem, he took time to notice as she reached for her coat, dropped to a conservative length that might have offered salvation if not for a careful slit rising to mid-thigh and adding a promise of long silky legs. With her hair piled and pinned in another elegant Victorian style, a glimpse of small diamonds in her earlobes, and a touch of cosmetics enhancing her vivid blue eyes and soft smile, the woman could have stepped off the cover of Cosmopolitan or Vogue. She was stunning, and he was in hell, his every sense quickened to breathe in the delicate female essence that was all Jenna Windrow.

Maintaining his poise, steeling his resolve, and almost grateful for his foresight, he'd escorted her to the limousine waiting at the curb. With two Federal Agents sitting rigidly across from them in the comfortably wide compartment, even idle chat was stifled considerably. Still, if he'd been forced to ride alone with her for two hours, Darius wouldn't have fared well. Still, he gazed at her too often, catching his thoughts spiraling in weird and wondrous directions that would never bear fruit.

In pure, unrequited bliss, he smiled at one observation or another, enjoying the spark of mischief in her deep blue eyes and the quiver of her lips. Not even their stoic companions were immune to that smile. More than once, Darius glimpsed them stifling smiles and glances. She was a temptress or an enchantress, and the Baron's observations fleeted in Darius's mind, effectively intruding to break her spell.

Hell. It was hell. Exactly as Darius knew it would be, exactly as the Baron had intended when ordering this circumstance. Look, admire, enjoy the play of soft interior light in her dark blue eyes and curved lips . . . he could almost feel the tension ebbing from his coiled limbs as he floated on the lyric of her soft, flowing voice.

Comfortably, naturally, without a conscious desire to seduce him, she'd repositioned on the leather seat alongside him, sitting sideways to face him and striking a pose that threatened every restraint in his libidinous system. Knees crossed, legs tucked as if riding sidesaddle on a trusty steed in true Victorian style, she rested close enough to whisper a brush of cloth at his pant leg, and her body heat registered despite all odds.

Not in eight years, not once, had Darius found himself more attracted, more physically aroused, more enthralled by a woman—and it occurred to him on that long and painful ride that she was oblivious of her innate wiles. Her smiles were honest, her laughter and lighthearted voice as natural as breathing, her physical attributes synonymous with her internal attraction. She wasn't a woman practicing her wiles. Not a woman attempting to worm her way into the boss's bed for personal gain. On a plateau that other women only dreamed of reaching, Jenna had found confidence in herself, a strength to rely on her intelligence and common sense. Undoubtedly, aware of her beauty, she suffered no need or desire to flaunt it or enhance it to lure a man.

In a paradox, Darius volleyed between heaven and hell, physically aware of her in every instant, enjoying the conversations that found safe territory in general politics, world affairs, and the weather. Speaking of the holidays lifted a higher shine in her lovely eyes, enhanced tenfold when she mentioned her family and the traditions abounding. Mother, father, sisters, grandparents, aunts, and uncles . . . the holidays at the Windrow house were never dull.

If not before those moments, Darius was lost in the moment, a casualty to her charms as she related some anecdote or another of her grandparent Windrows. English. 'Very proper and refined, I'll have you know,' she spoke loftily, mocking him and her grandparents. Losing rein, she laughed easily, waking him to her teasing. She had been mocking him—his reserve and accent, his dry wit and arrogance. But no dark sarcasm colored her words. She'd merely taken that tact to distract him from his internal thoughts as if she knew how badly he wanted to taste her lips.

Whether he'd sworn off such an action to spare himself torment or shame and possible penance, Darius never knew. Not in eight years had he kissed a woman as a beautiful woman should be kissed. He'd come close. Once or twice, if only to maintain the pretense of his reputation . . . but not once had he kissed a woman on the lips, held her in his arms, offered anything of the intimacy he'd once known and enjoyed.

His thoughts shaded, his gaze listed, he watched the darkness pass outside the glass, remembering . . . his vow. An oath and covenant which had damned him forever more. Had he fully realized the cost eight years earlier, he wondered what choice he might have made . . . and realized the futility. No choice. Nothing he could have done would have improved or changed the course of his life. The decision had been made for him. Oh, the Baron had been clever enough, allowing each of them to believe they possessed a choice . . . until the very end. Hours . . . for hours, they'd endured the taunting and chiding, the badgering. Like every other man in that room, Darius had rejected the reality, the horror. He'd believed he would survive if he held his council. The wretched game would surely end. A new day would shed clear light. The dawn would come, and he would return to his natural life—with his son in one piece. Like his son who'd already become a bloody sacrifice on a black altar, he'd been chosen and drawn into that wretched chamber, his life snatched, and fate sealed the instant he'd received that damned envelope and invitation.

Whether the words had been spoken the next day or days later, Darius couldn't remember, but the Baron's deep voice slid through his mind, low and silky, musing.

"Think about it, lad . . . remember who walked second into my chamber . . ."

Second . . . Darius remembered. Surrounded by strangers, each as curious and some even more tense than himself, he'd stood in that shadowy receiving room. Each of them held a copy of the scroll handed to them by a gaunt manservant as they'd entered the forbidding front doors of the Castle von Hendricks.

Second. He'd stood alongside the stranger from New York, a cousin he'd never met before entering that chamber. Like himself, the man had declined the offer for wine, his dark critical eyes panning the room and faces, judging the integrity of the conclave with alarm as high as Darius's own. Even now, Darius remembered that stranger's strength, the confidence of his pose, the intelligence behind his eyes. No fear. Where others had already begun to buckle to a weird fear and chided the scroll in hushed voices, Kevin Brock had stood his ground, silent and pensive, only more deeply curious as he'd plied George Halbrook with questions concerning his personal invitation—an urgent invitation of a legal nature. An estate settlement, Darius had learned later. Each invitation contained different criteria, each conveying urgency but drawing on a personal attribute to ensure each man would arrive. Twelve men. All bearing the surname. Brock.

A half step behind Att. Kevin Brock from New York, Darius had stridden through the second set of doors held aside by the same gaunt butler who'd escorted each of them through the dismal hall into the receiving room. Second, Darius had scanned the wide oval chambers. Floor-to-ceiling mahogany shelves carried books in ancient binders emitting a musty scent of aging paper. Perfectly round, an Asian rug, at first and second glance, resembled a serving plate with an intricate gold scroll at the edges and spread strategically in front of an immense mahogany desk wrapped in ancient intricate etchings.

Before that moment, Darius had never seen or met Amadeus von Hendricks. Via newsprint and library, he'd learned of the von Hendricks' vast financial holdings before leaving his flat in England and boarding the first ferry. Alarm bells had niggled at his neck as he'd stepped onto that rug, but he'd remained determined to demand his son's safe return—his son who'd been taken from his home. Stolen, in Darius's mind, although Sherri had packed a bag and delivered him into the hands of his grandfather . . . a grandfather who'd never existed in Darius's mind.

To either side of that desk, like bookends, two silver-haired elders had rested in velvet upholstered, wing-back chairs. Only later, Darius learned that one was a Baroness, Baroness Rebecca von Hendricks. The other, Baron Thaddeus von Hendricks, had stood as the acting patriarch of the empire. Behind the desk, the clean-cut image of an extremely powerful, young businessman had rested in casual repose, kicked back, simply watching them enter with an arrogant smirk curving his black, neatly cropped mustache.

Such was the beginning of the end in Darius's mind.

Second to enter, second to speak, both occurrences barely a half second behind Kevin whose lawyer instincts had clicked into high gear. Neither had consciously chosen their places in that conclave. They'd acted only by natural instinct and character to lead the collection—a pen of sheep, nothing more or any less—to the man who'd demanded their audience and brought some of them from halfway around the world.

If not by one means, then by another, the Baron would have brought them into that room. For Darius, the invitation had bordered blackmail, in line with his cynical nature and hot temper. No choice. If he ever wanted to see his son again as the letter had indicated, he needed to accept the invitation and follow the provided travel arrangements. Ferry and train fare . . . along with a legitimate recently issued passport with his picture and statistics in proper order. He should have known, should have suspected . . . nothing would have changed.

He hadn't traded his immortal soul, hadn't received even the luxury to barter with that intimate of all earthly possessions. Even that privilege had been lost to him, the decision snatched from his hands long before his birth. Not until he'd stood in that room, stunned and as horrified as all others, watching the second transformation . . . Not until he'd seen the first four Brocks step forward, deciding they were neither convinced of the Baron's words nor willing to participate in the loosely defined rituals . . .

Driven by either fear or righteous indignation, the four had raised their hands when the Baron had broached the question . . . *Who among you will refuse to participate?*

One, a mere boy, no more than fifteen, Samuel . . . the child had hailed from a village less than fifty miles from the castle proper. A child. Terrified and intimidated, and still high on whatever he'd ingested to bolster his courage and add a thrill to the train ride . . . Samuel Brock. A boy who'd been bullied and shamed into admitting he'd engaged a good Catholic girl in the backseat of her father's car—four times in the past year. No innocent. The boy had confessed to a conflicting value system, wanting to 'do it' more often, thinking about it often, becoming angry when the young woman limited their encounters to accommodate her needs rather than his . . .

Even now, Darius lamented over those moments as the boy had confided his hostility and agitation. Like Kevin, who'd just survived his own inquisition and personal torture, Darius had barely started to rise to the boy's defense before the Baron had moved to the next Brock and worked his wiles.

When the moment had come, minutes—or hours later—Samuel had stepped forward, just wanting to go home, to return to his parent's house and make believe everything he'd endured was a hallucination.

Four of them, Darius remembered, his mind fully entrenched in the past. Samuel, a mere boy with a scruff of long blond hair and an earring in his left ear; Earl, a cynic who believed the whole affair was no more than a glorified hoax designed to spice up the wealthy man's life; Ralph, a man who stammered his indifference to the affair, claiming he would 'just rather not be a part of it. . .'; Allen, a newly ordained Christian preacher who offered to pray for the Baron and wanted no part of ancient curses or covenants, no part of whatever evil import had brought them together.

Oh, and the Baron had thought that last amusing. 'Will you, now, lad?' he had asked with a feigned desperate note, and like a bloody zealot, Allen had risen to the challenge enthusiastically. 'Will you get down on your knees and pray for me here, now?'

Allen had knelt of his free will, and the Baron had turned his attention to Ralph, asking him to join his brother in prayer. Both men had lowered to their knees. Earl wanted no part of it; he'd considered even that request a hoax and stood his ground. But as Allen bent his head to the task, Earl and Samuel dropped, their knees buckled by an unknown source. Like a bomb detonating, those knees striking the carpet echoed within the room, ricocheting off the books and shelves, bouncing off the thick tapestry curtains to drape in elegant patterns over the narrow windows. And in a stopped wicked moment, Darius had suffered the vibration of the bomb through the soles of his shoes. The earth had shaken, a prelude of the moments to come and the unearthly power to spiral from that chamber.

Outside, night had fallen, but even in daylight, when Darius had first arrived, the castle proper had appeared bleak and dark, a twilight place of tall ancient trees and blackened stone. Stained by weather and blood, he later decided. And the blood had flowed then. With a mere word, a piercing glance, the Baron had enlisted the help of four others who'd pledged their participation in the ritual. They'd all been judged. By no mistake, no accident, the Baron hadn't enlisted either Darius or Kevin to ravage their kneeling, silent, and frozen cousins. Worried, and anxious, the four chosen men, perhaps believing they could gain their freedom by compliance, had loosened their cousins' shirts and sweaters, the blazer and jacket, baring four right shoulders as the Baron ordered. Not a muscle could those kneeling men move. Their backs rigid, their heads bent, they trembled by the sheer force of their ragged breaths—

"Darius?"

Jolted, Darius pivoted his gaze to find the deep blue eyes searching him worriedly, waking him fully to how deeply into reflection he'd fallen. Not in years had he allowed himself to remember those moments or relive that horror. After all else he'd seen, all else he'd endured at this damned lord's hands, he'd never needed to dredge those memories from the black depths. Why now, in the company of this stunning woman, he had only slight sense to realize. That night . . . that was the last night of his humanity. The last time he'd known honest compassion, if only through his ignorance. Without ever touching him, tainting him, the Baron had shredded his humanity and forced him into a shadow world where morals and integrity bedamned.

This woman, with her warm worried eyes and soft smiles, her innocent laughs and mischief, had reminded him of what he'd lost, how he'd lived before that damned night of nights. Looking into her blue eyes, he remembered how he'd once reveled in the company of a woman, how he'd enjoyed sitting across a candle-lit table or sharing a cocktail and idle chatter . . . the foreplay. He'd loved the company of beautiful women, loved the sound of laughter or sensuous voices. He remembered those later moments too, when he'd slid his hands through sheer cloth and nipped at necks, his passion heating swiftly as he rose the fires in his partners. Women had been his weakness and his strength.

'I would have preferred innocence,' the Baron had told him that day so long ago as a wry smile slivered through the bearded lips. Standing so much taller with his appearance changed, he'd poised, transformed into an otherworldly dominion. 'But perhaps there's something to be said for experience . . .'

"Did I say something to bother you, Darius?" the soft gentle voice intruded yet again.

Donning a slight smile, Darius shook his head, clasping her fingers that had touched upon his hand to draw him back. "No, Luv," he admitted quietly. "Perhaps you just reminded me of another time. A simpler time."

A different life where he might have taken her in his arms and kissed her with all the passion that had once existed inside of him. Instead, he leaned and brushed a chaste kiss on her soft cheek, drawing away far more slowly, more painfully than he would have deemed possible. "Reflection is not always good for the soul," he said quietly.

"You were married," she said then appeared to regret her statement. Collecting her thoughts and confidence, she held her faintly troubled smile despite his cloaked gaze. "I know it's not my business, I just wondered if that's what you were thinking about just now. If it's . . . the reason for your sadness."

How much more did she know about him, he wondered absently as the soft note of her observation touched him. Was it so easy for her to look into him, through him, to read the heaviness inside him and bring it to light? Sadness. Perhaps it was sadness. But not over a marriage gone awry. His marriage had gone bad even before the Baron had intruded. Losses. So many losses, not the least of which was his humanity. That he could even do what was required of him, that he could carry out this damned mission, was a testament to how much he'd lost.

With the dual agents, bodyguards engaged at Wharton's suggestion, hinged for a response, Darius forced a soft smile, "I'll admit, that's one of those memories I'd rather not dwell upon. And if it should cross your mind that I've fallen toward that end again, you have my full permission to land a telling blow with that lovely pointed shoe."

She smiled, not entirely relieved or convinced but apparently willing to drop the subject, probably with their audience in mind. "So, tell me about these cousins I'm to meet," she said with a change in tempo, a lightness of heart, and a spark of mischief in her eyes. "How are you actually related? And how close are you to the family?"

"Have you ever heard of the Scottish clans? Know anything about them?"

"You mean like Highlanders?"

"Aye, lass," he said with a mocked twist on his accent, a musing shine in his eyes. "You might compare my clan to one of those. I do, in fact, have several cousins who are rather entrenched in the Scottish heritage. I haven't a clue how they all connect, but as you may know, even the American Scotts remain actively involved and recognize their roots. My own are of similar design.

"Frankly, I've never met Adam Brock, or his parents, or however many others we'll meet. I've uhm . . . how to say this without sounding self-possessed?" he asked as if he needed to reflect, shrugging mentally, donning a slightly tainted smile. "Word traveled several years ago that I do a great deal of traveling. With all this trend toward genealogy and the like, the elders of my clan began contacting relatives far and wide. Somehow or another, I've rather inherited the post of family liaison or uhm . . . representative. Whenever it doesn't conflict with my other responsibilities, I make it a point to meet my extended relatives."

"I uh . . . I don't think I'm following this," she said lightly, a touch of amusement in her knitted brow. "You've never met these people, but you received an invitation to their wedding and decided to accept?"

"Had my schedule not changed, I might have settled for sending a card," he mused and shrugged. "Or I might have caught a commercial flight from Chicago to Cleveland and attended. You've no concept of the pressure some of my older relatives can apply. They've perfected the old-school belief that guilt is its own best weapon. It's rather a paradox for me," he admitted with a slight smile. "On the one side, I don't mind meeting these extended members. I never had a brother or sister. Never experienced that closeness you seem to enjoy and take for granted. To be in a position to meet these relatives offers me a sense of belonging, I suppose. On the other side, however, I think I've become something akin to the Scottish patriarchs who, I'll mention, are treated and revered with as much respect today as hundreds of years ago. Bluntly, Luv, don't be tremendously surprised if we receive the royal treatment. For some bloody reason that I can't begin to fathom, my relatives think of me as a blessing at these affairs."

Which was only too blasted true and far more obvious in recent years . . . though Darius had no trouble fathoming the cause. The Baron had plotted this course, had laid the foundations for these affairs years ago, and it amused that grandmaster of the game to see his humble servant revered as a damned prince. If the FBI hadn't figured this detail out long before now, the lads wouldn't likely catch on anytime soon.

Darius Brock never missed a wedding, rarely missed a birth, and more often than not, attended a Brock funeral on every visit to the States.

He was, or had become, the equivalent of a prince, a direct descendant of the lords who'd held title to lands decreed by a king—King Amadeus von Hendricks. The same bloody king, who'd dwelt in the castle and held title to a vast tract of land through the Romanian countryside four hundred years ago. The same king who held dominion and maintained a silent voice behind whatever governing body remained in attendance to this day. The Brocks boasted an extremely long history and a far darker connection to the von Hendricks than modern history would divine.

Not for a minute could Jenna doubt the words Darius had spoken in the car. From the moment they entered the banquet hall within the ultra-modern hotel, they were revered as royalty. Names and faces came at her too fast to grasp. Handshakes and pecks on the cheek were as avid as warm embraces that extended to Jenna with only slightly less enthusiasm. Within moments, they were escorted and ensconced at a head table generally reserved for parents and grandparents of the bride and groom. With a near duplicate performance of two days past, Darius fell into natural stride, smiling, chatting, drawing Jenna into conversations, turning grave when the subject warranted. Given a clear view of the bridal table, Jenna gathered their names—the bride and groom, Rita and Adam Brock, a couple not much younger than her.

Dressed in traditional white with a great deal of lace and a long streamlined bodice, the lovely young woman blushed prettily, her eyes bright and darting, her laugh echoing from the table as she spied the man of her apparent dreams. Adam Brock, oddly enough, resembled Darius a great deal. In his black tux, his dark hair swept into a tight wave, he wore the same dark eyes and firm jaw . . . And more than once, Jenna glimpsed the man studying his English cousin, who appeared oblivious, more intent on something one elder or another said to him.

In an odd moment, always a stickler for details, Jenna glimpsed Darius connecting with his cousin's gaze, and she recognized the slight glitch of curiosity in his eyes, the faint smile and acknowledging nod—almost as if Darius were a king offering his blessing and approval over a union.

Strange, very strange, but no stranger than Darius's reception at the Chateau. The man possessed an uncanny ability to stand taller while mingling and drawing others to him with natural charisma. And like the crowd two days past, this ensemble had awaited his arrival nearly as much as they'd anticipated this celebration.

"We're just so glad he could make it," the groom's mother confided to Jenna as if the woman meant to explain and apologize in the same breath. "Believe it or not," she giggled nervously and darted a glance toward the head table. "We nearly postponed the wedding . . ."

Jenna wasn't sure she believed it—not until the groom's father personally asked Darius to offer a toast directly after the best man muddled through a heartfelt speech. Having seen that expression before, Jenna stifled a smile as Darius covered his immediate dread and suffered to agree. Cute. The man made his living with his gift of gab, and behind his smiles, he absolutely dreaded this request. Their eyes locked only once as he received a refill of wine from a waiter, a prelude to his rise, and in that instant, Jenna conveyed her knowledge and saw the suffering behind his bemused smirk. He truly dreaded these moments, but with an ease that betrayed nothing, he rose with his glass in hand, his attention directed exclusively to the bride and groom. As if on cue, the couple tipped their attention to await his blessing. Smooth and confident, he offered approval and congratulations and spread his words to include the vast collection of Brocks. The words had changed, but the message conveyed the same praise he'd bestowed on the von Hendricks corporate leaders two days ago.

'. . . Darius the Great . . .'

Throughout the discourse, both bride and groom remained intent on him, the latter studying his cousin, possibly reflecting on their physical likeness or merely curious. Jenna supposed she might feel the same if faced with a distant relative who could pass for her sister if not her twin.

Listlessly, she thought of her cousins in Europe, wondering about her paternal grandparents who'd moved to the United States shortly before WWI. Her father was born here, but his older brother and sister had been born in England under Churchill's reign. Jenna's maternal grandmother had migrated to America in the first decade of the century; her American-born grandfather had served in the First World War. Both were in their mid-eighties. If she traveled to Europe, would she meet a parade of long-lost cousins and form an instant rapport? Could she experience a connection to those strangers like these Brocks felt toward Darius despite the miles and years—the cultural differences—between them?

The toast ended, champagne sipped, Darius slipped into the seat next to her and leaned, whispering in her ear. "As my most honest critic, be gentle when you tell me I bungled that ordeal, will you?"

She stifled a laugh and caught his shaded eyes, wondering if he'd meant those words even more literally than they sounded. Doubtful, he needed reassurance, but she offered it freely. "Very nicely done. I wouldn't be surprised if they ask for an encore."

Flashing a quick mocked horror, he leaned again, his voice like warm syrup at her ear. "Do not even breathe those words too loud, Luv."

Before he slipped away, she touched his sleeve, taking advantage of the opportunity and nearly losing her thought with the scent of his cologne. "I'd be more than happy to mention how much you love the spotlight, honey. It's no problem, really," she said in a much softer voice than intended.

Far too clearly beneath the florescent lights, his mahogany waves reflected a brilliant shine, falling over his ear, brushing his black collar. And drawing Jenna's eye. In a flashing instant, she imagined running her fingers through those silky strands and whispering intimacies in his ear. At the subtle vibration under her fingertips, she sensed his similar thoughts and gained neither satisfaction nor relief as he withdrew.

His dark eyes lanced her, locked, and he was no longer thinking about his speech any more than she was. Deftly, he managed, "I wish you wouldn't. . ."

But was he referring to her threat of suggesting an encore . . . or responding to her internal kibitzing?

The meal, the music, and the voices that rang through the hall offered slight distractions, effectively breaking the tension coiled between them. But not nearly enough to counter her lingering thoughts until she grasped the strangeness. Like the crowd Friday night, there seemed an unnatural tension growing and underlying the banter and revelry. Out of sync, Jenna smiled pleasantly when others approached their table and engaged Darius in mundane conversations until the music stopped.

Startled by the sudden silence, she turned her attention to the small orchestra across the room and caught herself doubting the conductor announcing the traditional wedding festivities.

First and foremost, the spry tuxedoed elder announced the bridal dance, beginning traditionally with the bridal couple and the solo dance as the orchestra played a classic love song. The four couples of the wedding party were announced, then the parents, grandparents . . . And somehow, Jenna wasn't surprised when she and her escort were nearly dragged into the growing collection. With a faintly embarrassed glint in his eyes, he held her at a respectable distance and managed to whisper, "I did try to forewarn you, Luv. I hope you're not too uncomfortable."

How does one respond to such a statement when she happens to be thoroughly content within the arms of an extremely handsome, reluctant celebrity?

"Not in the least," Jenna managed with a reassuring smile while sensing his genuine discomfort. The confidence and arrogance remained the same, his smile and charisma right on the mark, but there was something distinctly different between how he handled Friday night and this more social engagement. Paradox, he'd said in the car, and she believed that too. As much as he appeared to enjoy these strangers flocking to him, tugging on him, and surrounding him, he was reluctant . . . almost as if he felt unworthy of their apparent acceptance that seemed to enhance when the moment came to switch partners.

With her fingers snagged in the groom's hand, Jenna gained a close-up view of the likeness between him and Darius. Adam Brock's eyes were lighter brown and brighter, his smile wryer, his facial structure softer at the edges. Adam was not as intense, and his voice, though deep, lacked the resonance and timbre of his older cousin.

"Have you known my cousin long?" he asked as they swayed and stepped.

"Not too long," she answered.

"He's an amazing guy from what I've heard," Adam said while flashing a wayward glance over Jenna's shoulder, apparently toward his cousin, then back. "I probably shouldn't say this, but I don't like to see anyone getting in over their head." He barely paused and continued. "I don't think you should pin any hopes on him. As I've heard, he's a real lady's man and uh . . . not the kind of guy to get tied down, if you know what I mean."

Not the kind to be faithful, Jenna understood and smiled as she considered Evan Trevane's similar warning. "Thank you for the warning," she said smoothly and managed to offer congratulations before switching partners. When others joined the wedding party on the dance floor and the bar officially opened, Jenna slipped from the crowd and returned to her chair. Darius remained caught in the flood. A few tables away, the FBI agents rested, drinking coffee, watching the crowd and Darius with equal attention—a grim reminder that the man of her dreams wasn't a mundane character who hailed from Canton, Ohio. Both agents, looking more like Mafia bodyguards than legitimate officials, only added to the substance of traveling in the company of a celebrity. By no surprise, women approached him rather than the other way around. Doubtfully, all were cousins or even distant relatives, and apparently, too polite to decline, he remained in the mix.

When another Brock male approached almost warily, Jenna accepted the invitation for a dance and joined the throng on the crowded dance floor.

By what method Darius returned to her arms, she had no means to judge, but the relief slid through her as his hand clasped her fingers firmly and his other touched her hip. "I do believe you owe me a dance, Luv. No interruptions this time," he said smoothly and drew her closer by the sheer force of his gaze. "I promise."

He barely finished the words when the muffled ring interrupted, the tone cutting through the orchestra merely by proximity. Backing off, he looked down between them, and his eyes flashed quick dread with a distinctly unhappy smirk. "Somehow, I knew I shouldn't have said that," he said, appearing more apologetic as the second ring intruded. Sighing, he slid his hand off her hip and into his jacket. "If you'll excuse me . . ."

Almost as amused as she was disappointed, Jenna nodded and followed him off the dance floor, veering toward her table as he strode toward the furthest reaches of the room, already lifting the phone to his ear. One of the agents, Matlin, followed, prepared to dog him through the doors, but when Darius halted in a section of empty tables, Matlin stopped and maintained distance.

Darius wasn't on the phone long, though Jenna couldn't be sure how long. Rather than watch him, she fell into comfortable conversation with one of the older women at the table, a grandmother on the groom's side.

"The Brocks are a strange group," the woman spoke grimly, employing the privilege of age to gossip freely. "Was a damn shame when Adam lost his dad, though. Mirna—she does all right. And she likes Carl well enough, but I don't think she's ever really gotten over Abe. That boy you're with—he looks a lot like Abe. Carries himself about the same too. . ." Silver-haired, her face as smooth as stretched cotton with only fine webbed lines, the elderly woman wore a sorrowful expression as she trailed her gaze toward the couples on the dance floor. "Yea, damn shame about Abe not being here to see his oldest getting married, starting a family of his own." The woman continued as if exercising her right to appear maudlin. Her eyes came to Jenna with quiet sorrow. "Sometimes bad things happen to good people," she said quietly.

This was not a conversation Jenna might have anticipated, not on such an auspicious occasion. But the woman's sadness compelled her to ask, "Was it very long ago?"

Reflecting, she looked toward the dance floor where her daughter danced in the arms of a stocky man with graying hair and considerable age lines. Belatedly, Jenna realized the man wasn't Adam's father. She'd missed the last name during the introductions.

"About ten years now . . . both of them," the elder said absently. "Abe and his brother Bill," she continued and caught Jenna's gaze again. "Just about tore them all apart. Mirna, the kids, Bill's wife, and the boys . . . they were all close. Used to come by our house. Spent half the summers all together over at Lake Gilford right up until the summer of the accident. Nobody ever figured out what happened. The police said the brakes went out on Bill's pickup, but it sure didn't make any sense. Billy took care of his vehicles. . ." She seemed to catch herself falling deeper and brought herself up physically, leaning and patting Jenna's arm, forcing a smile. "That's not a thing to be thinking about right now. This is a time for celebrating. You young folks, you hold the key to the future. And that boy you're with, him coming all the way from England—that's something to be thankful for."

Jenna refrained from mentioning that Darius wasn't exactly a boy and he hadn't flown directly from England to offer his blessings. Somehow, she knew both comments would be ignored, and it lent her pause to notice that the old woman's opinion wasn't the exception but rather, the unanimous opinion of this crowd.

Watching more closely, strangely tense for no good reason, she recognized the eyes fleeting in search of him, and read the relief when they found him still among them. As if he were some blasted talisman or living totem in their midst. And it occurred to her, as the moments compounded, the majority truly considered his presence a blessing . . . or imperative?

Growing more uncomfortable, Jenna continued to scan the crowd, and by the time Darius returned carrying a drink in either hand, she wasn't entirely sure what to make of him either. Something had changed. Something very dark had fallen over this celebration, over this outing, and the curtain over his dark eyes only enhanced her unease. If she wasn't two hours away, if this were the Chateau, she would be headed for her car rather than smiling and accepting the gin and tonic from a man she neither knew nor entirely trusted.

"I do apologize for the interruption, Jenna," he said smoothly. "Modern technology can be a curse. I hope you'll give me another chance later," he said with a wink and smile. "I'm determined to finish at least one dance with you, even if we have to give it a go in stages."

She liked him, might even be falling for him, and that niggling detail offered no relief as she bantered with him.

'In over her head,' she considered, realizing the genuine warning in the groom's words. She suddenly felt certain that she was already exactly that, way in over her head with a man she'd just met. Something far deeper, far more powerful touched her when she looked into his dark eyes. She'd never been superficial, had dated men with less striking features, and believed herself fully in love with a slightly overweight commodities broker in Chicago—until she realized his love of money was more intense than his love for her. This was different. It wasn't just the intensity or the power in his quick brown eyes, not his physical charisma to quicken her pulse when he touched her.

In a startling revelation, she realized that what had seduced her at the onset was the same thing that disturbed her most at this moment. Something dark and extremely desperate hovered around this fellow. She'd seen it in the car, felt it again and again in his presence. Nonsense, she told herself as she watched him distractedly panning the crowded dance floor. If anything, she might be suffering a latent effect of the scene flashing neon in her mind—that of Lawrence Fradden collapsed like a shriveled balloon within the wing-backed chair. But even that seemed reflective of whatever ill-omen hovered around Darius Brock.

Seconds, only seconds they were alone, his attention barely turned toward her with a started word off his lips when another wave of cousins swarmed. One, a little girl no more than five or six, climbed readily onto Darius's lap as her father stood aside, shaking his head and smiling in bewilderment. Her mood shifted, instantly amused by the expression of unmasked surprise then delight in the dark eyes. Relieved, Jenna vowed to enjoy what remained of the evening.

"Mommy says you come all a way from England," the little girl spoke while plopping unceremoniously on his lap and lifting her bright brown eyes to him. "She says that's how come you talk funny."

Embarrassed flashes swam across the adult faces, but Darius had recovered, his mustache slipping into a more natural, genuine smile. "Ah, little lass, but you've not heard me talk funny lass. Now, an' 'ow's that, then?" he mimed in a perfect hackney accent, winding his charms on the lovely little girl who giggled delightedly.

She dramatized a roll of her eyes and said, "You dooo talk funny!"

With a stifled laugh, Darius switched to a Schotish brogue and started, "Aye, boot I doon't."

"Cheryl!" the mortified mother said and reached, scooping the giggling little girl away and apologizing profusely—unnecessarily. For a few seconds longer, the amusement lingered in the dark eyes before the curtain dropped, and he sobered, reassuring the mother and father. "No harm done."

However briefly, he'd been delighted, and Jenna remembered Wharton's mention of a son and daughter . . . alleging that Darius had forfeited his son to be reared by his employer while his daughter remained with the mother. By no surprise, the tension returned to his eyes, to his smile as he settled into conversations with other adults who drew chairs to the table to chat with him. For those few seconds, he'd forgotten whatever sadness lingered in him, had thoroughly enjoyed the little girl's company, and Jenna's heart ached for him, tempted to track down the mother and child and bring the little girl back to him.

With the conversations changing as swiftly as the faces and the music swirling in a wild collage, Jenna lost track of time, not certain how exactly Darius had disengaged them from the collection of his admirers and led her to the dance floor. They barely managed a few steps when the music tapered, and the band spokesman announced the bride and groom were about to cut the cake. At his dumbfounded expression and the disgust fleeting his dark eyes, Jenna laughed lightly. "Give it up, hon. We're destined to dance in stages."

"So, it would appear," he said dejectedly and led her to their table, excusing himself to visit the bar for refills.

After the cake-smearing enterprise, the garter removal drew a different crowd, and rowdy whoops echoed across the hall as the bride blushed prettily. After the single males had gathered and some lucky fellow with a crewcut caught the sexy ornament, the bouquet went sailing.

Neither she nor Darius had answered the call for singles to gather on the dance floor, which Jenna realized only when Darius ducked to whisper in her ear. "That should have been you, Luv."

Whooping and hollering, the young woman shook the bouquet in the air until the crewcut fellow twirled the garter and winked.

"I think not," Jenna said and flashed Darius a smile, accepting the drink and his return. If the man stood still for more than two seconds, someone approached, and Jenna wasn't surprised when another young woman arrived. Offering him catty smiles and remarks, she flirted shamelessly, which he appeared to accept in perfect stride. If Jenna was the jealous sort, this situation could be pure hell. Curiously, she found grace to take it in stride as well, aware of his hand resting on her shoulder, aware of his touch and reassurance that apparently conveyed a message to those who joined them. He danced, he chuckled, he talked and bantered, but somehow, he managed to return to her side often enough to keep her from feeling like a third wheel.

This wasn't exactly a date, she'd decided long before he'd arrived at her apartment door. The wedding invitation had included a guest, apparently, and he had preferred not to attend alone. If anything, he'd probably scanned those employee files at the hotel, considered his options, and invited her out of convenience based on her status and people skills. As she'd noted Friday evening, he touched when he talked, encouraging intimacy and assurance, engaging others like a magnet to draw them toward him, and she wasn't immune. A perfect gentleman, he played the part of an attentive escort and date, but Jenna knew the illusion.

By the time the newlyweds made for the door under a shower of laughter, Jenna was more than ready for the trip home.

Such was not to be anytime soon, however. If anything, the gathering around Darius grew more intense, the crowd becoming rowdier with the steady stream of traffic from the bar to the tables to the dance floor. Caught up in the activity, Jenna lost the thought of leaving, accepting an invitation to dance from one of the cousins, which began a series of dances, surprisingly, including one with the younger of the Federal Agents.

He probably hadn't been out of been out of the academy long. Clean cut, built square with capable shoulders on a lean trunk, Ryan Anders maintained a respectable distance between them. His blue eyes remained in constant motion even as he maneuvered them closer to the edge of the crowded floor. His ulterior motive became clear when he looked down at her, smiling a little too apologetically. "As much as I know you're enjoying yourself, miss, and I hate to put a damper on things, it would make our job a little easier if you'd stay out of the crush where we can keep an eye on you."

"I wasn't aware of being part of your assignment, Mr. Anders," she said honestly.

"We have orders to stay close to both of you," he said smoothly and glanced in another direction, his attention snagged.

Alerted by his quick change, she followed his gaze and found Darius sidled away from a small group across the room. He appeared to be reading a note that he'd flipped open. As always, with an eye for detail, she noticed one of the hotel staff already halfway to the door. Her attention remained fixed on Darius, but she glimpsed the second agent, Matlin, approaching him. At the same moment, Darius spotted him, started to flag him away, and then reached into his jacket. Another telephone call, as if that should be a surprise. Matlin paused as Darius lifted the telephone and began punching numbers.

18

"What the bloody hell is this?" Darius asked into the receiver, too genuinely disturbed by the folded note in his hand to be intimidated by the deep voice in his ear.

"I'd imagine it's exactly what it sounds like, lad," the Baron said smoothly. "With your rather vast following of the moment and considering the danger you're in, I didn't feel it would be wise to conduct our affairs in the usual manner. Aside from that, m'lad, there's really no reason. Your cousin's expecting you."

The only surprise should be his own surprise, Darius considered with a glance toward the federal agent, standing several paces away. Escaping and avoiding these lads for an hour had posed the single problem in his mind, but he'd worked it out. He'd planned to excuse himself and find a private room in the auspices of tending to a business emergency.

His cousin expected him?

"Be a good lad, inform your bodyguard of the invitation, and take him along. I'd suggest stationing him outside the door to the bridal suite—for your own safety, if not in good conscience, of course."

"Of course," Darius answered.

"Don't keep your cousin waiting long, lad. I have a sense he's been anticipating your visit for some time, and under different circumstances—had he been older, actually—he might have stood in your shoes. Quite a lad, this Adam Brock. Determined, not unlike another I know. Now, do run along and have a pleasant evening."

No other words could have convinced Darius more to the contrary and he didn't wait long to hear another jibe. Despite the silence at his ear, he nodded and mouthed more words, already moving toward Agent Matlin as he spoke a lame promise into open airwaves. "I'll take care of it first thing in the morning." Offering a parting amenity into the phone for the agent's benefit, Darius snapped the phone off and slid the device into his inside breast pocket. Lighting his natural curiosity, he darted his gaze off the note to Matlin.

"Appears my cousin requests a private audience," he said while handing the note to Matlin. "If you'd care to come along, I doubt I'll be long."

Matlin eyed the note suspiciously, reading the request. "Strikes me a little odd, Mr. Brock."

"The lad mentioned something about their honeymoon plans earlier," Darius said offhandedly and started toward the door, already tense behind his indifference. "As I understand, they're leaving for their cruise in the morning."

Let Matlin make of those words what he would. Darius had more disturbing thoughts to consider. Too many times, far too many times throughout the evening, he'd caught his cousin looking at him, studying him. In those moments, Darius had considered the speculation born of natural curiosity, but the Baron's implication had just voided that belief. Darius should have known, should have grasped the change over an hour ago when the groom's widowed mother had mentioned something offhanded about adjusting the wedding dates to accommodate a wayward visitor. Compounded by an overheard reference to the von Hendricks Corporation, Darius surely should have realized something else afoot. Another plan, another manipulation, a strategy designed weeks or months in advance. But to what end? What exactly did his cousin—this Adam Brock—know about a certain roving Englishman bearing the same surname and lineage?

Silently, Darius rode the elevator with Matlin on alert a half step in front of him, prepared to protect him from a frontal attack . . . as if such was bloody possible. Always from the side or rear, always from the shadows, springing to illumination in the blink of an eye. That was the way of most assaults, and this one, confronting Adam Brock, wasn't the exception. At least half the people in that damn hall had anticipated Darius's arrival, none doubting he would attend. Less than twenty-four hours earlier, Darius had heard these names for the first time. Less than eighteen hours ago, he'd received the invitation, delivered via overnight courier. Another blasted manipulation, another spontaneous deception sprung on him . . . but to what extent? To what end? And why at this precise junction? Was Fradden's demise scheduled as well? Was this whole blasted mess choreographed months in advance? Or had the pieces fallen into place by natural—or unnatural order—for maximum effect?

Matlin checked the hall in either direction before stepping fully from the lift and motioning Darius in the proper direction. Striding ahead, only annoyed with his escort's precautions, Darius followed the directional arrows on the next corner and continued through the carpeted corridor.

This wasn't one of the Baron's hotels, too modern, too conventional with basic light fixtures at every door, industrial wallpaper in a pastel design, and heavy-duty carpets running wall to wall. The doors appeared solid. The walls were likely constructed with acoustic material to lower the noise decibel, at least on this upper floor.

At the appropriate door, Darius barely knocked when Matlin nudged him aside and sent him a warning look. "Just to be safe."

Disgusted, Darius stood aside only until his cousin pulled the door open three inches and started a smile until spotting the agent. Nudging Matlin aside, Darius stated, "Wait out here."

"I'd better have a look—"

"I said, wait out here," Darius repeated, affirming his words with a warning glance. "I won't be long."

Moving into the bridal suite's entry cove, more irritated than he acknowledged under his cousin's blatant speculation, Darius scanned the immediate surroundings. An open arch to the left accommodated a compact kitchenette. Folding closet doors to the right likely held hangers, an ironing board, and sundry items. Directly ahead, a small sitting room provided a modern couch and television and sported a long set of drapes. His cousin's taut, smirked grin drew Darius's attention before they reached the living area. Whatever Adam Brock knew, it was more than he should. His gaze appeared haunted with as much dark amusement as anger.

Cordially, the young man motioned toward the sitting area. "Come on in. Make yourself at home, cousin."

A slight edge to that voice, Darius noted and nodded absently, striding forward and not entirely surprised to find them alone within the room. A champagne bottle and an empty flute occupied an end table alongside a provincial couch. Adam Brock held the matching crystal glass, and as Darius met his speculating gaze, the man offered a silent toast before draining the remainder of the bubbly. Not good. Nothing about this man's posture suggested the next moments would follow a routine.

"You asked to see me," Darius stated, adhering to the natural laws of etiquette and formality.

"How does this work exactly?" Adam asked in a low, modulated voice, his gaze more cynically amused.

"Pardon me?" Darius asked, a niggling dread touching the edge of his mind.

"How does it work? It's an easy question. And I have to admit, I'm curious," he said boldly despite a subtle hitch of anger mixed with alcohol. "I know the basics."

"Then you may know more than I do, lad," Darius said, positive he would take exception to this encounter despite the blasted rules. "What are you asking? Or rather, what have you already been told?"

"Rita and I have been together nearly five years," Adam said in a low voice, his gaze more haunted, more angry. "For the past two, we haven't taken precautions. By joint decision, we were ready to start a family. Truthfully, we weren't planning to take vows. I, personally, don't think a piece of paper makes a difference . . . or should I say, I didn't think so before about eight months ago. So how the fuck does this work, cousin? She's officially Mrs. Brock, which as I've come to understand, is a prerequisite for your service."

"With whom have you spoken?" Darius asked darkly, his anger ascending on par with the lads' arrogance.

"Networking," the man said with an angry smirk. "I know the concept. It's a people-to-people business, right? Like one of those get-rich schemes straight out of the roaring sixties. Something like a pyramid effect . . . and as I've been told, in no uncertain terms, you sit on the peak. So, now you tell me?"

Annoyed, Darius held the younger man's gaze. "I asked you a question, lad. With whom did you speak? And what exactly do you believe you know?"

"Oh, I left some things out, didn't I?" the man said tensely. "Like the fact that I went for some tests at Rita's request. As I said, we intended to start a family. Imagine my surprise to learn that's very nearly impossible? I won't trouble you with the details, cousin. You probably know them better than I do. Imagine my greater surprise when I received a phone call shortly after hearing the news of our family's unusually high rate of infertility . . . and heard an extremely troubling story?"

"Who phoned you?"

"A friend of yours, I'd imagine. The fellow's name was Halbrook. George, isn't it? An old friend of the family. So, here we are, cousin. You, me, and my wife stoned out of her mind as instructed . . . on what should have been the happiest night of our lives." He barely restrained his hostility in the pause but continued in a lower pitch. "I thought about adopting, you know? Simply coming clean with her and resigning . . . but it can't work that way, can it? Not only would we need to be married, but if I heard accurately, our application would be unconditionally denied forever. You, as I've been told, are our only option. Like the grim fucking reaper, a cloud we'll need to carry over our head for the rest of our lives."

The man knew too much and probably too little, Darius realized and felt the weariness stealing over him again. "Why don't we resume this conversation a few months from now?" Darius considered, refusing even a glance toward the closed connecting door. "I'm sure you—"

"You aren't leaving here until you do whatever the fuck you have to do," Adam said in a low, angry voice, his gaze spiraling between anger and desperation.

"Lad, I don't know who the bloody hell you think you're talking to, but I damn sure don't intend to humor you beyond this point," Darius stated with an edge, his gaze darkening to reflect his tone.

"I apologize," Adam said with a tempered edge. "Forgive me if I can't exactly find heart to be overjoyed with either your presence or this situation. The fact remains, if I understand this right, if I don't consent, then I forfeit the right to ever have a child. So, I'm stuck and if you walk out that door, you take whatever chances I have for a fucking normal life with you. So, I am sorry. This just isn't easy. I tried telling myself, it would be all right. I'd handle it. But I'm not fucking handling it very well, am I? I've offended you and pissed you off, and now, I should grovel at your feet to get back in your good graces. What do I need to fucking do here, cousin? Get down on my knees and beg you to screw my wife? Is that how it works? It's not bad enough that I've been instructed to watch as if this is some fucking lab experiment, but I must beg you for the fucking privilege?"

Darius shook his head, his thoughts spiraling in angry circles as his gaze listed off the more desperate angry eyes. "No, it's not how it works," Darius said quietly and turned his gaze to his cousin with his own desperation surfaced. "And it's as much a curse to me as to you that we're having this damned conversation. Obviously, my complacency and indifference have been noted and not appreciated by the powers that be. Thus, we are both damned. If I could change that, I would, but I can't."

"Then get on with it," Adam said in a lower, angry voice, his gaze changed, inanimate as if looking through Darius. The empty champaign flute lowered to his side, dangling precariously in his loose grip.

Starkly aware of the change, Darius studied the vacant brown recognizing the murky haze and pinpoint reflections within the wider black pupils. Not his cousin. The lad was no longer simply Adam Brock. Might not have been Adam when speaking his mind or displaying his desperation and anger. But no relief came with that revelation. By whatever means, the Baron had entered this game, and the stakes had just notched a degree higher. Shaking his head slowly, Darius held his focus on the frozen brown eyes.

"You heard me, asshole," the voice was Adam Brock's, the words were not. "Get on with it. I do intend to watch. I'm rather curious, you know? Like to see how well you perform."

"Damn you," Darius uttered.

A derisive snort slid off the lips. "Come now, you wouldn't want to anger your boss, now, would you? You have a job to do. Get it done. The fate of a nation depends on you. Isn't that how it works? Without you, the clan's dead. If you fuck up . . . oh, excuse me," the low voice chided but the lips remained automated, the inflect of emotion stolen from the face. "If you fail to fuck up, we all perish."

Abruptly alarmed, Darius studied the eyes. This shouldn't be possible. In a moment of crystal clarity, he knew this wasn't possible. Oh, the trance was right. Nothing out of sync about the more glazed eyes or the posture, nothing unprecedented in the lax features . . . but something was wrong. The words . . . something was wrong with the words. Something his cousin had said rang out of sync and abruptly, Darius knew, this wasn't the Baron behind these words, behind this trance.

'. . . isn't that how it works?' Not the Baron's words. If nothing else, Darius knew his 'boss' wouldn't attempt to conceal his presence in this grand hoax. His 'boss' would chide and taunt, would take great pleasure in exercising his control, but he wouldn't be fool enough to believe Darius doubted his presence. The indefinite line . . . 'Isn't that how this works?' By no means, would the Baron attempt to cloak himself with such a foolish question, and the Baron knew better than to believe Darius would fail to recognize the change.

How to handle this? How to handle this without risking Adam Brock's life? Or was the lad's life already forfeited? Could this enemy have already . . . too much control! Without direct contact, either physical touch or taint, Adam Brock shouldn't have retained the ability to answer the door and carry out the first half of this conversation. Without an internal connection, the lad shouldn't be capable of switching his tempo so swiftly, immediately!

When? How long ago? Weeks or months? Days? Hours? Could the Baron's adversary have followed the limousine to this damned hotel and waited in this suite for the newlyweds?

"We don't have all night, Darius. I think you better—"

Moving as if he intended to turn, Darius spun and threw the punch, clipping the jaw with a force to send the younger man staggering, sprawling into a single chair. Not wasting an instant, Darius moved forward, lifting his phone from his jacket, and already punching numbers. As the phone started to ring, he leaned and clasped his cousin's jaw, tipping his lax face, unconsciously searching his neck. The boy still wore his ruffled shirt open halfway down his muscled chest, the tie and cummerbund removed. Uncomfortably aware of the loose collar, Darius used only his fingertips to slide the cloth away from the right shoulder. His heart dropped a leaden beat as he found the dual pink scars not quite faded. New!

"What's happened?" the low dark voice slid into his ear.

"Your enemy's here," Darius said in an equally low voice. "And my cousin just became an expendable pawn in your fucking game. Dual fucking marks on his right shoulder. Fading even as we speak," he stated angrily and watched the marks evaporate on the muscled flesh. Fleeting, his attention darted between the marks and the trickle of blood gathering on the slightly parted, lax lips.

"I see," the low voice commented.

"How much? How much do you see, sir?" Darius asked angrily. "Where do your manipulations and this other bastard's end? Or does it? Am I wrong? Is my cousin now one of your chosen sheep? One of the branded? Will he wake from the bruise I just landed and ask me to fucking join him for a cup of tea? Ah, and while you're telling me that, perhaps, you'll tell me what I should do about your earlier command—"

"You're distraught, lad. Understandable. But don't lose your head," the Baron mused. "You're still with your cousin, is that right?"

"I've knocked him cold, but doubtful, he'll remain out for long."

"Well, if he's lost, he doesn't need a child to burden him," the Baron commented. "This might be a fine time to take your leave."

"I . . . haven't checked on his wife," Darius realized and glanced toward the closed bedroom door.

"Might not be wise to waste time with her, lad. Whether you have the master at hand or a soldier in your midst, the problem could be ehm . . . should we say . . .? Critical?"

"How . . . how much of this did you arrange?" Darius asked as he straightened, already moving toward the door. "Did you give this lad instructions to drug his wife? Did you give him instructions to watch? Were those your orders?"

"Possibly," the Baron said idly.

"D-don't do this to me, sir," Darius said in genuine despair. He was treading on dangerous ground, possibly overstepping his bounds, but he couldn't afford to remain in the dark. "If you intend me to leave here in one piece, I need more than suppositions. I need to know where your orders and this other chap's orders separate. Give me that, sir?"

"Are you still in that room?"

"Yes," Darius said as he stopped the door, reached for the nob.

"Stop, lad," the Baron stated.

Whether Darius froze by natural reaction to the tone, or his muscles gripped with an unnatural connection, he knew only his stopped breath, his stopped pose. As the low words spilled directly into his inner ear, he started backing away from the door.

His senses enhanced, he felt it then. Something . . . someone else inside this suite. "Oh, fuck," he uttered, his gaze darting to his cousin's fluttering lashes. Adam was rousting.

In the corner of his eye, Darius glimpsed a flash of motion and pivoted, slamming his jaw into an invisible force. Staggering, stumbling, lights sparking in his eyes, he stayed on his feet on route to the door with the phone still pressed at his ear. A low slimy laugh slithered from every corner of the room, a chiding voice. Blinking, darting his focus, Darius backed into a solid wall, not stopping, not slowing. In front of him, Adam Brock rose, and Darius glimpsed the vacant eyes as the boy advanced. Closer, a blur, a mere shadow passed, and fire ignited under a wicked strike at Darius's jaw, staggering him against the wall. He felt it then, a slice of pain through his skull as he lost dominion to the voice in his ear. Straightening, firming on his feet, he heard the words, his own low-pitched voice speaking conversationally as he continued sidling to the door. Who he was speaking to, why, Darius had no conscious thought; the voice was his . . ,

"You've had your fun, now, errand boy. Run home to your master and carry a message, for me, will you, lad? Tell this ill-begot, I will recover what is mine, but not until I have all that was ever his . . ."

In front of Darius, advancing in automated steps, Adam Brock glared vacantly through unmoving brown eyes. Likewise automated, Darius backed against the door and clasped the nob by no will of his own. In his ear, siphoning through his scattered, suspended thoughts, Darius understood the commands saturating his nerves, his muscles, moving him, his hand to find and twist the doorknob. Backing into the hall, he gained only a second, to grasp a thin, maniacal grin sliding into his cousin's lips. His system jolted as he snapped the door shut and a shudder poured through him.

A single command lingered, floating and dripping with rage, 'Now, get your ass out of that hotel.'

Matlin came off the wall where he'd been leaning, and Darius turned toward the elevator, already lifting his knuckles to his bloody lip, catching only a glance of the man's startled eyes. Over and over, the words slid through his mind, a warning, a threat, a command.

"What the hell happened?" Matlin demanded as he clasped Darius's elbow.

"He didn't want travel tips," Darius said in a low, nearly calm tone.

"Maybe you better tell me what the hell he did want?" Matlin snapped.

Darius continued to the lift, slamming the call button and freeing his arm from Matlin's grip. Reaching into his jacket, jamming the phone into the breast pocket, he found a handkerchief to wipe his lips.

"Goddamn it, Brock—"

In one motion, Darius pivoted, caught the man's lapels, and lifted him, slamming him into the wall alongside the elevator door. Looking into the startled, tense eyes, his own clear and hot, he stated, "If you intend to address me,

Mr. Matlin, I suggest you use the proper fucking etiquette. I have very nearly had it with American hospitality as well as ignorance." Belatedly realizing he held the agent on his toes, Darius snapped a curse and lowered the chap to his feet, almost carefully snapping the dark lapels into place. More calmly, he looked into the tense, startled eyes. "How the bloody hell was I supposed to know the lad would take offense to my offer to put him on a better luxury line?" he asked simply and turned in time to step into the parting elevator doors. Wiping at his lip, he caught the agent's wary gaze as the man stepped into the elevator. Forcing a faintly apologetic grin, he offered, "I do apologize."

"They probably have a first aid kit handy downstairs. We'll get you some ice," Matlin commented by way of acceptance.

"Not necessary," Darius stated. "But appreciated. I'd rather we collect our companions and depart before the lad decides to ignite a family feud."

The words had the intended effect. Matlin withheld any further suggestions and stayed on Darius's heels as they strode from the elevator. Before reaching the hall, Darius tucked the bloody cloth into his jacket pocket, grateful for the subdued light that further masked his mustache-shaded, swelling lip. Without wasting time, he spotted and motioned to his chauffeur with a nod, then collected Jenna from another ensemble of cousins. Bidding his farewells, the Baron's orders still replaying in his head like a recorder at slow speed, he helped Jenna into her coat and escorted her swiftly through the doors.

A soldier . . . if he understood the Baron's words before that assault, the entity he'd just encountered was a mere soldier in the enemy's army, but the bastard had the power to enslave Adam Brock. Refusing to buckle fully under the dread of that thought, Darius maintained a firm hold on Jenna's arm, his senses still humming, attuned to this maniac's presence.

No ordinary foot soldier, this chap, and Darius sensed the familiar essence. This was the same being who'd followed him from Jenna's apartment . . . playing a game? Or closing in? His attention darting as avidly as the agents, Darius steered Jenna through the front doors, barely glimpsing the chauffeur stepping from the driver's door when his own natural instincts firmed. How hard could it be? How much trouble to waylay this driver as the man had gone for the car? The Baron's words had probably only enhanced this devil's penchant for mischief, and suddenly, Darius had no intention of leaving his fate in the hands of another. Too damned easily, this stout driver could have been caught, turned. A two-hour drive, nearly a hundred miles of long dark highways through barren, snow-covered countryside.

Running his gaze over the chauffeur's lax expression as the man reached for the door, Darius decided—either this chap was a new recruit or half asleep.

"Change in plans," he said offhandedly and looked at Jenna with a half-smile. "How would you like to ride up front with me? I do so love to drive."

She looked at him as if he were slightly mad, but her gaze distracted, seeing his lip under the fluorescent entrance lights. Her gaze shot up, deciding, "Sounds like fun."

"Good," he said and looked to the startled agents, the dumbstruck chauffeur. "You lads can ride in the lap of luxury."

"I don't think that's a good idea . . . Mr. Brock," Matlin stated.

"Sir, I'm paid to drive," the chauffeur stated with a touch too much boldness. "My insurance won't cover you."

"Then you've lost a fare," Darius said while looking into the man's emboldened eyes. "Either I drive, or I send for a rental."

"Mr. Brock," Matlin stated. "Why don't we just step into the car and get rolling. It's late and we have a long ride."

In retrospect, Darius remembered the feeling inside that room . . . he'd stood outside the bedroom door, his back to the room entrance. He hadn't felt the presence immediately and the soldier hadn't entered through the bedroom door. Not even Raphael could move swiftly enough to open and close a door without detection. To get inside that room, behind him, the soldier would have crossed paths with Matlin. Not good. Not good at all! A damned trap! A death trap if he stepped into the limousine.

"Damn it," Darius said abruptly, his gaze flashing toward the doors, then to the agents, focusing on Matlin. "You're right. Unfortunately, I overlooked something inside. We'll need to go back for a moment."

Without awaiting a response, Darius turned, veering Jenna toward the glass doors, catching her more curious eye, and conveying what he hoped passed for a reassuring smile. Ignoring the estranged glances they received while passing through the lobby, Darius maintained his stride, keeping the young lady against him, the agents at his back as he led them into the still rowdy crowd. Spotting the elder cousin he sought, he waded through the tables and snagged the elder's eye before coming within reach. With the agents dropped back, Darius spoke smoothly and directly, "I need a car and a distraction from the lads on my heels, Daniel. Do you think you might lend a hand? I'll see the car returned to you tomorrow."

His cousin smiled slowly and nodded, responding mechanically to Darius's hand as if offering a parting amenity. In his other hand, which lifted to fold over their joined grip, he delivered a set of keys. "It's a Dodge, Charge, 89, parked third aisle to the left of the main entrance. We came in a side door, directly past the elevators. How soon do you want to leave?"

"Posthaste, lad," Darius said lightly. "And if you could detain these fellows for at least ten minutes, I'd certainly be grateful."

At his side, Jenna remained silent, merely darting her gaze between them with a faintly troubled line across her brow.

"Give me a minute, then," Daniel Brock stated. "Maybe stop and chat with my mum for a moment while I chat with our cousins."

"Thank you," Darius said lightly and passed Jenna another reassuring smile. He would have a great deal of explaining to do if or when they were safely underway. "Bear with me, Luv. We'll be leaving in a moment."

"Life with you is never dull, is it?" she asked with a touch of doubt.

"Sometimes, it's truly boring," he said and winked, turning her, and leading her toward Daniel's mother, a spry little woman with a lovely shock of nearly white hair and bright blue eyes. Within a minute, Daniel joined them, and less than thirty seconds later, Darius escorted Jenna from the hall with the agents blocked and lost within a rowdy crowd of revelers forming a train and shouting a rumba beat. As they hastened through the rear halls, bypassing the elevators, Jenna managed, "What's this about, Darius?"

"Soon, Luv," he promised. "Let's find our chariot and I'll explain on the highway."

They passed through the glass doors and braced against the chill. Hurrying them passed a strand of cars, Darius spotted the designated ride. Daring to believe, he inserted one of the keys in the driver's door and breathed a relieved humph when the lock disengaged. "Humor me, Luv, and slide across the seat from here." She did so smoothly, slipping across the seat with an economy of graceful ease to snag his thoughts as he slid behind the wheel and snapped the door shut. Not until he'd driven through the lot, bypassing the limo waiting in the covered portico at the main entrance, did he breathe a sigh of relief. Turning onto the highway, he bounced his attention from the windshield to the rearview mirror. No headlights turned onto the highway in their wake. Undoubtedly, his enemy, this soldier had relied on his new recruits and lingered on the sidelines. The chap might have discovered the diversion and might catch up, but a highspeed car chase wasn't likely this lad's style.

"Assuming you didn't just lose those agents for the heck of it, would you mind telling me why we just did that?" Jenna asked reasonably.

He glanced to find her watching him critically. "I have slight reason to believe that one of those lads wasn't exactly who or what he appeared, Jenna," he said honestly, letting a touch of concern affect his voice. "I owe you a few million apologies, only beginning with the most obvious."

"Which is?"

She needed fair warning, not that it would do much good or offer any protection. Uncomfortably, he glanced at her. "I've probably placed you in danger simply by finding you extremely attractive and not concealing that detail well enough." Only too honest, he considered and continued smoothly, "Had I known what the FBI assumed I knew two days ago, I wouldn't have taken the chances I've taken. That's not much of an excuse. Unfortunately, it's the most honest admission."

"What does that mean exactly, Darius?" she asked carefully, and he felt her gaze on him, searching him. "What do the FBI know?"

"In the course of my travels, I've apparently picked up a lunatic . . . one with a very dark obsession. Rather like a stalker, I suppose, and this chap seems to travel as quickly and efficiently as myself. I don't honestly know the details, other than to admit, Mr. Fradden wasn't the first person to die by ehm . . . unnatural means. I don't want to frighten you," he said honestly and glanced over. If her piercing gaze were an indication, he'd done exactly that. "But I want you to be careful and I don't want an argument when I insist on safety precautions on your behalf. It's ehm . . . rather obvious that I won't be able to conduct my affairs as naturally as I had intended."

"I don't understand," she said hesitantly.

"Jenna," he said quietly. "I travel in some extremely wealthy circles. If my suspicions are accurate, whoever this stalker is, he has financial freedom. Enough so, that he might have enlisted one of those lads we just left behind. If that's true, then I'll need to postpone my affairs. Become a hermit, for a time," he said offhandedly. "Unfortunately, that may extend to you, as well, Luv. Until I know what triggers this maniac, I won't take unnecessary chances where your life is concerned."

"What happened when you left the party?" she asked with quiet, impressive control.

"Had a bit of a misunderstanding," he answered and fell silent, concentrating on the highway signs momentarily. He needed to remember this was the USA. Unless he remained on the right side of the blasted highway, they might be in even more serious trouble.

"With Agent Matlin?" she asked.

"One of my cousins," he answered and continued to watch the highway and rearview mirror, pouring on a little speed and hoping to stay a fair distance ahead. By habit alone, he'd checked the maps before departing the Chateau, and though he might have navigated other routes, less-traveled routes, he doubted he'd save time or stay too far ahead of this soldier.

Adam lost. Adam living now under the control of a maniac, a monster without a face.

If Darius hadn't seen it, felt it, experienced it, he wouldn't have believed it. His cousin, his blood, an innocent who should have been spared, never to be directly touched by the damned curse . . .? Bad enough the whole bloody clan lived under the pall . . . If not to save others like Adam, what the bloody hell was the point of the sacrifices and oaths? The bloody covenant?

And Darius would rather not dwell on those moments inside that suite. Too swiftly, he relived the splitting pain, the loss of control in his limbs. Was it possible? Was he no different than most of the others? Had the Baron taken him years ago and left him with the mere illusion of freedom . . .? Or had he simply buckled to the overwhelming commands as easily as all others? With his senses wide open inside that room, his thoughts spiraling in search of an immediate escape . . . he was as susceptible to that deep, silky voice as all others in his clan. A phone call. With a phone call, the Baron could instill a temporary trance and suspend natural thought. But his thoughts hadn't been suspended. In some distant corner, he'd heard and understood the words, animated and felt his muscles responding to another's command.

Uncomfortably, he relived that strangeness to become cargo, a spectator inside his body. Belatedly, he shivered. Was that what it would feel like? Would he know . . . as he had said to Raphael? When or if the Baron ever took him, would he live in some small corner of his mind, aware of his loss of control, aware of the overwhelming power presiding over his body?

"Darius?" Jenna broke the silence, not liking the spooked shine or the tension in his handsome features.

Manic, he spied the rearview mirror before glancing at her. "Yes?"

"Did you mean what you said?" she wondered, needing to keep him talking if only to avoid thinking too deeply about his words.

"About?"

"Finding me attractive," she said and glimpsed his fleeting eyes before his attention riveted on the highway.

"You doubt?" he asked in a quieter tone.

Turning her gaze through the passenger window, she reviewed the past several hours—and days. Only on isolated occasions, she'd glimpsed something deeper, something genuine beneath his showman's persona. Interest, perhaps. Again eying him, she studied his troubled profile. Even in the dull glow of gauge lights, she glimpsed the hurt in his fleeting eyes. "You hide it well, Darius," she said quietly.

"There are . . . reasons," he said quietly.

"Your job?"

"My job," he agreed.

"Why did you really stop by my apartment last night?"

"I'm impulsive," he said offhandedly, his gaze still flashing between the empty highway illuminated in the headlight beams and rearview mirror.

"I don't buy that, sweetie. You think on your feet but you're methodical."

"You could be right."

"You're an irritating man, Mr. Brock," she said smoothly and caught his flashing dark gaze, sensing his wary curiosity in the soft glow of gauge lights. Let him stew, she decided and turned her gaze through the windshield.

At least the roads were dry despite the snow heaped to either side of the headlight beams. Scattered over rolling hillsides, barns and houses illuminated in dusk-to-dawn lights barely marring the platinum slopes to rise toward a mantel of charcoal gray clouds. Snow clouds. Just what they needed to end a lovely evening. The absence of traffic, the long winding stretches of two-lane barely . . .

She was riding in a borrowed car, in the middle of nowhere with a man who'd just told her—rather matter-of-factly—he had a wealthy, psychotic killer obsessed with him. . . . *Oh, and by the way, he might be after you now.*

To top off this grand evening, this extremely handsome gentleman hadn't even made a serious pass at her, not since asking her to remove her jacket and let her hair down to pose for his pictures. Then he dared to sound hurt when she doubted his admission? If she didn't sense an underlying tension in his posture, genuine restrained distress, she might consider the last hour a warped scheme to reap the present circumstance.

They were entirely alone for the first time since meeting. No bosses or associates to carry tales. No hotel staff to intrude. No police or federal agents hovering within earshot watching their every move. Not even another car on the highway, fore or aft. They truly were alone and after his announcement . .
.

Damn it, he truly was the most physically attractive, arousing man she'd ever met, and she hadn't shared an intimacy with a man in nearly a year. Whether he planned this situation, or merely manipulated certain circumstances to reach this end, mattered not in the least. They were alone . . . and if there was ever a good reason to break her golden rule, Darius Brock qualified.

Morals, high standards, principles, bedamned. Somewhere inside her head, the decision was already made, made hours ago when she'd rested in his arms on the dance floor. She wanted to kiss him and learn firsthand if his kisses were as fulfilling as the promise of his voice. She wanted to break the wall around him and touch him and be touched by him in return. Once, if only once, she wanted to lift the mask and meet the man who could heat her blood with his eyes or his touch.

The decision made, Jenna began unbuttoning her soft wool coat. With the heater blowing a steady stream of warm air under the dashboard, the car was warm enough. She slid her arms from the sleeves and let the cloth settle about her shoulders, catching only a side glance of his alert brown eyes. "I'm sorry I didn't take off my jacket for you the other night."

"I'm not," he said in a lower voice.

Watching his profile, she knew she held his attention. "I'm also sorry I offered you the couch last night, Darius," she said quietly and again received a fleeting glance, a started half smile. Without awaiting an invitation, she slid over the silk lining of her long coat. The car wasn't a limo where a wide gulf of leather had separated them, but by the time she rested against him, she'd gained his undivided attention despite his gaze on the highway. "You're not an easy man to understand and I wasn't too sure what to make of your advances. You have a natural talent to say one thing while alluding to something else." His long coat hung open, loosened if it had ever been buttoned. Jenna slipped her hand to his thigh, and his tension spiked in a subtle jolt.

His hand slipped off the steering wheel, dropping to cover her fingers, and for an instant, he might have meant to lift her touch away. Instead, his fingers closed carefully, folding over her hand. Tension ran across his eyes, haunted his rapid downward glance. "Jenna, this isn't . . . a good idea," he said in a deeper tone.

"No, probably not," she agreed. "But I've weighed the issues and options, and I'm not reckless by nature, I don't make important decisions without tallying facts, not in business or my personal life. Once I reach a decision, though, I don't believe in beating around the bush," she said quietly, watching his profile, gaging the slight tension. "We don't have a lifetime. We have what . . .? A day or two? Maybe just tonight? You don't stay in one place for long, and chances are, I won't be working at the Chateau when you pass through again. I don't appreciate the one-night stands. It's not a practice I condone or apply, but we won't have much more than that. Frankly, I'm as self-satisfying as you are, and if one night's all we have, I'd rather have that than nothing."

He was silent and almost too still despite his gaze on the highway. His left hand rode the steering wheel, gliding them around several long bends that might have been frightening at their present speed even in daylight. Only the tension of his hand conveyed his desire to match her own. Seconds, eons passed before his words slipped off his mustached lips at a painfully soft pitch. "Nothing in this world would I like more than to make love to you, Jenna. If you believe nothing else I've ever said or that you've seen in me, believe those words, Luv."

"But. . . ."

"But it can't happen," he said with a faintly desperate note, his hand clasped more firmly. "Having you here with me this evening . . .? It was more than I had a right to ask. More than I could have hoped for . . . and I can't explain that. Wouldn't know where to begin, even if I thought I could. For my sake, for your sake, Luv, I can't involve you in my life any deeper than you are, and I wasn't lying. I've already placed you at too great a risk."

She understood the sincerity in his voice as surely as the quiet desperation in his words, but if he'd meant to dissuade her, the opposite held true. Turning her hand within his grip, she twined her fingers through his in a more natural handhold, not lifting their locked grip from his thigh. Whether she reacted to his need or her own with the thought of serious danger, she knew only a desire to hold onto him, draw from his strength. Not again would she make the verbal offer or suggestion, but the invitation remained open. If or when he chose to accept, the decision remained his.

19

With the woman asleep against his shoulder, her hand relaxed within his grip, Darius volleyed between a collection of thoughts, none of which afforded any relief. To make matters worse and prolong his misery, heavy snow had begun to fall as he sped over the last stretch of country roads. Progress slowed; visibility declined. Barely, he identified the signs designating the Ohio-Pennsylvania line passing.

Not a firm believer in luck, Darius doubted the weather conditions would slow the advance of his pursuers, but he dared not push his own luck on the strange, slick roads.

With more than two hours to think, he'd reached few conclusions, none of which offered comfort or relief. If he couldn't keep himself safe, doubtful he could protect the young woman at his side. Neither solid walls nor human bodyguards could be relied upon with the nature of this damned enemy. No one he knew in this area could be trusted. Sooner or later, if he hid her with an acquaintance, she'd be found, and the Baron would likely have the information at his disposal.

Dangerous ground. Even fleeting a thought of hiding her from the Baron could be treacherous.

To truly protect her, he needed to sever all ties to her, all communication, all thoughts . . .

But just the thought of sending her away solo gripped his chest and staggered a heartbeat. Even if he sent her to fend for herself, she might encounter trouble, and then what? If the Baron's adversary caught her, she'd be lost; if the Baron found her, she'd be lost—if only to punish a certain renegade consort.

Either way, she was already lost to him.

No good solutions. No safe conclusions.

At the last minute, Darius recognized the glow of lights ahead and spotted the stop sign through the cut of headlight beams. After miles of staring into a kaleidoscope of flakes splattering between the swipe of windshield wiper blades, the sight of civilization disoriented him. Reading road signs, remembering the direction he'd glimpsed from the backseat of a limousine, he navigated the appropriate turn, following signs to indicate state Rt. 51. At the glimpse of a County Airport sign, his thoughts spiked, but he countered the thought before reaching the first set of blinking lights. Hiding Jenna on the Night Rider craft would be futile as well as foolish. The damn plane had become his home, more so than his flat in London, a detail to offer the only explanation for his momentary insanity . . . *Or verified just how fully he'd fallen into the Baron's service.*

Had he already lost so much of his humanity? Had he become no different from the ton of others who bent to the Baron's command without a thought of right or wrong?

The answers to his question scrolled through his mind, churning his stomach violently as he sped up the ramp to the four-lane. No damned choice. The best thing to happen to him in years was already lost, and he had no choice but to leave her fate in the master's hands. Humanity. His human nature was a curse, and as if to counter the thought, Darius pushed the car to a reckless speed, daring the ice to pitch him over a hillside. Only a fear of taking Jenna Windrow with him held him steady behind the wheel.

Time and again, throughout that long drive, he'd thought about his cousin . . . newlywed. On what should have been the happiest night of his life, Adam . . . and possibly his lovely bride . . . had encountered a fate worse than death. A fate even worse than what the Baron might have planned for them.

Humanity was a curse, and he hadn't lost it entirely.

The sting of tears threatened the corner of his strained eyes as he considered what sort of life his cousin might be forced to live. For another of his cousins to be enthralled was never supposed to happen. By unnatural law and the Baron's clearly defined rules, Darius had believed the hundreds of others of his clan would be spared. The twelve . . . the twelve had represented the whole. They'd been chosen, selected by the Baron to make the bloody sacrifices and offer retribution to protect all others. For no other reason, Darius had agreed. For no other reason, he'd forfeited his life willingly and fallen into the covenant of his own free will. And yet, Adam was lost. An expendable pawn lost in a game that could end by only one means.

Blood.

Human blood.

The Baron would play the game, and to bloody hell with how many lives might be lost, how many other pawns were forfeited. The bastard possessed an unlimited supply of pawns, and Darius could find no relief in his higher station. A knight . . . or a bishop. A rook, perhaps, capable of bilateral moves, none of which would see him safely out of range from another grandmaster in this bloody game.

He was human. He could be killed. Would be killed. He had only his damned human nature to avoid the enemy, and that would never be enough. He need only consider his aching jaw to know he'd encountered something more powerful and faster than him. In retrospect, he knew the Baron was right, though. If that soldier had meant to kill him, he would be dead or captured. For whatever reason, Darius had become the bait to lure this adversary into the light. How long this other monster intended to play with him remained the only question. Sooner or later, out of pure arrogance, this beast would come within striking range if only to smite the Baron and snatch his human familiar.

By whatever good sense remained, Darius slowed to a safer speed, cursing himself for his weakness . . . or was it sensibilities and damned compassion. Was he still so human that he dared hope for salvation? Or was it just the warm palm resting within his loose grip to counter his suicidal mood? His life, he could forfeit. Jenna . . . he couldn't take her with him.

Too much time to think . . . and not enough. Darius had solved nothing, and as the exit signs sped by, mere reflections of fluorescent green rectangles with the words lost under a white blur, he knew the futility of attempting to escape fate by rational plans.

Irrationally, he was a fantastic planner. He could scheme and connive with the best of men. Were he facing an enemy of human dominion, he harbored no doubts about the outcome. If he dealt with a natural enemy, he'd shield Jenna behind a protective wall of bodyguards, possibly send her on vacation to some pleasant island in the Caribbean with a promise to join her. A lie, of course, but he could arrange for her transport. With his personal funds—play money, as the Baron had once referred to the bank accounts at Darius's disposal—he could safeguard her passage and, ultimately, her life. Against a natural enemy, he would win. His arrogance would have it no other way.

How many kilometers had he put between himself and his enemies?

His thoughts turned in ever darker circles, Darius veered onto the appropriate exit ramp, belatedly aware of his speed on the icy slope. Cursing, he needed both hands to correct his mistake, and Jenna lurched awake as the car slid sideways onto the connecting highway. Touching the gas, Darius used the momentum of the slide, glancing at Jenna's anxious gaze. "Sorry, Luv. Didn't mean to wake you so rudely."

"I . . . we're . . . almost home?"

"I'm not driving you to your apartment," he said bluntly, feeling her more startled gaze. "You'll stay in the suite next to mine tonight, Jenna, and there are precautions I'll insist you follow. First and foremost, you are not to open your door to anyone—not the FBI, not room service, Mr. Mason, or hotel security guards. No one, unless I phone you directly and clear the visit in advance—"

"Darius—"

"No arguments, Luv," he said firmly and glanced over as he rolled between the pillared entrance to the Chateau. "Trust me, Jenna. Just for a little while, do as I say?"

Reluctantly, she agreed while slipping into her coat. Almost irritated, she commented, "I can't believe you let me sleep all that way."

Convincing himself to let her sleep had taken most of his willpower, but he refrained from saying those words aloud. Pulling under the covered portico just past the entrance, he shut off the engine and slid from the car, reaching her door before she stepped fully onto the sidewalk. Like the previous morning, federal agents arrived with Wharton in the lead, appearing more awake than the hour would dictate. Apparently, the alarm had arisen from Canton. Before Wharton could release more than an angry sound, Darius cut him off shortly. "We'll talk after I see Miss Windrow safely to a room."

In full command, Darius collected the keys to suite 608 and, with three agents crowding into the ancient lift, rose to the sixth floor without releasing Jenna's arm for an instant. Leaving the agents outside the door and stationing Jenna inside, Darius personally checked the suite, alert for any sound or sense of a predator. Passing through the sitting room into the bedroom and bath, he checked window latches, closets, and cubbyholes and returned to the main sitting area. After checking the cabinets under the slight bar, he rose and turned, colliding with the deep blue, deeply curious eyes. She hadn't moved from the door. She stood with her hands buried in her wool coat pockets, her head canted at an angle that would appear more coy than curious on any other woman. In the soft lamplight, her eyes as bright and alert as ever, wisps of curls scattered over her brow and down her temples, she was awesome, truly awesome. Without a clear thought, he moved to her, drawn into the blue depths.

One night . . . no lifetime together. Her words echoed through his mind as his hand lifted, brushing, touching against her raised chin. All the reasons slipped away, replaced by a desperate need. His head tipped and lowered, the touch of her warm, parting lips hitting nerves and igniting sparks through his system. A mistake. He knew the mistake before their lips collided. The barrier he'd wrapped around himself rippled. The clinical approach to copulation for the single purpose of reproduction—a safety mechanism designed to protect his sanity—blasted away in an explosion of desire.

Not in years had he tasted the breath of another or experienced the rush of shared need. Under the warm slide of her fingers at his neck, his body shuddered, quickening. He wanted to make love—

Startled, wary of a trick suddenly, Darius drew back, remembering another time, a distant time, the Baron's game.

He couldn't readily recount how many times he'd sensed a woman responding to him, believing in a flood of panic that she knew him and would recognize him. In a paradox, then, he'd jolted, fearing he'd made a mistake and broken through the woman's trance . . . while wanting fiercely to believe he was something more substantial than a phantom lover. Always, the moments came later, the disappointment and humiliation as the Baron taunted him, asking him how he enjoyed his encounter.

Looking into the clear, intense blue eyes focused on him exclusively, Darius knew only greater confusion and reluctance. He could be tricked. He could be deceived into believing she wanted him as badly as he wanted her . . . and yet, at the same instant, he knew the integrity of her desire.

To the passion in her eyes, the promise of her lips, he was lost. By no conscious decision, he accepted the gentle persuasion of her hand on his neck and touched down again, drawn into the heat of her kiss. No trick. No deception. This woman touched his heart, touched him more deeply, now, passing through the icy wall he'd built around himself. In wicked quick seconds, his restraints snapped, disintegrating like rusted iron. Neutral! He needed to remain neutral to female ministrations. With her fingers sliding into his hair, under his collar, his hands moved, heating a path at her neck, dispatching the wool from her shoulders. In his mind, he'd removed the soft black cloth a dozen, if not a million times in the past dozen hours.

Drawing her against him, he slid his hands over her shoulders, forcing her hands from his neck to her sides, dropping her coat at her heels. The moments jumbled, hands and fingers fumbling to free the cloth between them. Caution and wariness replaced the reluctance and desire of new lovers. Spreading kisses from her lips to her neck, his hands glided over her shoulders, his senses waking to the soft wisping breaths at his ear and the silky touch against his ribs and chest.

Lost. He was lost. He wanted to touch and taste every inch of her. Wanted to bury himself within her warmth and remain lost forever. Images of her poised, sleek, and pensive in the soft light of the dining room assailed his mind, drawing him deeper as his hands rode her hips and he lowered, tracing the imaginary V-line of her dress with his lips and tongue. Careful, wary, he remained lost in the wild abandon as she arched to his touch. Under his fingertips, her pulse rose, matching his racing heartbeat like a drumroll.

His gaze lifted, and he caught Jenna's flaming blue eyes looking into him, and for an instant, he doubted she knew him. Insecurity and fear flashed through his mind. His vulnerability and wariness threatened to cave under his need.

He rested on his knees, one of her hands locked on his shoulder, the other tangled in his hair, prepared either to draw him closer or rip him away. She wasn't pushing him away. Not lost in a trance. Her eyes held him, pinning him, promising and persuading him to continue.

Rocked back slightly, her taste on his tongue, her soft scent on his every breath, he took his fill of her glistening endowments. In another place, in another time, he would have risen then and lifted her, setting her down on his throbbing manhood, but at the very edges of his failing sanity, he knew the futility of his desire. He wasn't free, would never be free to make love to her as a man should make love to such a magnificent woman. His heart hammered a more leaden beat; his frustration warred with desire, lifting moisture in his eyes. Never more than at this instant could he regret what he had become.

With a restraint born of honor, he rose then, with the decision racing in his mind. Lifting her, he locked his lips over hers and carried her into the bedroom. His muscles trembled with a need too great to be entirely ignored. He would make love to her, could make love to her in every way but one, and on that fine line, he walked willingly, lying her on the soft quilt, stripping what remained of his clothes as she watched him with flames of desire leaping in her deep blue eyes. No words. Not a single word had she spoken either to voice her need or apprehension. Her eyes spoke volumes as he laid down with her; her hands and lips confirmed her consent with an abandon to drive him toward ecstasy.

Only for a second, they fumbled again like new lovers, Uncertainty blasted away under the force of desire. Over and under, they rode the same wave, exploring and touching, tasting and testing. In fleeting instants, Darius grasped the reality, not losing a thought or tempo as he reveled in the wonder of physical bliss. She was, without a doubt, the most sensuous woman he'd ever encountered, as confident and self-assured in bed as in all else, moving with him and against him, sliding down him and showering him with kisses to burn a path to his core. When he could withstand no more, when every breath became a gasp, he rolled her over and glimpsed her knowing smile, her fiery eyes as he administered the same erotic torture, driving her to a fit of heaves and breaths with his name whispered in soft hisses.

Racing. They were racing toward some ultimate place, a plateau, toward that moment of little death, and he was losing his battle for restraint. The forbidding reasons slipped further and further from his mind. Unless he stopped . . . unless he stopped . . .

The telephone ringing near at hand barely touched his mind, a nagging sound from some other place, some other life. Not now. Not here. But the sound persisted. Ringing and ringing, tossed into his mind like a lifeline in a roaring sea.

Cold sweat raced over him, pouring into his mind, his senses suddenly quick to realize, he rested atop this wondrous creature, his body arched for the final plunge. Chilled, stopped, he hovered an instant, then rolled smoothly, swiftly off her arched body, and continued to the edge of the bed, his hand already thrust to catch the phone off the base.

His breath halted, he snatched the receiver and brought it to his ear. No word slid past the constriction in his throat. No words were needed. He knew whose voice he would hear. As the deep, resonant voice slid into his frozen mind, his entire body gripped.

Disbelief vied for space in his compacted senses. Darius tried shaking his head, raising a denial, a protest, against the words pressing into his mind. He tried yanking the phone from his ear.

The words he'd anticipated, the demand, the outrage . . .? That wasn't what he heard. More frightening these words, this low silky command, the power flowing through his ear into his limbs.

Nooo!

'Finish what you've begun . . . lose your seed inside of her . . . finish . . . forget your vows. . .'

Trembling with the heat of need, Jenna watched him, saw him shivering. Unconsciously, she rolled and touched his sweated back, feeling the shudders pouring through him. Lying at an angle, she read the tension on his sweat-glistening face and saw the dark shine of moisture in his eyes as he gazed toward the telephone base. Beneath his quivering dark mustache, his lips parted, barely breathing. He was everything she'd suspected from the moment she'd met him, as fierce and determined in carnal pleasure as he was in his occupation. An artist. A gentle master who even now held her at the apex of desire, her body and mind heated on the brink of need to have him turning and returning into her arms. Under her palm, the chill shuddered through his lean muscles, and her hand slid down over his ribs, following the lean contour of his hip to his thigh. Only in a museum had she admired such a beautifully sculpted male anatomy, and he needed only to bend his elbow and tuck his fist under his chin to have posed for the sculpt. In wild, wet tangles, his hair curled over his brow and behind his ear, glistening and sparkling with the shudders. She wanted him off the phone. No other thought held more fully in her mind as she slid her hand at his thigh, catching his dark eyes shifting toward her.

He appeared lost or dazed as if he looked through her, and she remembered other estranged moments since they'd begun this encounter at the door. Vulnerable. For all his strength and confidence, an odd vulnerability . . . or innocence reflected in his eyes. Uncertainty and apprehension were the last emotions she'd expected to find in a man who could heat a woman with a glance or smile, and yet she sensed both.

Without uttering a word, he lowered the receiver to the telephone base and turned, his gaze locked on her, pinning her. A weird intensity crept over the mahogany shine. Her senses reacted to the change in him, and suddenly, she felt vulnerable on a primal level. Something had changed. He came over her, his hand touching her face with the same gentleness, his lips heated with the same desire . . . but his eyes. Something in his eyes had changed. His lashes dipped lower as their lips locked. She could barely see the rich, dark hue of mahogany aged to a glossy patina, but she saw enough to wonder if he even saw her now. Before she could fully collect her thoughts, he slid more fully over her, into her, and she lost her thoughts entirely as his mouth slid away, raining kisses down her chin and neck, sliding to her ear where his breath whispered in soft, heated puffs. In slow, animated motion, he carried them into a rhythm, rising and falling, drawing her toward him and slipping away.

Something had changed. Everything had changed.

At a base level, she suffered the conflicts inside of him, and for the first time since he'd kissed her near the door, she wondered if she was making a mistake. Too late. Far too late to consider stopping. Rising and falling, ripples of excitement and desire flooded through her, driving her to match his rhythm and meet him toward the peak of release.

No turning back, not for her or for him. Something had changed. Everything had changed. Whether to be free of her desire or to free him from his intensity, Jenna wanted it over and drove more fiercely against him, demanding an end, driving him toward his release. No regrets. With wild abandon, she took him completely and held him, looking into his murky gaze and seeing the strange bright light within the darkness of his eyes. He was there, looking into her, and she saw his confusion, his distress as they shuddered together, riding the waves of fulfillment.

His breath lurched as he sank over her, with her. His face ducked into her hair scattered on the pillows, his arms pressed against her ribs with his hands locked under and over her shoulders. Trembling. Her breath stifled in soft heaves, she drew in the scent of his cologne, the soft musk sweat and salt on her lips against his neck. Her arms quick about his ribs, her palms at his back, she rode his quivering muscles and hammering heartbeat. Confusion touched her mind only as the whispered words reached her scattered thoughts, soft words uttered and laced with a deep well of pain to penetrate her core.

"I'm sorry . . . I'm so sorry, Luv."

He trembled, now. A desperate note strained his whispering voice against her ear, and she understood only a need to hold him more tightly, to comfort him. Of all the reactions she might have anticipated, to hear the heartbreak in his voice and feel the tremors through him hadn't once crossed her mind. He was an artist, a practiced artisan in this endeavor. Never had another touched her in so many places or driven her to such heights, and yet, he sounded desperate, sounded hurt. Her hand slipped over her shoulder, finding his hair, holding his head as he continued breathing in soft panted breaths at her ear.

The hurt and sadness she'd seen in his eyes lingered in his voice now. If he were a lesser man, he would be sobbing against her with the deep ache of pain she heard and sensed in him. Instead, he held her more firmly against him. Their heartbeats joined, hammering. As if she were an anchor, he held onto her against a torrent of whatever torment wracked him.

He was hurt and desperate, and her revelation made no sense in her mind, not computing or comparing to the image she held of him, a leader and power in his own right. How was it possible? He was the epitome of male charisma and confidence. Other men bowed to him. Women melted at his feet. How could he feel so hurt and sound so distressed after what they'd just shared? How . . . how could he sound so tortured with regret?

Was his regret for her? Did he think she would regret making love to him?

Her thoughts racing, Jenna remembered offering him the couch, remembered countering his subtle advances. Did he hold himself to blame for breaking her defenses? Did he feel responsible for breaching her moral code? Did he believe she would demand more of him than this single night?

A smile played on her lips. She turned her head enough to capture his ear. "No regrets," she whispered to him. "We only had tonight. And that's okay." That she might never share a more wondrous experience again sent a pang of sorrow into her mind, but she withheld the heartache, refusing to consider the impact of this single night. She would make love to him again, right now, if she thought it was possible. Nothing—no one would ever compare. They had tonight, and that would need to be enough . . . and maybe he grasped that as well.

"I . . . I have to go," he whispered in a strained low voice.

"I know," she answered softly, withholding the ache of sorrow threatening her voice. As much as she wanted to hold him, keep him in her arms where he fit as if molded to her body, she knew better than to consider the possibility. Tonight. A stolen stopped moment in time. She'd known hours ago, had made the decision hours ago to share this night with him regardless of all the reasons she should have steered clear. He wasn't a man with whom she could share a lifetime. In the morning, he could be gone . . . and she couldn't afford to prolong this parting, not for him or for her.

"If I could hold you like this—" *Forever.*

Nothing he could have said would have stirred greater conflict. That wasn't a practiced line. Not a byline offered out of hand to any number of women in his black book. The ache in his voice resounded, as desperate and sincere as his apology. He'd felt something more, something deeper than a one-night fling. "You better go," she whispered, not sure how much longer she could restrain her sorrow or cling to her practical nature. Whatever this strange connection to him, this fierce attraction to him, he shared it . . . and consummating this bond might have been a mistake. If he stayed much longer, she might never let him go.

He rose hesitantly, lifting, shifting, easing off her and onto his side, and his eyes came to her, damp and wounded. "I—"

Jenna touched her fingers to his lips and looked into his eyes, suffering a sting at the fringe of her focus. She shook her head slightly, whispering, "No regrets, Darius."

His hand slipped between them, and he caught her fingers, brushing a kiss on her fingertips. With the dark intensity returned to his eyes, he spoke quietly, "No matter what happens, Luv, no matter what comes between us . . . know that what you've given me tonight was more than I could have ever hoped for. And more than I have ever had. I-I can't explain that, Luv, any more than I can explain why I've been in love with you since I saw you standing in the dining room . . . but it's true. If . . . if things were different, I'd never let you go. I-I didn't mean for this to happen tonight . . . or ever. I never wanted to feel like this, never wanted to involve anyone, much less another I loved . . . and it's too blasted late. I have fallen for you, and that's dangerous . . . for you and for me."

If not for the haunted note in his deep voice, she might be thrilled to hear and recognize the integrity of his words. Instead, a prickle lifted at her nape. He was being stalked . . . and she understood the warning and fear in his eyes.

"Things . . . so many things are beyond my control," he continued softly. "And I truly can't explain any of this . . . just know that I love you. That I will always love you." He leaned and brushed a kiss on her lips, then lifted in one motion, turning from her as he rose.

The words meant goodbye, and with every ounce of willpower, Jenna refrained from speaking any counterwords. She watched him collect his pants and nearly felt the wall rising around him as he stepped into the black cloth.

Pushing to his feet, he kept his back to her. By the time he half-turned, a black curtain had dropped over his dark eyes.

In a firm chilly tone, he ordered, "Don't open the door to anyone, Jenna. Promise me. If anyone demands to enter, ring my room next door. I truly don't know who among us is friend or foe, and until I know, neither of us is truly safe."

"I . . . understand," she said quietly.

His gaze held her a moment more before he nodded and turned, walking toward the door. In the entrance, he hesitated and looked back at her, his expression a study of determination. "When I leave, you'll need to lock the deadbolt. I'll set a chair by the door. Wedge it under the handle."

"Will you take similar precautions?" she asked, rising onto her forearm.

"I'll take precautions," he said and turned through the door.

Sliding across the bed, she pushed to her feet and veered to the bathroom to collect a towel. By the time she reached the doorway, he stood tucking his shirttails and pulling himself into a facsimile of order. He glanced over then sped a quick double take, and his gaze skimming downward. With an effort, he dragged his focus away and fumbled, sliding into his jacket and stepping into his shoes. Without consciously making the decision, Jenna strode to him, and he froze as she stopped in front of him. "You're upset," she said quietly, catching the dark shine.

"Slightly," he admitted. "This shouldn't have happened. I've jeopardized your life more than I care to consider. For that, I am dreadfully sorry."

"I'm not," she said firmly and clasped his hand, holding him within her gaze and seeing the emotions fleeting in his eyes. "I don't understand what I feel for you. I know you're not the kind of man who could settle down, and I thought that mattered at first. It doesn't," she said quietly. "No matter what happens, my door's open, Darius. If you ever want to see me again, you'll know where to find me."

"This . . . it's not fair to you, Jenna," he said while squeezing her hand gently, the sadness spilling through his dark eyes. "You deserve more than I could ever give you. You deserve a lifetime and that's something I can never offer you."

"I wanted tonight with you, and you gave me that," she said quietly. "Don't apologize. What we shared was too good to regret."

"You . . . are far too good for me," he said and tugged her gently to rest against him, wrapping his arms about her. Against her ear, he whispered softly, painfully, "I am damned, Luv, and I fear I've already damned you as well. For me, there's no way out, but I swear to the almighty, if there's any way to keep you safe, I'll find it." He held her a moment more and brushed a kiss on her cheek as he lifted, looking at her intently. "Lock the door when I leave . . . and trust no one, Luv."

When she nodded, he turned and lifted one of the armchairs, carrying it to the door with him. He looked at her only after he pulled on his coat and there was no mistaking the silent command in his eyes, or the implication in his final words.

Trust no one. Not even him.

20

Halfheartedly listening to Wharton's angry recital and lecture, Darius stood at the glass doors to the balcony, watching the night, while sipping a tall tumbler of brandy. He had more than enough on his mind without worrying about annoying or aggravating the FBI. A serial killer, Wharton had stated, while pointing out the dangers of Darius's stunt in Canton. According to the specialists in the Federal Bureau, they were dealing with a serial killer, and sooner rather than later, the maniac would come after Darius directly.

"Like it or not, this maniac could be coming out of your personal affairs," Wharton stated. "We have people checking into your business associates in all the major cities. We need to know more about your private life, Mr. Brock."

If only life could be so simple. If only Darius had attracted the attention of some purely human lunatic. Nothing could be that easy in his life, and the FBI remained the least of his concerns. Nowhere was safe. Not from the enemy. Not from the Baron von Hendricks. Sooner rather than later, one or the other would come in for the kill. Darius could feel the countdown toward an end, his end. He needed only to think about those moments inside the bridal suite to know how close he'd come to his demise. Uncontrollably, his muscles gripped with the memory of his cousin's glazed eyes . . . and his own lost seconds inside that room. The Baron had taken control. With a mere voice over the telephone, the Baron had slid into Darius's mind and taken control. Possibly to save his life . . . but neither comfort nor relief accompanied that thought. Not since standing in the receiving room of the von Hendricks castle had Darius felt more vulnerable than at this moment.

As the revelation had dawned when standing in that collection of his confused kinsmen, the revelation struck now. His life, as he knew it, was about to end. No other explanation, no other alternative existed.

In a paradox, Darius stood scanning the white haze through the glass. He'd wanted nothing more than to lose himself in Jenna's warmth, nothing more than to make love to her as a free man . . . but he wouldn't have stolen that pleasure and taken that liberty of his own free will. His vow. His oath. The Covenant. He would have stopped. Too many lives were at risk. Not even for a woman as magnificent as Jenna Windrow would Darius have risked breaking the Covenant and defying the Baron. He would have stopped and gladly suffered the humiliation of spilling his seeds in the sheets. By no mercy, the Baron had stripped him of self-control and forced him to continue. Mercy was no part of the Baron's nature. An omen, a sign. In those final seconds of copulation, Darius had realized the significance and understood the implication. His mission. His single purpose for which the Baron had spared him these past eight years had come to an end. Children . . . healthy male children had been born. As the Baron had promised, the Brock clan would perpetuate and prosper into the new century . . . Unless some damn fool broke his oath.

Whether that was a blessing or the greater curse, Darius had never decided. Too often, he regretted his service. As long as male Brock's existed, the curse would hover over the clan. But even as he considered that detail, he thought of the death toll.

Hundreds . . . literally hundreds had died. Accidents, suicides . . . spontaneous violence ending in death. Entire families had died in auto accidents and fires. To him, they'd been strangers. Even as he'd read about the accident on the Autobon where two entire families were lost in a single crash, the names had meant nothing. George Halbrook . . . the scribe, the historian, the genealogist who'd inherited the position to record the Brock lines . . .

Lost in thought, Darius remembered the moments inside the von Hendricks fortress. Days. Only a few days had passed since that fateful night. The Baron had kept all of them within the castle for several days, watching them, tormenting them, and letting them adjust to their new stations. Darius remembered those first days . . . remembered hovering over the desk where George Halbrook had huddled. Stacks of leather-bound tomes, some as much as three or four hundred years old, occupied every available space. Rather than the taste of brandy on his tongue, Darius caught the scent of ancient parchment and leather. The room where George would come to spend his life was undersized. The aroma was overwhelming within the windowless room. Tears had glistened on the portly cheeks. His eyes, behind window-pane lenses, were red and swollen with tears. Darius had felt no sorrow for the scholar. Only hatred . . .

'Why Dylan, George? Why my son?' That single question had brought Darius into George's compact cell. 'Why did you take my son?'

Gray head bowed, his stout frame trembling, George had huddled like a bird with its feathers ruffled against the cold. 'I didn't know what else to dooo, Darius . . . I didn't know any other way . . . I didn't believe . . . you have to believe me, I never believed any of this was real. I never would have hurt him . . . never meant to hurt anyone.'

'Why Dylan?' Darius had asked again, his fists locked in his jeans pocket if only to keep from wringing the stout neck. 'Why did you choose my son? There were others, goddamn you. You could have chosen a dozen others. Why did you take my child?'

For a long moment, the man could only stare at his open ledger, one of the newer registers if the pristine leather binding was an indication. Darius had glimpsed it, as well. Names, dates, columns of births and deaths . . . so many new dates in that latter column. Entire families . . . George had lost his brother, sister-in-law, niece, and nephew. All were lost in a house fire for which the authorities had no explanation. 'Your . . . your father,' George had said finally.

No other explanation was necessary. His father. A drunk. A derelict . . . a lowlife. For the sins of his father, for his own sins, Darius knew his son had been chosen, considered expendable . . .

Shaking his head absently, Darius caught up to Wharton's litany.

". . . I'm personally responsible for your safety, and I have no intention of hunting for you every time you decide to take a detour. If this happens again, or if you disregard my orders, I won't have any choice. For your own safety, I'll recommend revoking your visa and have you flown out of the country. In fact, for the record, I've already made that recommendation, and you should know, it's under consideration. No one wants an international incident."

"I'd imagine that's a legitimate concern," Darius said lightly and leaned against the door frame, turning enough to catch the man's heated gaze. "If I die on American soil, it could be a bit of a sticky wicket."

"I'm just saying—"

"You've made your point," Darius cut in. "It's late. I'm tired. I have no intention of departing in the immediate future. If you'd like to post guards in the hall, feel free."

Wharton looked as if he might like to say something more, then changed his mind, deciding, "I'll do that. And if you have any intention of departing, immediately or otherwise, I suggest you contact me in advance."

"Certainly," Darius said indifferently, holding the man's gaze another moment before drifting his attention through the glass. Doubtful he would need to worry about offering anyone advance warning. He had a feeling, a very bad feeling that his life was about to change again. The clock was ticking. A countdown had begun. Whether he would be changed physically or merely mentally remained the single mystery.

Halfheartedly, he considered how easily the Baron had stepped into his mind, wondered not for the first time if he'd already lost his humanness. He'd seen it done before. He'd watched as the Baron had taken control of others, forcing them to his bidding, had seen them wake from the trance without a conscious memory of what had been done to them or what they'd done. The Baron might have changed him years ago and suppressed that memory, allowing him to believe he held dominion over his mind and body. Perhaps, he'd worried these many years for nothing. It was possible, too damned possible, that the Baron had allowed him to consider himself free of the contaminant and let him believe he acted solely on his honor and volition.

Freedom to believe himself free.

Darius could imagine the Baron taking pleasure from that grand jest.

A genuine change or an awakening into the darker realm of the Baron's service, those were the only options for Darius's immediate future . . . and in an odd moment, Darius simply wanted it over. One way or another, he wanted the clock to run out, wanted the confrontation ended, the worry finished . . . And that was probably a mistake. For the pure hell of it, the Baron could prolong the inevitable. An end, any end, would be merciful, and Darius knew better than to beg for mercy.

Jenna.

His promise . . . to protect her.

Pushing off the doorframe, he paused long enough to draw the drapes, then strode to the couch, lifting the receiver off the phone as he settled onto the cushion. Only one way could he protect her. Punching in the room number, he leaned back and forced himself calm. She answered on the second ring, wide awake despite the hour. "I've found the only means to keep you safe, Luv," he said without preamble.

"What's happened?" she asked as if she heard the dread he attempted to mask.

"Nothing of significance, but what I'm about to suggest . . .? If there was another way, Luv, I'd take it," he said carefully. "I don't know how to explain enough of this for you to fully realize the danger. I will ask only that you trust me and do as I say despite how incredible and drastic this may seem." He paused only a second, hearing, feeling her doubt in the silence. "Do you have any ready cash available? Savings accounts? Checking accounts?"

"Yes, both," she said quietly.

"I . . . need you to disappear for a time, Luv," he advised. "And I do mean disappear. Take only cash. Don't use credit cards or banks. Don't check into hotels. Don't tell anyone where you're going. Don't take your car or borrow any vehicle which could be traced to you. For a time . . . hopefully only a short time, you must break all ties and connections to your current life. Don't visit or speak with family members or close friends. Don't tell them where you're going or when you'll be back. If you have someone—a distant friend, an untraceable friend—"

"I don't understand, Darius. What's—"

"I told you in the car, my enemy has a great deal of financial freedom and influence, Jenna. I need you to think about that and take it fully into consideration. This chap can enlist Federal agents in an attempt to find you, and I have reason to believe, he will try to find you if only to get to me." He barely finished the words when a prickle lifted at the nape of his neck, and his gaze slid toward the door. Something. Someone coming. "I ehm . . . I have to go, Luv," he said distractedly, his muscles reacting involuntarily, stiffening. "Do as I say, Jenna. Leave as soon as you can, and get to your bank as soon as it opens." As she spoke his name, he lowered the receiver, his gaze still on the door. Something . . . he felt something.

Pushing off the couch, he moved toward the door, his senses keening. He heard the weight shift on the floorboards and listened for the voices. No voices. He remembered standing inside the bridal suite, facing his blank-eyed cousin . . . a federal agent outside the door. He should have been safe inside that damned room. Right. Safe. A scratch or bite, a split second of eye-contact could enthrall any fully human man and hold him still for the taking and changing. Nowhere was safe.

If this enemy decided to come in for the kill, there was little hope for survival . . . but that wasn't how this game would be played. By these creatures' very nature, they would prolong the sport and take it to the limit. If this opponent was, as Darius suspected, of the Baron's ilk, the maniac would keep circling, playing.

Two years. For two blasted years, this maniac had been playing, and the Baron had probably known it for at least that long.

Muttering a curse, Darius strode to the bar and routed through the bottles, finding another bourbon. As he finished pouring a glass, another shiver slid down his spine, and his attention riveted toward the door . . . something was definitely circling, stalking.

In a cold sweat, Jenna bolted awake, halfway off the couch before she stifled the cry on her parted lips. Darius! She saw him, his image as clear in her mind as the armchair four steps away. Dead. He rested in a slumped heap against the base of the chair, his head rolled, propped at an angle to see slivers of glazed brown eyes beneath thick lashes. He wasn't alone. Shaded, as if a clever photographer had faded the background, she saw only Darius within a shroud of blackness, knew only a sense of human dominion surrounding him, hovering over him.

Dead. His arms and legs scattered in a crumbled tangle. One arm extended as if hanging on or reaching for his assailant. In slow motion, a film turning at its lowest speed, she watched his head rolling, his mustached lips parted, his jaw unhinged. For an instant, his lashes fluttered, a spark of life to start her heart beating again.

Insanity!

Heaving a breath, sinking into the couch cushion, Jenna shuddered from head to toe and drew her arms about herself, closing her eyes. A dream! A nightmare! Just another horrible nightmare driven by the sludge collecting in her subconscious. Darius was fine. He had to be fine. They were surrounded by Federal Agents. He was safe. Probably asleep. Shivering, she drew herself partway up and looked at the telephone. How many times had she done that? How many times in the past hour or two had she snapped awake and stifled a need to phone him? The sense of dread lingered, a sense of danger pulsing at the edges of her mind.

A man had died only two doors away . . . died horribly with hundreds of people within shouting distance. In freeze-frame, Jenna saw Lawrence Fradden slumped in the armchair, his head and body askew . . . but it was Darius's face flashing neon in her mind.

"No, damn it," she snapped and pushed off the couch, pacing.

Like all the suites on the top floor, this one offered all the amenities expected by the upper class, from the small island bar equipped with complimentary bottles to the small coffeemaker with packets of gourmet brand coffee. If only to offset her panic, Jenna collected the pot and strode through the rooms with a sense of purpose. In the bathroom, she muttered another curse. Making coffee didn't warrant the concentration of a rocket scientist but she caught herself filling the pot, spilling several drops into the sink, checking the water level against the fill line . . . adding another splash, checking, adding.

Organization and order . . . those were her stock in trade. Uniformity and conformity ran a close second.

Emptying her bank account and setting out on foot . . . slinging a backpack over her shoulder and sticking out her thumb? No charge cards. No rented cars. A bus ticket? Did he fully expect her to slip away from the Federal Bureau and try her brand of the government witness program? Disappear?

In theory, she understood his reasoning. If she vanished without a trace, whoever stalked him wouldn't find her . . . but in principle, the entire idea was absurd. Considering his intelligence, only two explanations existed. Either he was insane or desperate, and Jenna leaned toward the latter.

Something had happened in Canton.

Pouring the water in the pot and emptying the coffee packet into the filter, Jenna replayed the scenes in Canton for the millionth time, refusing to be sidetracked by how good he looked in a suit, how smooth he moved through a crowd. Very few intimacies had passed between them. They'd ridden for nearly two hours, chatting about little to nothing. They'd sat through dinner and festivities, resting less than a hand-length apart throughout most of the meal. He'd remained attentive, introducing her when necessary, including her in conversations if only by a flash of his dark eyes or brush of his hand on her shoulder. If she hadn't sensed something slightly deeper inside of him, she might have wondered if he'd chosen her rather than enlist an escort service. They'd spent nearly five hours together in that crowd, and he hadn't offered any sign that she was more than an attractive addition to warm his arm. If they'd returned in the limo, how much of those latter moments would have come to pass?

They hadn't returned in the limo. She remembered dancing with Agent Ryan, remembered the man warning her to remain at the fringe of the crowd. Across the room, she'd spotted Darius. He'd received a note or message, then he and Agent Matlin had departed for a short time.

Something had happened during that absence. He'd returned with a slightly swollen lip and an intensity in his mahogany eyes. In retrospect, she remembered the rush to depart from the hall, although, at the time, it seemed natural. He wasn't a man to dawdle once he determined his course. They'd nearly reached the limo doors when he switched gears in mid-stride, deciding first to drive . . . and she remembered a strangeness about the driver. Having spent enough time mingling in the company of wealthy patrons, Jenna knew how the working class deferred to the eccentricities of the privileged few. Under other circumstances, Jenna could imagine Darius reacting purely to his arrogance and finding another mode of travel. One does not deny a client of Darius Brock's stature, not if one values his occupation. With the memory of that agent adding to the fiasco by nearly growling his command to get in the car, Jenna shivered.

All wrong. That entire ordeal had been wrong, and Darius had known it, had admitted as much in the car, suggesting his apparent adversary possessed the financial means and clout to enlist assistance . . . even government agents.

Not for the first time, Jenna wondered what she'd gotten herself into, and the thought of what they'd shared in this room offered neither relief . . . nor regrets. Making love to him had been too . . . incredible to regret and to blazes with being practical or righteous. She hadn't made love to him to climb a corporate ladder or advance her social status. If an explanation existed, it lay in the primal instincts dictating male and female mating rituals. He was, without a doubt, the most attractive, physically alluring man she'd ever met. A work of art in erotica, and every bit as capable as he appeared. If she could live those moments again, she wouldn't change a thing. She'd known when he moved toward her. She'd seen the desire unmasked in his eyes, flaming with a wary shine, a primal shine. That look alone had blasted any doubts from her mind. He'd wanted her, needed her the same way a caged lion needed freedom. In setting him free, she'd found her own freedom. If she suffered any regrets, those lay in her current inability to recall every detail. Like riding a roller coaster or a fast horse, the sights had blurred, leaving only an impression of the excitement and thrill of the ride. Never . . . not in ten years of experience with men, had Jenna ever experienced anything to compare with those lost moments. He was a master, an artist . . . and at the same time, there'd come a moment when his mahogany eyes had lighted with surprise as if waking to something new, something incredible.

Shaking her head, she fumbled with a coffee cup and powdered creamer, reacting automatically to the sputtering coffeemaker in front of her.

He was in trouble. The sense of danger crept over her mind, tingling her spine. A maniac stalking him, killing people around him. The FBI had believed him a killer.

Her thoughts snagged, remembering Wharton in her dining room, asking her to help them, to get close to him. Of all the people who'd been inside that room, people who'd apparently known Darius for years, the FBI had come to her . . . and claimed to know he was attracted to her. Because of two dances? Because they'd chatted over dinner and drinks . . . talked about nothing of importance. She remembered considering Wharton an idiot and doubted she'd ever see Darius again, much less gain the opportunity to get close to him. Yet, only a few hours later, he'd arrived at her door. Hours later, almost offhandedly, like an afterthought, he'd invited her to his cousin's wedding reception.

In the limousine, they'd shared talk and . . . and she'd fallen in love with his half smile, the spark in his dark eyes when a genuine touch of humor emerged.

God. She had it bad.

What was it? A masochistic streak unbeknownst to her before this moment? With all the men in the world, with all the decent, basically sound males available, how was it even possible that she could fall for the only man who remained entirely beyond her reach? What was it? Not merely his physical appeal. She'd known dozens of handsome men, including at least two reasonably famous actors who'd lent her a second and third glance. No, not looks, though he suffered no lack in that department. What then? Power? Without a doubt, he was a powerful man. Financially, socially . . . physically. He moved with an unerring confidence and strength, arrogant and elegant, like a mountain cat on the prowl. Personality? His easy smiles and laughs in a crowd didn't count as personality. Alone in the dining room, he'd been less dramatic, a touch catty, a little reserved but still wearing the front of a happy-go-lucky executive. A front. Alone in her dining room . . . quieter, more reserved and pensive. He was a man with a great deal on his mind . . . and a great deal hidden behind his quick, dark eyes and arrogant smiles.

His sadness. The sadness behind that mask had touched her, reached inside of her, and touched her even now . . . And she knew why she'd fallen in love with that smile and spark. That was the man behind the mask. In isolated seconds, she'd glimpsed the man who'd been Darius Brock before a divorce, before giving up his son for adoption, before becoming the corporate executive who spent more time in the air than on the ground. Whatever the circumstances behind his rise to status, she sensed his unhappiness with his current lifestyle . . . and that sadness had existed before the murder down the hall or the awareness of a killer within his circle of acquaintances.

Unfortunately, nothing in her thoughts or revelations improved her current situation. He wanted her to disappear, to vanish, from her life, from his life, indefinitely. He hadn't even hinted at how long she should remain gone, no mention of meeting at some other time. Just leave and don't come back. Don't phone family or close friends. Just go away and stay gone . . .

Until news of the killer's capture became a media circus? Was that an implied understanding? Had he left it to her discretion, her intelligence to judge how long she should remain invisible? To wait for that sign?

Impossible. Even if she believed the idea was feasible, she couldn't do it, wouldn't, which was exactly what she would tell him in the morning. She wasn't walking away from this, from him, knowing, sensing the very real danger hovering around him. Whether they would ever share another moment of intimacy made no difference. She'd known last night, she wouldn't come between him and his life, wouldn't ask him to choose. She wanted no more than what they'd already shared. A single night of bliss.

Naive, by no means, Jenna refused to romance any notion of a long-term relationship with a man who probably harbored a woman in every port. She would slip from his life when the time came, would let him go without strings attached . . . but by God, she wouldn't walk away until she knew he was safe.

If he believed otherwise, he had another thought coming.

Carrying her coffee, she strode to the couch, again glancing at the phone. More than anything, she wanted to dial his room and hear his voice. The silence in the room, a near duplicate of the room where Lawrence Fradden had met his end, sent a tiny shiver down her spine. She should have asked him to stay with her, should have asked to stay with him. Sitting alone, even with the doors locked and braced, offered no blasted relief. Maybe she should have tried out the terrified female routine, which wouldn't have been too difficult to fake. She was scared. For herself, for him, for all the others who might be caught unaware as easily as Lawrence Fradden.

The sense of something stalking through the hotel, possibly hunting another victim, sent another shiver through her limbs. Someone else was going to die. She knew it. Felt it. Sensed it on every level and never cursed her unruly sixth sense more than at this moment .

21

S howered, dressed, and too awake to consider lying down, Darius paced inside the compact room that seemed smaller than usual. If this were a normal night in his unnatural life, he would be cruising the damned city searching for an after-hours club if only to find an illusion of companionship. Nights. Between the middle of the night and dawn, that was the worst time of the twenty-four-hour stretches. And this was ridiculous! If this was a countdown to his end, if a bloody monster awaited around the corner to attack . . . he'd made love to Jenna. His vow was already broken by no fault of his own.

Without a conscious decision, he reached the telephone, lifted the receiver, and punched the room numbers. Heart skipping a beat, he waited through two rings before the soft voice erupted, lifting a quiver on his lips. "Are you awake?"

"Yes." More awake.

"Good. I'll be over," he decided and replaced the receiver, striding toward the door without a second thought. Sanctioned. For whatever reason the Baron had allowed him to breach the rules, the rules were broken, and only a damn fool would look a gift horse in the mouth. As Darius opened the door, the agent rose from his leaning pose and nearly stepped into the doorway. "So sorry. Didn't mean to wake you," Darius said with mild sarcasm and sidestepped around the agent, striding toward the second agent less than a dozen feet away. Without more than a glance at the more curious man, Darius rapped his knuckles on the wood and heard the rattle of the door handle and drag of the chair legs. She'd followed his directions. Damned futile directions, but not nearly as foolish as the latter set of directions and solution he'd offered.

"Darius?" she asked through the door.

"Yes," he verified and heard the clatter of the deadbolt. Smart lady, this Jenna Windrow. As the door started opening, he drank in the long, shadowy length of her, scanning the same sexy dress he'd removed a short time ago. She'd taken a shower in the interim. He caught the fresh, flowered scent and locked her gaze as he moved forward.

Once was not enough. Once would never be enough. And if he was headed for hell, he might as bloody well have a good reason. He stopped in front of her, caught her hip, and slid his other hand to the nape of her neck, capturing her parting startled lips under his own. Warm current, an anxious breath, she relaxed under his touch, and his senses swam with the heat of her response. Lifting, he looked into her deep blue eyes. "Come back to my room with me?"

"Alright," she agreed.

Smiling slowly, he clasped her hand, keeping her in his gaze as he nudged the door with his foot and backed them into the ancient hallway. She wasn't the type to tease or play coy. Her eyes carried an intensity, a desire to match his. Once was not enough. Not for her either, if her soft smile and flush were any indication. Ignoring the agent who followed them and the other who stepped aside at the door, Darius maintained his handhold while unlatching the door and ushering her inside ahead of him.

Freedom. Freedom to believe himself free . . . for one night.

Inside the door with the deadbolt fastened, he looked down at her. Restraint. With a fleeting thought of how he had lost himself in those first seconds inside her room, he held himself in check. Normalcy. A date? He hadn't entertained a woman, engaged in a natural mating ritual in so blasted long . . . "Can I get you a drink?"

"A . . . glass of wine," she decided, apparently humoring his belated attempt at civility. At the corner of her lips, a slight smile quivered, and he nearly lost himself again as her amusement quickened, crinkling the corner of her eyes.

Backward, entirely backward, this touch of sophistication, and by her stifled smile, she was attuned to his blundering. With an effort, Darius withdrew and turned, moving behind the bar, his gaze darting to find her following, arriving at the counter across from him. In the lamplight, her hair glittered bronze in flips and sparkles to enhance the shine in her livid eyes. She was stunning. As relaxed and confident in her sexuality as she was in business, a touch of genuine class held him nearly enthralled as he reached absently for the wine and glasses. Whether he wanted to make love to her again or merely stand and admire her, reveling in the light that seemed to glow around her, he couldn't decide. Not another woman had ever captured him so completely, so deeply. Keeping his hands off, keeping his distance over these past three days had ranked among his most difficult undertakings. He wanted . . . wanted just to know her. Damned fool, he knew the improbability, the impossibility. They would never share that much time together . . . but she wasn't a tumble and walk away.

"What are you thinking?" she asked quietly.

"That you are the most incredible woman I've ever had the pleasure to meet," he said and darted his gaze to finish pouring the wine. Setting the bottle aside, he lifted both glasses and circled the pillar to join her on the receiving side of the counter, delivering the glass into her hand. "I owe you an apology."

"No, you don't."

He nodded, entirely sober. "The way I've treated you . . . it's unforgivable, and I am sorry. I can only admit, I haven't felt this way about any woman in so long . . . I truly don't even know how to apologize."

"Why don't we start over," she said with a soft smile, understanding in her eyes. "Things . . . everything's been moving so fast the past few days. Tonight, it just seemed like a natural progression."

He lifted his hand, brushing the back of his fingers over her cheek, recording every soft curve and nuance of her lovely face. How had it happened? What was it about this stunning woman that touched him? He'd met beautiful women. He'd crossed paths with thousands of women all over the world, but none had ever reached inside of him with a glance or a smile. None had ever turned his world on its ear and his heart inside out. "If I had a lifetime to spend with you, it would be too short," he said quietly. "But I truly can't even offer you that, Luv."

"To the here and now?" she suggested and lifted her glass, holding his gaze.

"To the here and now," he agreed and touched her glass, taking only a sip of his wine without lifting his gaze. She was doing it again, looking into him, and he couldn't pull away, wanted not to pull away. He hadn't felt closer, more connected to another . . . not in his lifetime, not before the Baron, not after.

She clasped his hand, keeping his gaze as she turned.

Accepting her lead, he followed her to the couch and settled into the corner, content to watch her ease down to rest beside him. She slipped off only one shoe and turned sideways, one leg folding under the other. His gaze distracted to the slender limb, but as he reached, her free hand caught his fingers, halting him and drawing his attention to her eyes.

"There's something we need to talk about," she said quietly, soberly.

Probably more than one thing, he knew and nodded slightly, waiting.

"I thought about what you suggested on the phone, Darius, and I've decided, I can't do it. Won't—"

He parted his lips, intending to agree. His better judgment and common sense kicked in. He couldn't protect her by sending her away alone. Before he could speak, she continued hurriedly.

"I don't know if my staying will help or hinder," she stated. "I just know I can't leave you to handle this alone. And don't take that wrong. I've seen you in action. I know you didn't rise to your position by being careless or inefficient. If anyone can stop this apparent psychopath, you can. I just can't take off for parts unknown while knowing that your life could be in danger, and please don't ask me to explain that, Darius. I know we just met. I know I have no right to feel this way about you . . . I don't expect any commitment or strings," she said candidly. "But the fact remains, I need to be here with you, for you, for as long as we have."

"I . . . reached a similar conclusion," he said quietly. "As much as I thought I could protect you by putting distance between us, I realized the absurdity. You . . . you truly don't know the extent of the danger, here, and I doubt I could even explain it fully. That's . . . probably one of the reasons I brought you here," he said honestly. "As much as it grieves me to admit, I've decided the only way I can even attempt to keep you safe, is to keep you close. If I live to regret this, I will live in hell, but I must ask you, Luv . . . stay with me?"

For a long moment, she studied him, searching him intently before she spoke softly, "There's so much sadness in you."

Her words hit him hard, the truth of such a simple statement driving an ache across his mind and through his chest. His gaze listed off her too-perceptive gaze, fanning the room. "No more than in any others, I'd imagine."

Her grip firmed, drawing him to the warm understanding in her eyes, a disheartened curve in her lips. "I will stay with you, Darius."

Drawn, he started to lean toward her, lifting their gripped hands.

The telephone blasted, amplified in the silence, startling and gripping him in an instant panic. The Baron! Another trance! Pivoting his gaze, he stared at the harmless instrument that appeared as dangerous and lethal as a coiled snake. No choice. He had no choice. Ignoring that ring could not bode well for his future . . . but the countdown. It rang again, jolting his coiled muscles.

Fear. Cold, incontestable fear spilled down his spine. No choice. One does not ignore the summons of Baron von Hendricks, not if he wants to survive a few more days. Tense, he freed his hand and reached, never dreading his actions more. Pulling the receiver to his ear, he spoke in a dead calm. "Yes?"

"Darius!" the voice shouted, a cry of panic and hysteria to lurch Darius physically. Reflexively, he snapped the receiver away, then back to his ear on Raphael's second cry. "Darrriuuus!"

"I'm here!" Darius stated, riveted, attuned to the sob and terror in the young voice. "What's wrong? What's happened?"

"Was awfulll!" Raphael cried, half-screamed. "Hoorrriblle!"

"What? What, lad?" Darius asked, his neck prickling and muscles gripping. Unconsciously, he leaned forward as if he would spring to his feet. "What's happened?"

"I sssaww it! On the telly!" Raphael cried and whined. "Awwefull! Horrible!" he shouted with a rising edge akin to anger now. "Aunt Rebecca laaaughed a mee! She laughed! Oogly! Oogly. Ooooogllly!" he cried with a return to natural fright.

"Slow down, lad," Darius said carefully despite his hammering heartbeat. "What ehm . . . what was ugly?"

"Where are you!" Raphael demanded.

"Lad, you phoned me," Darius reminded him gently. The lad was definitely in a state.

"Oh," he said, heaving a ragged breath before snapping. "Why! Why are you still there! You shouldn't bee there!"

"What did you see, Raphael?" Darius asked carefully, knowing the boy's temper could shift in a blink. He could almost feel the li'l devil's rise toward sobs and lingering tremors. "What was so horrible?"

"Th-they p-poot a ssstake in him," Raphael stammered and whined. "Th-they're gonna come after mmmeee next! I'm knoowing it! I saw them! They're coomin for mee next! Am I oogly?" he pleaded and demanded. "Am I, Darius? Am I oogly like all the oothers? Do you think sooo?"

"No, lad," Darius said, only beginning to grasp the child's fright.

"You asked mee!" he cried angrily. "Why did you ask me aboot the oothers? Why did you make me watch aboot the oothers! I don't like you anymore! I hate you, Darius! You're cruel! Cruel and mean as all oothers! You made me watch! Asked me aboot the others. The hunters! They'll coome for me next," he whined in a lowering tempo, a more lamenting tone. "I'm doomed. They'll coome here after me. Pappa's away. Aunt Rebecca willnae save me. She'll let them. She'll watch them drag me to the blooff and drive the stakes in my hands. Aye, then my chest. The sun will coome up then, and they'll be nae more than ashes left to me."

The pain and fear in the young voice carried through the line, and Darius battled his emotions to think, to work out the rising and falling litany. "What . . . what were you watching, lad? Will you tell me, now?"

"Aye," the morose voice uttered, and Darius held the receiver tighter, closer to his ear. "Was aboot us. Aboot pappa and me. Vampires . . . that's what they call us boot . . . boot the ones they showed on the telly . . . oogly. Do I get ooogly, Darius? Am I as oogly as those ones on the television? Aunt Rebecca . . . she says I'm handsome boot she's a liar. All people are liars. Horrible liars. Dinnae lie to me, Darius," the voice lamented, downtrodden, depressed, and resigned. "I cain take it. Tell me . . . am I an oogly thing like the oothers?"

"Will you believe me, lad? If I tell you the truth, will you trust me?"

"Aye, maybe," Raphael grumbled.

"You are the most handsome li'l imp I've ever had the pleasure to know," Darius said honestly and woke suddenly to the woman seated at his side, listening. No matter. This was Raphael, and Raphael needed him. "I wouldn't lie to you, lad—"

"Soomeone's . . . there with you," the words came deftly. "Who, Darius?" the voice animated slightly, interest overriding his emotions. "Who's this with you?"

"A friend, lad," Darius answered, controlling his start of worry and realizing his mistake an instant too late.

"You hate me too," the voice came with an edge.

"Don't. Couldn't. Wouldn't," Darius said in clipped words, hoping to offset the mood swing. "If I had anything to do with your distress, lad, I am sorry."

"You doon't want to talk to me either." The sentence punctuated with a clamor, then a static hiss of disconnection.

"Damn," Darius said absently and glanced off the curious blue eyes as he reached and touched his finger to the disconnect button. Waiting ten seconds for the line to disengage, he released the button and dialed the long number. Looking over as he sat back, he caught the more curious blue eyes. "Rather urgent business, Luv. Give me a moment?"

"Certainly," she said quietly.

As the ringing started, Darius turned his attention to lifting his wine glass. Too many desperately lonely nights, he'd spent on the phone with this little hellion needing the young voice as desperately as the child needed him.

On the fifth ring, the voice grumbled, "What do you want?".

"Your telephone manners leave a great deal to be desired, lad," Darius commented.

"Aye! And is it your business, then? Do you think you can tell me a thing now?"

"Raphael," Darius said in a tempered voice. "I love you."

Stopped, silent.

The silence lingered so long that Darius began to wonder if the child had learned his father's trick to hang up in total silence . . . but he felt the ear across the miles. "I do, you know."

"I . . . I'm sorry," Raphael heaved on the brink of another sob. "I am wicked. Wicked and evil joost like those oogly things on the telly. I dinnae even deserve to have a friend."

"Raphael, what you saw on the television . . .? Was it a movie by any chance?"

"I doon't think so," he said with another wary, worried note. "Was like all the oother things I've seen there. Violent. Aye," he said gravely. "The world is a horrible place now, Darius. I'm afraid for you. I don't like you being so far away all the time. If they catch you, they'll kill you, too," he said with a touch of fear. "They're hunting for us. Doctors and the like. If they catch you, they'll kill you joost for being our friend."

The truth in those words was difficult to deny, and in a weird moment, Darius wondered how much of the boy's words had come from the apparent horror movie. Was this a masked warning? A premonition? At times, the devil-damned imp possessed an uncanny ability to see into the future and grasp the heart of a situation despite the lack of knowledge. "Don't be afraid, lad."

"You still want to die," the words erupted candidly, factually. "I don't want you to die, Darius. I know you want to. I know why you want to. Boot I doon't want to lose you, too. It's been soo long," he said sadly. "Time goes so quickly. It seems like only yesterday . . . but for you, it has been a lifetime, hasn't it? You are going to die too yooung, my friend."

The receiver lowered far too quietly, no clamor or clatter of emotions. To the static at his ear, Darius drew from his grip of tension and suffered a chill, a shudder. Lowering the receiver to its cradle, he pushed from the chair, unable to sit with the tension coiled through him. Dying. The cessation of life. He often thought about it. Wanted that end. Needed it to break free . . . but would there ever truly be freedom? His end. He wouldn't die quietly. A violent bloody end, he'd known that for eight years. Whether he died at the Baron's hands or the hands of this new threat, it mattered not one way or another. He would die violently. Badly.

Without a conscious thought, he strode to the balcony door, stood looking through the part in the curtain. The night. The darkness. His life. Young. By any measure of the years, thirty wasn't that old. He felt older, though, and his thought offered no comfort or relief. At thirty years old, he felt weary and resigned, ancient. And across the ocean, a child existed who had never truly lived at all.

At the hand touching his arm, Darius flinched and looked over, blinking against the sting at the corner of his eyes and looking into the deep blue eyes. Too late to mask his emotions, he made only a slight effort to smile and failed miserably if her greater sorrow was any indication.

"Was . . . was that your son?" Jenna asked quietly.

He shook his head, feeling only worse and turning his gaze through the dark glass. Daylight was still so far away. Winter, he considered absently. Here, the winter solstice had come, and the darkness would linger longer. A few hours . . . a life could be lived or crushed in that many hours of darkness. His had ended eight years ago in far less time.

"Do you . . . ever see your son?" she asked.

Looking over and down into her, he felt the curtain dropping, the chill wrapping around his heart. Dylan. "Who uh . . . who told you I have a son?"

"Agent Wharton," she answered and held his faintly startled gaze. "He and his associate paid me a visit Saturday."

"You mentioned that," he said lightly. "What else did they tell you?"

"That you were a murder suspect."

Far more critically, he studied her and realized the absence of fear, the absence of doubt. Recalling how smoothly she'd opened the door to him in the dead of night, he wondered, "What made you decide they were wrong?"

"Intuition," she said without reservation, her gaze as sober as his. "And observation."

"Excuse me?"

"I really don't have a concrete reason,," she said quietly. "I tallied what I knew and what I felt, and I knew they were wrong. You may be hell in a boardroom, and God knows, you hide behind those handsome smiles, but you couldn't take a life."

"What did they tell you about me?" he wondered.

"Highlights," she said lightly. "They . . . were attempting to convince me to work with them."

"I'm not sure I understand," he said curiously. "What exactly did they want you to do?"

"I will answer you," she said soberly, her gaze intent. "But bear in mind that I told them to go to hell."

Watching him for the reaction, aware that he might hold her words against her, Jenna told him about the FBI's proposition. The man was no fool. Presently, she stood exactly where Wharton had wanted her, close enough to watch him, learn something about him, find evidence to bury him. The fact remained, she knew he wasn't the killer and had no intention of telling Wharton or anyone else a thing. Finished, she stood looking at him, aware of his tension despite the cloak over his dark eyes. She wasn't about to point out that he'd come to her door, invited her into the office, and ultimately into his life with the wedding reception. He was bright enough to work out those details for himself. Unwavering, she held his gaze, willing him to trust her as much as she already trusted him despite all rhyme and reason.

"What did they tell you about my son?" he asked after a moment.

Of all the questions she might have expected, that was the last. Remembering, she answered, "You gave him up for adoption."

Hurt flickered a half second before he turned his gaze through the glass again. Even in partial profile, he appeared distant. The curve in his mustache wasn't a smile. Sadness. She felt the sadness and pain behind his handsome eyes.

"What's his name?" she asked quietly if only to break through his sorrow.

"Dylan," he answered.

"You didn't answer me, honey," she nudged gently. "Do you ever see him?"

"No," he answered in the same vacant tone.

She'd heard the child's voice in those first seconds on the phone. He'd been speaking to a child, and the affection in his voice, the concern in his words . . . the simple honest admission of love. If not his son . . . "Who is Raphael?" she asked quietly.

In slow motion, his gaze turned, and a faintly disheartened shine lingered in his eyes. "I . . . don't discuss my private life, Jenna," he said quietly. "And please don't misunderstand that. I don't believe you'd run to either the FBI or a reporter for some tabloid to exploit my endeavors. I'm . . . I suppose you could say I've vowed silence that falls under a liability clause." He paused a half second with a glimmer of thought and a suddenly more disheartened expression. "Suppose that explains why I truly don't share any intimate relationships. A running dialogue of corporate stats and economic trends isn't conducive to personal investment. I'm sorry."

She'd learned more about him in the last half hour than in all the hours past, and he was no longer the stranger who'd swept into the banquet hall with a salesman's smile and an uncanny intensity. If she learned absolutely nothing else about his past, his life, she knew at this moment, it wouldn't matter. Words would neither enhance nor hinder what she felt for him by the simple honesty in his eyes. With little more than a sidestep, Jenna slipped closer and slid her arms about his waist. Intimacy wasn't words. Intimacy was the simple act of acceptance that she felt for him, and as she hugged him, she caught his faintly startled eyes as he slid his hands about her, returning the embrace. "I won't ask anymore," she promised quietly, holding his dark eyes at an angle. "Just don't hold me at arm's length in every way if you can help it."

"If it were in my power, I'd hold you this close forever," he said quietly and drew her closer against his solid length as he lowered his head.

The power in his coiled limbs and the heat of his kiss ignited the same quick sparks and anticipation, but she sensed his restraint, his desire to take these moments slower. Backing from the kiss, she clasped his fingers, seeing his doubt and sudden wariness. For a man who could make love like a maestro, he was not as trusting or confident of himself as his talent indicated. Keeping his hand, she drew him from the window and led him to the couch. Slow and easy, she wanted to see him and needed to remember these moments, no matter how long or short.

A sense of urgency niggled at her mind and body even as she gleaned the heat of his eyes and suffered a flashing, instant memory of his body crumbling and head lulling. No! He was here. Safe. Alive. No other thought moved her more effectively to settle onto the cushion at his hip. Her hand slid over his sweater and into the nook of his neck as she rose to capture his lips.

And the damn phone rang again! His muscles jumped, jolting her with equal intensity. Settling onto her shins, she read the alarm in his eyes. "I . . . think you better answer that."

He nodded absently, appearing as dreading as she was annoyed. With the same wariness he'd answered every other call, he voiced a simple, "Yes." Nothing of expression touched his face, but she glimpsed the flash of dread in his eyes a moment before he looked to her and held out the receiver. "This one's for you," he said simply.

Curious, and abruptly more alarmed, she clasped the receiver and brought it to her ear. "Yes?"

"Lissstennn. . ."

22

Long after the receiver landed in its cradle and Jenna slid to lie on the couch, Darius sat in the single armchair, drowning his frustration in several glasses of wine. Even asleep, she was beautiful, and with a great deal of reluctance, he'd brought a blanket to cover her. He had known. Should have known better than to believe the illusion would last. For the moments he'd spent with her, he should be grateful. Holding her, kissing her . . . even just sharing a toast and touching a glass without a room full of spectators was a privilege for which he should be grateful.

He wasn't grateful. Half sick, tense, angry, he continued to watch her. With her face tipped at an angle, the shadows played across the lovely contours, enhancing the sleek lines, adding depth. She'd passed from trance to natural sleep. Her lashes fluttered in the dream stage, flickering in the shadows above her cheek. Her brow furrowed faintly, as if troubled by whatever mind-scenes played behind her rippling lids.

Nothing decent, nothing good ever came to him without exacting a cost. More than three days past, Darius had known he would pay for his attraction. Kindness. Mercy. Neither word existed in Amad von Hendricks' vocabulary, and Darius shivered internally. What exactly he'd done to deserve this new trip through hell, he couldn't fathom, and it grieved him more to realize—the Baron never needed a reason. Human suffering was his hallmark, and the Brock clan remained his favorite source of entertainment. For all Darius knew, Amad might have chosen Jenna Windrow with the explicit purpose to drive him toward the peaks of anxiety.

Nothing remained beyond the realm of possibility, not with the Baron von Hendricks. In his current distress, Darius could believe the Baron had deliberately sought and placed Jenna in this hotel. She'd worked here only six months, had arrived shortly after Darius's summer visit. Nothing remained inconceivable. He might have done something months—or even years ago—to annoy the master of misery. To the Baron, time was irrelevant. What was a few months or years to one who held eternity in his grasp? The Baron planned and plotted his private manipulations, the spice of life, as carefully as he designed his business strategies. The missing wine, this deadly opponent, Jenna . . . could Darius afford to believe these circumstances were a coincidence? Where did fate end and the Baron's plot begin?

Up and pacing, caged, Darius stalked around the room and returned to hover over the couch, watching the fluttering lashes, controlling his urge to reach and touch the shimmer of bronze-flecked hair spread over the cushion. Hell. This was hell, to stand so close and so damn far away. He knew better than to touch or attempt to awaken her. No explanation or lengthy command. Simple, direct, 'Hand the phone to your mistress.' Not even a blasted 'hello.' Just that simple order, and Darius remembered the ache and dread, the leaden beat of his heart. Helplessly, he'd obeyed and watched the deep blue eyes glaze, misting and fading. He'd seen it a hundred times, but he hadn't suffered such pain and sorrow in years as he had this even watching Jenna glide under the trance. Animated, sightless, she'd handed him the receiver, then turned and lay prostrate, her empty blue eyes like clear glass, staring at the ceiling. The Baron had hung up before Darius lifted the receiver to his ear. No words were necessary. If he wanted to make love to her, he could, but it would remain a one-way affair.

"Damn you," Darius uttered, not sure whether he cursed himself or the Baron as he backed away from the couch, turning, pacing. Grateful! He should be only grateful for the memory of their lovemaking . . . even if those final moments were lost in his conscious mind. He wasn't grateful. The experience had reminded him of what he'd missed for so long, had rekindled the distant memories when he'd enjoyed the company of women. Damned young fool that he was, he'd taken those encounters for granted. A few laughs over dinner or wine, a trip to a bedroom . . . or a blasted backseat. He'd conceived his son in the backseat of a battered Benz.

Settling onto the single armchair, Darius leaned back, his thoughts turning, his gaze again focused on the lovely woman sleeping so soundly across from him. How was it even possible that he could feel so deeply for this woman? Did it matter? He knew what he felt. If left to his own devices, if only to hold her safe, he would have stayed away from her. And therein lay his mistake. The Baron had looked into him, through him, and found the spark. An opportunist, this master of misery.

Shaking his head, uttering a curse, Darius reached and collected his wine glass. Human weakness, human frailty. Vulnerability. As much as he appreciated his human condition, at times, he almost envied Amad for his lack of the same. How much easier life would be to glide through the world without serious investment . . . and as he considered his thought, Darius knew his lie. For eight years, he'd lived that lie, clinging to his singular belief that he felt nothing. No emotional strings or attachments. Only by sheer force of will, he believed himself immune to compassion, believed he felt nothing for any member of the human race. In place of his biological human son, he'd come to love Raphael. For his safety, his sanity, he'd formed that human bond, the connection. Raphael could be hurt, could be tortured. At any moment, the Baron could severe their relationship and forbid their friendship . . . but the child would survive.

Safety in loving Raphael, Darius knew. No matter what happened, Raphael would survive. No others held that luxury or privilege. At the Baron's whim or whimsy, human lives could be taken or prolonged for extended misery, but Raphael's living essence would be spared.

'. . . But for you, it has been a lifetime, hasn't it? You are going to die too yooung, my friend.'

The sadness and pain in that child's voice touched Darius even now, shivering him internally. A prophesy? Or a child's fear? In all these years—a lifetime—Darius had never truly worked out Raphael's nature or talents. From hellion to prophet, the child could swing in an instant . . . and in an odd moment, Darius understood why the Baron would spare the li'l devil. What the child had been in life—his innocence, his purity, his great capacity to love and need to be loved—all had remained inside the boy. A lodestone, this little damned imp. He could rise a man to laughter or drop a man to tears . . . and Darius couldn't blame the Baron for exacting such a wretched toll on the Brock clan for what had been done to his child. At a gut level, Darius knew what his reaction would have been, needed only to think about Dylan to realize the hatred festering and burning in him even now.

Jenna was wrong. His gaze listed, absently, studying her serene expression. He could kill. He would have killed George Halbrook within that little room long ago if the Baron hadn't appeared in the doorway and dragged him away. Never had Darius come closer to taking a life. For his son, for the injustices and injury against his son, he would have killed Halbrook and all the others who'd conspired against him.

For her, now, he would take a life if it came within his power.

Was he as much a monster as the monster himself?

"Hell," he uttered and pushed to his feet, pacing before he truly caught up to his actions. Tense and agitated, he continued to pace, feeling as trapped and contained as a tiger in a carnival cage.

Murder. Missing wine. A monster stalking him for two blasted years . . . and him, unaware. Huge surprise. For years, he'd traveled from one stage set to another, walking in whatever shoes the Baron placed before him. A grand masquerade, this dual life, but he fooled only himself to believe he shared an attachment to the world around him. Stock market, market analysis, business journals, economic conditions . . . he kept abreast of the financial trade and social conditions if only to conduct his affairs with a degree of intelligence. If Wharton's enlightenment held a grain of truth, by the time any of those bodies had been found, by the time the media announced the grizzly details, Darius had been long gone. They had, however, died when he was still in the vicinity. A setup then. To have him sitting where he was now? Trapped and apparently still suspected of the crimes? Only the Hendricks Corporation and his own clout had stifled the FBI's serious intention to indict him for murder. The media would have torn him apart and seriously damaged the Hendricks Corporation's reputation. Homicidal maniacs employed in the top rank of a company which spanned the globe might send serious shock waves through the current financial figures. He was too well known, his face and name too familiar within the affluent circles to orbit the various satellite companies.

Had this maniacal enemy planned this endeavor with that intention? Was the plan so complex? Or was it somewhat more personal? Were these deaths nothing more than a slap in the face to the Baron von Hendricks? Surely this enemy knew the Baron's capabilities. To believe these deaths were a surprise to the Baron was a fool's dream. Darius knew the master of misery had lied. A game. A mere game. Amad had probably known about this beast from the first murder and simply chose to watch and wait.

Remembering Raphael's call Friday night . . . the mention of the Baron's rage, Darius suffered only an instant of doubt. All part of the bloody game. Complexity was a word the Baron embraced. In retrospect, Darius imagined Amad raging for Raphael's benefit, knowing damn well the lad would break eventually and phone his human familiar. Timing. Even the timing could have been controlled. Darius remembered Raphael worrying about making that phone call. The Baron could have enlisted his great-great—however many greats—granddaughter to play on Raphael. If ever there was an old woman to send ice through a man's veins, Rebecca von Hendricks was such a one. Just a thought of her sent a cringe through Darius's muscles. Human, fully human, that old shrew prided a heart of stone and wore the glaze of something long dead in her graying eyes. If not the physical aspects of her ancestor, she'd inherited a great deal of his nature. Human, fully human . . .

Primly, she'd poised like a grandam at a banquet in her honor, stationed in a high-backed ornate chair to the left of the Baron's desk. Silver hair swept into a matronly style, her lined lips wrinkled with just a tweak of a smile at the corner. She'd appeared as harmless as all else inside that room, just a nice old lady with a curiously darting gaze. Darius had glanced at her, barely lent her a thought, but later . . . later he'd recognized the concentration in those pale blue eyes, the heat of her anticipation. A banquet all right. A bloody feast. And that old bitch had sat watching and anticipating the slaughter, a critical observer, a thrilled witness. The titled Baroness was every bit her father's daughter.

Without any trouble at all, Darius imagined her participating willingly in this latest endeavor. He imagined her hovering over Raphael, keeping him from the telephone until just the right moment. Like no other mortal, that shrew worried the li'l devil in her keep. The bitch. She probably had laughed at his childish terror, had probably neglected to comfort his fear over a blasted movie. In fact, she'd probably deliberately found the movie . . . maybe rented a damned video . . . and played it for Raphael to scare the hell out of him. For all the little lad's years, he wasn't in tune to the world beyond his immediate realm. A break in his natural progression, Darius knew. The boy was isolated, forced to dwell in the family manse, protected, or was it imprisoned, with no clear sense of the world around him. The lad had no blasted way to judge between a newsreel and a fictional rendition of life, and this wasn't the first time he'd phoned in a state of hysteria over something he'd seen on the damned telly. Not all that long ago, the lil devil had seen a depiction of nuclear war and it had taken over an hour to convince him no bombs had landed and incinerated entire continents.

'Come home! Come home! Come here! The dungeon! We'll be safe! Come!'

"Shit," Darius uttered, shaking his head, pacing. Caught between a smile and a frown, he continued pacing, remembering. Raphael had cried and raged, demanding his return, promising sanctuary, safety, survival. They could last a hundred years, two hundred years the child had promised, failing to consider the semantics. He could last a hundred years, might very well survive a nuclear holocaust . . . as long as he kept a herd of humans alive. Something of Darius's thoughts had registered, then, and the child had raged and wailed that much harder.

If ever a more tortured old soul existed, none greater than Raphael.

Depressed and still angry, Darius shook the thought away and tried to concentrate on his current dilemma. To believe himself or Jenna safe was a fool's dream. They were penned. Outside the door, two Federal Agents stood, but neither would fare well if the enemy attempted another frontal assault. Nowhere was safe. Just the thought of Adam Brock's fate confirmed his thought.

Adam was lost. Undoubtedly, his new bride would meet the same fate. If not already, then soon. They were prisoners of war and instead of worrying about his damned love life, the Baron might have phoned to discuss that assault and these new developments. What would become of Adam Brock now? Or the dozens of other Brocks in the Canton area? Would the enemy merely be satisfied to have taken him, used him, or would this bastard continue to use and torture Adam?

As much as he preferred not to think about his cousin's circumstances, Darius couldn't shake the endless possibilities. Adam could be used, could show up on the hotel doorstep in the morning and demand an audience as if it were the most natural thing in the world. Or worse, the lad could pack up his drugged bride, climb into a car and drive full speed into a cement abutment. A casualty of war. Would that be worse or better than the alternatives? His cousin was lost, his immortal soul chained to a monster, his mortal life changed forever. Not another moment of true love or happiness would his cousin know. Even if this beast simply played inside the lad's head, Adam would never know another moment of peace or joy.

His thoughts traveled full circle and his resolve snapped, halting his infernal pacing and freezing his anxiety. Rather than the hotel line, he routed in his discarded jacket and used the cellular phone, dialing the long series of numbers on a direct line to the hotel on the Sound. Hoping, half-tempted to pray, Darius stood, stopped just inside the bedroom door, listening to the start of ringing in his ear. The Baron could leave him hanging.

Prolonged misery was always the best misery. All too well, Darius knew the dual-edged sword of his human nature. He wanted answers, needed answers, but unless the answers would benefit the Baron, none would be forthcoming. The chap could be sitting in that suite, merely listening to the telephone, enjoying Darius's anxiety.

Or he could be away from the suite . . . on his way to Pittsburgh.

The countdown.

"Damn it," Darius uttered and snapped the phone away, ending the call. Pacing halfway across the living room, his gaze fleeted to Jenna and he halted. Kevin. If he phoned Kevin . . . at least he might learn something about the damned wine. If he could track the wine, he might find the enemy. Doubtful. More than likely, he would get himself killed making the bloody attempt, but anything would be better than idling about and waiting for this enemy to strike again.

Flipping the phone from hand to hand, a habit which all too often accompanied his pacing, Darius caught it and nearly stabbed the first number on the keypad. The ring jolted him, startling a curse off his lips as he jabbed the appropriate key. "Yes!" he snapped.

"A tad edgy, are you?"

"Yes," he said in a tempered tone, as much relief as dread racing through his mind.

"Doubtful I've returned your call to relieve your troubled mind, lad. A pity, but a fact of life," Amad mused.

A fact. Now that Darius had the Baron's attention, the entire idea lacked appeal. No relief would come from this end. Frustration and anger slid through his mind. "How the bloody hell am I supposed to fight this enemy? You want me to keep myself alive. Tell me how! Or is that the joke of this entire ordeal? The grand jest? Should I resign to the fact that you've given me orders to keep myself safe for the sole purpose of damning me further when I fail to do so? Should I expect to land in this enemy's clutches, suffer all manner of ill, then return to your keep for the final hell? Is there any fucking thing I can do to stop this? Change it? Avoid it?" *Ohhh, hellll!* "I'm sorry," he said quickly, tensely. "For all the bloody good that will do, I am sorry. I just don't know what you expect of me. I don't know how to help in this battle, and I feel so damned useless locked up in this suite. Is there . . . is there anything at all I can do to keep myself safe? Would it even help if I found Fradden's killer? Or your wine? Or am I truly just the carrot you're dangling to snare this bastard?"

"You are in a state, lad," the deep voice idled.

"You . . ." The memory came, blasting to the foreground of his mind. He'd read the scroll, the story, written as if it were a fable, but no fable was that tale. "You've stood where I am now, sir," he said carefully, remembering the mention of the stakes, the ropes bound at the wrists, the forest sounds. As if the memory was his own, he suffered the tension of the night closing in on him with the nocturnal sounds haunting the edges of his mind.

"You . . . you do know what I'm feeling. As a man, you stood chained to the posts, the bait, an offering and sacrifice to something you couldn't understand. Had I lived then, I couldn't have been a party to that . . . wouldn't have been if I was the same man I am now or was before I answered your summons. That's no consolation, no attempt even to beg your mercy, just . . . . just an explanation. If you've stood me at this stake to make amends, to exact the punishment against my clan, if this is your revenge then I'll accept my due and I won't ask for further advice. I will suffer this madness as you did and attempt to survive it. But if there's a chance, even a slight chance that you expect me to survive, if there's some way I can truly battle against your enemy, then tell me how."

"The dawn draws near," the low voice idled. "Open the windows to your soul, lad, and watch its advance. Revel in the light. Feel safe in it," the voice said with a low scathing edge. "Live today as if it's your last, and rest assured, the darkness will come . . ."

Few other words could have affected Darius more deeply or verified his belief more swiftly.

At the window, the curtains parted, he stood and watched as the sky silvered, brightening slowly. No sunlight accompanied the ebbing darkness. A thick gray mantel of cloud shaded the hills but even the faded light bothered him, needling his staring damp eyes. He'd survived one more night, but he wondered if that had truly been his last. In the daylight, he was safe, or reasonably safe. If his cousin came, death could be short. He was human. He could be shot, strangled, knifed. Doubtful anything would be that simple or short. Whoever this enemy was, he shared the Baron's desire to play the game.

The light was safe. Daylight. Natural light.

If he'd been weary days ago, he was exhausted now, but sleep wouldn't lift this heaviness in his mind or limbs. He was a carrot. Or a sacrifice. As helpless and desperate as the man in the fable that each of the twelve had been forced to read. A pre-requisite, a prelude to the madness to come. Even as he'd read the scroll, Darius had suffered an empathy with a man who could be wrongly accused and condemned . . . as confused and desperate for an explanation then as now. What had he done . . .?

No answers would be forthcoming. The order . . . to live today as if this was his last.

At the sound, stirring at his back, he blinked the spots away and turned in watch Jenna push aside the blanket, rise onto her hip. If this was to be his last day, by damned, he could think of no one with whom he would rather share his final moments.

Her brow troubled and blue eyes murky with sleep, she sought and found him as he started toward her. "I . . . .?"

"Good morning, Luv," he offered with a smile.

"I . . . Good morning," she said, doubting until she spied the daylight through the parted drape. Not fully awake, confusion lingered in her cloudy eyes, but how much of her current distress lingered from their midnight caller.

Without slowing a step, Darius reached the couch and leaned, brushing a kiss on her lips. Fully enjoying the startled flicker of delight in her waking eyes, he cupped her cheek, musing, "I believe I better ring room service and have several pots of coffee delivered."

"One would help," she agreed as he withdrew. Tugging at the blanket, untangling her long legs, she appeared disoriented and agitated while climbing from the cushions, tugging at her long black hem. "I need to get out of this dress," she nearly growled then halted and darted her gaze upward.

Oh, and he would like nothing better than to help with that enterprise, and she read his mind if not his interest. Rolling her eyes, a smile playing in her lovely lips, she decided, "I probably should have phrased that differently . . . What I should have said is, I need to get home."

"I rather liked your first idea," he said lightly and collected the telephone, winking at her before punching the call buttons for the kitchen. A single day. Lived fully. Could be more than he'd lived in the past eight combined. To hell with a monster, the darkness, the investigation!

Dumbfounded, Jenna listened to him order breakfast, halfheartedly wondering how many people he'd invited to join them. If he hadn't ordered one of everything, and two of some things, he'd certainly come close. Not quite awake, she retired to the bathroom, intending to wash the sleep from her eyes and take care of business. Nothing made sense in her fuzzy mind. She couldn't remember if they'd made love a second time. She remembered her intention to do exactly that, but the details skipped away . . . and asking Darius wasn't an option. He appeared content, almost happy? Or hyper, she considered when she stepped from the bathroom and nearly ran into him.

"Blast," he said with a slow donning grin. "I'd hoped to hear the shower running."

The foreplay had ended, the doubts eliminated. He'd apparently intended to join her in the shower, and she wouldn't have minded one iota if she had a change of clothes. He'd already showered, she noticed, awake enough to appreciate his tall lean length. This once, he wore casual attire. In black jeans and a charcoal cashmere sweater over a gray collared shirt, he remained the epitome of elegance . . . and she, again, felt like a blasted wet dishrag. "My apartment . . . ? A half hour . . . ?" she offered

His eyes darkened, nearly to black and his smile enhanced, twitching his mustache. "We'll leave after breakfast," he agreed simply and settled for another kiss. Long, slow, and deep, that kiss to snatch the beath from her lungs. "On second thought," he said as he lifted. "We'll leave now and dine later."

With the same pent-up energy and split-second decisions as last evening in Canton, he moved now, gathering his coat as she stepped into her shoes. Before she considered how they'd deal with the FBI escorts, he led her into the hall and sent one of the men to the next room to collect her coat and handbag then guided her toward the elevator with the other agent following. His hand slipped into hers, and he stood almost entirely shielding her from the agent, winking and smiling down at her.

Something was wrong. Something was seriously wrong, but if she intended to work out the problem, she most definitely needed a cup of coffee . . . if not an entire pot. Gathering her wits in the elevator, if only with a thought of encountering other employees, Jenna suffered an instant of self-consciousness before she shoved it aside. Regardless of what rumors would fly, an upward glance into his fathomless dark eyes countered any regrets.

Barely, they stepped into the elevator's alcove, when Agent Wharton and three others converged on the opening, nearly blocking the lobby entrance. Without preamble, Darius crowded the men, backing them into the lobby as he wondered, "Reasonably quiet night?"

"For the most part," Wharton stated. "Going out?"

"We are venturing out, Agent Wharton," Darius began. "If you'd like to enlist a team of your associates to follow, I won't mind."

"I think we already discussed this, Mr. Brock," Wharton stated. "If you have business to conduct, we'll need to discuss precautions and safeguard your route."

"As much as I know this will annoy you, Agent Wharton, I have no intention of following a schedule or plotting a designated course." With his lofty English accent pronouncing the word 'shed'yule,' his natural arrogance enhanced tenfold. "I'll cooperate to the extent that I will let you know, when I know, where I intend to go. Our first destination," he said with a flashing downward glance and wink to Jenna and back to Wharton. "Is Miss Windrow's apartment. She and I, as you may note, will be traveling together. How long we'll remain at her loft remains to be seen."

"I'll have a car take you over and we'll—"

"I have a car in the parking lot, sir," Darius said in a quiet tempo. "As I mentioned, if you'd like to appoint a few lads to follow, I won't mind, but I do intend to drive my own vehicle and unfortunately, it's equipped with only two seats and the boot. I will keep you informed as well as I'm able, but frankly, I don't intend to spend the day idling about and awaiting you to break this case. For whatever reason, I've found myself with a day to do as I damn well please, and I do intend to take full advantage. If you must reach me, if anything develops from the information Jenna and I collected for you yesterday, then do ring me up."

"Do you intend to visit any of the Hendricks subsidiaries?" Wharton asked temperately.

"At the moment, no." His voice and attention shifted, distracted.

Jenna followed his gaze to find Mason, appearing haggard and grim, ambling toward them.

"Mason," Darius acknowledged and eyed the elder man with an unnatural intensity. "Lad, you look as if you need a dozen hours abed. Surely you haven't been up these past three days?"

"I'm just coming in," he said, and his gaze darted off Darius. "If you'll pardon me for interrupting," he said lightly and looked to Jenna. "I'd like a word with you."

In all the chaos of last evening, Jenna hadn't even considered her work schedule! With a glance at her watch, she realized what he meant to discuss. In her mind, she'd already resigned her position, but protocol dictated. She'd offer a two week notice and train her replacement. "Of course." She barely started a step toward him when Darius caught her elbow and her gaze. "I think we'll need to change our plans," she started.

Pivoting his focus to Mason, Darius spoke smoothly, "Miss Windrow and I will be departing in a moment, and if her absence should leave you shorthanded, I suggest you ring someone to fill her position for today," he barely paused, considering. "In fact, considering the probability of extended official protection, you may need to arrange your schedule for the next several days. I'm certain Miss Blythe would be happy to assist, and if questions arise that only Miss Windrow can answer, you may contact her via my personal number. Do bear in mind, it's a business phone and limit your calls to urgent matters if you please."

Mason wasn't happy, but then, he was rarely happy. Presently, though, Jenna shared his immediate distress, neither appreciating the swift intervention or the mention of protection. The thought of Lisa Blythe filling her position—even for a day—added to her irritation. Before she could raise a protest, Mason rushed an apology, and two seconds later, her coat arrived.

Darius wasted no more time, helped her into her coat, and started them toward the door with an entire troop of agents hustling and taking quick commands, scattering.

Likely aware of the chaos abounding fore and aft, Darius continued toward the entrance, merely flagging a hand to signal Henry at the doors. He barely needed to slow their pace to escort her through the opening doors.

A cute smile tilted the corner of his mustache, a glitter rose in his mahogany eyes as he escorted her through the second doors and into the crisp morning air. "You did suggest I should take a vacation."

Three nights ago, sitting in the dining room, a lifetime ago. "I'm surprised you even heard me," she said as she accepted his lead into the parking lot. In proper form, he maintained the touch on her sleeve, prepared to catch her if she teetered on her high heels or slid on the sidewalk. Which wasn't likely. Under the glow of neon entrance lights and coach lights, pavement and lanes carried a wet sheen to evidence the maintenance crews working around the clock. Not losing her thought or attention on her escort, Jenna commented, "And as I recall, I mentioned you looked like you needed a break and a genuine rest . . . Did you get any sleep at all last night?"

"Time enough later," he said lightly and might have finished, 'When I'm dead.'

A shiver slid through Jenna as she sought his expression. With the entrance lights behind them, his features remained shaded,

They needn't travel far. They barely passed the handicap spaces before reaching his Mercedes that remained camouflaged under a layer of frost and patches of ice. Halted at the passenger door, he wore an expression of dumbfound.

"Look at this," he said as he surveyed the car, then skimmed his fingernail over the passenger door glass. Wearing a slightly sheepish expression, he looked at her. "I probably should have enlisted someone to heat and clean our ride before bringing you out here."

"You, sir, are spoiled," she said and smiled at his more dumbfounded expression. "And on the outside chance that you've never scraped snow off your own car, I'll be glad to show you the technique, providing the car's equipped with a scraper. If we use our fingernails, we'll be here most of the day."

He considered a half-second, smirked and fumbled his keys into the crusted slot, unlocking and opening the passenger door. As Jenna leaned inside to search for a scraper, she heard him fumbling, then punching numbers. Seconds, mere seconds later, still looking behind the driver's seat, she heard him speaking, "Be a good lad, Mason, send out one of the bellhops with a ehm . . . a scraper for the car . . ."

Good God, the man truly was spoiled! Jenna turned on the seat and looked out and up in time to see him smirking, disconnecting the phone. Without a word, he touched the lock button on the door and nudged it shut between them before she could voice a word.

Seconds later, he slid behind the wheel, arranging his long coat and slipping the key into the ignition, Still wearing the same bemused twitch in his lips, he avoided her gaze.

"I do believe you have it in you to be a real smart aleck, sir."

His smirk deepened and he looked over with a mocked innocence. The tip of his head added a touch of mischief to the entire arrogant pose. "Not I, miss. Merely exercising practicality."

"You don't have a scraper," she decided, enjoying the light in his dark eyes, the smile in his lips.

"Truly, I have no idea," he said lightly. "The car was warm, clean and already purring when last I slipped behind the wheel." He shrugged, barely paused,

"But I suppose I should admit, I exercise my right to avoid tasks which I can pay others to perform."

"You are spoiled," she said with a stifled laugh. "But I can certainly see the practicality."

His eyes sobered a tad as he reached across the thin console and clasped her hand, drawing her closer with the mere gesture until their chilled lips touched. Still holding her gaze, he leaned back into his seat and smiled quietly. "If you could do anything you wanted to do today, what would be your desire, Jenna?"

To spend the day in his arms, she nearly said aloud but the words weren't necessary. His dark eyes sparked and shaded within the gray light. They rested in a cocoon, encased in ice, with only the engine sound vibrating and blocking out the outside world.

"Other than that?" he asked with a slightly teasing note.

"Hmm, I'd need to think about it," she said idly, reflecting, teasing in return. "I do have a Christmas list to fill. I suppose, as an alternative, that would have to do."

"Shopping," he said with a bemused smirk, lifted brow.

"Actually, that's the last thing I'd want to do," she laughed. "I tried it for a little while Saturday, the stores are already a madhouse." Looking into his pensive eyes, she lost her thought, realizing he was serious and asking for a reason. "My turn. What would you want to do?"

"Other than that . . .?" His voice drifted. "Therein lies my travesty, Luv. I've not had such a day in so long, I haven't a bloody clue what to do with it."

Far more critically, she studied him and read his honesty and faint distress. He was serious. He fully intended to spend the day away from work, away from the tension . . . with her. "What sort of things do you like to do?"

The scraping started at the back window, jolting them but his thought remained on the question. His gaze listed toward the crusted window shield. "I . . . I truly don't know," he said and looked over, more troubled. "Does that sound incredibly strange?"

"Do you like sports?"

"Not particularly, though I manage to catch a game on occasion," he said offhandedly. "Box seats. Business meetings with a twist. Perks, and all that rot," he added with a touch of disgust. "Do you enjoy sports?"

"Considering the fact that I come from a family of fanatical Steeler fans, I'm almost ashamed to admit, no. I don't generally enjoy sports." She considered and nearly mentioned the symphony or an opera before considering the early hour. "We—"

"Your family lives nearby," he said idly and held her gaze as she nodded. "I'd like to meet them," he decided.

Surprised, she studied his sincere dark gaze. In rapid clicks, she considered the humble homestead . . . and how long it had been since she'd introduced a man, any man to her family. Not since college . . . her first year of college. The guy was a first-year med student, and her parents had welcomed the introduction until deciding he lacked personality. Faintly amused at the thought, she read his slight discomfort. "You have no idea what you're asking for, ."

"They wouldn't approve?" he wondered hesitantly.

"My father would probably faint the moment you opened your mouth," she mused.

More reluctant and wary, he studied her.

"Your accent, Darius," she explained with a stifled laugh. "I'm exactly half English, which is a running battle in my family. My paternal half is extremely stereotypical English, very proper and reserved—like you, I might add. My mother's a hotheaded German. The combination never ceases to provide comic relief in my family. They would absolutely adore you and pester you to no end . . . and if you'll promise not to hold them against me, I'd love to take you to meet them. Just bear in mind, they don't fully approve of either my profession or my independence. If they try slapping you over the head with a wedding bell, just duck."

The smile crept into his lips and enhanced the sparkle in his eyes. "You are a woman of rare candor, Jenna, and I do believe I could listen to your voice the day through."

That pronouncement was mutual. The command in his deep voice—enhanced a hundredfold by the clipped notes and occasional English quips—matched every ounce of his lean powerful body. "Say schedule," she said and caught his slight hitch of doubt. "Please?"

"Shed-yule," he said carefully.

Jenna stifled a laugh and squeezed his hand. "Do you have any idea why you're begged for an encore every time you're conned into making a speech?"

"Conned is extremely accurate," he said and glanced distractedly at the boy cleaning the window in front of him.

"It's your voice, sweetie," she said lightly and caught his lifted, skeptical brow. "It is. Between your accent and the pitch of your voice, you hold an audience spellbound whether giving a toast or an introduction. You have an incredible talent for mesmerizing an audience, and I think I fell in love with you the moment you began speaking through that microphone on Friday night. Do you . . . truly despise public speaking as much as it seems?"

"Loathe it," he admitted with a spark which by no means concealed his honesty. Her words, her admission . . . love. He continued smoothly, "It's one of the milder tortures of my occupation, but the least, by no means."

"You love people," she said lightly and noted his flash of doubt and surprise. "You do," she said simply. "And they're drawn to love you in return," she added, remembering how he moved through a crowd, touching, smiling. No matter how hard he attempted to maintain his distance, no matter the casualness of his smiles, his need to touch and be touched was as natural as breathing. Where she'd believed that talent a perfected art on Friday, she knew better now. No intimate relationships, he'd admitted in the early hours . . . and in lieu of that absence, he formed instant relationships on contact. She was in love with him. The sound of his voice, the touch of his hand, the rich mahogany shine of his eyes beneath thick long lashes.

With an effort, she returned to the conversation. "If you truly want to meet my family, Darius, I'd love for them to meet you, but this is your vacation," she said smoothly, holding his dark eyes. "There are all sorts of things we could do, places we could go. Pittsburgh's not New York or Chicago, but we have theaters and museums, Christmas displays galore, planetariums, a Science Center with fantastic displays . . . or we could do nothing at all."

"All of it," he said quietly, his gaze uncannily tense. "I want to do all of it. See all of it. Then do nothing at all. And I want to meet your family."

23

I f Jenna had doubted his decision in those early moments just after dawn, the doubt had vanished. Aside from an hour in her apartment and another brief sojourn in her parents' homestead where he'd captured the hearts of her mother, sister, and father, they hadn't stopped. Weaving through traffic, as efficient behind the wheel as in all else, he'd sped through the city from Northside to Oakland, back to the Point where the Ohio, Monongahela and Allegheny Rivers converged. With the chilled wind off the rivers and ice over the fountain base, they hadn't stayed long at the Point—just long enough for Jenna to read his wistful expression while watching the muddy river flow as if searching for an old friend. His hand gripped hers with enough warmth and strength to defy the chilly air in those moments, and his eyes carried such a well of sorrow, Jenna moved naturally under his arm and held him about the waist, searching the river for whatever he saw there. He smile returned by the time they reached the car, undoubtedly as amused by the four distraught agents as he was delighted with the walk down whatever lane his memory had traveled.

Shortly after noon, they'd stopped for lunch at a small pub downtown. The scent of burgers had caught his attention, or so he'd claimed when swinging off the one-way street and circling the block to find a parking garage. College students sped on the sidewalks, books and backpacks in hand, ragged jeans, and wild hair . . . and Jenna sensed it was the atmosphere he enjoyed after catching him watching a particularly bizarre collection of students. With buzzed hair and dangling earrings on males and females alike, the menagerie bounced and bantered while passing the Mercedes' front bumper. With a lifted brow, bemused smirk in his mustached lips, he idled a laugh and met her gaze, thoroughly delighted as he admitted, "I don't believe I was ever that young."

"You were probably that young, just not that insecure," she returned. *And too naturally arrogant to deny the truth in the words.* Doubtful he'd ever run with a crowd or sought his identity in the latest trends. By his manner, he'd stood alone for an extremely long time.

The pub catered to businessmen and executive-style woman and by no means, carried the latest health kicks to offer carrot juice. Tomato juice, perhaps, in the form of a Bloody Mary. Within seconds after stepping into the candlelight atmosphere, Darius glanced at the nearest business attire and overheard enough of an intense politically oriented conversation, to change his mind and reverse course. Turning his back on the maître d, he nearly rammed the Federal escorts through the door, speaking in a low tempo to mention they weren't staying.

On route to the car, they walked hand-in-hand through waves of pedestrians bustling in either direction. Overhead, the sun reached its zenith and arrowed brilliant streams onto the street between the PPG Place skyscrapers. With a sudden halt, Jenna stumbled a half-step ahead and flinched with the quick, fierce grip on her palm. A split-second, no more. His grip released and he ducked his head, already veering into the shade at the nearest gray stone wall. Against the granite, he leaned, uttering curses under his breath, rubbing his eyes with the heel of one hand while the other fumbled in wool coat pocket. With two alarmed agents crowding around them, Jenna refrained from asking, more concerned with the tension in his face and watering eyes before he donned a pair of dark sunglasses. In a few ticks, he recovered, and they continued the half-block to the parking garage.

"Light sensitive," he admitted in the car, appearing even more sexy wearing Ray Ban glasses. "And now you know one of my deep dark secrets," he said with a twitch of a smile in his still tense lips. "Give me an overcast sky any day of the week and I'll sunbath until hell freezes. Hit me with a full—unfiltered—dose of UV rays and I'm as blind as a bat."

"Have you ever had your eyes checked?" she asked naturally, and he laughed as if the thought tickled him.

"No one's ever asked me that before," he said with a lingering amusement and more natural smile. "But yes, I've had my eyes checked. Twenty-twenty so long as I refrain from looking directly into a sunray. An anomaly I've suffered since childhood," he said and closed the conversation without elaborating or mentioning his vow of confidentiality regarding the von Hendricks Corporation.

In a comfortable silence, they traveled back across the river and found a café on the Eastside, one he'd likely spotted in passing. A riot nearly ensued when all four Federal Agents, mad as hornets, converged on the café and crowded outside the booth. Unwisely, the eldest of the quartet leaned into the booth, snapping warnings regarding Darius's evasive driving tactics.

How many times Darius lost their entourage, Jenna had lost count. At least twice, Wharton had phoned and demanded to know their location which Darius had provided, along with an apology.

He wasn't inclined to apologize to the fellow who leaned into the booth, intending to intimidate him. In one smooth motion, Darius rose off the bench, backing the fellow a step, and stood face to face, three inches taller, glaring down into the slightly older man's eyes. "Who the bloody 'ell do you think you're talking to, sir?"

"If you try to lose us again, Mr. Brock, we'll have no choice but to take you—"

"If I were trying to lose you, I'd have lost you," Darius stated in a tempered low tone. "And if you continue to annoy me, I will most assuredly do exactly that and you will need to explain to your senior agent why I'm not answering my phone when he tries to reach me."

The cook, a stocky hairy fellow wearing a grease-stained apron over a T-shirt pulled taunt over muscled shoulders, stepped from the kitchen. The fellow appeared more fit as a bouncer in a pub than a café cook as he joined the gathering. Sidling to Darius, he spoke while wiping his meaty hands on a soiled rag, "These guys giving you some trouble, dude?" With his native Eastside dialect, and Darius's distinct English accent, they wouldn't likely understand each other but no words were needed. In a split second, the cook judged the department-store-rack black suits and decided, "If you guys ain't gonna order, then you better step ou'side."

When the tempers cooled and Darius slid into the booth, the cook departed, but returned moments later with a complimentary sample of the house special—kielbasa and sauerkraut on a fresh baked hard roll—which Darius downed in four bites. The man loved food, Jenna decided as she watched him annihilate a double burger, an immense order of fries . . . and another 'house special.'

Making a point to look under the table, she ran her gaze up the length of him and met his curious eyes. "You really don't slow down for two seconds on an average day, do you?"

"Pardon me?"

"You must have the metabolism of a marathon runner to stay so fit."

He caught on and smiled slowly, his unshaded eyes glimmering, "Tell me the truth, Luv, did you deliberately ignore Blythe's occasional snipes at the table Friday night?"

She remembered and matched his smile, "Truth, huh?"

"Please."

"Lisa can't sniff food without gaining five pounds. A fact to which I've been privy for quite some time. I uhm . . . don't have to watch what I eat which drives her bats."

"Metabolism," he mused and appraised her with his gaze heating. Mischief lighting in his eyes, he glanced at her cleared plate. "Possibly we'll find a buffet for dinner. Between us, we should manage to clear the bins."

"I asked for that, right?" she mused.

"I've seen parts of the world where children are starving, where mothers don't eat enough to breast feed their infants." His gaze dimmed with the admission; his voice softened. "I've seen strife," he said quietly. "And it drives me to wits end to see any man or woman pick at a plate and leave it half full. To bloody hell with that false coyness. I loved watching you down that steak," he said with a renewed wry smile. "If I wasn't in love with you prior, I was lost then."

They kissed then, oblivious of the cafe patrons, the agents, the matrons several booths away who flushed crimson and tried not to stare. Only as they strode from the cafe and Jenna glimpsed the women's gazes, did she consider the length and heat of that connection. All three elder women smiled, red-faced, approving and nodding to her with a glance toward Darius which spoke volumes. 'You're one lucky girl.'

In Station Square, despite the frustration of the agents, they strode through the shops and to Jenna's shock and mild distress, Darius bought a diamond necklace and matching earrings. With his casual insistence, he refused to depart until he assisted her with the necklace clasp, admiring the glitter at her open collar. She'd dressed casual in his reflection, wearing jeans and a v-lined blue sweater over a dark blue blouse, ankle boots styled for hiking rather than snow, but her ensemble had nothing to do with her discomfort while donning the diamonds. In the car, still troubled, she looked into his perceptive brown eyes and read his dismay. "I love them."

"I'd believe that more if not for that little kink in your brow, Luv," he said quietly, sorrowfully. "I hadn't meant to upset you with a gift. I . . . needed to give you something, Jenna. You've given me so much more than I had a right to expect." Heart in hand, he held her gaze. "Please, don't be angry with me."

"I'm not angry with you," she said honestly. "I'm just a little . . . a lot stunned," she corrected. "I feel like Cinderella, and I don't know how to handle this. I don't need expensive gifts. I love just being here with you."

"Diamonds are forever, Luv," he said soberly, his gaze intent. "Please accept them and whenever you wear them, think of me?"

He was leaving. He would go away, and she wouldn't likely see him again. No matter the love they vowed or the moments they shared, they only had today. In his eyes, in his voice, the pain of his departure lingered. She would keep the diamonds, wear them often, think of him, forever. Tears stinging her eyes, Jenna moved to his mere suggestion and wrapped her arms around him.

Breathing in the scent of his cologne, she recorded every detail, from the brush of his hair at her temple, to the strength of his arms about her, to the twist of their bodies parted by the narrow console which might have been a gulf between them. If only she could hold him like this forever, but they only had today. "I do love you and I love your gift, Darius," she said when she found voice. "And I will never stop thinking about you or loving you no matter what tomorrow brings."

Sorrow flashed in his eyes, but he smiled faintly, accepting her vow.

By mutual, silent consent, they refrained from mentioning their parting, refused even to allude to that coming event, but it was never far from their minds, hovering like a dark cloud on the horizon.

As carefree and close as new lovers, they held hands while meandering through the museum, declining the guided tour, impressing one another with their shared knowledge of art and history. The Renaissance era fascinated him, Darius admitted, and Jenna believed him after he stood for several moments, absorbed in a sixteenth century painting. Bearded men and hefty women engaged in a banquet festivity, frolicking nearly to the point of cavorting on a hardy table and chairs.

For an instant, when he drew from the painting, he appeared disturbed, but his smile returned smoothly. "I've often wondered if the women were truly as voluptuous as they're depicted or if most painters needed bifocals," he commented. "If not the latter, we've created a society of anorexics."

"You may blame that on our ancestors if so" Jenna pointed out. "I think either the English or French designed corsets and women had no choice—lose weight or suffocate."

In front of a Victorian print, he stood fondling her hair and looking into her with a contented smile, "You have the style to have posed for these artists . . . and you would wonder why I couldn't resist capturing you on camera? If I were a painter, I'd hock my soul to have you pose as my model. Camera shutters are far too swift."

"It's not fair, you know, my dear," she said lightly. "You have all those pictures of me, and I don't have a single one of you. Sometime today, I am buying a camera, even if it's one of those throw-aways."

The conversation was cut short then by Agent Baines and Rutherford, neither wasting any time for lengthy explanations, merely shuffling Darius and by extension, Jenna toward a safe nook as the other team checked the area. Less ruffled by the possible danger than the interruption and delay, Darius barely awaited the 'all clear' before starting the procession toward the door. In the car, relaxed but still faintly annoyed, he scoffed at the agent's suggestion that someone had been following them. "They just don't appreciate fine art, Luv. I believe they were bored and needed an excuse to hustle us along."

The experience remained yet another reminder of the circumstances that had brought them together and would inevitably pull them apart. If not for Mr. Fradden's untimely end, Darius would have boarded his plane and continued his given course. The photo session would have been their only memory, their single encounter. As much as she hated the circumstances, dreaded the thought of him leaving, feared the danger, Jenna couldn't regret whatever had allowed them to be together even if only for a little while. With the tension hanging like a pall over the car, they drove in a brief silence, not entirely plotting a course, not searching a new destination.

At a camera store in Oakland, they stopped and bought a camera—not of the throw-away variety. Watching him fiddle with the camera, Jenna relaxed, amused. He looked like a child with a new toy and after he'd snapped more than a dozen shots of her, warding off her attempt to catch the camera, she laughed uncontrollably and shook her head. "I don't think you like to share. Not one bit," she chided, and he flickered one of his more comic innocent smiles.

"I do, Luv, I just haven't worked out the details," he smirked. "It's rather difficult to share every frame with you while holding the camera."

He worked out the details, much to the younger agent Rutherford's dismay, and Baines' annoyance. On the street in front of the camera shop, Darius enlisted the agent to snap the first shot of them together, locked in a joined pose, arms over and under. Neither had looked at the agent, their eyes locked and held at an angle. Rutherford was a good sport. He caught the second shot of them locked in a fiery kiss without an order or request.

"We should go back and do everything again," Darius commented in the car as Jenna fidgeted with the camera. Playing with the controls, she familiarized herself with the features and adjusting the electronic zoom lens. She captured him in a side glance, a pensive tip in his mustache, the dark glasses covering his eyes as he commented, "I'd like to have this entire day to live over again."

Whether he referred to capturing their adventures on film, or meant something else, remained a mystery but his sadness drew her. Clasping his hand, she held him tight, and his tension slipped away, his mustache tilting into a natural smirk. "Anything's possible, Darius," she said quietly, unwittingly drawn to experience the pain of their parting. "You pass through this area a few times a year," she said with inspiration. "I . . . 've decided to take your advice. I won't continue working at the Chateau Suites, but I'll probably stay around here," she said honestly. "You know how to find me." The 'if you want to' remained unspoken.

For an endless moment, he held his attention on the traffic ahead, the curve of his lips poised in a frozen half smile. "There's nothing that would give me greater pleasure," he said after a time. "But I can't make any promises, Jenna," he said more quietly. "And I won't ask you to wait for something that may be impossible. We have today," he said in a far more controlled, deep voice, his expression enough to convey his sobriety without the need to see his eyes. "If I had a lifetime, I'd want to spend it here with you, but we truly don't have that luxury. My life . . . it's not my own, Luv. I can't walk away from my occupation. It's . . . a commitment I made, and a promise I will keep."

"You don't like what you do," she said quietly.

A smile twitched his lips. "Not always, no," he admitted quietly. "But it's a part of me, now. I wouldn't even know how to begin another life or to live it," he said as he turned his attention to the traffic ahead with the first blast of a horn behind them. "Upon a time, I envied people who held positions of power, who could afford to travel around the world. Wealth and power, I always believed, meant freedom . . . and therein lies the greatest misconception of my life. With wealth and power comes responsibility. Commitments. Demands which seem almost impossible to fulfill. But it's truly not something from which I could walk away."

Not even for her, she understood and squeezed his hand. "I haven't, and wouldn't ask you to, Darius," she said quietly. "I wasn't kidding when I said, no strings. I won't ask you for a lasting commitment or any long-term plans. But I won't lock the door if you come knocking, nor hang up the phone if you call. When there's time, if there's ever time, I'll be here."

"That's not fair to you, Luv," he said deeply. "None of this has been fair to you but I can't bring myself to apologize. Having you with me today has meant more than I could ever admit. Nothing in my life has compared, and I'm a self-indulgent rake. Don't love me, Jenna. I'm not kind or considerate. If I call, hang up. If I knock, bar the door. Even knowing I could bring you only heartache and pain, I couldn't stop myself. You, Luv, you have to be strong for both of us and when I leave, hate me for whatever grief I cause you."

If the words were not so filled with conviction, she might think him jesting, but nothing of humor touched her mind. He meant his words. "I'm not that strong, darling," she said sincerely. "And I could never hate you. No regrets. No grief. There's nowhere I'd rather be than with you today, and if this is truly all we'll have, I don't want to waste another moment thinking about what the future holds."

"It's getting late," he said almost absently.

Not that late, she might have mentioned, barely a little past four.

"There's a place . . . an overlook. I remember finding it on one of my trips, rather by accident. The view over the city was incredible," he glanced over. "Cast iron rails and coin operated telescopes. Would you know where it is and how to find it?"

"Mt. Washington," she said and sought street signs to gain perspective before offering directions.

Situated on the brink of the highest hill surrounding the city, Mt. Washington offered a view of the Point and bridges, and the collection of skyscrapers and towers. They found a parking space on the street and braced against the chilled wind across the ridge, Pulling their coats together, they walk alongside the cast iron fence toward the nearest overlook. A decorative fence, that cast iron rail, providing a guide rail, nothing more, and offering only an illusion of safety from the steep cliffside.

Despite the gray dawn, the sky had transformed into a rich blue canvas, with white clouds drifting and contrasting beautifully with the chilly wind. A summer day could be no more lovely and with the last tilted sun rays lancing the windows and glass towers, the city sparkled in rare magnificence. Around them, against them, powdery snowflakes twirled like silver dust, lifting and spraying off the bluff through the black rails. Pale blue and salmon hues, splashes of pastel pink and orange danced across the horizon in every direction as if stroked by a painter's hand.

Whether the incredible sunset sky or the image of Darius held her more enthralled, Jenna remained fascinated. He'd stepped to the edge of the overlook, his hands shoved into his coat pockets, the black cloth whipping against his shins in a wild dance. His hair lifted and tussled, falling over his brow and across the top rim of his dark glasses. The curve in his mustache reflected as much awe as sadness, no honest joy in the cut of his jaw or haunting features. Preoccupied and overwhelmed, this pose, and Jenna remembered her camera in time to capture him in this moment of stillness. Almost slowly, he turned his head, lifting his hand to the glasses, lifting them to catch her gaze, and she snapped the camera a second time, catching the rise of his brow the flicker of his distracted smile.

"I've created a monster," he mused and sidled toward her, needing little more than a deeper smile to slip the camera from her hand. "And I do believe it's my turn."

They were not alone on the overlook. Another couple with three young children traveled from one lookout station to the next. Undoubtedly, tourists or wayward family members visiting the city and relatives for the holidays. The voices were lost in the wind, but an occasional word cleared enough to judge the father the authority. From one viewfinder to the other, he pointed out the triangle of the rivers, the more famous buildings, the history of the steel city, while holding one child after another to spy through the viewfinder. Without reluctance, Darius interrupted the fellow in mid lecture, and enlisted him to snap a few photos, lending Rutherford a break from photographer duty.

A half dozen paces away, the agent stood, watching the street, undoubtedly cursing the cold and Darius's whimsical attitude toward his safety. Further away, stationed in strategic proximity, the other three agents stood guard, no more interested in the view than they were happy with their current assignment.

Posing, leaning against Darius and looking out at the city, Jenna sensed his mood transitioning, his more pensive expression. They were running out of time. At the fringes of her mind, she heard a clock ticking, a countdown accelerating with the descending sun. Long after the camera returned to them, they stood against the chill. Unconsciously, Jenna turned, leaning back against his chest, accepting the warmth of his coat which he'd opened to wrap her within his arms against the wind. Only her cheeks and ears suffered the chill as they stood, melded together, watching the colors twining and blending to a dimmer shine across the sky. On the tangle of highways and bridges below, headlights ignited. The city lights flickered on the surface of the rivers to shine like wet tarmac rather than water. Together, they watched a barge glide through the junction and continue down the Monongahela directly below them.

"I lived near the docks," he spoke in a reflective low tone. "I loved watching the ships passing or mooring . . . freighters and steamers . . . the cruise ships. I've never taken a cruise," he said almost sadly. "A childhood fancy . . . a daydream. I told myself I'd one day travel to America on a great luxury liner and I'd have stewards attending me hand and foot . . . and that probably stemmed from a tussle I'd had," he said with a slightly wry note. "Run o'cross one of the ship's lads coming off a gangway and he landed me a stout blow, so he did," he spoke with a faintly different affect in his accent, amusement in his tone. "Him, all spruced up in his uniform, probably no more than a bellhop or a waiter . . . I got even though," he mused. "Probably wasn't more than seven or eight at the time, and while he was busy clouting me for bumping into him, I pilfered his wallet."

Doubt touching her mind, amusement rising through her eyes, Jenna tipped her head and found his dark eyes sparkling with mischief. "You didn't."

"Gospel truth," he said with a contented smile. "I had talent . . . not that it did much good with that chap," he mused. "In hindsight, I know he had a great deal of money on hand. At the time, I considered the strange paper useless. Even if I'd recognized the currency, I couldn't very well have walked into a currency exchange. Tossed the entire wad in an alley and barely had enough genuine money to buy a gumball."

Laughing, she turned within his protective fold and wrapped her arms about his waist, looking up into his likewise laughing eyes. "A pickpocket," she laughed. "Were you ever caught?"

"Not once," he said arrogantly, teasing with his eyes. "I had sense to retire that talent before my luck ran dry . . . and now, you know another of my deep dark secrets."

"Hmm, a child prodigy. Sleight of hand . . . That explains a great deal about you," she said with a thought of how easily his hands had slipped around her more than once.

No longer thinking about his early exploits, his eyes shined with a darker intensity. "Does it now?"

"Most assuredly."

"We should probably get out of this wind," he said and sent another wistful glance off the overlook, panning his gaze and drinking it all in as if to capture every detail on a filmstrip. Sighing, he brushed a chilly kiss on her lips before moving them. "Dinner," he said on route to the car and glanced at her, chuckling. "No buffet, Luv. Somewhere we might find soft music and a dance floor . . ."

They found just such a place and despite their attire, the maitre'd seated them swiftly, not quite as accommodating for the pair of suited agents who followed them inside. More than once throughout the morning and afternoon, his phone had rung, and he'd stepped aside to carry on conversations and conduct his affairs. When it rang within the booth, he uttered a curse under his breath and took the call, not saying more than a few words before dunking it into his coat pocket. He appeared more disturbed than annoyed, even with the candlelight playing in his eyes.

"A problem?" Jenna asked, wondering if that might have been Wharton again.

"Not one to intrude on dinner," he said idly and turned his full attention to the menu.

He'd been serious about taking the day off. He hadn't spent much time on the phone regardless of how often it rang. 'All of it,' he'd said at the onset, and he meant those words literally., intending to make up for lost time and experience a lifetime in a single day.

Over an immense dinner, they fell into easy conversation, discussing music, art, and touching on literature. The subject turned toward politics briefly, and he admitted to meeting several top political figures in the US. By silent agreement, they skirted any mention of partings, murder investigations, psychopaths. They danced, melded together as a single body, sharing the dance floor without a single interruption, not via the phone line or the other couples crowding around them.

At the edges of her mind, however, Jenna sensed the day ending, and knew, he felt it too. The tension that they'd successfully held at bay crept over them, rising with every tick of the clock. In a weird balance, the conflicts lingered in the dark eyes. As much contentment and pleasure as sorrow and distress flickered on and off between his smiles.

"We need to go," he said in a near chilly tone, and she felt it then, the sheer force of the man who'd captured her heart and held her in his grip for the past dozen hours. She might not fare well in the coming moments, but he would adhere to his decision, to his responsibilities.

In silence, they returned to the car, and Jenna's thoughts raced with questions, questions she could have asked, should have asked. Only as they rolled through the entrance of the Terrace Estates, she considered how easily she'd rejected any thought of his departure. Where would he go next? What would they do next about this maniac in his shadow?

As if his thoughts spiraled on a similar wavelength, he stopped at the curb and dispatched the engine. Clasping her hand, he half-turned and caught her gaze. Even in the dim light, she couldn't mask the wet shine threatening her eyes, but she refused to buckle to the gripping pain.

"I'll walk you up in a moment, Luv, but there's something I need to discuss with you."

She nodded, knowing their goodbye would never be spoken. "Police protection."

"If I thought I could keep you safe by keeping you at my side, I wouldn't hesitate to make that suggestion," he said quietly. "I've wrestled with this all day, and I've reached only one conclusion. You won't be safe until I'm gone and even then, there's no guarantee. I truly can't protect you. I can only warn you, Luv. And don't mistake this or dismiss it out of hand. I told you early this morning and last evening, trust no one, and I need you to understand that fully. Do not return to the Chateau Suites, not for any reason, not tomorrow or the next day. Knowing your sense of commitment, I know you'll be tempted to adhere to the natural order of a resignation. Don't. Don't even phone to make your resignation official. I'll handle it."

"Darius—"

"Listen to me, Luv. Just listen," he said quietly, his gaze intense. "When I take you upstairs, I'll see that your apartment's safe and I won't have a choice but to order two of those agents to guard your door. Don't open that door after I depart. No matter what they might ask or say to you, don't let either enter." He paused only a second, and continued, "I don't know how to make this clear to you. This enemy . . . I have reason to believe, he dwells within the Hendricks Corporation and greater reason to believe, he'll only strike after dark. That information is privileged, Luv. Don't mention it to the FBI or anyone else. Just take greater precautions in the night for a while and cut off communications with anyone affiliated with the Hendricks Corporation. When I'm gone, you should be safe, but don't take any chances. In fact, if you could move out of this building, put distance between yourself and the Chateau, it might lend you an advantage. If there's any way possible, I will protect you as I promised, but I've never been less sure of my ability than I am at this moment."

"You can't . . . you can't go back to the hotel, Darius, and I'm not—"

"Jenna, I don't have a choice," he said smoothly. "And please don't ask to come with me or stay with me. I . . . I don't intend to stay there long," he said quietly. "With any luck, I'll be gone before midnight if not sooner. Don't inquire at the hotel. If you need to know, Luv, contact the airport and inquire about my plane. If it's not there, you'll know I've gone and hopefully, taken the threat with me."

"I . . . I'm afraid for you," she uttered, feeling the tremors she'd fought throughout the day.

"Not half as afraid as I am for you, Luv, trust me," he said with an attempt to smile and a tug to bring her into his arms. Against her ear, he whispered, "If I could change but a moment in my life, it would have been the moment I fell in love with you. If only to have kept you from harm's way."

24

The waiting was nearly over, Darius knew if only by the calm pouring through him as he left Jenna's apartment. No one had been inside her flat, not that he could determine, but his capabilities were impotent against these enemies. She wasn't safe. Nothing could he have done differently to keep her safe, and that reality only enhanced his readiness to meet his end in this coming confrontation. To have spent one such wondrous day was more than he could have hoped, more than he would have believed possible a day ago. In a bitter conflict, he lingered on the brink of genuine gratitude toward the monster who held his leash. Two-edged. No kindness without dire agony. He'd loved every minute of the day . . . and hated it with equal integrity like any normal man with a death sentence hanging over his head. No tomorrow. Never again would he experience the pleasure to hold a hand or gaze upon a magnificent sunset. To love a beautiful woman. To feel her love for him. If the Baron had meant to rekindle what was human inside him, the fellow had succeeded. Darius remembered now what it was to live, to love, to be part of a world where children danced in swirling snow and lovers swayed on a dance floor.

If he had any good sense, he'd jam his foot to the floorboard and ram the stone pillars head on. Instead, he coasted through the arches and sped toward the main entrance. He'd given his word, vowed his loyalty. If he broke that oath now, everything he'd done over the past eight years would be for nothing.

He would finish what he'd begun, accept his due as he'd declared hours ago.

Climbing from the car, he locked it by habit, barely glancing to his hurried escorts, more intent on the shadows gathered between the nearest parked cars. He hadn't lied to Jenna when mentioning the local monster resided in the ranks of the von Hendricks Corporation. Either a hotel employee or one of those in a subsidiary division had removed Fradden from the living realm. If not the killer personally, then the chap had a spy in the ranks which was just as bad. Too easily these beasts could mingle and mix, cloaking themselves to pass for entirely human entities no differently than he'd traipsed on the edges of the natural realm for these eight years. The difference was, he was still entirely human, whereas these half-living beasts could recruit an army with a bite.

The Baron had enlisted that method for years, monitoring his entire network around the globe. In every key location, the Baron had placed his recruits. Offhand, Darius could name several in the local area, only beginning with Mason Gordon who'd probably been in the Baron's thrall for the past fifteen or twenty years. Like so many others, Mason retained no conscious recollection of his taking. He moved through life, believing himself responsible for his actions, maintaining a pretense of normalcy through ignorance, harboring no concept of how or why he'd lost his zest for life.

Passing through the held door, Darius nodded to the doorman who might be another of the Baron's vassals. The chap was old enough, likely beginning his natural service when Amad had globe trotted, posing as Thaddeus von Hendricks, and then the son of the same. Twenty—thirty years ago, before Darius had drawn his first breath—the Baron had personally handled his affairs, building an empire, expanding his power. Interchangeable, the Baron had used Thaddeus, a legitimate living heir to the von Hendricks family, taking the man's place and trading identities. The old coot was still alive if his existence could be considered life.

And Darius shuddered uncontrollably with the memory surfacing as he stepped into the lift.

The longest night of his life . . . the last night of his life, Darius corrected as he remembered the moonlight. . . the cool air. The confusion. So much had happened. So many ups and downs and inconceivable enlightenments. When the Baron had dismissed them, he and Kevin, Darius had known only dull relief, too lost in confusion even to fear for the others they'd left behind. They'd received orders . . . he and Kevin were to visit the resting place of their ancestors . . . Raphael was to escort them, introduce them . . . and Darius remembered half believing he would see a corpse rise from the earth and hiss a wicked 'ello....

In the quick of night, the stroke of midnight merely a memory echo, they bolted through a side entrance, both running to keep pace with the strange child who'd launched down the hall at lightning speed. A half step behind Kevin, Darius slammed into his cousin when the chap halted. Caught in the moonlight, the youngster backed a pace, his silver-flashed eyes wide with fright. Kevin barely started, "If we're to see—"

"The path through the hedge!" *the child huffed still backing away.*

"Slow down, boy—"

"No!" *Raphael demanded and pivoted, trotting ahead but allowing them to keep pace.*

A wild race, darting in and out of shadows, Darius remembered as he fumbled with his keys outside the door of suite 606. They'd lost sight of Raphael again and again before he'd fled into the high hedge and disappeared into the maze garden that spread from the rear of the stone manse. A trick of the moonlight, the shadows. Even after everything he'd seen, Darius remembered doubting the child could simply disappear or fade from his sight. Huffing, heaving, he and Kevin had stopped at a junction in the labyrinth, basked in the moonlight. Nocturnal sounds drifted from some higher plane or deeper forest. Nothing of civilization touched them, and Darius was a man accustomed to the sounds of human occupancy. He'd grown up on the streets of London, not in the woods or wilderness. *If not for Dylan . . .*

Inside the suite, Darius ambled behind the bar by routine alone, absently watching as his escorts moved about the room, into the bedroom, searching and securing the suite as Darius had done personally in Jenna's flat. No need here, he might mention if either asked. If the beast hid within the room, they might or might not hear the battle from outside, but they'd never reach him to save him regardless.

Inside his head, he heard his huffed words from so long ago, remembered the disbelief and fear vying for space inside his mind even then. 'This . . . we're 'aving a nightmare . . . that's it, isn't it?'

'Unfortunately,' the stranger who'd soon become his only fully human friend and confidant had spoken with an equal heave and huff. 'I don't believe we'll wake from it.' *He turned slowly, searching the paths, seeking the slight shadow which had led them into the maze.* "Where is he?"

"Who gives a fuck!" *Darius heaved.* "We should be trying to get the bloody 'ell out of 'ere! Contacting the authorities! Something!" *There were men inside that room, and already, the others had been taken for slaughter! His son was inside that towering black fortress!*

Kevin wheeled on him with a speed to stumble Darius backward against the hedge. "If you have half the mind you arrived with—cousin," *he hissed the word with a bitter edge.* "You better use it! You just sold your soul to the devil and if you even think to break that covenant, I'll kill you myself!"

"Goddamn it man, there are lives—"

"Our life as we knew it is finished. Over, Darius," *Kevin hissed in a soft voice.* "We will not wake when the sun rises and forget what we've done. God help me, I know what you feel—how you feel—but it's done. We . . . you and I, we're like the Jews on the night of the Passover, boy . . . But it wasn't God's hand to have spared us. Now, unless you'd like to go visit our new employer and mention we've lost his child, I suggest you pull yourself together and help me find him."

"I'm in a fucking nightmare," *Darius huffed softly but he moved, following Kevin's chosen course into the maze, searching.* "I'm lost in a fucking maze . . . under a full moon. . . trying to find a demon . . . to walk me to a fucking cemetery . . .? A nightmare or I've already died and gone to bloody 'ell—"

"Word of advice, cousin, take care in what you call this . . . child. Like father, like son."

'Then I 'ave gone to 'ell . . . none of this is real.'

The child appeared seemingly out of nowhere on the path just ahead. Barely, Kevin called, "Wait!" *Following, Darius ran in Kevin's footsteps to catch up and the child merely watched, waiting for them to draw close enough to see his direction. Silver light danced on his inky black curls and caught reflections on the black jacket. He'd worn a suit inside that hall, had appeared as prim and proper as any child of the upper class. Without a sound, he fled through another opening before they could reach him, but he hesitated a short distance ahead.*

Following, running, Darius had no time to consider the speed of the child's flight with his concentration shattered. He found the opening through which the boy had fled, an ancient wooden door leading into a tunnel through what could only be a solid wall, the castle bailey. On the other side, the hillside rose, scattered with trees, a path bright with the moonlight, marked by ragged hedge and brush.

They heard the voice first, a seething low hiss on the cool breeze. None of the words reached them but they both slowed to trot, alarmed. What other horrors could await them on this night of horrors, Darius couldn't fathom, but as they advanced, more of the sounds amplified . . . and Darius remembered the old man, recognizing the scratchy voice.

Thaddeus von Hendricks. The chap had poised as still as a granite sculpt in a chair alongside that wide ornate desk, seated at the righthand of the man who'd transformed into a monster. Jutted chin, his face chiseled with deep crevices, the old man had maintained a dignified pose throughout the first hours of the madness, but he'd aged sitting in that chair. Crumbling line by line, his gaunt shoulders slumped, sinking until he'd rested with his elbows on his knees; his thick wiry gray hair stood on end, spiked between his spindly fingers. The family resemblance between the ancient and the monster was unmistakable. An aged rendition of the same face, the same hair and eyes, the same arrogance. Far too late, that ancient had acted on his outrage, railing curses at the younger, issuing threats...

The same voice seethed, now, hissing cruel words, curses and cackling laughs, clearing in broken quips as the feeble voice rose and fell in violent pitches. ". . . never be loved . . . Satan's bassstard . . . disgusting soulless little beast, those are the words I would have spoken a thousand times as I held you pretending to love you . . . Not again will I humor you, beast . . . I would kill you—"

A half step behind Kevin, Darius rounded a shaggy hedge, seeing first the hulking, spindly man who'd lurched toward the monster in that hall, knife in hand, fire blazing in his pale eyes. Whether he was merely a man or another rendition of the monster, Darius hadn't decided then, couldn't decide, now. Moonlight glowed on his wild tangled gray hair, but his shape reflected the posture of a bent, petrified tree trunk. With the full-moon glowing, the hillside might have been basked in sunlight for as clear as the images appeared. And too swiftly, Darius recognized the stout granite stones scattered and jutting in the lower bush. They'd reached the cemetery. With no more than a darting glance, Darius realized the elevation they'd traveled, seeing only black rolling and rising hills climbing even higher toward the platinum twilight. No stars. In the brilliance of the moon, not a single star glittered. Surrealistic, the light showered around them and glistened in the wide round eyes as the ancient head turned toward them.

"So good of you to join us, gentlemen," *the voice sounded natural, now, an aging sophisticate welcoming a visitor into his parlor for a spot of wine and a chat.*

Only more disoriented, Darius darted his gaze and found the child then, a dark mass huddled against a listing stone. Under the feral red-shine, Darius's blood ran cold, his thoughts spinning toward all manner of dangers to be found in the wild, reaching only one quick thought. A wolf . . . a wolf crouched at the headstone!

"What's . . . what's wrong with the child?" *Kevin recovered first, advancing on the pair, sounding far too normal in a world gone mad.*

"He's sulking," *the elder said in a twisted note of piety and sarcasm. He straightened his posture, recovering his dignity and poise, turning, and speaking more naturally.* "I nearly forgot, we have orders, don't we? I'm to show you the graves of your dearly departed—the Devil's familiars whose place you shall perpetuate in the annals of history . . . Come along, boys. We mustn't disobey the master." *He paused then, rolling his wide eyes from one of them to another. A smile skated into his lips and deepened the trenches in his cheeks as if he might be enjoying a silent joke.* "And he is, you know? Your new master—the Devil."

He stood, now, still smiling that twisted gnarl as he turned his focus toward the cowering child. His tone changed, the lines softened with an echo of sorrow—

"Everything seems to be all right."

Yanked from the memory, Darius jolted slightly as Rutherford halted in front of him. Too deep in the memory. Darius couldn't recall moving from behind the bar, leaning at the pillared post. Orienting, he met the man's critical gaze, aware of the chap's curiosity. They were close to the same age, but this agent appeared younger with his neatly cropped hair and concern etched in his rigid face. "I'm sure everything's fine."

"Are you alright?" Rutherford asked carefully, wisely doubting it.

Reading the discomfort, Darius understood the man's conflict. They hadn't exchanged more than a dozen words throughout the day, nothing of a personal nature to suggest concern or genuine interest. Humanity, then. To reach out to another with a simple question, a natural empathy and desire to offer comfort. The man's occupation stood in conflict with his nature. "It's been a long day," Darius said by way of explanation, wondering how bad he must appear to gain this mate's solicitude. Pushing off the post, managing a slight apologetic smile and including Baines, Darius commented, "For whatever it's worth, thank you gentlemen for humoring me today."

"We'll have a team set up outside the door," the elder chap stated crisply. "You shouldn't have any problems tonight."

If he faced ordinary men, an ordinary killer, Darius might agree. The security inside and outside the hotel had tripled, and the Bureau hadn't attempted to conceal that detail. To them, making Darius Brock the bait to catch a psychopath hadn't entered the realm of possibility. If they could have placed him in a safe house and thrown a net of security around him, they would have done so or escorted him personally to the airport and put him on his plane. They were pawns. Merely human pawns to sweeten the pot in this game. They could be knocked down and removed from play as easily as the knobbed pieces on a Chessboard, a mere distraction and entertainment for the masters of this game.

Nothing of his internal thoughts surfaced as Darius ushered them to the door and fastened the locks, sliding the deadbolt home. Carrying his drink, he paced a moment, considering the sensibility to attempt arming himself and nearly laughed at his foolishness. He had no weapons to fight this enemy. If it came to kill him, he would either die or survive by the Baron's design. A quandary this, Darius mused while bringing his cellular phone from his coat, settling on the corner of the couch near the land phone. To escape one monster, he needed to rely on another. His weapon, the bloody telephone. His only hope for survival rested within the Baron's realm, and therein lay the true quandary ... survival ...

"I pity you, gentlemen," Thaddeus spoke solemnly, his gaze locked on Kevin who held his spindly arm, halting another physical strike.

Still stunned, Darius rested in a stooped pose, his gaze fleeting off the boy cringing against at the stone. His soft sniffs and snivels were as human as any natural child. The child was hurt, physically hurt. In a paradox, Darius glanced between the injured lad and the maniac who'd struck so fiercely, unexpectedly.

The old man was a monster. Clearly, Darius understood that much, having heard the soft lulling notes, the sympathy and sorrow in the frail voice. He'd fallen for those words, believed the elder meant to comfort the frightened little beast, and even that detail had disoriented Darius. He'd watched the child creep from his huddle, advancing warily, worriedly; his immense twilight eyes darted fearfully to Darius and Kevin. At the last instant, when the boy would have flown into the elder's proffered arms, the old man had balled his fist and sent the child sailing. By reflex alone, Darius had lurched toward the boy as Kevin, nearer the old man, had caught the elder's arm to stay the assault. The child was frightened of him. By instinct, Darius understood the child's fear . . . and he'd appeared as a child, a hurt and sobbing child cradling his undoubtedly bloody mouth and battered cheek. In the moonlight, his eyes reflected a silver light as if genuine tears glistened on the surface.

"You've made a pact with the devil himself," *the old man continued in a soulful, conversational tone, drawing Darius's gaze to the gnarled face.* "You should have let him kill you . . . all of you. If I'd known sixty years ago, what I know now, I'd have tried to kill the bastard myself. It's too late for me, but you two . . . if you were smart, which I have reason to doubt," *he spoke arrogantly.* "You'll drag that monstrous little bastard from his bed one day and toss him into the noon sunlight. He's no child. Never be fooled by his smiles or giggles. He's the devil's own seed and if you destroy it, the devil will die as well . . . Levine Brock knew that. You should regal him as your savior, your hero, accept what he attempted to do for all of you and follow his lead. You two . . . you can stop this plague of evil. Break your vows. If you truly want to help your family, break your vows, and set yourselves free . . . kill the seed, the devil will follow. The hell you will live is not worth the price you will pay . . ."

The ranting of a madman, Darius had believed then, and as he sipped his bourbon, he knew the accuracy even now. If he'd known then, standing on that bluff, what he learned a short time later, it was Thaddeus von Hendricks he would have killed . . . but that was so easy to believe in hindsight. Like every other memory from that long black night, the moments on the bluff were shrouded in confusion and fear. Who was the monster? The little beast sobbing with such abandon that it nearly broke Darius's heart to hear him . . . or the fully human old man who'd repeatedly struck that little beast, battering the weird child again and again? In singsong rhythms, the decrepit elder had lured the little fellow from the stone, twice more. Thrice in all, Darius remembered. Three times, he and Kevin had watched and listened, lost in their confusion to hear that old man apologize and play on the child's desire for comfort, luring the boy from his huddle only to strike the child a wicked blow. The von Hendricks were truly cursed. Alive or dead, they were monsters.

His heart had ached for that boy who'd been so dreadfully afraid of him and Kevin, too afraid to run to them for comfort where he might have received what he'd desired. As drawn as a miller to light, the boy had flown to his alleged 'grandfather,' buckling to his child's fright, only to be battered and struck again.

Suffer the children, Darius considered with a lingering ache of sorrow. He knew Raphael's story. He'd learned the boy's beginning and short end on that bluff so long ago. Even in life, the youngster, a direct descendant of the von Hendricks bloodline, hadn't lived an easy life. That he'd remained so innocent and reached his eleventh year with his innocence intact was still a mystery and a miracle. Conceived first in the throes of true love, then again in the fires of hell. Were the details recorded, Darius wondered? If he went to the seaport city in Scotland, would he find records of the murder of Raphael's father? The man had been hanged according to the tale Raphael had told, as told to him by the Baron. A great-great nephew of Amad von Hendricks, the chap had fled the palace to make his way in the world, and ended his life hanged on a cliff on the banks of Scotland, victim of the same circumstance that had condemned the Baron two hundred years before.

Darius hadn't asked Raphael's mother's maiden name, feared even now, he might know the answer. History, like damnation, repeated itself. She'd probably been a Brock. Her father, her brothers—Brocks. The Baron had never said, and Darius had never asked, but he still wondered. Had the Brock clan murdered Raphael's natural father as the clan had attempted to murder Amad so many years earlier? A probability. The families were so interlocked, interwoven, destined by black fate to twine and twist, condemning and damning each other again and again.

Thaddeus was a fool, a damned fool to believe there would ever be a means of breaking this curse . . . if anything, that old man's wickedness had only strengthened the curse. Because of that black-hearted human and his twisted human nature, hundreds of Brocks had died. A conspiracy, a plot. Damned fool. After all his human years in the Baron's shadow, the idiot learned well, but missed the most important clues of the Baron's nature. The Baron thrived on plots and conspiracy, enjoyed no greater thrill than to simmer the pot until he drank his moment of triumph.

His thoughts turned full circle without relief. The moment of triumph had come. In two-hundred-year cycles the curse repeated itself. In two-year cycles, the Baron played his games. For two years, the Baron had permitted the curse to spill through the Brock bloodlines, undoubtedly enjoying every lost life. Two years. Was there symbolism in that number? The Baron and Raphael. A year for each of them. For two years, the Baron had granted the child suffer the full wrath of Levine Brock, the fool who'd conspired with Thaddeus von Hendricks. For two additional years, the Baron had festered, awaiting George Halbrook to act.

For two years, the Baron had allowed this latest plot to fester, and Darius chanced to wonder if it might be a Brock behind this conspiracy. Had one of his clansmen suffered the change? Had one survived more than his natural years?

The idea seemed impossible. If nothing else, Darius knew the Baron stood by his blood oath, and again, it had been Raphael who'd offered insight to realize, despite all rhyme and reason, despite the wickedness inside the Baron, the monster clung to his word as deeply and completely as any nobleman. Once vowed and sealed by blood, the Baron would keep his promise. He'd been a nobleman, a man of honor, an innocent when he'd been wrongly accused and condemned. Blood. Nobility. Amadeus von Hendricks would have been a king in his castle, an honorable king, a decent man . . . if the evil hadn't first manifested in the Brock clan and destroyed him.

Darius shook his head, swirling the bourbon in the bottom of the glass. His ancestry grieved him. He was never certain now if he lived this hellish life to save his clan, or simply to make amends for the injustices against an innocent decent man. As much as he loathed the Baron and all the evil wrapped around the monster, Darius suffered a sorrow for him, an empathy with him. In shining moments, Amad was the man he would have been, and how it must torment him to battle his wicked nature to extend a kindness.

Tortured. To bear so much natural decency locked inside and to battle oneself just to offer a kind word or allow a mercy to slide through the cracks of wickedness . . .

If Darius could travel backward in time, he might slay the Brocks who'd ambushed the young Lord von Hendricks and dragged him from the bailey. A plot. A wicked black plot to remove the heir apparent to the throne. Trusted servants of the von Hendricks, those black-hearted Brocks.

As the scroll had detailed and George Halbrook had later verified, two Brock brothers had held the highest positions beneath the king, an aide and the castellan. Amad had been in love with the castellan's daughter, had planned to marry her when she came of age. He was a young man of honor and high breeding, hadn't once touched her in a carnal sense. He hadn't known she was with child when the Brock's rallied and dragged him from the keep. They'd beaten him with fists and whips . . . and took him into the woods, tethering him in a place from which he was never expected to return. Bleeding, they'd left him tied to wooden stakes, a sacrifice to some wicked thing of legend. Murder, by no other definition. Perhaps, only two or three of the elders had believed something more existed in those wild black forests. No man rode alone into those hills and ever returned. They left their prince half alive, dripping his blood to flavor the chilled air through the woods to draw the natural predators. But Amadeus von Hendricks hadn't returned as a man when he'd entered the village two years later. His father had died believing his beloved son had raped and created the monstrous child which the Brock maiden had birthed . . . a child created instead, by the king's trusted aide, the maiden's own uncle . . .

'. . . And I should be merciful?' the Baron had seethed on that night only eight years past. 'Twice, your clan has conspired against me . . . threatened to destroy me and threaten all that was mine. And I should be merciful . . .? I would rather burn in eternal hell.'

The words slipping through Darius's mind prickled down his spine even now. God have mercy on his soul if this was another conspiracy designed by a Brock.

At his silent cry toward that most elusive of all beings, Darius shivered again and pushed off the couch, unable to remain still any longer. If he'd ever believed in an almighty savior, an ethereal being of true light and mercy, he'd forfeited that belief long ago. Nothing could save him. He was damned to live and damned to die . . . and the clock was ticking.

He felt it. A strangeness. The prickle hadn't ebbed from his spine, an awareness and alarm touching him at the very core. Which would come for him? That remained the only question in his mind, a luxury perhaps, an awareness the young lord of so long ago hadn't been granted. Amad von Hendricks had hung in those ropes, knowing the forest animals would finish him, undoubtedly wanting an end to his human suffering as deeply as Darius wanted his own end now. A luxury, to know he had two choices. To be killed by Amad and have his awareness snatched from his mind, to become a sheep in the keep, or to be killed by an unknown monster prowling through this hotel even now. Darius felt it. Something creeping at the edges of his awareness. A touch of the Baron's influence so remote as to remain natural throughout his life, this heightened awareness. A sixth sense.

Which would come for him?

The Baron?

Or this soldier from the enemy's camp?

Or the enemy, personified, come to make his claim?

A living man against monsters, he would never survive ...and abruptly, Darius knew . . . the Baron was here. If not outside the door, then on his way.

A damned fool, Darius considered as he moved to the door, silently throwing the bolt open then moving toward the bar. Absently, he glanced at his watch, surprised that so much time had passed.

11:31.

By his calculations, he had little more than thirty minutes of life remaining.

Belying the Baron's order to live this day as if it were his last, Darius had understood the implication and the promise. One more day, his last day with the freedom to believe himself a normal man. A single day to live as he hadn't lived in eight years, reveling in the light and life abounding. A kindness and a cruelty. No illusions. He stood at the left hand of a vampire, a human familiar, free for a day to grasp the complexities of the life he'd lost, to kindle the shallow hope and desire for life. All of that would be snatched away, and his only hope lay in the single desire not to be living and breathing in the morning, never to feel again what he'd lost in this madness bequeathed to him.

For the sins of his forefathers, for the acts of wicked strangers long ago departed . . . but that was a lie. Not centuries . . . Levine Brock had lived ten years ago. Whether that bastard still lived remained a mystery.

Despite his effort to remain calm, despite the futility of worry, Darius's hand shook as he gulped his bourbon and set the tumbler aside. Drinking wouldn't help. Nothing would help. By now, he should be immune to fear, should merely accept the inevitable. He should bloody well know the Baron had allowed him to sense the coming moments only to stand him on edge. He felt like a damned child again, one who knew he'd face the wrath of an extremely angry parent . . . and it was no consolation to realize he was exactly that when compared to Amad von Hendricks. Thirty years vs four hundred.

By the time the lock tumbled under an external key, Darius rested controlling the urge to panic. By force of will, he leaned back on the couch cushion and ran his fingers through his scattered damp waves, reaching, collecting his tumbler off the end stand. The moment had come. He would accept his due.

In a position to watch the door, Darius needn't shift more than his gaze when the Baron entered. He was connected, whether by blood or merely extended exposure, he never knew but he'd recognized the bond between them nearly at the onset—that too, beyond his control.

Just inside the door, the Baron paused, and Ted helped him off with his long black coat, the same coat he'd worn two nights ago when arriving at the Grand. The door had closed and locked, leaving a half dozen anxious federal agents in the hall. Even as Amad slid from his coat, his dark blue eyes leveled on Darius.

Uncomfortably, Darius met the gaze, resigning to the inevitable, neither deceived nor relieved by the smile flickering in the thick black mustache. Another prickle lifted as Darius noted the jaw thickening. Frozen in as much natural surprise as heightened awareness, he watched the thick bristles breaking and spreading on the firm chin, a beard forming and lengthening to spill between the black lapels of his tailored suit. In split seconds, the transformations were complete. Openly, Darius stared at the much younger version of the Baron

Amadeus von Hendricks. Long and thick, his black hair tumbled over his suit collar, his blue eyes glittered naturally with a cobalt shine beneath thick black lashes.

Belatedly, Ted stumbled a quick backward step and stared up at the stunning, handsome image with nothing slight of adoration.

This image, this younger bearded version of the Baron . . . Darius had seen it only once before, on a night eight years earlier. The Covenant. As the Baron had rested behind his desk, discussing the broken covenant, he'd transformed, lending each of the twelve the first indication of something beyond the natural realm. The significance of the change now was clear. The Covenant. The change could only verify his belief that his service had ended, and some aspect of the covenant had come into consideration. He'd disobeyed no commands, had fulfilled his oath. Not of his own free will had he laid with Jenna and consummated his love for her. This opponent, this enemy . . . another Brock had broken the Covenant?

With a graceful elegance, the Baron continued forward and sidestepped, settling smoothly into the single armchair directly across from Darius.

The waiting was over. Only that thought held firm as Darius lowered his gaze and fumbled absently with a cigar which he couldn't recall bringing from his shirt pocket under his sweater.

"You've had quite a day, lad," the voice carried a touch of an ancient accent, the depth of that single statement bearing as much sarcasm as threat. "But you look no worse for the wear, I'm noting. A bit pale. A tad distraught. A little . . . guilty, perhaps?"

Darius returned his gaze without reluctance. "I'm not guilty of breaking the oath I made to you," he said quietly, calmly.

"Technically, I suppose you're right. You did seem to exercise a great deal of restraint. I'd rather thought you'd attempt to spend your day tumbling your mistress. Quite impressive, I'll admit," he said with a smile.

Remembering the battle to avoid doing exactly that, Darius withheld his thought, turning his attention deliberately off his emotions to the more immediate concerns. The night past, the bridal suite where he'd nearly lost his life . . . "I owe you my gratitude." *For one more day.*

The brow lifted in a skeptical notch; the bearded lips curved mocking a curious kink. "Your gratitude? For what, I wonder?"

"Saving my life last night. Giving me today."

Amused, the Baron studied him. "I had the impression you resented my intervention, m'lad. You've been in quite a quandary since that little tussle—if not long before it. I happen to believe you would have preferred engaging in physical combat last night. In fact, I think you might have enjoyed sticking your neck out for the chopping. And therein lies my own quandary."

"I can live like this indefinitely," Darius said quietly, his gaze unwavering, thoughts turning. The Baron knew the futility rising inside of him, knew his desire for an end. "You can see to that I know well enough. You can force me to live with questions and fears. You can keep me alive just to torment me and perpetuate my misery until my life expires by natural causes. You can drive me to the brink of insanity or over the edge because I'm still human enough to endure natural impulses and emotions. I can live like this for as long as you grant me . . . and therein lies my futility. I can't die. I can't fully live. My entire existence is beyond my control. If I believed for one bloody instant that I'd escape this madness through death, I'd have taken my own life years ago . . . and you know it," he said and listed his gaze to find Ted staring at him from across the room. Futility. They were all so bloody trapped.

Shaking his head, Darius dropped his gaze and tossed the pack of cigars on the end stand. "When . . . when is it enough?" he asked as he fumbled with the cellophane wrapper on the cigar. His gaze lifted with a quiet strength and intensity. "Will it ever be enough? Is there ever to be a moment when any of us will know peace? Or are we all truly damned to live forever in hell whether here on earth or on some unnatural plane of eternity?"

"Hmm, you truly are in a quandary, lad," the Baron idled, his smile tainted.

"You've taken anything and everything that's ever meant anything to me," Darius said quietly, no longer afraid or worried. "You've made me live every day in fear of consequences which I don't even have good sense to grasp fully. I have only my experience to judge where my future will lead, what penalties I'll pay for mistakes that I haven't sense or ability to avoid. In one respect, I know I've had it easy thus far, and I am grateful. In another, I know I live on borrowed time. Sooner or later, my life will change, and I can no longer cling to the hope that it will improve. A fate worse than death awaits me, and you want that I should live as if I have tomorrow? I have nothing . . . nothing good awaits me and you wonder that I should anticipate death?"

"And to think, I believed I was being kind by commanding you to break your vows," the Baron sighed and shook his head.

"You did so to torment me further," Darius said knowingly, his gaze unwavering despite the ache in his chest. "I've fought against emotional involvement. I never wanted to feel the kind of hurt and fear that comes from loving another. Only one . . . only Raphael could I allow myself to call friend or love, and only then because I know you'd never destroy him entirely. You can take him from me, but you can't hurt him as you can and will all others."

"Certain of that, are you?"

Darius nodded, refusing to buckle under the low threat and challenge of the voice. "In your way, whether you love him as a son, or love to torment him, you do love him. You'd hurt me to hurt him, but he would survive . . . and I'm resigned to being at your mercy. I can't stop you. I can't protect myself from whatever you plan next for me any more than I can fight this opponent, your enemy. I'm damned and doomed and with every word I'm speaking, I'm forced to believe I'm digging my own grave," he said in a moment of dread and greater futility. Dragging his gaze away, he flicked the lighter and dragged a flame into his cigar.

"You know the lie in your words," the Baron mused. "That's one of your more intriguing qualities, my lad. To me, to yourself, you're a fantastic liar. Fortunately, I have a vast understanding of your nature. Even as you speak your lies, you tell yourself you believe your words."

Darius nodded and looked to the bemused, near human eyes. "I'm living the lie to the best of my ability, and you know my nature. I think . . . I do think you know I can't take much more of the life you've granted me. My survival means very little. You hold the survival of my clan over my head, and there are moments, too frequent moments, when I believe I would bless them by destroying them. If I've done so already, if by my honesty, I'm doing so now, not even that can I fully regret. That you're here is slight consolation. I'd rather die at your hand than that of an enemy, and with that admission, I've probably damned myself more. There's no way out of this for me, mentally, physically. I can't protect myself. I can't protect the things that still might mean something to me. If this was truly my last day and you've my end at hand, I can be only grateful."

The Baron smiled more deeply, leaning back more comfortably and merely studying Darius as he lifted his shiny oxford over his knee. "You know better than to believe that announcement comes as a surprise to me, Darius. I've sensed your conflicts from time to time. By your nobility, and on your honor, you'd not destroy the lives you've created. For all your cynicism and deceit, your greatest lie is simply this—you have a grand capacity for compassion. Oh, hide it well, so you do, lad, but that simple truth belies your every action. Deny your love as you will, but that changes nothing. You would take your own life before you'd take the life of another, and in the same respect, lad, you wouldn't take your own life knowing it would cost the life of so many others. A quagmire."

Darius shrugged. "Futility."

"Courage," the Baron said offhandedly and reached in his jacket, extracting a thick cigar. With a glitter in his eyes, he smirked. "Your courage is another trait I've always found rather fascinating. I gave a near impossible task and placed you in a position that tested your strength to the fullest. Few others could have risen to the challenge, and you—you little devil—not only accepted that challenge but managed to prosper in the face of adversity. That's commendable."

At face value, the words could be a compliment, and Darius chose to acknowledge them as such. "Thank you."

"Ah, and there's yet another trait, I enjoy," the Baron mused. "You defy your natural aversion to be humble when you believe the situation warrants. For the most part, lad, you are courageous. Few others have the audacity to speak to me as you do, knowing me as you do. And perhaps, this is a good time to mention, I've never tainted you by blood, lad. What you've done, what you've thought and felt, those are by your own design. I won't deny that I've sometimes looked through your eyes or sensed your difficulties when times became particularly troubled. As I told you once long ago, there's a little part of me in each of you. I was never particularly morally sound, lad. Tumbled with more than a few of your grandmothers, to be perfectly honest." He smiled wryly and shrugged, "Suppose, technically, you're already my grandson, and thus, lad, you were damned before I ever brought you physically into my realm."

Darius knew at least the partial truth in those words, recalling a similar explanation three days ago, and even now, his sixth sense jangled a warning through his system. The end. An end was coming. Too many compliments. Too many reflections. Darius would have preferred seeing, feeling the Baron's anger.

A smile twitched the bearded lips; the Baron glanced over his shoulder to Ted and commented, "We could use a drink, lad."

Wariness creeping uncontrollably over his mind, Darius glanced to his cousin as the young man draped the coat over a chair and hurried around the bar counter. How had Ted survived? How had any of them survived within this madness? A world existed where businessmen were simply human, where curses were merely words slipped off angry lips, where blood red wine was a compliment to dinner, not a convenience to cover those occasions when the Baron dined within the natural realm. Darius remembered that world again now, thanks to the Baron's gift of a reprieve. A world where he'd scoffed at the mention of monsters, assuring there was no such thing, and laughed at the thought of the devil walking on two legs in the shape and image of a man.

The Baron emitted a humph and his dark blue eyes glittered. The smile was indication enough.

"I won't apologize for thinking," Darius said quietly.

"Wouldn't expect you to, lad," the Baron mused.

"It is over for me, isn't it?" he asked indifferently. "Tonight . . . it's not my imagination that my service is truly ended."

"You have a great deal to offer," the Baron said offhandedly, a smile playing in his lips.

"My blood."

The Baron stifled a laugh as Ted hustled from behind the counter carrying two filled glasses. Without more than a nod, the Baron accepted one then motioned Ted to deliver the other to Darius.

With a glance to his ashen-faced cousin, Darius accepted the glass and locked his gaze firmly on the Baron who held his glass in a position for a toast.

"To change?" the Baron mused.

Darius shook his head slightly, not fully lifting his glass. "I'd rather drink to death."

"To change," the Baron said more firmly, something of his amusement fading.

"I'd rather be dead," Darius repeated.

"You are a stubborn little devil, Darius," the Baron said with a more cynical smile. "What say we drink . . . to your health?"

"To the cessation of the same," Darius said and tipped his glass smoothly, toasting and drinking a gulp without lifting his gaze from the cobalt shine.

With a sly smile, the Baron tipped his head in affirmation, tilting and sipping from his glass. He drew no more than a swallow before setting it aside. "You are worried, Darius, and I won't even attempt to ease your mind," he said soberly. "With the transgressions last evening, we have a serious problem."

No more cat and mouse, Darius understood and nodded slightly, his gaze listing.

"I told you the evening before last, I wouldn't be kind if you were lost to another."

"I wasn't," Darius stated and met the Baron's gaze. "You saw to that."

"You were lucky," the Baron commented indifferently.

"You were there," Darius stated.

"I'll admit, I was rather interested to see how you'd handle your cousin," the Baron commented. "You've become rather complacent of late. Had things gone as planned, you would have been angry, possibly a bit shaken, but I truly didn't count on losing your cousin."

"Then his words . . . him drugging his bride? That was by your design?"

The Baron shrugged, smirking. "You've become complacent," he repeated. "I'd hoped to liven you up a bit. Add a touch of spice to your life." He shrugged. "I understand boredom, lad, and drudgery," he said with dry dark humor. "I rather sensed you mounted the madams with the same excitement as you pull up your pants. Fate, however, conspired against you more than I ever could," he said with a wry smile. "Had I known you merely needed a touch of true love, I might have arranged a different strategy. As it was, fate shined on you twice last night, Darius. If I'd not been eavesdropping, I might not have come to your aid. Thus, you might have been lost to another."

"I . . . assumed the entity I encountered was merely a soldier," Darius admitted, slightly tense and alarmed. "Are you saying—"

"He was, lad, but therein lies our current dilemma. This soldier possessed a great deal of power . . . a bit more than I would have expected, in fact. Very nearly a full changeling," the Baron commented and reached again for his wine. "Undoubtedly, the same fellow who drained our unfortunate friend, Mr. Fradden."

"Then he truly would have tried to take me?"

"I have reason to believe he would," the Baron said and sipped his wine, his gaze holding Darius with a purely human shine. Lowering the glass, he continued, "In the broader scheme of life, Darius, you are still a naive child. You understand my nature and possess an innate instinct or intuition. You know things exist beyond your natural realm, but you don't truly understand those anomalies. That's not intended as a criticism. Merely a fact. Thus, I will explain . . . This soldier, as I said, is very nearly a full changeling. At this stage in his progression, he could have taken you as easily as he took your cousin. By his enhanced nature, he would have done so simply to rebel against his master. Were he mine, I'd kill him," he said without compunction. "But my adversary may feel differently, might not give a damn how many of us he creates. Personally, I'd not let any of my underlings rise to that extent of power which tells us at least something about my opponent."

"Obviously not that he's compassionate," Darius commented, and the Baron smirked.

"Obviously," he agreed. "He's foolish and careless, and quite possibly, still naive to his change. The latter disturbs me for the obvious reason—I haven't created any others recently."

"Could . . . Raphael have?"

"I'd have known," the Baron said simply, surprising Darius by answering. "And you should have known that without asking," he added, his gaze intent. "My lad might be a full changeling, but he's a fledgling still. Very little can he withhold from me."

The Baron knew about the favor and the promise. Under the intense gaze, Darius refused to buckle but his neck prickled. The Baron would never permit his son to fulfill that promise, not now, not ever. No words needed spoken. Darius felt his single escape route closing, his single hope ebbing. *No end.*

"Do you recall the vows you spoke, Darius?" the Baron asked quietly.

Every word. Darius nodded slowly.

In slow motion, the Baron dropped his foot to the floor and set his glass aside. "Come here, Darius," he commanded in a low voice.

Heart slamming a leaden beat, Darius set his glass aside. No request. A simple command . . . and he'd vowed to obey. Tense, as tense now, as eight years past, he rose smoothly and stepped forward, his gaze darting off the blue eyes, dropping to the floor as he halted within arm's reach of the bended knees. An end. A change.

"Kneel, lad," the Baron commanded.

Against every ounce of desire, Darius obeyed, sinking to his knees as he'd lowered a lifetime passed.

"Renew your vows, Darius," the low voice ordered.

25

His vows, his curse, the words that had damned him and condemned him to a life of hell . . . and Darius was no more capable of rejecting the command now than eight years ago. In a low deep voice, he spoke the oath from memory without a need for the Baron's assistance. "I, Darius Brock, vow from this moment forward to serve, to protect, to guard . . . the Baron Amadeus von Hendricks. All that I am, all that is mine, I place in trust to his hands . . . Upon my blood, the blood of my clan, I pledge to obey, to follow, to abide by the laws he lays before me . . . Henceforward, I am bound by this Covenant . . . Should ever I betray his trust, all those bound by my blood will be forfeit. Thus, I vow and enter into this pact as an honorable man . . ." Only memory pain flashed from his thumb where Kevin had scored an ornately etched blade across his flesh.

In a low voice, the Baron continued, "I, Amadeus von Hendricks, accept the blood offering . . . to govern the clan of Brock in a manner I see fit. As the clan has twice betrayed me, I make no promise to be merciful upon this generation. All those who live and breathe in the moment of this agreement are henceforth mine to do with as I will . . ." He stopped there, though many more lines had followed on that black eve of a lifetime past. "Do you abide by these words still, Darius?"

Head bowed, he nodded slowly. "You know I do." To the shadow coming toward him, Darius refrained from flinching, felt only a greater ache of dread as the chilly fingers lighted under his chin and drew his face from the bow. Older, no wiser. As helpless now as eight years earlier. He'd seen too much even then to deny the power behind the cobalt eyes. Under the intense blue gaze, Darius suffered a knot of fear. No man had ever frightened him. No mortal man had ever intimidated him. The Baron Amadeus von Hendricks was not a man and as if to verify those words, red flashes sparked within the blue glass orbs.

"You have served me well of your own free will, Darius," the low voice stated. "You have proven yourself an honorable man and amended many of the injustices against me. Thus, were there another way to protect you, I would. By my own vow, lad, I am bound. A two-edged sword, that oath to govern your clan and accept the responsibilities of all that you placed in my trust. Understand, Darius, this is not a punishment or a misery I'd have planned for you. My word as my bond, I'd never meant this end for you."

"Don't do this to me," Darius uttered softly, his every sense awake and pleading from the depths of his tarnished soul. No end! Not an end as he had hoped!

"We are both trapped by our blood and our vows, my lad," Amad said quietly, and brushed his thumb over Darius's jaw. A nearly human sadness crept into his handsome face, his eyes softened to a more natural blue but still the tiny sparks of red flared around the black pupils. "Upon a time, I was as human as you are, now, Darius, and through you, I've seen something of myself. More than any others of your clan . . . or my own," he added with a touch of weariness. "I've seen myself in you, so and perhaps, you are already more a part of me than even I've realized. Were I you, I'd doubt me as you doubt me now, lad, but look closely. You have in you a talent to recognize the lies I've always spoken. Look now, lad, and realize, it was no punishment that I allowed you to lie with your mistress or visit the land of the living one last time, but the only reward I could afford you."

The truth of the words touched him, but offered no relief, only a greater misery. An end. His end. It wasn't merely his blood to be tainted and taken. "I . . . have never begged you, sir. Not once have I begged a mercy or kindness . . ." And he couldn't beg even now. Not when the futility loomed large in his mind. "I . . . can only ask of you . . . don't do this to me. Don't take what little remains of my humanness. With everything that's inside of me, I'll battle this enemy and keep myself safe in your service."

A faint smile touched the bearded lips. "Thus, lad, I'm counting on," the Baron said quietly and withdrew his hand, sitting back more fully in the chair. "The problem is this, Darius, you have no weapons to battle this enemy. You are vulnerable. As much by your natural scent as the position you hold in my service, you've become a target and a prize to be won." He shrugged by his tone; his head tilted slightly. "You do know me, lad. Thus, you know, I won't play this game fairly. Remove your sweater, Darius, and roll up your sleeve."

The words were spoken so smoothly, nonchalantly, Darius nearly missed the command entirely. Under the intent gaze, he caught up to the words and shuddered in a quick chill. His head shook slightly even as he began to obey, and his heart thudded a more leaden beat. "Would . . . would this change if I truly begged?" he asked with a slightly more desperate note. "I'm . . . I'm on my knees. If I begged—"

"You don't have it in you to beg, Darius," the Baron said quietly, a half-smile in his bearded lips. "That you'd even ask before forfeiting your arrogance and groveling, is only more proof of your arrogance, as well as your intelligence. You know the futility. Keep your arrogance."

"W-will I have it still when you're through with me?" he wondered as he dropped the sweater to the floor at his side.

For a long moment, the Baron studied him, looking into him.

Nothing could Darius hide, and his fear was genuine. He'd seen too many others after the Baron's taint. Sheep. Mere sheep to plod on whatever course the Baron set for them. Darius had seen them, too many of them, living their lives, oblivious of what had become of them, most unaware of what they'd lost. He'd known though. He'd come to recognize the lack of ambition and volition, the lack of vitality. They were sheep, plodding through life without a will to live and no compunction to die. A worse fate, he couldn't even imagine.

"Your right sleeve, Darius," the Baron commanded.

Tense, and suddenly, angry, Darius unfastened his sleeve but in a moment of madness, he pivoted off his knees, onto his feet and backed away, shaking his head. "No," he stated and shoved his fists in his pockets, backing and sidling from the circle of chairs. "I . . . I can't. Won't. Kill me. Kill my children. My clan. I don't give a damn. I can't . . . I can't take this command. I'd rather be dead."

"Darius, come here," the Baron said smoothly.

"No," he stated as he backed into the wall and firmed his balance. "I've followed every rule. Accepted every command you've ever given me. Against everything inside of me, I've never deliberately defied you but . . . but I can't take this bloody command, not of my own free will."

"I've not mentioned your free will, Darius," the Baron said quietly, merely looking across the distance, making no move to rise or advance. "Nor will I. That, I'm afraid, has resided in my keep for the past eight years, lad. At this moment, you have only two choices. Come to me as a man and abide by your oath. Or be dragged forth like a stubborn colt on a shank and I will see that you abide by your oath."

In split seconds, Darius knew the futility of his stubbornness, of his defiance. The decision was made. No escape. Whether he walked across the room and faced his damnation on his feet, or walked in trance, the outcome would be the same. He'd lost. He'd lost whatever remained of his free will and his life years ago. He'd spoken the oath . . . had sworn on his blood and the blood of his children . . . to abide. No choice then. None now.

Angry but resigned, Darius lowered his gaze and dragged his hands from his pockets. Futile and foolish. Shivering internally, he began rolling his sleeve up his arm, only vaguely realizing the strangeness in this command. The shoulder . . . always on the shoulder. The mark, the change, the taking . . . initially, he realized as he forced himself forward. The initial mark on the shoulder, like a brand . . . but later. . . when the Baron chose to dine . . . when Raphael dined. The forearm . . . they both drank from the forearm. Stopped, Darius looked at his muscled forearm then slowly shifted his gaze into the red-flecked blue eyes. No command was necessary. Not a single word. Hand fisted, Darius extended his arm and stood firm.

Leaning slightly forward, the Baron clasped Darius fist and tugged slightly, flashing his gaze downward in silent command.

By his nature alone, Darius lowered slowly, defiantly, holding the inhumane gaze with a force of will as he settled firmly, smoothly onto his knees.

The Baron's smile quivered and grew as he yawned.

Heartbeat quickening, Darius held firm as the incisors lengthened. In slow degrees, the red shine spilled over the dark blue eyes. Feral . . . the eyes shined feral within the lamplight, and it was too late to pull away, too late to reverse a conscious decision. Darius suffered the tug of the Baron's will inside his mind. His balance firmed under an external force. To his throbbing heartbeat and pulse, Darius rocked. His breath halted as the shag of long black hair lowered and the furry lips yawned wider. *No . . . no . . . ahhh, noooo!*

'Yessss,' the single word accompanied the quick, fierce pain shooting up Darius's arm and lurching through his muscles.

Conscious, fully conscious, Darius experienced the burning sensation rising, expanding, racing through his elbow joint toward his shoulder. Suction. His blood racing, pulse staggering, he swayed physically and believed himself pulling away, knew he needed, wanted to pull away. Still, he rested frozen, awake to the reality, the horror. His blood . . . the Baron was taking from him, drinking his blood . . . and it was worse than he'd imagined. Worse than he'd feared. Flames! His arm could hurt no worse if his flesh had caught fire, but this agony ran deeper, raced through his every tiny vein and nerve fiber, cut through his bone marrow, and lanced his shoulder. Awake, fully, his chest caught fire; red hot spikes lanced his heart, staggered the raging beat until he knew death . . . death . . . coming. Dying! He was dying! Not even the trance could stifle the gasped breath and sputtered cry. Nothing had ever hurt like this! Nothing!

Ssstop! Stttooooppp!

Jolted, Jenna came off the edge of the bed, already standing as the word slid off her lips, a desperate cry, "Darrriusss!" Cold sweat lifted, spilling, filling the silky nightgown and clinging the cloth to her spine as a more clammy sensation rose tremors quaking through her taut limbs. Darius! The nightmare! A familiar nightmare! Again!

Moving without conscious thought, she grabbed her thick robe off the end of the bed, awake to the soft light spilling through her bedroom door. Her apartment. But in her mind, she saw him still, his body crumbled. Dead. Magnificent, his body slumped on a dark carpet, brightened by a shallow glow of lamplight. Around him, the darkness hovered as if a photographer held the focus on him alone. Darkness. Cloying and chilly, black shapes spread from his ashen face, but his face remained illuminated. Head rolled and held aloft by an unseen entity. His beautiful brown eyes stared, sightless, empty beneath the fan of thick black lashes. Ashen, nearly gray, his complexion glowed; his mustached lips parted in a silent scream. Dead. His arms and legs scattered in a crumbled tangle. She saw his arm thrown outward, upward, glowing in the circle of light . . . and a crimson trail glistened, spiderwebbing over that powerful limb. His wrist slashed—

Swallowing a cry, Jenna sped across her room, pulling on her robe to ward off the frozen breath around her. Too vivid! Too lifelike this image sailing, hovering, and freezing in the foreground of her mind. A nightmare! Just a nightmare!

Heaving breaths, trembling fiercely, she reached her kitchen. Nothing of the soft neon nightlight touched her, no warmth from this low beam. Before her hand reached the overhead light switch, she halted, remembering the surveillance . . . the FBI. Backing away by force, she turned and gathered the robe around her, turning more, searching. Her apartment. This was her apartment. Her refrigerator humming softly, a fan motor running. Heater vents emitted a tiny clink that threatened to drive her crazy long before this waking horror had heightened her awareness. Without a clear thought, she moved to the vent and might have kicked it—caught herself before stubbing her bare toe.

"Oh God," she heaved and the hysteria in her voice startled her to swing away. What—what was this insanity!

Panic still too keen in her mind, she pivoted and stared at the clock on the coffeemaker. Eyes wide, round, she stared at the numbers as if they were written in hieroglyphics. Seconds, possibly minutes past before the time registered and she drew a short cry . . . 12:00. Midnight. Exactly midnight! A shudder rolled down her spine. Dread, fear, and horror clawed at her every mental fiber.

No. She would not, could not let herself think about this! The numbers, the time meant nothing! But she was still watching when the digit flipped . . . :01.

Darius was dead. Not on a plane. He was dead. As if something inside her heart ripped, she knew the certainty. Tears lifted and spilled, flowing down her frozen cheeks, her lips parted.

The nightmare . . . not a nightmare. A premonition.

Nooo!

In a flashing instant, she locked onto the image, and saw him, crumbled, broken . . . reaching for his assailant with his bloody arm. Not his wrist, the blood trails spilled down the ashen flesh toward his elbow . . . and something held him. Poised within the neon glow, Jenna shuddered and stared internally . . . a flicker of lashes. Lips parted . . .

A spark.

Unconscious of her decision, she lurched into motion, and reached the living room, already grabbing the receiver. The FBI! They were in the hotel! They would—could save him still! She had to phone . . .

Her finger halted on one of the keypads, holding the number down, frozen. His words . . . the words he'd spoken in the car. '. . . Cut off communications . . . speak to no one in the Hendricks Corporation . . .' If she needed to check . . . his plane. 'Call in the morning and ask about my plane . . .'

Trembling more fiercely, Jenna released the button and clamored the receiver to the phone base. He'd made her promise before leaving this room. She'd promised. How could she break that single promise . . . over a nightmare? A dream?

As if the life drained from her limbs, she sidled and sank onto the couch, catching her head in her hands. The tremors, aftershock tremors, spilled through her system. Her heart hammered quick painful beats, stifling her breath. "God help me," she uttered, on the brink of a sob. If what she felt was real . . . she couldn't bear the thought.

In memory flash, she saw his smile in the candlelight . . . the intensity of his eyes . . . felt the warmth of his embrace as they'd stood on Mt. Washington, melded together like a single monument braced against the cold. Not possible. He couldn't be dead. Too smart. Too strong to have been caught and killed by a psychopath! Whatever this madness, she could not, would not believe it!

A nightmare driven from the sludge of her subconscious . . . The dumping ground of the mind, someone had told her. She'd gone to bed in fear for his life. She'd spent the past three days fearing for his life and feeling his ambivalence. How could it be otherwise that she would wake with such a terrifying image?

A nightmare, nothing more . . . but one certainty remained. She wouldn't even attempt to sleep again before making that phone call. At first light—at first light, she would phone the airport . . . then she was getting the hell out of this apartment, going to her parents' house, visiting her sister . . . something. She wasn't staying alone in this apartment at the mercy of wicked nightmares. If nothing else, the sound of a human voice would be a comfort . . . and she did hear voices suddenly, soft lulling voices at the edges of her mind...

Darius heard the sighed breath at the edges of his silent scream, felt the world spinning and his head sinking, his body collapsing. Heaving breaths, short soft grunts, he clung to his consciousness as he sank against the black clad legs. A hand caught his head, steadying his thudding skull. Conscious, barely, he heard the low silky words.

"Better. Much better . . . relax, now, lad . . . Nothing to fear . . . Open up, child..."

Not a child, the words weren't meant for him, but something touched his lips. Through a haze, he gleaned only shadows, an immense shadow from which he meant to shy. Bitter, the taste touched his tongue and he sputtered, attempting to pull away. *No . . . no mooore!* A futile silent cry, a desperate cry. His own, Darius understood as the hand clasped his head and held him more firmly. Fire, the taste on his tongue spread like fire and his entire body convulsed in a spasm of shock. Without a conscious thought, he lurched and nearly broke from the firm grasp. Choking, suffocating, he sputtered and tried to spit the burn from his mouth. Only dry heaves caught in his throat and jerked him within the small compact circle.

"There now . . . All finished, now, lad . . . Just catch your breath, my lad."

Shaking his head, he awoke to his muscles thickening, gathering. His sight cleared more rapidly. He rested in a clumsy fold between the Baron's shins, his head still pressed and held against the knee. "No . . . no . . . fuck," he heaved and jerked, picking himself partway up as the burn continued spilling through his system, shaking him, jerking him from the inside out. On his hip, he halted, holding his right arm in a cradle against his waist, dropping his head more fully against his raised knee, rocking with the breaths. *Hurts!* His arm. His shoulder. His chest. Even his toes within the soft leather shoes. *Hurts!*

Of course it hurts, my lad, but that will pass.

That voice . . . the voice! The words were inside his head! "N-no," Darius heaved, and his head rocked in denial, rejecting his thoughts, his revelation.

Careful, son . . . to reject what you know is true will only threaten your vision of reality.

Unconsciously, Darius snaked his hands upward and caught his head, his ears between his numb hands, rocking his head. "No."

A larger hand came over his head, freezing him. *Accept my voice, Darius. Accept what you know. You have questioned the change. You suspected the nature of this change. Accept and adjust, lad.*

Nooo! I don't hear you! I do not hear your voice in my head!

"You've undergone a change, lad," the Baron's deep silky voice cut through Darius's palms, echoing inside his head as if through a tunnel.

Darius choked a breath as if gut punched. Hot tears burned behind his closed lids.

"My boy, I don't expect your gratitude, but I will demand your acceptance."

"No."

The Baron sighed, his voice slightly amused, "So, and you are stubborn even now. Stubborn, defiant . . . obviously, a tad unruly. Odd, don't you agree, son? I would think a sheep to bear less volition. I'd venture to say—a sheep would resign to its fate and simply nod doggedly. Ah, but you defy me even now."

The words taunted, making no sense in Darius's scattered thoughts.

"Sit up now, lad. Let me have a look at you."

Go to hell! Darius screamed silently.

"Is that any way to talk to your pappa?"

You're not . . . no. Not possible. Darius refused to acknowledge the possibility, but before he quite caught up to his motion, he stared up at the Baron. All too clearly, the more human eyes glowed, the mustache twitched . . . and in a flashing instant, Darius knew he hadn't consciously obeyed the command to lift his head. The change . . . he had undergone a definite change.

"Indeed, you have, Darius," the Baron said in a low musing tone. "You are more—and less—than you were when I entered this room. The sooner you accept and introvert the change, the easier this may be for you."

"Wh-what h-have you done to me?" he heaved softly, half fearing he already knew.

Rather than answer, the Baron reached into his jacket and Darius glimpsed the reflection of silver an instant before his hand shot up and caught the projectile tossed to him. Lowering his gaze, he opened his fist and stared at the silver spoon . . . the same small ornate style spoon that he delivered to the Brock infants. He shook his head in denial even as he grasped the implication. A son . . . the Baron's son. A vampire son . . . Raphael. "No," he stated and lifted his gaze to the glittering blue orbs. "Not . . . I'm not. . ."

"No, not entirely, Darius," the Baron commented idly. "You're something of a fledgling, and I'll mention, still bound by your oath. Slightly more so, in fact. You're bound by my blood."

Impossible! The words. The spoon. A trick! He wasn't . . . couldn't be . . . wouldn't have been changed to that extent! Without a conscious thought, he rose off the floor, his gaze darting. His cousin drew back against the end of the counter, staring at him wide-eyed. Nothing had changed! Warily, Darius bounced his gaze to the Baron who simply watched him. Turning, Darius paced toward the couch, toward the window. He wasn't a fledgling vampire! *A sheep . . . or a cow.* The Baron had fed off him no differently than the chap fed off the servants in his keep...

Even as Darius considered that thought and his anger kindled, he awoke to a greater strangeness . . . a very definite strangeness. Where he'd always sensed when someone watched him, he felt the eyes now . . . and heard. He heard an echo of his cousin's fear and dread . . . fear of him . . . dread for him. The Baron had fed. *Changed.*

Stopped, poised as if to take flight, Darius heard and sensed, felt the human presence beyond the door. One or another of the agents shifted his weight on a chair, another sighed. Keening, Darius caught Jenna's scent on himself, the soft fragrance enhanced and rising through his nostrils touching off memory flashes inside his mind. He shook his head . . . felt . . . he felt the Baron watching, felt the presence as if another entity hovered at the edges of his mind, listening, looking into him . . . *sharing his every thought!*

Turning slowly, Darius met the Baron's gaze. *You're inside my head.*

"A detail you'll need to accept, Darius."

"What if I can't?"

"You don't have a choice, lad," the Baron said simply. "I share your thoughts, and I have no desire to conceal that detail from your consciousness. In fact, son, I fully intend to enjoy your current distress."

"You fully intend to drive me stark raving mad," Darius stated as his insides trembled with tension.

With a humph, nearly a laugh, the Baron mused, "You're too arrogant to fall into madness, son. Trust me. No matter how miserable you are, you'll maintain your sanity."

"That should be a relief?"

"You know better."

"This is . . . my comeuppance for attempting to defy you?" he spoke if only to offset the strangeness pulsing inside his mind.

"I'd no more punish you for that than I'd hold a bird responsible for having wings," the Baron smirked. "If the bird was mine and attempted to fly too often, however, I'd be forced to clip its wings. Thus, my son, you've been grounded."

"I'm a sheep," Darius said distractedly, his gaze listing. Too many sensations. Between the sounds and smells, the alien presence inside his mind, and the effort to carry on the conversation and work out the details, he lost his concentration. Something . . . he wanted something. Or *felt* something. *Fear, possibly. Confusion.* Or was it something physical to tremble him more fiercely?

Whatever this strangeness, he knew a growing agitation inside himself . . . and it worried him, if not genuinely terrified him.

Pacing . . . he caught himself pacing to the end of the couch and halted, driving his fists into his pockets as if to hold himself together. An explosion. Something inside of him threatened to explode. Tension spiraled through his quivering system, his anger rising at an equal speed with his ascending fear. He wanted this stopped! *Needed . . . needed this stopped!* Out of control! He was losing control! *Something!* He needed—

Barely, the thought crossed his mind when he stepped and swung. A split second before his backhand connected with the lamp, an arm looped over him and wrapped around him lariat style, cinching his arms to his sides. Yanked backwards, he staggered within the fold. Heaving ragged breaths, Darius struggled to break the fold. Stepping, pitching within the lasso of arms, he staggered the solid form at his back.

"Enough, lad. Settle," the deep voice cut in close to his ear. "Calm down and listen . . . listen . . ."

Stillness . . . a preternatural stillness crept through his raging system, into his mind, but he heard . . . he heard the voice spreading inside of him, saturating him, and he understood the wordless sounds. A fledgling . . . not fully turned. No longer fully physically human . . . a soldier. Caught halfway between life and death, a foot in either realm. Bound, joined, his every thought and impulse at the Barons' immediate disposal. He'd retained his human nature. Could think. Feel. Enhanced. Bright light sensitive . . . avoid direct sunlight, shade his eyes, continue to wrap himself in dark cloth . . . buy a hat.

Tears spilled from under his lashes, falling silently as the sounds and impressions continued filling, saturating his mind with understanding. No longer fully human. Changed. More changed than any others he'd ever met. The Baron had taken from him . . . and given something of himself in return. Connected. His every thought and action . . . shared.

Only half aware of moving, Darius settled clumsily onto the couch cushion, his arms free. Dropping his elbows to his knees, his muscles quivering and senses spinning, he caught his head between his hands. He'd never wept openly, not in sorrow or pain, not in joy. Not even as a small child that he could remember . . . but if he could, he would now. Worse. This was worse than he imagined. *A new dimension of hell.* And he recognized the Baron eavesdropping on his silent misery, sensed satisfaction in the presence. The Baron hadn't changed him for spite . . . he'd acted on practical reasons . . . but the devil would take his due and enjoy every instant of this new torment. Torture. To have every moment, every thought and action monitored, governed by another . . . torture.

In heated waves, anger and pain assailed his mind, rising and falling, high and low. No stopping it. Control . . . his self-control had shattered. Under the weight dropping on his head, Darius lurched mentally and might have shied physically, but an internal command halted him, held him . . . and Darius grasped that complexity as well, understood the significance in this gesture, the verification. Nothing could he deny or defy. As badly as he wanted to escape that hand, not even his muscles would lurch or jolt at his command. The Baron's will held him internally. No voiced command, not in his mind, not in his ear. As easily as the hand gripped Darius's head physically, something far darker and deeper, held dominion internally.

The Baron was inside of him.

And outside of him.

The hand scuffed Darius's sweated hair in a gesture of mocked reassurance and comfort. In a horrible moment of crystal clarity, Darius grasped the paradox. He wanted, very nearly needed to accept that comfort . . . and at the same time, knew the black humor behind the feigned affection. Forever . . . forever he'd been alone. Relying on his strengths and weaknesses, depending on himself to survive mentally, physically. He wanted that hand gone! Wanted . . . needed to handle this alone, as he handled all things. But even as those thoughts surfaced, Darius suffered the sensation of the hand becoming an extension of himself . . . an extension of his mental aspect, a lifeline to calm and console. Never had he known a greater confusion or conflict. Not him. This was not happening to him . . . but when the hand tugged him sideways, he moved without resistance. Waking . . . waking fully, he knew himself resting against the Baron's broad chest, felt the arm wrapped over his shoulder, embracing him, holding him like a damned child. Never . . . not in his eight years of service had Darius embraced the Baron. Others had . . . Teddy had fallen under his spell at the onset. Brian loved and hated him. Kevin . . . the oldest of the twelve, the strongest of the twelve . . . Kevin had broken down . . .

They'd been seated around the long banquet table . . . all of them together again for the first time. At the head of the table, the Baron rested, chatting, outlining their future, taunting and testing them even then . . . . breaking them. Back and forth, the word games, the prodding and probing, the torment. Darius remembered his confusion at that gathering, his shock and horror as he'd awoken to the Baron's plan for him. Kevin . . . . the leader among them, the strongest, the chosen . . . to sit at the Baron's left hand at the table, directly across from Raphael who'd simply poised like a proper child and listened, watching the Baron's manipulations.

'. . . With my clan as my witness,' Kevin had spoken at the brink of frustration and pain. 'Give us some sign of your mercy or I'll drive a knife through your black heart and end this misery for my clan . . .'

No mercy. None. Beneath the table, Darius had kicked his cousin a fierce blow to silence him, as Kevin had kicked him to halt his rising temper and shock at least twice during dinner.

The Baron had ignored the threat . . . simply continued to taunt, turning his attention toward the youngest Brock at the table. Sam . . . Darius remembered Sam sitting toward the center of the table, his blond strings hovering over his barely touched plate, his young face twisted in a mask of physical pain. What had been done to that boy, a child of no more than fifteen, should never have been done to any man. Mentally, physically, the boy had been destroyed. As helpless as all others, Darius remembered his sorrow and shame, to look upon the sobbing boy . . . and he remembered the fear for his child, for Dylan who'd been held somewhere within that black manse.

The Baron had shown them his . . . *mercy*. Eight of the twelve had risen to their feet without a word and marched around the table, their eyes glazed and faces lax. He'd taken from them, had changed them during the night. Only four . . . only one third of the twelve remained untainted and sat, stunned and stricken to silence, watching as each robotic man strode to the Baron and bowed, then returned to his chair without a conscious thought. Even Sam had plodded without a visible sign of distress, his contorted face pale and lax lips parted. 'Should I keep them here then, Kevin? Consign them to the dungeon and continue to take from them after the sacrifices they've offered me? Or should I allow them to forget what's become of them and let them live their lives as I planned?'

Belatedly, Kevin had realized his temper . . . and his threat of betrayal. In split seconds, beneath the twilight shine in the dark blue eyes, Kevin had realized the cost of his words, his conviction. He'd understood his mistake to threaten the newly formed Covenant. His arrogance, his conviction, his horror to be responsible for the life and death of so many . . . For the first, and only time, throughout those long, horrible hours, Kevin had crumbled.

Darius heard those sobs even now, low, tortured sounds, like a child as Kevin had dropped his head and buckled forward. His forehead had landed, leaden on his fisted hands on the table. Darius had heard grown men cry, drunks and derelicts in alleys, family men sobbing on a bar stool after too many pints. Never had he heard a more desperate, deeper sorrow, a more mourning sound . . . and something of himself had broken with Kevin. He'd reached. He'd meant to clasp his cousin's shoulder if only to stop the sounds, but the Baron had risen smoothly and deflected Darius's hand by gesture and gaze. The fate of their entire clan had rested on Kevin's shoulders at that table. Darius had understood the man's pain and resignation. Kevin had never lost an argument, never lost a case in a courtroom . . . His confidence and arrogance had held firm throughout those long horrific hours of the night. To have lost, to have forsaken his entire clan, to know the Baron could and would take his due from hundreds of innocents . . . Kevin had buckled under the weight of what his words could cost. To lose his life had meant nothing to Kevin Brock. He would have forfeited it gladly to spare so many others . . . but to lose his life knowing he'd condemned their entire living clan to a greater hell . . .

The Baron had expected nothing less than Kevin's collapse. Like a father, the Baron had clasped Kevin's shoulder and drawn him sideways into an embrace, holding him, comforting him, and drawing him slowly from the very pit of despair.

With the memory quick in his mind, Darius awoke to the same arms wrapped around him, now, to the strength of the hold . . . and his own confusion. Whether he'd brought the memory of Kevin to the foreground, or whether the Baron had driven it to the surface, Darius knew only the greater pain rising through him. Kevin had folded, and clung to the Baron, and they'd all shared that collapse, knowing there was nowhere else to turn. They were at the Baron's mercy or misery. Their lives forfeit.

His life was forfeit now. No turning back. No hope for salvation. Lost. He was lost. Against his nature to stand alone, Darius battled, wanting to escape the strength of the embrace, needing to stand on his own feet and find some semblance of his sanity, reality. No comfort to know the Baron hovered at the edge of his mind, sharing his confusion, feeding on the conflicts raging through him. On a dual plane, Darius knew his foundations crumbling, buckling to the greater force inside of him, and knew he had nowhere else to go, no means to escape. His life as he'd known it . . . his freedom to think and feel, to be human . . . the last of his humanity was gone.

A monster . . . he was a monster, now. A mere extension of the devil he'd loathed and feared . . . and not for an instant could he forget or ignore the alien presence eavesdropping on what little remained of his humanity. No escape. Nowhere to hide. Not physically. Not mentally. His every thought . . . action . . . emotion...

26

"Worse things could have happened to you, son," the deep voice intruded, breaking through the rising hysteria and halting Darius on the brink of a sob. The hand moved in a gentle motion over his chilled fingers and scattered hair. "Far worse things, in fact," the Baron continued smoothly. "Better the devil you know, lad," the low voice mused. "Never a more fitting cliché than at this moment, eh?"

Darius shared nothing of the humor in the voice, knew only his greater distress.

"Odd, very odd," the deep voice mused. "I've not felt such a fresh kinship and affection in years." With a deliberate, elaborate breath, the Baron ducked and sniffed at Darius's available hair, sighing satisfaction. "Just a touch of my scent in you, enough for my enemy to know in whose keep you remain. Scents, Darius. If not immediately, you will grasp the complexity of life's flavors. In time, you will identify those scents. Where you had only your innate talents to judge a man's integrity or corruption, you will know more swiftly, now."

Raphael had told him about the scents . . . and the hunger to accompany those scents. Blood. Hunger . . . he was hungry, he realized in a fleeting instant not certain from where the thought originated.

"A natural reaction," the Baron commented.

No mercy, Darius realized even as he moved to an internal and external command, settling more smoothly against the arm and broad shoulder. In his mind, he suffered an impulse to rise and move away. His body remained relaxed and limp. His hand slid off his head, lowering to rest against his thigh. No mercy. He knew the greater force inside of him, holding him still. Only his head rolled, his senses shying as the Baron moved through his line of sight, reached to the end stand and lifted the barely touched wine glass. *No. Don't. Don't.* But his words were futile. His dark eyes heated, Darius looked into the bemused blue eyes as the Baron lifted the wine glass. Unwittingly, Darius parted his lips, rejecting the internal commands only in his mind as he swallowed the bittersweet liquid poured down his throat. Why? Why was the Baron forcing him to endure this? But even as he questioned, the answer came. A force of will. *The verification.* The Baron hadn't lied. He would enjoy every moment of this torment. The blue eyes glittered with a satisfied shine, arrogance and amusement emanated from the slight twitch of a grin, A mocked innocent grin that Darius saw and understood too clearly.

"Paternal instincts, son," the Baron said in quiet comfort. "For all intents and purposes, you're a newborn. Only fitting a father should feed his infant, wouldn't you agree?"

Do I have a choice?

The Baron stifled a laugh. "No, I don't suppose you do, son. And I might also admit, I rather enjoy having you humbled for a change. Even now, fully in my keep, you'd like nothing more than to defy me." He lifted the glass again, forcing swallows into Darius's mouth. Smirking, he commented, "I might also mention, lad, you need to adjust and accept this change inside of you. At times, I may be inclined to take control. Considering your defiance and your confounding nature to lead, those moments shall be the most difficult for you. No longer does the decision lie within your grasp to obey. No longer shall you think before you act on my command. I have put something of myself inside of you and my will is the reigning entity. Battle that detail as you like—you won't change it."

"I have never defied you, never disobeyed your direct orders or command," Darius spoke aloud, his gaze steady despite the ache sliding through his mind. "Why . . . why have you done this to me? What have I done to . . . deserve this torture?"

Head canted at an angle, the Baron spoke smoothly, "Are you so sure this is a torture, lad?"

"You've taken what was left of my humanity."

"I've given you something in return," the deep voice cut in, the eyes turned nearly twilight. "Consider it a curse, or accept it as an honor and privilege, lad. That choice remains yours, and do not misunderstand me. You have retained enough of your humanity to make choices for yourself. You are bound to me, by oath and by blood, yes. When your decisions conflict with my own, you shall know the force of my will inside of you. What you need consider and grasp fully, is the essence of the change and the gifts I've bestowed upon you. Oh, make no mistake—you will feel differently about some things. Enhanced, lad. Everything around you and inside of you shall be enhanced, from your six senses to your emotions . . .

"But you are not much different from what you were," the Baron said quietly. "There has always been an intensity within your nature. You take that sense for granted. I've known that since I first laid eyes on you. Scruffy," the low voice mused, the eyes sparked with mischief. "You were a scruffy boy. A renegade without direction. Brilliant but stifled by social and moral conditions. Oh, but the intensity and strength inside of you was well within my power to observe and taste. I thoroughly enjoyed cleaning you up, granting you polish. You defied me even in that simple undertaking, refusing to accept what you became in my keep. A masquerade, isn't that what you've forced yourself to believe? That you are merely masquerading as an executive? You've seen yourself as little more than the same scruffy child who raced through alleys and perused crowds pilfering wallets. A grand jest, you believe even now. You've never felt yourself worthy of the accolades and respect that others shower on you. You've clung to the belief that I rose you to the position of prestige through my dark nature to defy society—you, a slum rat, mingling and mixing with the ton, whether on your homeland, or on foreign soil. Humph," the Baron mused, his dark eyes glittering.

"And you think your current conflicts something new?" he commented. "You've lived in conflict with your nature longer than I've had you in my keep. Nothing's changed in your nature, lad. Trust me. If anything, you may find yourself drawn closer to what exists inside of you. Doubt me as you will, but ask yourself . . . have I controlled you before this night? You have inside of you the power to recognize me inside of you. Ask yourself, lad. Did I control you when you stood in boardrooms and made decisions to effect hundreds? Did I take over inside of you when you stood with a microphone? Did I control you each time you strode through another bedroom door, defying your moral outrage, and fulfilling the Covenant to propagate your clan? How many others do you think could have done what you've done? Could have carried out this endeavor that you consider a masquerade? Blimey, lad, how many others could have overcome their fear and strode to me as a man a short time ago?"

"I didn't have a choice," Darius stated.

"You had a choice," the Baron said soberly. "You could have broken into a sobbing fit and cowered against that wall. In which case, I'd have brought you forward, made of you a thrall and consigned you to pasture. Frankly, that wasn't an option. I know you, Darius. I chose you for your strength, your courage, and your intelligence. A bit on the unruly side. Hot-tempered. A tad cynical and sly . . . but a man who weighs his options and chooses his path with a clear head. In your confounding way, you're an honorable man . . . and a man still, Darius," the Baron said smoothly. "One with some new talents and weapons to protect what is mine, as well as yours. No longer will I abide your desire for death," he commented with a touch of amusement. "My will to survive is inside of you, now, merged with your natural desires. You may find it a tad uncomfortable. I know how close you've come to convincing yourself that death was an option. That option is gone. You will fight to survive regardless of what enemy you encounter with everything that's inside of you."

A thought of Raphael fleeted through his mind.

The Baron shook his head slowly, smiling more darkly. "You know what's happened to you, Darius. You are not one of the blind sheep in my throng. Raphael may attempt to fulfill his promise to you—my lad's always had a sneaky side to his innocence—but you no longer possess the ignorance to allow him to succeed." A smile played more deeply in the corner of his mustache. "Frankly, I'm rather anxious to see how the two of you get along when you meet. For all intents and purposes, I've made you brothers. Considering how much he's loved you hence, you may find yourself the object of a great deal of attention."

Knowing how much the Baron enjoyed tormenting his son, Darius suffered an inkling of the implication. Another side benefit of his change, he realized and chanced to wonder, "Did I seal my fate by asking for his promise?"

"I could leave you to wonder, but you've enough to trouble you at the moment," the Baron mused. "So, I'll admit, Raphael was no part of my decision to ascend you. A side benefit, as you guessed. The lad's been pining and depressed since I took his pet away."

Dylan! A pet. "Damn you," Darius uttered.

The Baron smiled and laughed in a humph. "There's the lad I know and love. Coming around nicely, so you are."

Darius felt the release and in a single motion rose from the lax pose, not stopping until he stood several paces from the couch. Turning, he watched the Baron throw his arms wide across the back of the couch. A normal-human pose. The laughter continued to shine in the dark blue eyes. The smile quivered with a sense of triumph and satisfaction. In split seconds, the beard ebbed, and the thick shaggy hair retracted to a more natural, modern style, not too long or too short. Dressed in his tailored black jacket over a dark gray polo shirt rather than chambray and tie, the Baron could pass for the considerably young tycoon who'd made the cover of several prestigious magazines and appeared in countless business journals. Amad von Hendricks, heir to a dynasty with a network spanning half the globe . . . and a monster behind the purely human mask.

His thoughts were not his own. Darius read the greater amusement behind the twilight eyes. "I . . . can't control what I think."

"Wouldn't expect you to," the Baron mused. "But bear in mind, you may reap what you sow."

"What happens now? What's next?"

"Be specific."

"Your enemy. The game. The murders. My occupation. Will I need what you need to survive?"

"Blood, do you mean?" the Baron mused.

Uncomfortably aware of meaning exactly that, and more aware of a gnawing emptiness inside himself, Darius nodded warily.

"I wouldn't advise ordering a steak well-done," the Baron mused. "But you needn't worry about traipsing through alleys and catching rats to be sated."

Not entirely relieved, Darius ventured a glance toward his cousin. In a heartbeat flash, he read the boy's sorrow and intimidation . . . but how much of that was different? Teddy had always been wary in his company. Intimidated. Squirrelly, Darius considered, more agitated by the pale blue eyes darting away from him, darting to the Baron . . . for comfort? "What the fuck do you think I'll do? Bite you?" Darius snapped.

"I hmm . . . Darius, no," Teddy stammered slightly.

Now, the boy truly was worried . . . and Darius caught the scent, an odd scent to keen his senses. *Fresh.* Spring scent, as near as he could determine. His gaze flashed off his cousin toward the drawn curtains. Winter beyond the glass. Snow. He caught that scent too, but this other . . . *fresh.*

Something stirred inside him. Longing. Desire. He breathed more deeply, fleeting a thought of a meadow in full bloom, a warm breeze. . . *a water scent* . . . like the scents he'd caught on the docks where he'd played as a child. He remembered the docks, the tangy scent of fish . . . but every once in a while, when he sat on the edge of the dock, a scent would spin off the water. *Fresh. Alluring.* A woman's scent, he considered in the next instant, a soft, wispy fragrance to stir him. Distracted, he sped his gaze about the room, recognizing the Baron's distinctive musk scent and an undertow of lemon polish, cigar smoke. Fragrances were enhanced. He still tasted the wine on his tongue and drew an aroma from the glass. This other though . . .? *Where the bloody hell was it coming from? And why the hell did it stir such strange sensations through his lower regions?*

Tense and alarmed, Darius looked at the Baron who studied him with a bemused shine. "Where . . ..?"

In a slow turn, Darius followed the Baron's shifting gaze.

Arms folded across his chest as if holding onto himself, Teddy stood leaning against the stout post at the end of the bar, attempting to appear casual and relaxed. His eyes betrayed him, darting warily from Darius to the Baron, back and forth. His soft pale face flushed; he bit his lower lip in a nervous habit.

Darius ran his gaze down the slender length of the albeit relaxed body, seeing, sensing the tremors within the dark blue jacket and slacks. Handsome . . . the boy was handsome. A Brock despite his soft features, Darius noted arrogantly. Long blond waves, long thick lashes that couldn't quite curtain the worried shine, soft full lips. Effeminate features, Darius considered as he moved toward him. More worried, Teddy locked his slightly wider eyes on Darius and struggled to maintain his relaxed pose. *The scent . . . the soft wispy fragrance . . . alluring. Sensual . . . sexual.* Darius stopped short less than three steps from his cousin and looked into the worried, innocent eyes. With his word echoing inside his mind, Darius drew in the scent and the cheeks flushed more pink; the full lips quivered.

"Goddamn," Darius uttered and stepped back with his revelation. Turning in a quick spin, he landed his heated gaze on the Baron who idled a low dark chuckle. Shaking his head, Darius flashed another wistful glance toward his flushed cousin, then back to the Baron, caught in his paradox. *A virgin! The scent of a virgin!*

Still chuckling, the Baron glanced off Teddy to Darius. "I wondered how long it would take you to work out that fragrance. And I'm not a bit surprised you'd react and recognize that scent." Amused, he looked at Teddy. "You may need take care around your cousin for a time, lad. He doesn't quite hold a rein on either his appetites or his nature and you are a temptation and distraction, he can do without." As an afterthought, he dropped a hand and patted the cushion at his side.

Despite the conflicts, Darius watched his cousin sidle further away and hurry, navigating a roundabout course to reach the Baron. The boy settled smoothly on the cushion at the Baron's hip, appearing only relieved when the hand dropped to his shoulder. Annoyed, if not genuinely angry, Darius glared at the wary boy then lanced the Baron with a heated shine. "I wouldn't have touched him."

"We may debate that notion in time," the Baron said idly. "At the moment, there are things we need to discuss."

The answers to his earlier questions. Darius nodded, moving unconsciously to slip into the single armchair nearest the door, catercorner to his cousin. Distracting, that scent, and the wary shine. Considering the boy's preferences, his obvious attraction to the male gender and the Baron in particular, Darius's anger and disgust rose, his glare intensified. He'd like nothing better than to slam a fist across the boy's jaw . . . and his thought disturbed him abruptly. He'd never judged others . . . never reacted to prejudice. Each to his own. Where was the sorrow and pity he'd known for the boy two evenings past? "Damned fool," Darius growled.

"Lad," the Baron sighed, drawing Darius's attention. "You need to find a balance and attempt to pay attention."

"Fine, then. I'm listening," he stated firmly.

Again, the Baron sighed and shook his head, amused. "Not entirely, but I think that may change in a moment . . . Jenna Windrow."

His attention riveted. Images of the afternoon—and night past—flashed in his mind, heating his body head to heel. The taste of her, the scent, the feel of her warmth. His senses quickened; muscles gripped. His promise to protect her . . . He would keep his promise. Had kept . . .

The Baron heard every word, knew every thought.

A shiver slid down Darius's spine. He'd given her an order to sever all ties, to save herself . . . from the maniac they'd encountered in Canton, from the Baron, from himself. He'd known he wouldn't last . . . hadn't for an instant considered the extent of the changes he might undergo. Blind. He'd expected to be rendered blind. Had anticipated an end to his conscious existence. He was all too aware . . . and waking more swiftly to the enhanced essence inside of him. Caught in a paradox, he wanted her to go and be safe . . . and wanted to keep her within his reach. He wanted to feel her in her arms, needed the warmth of her voice and the heat of her eyes looking into him, touching him as no others had. He wanted her safe, safely away from this madness that had become his life.

His heart in his hands, desperation pouring through his mind, he met the Baron's studied gaze. A reward. The Baron had considered her a reward . . . an act of kindness . . . a final human encounter with the present circumstances in mind.

What if . . . what if that encounter bore fruit?

Not for an instant had Darius thought to use protection. For the first time in years, he'd been entirely lost in the physical aspect of propagation, had loved her and made love to her as a normal man. Not in years had he shared such a wondrous encounter, to tumble in wild abandon with a woman who'd met him with equal fervor. Never again. In a stopped instant, Darius knew he would never again share such a pleasure. If she'd deserved more than he'd offered before, she deserved nothing of what he could offer now, and fear touched him at his core.

Whether he loved her or loved the feelings she'd stirred inside him, it made no difference now. He loved her still . . . and she would be his weakness. Was his weakness . . . just as Dylan had been his weakness for all these years. "Don't use her against me, sir," Darius said in quiet dread. "Don't bring her any deeper into this. Let her go—"

"You know better, lad," the Baron said in a low tone. "And if you think with your head rather than your heart, you'd know it's not merely my wicked nature belying that fact. She is involved. She became involved the instant she caught your eye. A pity love should strike you this late in the game," he said indifferently. "Does she feel the same about you, I wonder?"

Doubts slid through his mind. She'd known . . . by whatever innate sense inside of her, she'd known they would never share a lifetime. A one-night stand. A single day to love her and be loved by her. Did she truly know how short their moments together could be? How little time he had left to love her? She'd admitted loving him, falling in love with him. In her eyes, he'd seen it . . . but had it been real? Or was she . . . no different than the countless others who'd reacted to him? Had she played with him, teasing him with the technique of a practiced skill, simply to share a few pleasant hours between the sheets . . . or to snare him for the illusion of wealth around him?

"Hmm, so, you have been rapt in your emotions with little regard for hers then," the Baron mused. "Don't suppose it matters. You're a single-minded little beast, and with what I've given you, even less trusting than before. I'd think, just to satisfy your curiosity, you'd want to keep her at your side."

"I don't want her hurt any worse," Darius said quietly, honestly. "It . . . it doesn't matter what she thinks of me, what she feels for me. I am self-satisfying and self-centered enough to believe that what I feel for her is enough for both of us. I don't want her hurt. Don't make me hurt her . . . don't hurt her to hurt me. You have me. Let that be enough, this once?"

"Ahh, m'lad, if life were only so simple," the Baron sighed. "But alas, that's not to be. Think with your head," he said again, his blue eyes indifferent. "I've given you an advantage over the beast stalking you. It's an advantage from which your newfound love might benefit as well. Do you think she's capable of fending off this beast alone?"

"If I'm gone from here—"

"She wouldn't last two days. Our mutual enemy would take her for spite. Think with your head. Forget that you are changed. Remember your human-ity. Your vulnerability. Is she safe from the enemy stalking you. . .?"

No.

"Slam your head against a wall if you must, but credit where credit's due. With what I've given you, you are far more capable of protecting her than you were an hour ago. I won't attempt to disillusion you. Not again will you tumble with her. A pity and pure hell, I know," the Baron mused. "From the unique perspective which you afforded me, I'd have to say, the woman's more than adequately equipped to pleasure a man for hours. Unfortunately, you're no longer entirely a man, Darius. And it grieves me to mention, should you lie with her now, you'd taint her, as well as the offspring you might have placed in her womb."

"I . . . I'm impotent, now," he said absently.

"You may find this difficult to believe, lad, but honestly, I haven't a clue," the Baron mused. "We may need to have you tested just to satisfy that curiosity."

A lie.

"On the contrary, Darius," the Baron chastened, still amused. "I haven't created a son in more years than I can remember. None since Raphael, and sadly, the lil' lad never reached the age of sexual interest. He thought about it once . . . went through a horrific stage where he attempted to become a man despite his childish nature," the Baron mused. "Unfortunately, his young body refused to cooperate with his equally young mind. Scared the bloody hell out of himself and sulked for a time. Prior to Raphael," the Baron hesitated and let a deeper glitter of amusement rise. "None of my bound sons lasted long enough to test the integrity of their encounters."

For the second time Darius caught the implication. His days were numbered. And suddenly, he understood the Baron's mention of his will to survive. Where the thought might have pleased Darius no more than an hour ago, a prickle of doubt affected him now.

A more natural smile slid into the black mustache, emitting a glimpse of straight white teeth. "No need to fret in advance, lad. I've clipped your wings; not given you license to fly. My other lads were generally mistakes, which shows just how long ago it's been. You, a pity though it may seem, no longer retain the ability to defy me to the extent that I'd take your life."

27

S hould he be grateful for that reassurance? Or more annoyed? Darius understood the words, if not much else about the changes transpiring inside him still. That he could even carry on a reasonable conversation was something of a surprise. In every instant, the Baron knew his thoughts. Knew his actions before he fully realized them. No defiance. Even his thought processes could be stifled and changed.

"Darius," the Baron interrupted and drew his gaze. "If I'd wanted a robot, I'd have taken less of you and given nothing in return. Your thoughts are your own. You may annoy me, in which case, I will undoubtedly intrude, and you will know my intervention. But I rather like your quick wit and temper. Those, you shall retain."

"Nothing will ever be normal for me again, will it?" Darius asked quietly. "I'll never know another moment of peace. By no bloody fault of my own, I've lost whatever human rights and privileges remained to me. You've left me with the ability to think and to breathe, but you've removed even the human condition to feel the futility and resignation that would have been my due. To be a robot would have been a bloody blessing. You allow me to know, to understand, to grasp fully what I've lost . . . and you want me to be grateful for this? I should feel privileged? Consider it a fucking honor? It wasn't bad enough I've been no more than a prize stud in your stable, now what am I? And don't bloody tell me your son or expect me to believe it. I'm not dead. I'm not alive. I'm not half the man I was a bit ago. So, what am I? Truly? What the fuck am I and what do you expect of me?"

"You can ramble on and rage, and you would wonder at your humanity?" the Baron mused and shook his head. "Perhaps, in time, you'll find your new self, lad," he commented and turned his attention to Teddy. "Why don't you ring room service, m' dear. With the stir we created with our arrival, the griddle should be hot and staff hustling. Three hardy helpings of steak and eggs. Two rare. One medium."

"Yes, sir," Teddy said and scooted sideways.

Blind obedience, Darius considered with an edge, and the idiot obeyed out of pure love and adoration. Shaking his head in disgust, Darius caught the Baron studying him again and held the gaze with his anger. "If you don't appreciate my thoughts, change them," Darius stated and glimpsed Ted's quick fright and fear for him. "Asshole," he commented offhandedly toward his cousin and pushed from the chair. Apparently, pacing was permitted. Tense and agitated, Darius strode from the circle of chairs, striding as far as the curtains and slicing his hand through the thick fold to look out at the night. By sense alone, he knew daylight remained a long way off. Daylight. Sunlight. He shivered and let the curtain fall, sensing the presence behind him even as he turned.

The backhand ripped across his face, lifting him off his feet in an explosion of white light and pain. Blood—he tasted his blood even before he slammed into the sidewall and collapsed in a heap of scattered limbs. Heaving, blinking spots and unemotional tears, Darius shot his hand to his throbbing jaw as he collected his legs in front of him and forced himself to his hip. Above him, several paces away, the bleary image of the Baron posed, arms folded loosely across the broad chest. Only in his mind, Darius heard the deep voice.

I'm no more tolerant of your sarcasm now than any time past, lad, the words seethed. *Perhaps, even less so. You've a mind and talent to restrain your temper, I suggest you use it. Now, stand up.*

A little clumsily, Darius obeyed the silent command, blinking the water and spots away warily, keeping the Baron in his sights. Compared to the Baron's strike, that assault on his jaw in the bridal suite had been a lovetap, and the revelation offered no quick comfort. Never before had the master touched him physically. Emotionally, mentally, the Baron had battered him more often than Darius cared to remember . . . never physically. The power behind that hand was every bit as fierce as the lord's size suggested. "I'm . . . sorry."

"Don't humor me," the Baron commented and stepped forward, backing Darius fully against the wall. At arm's reach, Amad halted and lifted his hand, clasping Darius's wrist and tugging his hand away. No anger in the blue eyes, merely speculation and inspection. With thumb and forefinger, he clasped Darius jaw and tipped his head for a better view. Looking into his eyes, the Baron commented, "Enhanced, lad. Everything you feel, now, shall be enhanced. Part of the curse and a counterbalance to compensate for the fact that you won't hurt for long."

The truth of the words sank in as Darius realized his lip had already sealed and the pain ebbed to a toothache thud, fading rapidly.

"You haven't forgotten your early years," Amad said smoothly. "You were a brawler. A street fighter. A ruffian, by no other word. So, and we'll test your memory, eh? Awaken some of the instincts you've put aside too long." Barely pausing, he backed away and motioned a single finger for Darius to follow him into the more open spaces. Standing an arm's length away, Amad shifted his head, availing his jaw, his eyes glittering. "You'd like to strike me, boy. You've wanted to strike more than a time or two. Now, and you have my permission. Call on all that anger you've banked and strike me if you can."

"I can't," Darius stated despite the accuracy of the words. He'd wanted to strike, had romanced that notion a million times and knew the futility then, as now. "I am bound and I'm no fool," Darius continued carefully.

"Hmm, I've always been forced to offer you a choice. Suppose that hasn't changed," the Baron commented. "Choice . . . hit me like a man or I'll turn you over my knee and whip you like a child, infant son."

"Damn you," Darius uttered, considering the choice. No choice at all. With a half step and twist, he drove his fist upward—and punched open air. Gone! The Baron had vanished. Collecting his balance, Darius pivoted on his heels, searching, darting his gaze off his cousin who'd scrambled off the couch and returned to his post at the bar. Gone! But not entirely. Darius sensed the presence close by, and continued to turn, searching the shadows, remembering his similar effort in the bridal suite. This was not a soldier. This was the Baron von Hendricks, and the fellow could move faster than light. Heartbeat quickening, anticipating another blind strike, Darius backed slowly toward the wall, doubting that would help.

A little slow, lad, the low voice slid through his mind, offering nothing of direction to follow.

"Lucky for me then—" Darius barely finished before the arms wrapped around him, pinning him from behind. Heaving a quick breath, he tried twisting away by instinct and reflex, and the chilled lips brushed against his cheek before he staggered free. Gone! Gone again. Not even a glimpse of the arms around him or the head over his shoulder.

Pivoting, Darius landed his back against the wall and darted his gaze, searching. Nothing moved in the room. No shadows out of place. Across the room, Teddy had adopted another casual pose, a curious smile on his full lips as if he wasn't certain whether to be worried or amused. Not amused, Darius scanned the stillness, feeling the presence, listening, sensing movement. To the body animating against the wall, leaned casually within an inch of his shoulder, Darius lurched and sidestepped. His fiery dark eyes lifted to meet the bemused twilight shine.

"I may end up turning you over my knee yet, son," the Baron said in mocked sorrow. "I've had better sparring partners in a whorehouse."

"What do you want from me?"

"Hmm, can't you guess?"

He could but no relief came with the revelation. Even if this was to be a training session, or a lesson, he wouldn't fare well against this master of wicked tricks. "I don't have your talent. That's a given," Darius said carefully, putting another step between them and nearly backing himself into the deep corner of the room. "Not to mention, you know what I'll do before I do it."

"So true, but whoever said there were rules to this game?" the Baron asked, making no move to rise from his nonchalant pose. "Do you think then, when my enemy or his soldiers come after you, they'll play fair? Did the fellow announce himself before hitting you last night?"

"I had a slight advantage to sense a strangeness inside that room," Darius pointed out. "I don't have that advantage here. I know you and I'd be a fool to think I could match your skill."

"So, if my opponent comes at you, you'll forfeit because he's stronger?"

"You know what I meant."

"Hmm, so I do. I've intimidated you for the past eight years. You fear me, regardless of how you loath to admit that detail even to yourself. Because you fear me, you've limited yourself. Lived with the restraints I've placed on you, too. Convinced yourself, you don't stand a chance against me."

"And you'll tell me I'm wrong?"

"No, don't suppose I will. You'd know the lie. Unfortunately, Darius, you'll either tap your anger and improve your skill in the coming moments, or . . . sadly, I'll beat the living hell out of you."

So calm and simple that benediction. And before Darius could rise to the fear, the Baron stepped off the wall and vanished in a gray haze. Far more tense and worried, Darius sought the stillness again, breathing in the scents, listening. Motion. He felt motion, the air currents shifting. Fear. He drew back. Too late. The slap cut across his cheek lifting welts and spinning him in a half turn to slam the outside wall. As he stumbled to catch his balance, a hand locked on his upper arm and tugged him, throwing him halfway across the room. Barely, he landed on his hip and hands when he scrambled off the floor. Spinning, his senses quickening, keening, he sought the currents, the scents. A phantom. The Baron had become a phantom, and the stillness in Darius's mind was no relief. No taunting words. No presence. Alone in this half-human, half-monster shell, he knew his human half could be hurt.

He felt it again—the presence—spun and blocked his face in one instant and buckled under the ramrod strike at his waist. Breath blasting on impact, his knees caved, his shins slammed the carpet. Folding, wrapping his arms at his waist, his head ducked, thudding the floor. Senses spinning, white hot pain flashing through his stomach and chest, down his legs, Darius knew his mistake with the weight landing over him. In a wild panic, he struggled against the hands and clamored to his feet. Futility spread through his mind as the arms circled and held him, pinning him. Heaving, shaking his head, he stopped struggling.

Against his ear, fully animated, the Baron hissed softly, "Quit again, lad—let me catch you like this again—I'll take you to the floor and bed you like a cheap whore. No holds barred, m' lil hellion. Fight like the lil bastard you are, or I'll make you a bitch."

The arms broke and vanished and Darius spun, anger rising in equal measure with his fear. With the words ringing in his ears, he moved smoothly, swiftly, turning, heaving, searching. At the brush against his shoulder, he spun and swung, catching only a hazy outline as the head ducked from his fist. He wasted not an instant, ducking, pivoting, tracing the air currents with a force of anger and a need to survive. As the arm swept across him, he veered and spun, driving his hands, and slamming an invisible wall. Ramming his full weight into the drive, he recognized the staggered step. No time to think. Action. Reaction. A hand ripped across his jaw, staggered him, spraying white light through his dark eyes.

Not stopping. Not getting caught. No other thought held more firmly as Darius pivoted and collided with the solid invisible wall. Jabbing his fist skyward, his knuckles exploded in red hot pain, snatching his breath as a low deep laugh vibrated within the room. Action. Reaction. He followed the laugh, the scent, spinning and ducking, colliding. The arms spiraled around him, and a crazy wild panic raged through him when his knees buckled and the weight drove him forward, headfirst toward the floor. Twisting, he pitched off his knees, bucking and rolling over the solid form. Animated, the Baron rose at the same time, swinging and chuckling, landing a blow to Darius's jaw and pitching him several steps. Pivoting, Darius swung, and his wrist caught in a chilled vice, his fist halted in midair. With his fist trembling a hair's breadth from the firm jaw, Darius glared into the likewise shining eyes.

"Hmm, so and you do know how to fight," the Baron mused in a natural deep pitch.

Not trusting the pause, not foolish enough to believe the fight ended so swiftly, Darius pivoted and rammed the Baron with a speed and force to stagger the man/monster. No holds barred. That was a term he understood, and with a ferocity restrained for too many years, Darius broke the hold on his wrist and slammed a fist into the washer board ribs. Pain flashed through his wrist and arm, but he came up swinging, following, tracking the vanishing image, stalking, and advancing with a sidling walk. He felt him now. Sensed him. Followed the brush of soles on the carpet, shift in the scents. Whatever this weird waking talent, Darius suffered a horrible instant to realize—he liked it. Awake. Wide awake and breathing in soft wisps, he poised, tracking the Baron in a small circle around him, saw his cousin watching but lent no thought to the impotent spectator. Anger, hatred, rage flowed through him in waves and focused entirely on this phantom enemy.

Several paces away, the Baron dropped his cloak and became fully visible. Arms crossed at his chest; a smile quivering in his mustache, he commented, "A slow start, but a commendable quick study, son. Go get a shower. You smell like smoke, sweat, and sex."

Not ready to quit . . . only that thought held firm as Darius moved with a sliding step, circling, his gaze steady on the bemused blue eyes. Barely, he started a forward motion, when his muscles slipped from his control and he lurched, rocked, halted.

"A lesson," Amad said in a low calming tone. "You've satisfied my curiosity and fared well in this session. If . . . or when a situation develops, you'll hold your own. Take a deep breath now and recover, lad. I've no intention of engaging you in a serious battle. As your common sense told you, I have too many advantages over you only beginning with the fact that I could hold you as still as stone and rip your heart out."

Whether the words saturated his mind internally or externally, Darius introverted the base truth and lost his rage behind a wave of genuine thought. He was held as still as stone and if the Baron had meant to hurt him, he would be dead. "I won't win against another of your talent," he said absently.

"As a man, alone, no," the Baron said simply. "Thus, if such a beast attempts to take you, lad, you and I will move as one. This lesson . . . session, we both learned something of the other's nature. You are, as I suspected, a physical beast with a commendable talent. And despite what you believe, Darius, you've taken the change well." His gaze slid downward and lifted again slowly until their eyes locked. "Go get cleaned up. We'll discuss your new station over dinner."

With the freedom to move, Darius accepted the command in the form of a suggestion and strode toward the bathroom. Alone, but not entirely alone in the bathroom, Darius stripped swiftly and stepped into a hot shower. Strange . . . changed. Even something as natural as showering seemed somehow different as if he stood outside his body.

Alone with his thoughts, the revelations scattered, racing in circles. Under the spray, he stood for a long moment, watching the water spiral off his bare forearm. The marks had vanished, but he remembered glimpsing the dual punctures in the muscles. He shuddered with the memory of fire raging in his arm, the horror racing in his mind.

Shaking his head, his thoughts veered again, touching on Jenna. Did she truly care for him? Would he keep her? Could he? Kevin . . .? Would Kevin blame him, condemn him, fear him as Teddy seemed to fear him now? Raphael. Would Raphael truly attempt to fulfill his promise? Dying was no longer an option . . . a will to survive. For what purpose? Toward what end? For the mere sake of breathing?

By the time Darius stepped into his jeans and pulled a sweater over his head, he'd gained only more questions than answers. Stopped. He stared at his reflection in the mirror above the sink. Nothing of the change appeared in his reflection but he wasn't the same man . . . not the same entity who'd entered this hotel three nights past.

Your dinner's arrived.

Jolted, Darius darted his gaze toward the door before realizing the voice had originated in his head. A little clumsily, he collected his shoes and socks, and stepped through the door as the scents from the small table woke him to a gnawing hunger. The Baron and Teddy already sat at the table. Darius dropped his shoes near the couch and joined them, slipping into the available chair, already lifting one of the two closed silver lids. Without more than a fleeting glance to the sunny side up eggs, Darius assaulted the thick red steak, slicing a single sliver and filling his mouth. His appetite hadn't changed. As he chewed, he diced and sliced. Good. Not great. The meat was red, barely touched brown at the outer edges. The juices swimming in the sunken plate . . . warm . . . red . . . fantastic! Swirling the chunks of steak in the juices, he paid little heed to the spectators, his concentration on the single pleasure.

Nearly finished, he slowed enough to glance at his cousin's faintly dismayed gaze. The Baron relaxed back in his chair, swilling a wine goblet, and smirking with a faintly bemused shine in his eyes.

"You . . . you're not eating?" Darius asked.

Stifling a sound, like a laugh, the Baron flickered red darts through his eyes and commented, "I've had plenty to last me a little while."

Stopped, Darius realized the implication, insinuation. Him. His blood. Distracted and not quite as hungry, Darius dropped his gaze to his plate . . . and truly studied the nearly red juices, the raw, barely warm chunks of meat. In a paradox, he considered pushing away from the table and suffered a painful desire to finish.

To add to his misery, he glanced at his cousin in time to see the boy take a near dainty bite of egg off his fork. Irritated, Darius glared across the table, watching the blue eyes flicker toward him and away, noted the hand and fork tremble slightly while lifting another delicate bite. Dainty . . . and scented . . . and soft around the edges . . . and meticulous. Teddy had been born and raised with a silver spoon. Proper, mannerly, a study in social graces . . . and as gay as the day was long despite his lack of experience. To add to the absurdity, the silly fop had the audacity to fall head over heels in love with the Baron von Hendricks, and the Baron tortured the little idiot by making him a manservant and driving the boy to the brink of hysteria and humiliation. Aggravated and angry for no clear reason, Darius turned his heated gaze to find the Baron still watching him. "Why don't you just tumble the lad and get it over with?"

Across the table, Teddy choked on a bite of egg and the Baron chuckled.

"Seriously?" Darius asked with an edge. "Just put the silly little boy out of his misery and wake him to the dark side. He lives for you, now. That wouldn't change."

"You are in a mood, lad. A tad jealous, perhaps? Or is it more basic, his scent's driving you a trifle mad?"

"It's the way he eats his bloomin' eggs!" Darius snapped and shot his gaze to Teddy's startled blue eyes. "Dump them on your fucking toast, add ketchup or tabasco and eat like a man. You'd probably gain a few pounds if you ate faster. You're too fucking thin."

"Darius," the Baron mused. "Do remember your manners. Granted, you weren't born with them, but I taught you the basics."

"Right. I eat with a fork," Darius growled and stabbed a chunk of meat, aware of an internal tremble, a vibration. Flipping the fork, he bit the meat off the upside-down prongs and glared at his worried cousin as he chewed. A smile slid into his mustached lips. "Was there ever a time I didn't scare the bloody 'ell out of you, lad?"

Almost sadly, Teddy turned his pale blue eyes to the Baron. "May I be excused, sir?"

The Baron leaned and patted his arm, "Have no fear, m' dear. He's too busy with his steak to consider biting you."

"I . . . I don't like to see him like this, sir," Teddy admitted with a rare boldness and a more disheartened shine toward Darius. With his singsong French accent on the English words, his voice maintained an irritating femininity. "I know you can't control what's happening to you, Darius, but that doesn't make it any easier. You were neve-air deliberately cruel."

"I'm not being cruel now, lad. I'm attempting to offer you practical, sound advice," Darius stated in a guarded, solemn tone. "I've bedded enough women to know I prefer a little meat on the bones."

Teddy flushed a deeper red and dropped his gaze to his plate.

"Shit," Darius stated and darted his gaze to the bemused master. "Obviously, there's no hope for the lad. The mere mention of sex turns him red."

"The steak isn't enough for you, is it, lad?" the Baron asked.

"It's all right but I've had better," Darius said offhandedly and turned his fork more naturally, lifting another ample bite.

"Son," the Baron said gravely and drew Darius's piqued gaze. "You're flavoring your meal at your cousin's expense. I don't particularly mind as we're dining in private, but should you attempt this bit of spice in mixed company, you might lose your appetite when the heads start to turn. Think. And do try to exercise a tad more control."

Stopped again, Darius played the past minutes through his mind and as if the Baron had prophesied the outcome, Darius lost his appetite. He hadn't thought about the words, not the cruelty belying the jibes he'd tossed at this innocent . . . fully human cousin. From some shadowy space inside him, the sorrow rose with enough regret to sting the corner of his eyes as he turned his gaze to the Baron. "H-how . . . how do I control this? I . . . he was right. I'm not in control . . . and if I can't control this . . . the last of the life I've known is lost. I . . . how the bloody hell could I mingle in the circles you make me move if I can't even sit down to a dinner without being . . . crude and ill-mannered? What would I say with a bloody microphone in hand...? Good evening—fuck you? Mercy. This isn't good. Maybe you better finish your dinner, sir, and find another able body to fill this post."

For a long moment, the Baron studied him then decided, "Finish your dinner. We have a few errands to run."

28

As a last resort, Jenna found a radio station, a rock n' roll station that played a fair mix of classic rock from the seventies and eighties. Whether the music or the nighttime disk-jockey's low, sexy voice offered more comfort, she couldn't decide. The disk-jockey spoke often enough to lend an impression of companionship, taking calls, chatting with other lonely souls in the quick of night. He'd need only an English accent to sound like Darius. The mood, the tempo of his voice, the rhythm of that deep baritone resonance . . . he would sound like Darius.

In the soft light from the stove, Jenna sat at her kitchen counter with a variety of Christmas cards scattered over the butcher block top. Another last resort. A distraction from the panic that had stolen over her and held her muscles on edge. Neither the music nor the drone work of writing Christmas cards helped completely. She'd never feared for another more, nor felt so helpless and alone in that enterprise. Catching up on Christmas rituals, hoping beyond hope to rise above the ache of despair, she sat mulling over the stacks of cards, concentrating as if her life depended on which relative or friend received Santa Claus vs the nativity scene. Addressing cards had seemed like a good idea when she's brought the boxes and her address book from the buffet.

Three cards stood on the addressed stack, the culmination of her effort over the past hour—her parents, her sister, and her Windrow grandparents. And she'd devoted about thirty seconds to each of those choices. If she'd anticipated the burden of matching cards to faces, she might have ordered a couple boxes of the same design with her name pre-printed after the internal verse.

A roll of preprinted return address labels rested alongside the blank envelopes . . . and her attention caught on the address, her apartment address in old English script. He'd told her to move—to put distance between herself and the Chateau.

Heart aching, her focus drifted to the Christmas tree positioned in front of her balcony doors. How long would this last? This sense of doom and despair? She'd always loved the holidays, never minded the shorter winter daylight or suffered from SAD like many of her colleagues. This was different. As if a single moment had collapsed her world and the weight of it threatened to destroy her.

To hell with sending cards! To hell with receiving cards!

"To bloody hell with Christmas," Jenna snapped in a reflection of Darius's smooth English curses—the equivalent of saying 'fuck it.' Jolted by her voice slicing through the disk-jockey's intimate monologue, Jenna bolted upright from her slump. This was not her! She'd forever been an optimist . . . but hot tears stung the edges of her eyes. Blinking at the blur, she focused a split second on Santa's jolly face then swept her arm across the counter.

In a blurry kaleidoscope, Santa and the holy family swam away. Red and green ink pens took flight. The two boxes and lids caught the force and clapped against the arch to the living room. One lid flew far enough to bounce off the end table in the joining room.

Folding her arms on the cleared counter in front of her, Jenna dropped her head on the soft terry cloth and heaved an angry breath, swallowing the threat of a sob. Ridiculous! This was ridiculous! Darius was alive and well. Might be sailing across the Atlantic back to his home, his life, his world. Whatever dark portent of that nightmare, she couldn't afford to believe it, not if she intended to retain her sanity until morning. If something had truly happened to him . . . she might have heard. Would have heard. The disk jockey standing in place of a real friend would have told her. The death of Darius Brock would have made the news—

"Stop it!" she heaved; her voice muffled. "Don't . . . absolutely do not . . . do this."

The blast of the telephone jolted her upright. Already in motion, she spilled off the stool, barely collecting her balance afoot. Heart hammering, panic and hysteria exploding, she spun her focus toward the stove clock . . . 2:18. Two hours! She had been awake over two hours . . . two hours was time enough for someone to have found—

"Nooo!" she heaved as the telephone blasted again and she launched, jack-knifing around the counter. The telephone stood on a side table near her apartment door. Barely, her fingers touched the receiver before she halted, frozen with a sudden epiphany.

2:18. If this was news about Darius, from whom would it come?

A chill slid down her frozen spine, her breath halted in her throat. In slow motion, she retracted her hand and hugged herself as the phone sent another grip through her limbs. Three rings. She'd set the answering machine for three rings. A click erupted; a button flashed. Her lofty voice ignited, echoing in the stillness, direct and to the point, deliberately clipped in secretary style. *Who would call? The police? Agent Wharton? Mason? Some other affiliate . . . Evan*

Trevane? Evan had left three messages for her throughout the day. All business messages, resigned to missing his chance with her, but wanting to speak with her . . . follow up. Would Trevane call her now . . . ? Two in the morning. Would . . . *a psycho call?*

From the machine, her voice ended the instructions, and the machine emitted a signal whistle to begin recording. For an instant, in the silent pause, Jenna's muscles gripped.

"If you're awake, Luv, do pick up this phone," the deep voice ordered.

"Oh-mi-God!" Her hand snatched the receiver. Her index finger slammed the button to halt the recording. "Darius!" she huffed on a breath. Thrilled. Relieved.

"In the flesh, Luv," his voice was deeper than the disk-jockey's. Richer. Fuller. "Do hope I didn't wake you."

"I . . .well, no. You haven't. Are you alright?" she spoke on a breath.

He hesitated then sounded slightly amused, "Better than alright, Luv. Much better. I ehm . . . I don't know exactly how to say this or ask this. It never occurred to me. Twenty-twenty hindsight. Always the best kind."

He sounded strange, distracted. "Honey, what's wrong? What's—"

"Nothing, Luv. Everything's right, in fact. If I sound a tad nervous . . . I've never quite been in this situation before now. I've never been in love."

Her heart leapt with the simple benediction; the words so quiet and controlled. A smile slid into her lips as she lowered unconsciously, gripping the phone to her ear. Relief and joy spread through her overwound system. "Darius, I love you too."

"I hope so, Luv. I want to believe that more deeply than in life itself," he said in a slightly wary tone. "But . . . well, I'm stalling miserably here. There's something I need ask you, Luv, and I'll need your answer immediately. Actually, I don't know that I'll truly even await your answer," he said in a dry tone. "I've come up with the only reasonable solution to our current distress. I can't leave you and I can't stay here with you. I have orders . . . and a request from your hierarchy to leave the country. Therein lies my dilemma, Luv. I truly can't leave here believing your life's in danger. The solution then. I want you to come with me."

Her thoughts riveted, halted, stunned those simple words.

"I know it's sudden and a shock, Jenna, but I realized this evening, there's no reason, absolutely no reason why we need to be parted. I have fallen in love with you, and I've never spoken those words to another. Come with me."

"I . . . I don't know what to say," she uttered honestly, her senses reeling. He was asking her to leave with him, to drop everything and . . . and what? Go where? Where would they go?

"Simply say you'll come, Luv," he said in a low sensuous tone. "Say you love me enough to come with me."

"Darius, I'd . . . where would we go? What would I . . . for how long? How long would we be away?" she asked with the voice of reason rearing its ugly head. As much as she loved him, she knew so little about him, his life. She knew he traveled, kept an apartment in London, but he had admitted not spending much time there. Was he asking her to live with him? Go to London?

"We've been given sanctuary, Luv. We'll stay at least through the holidays in Europe. Depending on the success of your authorities, we may return to this country within the month."

"You said . . . you need my answer immediately," she said while skimming her gaze unconsciously toward the scattered cards on her kitchen floor. Her head spun with the details, the arrangements to make before agreeing to his offer. The holidays. Her family. She needed to contact her landlord, make arrangements for her mail collection . . . Her sister or mother could handle that. "How soon would we leave?" she asked quietly.

"I'll pick you up . . . six o'clock."

"This evening?" she asked, hoping to God he didn't mean—

"This morning, Luv. I am sorry for the urgency. My flight's scheduled to depart—"

"Darius, I don't even have a passport."

"Not a problem, Luv. I'll take care of it. If you'd simply pack . . . warm apparel. We'll be spending a bit of time in the mountains."

"I . . . I don't think . . . Darius, I'm not this impulsive. I can't just pack and leave—"

"Do you trust me?"

Stopped, she considered those words. In fleeting glimpses, she relived every moment she'd spent with him throughout the day, and realized she did trust him. And what was more important, she loved him. Despite all good sense, she knew at this moment, she would drop everything and leave with him. "Yes," she said quietly.

"Say you'll come with me," he said softly. "I know it sounds insane and impulsive. And I know what I'm asking of you . . . but I need you with me, Luv. I need to know you're out of harm's way."

Not once had he alluded to running away together. By mutual understanding, they'd agreed. One day. Not a lifetime. A singular pleasure, a moment stolen for themselves. His career, his occupation . . . he'd stood overlooking the City of Pittsburgh and admitted he couldn't offer a lifetime. He'd warned her to run away, to put distance between herself and the Chateau. Trust no one . . . but he was asking her to trust him . . . and there could be only one answer.

She'd never become so completely, deeply attached to another and the time factor, bedamned. If only to investigate and fully experience what she felt for him, she would accept his invitation. She maintained a sizeable savings account, has banked enough to carry her for a time. If this was a mistake, she would handle the consequences solo, as she handled all things, holding no one else to account.

The silence on the phone lingered. She sensed him waiting, his breath held for her answer. "I will come with you, Darius, but . . . but there are arrangements I'll need to make before I leave. I'll need to speak to my parents and stop at the bank—"

"You can't, Luv," he said quietly. "Not from here. It's better . . . safer for both of us if we don't inform any others of our activity. We can manage your affairs over the phone once we're in the air or when we land. I know this is a tad frightening, Luv, but the arrangements are out of my control and the precautions are for our safety. Trust me, if I could give you more time or make this easier, I would. Don't phone anyone. I'll come for you personally. Don't open your door to any others, not for any reason."

"Now, you have worried me just a little, honey," she said honestly, her neck prickling with the alarm. "Has something happened?"

"Nothing I can explain at this moment, Luv. I'll tell you everything when I come for you."

He was safe, alive. Nothing else mattered. "I'll be ready," she decided. "See you then, Luv."

Replacing the receiver, Darius withdrew his hand. The shadow of a spectator lingered at the fringes of his consciousness, adding to the heaviness in his mind. No choice. Whatever part of him that had often rebelled and attempted to defy a command had been overruled. As much by the influence inside his mind as his desire to have her with him. A paradox.

"You have a natural talent for seduction," the Baron said with as much approval as amusement, aware of Darius's conflicts. "That's not necessarily a bad thing, Darius."

Warily, Darius watched the Baron rise from the armchair. His own body rose in the same moment. Control. No control. Mildly disoriented and distressed by the strangeness to respond to the silent impulses, Darius still held the blue gaze as he stood. "You will hurt her . . . or you'll make me do it."

"She's safe for the moment," Amad said in a silky tone, his smile slippery. "More so than she was before your call. Nothing else should concern you at present."

Without a clear thought, Darius started moving as the Baron turned toward the door. "Where are we go—"

Silence, now, lad. Watch, listen, learn. We'll test your new talents in due time.

Distracted by the Baron's veer toward Teddy who rose smoothly from a chair at the table, Darius reached the door and paused. The Baron towered nearly a full head taller, hovering over the slender boy who peered up at him like a small adoring child. Annoyed at a base level, Darius watched by no will of his own as the Baron ran a finger along the boy's upturned jaw. The soft cheeks flushed, and pale eyes flickered. Enhanced, the scents flavored the air as the Baron ducked his head and spoke in a low silky whisper against Teddy's ear.

"If anyone should call for either of us, m'lad, do tell them we're not to be disturbed and we'll return their call."

"Ou-oui," Teddy said breathlessly.

As the boy's eyes flashed nervously, Darius turned his gaze to the door, concentrating on the single order to 'listen.' He heard or sensed the Baron kissing the boy's cheek and in an odd moment, Darius suffered the slight edge or irritation. Impressions and instinct prickled him with a warning, a greater force drew him to spy the heated blue eyes and feel the intensity inside and out.

"So, and we learn something of your new nature, lad. Stubborn and defiant even now, but do not test your wiles on me."

"I . . . wasn't aware of doing any such thing," Darius admitted. A raw discomfort spilled through him, shivering him and lifting gooseflesh under his collar.

Amad smiled slowly, leaving no doubt he had manifested the discomfort. "And now you learn something of my nature," he said and gestured toward the door with a purely physical nod.

Where natural impulses and the Baron's influence parted, Darius had no idea. He opened the door, stepped aside to let the Baron pass and watched as all three Federal agents turned and froze, their gazes locked, eyes glazed. By instinct or experience, Darius had known this aspect of the Baron's nature, not surprised when the three agents returned to their relaxed positions, seeing nothing. Without a spoken word or any cloaking device on a physical level, Darius followed the Baron in the opposite direction of the elevator, toward the stairs. Not a single agent glanced at him or acknowledged him as he passed. Watch, listen, and learn . . . as if the words were part of him, a mantra inside his skull, he introverted the feeling of invisibility, glancing over his shoulder to note all three men stationed as before, oblivious.

Humans are the greatest predators on earth, save myself of course, the Baron's words slipped through Darius's mind as they descended through the stairwell. *You have in you, that talent enhanced a hundredfold . . . breathe in the scents. Find him. You know his scent . . . find your assailant.*

On a primal level, Darius could no more reject those words than he could deny his willingness to obey. Something had changed inside of him. Images of Adam Brock assailed him. His vulnerability of the evening past woke a greater strangeness inside of him. A scent . . . an alien scent had flavored that suite, but while his conscious mind had rejected that scent, oblivious, his subconscious had retained the flavor. Animal instincts. Primal. Whatever this change, it had affected him at the core of his humanity. As a hound searches and catches the scent of a fox, he was so endowed.

Traces, only echoes of an old scent lingered as they descended through the stairwell. On dual planes, Darius understood, the beast had passed this way before, had traveled this route to reach Lawrence Fradden three nights past. Where the investigators had only theorized without physical evidence, Darius knew without a doubt, and found himself poised on a landing, halted at a door where a gold plate marked the second floor. Stronger. Enhanced. An essence of the beast touched him. The same but different than the musty odor that rose from his pores, an extension of the man/monster idling near him. No explanation or defined odor reached him. The difference between roasting beef and roasting lamb . . . or even less distinctive, the scent between raspberry and strawberry jam. Would every scent and aroma reach him with a aroma to stir hunger?

Distracted, Darius stood, breathing the scents, a hound to a fox, searching the trail. Hungry. The beast had passed this way, not long ago, and it seemed, now, the scent came from every direction. Above and below, stronger near the door. He ventured a step closer, uncertain, more distracted. Like a hunter awaiting his hound to bellow, the Baron stood aside, waiting, listening, alert. Bringing his gaze about to find the cobalt eyes watching him, Darius nearly spoke aloud, his words spilled across his mind, *Do you smell him?*

He touched you. Find him.

He's been this way. I can't tell how long ago.

Follow the scent.

No assistance, Darius realized. This was yet another lesson, session. Reaching a decision, Darius started to reach for the door and thought better of touching the handle with his bare hands. Using his sweater, he clasped the nob and forced the door open an inch, listening, waking more to other scents, other flavors. The human race. Hotel guests asleep. Scents. So many damned scents suddenly. The images flickered in his mind from small children to adolescents, from elder women to young men. Impressions of age and wisdom, frivolity, sloth. He smelled liquor, drawing in the aromas of whiskey and beer, dereliction which awakened yet other memories and images inside his mind, his childhood. He knew these scents, recognized these flavors from some dark and primitive place inside of him. How was he to concentrate with so many distractions and images, so many memories clicking and heating inside his mind. Fleeting, he remembered the sailor he had mentioned to Jenna, recalling the moments on the mount, distracted by yet another fragrance inside the hall, a flowery scent to keen him toward another primal sensation.

To his panted breath, he awoke slowly and withdrew into the stairwell, pulling the door closed and dropping his gaze into the shadows between himself and the door. Awakening. He was awakening to something far darker, and deeper inside of him. At the core of his consciousness, he suffered a conflict of fear and anticipation. Humanity. Just the residual scents of humanity affected him, now.

What you seek is no longer human. Realize the difference. Catch the scent.

A father teaching his son to hunt, a hunter training his dog to track, both images vied for space in Darius's heightened awareness. The hunt. The killer. His enemy. Survival instincts sped toward the surface; his senses keening yet again to capture the essence of his enemy and it was an unnatural scent. An anomaly to the natural scents. Something rotten. Something dead . . . but not necessarily offensive to his senses. What kind of beast had he become?

Both the hound and the fox. He stood, frozen. Or was he something even worse? A wolf on the scent of another wolf.

Moving, without conscious thought, he turned and continued down the steps, drawing in the scent and heightening. He did smell this monster. Enhanced, the rancid odor stung his nostrils as he reached the first level and on a conscious level, Darius understood this beast lingered in this lower realm. Whether he thought of a bakery scent where the aroma of fresh baked bread lingered constantly or considered a more feral aspect to know he entered this monster's territory, he stood breathing in the spoors at the door.

Consciously, he introverted what he knew, his thoughts racing over the more practical knowledge imbedded in his human psyche. An employee . . . someone with access, opportunity. Someone who could wait and watch, a non-entity to linger at the edges of the hotel's order. He had considered those details, had scored the employee list with Jenna, checking all employees on duty Friday evening. Some he had already known, but she had added insight to others. Knowing what he did about the Baron's nocturnal habits, nightshift employees seemed the most likely. He hadn't known about soldiers or ranks of this unnatural condition, had fully believed he faced another of the Baron's full talent. If this beast could travel through half-light, the possibilities broadened.

Doormen . . . he eliminated with a thought of the swing-shifts and the nearness to the light. Bellhops, he overruled on the instant with a thought of how often those lads would pass through the upper floors. Not strong enough those scents at the upper doors. A ground-floor employees. Security guards . . . a clear possibility. Cooks . . . registration desk clerks . . . anyone in the administration wing . . . waiters and waitresses . . . bartenders. His thoughts raced, remembering those moments with Fradden in the dining room, the attention they'd drawn. The enemy had stood inside the dining room with a bird's eye view of that encounter. Even if Fradden had been unconsciously connected to the master opponent—

Fradden was mine.

The simple admission halted Darius's thoughts before he realized how fully the Baron had entered this game long before today. The missing wine . . . the Baron had known about that ordeal, had sent Fradden here as a pawn. The enemy was inside the dining room, observing, waiting. A waiter . . . a waitress . . . a cook . . . a bartender . . . and abruptly, Darius knew who exactly carried this scent, understood fully, completely . . . and his rage rose by a will of its own, heightening at a speed to give him vertigo.

Ah, so you've caught a taste for the hunt. Shall we see then?

Yesss, the word hissed through his mind even as he swept his sweater and hand to the door, pushing it open and keening for every sound. No one stood or moved in the rear hall. Distant, the generators hummed from the pool area, wafted a tangy flavor of chlorine to nip his tongue. Moving with a speed and agility that might have given him pause only a few hours earlier, Darius sped silently through the dim lighted corridor, drinking in the scents from the kitchen where the aroma from his dinner lingered. Voices echoed from some distant place. Intent, Darius tracked that unnatural scent within the more human flavors. At the sense of human occupancy in the lobby, he slowed and stopped just shy of the arch. Jenna's scent . . . he recognized her wispy scent and nearly turned to search for her before he realized her overwhelming fragrance within the entire realm. No more than a foot from his flared nostrils, a strand of artificial pine garland strung against the arch, and she had touched this strand, might have taped it in place and arranged the tiny gold bows with her own hands. In total conflict, Darius poised, remembering his humanity even as his rage flowed, his desire for the hunt boiling at his core. What was he doing . . . what would he do when he caught this monster . . . ? Even as he questioned, he knew the answer . . . the hunter stood at his back and inside his mind.

To the Baron it was a game, a mere training session . . . a sport. The hunt. The kill.

Leaning against the wall, trembling with the force of his conflicts, Darius turned his wary gaze to find the Baron merely watching him. *I am the hound.*

A hound with a conscience and morality, the words slid through Darius's mind, troubling his brow even as the smile snaked into the black mustache and red flickered in the Baron's eyes. *Find our enemy. Discover the truth if it's to be had. Move swiftly and stay at my heels as we pass through this arch.*

The words were unnecessary. Even as the Baron fled past him, Darius followed without a conscious thought. In a fleeting glance, he glimpsed the agents positioned in the lobby, both lounging on the leather couches around the softly crackling fire. Another less obvious, stood near the registration desk, chatting with the night clerk, flirting. Not one of them reacted though Darius sensed the young woman's chill on a base level. In the Baron's shadow, he passed through the open arch into the administration wing, and without a clear thought, Darius again took the lead, slowing as he passed the first three doors, slowing. Here. The scent was here, overwhelming and spiraling anger and rage through him, quickening his need to find this beast. Like a rodent rotting in an alley, decaying beneath a pile of rubble, the scent lingered at every door, pausing him.

He had found the beast's lair inside this hotel . . . found the beast.

So, you have, the syllables slid together, prickling and alarming, sinister.

With short hair lifting under his collar, Darius realized the change, already half afraid of what he would see by the time he started to turn. Only once, he'd seen the Baron transforming, only once experienced the cold terror beneath the purely feral shine. Frozen now, he looked into the red glowing eyes and his muscles constricted, recoiling. Even without reflected light, the flaming orbs shimmered like molten glass, the natural color washed away. Taller, broader it seemed, the Baron hulked. His human features enhanced, changed merely by the intensity of flared nostrils and hooded brows. Human essence hung like a cheesecloth cloak, an illusion which threatened to shatter. At a gut level, Darius suffered twinges of fear, but something in himself held firm, a kindred touch, an understanding. His humanity suspended him in a state of vulnerability, but those eyes were inside of him, outside of him.

The rooms are empty, the words pricked like shards of glass. Feral eyes spiraled away, and head lifted, canted. Listening. Drawing in the flavors far more swiftly and deeply, the bristled lips twitched. *But the beast was here recently,* the slivers continued, stinging inside Darius's mind, sending a flinch through him. Words . . . just words, but the sounds truly pricked, needling as if scraped over raw nerve endings. Shuddering uncontrollably, Darius meant to withdraw his gaze, but again the eyes lowered, catching and probing inside his head. *Desssperate . . . I sssense itss feear . . . itsss masssster's tooo farr away and it knowwws, I'vve comme. Traack it . . . find it. Nnnowww wwwhelllp.*

A fledgling or a whelp, Darius was no match against the forces moving inside of him, through him. As if stung by electric current, he launched, connected to this shadow of human occupancy. Through an unlocked door, he passed smoothly, not hesitating to spring the locks on a window and send the glass rising, the screen snapping under his push. At the edge of his mind, he knew he passed through Jenna's office . . . her office . . . tainted by that scent . . . her door unlocked . . . Jenna . . . a desperate beast on the loose . . . with free run in her office.

Jenna!

29

No longer listening to either the disk jockey or music filtering from the wall speaker near her bedroom door, Jenna stood scanning the scattered piles of clothes covering three-quarters of her flowered bedspread. Packing for a month didn't mean she needed her entire wardrobe. One would think, with all her exposure to seasoned travelers, she would understand the concept, but that revelation didn't make the chore any easier. He'd said to pack warm apparel; they would stay in the mountains. A sanctuary. What did that mean? Would she need a ski suit? She had plenty of wool slacks and skirts, sweaters, jackets . . . but heavy clothes occupied a great deal of space. Would they dress casual more often? Should she take a pair of spiked heels or settle for flats and boots?

Packing was not the issue, not the problem. In a stopped pose, Jenna skimmed her fingers through her scattered hair and sent the entire mound over her shoulder. The problem remained with her doubts, her anticipation and anxiety. She'd never done anything quite so . . . well, maybe she had done something slightly irresponsible before now. According to several aunts, uncles and cousins, she'd been an irresponsible idiot to walk away from college and work full-time in a hotel. Had they asked, she might have mentioned, a career in college wasn't the equivalent of an education based on experience, and if one intended to someday open her own hotel, one needed a great deal of both. She had both, along with a decent financial portfolio when she decided to make the plunge. She wasn't frivolous, impulsive, or irresponsible . . . but she'd never felt toward any man what she felt for—and with—Darius. If what they shared was merely a bright flaming candle to burn out swiftly, she needed to know in advance. She refused to live a life of 'what ifs' and 'should haves.'

'. . . Seize the day . . . A life without love . . . It is better to have loved and lost than never to have loved at all . . .'

Tamping the running dialogue of clichés, Jenna muttered a curse and again attempted a more thorough inspection of her scattered collection. Ancient travelers had the right idea. In every blasted book and movie she'd read or seen pre-dating the era of air travel, the authors referred to steamer trunks. Those folks truly had the right idea. They packed for a damned month or a lifetime every time they boarded a ship, train or stagecoach. Modern economy . . . economizing meant taking a single satchel and buying whatever the hell one might need when she reached her destination. Unfortunately, without a firm destination, she couldn't rely on that blasted luxury. For all she knew, they might fly into a tiny little airport outside a village and catch a rattling bus into the mountains . . . or worse, climb aboard mules—

"Good grief," she snapped, annoyed with her runaway thoughts. They weren't destined for the blasted Amazon or the Indies. She could rule out camel and elephant travel. Pack animals of any breed. Darius Brock was not a fellow to forfeit his life of luxury and opt for an alternative source of travel . . . or turn into Daniel Boone the instant they touched his homeland. England. She had always planned a vacation in England. If she remembered her geography, however, England wasn't generally considered mountainous unless one headed for the Highlands.

"Alright, let's handle this in a practical manner," she said firmly, speaking aloud if only to shove the wild rambling from her mind. "Wool slacks, skirts, sweaters . . . only the soft wool," she decided. Settling onto a shin on the bed, she began sorting. A charcoal gray slacks suit, she set aside for traveling. When complimented with a pale gray silk, the suit never failed to wear well or appear decent regardless of how harried she became. Practical and sensible, and if she wore the jacket, she'd conserve space in her luggage. Wool was the most practical material for both cold climates and limited space, far more feasible than attempting to mash the long, furry woven fabrics into a bag. Holding up one such design with a thick furry collar and patterned weave, Jenna debated for a second. She wasn't fond of bright red, but Christmas was less than two weeks away.

"Damn it," she muttered and folded the sweater, stacking it on a pile of 'definite maybes.' If this continued, she might not be dressed by six o'clock, much less packed. Already twenty minutes of the three and a half hours had slipped through her fingers, and she'd only accomplished making a mess of her bedroom and closet. If she left the room like this, whoever came to collect her mail would believe she'd battled for her life and probably imagine her massacred somewhere within the debris—

The sharp buzz erupted from the wall speaker, halting her thought and riveting her attention. Not six o'clock already! Impossible! Her attention spun to the nightstand, reading the clock but not entirely relieved as the buzzer sounded again. Darius? Had he come early?

Sliding off the bed, Jenna strode to the buzzer and hesitated with her finger hovering an inch from the intercom pad. He'd said not to let anyone into her apartment. Don't answer the telephone—let the answering machine screen the calls. The door buzzer offered no such luxury and unless she at least spoke to the caller, how the blazes was she supposed to buzz him in when he arrived? Sighing a breath, she pushed the button, "Yes?"

"Jenna!"

Muscles jumping, Jenna snapped her hand off the pad. Panic in that voice, a voice she recognized all too swiftly. Not a voice she wanted or needed to hear at this moment, if ever.

"Jen! Please," Lisa heaved, her voice quaking and panic inflected in every word. "Pleeease! I know we've never got along that well but please," she strained on the brink of a sob, hysteria rising. "I don't know where else to turn! I'm . . . I'm scared out of my wits! I think—I knooowww someone's trying to kill me!" she cried.

Heartbeat quickening, fear fluttered the nape of her neck. The killer! After Lisa! "S-slow down, Lisa," Jenna said with a tight rein on her rising panic. "Tell me what's happened."

"Ohhh, pleeease, let me come up!" Lisa hissed and whined, her voice inflected with the furtive notes of someone trapped, terrified. "Buzz me through! Pleeease! I can't stand in this doorwaaay! Heee'lll see me! He's folllowing me! I know it!"

"Alright, just calm down. I'll buzz you through," Jenna said and touched the lock release. Now what though? If Lisa came up . . . federal agents stood right outside the door. They could do something. Take Lisa into protective custody. Something. This snippy young woman was definitely not Jenna's problem. Why Blythe had even come here for refuge posed as a mystery enough. With that in mind, Jenna strode through her rooms to the door and lifted the receiver. Darius had said not to contact anyone in the hotel; however, he'd exempted himself from that list. She dialed the direct number into the suite, hoping, praying he picked up quickly.

"Oui . . . yes?"

Startled, stopped, Jenna stared down at the phone base, wondering if she'd dialed a wrong number. Impossible? "Is uh . . . this room six-zero-six?"

"Ye-es?" the curiously soft voice confirmed and questioned. "For whom are you calling?"

This was't a voice she'd heard before. Having heard more than enough French-Canadians in Chicago, she recognized the accent. Male or female, though? "Darius Brock."

"Ahh, oui . . . yes. You are ehm . . . Well, he's rath-air biz-zee at the moment. Who may I ask, is calling?"

"I ehm . . . Jenna Windrow."

"Oui . . . yes. I will have him ray-turn your call as soon as he is fin'eshed."

Who the heck was this? Male or female? She couldn't be entirely. The words were soft, almost whispered but not quite. Good grief. Before she could quite catch up to her thoughts, she heard the line disengage and lifted the receiver off her ear, looking at it as if the answers would jump through the tiny little black holes. Not entirely rude, this soft voice, but certainly not entirely friendly or considerate. She hadn't even gained the opportunity to mention the urgency.

Replacing the receiver, she looked at the door, unconsciously fumbling with her belt, folding the robe more securely. Blythe would be outside that door at any second. Deciding, Jenna moved closer to the door, leaning at the wall, almost annoyed by the effective acoustics in the modern complex. Worrying the side of her gum between her teeth, she strained to hear the hum of voices or vibrations of footsteps and heard nothing. What was Blythe doing here, of all places, in the middle of the night? Was she seriously stalked, chased? Was it possible the stalker had come after her? No good reason for that possibility came readily, but then, Jenna hadn't entirely decided on her own danger. By proximity, it was possible. If she'd become targeted through Darius, then it was possible that Lisa was also a target. Lisa had done everything but climb his trunk Friday night, and to hear Blythe talk about him, they'd shared an intimacy on each of his visits

Jenna hadn't asked him, had preferred not to know if those rumors were true, but she remembered a few occasions when he'd mentioned Blythe. Only this afternoon over lunch, he'd asked about Lisa, amused at Jenna's passive-aggressive techniques. He hadn't sounded fond of Lisa . . . and what if that was how he operated?

No. This wasn't a thought to consider a few hours before jumping on a plane with him . . . but Jenna remembered the absence of emotional investment in his voice, the bemusement in his eyes. What if he dumped her in Europe and six months from now, she meant no more to him than Blythe? No. Something . . . sincerity. He might have lied with words about loving her, but his eyes had carried the integrity of his professions. If he . . .? Damn it. If he was the type who fell in and out of love, loving each one as if it was the first . . .? He was no stranger to the bedroom.

The knuckles rapped the door, snapping Jenna from her introspection, waking her to the poison in Blythe's mere arrival. "Yes?" she called through the panel, moving to spy through the safety lens. The face of Agent Reichly occupied the lens, his eyes magnified, darted as he spoke.

"We have Miss Blythe out here, Miss Windrow. She said she's already spoken to you and she's clear to come in if you'd open the door."

Alarm niggled at the nape of her neck. Clear to come in by whom? Why were they even suggesting she come into this apartment? Why weren't they issuing an alarm with Blythe's panic?

Something wrong here. All wrong. Jenna looked at the stone sober face, needing to close one eye to keep the man in focus. He certainly didn't appear too shaken up. What was this? What was Blythe up to?

The note. That damned note on her windshield. If Blythe had come here to cause trouble, lying about her current danger . . .? "Agent Reichly, I think it'd be a better idea if you call for—"

Reichly lurched sideways and a face magnified in the tiny circle; a single blue orb pierced the circle . . .

Abruptly confused, Jenna settled clumsily on her couch. Blinking, she focused as Lisa bolted the door across the room, turning. She wore black. From stretch black pants to a fitted black jacket, she stood in sharp contrast to the pastels of Jenna's apartment. With her shape defined, she poised with hand on her waist as if posing for a centerfold, enhanced tenfold by the open jacket and low-cut blouse exposing white bulging mounds. With her neon blond hair stuffed into a black knit hat, she appeared even more peculiar and the smile creasing her ruby red lips added to the carnival appearance

"What . . .?"

"I can't believe you weren't going to let me in," Lisa said as she trounced forward. Her eyes darted around the room, speculating, inspecting. With an odd shine in her pale blue eyes, she smiled down at Jenna. "We girls have to stick together. Don't you know that, sweetie-pie? I mean when you get right down to it—"

Remembering the performance through the buzzer, Jenna cut in, "So, it was an act." Nothing of hysteria remained on the heavily made-up face. From the painted porcelain color of the flesh to the thick black outline around her eyes, she'd dressed for effect . . . probably to stand on Liberty Avenue and turn a few tricks. Recovering her thought, Jenna continued, "I don't know how you managed to get in here . . ." And pushing to her feet, she stated, "But I think you better leave."

"You did get my message, didn't you?" Lisa said with a serene smile, halting near the center of the room.

Heat rising in Jenna's eyes, she stopped within a few paces. "If you mean that adolescent attempt to scare me, I'd imagine I did."

"You haven't seen scared, bitch, but you just might," Lisa hissed softly.

Her eyes . . . there was something wrong with those eyes. With only the shallow light from the kitchen to lance the shadows, the shine seemed far too intense. Uncomfortably aware of the time lapse between speaking with Reichly and sitting on the couch, Jenna studied the oddly plastic face in front of her, the scathing smile. "What is this, Lisa? What are you doing here?"

"Just tying up a few loose ends," she said offhandedly, her smoker's voice adding an almost masculine bent to the words. Without invitation, she started moving again, striding toward the kitchen entrance. "So prim and proper."

Jenna reached to halt her and suffered a quick disorientation when her hand missed its mark and Lisa passed into the kitchen. Confused and becoming slightly more irritated, Jenna followed. "I don't know what the hell you think you're doing here, Lisa, but I suggest you—"

The woman spun with a speed to halt Jenna in her tracks. The face twisted; the lips curled in a more definitive snarl. "I've about had it with you, bitch. In fact, I have had it with you. You've been sashaying around like you own the fucking world, and it's about fucking time somebody gives you what you deserve."

Blythe was crazy, no doubt about it. But just how crazy? And how the blazes had she gotten into this apartment? Past the Federal agents? Through the damn door! How had that happened?

"Ah, getting a little worried now, huh?" Lisa chided and bounced a forward step. "You should be, bitch. You should be real worried about now. Because I'll tell you," she said and shifted closer in an eyeblink.

Jenna jerked and started a back step. Her neck caught in a startling strong grip, bruises erupting on impact. Awake to the enlarged hand, the tiny black eyes magnified at close range, Jenna knew an instant panic. Insanity blazed in those eyes. Hatred. Menace. Hands flying, Janna clasped the black clad arm and intended a push. Both hands halted. She stood, frozen, paralyzed, looking into the beady glaring eyes. In her ears, her heartbeat throbbed; the pulse quickened and slammed under the bruising fingers.

"Oh, I'm not gonna kill you, bitch," the scathing voice promised, whispering. "I'm gonna do something a whole lot better . . . and worse, miss goody-two-shoes. A whole lot worse for you. Cause see? I just don't like your attitude," the slinky voice chinked. "You think you're something special. You think . . . hell, you think your ass is gold. Well, you ain't shit, bitch. You're nothing in the broader scheme of things. Just some fucking tramp who'll spread her legs to get ahead as well as the next gal. And that's what you're working on now, huh? You think you have a chance with Darius. You fuck him and you'll have it made, and that's the biggest fucking joke," the laugh in the voice offered nothing of humor.

Looking into the glowing eyes, the crazy shine, Jenna could only listen, too stunned by her immobility and the pain in her neck, the pulse in her body, to think clearly, reasonably. She wanted to rip Lisa Blythe to shreds. Would like nothing better than to slam the crazy smile off the thin red lips. Instead, she watched as the lips drew back over sharp white teeth like a clown's painted face. A grizzly clown, a sinister clown. Lisa Blythe was crazy . . . and she was something else. Something . . .

"That really is, you know?" Lisa taunted, warming to her game. "Darius the Great . . . that's his pet name, ya know?" she chided. "And that's all he is, bitch, a fucking pet. He's got a collar around his neck and when his master feels like jerking his chain, he jumps. You want to hear about that, too? I know all about it now," she said with a soft cynical laugh. "I always figured the bastard was gay. Figured he was in the fucking closet. Big macho bastard like him and he doesn't want to fuck around? Makes a girl wonder. Bet you wondered, huh, bitch? Wondered why he didn't jump soon's you started wagging your scrawny ass in his face."

The chiding had the opposite effect if Blythe intended to frighten her. Jenna's temper rising, her pulse slowed and her thoughts turned in weird circles to suffer a dark cynical amusement. Darius hadn't made love to this crazy bitch . . . and Jenna knew without a doubt, the man was fully capable and straight.

Something in Blythe's eyes flickered, sparks lifted, the smile drained slowly away. "You fucking whore . . . you fucking—" She drew back, releasing her hold.

Before Jenna could fully swing away, the hand ripped across her face. Lifted, thrown, Jenna slammed against the edge of the arch, reeled and skidded down the wall alongside the buffet. White hot sparks splashed over her eyes, blinding. Fire flashed from her jaw, her shoulder. This maniac would kill her! Meant to kill her! The reality sank in behind her shock and Jenna scrambled, blinking spots and finding the black, bleary image poised only a few steps away. Survival! Without a clear thought, Jenna swept her hand and latched onto the brass candlestick on the buffet, already pivoting, swinging wide as if wielding a wooden bat. The black slender limb shot toward her, and Jenna felt the connection, heard the startled breath as the entire slinky black form darted and vanished.

Vanished?

Shock stopped, trembling, Jenna darted her gaze, barely aware of her hand lifting, touching her lip. Her fingers came away wet, the only visible sign of Lisa Blythe's existence, but she was here. Turning slowly, Jenna panned her wide-wary gaze around the kitchen, toward the living room. The hallway. Light from her bedroom lamp spilled across the beige carpet, brightened the walls. She had a clear view into her bedroom. With a rare tunnel vision, more in line with a dream scope, Jenna peered down the hall, still turning, looking into her dining room. The FBI were outside the door . . . unless they were dead. At this moment, she could believe them dead. Could imagine herself dreaming. Where was she! Where was this lunatic? She couldn't have vanished. Unless this was one of those lifelike, waking nightmares. A hallucination. Nothing felt right, nothing felt real! But her shoulder throbbed. Her lip pulsed spilling more salty fluid. Running her tongue over her rapidly puffing lips, she tasted blood . . . and in a halted instant, she knew the danger. An association to blood . . . this maniac wanted her blood!

Life or dream . . . neither mattered. As long as she remained locked into this weird world, she wouldn't forfeit her blood to this lunatic who posed as Lisa Blythe. And was it any surprise this dream-monster would wear that bitch's face? Subconscious sludge! Lisa Blythe fit into that mold nicely!

"Where are you—you bitch?" Jenna seethed as she scanned the shadowy spaces, keen to the silence. "Come on, you chicken shit little slut!" she taunted. Bedamned if she would settle for anything less than a few good whacks at this menace. Six months of irritation festered in her subconscious, and she wasn't about to miss this golden opportunity to kick Blythe's ass. Blood. "You want my blood, bitch? Come and get it."

"We should have done this months ago," Lisa said, and Jenna spun to find her leaning languidly against the refrigerator. A smile curled her lips; her eyes flickered with that same weird light. "A little more than meets the eye, here, huh, Toots?"

Toots? "You really are . . . psychotic. And to think, all this time . . . I just thought you were hard up. I mean, you'd have to be pretty desperate to go to bed with Mason just to stay on the payroll."

Like a cat uncurling, Lisa started off the refrigerator door and Jenna didn't wait. Didn't wait, didn't hesitate. Launching forward, swinging the brass candlestick, she caught the fading image on the shoulder, and knew the ineffectiveness too late to correct her balance. Rammed sideways, she slammed her hip against the cabinets under the sink and the fingers clawed into her hair. The burn spread over her scalp as her head wrenched, her neck kinking with the whiplash effect. Red! She saw the red shine glowing over her and started to swing. Whether she stopped in shock, watching the spikes growing from under the curling lips, or froze under the gaze, Jenna knew only the impact of her knees caving, arm falling. The candlestick clattered in the metal sink basin. Now would be a good time to wake up from this dream!

"You're mine, bitch."

Cold . . . a bone chilling cold had slid through his flesh and settled in his core, but the anger kept Darius moving in the Baron's shadow. Over and under, they sped through the tangle of saplings and snow laden mounds. Barely an imprint he left in his wake. The scent of this beast flowed on a parallel course, the same path. Toward the back of the Terrace Apartments, they emerged from the woods and Darius needed neither direction nor scent to fly toward the building where Jenna dwelt. No time to waste. He passed the hedges at the rear, barely glimpsing at the blacked out glass of patio doors. A half step ahead, he jumped from the rail of a low balcony to the roof edge of the second floor. No time to waste! She was in trouble!

With the skill and talent of his youth, he shimmied and climbed, rising to the next, scaling the balconies like fire escapes. The Baron sailed over the balcony rail a half pace ahead, and for a split second, Darius feared they were too late. As he launched toward the wide panel of glass doors, his muscles collapsed and his knees landed on the cement floor as if a hammer slammed his head. Heaving a hurt breath and buckling uncontrollably under the pain, he understood the weight of the intervention.

Nnnnooo!

Silllennnce.

Trouble! She's in trouble! Don't wait! Letttt gooo of me!

Lissstennn!

He did listen, heard the soft voices at the edges of his mind, heard the scathing soft voice hissing taunting. Jenna? Jenna's voice? Taunting the monster? Caught between surprise and admiration, doubt and the bone chilling cold that reached into his lungs, burning his every breath, he tipped his head, lifting slightly. The Baron hulked at the door to the balcony, apparently listening as well. Taunting? Darius doubted the words, the boldness. Was she crazy? Had he fallen in love with a madwoman? Or was she more courageous than he could have anticipated?

Youuu have fine tassste. But she hasss no idea what she's up aaagainssst.

We have to . . . you have to . . . plllleeease!

Now you beggg? The prickly voice chided with a sigh of disgust in the ethereal realm. *Ahh, but alasss, you havvve a point. Commme. Ittt's timmme.*

Up and moving, barely aware of his stealth, Darius adhered to the internal command, sliding through the parted glass, not entirely sure how the Baron had managed that trick to unlock the door. He heard Jenna baiting Blythe as he slipped behind the curtain following the Baron and skimming past the branches of the Christmas tree. He smelled the blood, human blood mixed within the overwhelming musty smell of the vampire. Moving, sweeping from behind the curtain in the shadow of the Baron, he saw Jenna step and swing. More clearly, the black phantom darted and pivoted, slamming the white frocked body against the cabinet and catching the fiery bronze hair. Only in his mind, Darius snarled rage and battled to snap the unyielding control in his limbs. Chained, collared, he was as bloody helpless as a hound on a leash, at the mercy of the master who swept around the corner and rose over the tangle of black and white images. For a frozen instant, as the blond head plunged, fangs protruded, Darius's heart stopped

In the next instant, the Baron caught the head in his massive hand as if catching a softball, halted the action, and wrenched the head back. The red eyes bulged, a cry started off the yawning lips and fear blazed neon as it lurched to break free. With the immense fingers curling about the blond hair, the nails extended, sinking, The hauntingly human face twisted, the feral shine doused under a wave of terror and pain. Like a rattler striking, the Baron lunged and plunged, his black mane falling over the painted face. Cringing within his frozen frame, Darius heard the scream of pain. A hundredfold, the rancid scent permeated the kitchen, nearly taking his breath away with the stench assaulting his nostrils.

Release the woman, vixen. Only in his mind, Darius heard the hissing words sliding, pricking and stinging inside his own skull.

Jenna's eyes flared wide, blinking. Within microseconds, her eyes glazed and misted but her hands groped to the sink, her body unbending rising. Her head tilted into a more natural position. By reflex, Darius lurched toward her, his every sense to catch her, help her. Blood on her lips! His action halted and his gaze lifted unwittingly to find the Baron rising, licking a black taint off his lips, looking into him.

By reflex or impulse, Darius reacted and caught the limp body flung sideways against him. Uncontrollably, he wrapped his arms around Lisa Blythe and stood frozen, his senses reeling in conflicts of rage and outrage. This wasn't the body he wanted to hold! Not the woman he wanted against him. This half dead thing hung against him, head sagging over his muscled arm, a slight body emitting waves of noxious odors. He could only watch as the Baron turned his attention to Jenna.

Poised with her back against her pristine sink counter, Jenna stood with her hands fisted, gripping the ends of her terrycloth robe belt. Her head tilted in a natural slight bow staring at the center of the floor. Beautiful, she was so incredibly beautiful. But hurt. A spot of blood smeared her delicate chin, still glistening, wet. A thin red line nicked her upper lip on the left side. Her lips already puffed, and a red handprint welted the lovely cheek. Her left eye watered, spilling a trickle of tears. The right remained clear. Beautiful! Hurt! She was hurt! Could be hurt worse!

Almost human, Amad stood to one side, possibly deliberately lending Darius his view. A full head taller, he looked down on the bronze hair, lifting his hand to Jenna's delicate chin and lifting her cameo face from the bow. Heart hammering, Darius watched the Baron caress the smooth cheek then moved his thumb, lifting the smudge of blood off her chin, carrying the smudge to his lips. She was still in danger. Darius cringed internally with the red flashes in the dark blue, nearly human eyes. With his breath panting drawing the aromas past the smell off the thing in his arms, Darius battled the hold inside of him. Never more chained or tortured, his rage rose. And in slow motion, Jenna's hands unraveled the belt. The cloth parted revealing a champagne-colored silk gown; a touch of lace dipped into the valley between her full breasts. Memories blazed in his mind from a single night past, heating and haunting him as he stood frozen, raging silently. Even the presence inside his mind, the observation countered nothing of his torment. His heartbeat hammered as the Baron traced a path along the lace with his index finger and dipped lower, deeper within the V. Not even this could he spare her! She wasn't safe! Would never be safe in his keep when he rested more completely entrenched in another's keep.

In one smooth motion, the Baron dipped and lifted her smoothly into his arms, sweeping her off her feet. Lancing Darius with a glance to sting and burn, the Baron strode from the kitchen, carrying her into the hall, to her bedroom.

As the Baron had promised, his emotions were enhanced and with every passing instant, rage flamed higher, igniting images of what he would like to do to the beast hanging limp, unconscious in his arms. Even when he'd believed her a woman, he'd considered her a conniving slut, a wicked little tramp with a singular talent for lying on her back. Whether she'd obeyed orders she couldn't refuse, or attempted to ascend beyond those orders, neither mattered in his mind. She had killed. She'd marked Adam and taken his will. What she might have done to Adam's new bride, Darius had yet to learn and preferred not to know. No news was the only good news he'd ever received. Messengers brought chaos and pain. This bitch brought damnation . . . for him, for Jenna, for Adam. He wanted her dead and with every moment the Baron spent in that back bedroom, Darius rage rose. If he gather his limbs, he would crush her . . . or break her neck . . . or . . . or . . .

"None of those methods would prove effective," the Baron said in contented tone as he strode from the hallway entrance, a smile playing on his human lips.

Silent. Seething internally, Darius had no control over the hatred pouring through his mind. He wanted this slut to pay . . . pay . . . *pay!*

Reminds you of your mother, so she does.

The simple sliding, chiding syllables inside his head halted Darius more effectively than the Baron's presence looming large in front of him. No response. His thoughts had grown suddenly as silent and still as his muscles.

Ah, but I have your undivided attention now, the voice chided, and a glitter of amusement lifted in the cobalt blue eyes. *Now, what to do with this little vixen? Breaking, crushing, killing the little beast is slightly more complicated than it seems. More complicated in this modern age. There's almost nowhere one can find a quiet place free of spectators. The world has become so small compared to centuries past.*

A sigh slid through Darius's mind almost in harmony with a sense of the internal order to collect the beast more naturally into his arms. Dead weight settled in his arms, her limbs dangled, flaccid. Halfheartedly, he wondered if she'd already perished under the Baron's bite, but his question remained unanswered. Silently, he followed the Baron through the kitchen arch into the living room, to the door. Curious, aware of the men on the opposite side, Darius glimpsed the startled eyes turning toward the Baron before both men froze in a half turn. Experience and instinct offered the explanation as both agents lifted an upturned palm toward the Baron as if offering him a drink from their cupped palm. He drank from their flesh, sinking a single fang through the muscle under the thumb on one, taking from the wrist of the other. Licking the blood smears, he finished the taking, granting nothing in return.

Not privy to the silent exchange, equally enthralled, he accepted the silent command to follow as the Baron continued into the hall. Neither agent lent him a glance despite the body dangling in his arms. Silence. Not a single mind or body stirred on the entire floor. If anyone moved within the apartments, no sound breached the walls as they stopped at the fire escape doors.

To the human hand clasping his shoulder, Darius jolted, and his muscles freed once again. A natural shudder rolled to his soles and his wary dark gaze lifted to the cobalt orbs studying him inside and out.

Quite a night, we've had, lad. What say we take the stairs and jaunt back to the hotel? Your cousin worries so when I'm away too long.

He wanted nothing more than to return into Jenna's apartment, to see her, touch her, and knew the futility before he fully formed the thought. *Is she safe, now? Will she be safe here?*

Is anyone ever entirely safe? the low voice said with a whimsical note, and the hand nudged him through the fire escape door.

No relief would be forthcoming, Darius understood. The night was still young. His misery not soon to end. *What are we to do with Blythe?* he asked silently.

Ah, I'll think of something. You needn't worry.

No relief or answers in that area either, Darius understood but he continued to stew on the questions and fears as they descended through the stairwell and passed through the fire exit doors without making a sound. At a trot, they sped across the lawn and dipped into the deeper shadows of the woods. The cold . . . the cold reached into him again, more intense without the distraction of the hunt in his mind. Shivering internally, he held the limp woman closer, knowing the futility of drawing warmth from her frigid limbs. Ducking the snapping branches off the Baron's shoulders, he gained sense of their direction veering away from the hotel. No answers. No relief. His thoughts turned in slowing circles, retracing every detail, wondering, heaving condensation, he asked, "Wh-what will happen to Adam . . . will she . . . is he lost to the other?"

"Let me worry about your cousins, Darius," the Baron said without a hitch in his breath or stride. "You've enough to keep you occupied mentally for a time."

The cold seemed to lance every fiber of his sweater and jeans, sinking like icicles into his pores, cutting into his bones. Every step sent prickles and pains from his toes. His fingers were surely numb, frozen against the chilled shoulder and knee cradled in his arms. Catching fire on every breath, his chest ached, and his pace slowed more with the shudders quaking through him.

Weakening. Physically weakening, Darius staggered a step and nearly lost his hold on Blythe as he slammed against a tree trunk to catch his balance. Pain ripped and burned like dry ice through his fingertips. Heaving softly, huffing pained breaths and sounds, he stumbled again, breaking a hand free, unconsciously clasping Amad's jacket. Dying! The temperature had dropped a hundred degrees! No other explanation reached his reeling, failing mind. A man could die in zero-degree weather . . . no coat. A wind chill below freezing. His breath turned to icicles inside his throat, driving gasps from his parted lips. *Hhhheelllp! No coat! Freezing! Human! I'mmm stilll hummman! Weee have to runnn! Sssomething! Helllp! Orr dooo you wwwant meee deaaad? Isss mmmy ssservice ennnded? Finnnding Blyyythe!*

The Baron stopped in a half turn and clasped his arm, holding him steady by purely physical force. "Lad, you are in a state," the low voice mused. "I can't even be comfortable in your head. You've very nearly frozen me out."

Ddddyyying! Darius cried silently, unable to slip breath or syllables off his tongue. Swaying, quaking, he clasped the jacket sleeve if only to stay on his feet, wedging Blythe and himself against the solid capable build. If he fell, he would never rise. The Baron would leave him here to freeze to death alongside Blythe! *Ddddon't!*

"Freezing is one of the more pleasant ways to die, Darius. Are you sure you want my help to reach the warmth of the hotel? A few more minutes, you'll be asleep and drifting toward eternity. Truly. You're over the worst pain. Wouldn't you rather I leave you here in peace?"

Nooo! he cried in more quick anger and fear. *Warmth! Help! Human! Life! Liiifffe!*

"Possibly, we should get you inside after all," Amad mused. "As much as you may feel as if you're dying . . . I lied to you, lad. You wouldn't die even if I left you here until the dawn any more than that wench could die of exposure. And you haven't passed from the physical distress. It's one of life's little discomforts in your current physical state, Darius. I won't humor you . . . nor carry you, m'lad. You will walk. Sad to say, you need to adjust and learn from this experience as well. I won't have one of my executives running about wearing parkas and gloves on a cool summer night." Undoubtedly only for practical reasons, the Baron clasped Blythe, ripping her from Darius's hands and tossing her like an empty sack over his broad shoulder. Her head thudded against a branch, but Amad appeared not to notice. He merely continued onto the narrow wooded path, a deer path, perhaps.

Walking hurt. Every step burned and took Darius's breath away as he began walking again, clinging to Amad's sleeve. Barely, he grasped the anomaly of the tangled briars and saplings passing. Not much moonlight, but the images remained vivid, daylight vivid. Distracted by half, he remained more intent on his grip, aware of his icy fingers clasping the sleeve, and sending fire into his arm, his shoulder . . . reaching into his shoulder, collarbone, and neck. And by his nature, he struggled to collect the details.

Pain . . . discomfort . . . his current physical state . . . half dead. He was only half dead. A connection . . . his blood . . . thin?

"Ah, you are a bright one, Darius. I always knew that, but it's a fine pleasure to listen to your little wheels spinning and grasping at concepts you've never needed to consider."

Physical discomfort . . . the outside temperature was cool, crisp . . . but not even close to a hundred degrees below zero. As much as he grasped the concept, nothing of relief touched his mind. He was walking. His bones weren't actually frozen. His limbs wouldn't break with the icicles in his veins no matter how his every step threatened to shatter him.

A low chuckle slid from the shadowed figure beside him. "Therein lies the truth of the matter, Darius. You won't regulate to temperature as well as you once did. That chill you feel . . . it won't ebb swiftly. You will be uncomfortable from time to time. A natural process, I assure you. Even the meek in my flock suffer the twinges of this condition. I won't warm them. I won't warm you. Keep walking . . . or should we hasten this pace a tad and find a warmer climate a little more swiftly?"

Not even a whisper of a response touched his mind. A safety device. Silence. Silence. Silence. No reaction. No reaction.

The Baron chuckled more deeply. "If it doesn't matter to you, lad . . . then the decision's mine and I did mention your cousin's needs."

Bassstard! Darius hissed silently, but nearly buckled to the scream as they broke into a jog.

30

As Darius had known, they weren't traveling a direct route to the hotel. Shivering and quaking despite the run through a tangle of forest that might have heated his blood in the past, Darius stood heaving chilled breaths, watching as the Baron stepped into a small clearing within the moonlight. Lisa Blythe was dead . . . and in a wrenching moment of humanity, Darius found no consolation to realize she'd been more than half dead before the Baron touched her. His own condition . . . his own fate stared him in the face as he watched the Baron lie the woman down, sprawling her on a patch of snow. Amad owned this forest stretching from the hotel perimeter. Belatedly, Darius recalled the land developers occasionally reaching out to him over the past several years, asking to purchase sections of the two hundred vacant acres. As Amad arranged Blythe on the east facing surface, Darius wondered if the Baron maintained these holdings for this sole purpose.

Without conscious thought, Darius obeyed the internal command, meandering on the edge of the clearing in search of a fallen branch, not entirely certain what the Baron intended. Choosing a stout branch on impulse, Darius carried it to the Baron who stood over Blythe, then set off again, responding to a silent command. Suffering the vertigo in his mind, Darius worried over this separation of mind and body. A severance at the primal level. Conscious, fully coherent, and curious, Darius scrounged in a cover of dead leaves and watched his hand dig a fist-sized rock from black muck.

A stake and a rock. His body returned like a well-trained mutt, delivering the rock into the Baron's much larger hand. After all else Darius had seen and learned in the past eight years, the revelation lent him another sense of vertigo. A stake through the heart, like some wretched fictional tale in a movie . . . Raphael. Another lesson . . . or a genuine means to an end which might await him in his future? Was the Baron attempting to torment him, reduce him to the child's fear, or was it even more basic—confirmation that the Baron had truly known about the promise Darius had asked of Raphael? A sign of how much he truly knew about the boy's occasional contact.

His attention riveted by no control of his own, Darius watched Amad score the end of the stake and place it over the area of the woman's heart. She hadn't moved or twitched. Her long fake lashes hung at half-mast; her sightless eyes peered through slits . . . seeming suddenly to be watching the Baron. Shivering internally, Darius cringed at the dull thud amplified with the first strike of stone on the stout branch. The eyelids snapped wide open and eyeballs bulged; the thin lips parted but no sound emerged. She moved . . . she bloody moved as the Baron slammed another solid whack on the stake. Her body jerked in spasms; her fingers curled until the jagged nails bit into her palms as she struggling to rise off the earth. Her tangled blond hair swung with her head twitching and twisting under the moonlight. Whether time had slowed or Darius suffered the first stages of exposure, he stared at the stake, horrified . . . until he realized the absence of blood around that wood and the pale gray face contorting. Was it even possible . . . had the fictional world carried a grain of truth? Was this the only means of killing something already dead? His mind turned in slow circles, frozen in stark horror as Amad continued to drive the stake through the woman's dead heart. Scalp crawling, he recognized the pitch changing as the stake met solid earth beneath the writhing figure. In more hollow thuds, the stake descended.

Done—it was done, finally. Smoothly, the Baron rose and tossed the rock almost leisurely toward the surrounding brush. Far away, sounds of life echoed, amplified, and Darius imagined a tractor-trailer passing on the expressway. Normalcy. A world of ordered normalcy lingered just beyond this clearing, and in another weird vertigo, he suffered the impact of his separation. He was no longer any part of that world. The illusion had shattered entirely by the time he lifted his gaze from the still jittering woman to find the Baron's blue eyes looking down at him, lanced silver in the moonlight. Numb. As much from shock as the cold, now, Darius woke to the sting of tears in his eyes, not certain for whom he meant to weep, Blythe, himself, or the whole human race, the majority of whom remained oblivious and ignorant. Monsters. He was the monster.

"A pity you need learn another lesson, Darius," Amad said quietly and lifted his hand. Under the chilled index finger skimming over his jaw, Darius shivered uncontrollably. "But alas, you need grasp the reality of your condition. Curious and courageous, son. Fine traits," he idled. "Have your answers and reach your conclusions. There's enough shade to see you back to the hotel when the time comes." Barely pausing, he commented, "Enjoy what remains of your new day, m'lad."

Tense and alarmed, Darius watched the Baron turn and in a split second, Amad vanished. Not even a whisper of snapping branches or footfalls marked his departure into the woods. Alone. Entirely alone, Darius backed away from the twitching woman, turned clumsily and made his way into the darker shadows of barren trees and tangled vines at the edge of the clearing.

Insanity! Surely, he had gone mad! He couldn't be standing less than fifteen feet from a woman who should be dead and struggled as if she would rise off the stake at any moment. Not a woman. A vampire, he countered and shook himself to his frozen toes to realize the greater insanity. A myth, a fairytale, folklore passed down through generations with the sole intent to frighten small children in the dark . . . He had believed that once. At a base instinct to survive, he'd rejected his reality time and again, forcing himself to believe he remained a company executive for a ruthless employer. Even the memory images of horror from that long-ago night had dwindled with time, allowing him a reprieve from the madness he was forced to live.

Leaning against a tree trunk, shivering, his hands shoved into his pockets and frozen in fists, he stared at the half-human thing twitching on the ground. Again and again, he attempted to deny the reality aside, clinging to the thought of a nightmare. Practicality, logic . . . conscious thought slid through his quaking mind. He stood less than fifteen feet from a woman who'd been a part of the living world. Like him, she'd held a position in the von Hendricks Corporation. In the natural world, this was murder, and already, the American government had believed him a murderer. If he was caught here . . . if physical evidence led from this woman's corpse to him . . .

Suddenly, Raphael's fear of that bloody movie seemed far more reasonable and practical than Darius cared to consider. If any others truly learned—and believed in the existence of vampires—they would be hunted down and killed. What remained of his heart hammered a quicker beat as he considered himself lying pegged to that snowy bed, a stake through his heart. The Baron had drained her . . . no differently than she'd drained Fradden . . .

'. . . he was mine.'

Damn him! Amad had known, as much as three days ago, Amad had known Lisa Blythe was Fradden's killer! Through Fradden's eyes, the Baron had undoubtedly seen the face of a killer . . .

Stifling his thought, starkly aware of the silence inside his mind, Darius suffered a new shiver. His thoughts were no longer his private domain. In every instant, the Baron remained privy to his internal kibitzing, and what were the ramifications if he ventured an accusation? Still, his revelation spiraled. The Baron could have taken care of Blythe . . . the Baron could have avoided changing him. What had he done to deserve this end? To be double-damned?

What mistake had he unwittingly made to stand in this frigid air and suffer these maddening reflections as his body chilled to a block of living ice?

What the bloody hell did I do to deserve this? He screamed only in his mind, but no answer came. Silence. Internal silence lingered after his scream.

External, the sound reached him. Not breath nor even an attempt at voice. A primal groan emitted from the writhing body, barely a whisper in the stillness. Blythe should be dead! She lay sprawled with a stake through her heart, pinning her to the snowy slant of a hill. And still, she made a sound to send another shiver down Darius's frozen spine. Alive. Living dead. And inside himself, an alarm niggled, hearing distant sounds of car engines passing more frequently on the expressway a mile or less from where he stood in black shadow.

The moon. Moonlight slanted through the branches around him, and in a mild start of panic, Darius searched the tangle overhead, searching that silver obelisk. Mercy! It was nearly gone and at a deeper level, a primal level, fear niggled. He'd lived in shadows for years, but he'd never feared the daylight, confident that he could walk into the morning light without serious harm. Something had changed . . . a great deal of something had changed. With the first hint of daylight silvering the sky, prickling discomfort sped through his ice-encased limbs. '. . . buy a hat . . .' Had the Baron lied? Would the sunlight incinerate him? Was this lesson to be his last? Had Amad left him here, like Blythe, to kill two birds with one stone?

With nothing more than a sweater and jeans, tempted to believe he stood encased in icicles for as cold as his flesh felt, he knew himself fully changed. A vampire . . . fledgling. Mercy! He could be murdered by the bloody elements, and if the Baron chose to kill him, he knew better than to believe he could turn and run for safety. Doomed and damned. Possibly he should merely accept his due and step into that clearing, lay down alongside Blythe and offer himself to the light. In the next instant, he knew the futility on two planes—not only could the Baron stop him . . . a mere thought of Jenna held him immobile. Whether he was more or less capable of protecting her now, the fact remained . . . he needed to try.

What of their plans? The trip? At 6: a.m. he was supposed to pick her up, to take her to Europe with him . . . and he had been a fool even to believe that possibility. If Amad forced him to carry out that plan, it would not be to ensure her safety or allow him to become a part of her life.

Futility, fear of the advancing dawn, frigid air and Lisa's soft mewling sounds combined. Sinking against the tree bark, his knees buckled fully for the first time. Emotions he hadn't allowed himself to feel, sensations of vulnerability he'd known as a child, reared anew in his swirling senses. He was trapped. A vampire's familiar, more, now, than eight years passed when Thaddeus von Hendricks had voiced those words. Since that night of horror, Darius had known his life would be forfeit; he'd known Kevin's lie in his mention of the Passover. They would all die—or live eternal hell on earth and in the hereafter. As he had known long before last night, he remained another sheep in the Baron's herd, slaughtered and condemned. If he was forced to lie down alongside Blythe, it would be a mercy, and he knew better than to hope for that swift wicked end. Inside himself, the chains of bondage had tightened more effectively than a choke collar around his neck.

If only to torment him, Jenna filled his mind's eye. In a whirlwind, he recalled every natural instant he'd spent with her, cursing himself more thoroughly for not taking full advantage. If he'd run away with her . . . damned the reality and the knowledge willed to him. Nowhere could he have taken her where Amad wouldn't have tracked him down and made him suffer a more wicked fate for his treachery. To cross Amad, living or dead, would be a fate worse than death . . . and he couldn't have betrayed Amad then any more than he could, now. His word. His bond. His oath and his honor.

For the sins of his fathers, he was damned and not even his love for Jenna could set him free from that reality. He did love her, had loved her from the instant he'd sat in that blasted dining room, loved her enough to want her free. How could fate have played such a wicked trick on him? How? After eight long years, how had she arrived in his life when his life was ending?

No answers, only misery compounded every passing second as the greater prickling of alarm tweaked the edges of his mind. Daylight. A gray haze had replaced the silver shine of moonlight and five yards away, Lisa Blythe, dead to the natural world, writhed and moaned. By no will of his own, his moist eyes lifted and found her within the gray light. Dressed in black, she appeared no more than a hazy silhouette, her long thin legs jittering, her arms bent. Ashen, red-tipped fingers clawed and scraped the black cloth at her waist. Her head twisted, a ghastly mask, tilted toward him surrounded by the neon mat . . . and her eyes, as black as her thick fake lashes, found him in the shadows, glaring at him.

Shuddering suddenly, Darius suffered the probe like tiny spikes against his eyes, and something inside himself rose to thwart her invasion. Even now, more dead than alive, she sensed his presence, and in a violent shiver, Darius understood her raging command, her demand as well as her terror. She wanted him to set her free!

Heellllp mmmeee, the distant cry pervaded, touching him to stare more blindly toward her black slitted eyes. *Cccommme and pulll this staaake outtt! Helllp mmmeee, Darrriusss! Weee cann essscape him! I'lll helllp youuu! Ssset yyyouuu freee!*

She had heard! Somehow she had heard his thoughts as easily as the Baron.

An abomination! A murderess. A vampiress! A fully changed vampire! In a fleeting instant, his mind woke to the daylight, his fear ascending. He'd never fully believed others existed. In his limited world of horrors, he'd forced himself to believe that Amad and Raphael were the only ones of their kind . . . and knew he needed that belief to survive. With his present condition, and rising discomfort, he understood clearly. He could be damned more fully, cursed to live . . . forever?

I'lll ssset youuu freee Darrriuss, Blythe promised in a distant echo within the ether. *Helllp mmme! I'lll ssset youuu freee. Youuu coullld beee wwwith Jennna forrrever. Freee offf a masssterrr. I'lll helllp youuu! Commme tooo meee, nowww.*

Her words touched him, but rather than welcome her wily attempt to seduce him, the words offered the opposite effect. He understood her promise to set him free, her intention to change him fully. Free. He could live with Jenna forever . . . right after he drank from her and changed her into an abomination, snatching her life from her. Never! Never would he condemn his love to live this hellish existence.

More anxiously, Blythe's words slid through his rage, and he grasped her fear. His own fear ascended on equal planes as daylight crept across the sky overhead. He'd missed the six a.m. deadline . . . and by his quickening shudders and prickling, sunrise wasn't far off. How would he return to the hotel? Was this truly his end? Could it be so simple? So quick? In stark contrast to the light, his vision blurred as it had a day passed on a sidewalk in Pittsburgh. But he'd walked in sunlight then, had reacted to the tremendous brightness for which he was unaccustomed. No sunlight yet. Gray, the light crept overhead and even lifting his gaze toward the sky rose the tears to prick his eyes. When the sun rose fully, he would surely be blind! And how was he to return to the hotel undetected even if he managed to survive?

Helllp mmmeee! Blythe screamed and her blurry form writhed in greater frenzy, struggling to turn, to extract her body from the stake. Her hands had found the protruding shaft, and she battled against her drained limbs, tugging at that shaft.

In a blinding epiphany, Darius realized the stake was no more than a pin to hold her in place . . . the sunlight would send her to hell. And as he watched, unable to retract his blurry gaze, her words rose to panicky screams. Promises, masked in terror, she tried luring him from the bushes where he rested in shade and shadows. By the time the first sprinkles of sunlight crept lengthwise through the surrounding woods, his internal battle had begun, his fear rising equally with his physical distress. As if he were wrapped in a cake of dry-ice, fire and frigid spikes scattered over his quaking limbs. Even if he wanted to move now, his limbs had molded, melted into a fiery vat. He couldn't move! Could barely see the writhing image splayed on the white bed which brightened more to blind him. Only at the fringes of his mind, he heard the crackle of branches and footfalls, and any thought of getting caught or arrested vanished as he heard the silent, primal scream.

31

With a single name whispered on her lips, Jenna awoke. Within seconds of clearing her foggy mind, she found the spot of blood on her pillow and the overturned lamp lying at an angle against her headboard. Nightmares . . . only impressions of the nightmares lingered now, and a single thought moved her. She needed to know Darius was safe! With the started motion, she gasped against more aches and pains, waking to her stiff neck and thudding pain in her shoulder. How she'd even fallen asleep remained a mystery. Whatever demons she might have wrestled in the nightmares, she'd rather not know.

Daylight glowed against the curtains of her balcony door, sunlight trickled through the window above the sink, brightening the kitchen . . . but neither offered a shred of relief. Without clear thought, she reached the telephone on the wall, found the phone number she'd jotted on a notepad in the wee hours. Talking hurt. Gingerly, she touched her lips, almost stunned to feel the puffiness. Her present state offered new meaning to 'a rough night.' Concentrating, she managed to ask if the von Hendricks' plane was still at the airport, and a droll female voice put her on hold. Tense, irritated, finding more aches and pains, Jenna waited, tempted to panic before the voice returned and verified, the plane had departed at six thirty. Thanking the operator as the line disengaged, Jenna moved to the couch and settled onto the corner. She should be relieved . . . glad to have him safely away . . . but the feeling of abandonment stole over her. She would have gone with him . . . was it only in a dream he'd invited her and she'd accepted?

Disoriented, she sank into the cushion, scanning her living room as if she were suddenly a stranger in this room. Against the sunlight streaking in her kitchen, she squinted, remembering those seconds downtown when Darius had suffered near blindness under a stroke of sunlight. Her eyes adjusted slowly with the lingering haze of sleep. Clearly, she scanned her kitchen . . . and felt an absence, caught a chill.

Nothing felt right. Nothing felt real. Even that call to the airport felt wrong, as if she'd acted on some stupid impulse. No promises. Darius hadn't made any promises to her, hadn't even hinted that he wanted anything more than what they'd shared.

A fun interlude. A pleasant break and distraction. A stolen pleasure when opportunity had knocked, and she grieved to consider the circumstances, granting them the opportunity to steal that pleasure. A murder. If Lawrence Fradden hadn't lost his life, Darius would have flown out of her life as swiftly as he'd flown into it. He was gone now. She might have felt his absence without ever making that call.

Something was missing.

What to do now? He'd said to sever . . . or had he? Even those moments seemed hazy and surrealistic in her mind. Had they sat inside his car . . .? She remembered them entering her apartment, could almost taste his cologne on her breath and lingering in the air, stronger than the pine scent of potpourri on her sideboard.

Uttering a curse, she pushed slowly off the couch. Sitting, struggling with the haze of sleep and lingering nightmares wouldn't afford her any relief. What was done, was done. No promises. She hadn't asked and he hadn't offered. The opposite held true. On the bluff overlooking Pittsburgh, he'd verified her belief at the onset. He wouldn't forfeit his career, wouldn't consider leaving his occupation, grounding himself in a relationship, and abandoning his responsibilities . . . any more than she'd consider becoming extra baggage to traipse around the world attached to his hip. A month or two though . . . His intensity and commitment, his power, was as much a part of his allure as his handsome dark eyes and hair. She could love him, would miss him desperately if her current state was any indication, but she'd known at the onset, she could never have him entirely.

By routine, she turned on the coffee pot and returned to her bedroom. A shower would never soften the edges of her physical distress. When she felt the worst, she dressed the best if only to improve her mood. Bringing a gray wool suit from the closet, she routed through the hangers and found the coordinating gray blouse. A sensible ensemble, a ready-for-anything ensemble. She would be ready for whatever fate deemed for the day . . . right after she soaked in a hot tub and held an ice pack to her lip. Explaining the result of the night's distress could be the most difficult, and embarrassing. To hell with appearances or explanations! She barely finished the thought when she spied her reflection in the vanity mirror, fingering her slightly puffy lip. A tiny cut slivered her top lip. Not much more than a paper cut or an effect of chapped dry lips. Considering how often she and Darius had kissed . . . maybe she would leave the puffiness a little longer and let imaginations run wild. She could cover the pink tint on her cheek where the lamp base had slammed her. With a wry smile sliding into her lips, twinging just a tad, she considered running across Lisa Blythe . . .

Soaking helped. Routine helped more. By the time she finished her morning ministrations and molded her hair into a flowing, loose style of curls, she felt better, looked better. The classic business executive prepared to meet another day. With a first cup of coffee downed, a second poured, she strode through the living room and halted as she reached for the locks. A flutter of anxiety lifted at her hairline, prickling her collar . . . whether she saw her fingers disengaging the lock or suffered a thought of the agents, a warning, she couldn't decide. Muttering a curse, she toggled the lock and opened the door carefully as one of the agents turned. "Uhh . . . good morning."

"Good morning, miss," Reichly said formally, and she pushed the door open in invitation. The second agent turned partway and met her gaze, his brow faintly troubled and pale eyes murky, red from too many hours of standing in the hall.

This was ridiculous, making them stand in the hall like palace guards. Forcing a slight smile, she decided, "You both look like you could use a cup of coffee. Why don't you come in? I didn't think you'd both stay all night."

"We were relieved for a while," Reichly supplied and accepted the offer first. The second man held the rolled daily which she'd intended to collect off her threshold. He handed it to her with a wan smile. "Think this belongs to you, miss."

"Yes, it does," she said and accepted the paper, letting him close the door at his heels. His name came to her as they strode into her kitchen. Miller—Agent Miller. If she had heard either man's first name, the memory eluded her. Motioning them to make themselves at home, she poured two more cups of coffee, not surprised when they drank it black. Real men drank their coffee black, as if adding cream could detract from their macho image. Federal agents needed to be tough, she supposed . . . or they couldn't waste time with luxuries. Delivering the cups, she glanced between them, reading tension on Reichly's face, in his eyes. "Is everything all right?"

"There's a situation back at the hotel, but it's under control," the agent said gravely. "Probably nothing serious."

"You do realize, you can't say something like that and leave me hanging, right?" she asked with a niggling fear at the nape of her neck. "What's the situation?"

Miller glanced at his partner as if doubting the man's judgement. Stocky, Miller wore the build and conviction of a dedicated weightlifter, not quite a bodybuilder. His dark jacket rested over his square shoulders in a natural fit.

His tie knotted in perfect alignment with his shirt collar. His eyes were quick, too quick and pale, less murky.

Jenna turned her attention to the slightly dismayed, slightly older and more slender face. "What's going on?"

"Probably a false alarm," he said with an attempt to sound casual. "One of the morning employees didn't show up for work, didn't call in sick. At this point, we're checking any and every discrepancy. She probably just slept in or had car trouble. I'm sure it's nothing."

"Who . . . who didn't show up?" she asked tensely.

"Miss, I really didn't mean to worry you," he said with a natural apology in his tone and gaze. "I'm sure we'll find her safe and sound."

Jenna hesitated and reached only one conclusion. If she wanted answers, she needed to go to the source. These two had orders apparently. Slipping off her chair, she sidled and lifted the wall phone, dialing the direct line to the Chateau's front desk. Lucy Perrel, the steady daylight clerk, answered with a feigned perky note. "Lucy, this is Jenna. Is Mason in his office?"

"God, I'm glad you called," Perrel said with a breath of relief. "We weren't sure what to make of you not showing up, now Lisa's not come in and after last night . . . God, this place is a mess. Mason's . . . Mr. Mason's in his office, Jen. He's with that man from the FBI. I could connect you. I'm sure he'd want to hear from you."

"What happened last night?" she asked distractedly.

"God, you wouldn't believe it. When Lori told me . . . I wish I'd have been here!"

"Lucy, what happened?" Jenna asked more firmly, her attention riveted.

"Baron von Hendricks—theee Baron Amadeus von Hendricks was here!" she said with a new height of hysteria in her voice. "I've worked here for almost ten years, and I've never seen him. According to Lori, he came in just after she came on duty. God, she said he's even more impressive in person. Anyway!" she continued with a softer, conspiratorial whisper which suggested someone approached the desk. "He spent most of the night in meetings. Lori said it was like getting a visit from the President. Even the FBI guys went nuts. I swear, we had about fifty of them still here when I came in. Talk about security! We're down to about a half dozen again, now. I can't believe I missed all the excitement. Anyway, they're gone, but boy, that guy doesn't mess around. I think Mr. Mason . . . Well, anyway, things are still hectic. I can't believe Lisa didn't come in today." A slightly amused note entered the soft breathless voice. "I'm almost tempted to think, she heard about this and tried catching up to them at the airport."

Some things were simply understood and too hard to ignore. If Lisa heard about the head of the company's visit, she would have attempted to catch the fellow's attention. If she'd failed, she might have decided to take the day off out of spite. Damn it. With everything else Mason needed to handle, he couldn't afford to be shorthanded by two. "Luce, don't bother Mr. Mason. I'll be in shortly."

"I thought you were taking a couple days off," Lucy said in a tempered voice, a hint of concern. "I know the FBI are worried that you could be . . . in danger. Honey, don't come in. I'm sure Lisa will show up in her own sweet time. This isn't the first time—"

"Luce, just hold down the fort. I'll see you shortly."

Even as she hung up the phone, she heard an echo of the deep voice warning her . . . but no clear thought accompanied the words. More clearly, she heard her decision to resign her position with the company. She would put in her two-week notice . . . just as soon as this mess was cleaned up and the Chateau was running smoothly. She'd never run from a damned fight in her life, had never walked away from a commitment or an obligation. And she felt both toward the Chateau. At some point, she'd submit her notice and walk away, but not with so many loose ends.

Neither agent attempted to alter her decision, both merely agreeing and following, ever watchful as she gathered her purse and coat, her car keys from the hook near the door. Reichly intruded only to mention she would be safer in their car . . . and he must insist she ride with them.

In front of Darius, sunlight poured through tree trunks and barren branches, slashing the clearing like a sword . . . and in a blinding explosion, like a match striking kindling, the fire ignited. On and on, the scream echoed from the leaping flames. Tear-blind, he stared at the flames . . . imaging. the hand of God sending this abomination into the fires of hell. No other thought held firm as the light disintegrated the blackened image, swallowing, incinerating the cloth, flesh, and bones. The screams silenced, echoing only inside his mind where they might haunt him for all eternity, an open conduit to hell and damnation.

Gone. Lisa Blythe, or whatever remained of her earthly presence, had vanished, reduced to a smoldering black blur against the whiteness. Choking breaths of fear and pain, Darius ducked his head fully to bury his face against his knees and thighs, breathing in the earth scents as he wrapped his clothed arms over his head. Even within the shadows, the heat of that sunlight touched him. The world around him compacted and pressed. Without clear sense to wonder who, he knew only quick, panicky relief as a heavy dark cloth dropped over his shoulders and someone clasped his arm, tugging him. A brimmed hat fell over his head, shading his eyes. Manic, he tugged at the heavy cloth, folding again, and waking to his mobility to wipe at his flooded eyes and drenched cheeks.

Gloves, he grasped when a gloved hand tugged at him, shoving leather into the deeper shadows under coat and hat. Gloves and dark glasses . . . and he pulled them on swiftly, welcoming the relief, the reprieve, the mercy of whoever stooped near him.

"Catch your breath," a strangely familiar voice coached. "We'll head back in a moment."

One of the federal agents, Darius realized as he knelt shivering and gasping chilled breaths, his eyes clearing behind the dark tint, his fires cooling below the brimmed hat, within the gloves. Rutherford—Agent Rutherford—one of the two agents who'd stood outside his door only the night passed . . . the same agent who'd shown him a sliver of compassion. Through the dark tint, still lost in his fear of looking toward the light, Darius squinted and watched in stark dumbfound as the man strode about the clearing, kicking at the blackened snow, using bare branches to sweep at the footprints and outline of charred earth. Lisa Blythe was no more. Even her blackened outline had erased from the charred earth. The marred clearing looked more like a stomped campfire than the site of a cremation.

By the time Rutherford returned, Darius had climbed afoot, but he needed the tree trunk to keep his balance with the wicked tremors in his limbs. Mentally and physically exhausted, chilled, Darius caught the dark eyes studying him, speculating.

"Can you walk?" the agent asked.

Did he have a choice? Managing only a nod, Darius pushed off the trunk, following the shorter man's lead to step over a felled log. If the Baron intended to prove the reality along with his power, he succeeded admirably. Blythe, nearly a full vampire had returned to dust, and a Federal Agent had just destroyed the evidence. By no surprise, Darius remembered the words, 'If he was one of mine, I'd kill him. . .' Blythe could have been one of Amad's. She'd worked in the Chateau for at least the past eight years. As much as three days ago, Amad would have known she killed Fradden . . . and Amad could have issued that order.

The father of lies . . . dangerous thoughts, Darius knew and shuddered more with a thought of the Baron eavesdropping. His thoughts were no longer his own . . . or perhaps, his thoughts were his own, but no longer private. At any moment, he expected to hear the voice or buckle under an internal blow despite the conscious sense of a spectator. Physical pain dragging at his limbs; every step remained an agony with the heated spikes in his frozen limbs. Staggering a step, Darius resigned, accepting the agent's hand on his arm. By instinct, Darius ducked his covered head more deeply as the sprinkles of sunlight lanced the bare branches overhead. Even through the thick cloth and heavy hat, the heat touched him, worrying him. Whether he shook from the physical pain, the ice in his limbs, or the exhaustion compounding with the oppressive sunlight weighting the world around him, he retained no clear grasp. An instant of genuine terror ignited as they reached the rear parking pavilion where he would need to cross a short stretch of brilliant sunlight.

Belatedly, he heard the car engine and glimpsed the black stretch limo cutting across the parking lot, creeping at the edges of the pavement.

Dull sunlight filtered down between the buildings, not quite as intense as Jenna would have imagined. Her Lincoln still wore frost from the day before, not unlike most other cars in the parking lot. Almost sadly, she noted the absence of Matt Cord timing his departure to coincide with her own. His new Grand Am rested in its usual spot alongside her Lincoln, its glass frosted, and roof encased in ice as thick as the coating on her car. Not until she slid into the backseat of the agent's rental, she chanced another glance at Cord's car. A glance at her watch niggled alarm at the edge of her mind. Matt worked steady daylight at an advertising firm in downtown Pittsburgh. He'd once mentioned leaving early every morning to avoid traffic. A lie, Jenna knew. He timed his schedule to match her departure.

Had he awaited her this morning? Changed his mind at the sight and presence of the FBI escorts?

Men were such fickle beasts. The whole lot of them, from the arrogant and sophisticated, to the mundane and insecure. And they had the gall to consider women mysterious.

Making a mental note to check on Matt later, Jenna turned her attention to the more immediate concerns. Depending on who'd covered for her the day past, she'd probably find her desk a disaster, and even if Lisa came in, doubtful she'd lighten the load. More than likely, she'd create a new level of chaos . . . and Jenna caught herself silently cursing the woman with an unnatural anger. Unless she intended to beat the bloody hell out of her on sight—

The echo of Darius's words, his voice, halted her anger almost as effectively as her shock to focus so much rage on Blythe.

He was probably somewhere over the Atlantic by now. Was he thinking about her? Would he think about her? She caught herself fingering the diamond earring, her gaze listed through the glass, not actually seeing the passing wooded lots or the houses scattered within the trees. How long would it take? How long before her every thought stopped spiraling his image and voice through her mind?

For a split second, she saw him poised, holding Lisa Blythe in his arms, and her thoughts jack-knifed, her every sense keening. Fear. Unaccountably, fear touched the edges of her mind far more readily than jealousy, but as she tried to recover the image, she lost the thought entirely.

Muttering a curse, she stepped from the sedan with the agent holding her door and panned her gaze over the grand entrance. Coming home . . . that sense of coming home registered. More familiar than her own apartment, this grand old hotel triggered that distant sense of homecoming, a mix of sorrow and joy. Contentment enhance tenfold as she passed through the glass doors, smiling to George who returned the amenity with a pleasant, "Good morning, Jen."

How could she walk away from this contentment? How could she—

"Jenna!"

Muscles lurching, she pivoted her gaze as Evan veered his direction across the lobby, heading in her direction instead of the executive wing. He appeared nearly as worried as shocked to see her. His pale blue eyes darted swiftly over her, taking her measure as if to judge her health. A smile quivered into his taut lips, his eyes locked onto her and before she could grasp his intention, he clasped her shoulders and tugged her into a manic embrace.

"God," he heaved against her ear, his arms conveying a strength and integrity to add to his words. "It's good to see you. I've been going out of my mind worrying about you."

She would feel no more or less effected by his arms if she hugged her own brother, but she returned his embrace, amused by his statement. "I'm fine, Evan."

He drew back, holding her shoulders, looking down into her searching—then knowing. His ebbed into quiet sorrow. Darius was gone. "You are fine, darling."

"And a little late for work," she said, refusing to acknowledge what he read in her eyes, in her heart. "As I've heard, things are a little hectic this morning. If you'll excuse me?"

"I was just on my way to see, Mason," he said and withdrew his hands. "I'll join you, if you don't mind."

"I don't mind," she said, tongue-in-cheek, considering the absence of choice. A perfect gentleman, this fellow who'd stepped quietly aside in the presence of Darius. He touched her arm in a gesture of comfort rather than possession that could pass for gallantry. He did know. By whatever male instinct governed the species, he knew she'd fallen for Darius, and likewise knew the futility of such an affliction, neither threatened nor jealous by his understanding.

As he escorted her through the arch into the administration wing, he glanced down, a faint smile in his eyes, in his bearded lips, he wondered, "Would you mind terribly if I ask you to join me for lunch, or dinner this evening?"

"I wouldn't mind if you ask," she said while fumbling with her keys at her office door. "Unfortunately, I don't think I can afford to make any plans at the moment." She found the key to her office and slid it into the lock. "I'll probably be swamped with—"

"Jenna," Evan spoke almost as the same moment as she felt the lock's reverse pull. His hand still riding her arm, he looked down into her startled eyes and started, "You'll have to take time out at some point . . . what's wrong?" he asked more curiously.

She dropped her gaze to the lock and tumbled the works free, already reaching for the nob. "My office was unlocked . . ." And the cold chill was as much a natural phenomenon as a cutting edge in her mind. Across the room, the louver blind hung at a cockeyed angle; the windowpane stood open; the screen hung by a tangled thread. A flutter of paper drew her gaze to the floor where printouts and mail scattered, apparently blown off her desk. "My God," she uttered and shoved the door more slowly inward, scanning the room in slow degrees, searching for any other signs of disaster. Nothing else appeared disturbed.

Evan clasped her arm more firmly, halting her from a forward step.

Reichly and Miller moved in tandem, nudging her into a protected position while scanning the room. "When were you in here last, miss?" Reichly asked methodically.

"Sunday morning," she answered while starting another step into the room.

"Do you always keep the door locked?"

Collecting her thoughts, she caught up to the question, understood the agent seeking a time frame for this intrusion. "I do," she answered hesitantly. "But that's more of a habit than a necessity. Anyone on the administration or maintenance staff has access. Finding the door unlocked isn't a shock." She'd decided months ago to lock up any classified information and leave nothing of personal value lying around. Too many people had access, and this wasn't the first time she'd found the door unlocked. Turning her attention into the room, she glanced off Reichly and motioned him inside. "Let me look and see if anything's missing."

Reichly agreed tentatively and sent Miller to locate Wharton.

Things were moved. Her chair no longer rested under the desk, but rather stood at a cockeyed angle. The fold-away bed was gone by no surprise, a sign of maintenance efficiency. At least one desk drawer remained open an inch, but it contained only odds and ends, nothing of value or significance. Her file cabinets remained locked, the computer off, but the keyboard rested at an angle as if shoved precariously against the hard drive. Someone had rested at her desk. Pencil holder, her ceramic knickknacks, the framed family portrait, even the phone base and address index holder stood in odd locations. The cleaning staff might have rearranged the whatnots, but in a moment of certainty, Jenna knew the explanation wasn't so simple . . . nor entirely a shock. Lisa Blythe. The woman might not make a special trip into the hotel to enjoy the office, but if she'd worked yesterday . . . without a doubt, Lisa would seize the opportunity to mettle and . . . scheme?

The open window remained the only serious mystery. Stepping into the chill, Jenna halted without Reichly's intervention. The windowpane remained in one piece. The screen folded outward, mangled, and ripped from the casement.

"Is there anything missing?" Reichly asked.

"I'd have to go through everything to be certain, but on the surface, it doesn't look like it," she answered and before she could form further judgement, several other agents arrived, shuffling her into the hall. Mason had joined Evan and with a glance to the more haggard gray face, Jenna felt for him. A murder, a hotel to run, a visit from the hierarchy, a remiss employee and now an apparent break-in . . . or 'out,' as it appeared. "Mason, I'm sure it's nothing serious," she said quietly, touching his arm in reassurance. "Nothing's missing."

Far more grim and gaunt than any time passed, he tried a smile and managed only to appear more ghastly than reassuring. "I'm sure everything's fine," he said and sounded as if he were the captain on a sinking ship.

Doubtful Mason had rested at all since this had begun three days ago, and guiltily, Jenna realized her own negligence. As second in command, she should have stood at his side and relieved part of the burden to keep the hotel running smoothly. If not for Darius, she would have done exactly that. He'd taken the decision from her hands, under the pretense of keeping her safe, and as much as she understood his reasoning, she couldn't accept that excuse entirely. While Mason had suffered the weight and responsibility of this disaster, she'd spent two of the most wondrous days of her life. Looking into Mason's weary eyes, judging the dark patches and thin red veins magnified on his pudgy cheeks, she reached only one conclusion. It was past time for her to return to the real world, the world she understood, business and hotel management.

"You shouldn't be here, Jenna," Mason started.

"On the contrary, there's no place else I should be," she said smoothly. "Why don't you go on back to your office and I'll handle this. As soon as I straighten this out, you can brief me on whatever's on the agenda, then I think you better consider going home and getting some sleep."

"I couldn't possibly think about sleep right now."

"Give me an hour to get things in order," she said quietly. "Then you better at least attempt to think about it."

32

More grateful for the tinted glass than any time passed, Darius rested in the rear compartment, waking more to the changes inside himself. Even gazing through the dark glass too long stung his eyes, and despite the solid black panels around him, the mere thought of sunlight ignited an internal tremor. By the vibration of a jet engine overhead, they'd reached the airport, and for a few wicked seconds, he dreaded the thought of seeing Jenna . . . nearly as deeply as he needed to see her. For her, he would combat his distress. No other thought held dominion in his reeling mind as the car sped into the shadowed hanger.

This was not his craft, not the Nightrider craft which had become his home, but he recognized the Baron's insignia—an immense raven scrolled across the fuselage. With the hanger doors closed in the limo's wake, the shade descended offering scant relief as Darius climbed from the car. Behind the dark glasses, he glimpsed the chauffeur collecting his overnight bag from the trunk and despite his apprehension, hurried toward the lowered steps. On the stairs, his steps faltered, his senses keening to the scents . . . and waking to the absence of the single scent he sought.

Jenna hadn't passed this way . . . nothing of her essence lingered here. The Baron's musk scent . . . Teddy's springtime essence . . . the Baron's private pilot who wore only a faint trace of the Baron's essence beneath the heavy aroma of cigarette smoke. Nothing of Jenna's essence touched him, and what remained of his heart hammered a wicked blow as he continued his ascent, passing through the small, enclosed space at the door.

Candle watt lights glowed from modern fixtures along the upper curve of ceiling, basking the only two passengers in dusk shadows. Far more solid and dark than his own craft, the Baron's chariot reeked of wealth and sophistication, from thick padded chairs to accommodate a half dozen passengers, to thick velvet drapes despite the absence of windows. Like his own craft, this one carried a kitchenette, undoubtedly stocked with the essentials from wine and caviar to a full gourmet meal, as well as a wide desk equipped with the latest technology. At any given moment, the Baron could conduct his natural affairs from this mobile cabin, but presently, he rested in one of the leather chairs, merely appraising Darius with a glimmer of a smile. Teddy sat toward the rear, already buckled into a seat, or so it appeared by his posture.

"Do, relax and come sit," Amad said and signaled to the empty chair nearest him.

Jenna. That single name lingered in his mind as Darius obeyed the command, settling into the seat at the Baron's side. Whether he was relieved by her absence . . . or heartsick, he couldn't decide. Not daring to react, he fumbled with his seatbelt, jolting slightly when he glimpsed the shadow of motion in front of him. Halted, he stared at the Baron's offering, recognizing one of the photographs of the Chateau . . . a picture of the lighted entrance, unnaturally clear in his line of vision.

In a flashing instant, he remembered rolling through the stone pillars . . . halting just inside the entrance . . . gazing on the lace of white lights. He remembered his shock, his awe, to find the Chateau so well lighted and magnificent . . . He remembered venturing out into the night and adjusting lenses, capturing the grandeur on film, positive he would never see such a sight again. For Raphael, for himself . . . he'd captured this gift of light. Nothing of either sorrow or joy touched him at this moment. A memory of an emotional high . . . and low. He felt nothing now. Only a mild curiosity to view the candles in windows, the arches glittering . . . or possibly he did feel something, something akin to anger that he would never fully appreciate such a spectacle again. The chill lingered, but it was no longer merely inside his bones. The cold ran deeper, suturing his bone marrow.

"No reason why you shan't hold on to these for a time," Amad said pleasantly.

Deftly, Darius accepted the stack of photographs, knowing at a gut level, not another of Jenna's photographs rested in this collection. His gaze lifted, finding the Baron in a haunted gaze. "The plans changed."

"You needn't worry, lad," Amad said smoothly, a wry smile slipping more deeply into his mustached lips. "I've made other—more proper arrangements for the lass."

Leaden, his heart dropped and his gaze slid to the photograph in his hand as if he could truly hide the dread in his heart or head. Around him, the craft vibrated with the engines igniting and he'd never dreaded that sound, that sensation of departure, more than at this moment.

His gaze turned toward the Baron, catching the human eyes studying him inside and out. For his sanity, safety, he maintained only the curiosity in his mind. No answer forthcoming. The silence within that hovering presence in his mind verified his thought. In an uncontrollable instant, Darius asked, "Is she safe, now?"

"Redundant, lad," the Baron said in sighing disappointment. "And a word of advice, I'll offer, not that I believe you'll take it," he continued, his gaze steady. "You serve only one master. Snap the chain of this spell the lovely witch cast upon you. You won't see her again. You won't hear from her or about her beyond this moment. What becomes of her is beyond your control and should no longer be your concern. A warning though, son, if you annoy me too deeply with this burning lust in your heart, you may yet alter her course, and I probably needn't mention . . . not for the better."

Hatred and pain flashed neon through Darius's mind as the full weight of the words sank within his altered mind. As much as he knew he should heed the advice, he knew the futility . . . and it was Dylan all over again. If he could hate her . . . if he could truly hate her for the misery that she might yet bring him, he would.

Instead, the heartache settled more fully through him. As he'd never seen his son to explain, to comfort, to hold . . . he would never see this enchantress who'd slipped into his chilly heart. If she hated him, if she came to hate him . . . he could never blame her. As he'd abandoned his son, his daughter, his life . . . he would abandon her now. Never to know if she survived. Never to know if she' had truly loved him. Never to hear that soft warm voice again. Like a knife in his heart, only the questions and desire would remain, unrequited.

And there would be no end to the misery in his mind or heart. If not much else, he knew the integrity of that singular belief. No end for him. Enhanced, he would suffer every instant of misery and already the pain of her absence spread as the distance grew between them. That his last image of her would remain the sight of her in the vampire's arms, blood spots on her lips, only drove the knife deeper into that precious of all organs. He had put her there. By falling in love with her against every odd, he'd condemned her and consigned her to hell on earth.

The break-in truly had been a break-out. At some point during that torturously long night, someone had dashed through the administrative wing of the Chateau Suites Hotel and fled through the first open office. The miscreant had ripped out the screen, unlatched the window and left the pane gaping wide open. The night's breeze had sent folders and whatnots sailing off Jenna's neat desk.

Speculating, the agents believed the killer had slipped into her office, possibly to avoid hotel security, a staff member, or the FBI. Whatever the killer's intentions, his plan had run afoul, and he'd departed hastily through the nearest window. The crime scene technicians hadn't lifted prints from either the window or sill. Fingerprint dust smudged her desk, drawers, cabinets, keyboard, computer and every other possible surface, and the techs had lifted dozens of prints . . . Likely matching staff members.

Two hours passed before Jenna turned her attention to hotel operations. . Rather than the pool of the administration office, Mason ensconced her in his office, briefed her on the most urgent problems, then took her advice and departed.

With quiet efficiency, Jenna sorted through the most immediate concerns, most of which dealt with customer service and maintenance, including some problem with the sauna, and not excluding a dozen return calls over several scheduled activities. Within a few hours, interrupted a dozen times by either reporters attempting to secure an interview or update, or guests complaining over the inconveniences they'd endured, Jenna sent a message through Lucy at the registration desk to screen the calls and put through only the most urgent or irate callers. Designating authority, she promoted Bonnie Schwan from kitchen staff to manager and put her in charge of the evening banquet. She sat down with Arlen Dawson, chief of maintenance, and Jim Radler, chief of security, respectively, and enlisted Evan to calm a current guest's agitation over an incident with the FBI. The man hadn't appreciated getting frisked in the lobby and even Trevane's polished skills had barely appeased that fellow. Jenna could be only grateful to the Pittsburgh office for lending Evan to handle the Chateau's public relations crises. If she had to deal with the guests and media circus, along with the FBI and the hotel's normal business, she'd surely lose her mind.

Keeping in contact with Agent Wharton, she learned little of consequence. Lisa Blythe had neither showed up for work, nor returned to her apartment. Within their legal grounds, the FBI and local police had searched her apartment, only to discover Blythe had extremely weird tastes and few housekeeping skills ... the latter of which countered any clear indication of her present whereabouts. Her larder, as one agent indicated, was nearly bare, save for a few frozen goods and a few bottles of cheap wine.

Jenna listened to the updates with halfhearted interest, positive the woman would trounce into the hotel at any moment and be entirely thrilled with the added chaos in her honor. Doubtful, her thrill would last when she learned the extent of the invasion of her private—weird world. Even one of the agents had commented on Blythe's duality by the condition of her apartment, and more often throughout the day, Jenna heard other references to Lisa's world. Black shutters and thick, double-tiered curtains, a bed draped in a black shroud like mosquito netting, reading material and instruments suggesting . . . sado-masochistic perversion? A great deal of material suggested an interest in black magic and the Middle Ages.

The woman was more twisted than she'd appeared, but in a moment of critical thought, Jenna wasn't surprised.

Shortly after noon, a controversial lead developed when an astute local officer spotted Lisa's brown Nissan parked behind a boarded-up gas station a mile from the Chateau. A touch of worry fluttered across Jenna's mind, but she had more than enough to keep her mind occupied. Over a short break, decreed by Evan who killed two birds with one stone, bringing sandwiches and updating her over the disgruntled guest, Jenna listened to his speculation concerning Blythe's abandoned car.

"No sign of foul play," he commented. "That's always a good sign. Knowing Miss Blythe as I do, I wouldn't be a bit surprised to learn she planned a rendezvous and she's currently occupied with one of your married underlings. According to the Bureau, she was last seen here in the hotel around noon yesterday."

"I'm sure she's fine wherever she is," Jenna said offhandedly. "But if you truly think that's a possibility, maybe we better mention it to Agent Wharton and have him doublecheck any of our male staff on duty yesterday . . ."

The second less controversial lead and more damning evidence, arrived via a phone call to Agent Wharton which was patched into the manager's office where he'd stopped for another update. Even in his generally unreadable features, whatever words he heard flickered doubt and curiosity. "If it's not on the way to the lab, get it sent, now. And I suggest you get someone from the DA's office involved. I want that place turned over and our forensics team in there."

"What was that about?" Jenna asked and for a long moment, Wharton sat across the desk, taking her measure, reaching a conclusion.

"One of the local detectives over at Blythe's apartment," he answered with a tempered edge. "Apparently, he has some kind of hobby or he's an amateur wine connoisseur. He was looking over her selection when he noted the color was wrong." Rising out of his chair, he continued, "I'm not exactly sure what this indicates, Jenna. I'll keep you informed."

Without truly telling her a blasted thing, Wharton slipped out of her office, and she nearly followed She had enough to keep her busy, and as if to verify the thought, the phone emitted another signal and drew her back into hotel business. Caught up in her affairs, she didn't stop to think about the investigation, spared only a few uncontrollable thoughts to wonder where Darius was now? Was he thinking about her? Would he ever think about her?

Too busy to listen to gossip or rumor, Jenna was on route to the lounge to discuss the details of another banquet with Tony when Rita caught up to her. Reacting to the spooked shine in the older woman's eyes, Jenna halted, awaiting a mother and her two sons, dressed for the pool, to pass. "What's wrong?"

"I . . . we just heard on the radio, Jen! There was a newsbreak. I don't know what to think—it's so . . . God, I can't believe—"

Alarmed, Jenna clasped the stocky woman's arms. "What's on the news? What's happened?"

"They're saying Lisa Blythe could be responsible for Mr. Fradden's murder! They didn't come right out and say it, but they're implicating her. They put out her description—"

What affected her more, the thought of Lisa as a murderer or the thought of Wharton letting the press have that information before giving her fair warning, she couldn't decide. Angry, she turned and directed Rita to follow. "We better get security to the lobby. If that's true, we're in for another media siege. Goddamn it, how's this even possible?"

"God, I always knew she was weird," Rita huffed, keeping pace. "They said something about some kind of cult involvement."

"Terrific," Jenna stated. "Enter another faction of lunatics . . ."

The first wave of a media circus came through the doors only moments later, by which time Jenna knew the accuracy of the report. Apparently, Lisa had concealed quite a few other quirks, only beginning with a wine bottle filled with blood. Wharton had personally issued the APB and begun a more serious, intense search to find Blythe and included circulating her picture to the visual news media and sending agents to the airport and bus terminals, rental agencies and nearest car lots with a copy of her photograph. The media knew as much as Jenna knew, and despite her annoyance, she joined the throng in the lobby to verify her ignorance. In a crisp cool tone, she mentioned harassment charges in regard to either guests or hotel staff members, agreeing to issue a statement on behalf of the hotel as soon as information became available. Evan came to her rescue, sequestering her in Mason's office where they contacted the hotel's legal firm, Mason, and the American based Hendricks offices under whose umbrella the Chateau resided.

In a swiftly well-crafted statement to the press, relieving the hotel of liability or culpability, Jenna made her debut under the heated flashes and strobes of the press. With gritted teeth concealed behind a sober mask, Jenna admitted that Miss Blythe was an employee for the past nine years and held an assistant manager's position. Regardless of the police reports, the hotel reserved its judgment of either Lisa's guilt or innocence.

Long after dark, Jenna sat with Agent Wharton in Mason's office, no longer doubting Lisa's guilt. How exactly she'd physically managed to break Lawrence Fradden's neck remained the only real mystery.

According to Wharton, his agency had uncovered a circumstantial association between Blythe and a group of satanic followers based in California. "One of those budding vampire cults," he said grimly. "They run around in Halloween masks year-round, wearing black, chanting oaths to a dark lord or some shit." More than twenty-six months earlier, Lisa had taken a vacation/business trip to California, attending a conference where Darius Brock had spoken. "We have reason to believe her obsession began then," Wharton said grimly. "For all we know at this moment, she had members of the group watching him every time he came into the states. We know she's placed and received several calls from California as well as Chicago. Our specialists are working up a profile, but it's not that hard to figure out. She gets obsessed with this guy and knowing him a little, I can imagine how he might have reacted."

Jenna caught herself wondering what Wharton thought of how Darius had reacted to her, and he apparently read her discomfort.

"Let's face it, Miss Windrow," he said carefully. "Mr. Brock wouldn't have been attracted to a woman like Lisa Blythe. He has far too much class to settle for anything less."

Wharton wasn't a fellow to pass out flattery or compliments loosely. Appreciating his effort, Jenna smiled slightly but gained no genuine relief. Darius would never settle for any woman.

"We're still piecing it together," Wharton stated. "But the time factor's right. The murders started about four months after her trip to California and according to our records, he was in Pittsburgh about a month before the murders started. What exactly she intended to gain by setting him up or bringing the cult into this ordeal is still up for debate."

"You're saying she's not the only killer?" Jenna realized with a cold chill.

"It looks that way," he said gravely.

With the details sinking in, she shivered. "What happens now? What happens if you don't find her?"

"We'll find her, Miss Windrow," he said simply. "It's just a matter of time."

"You believe I'm still in danger," she realized.

"We won't take any chances," he half confirmed. "Until we have her, we'll keep a team with you around the clock."

Jenna considered the words before deciding, "I live in a secure building, sir. If you'd like to have your agents escort me to and from work, I won't argue, but I really don't want any full-time bodyguards either outside my door or in my apartment."

"Miss Windrow, this woman's dangerous and she's obsessed with your friend. Give us a few days. If we can't find her, we'll make other arrangements. Right now, we have to believe she's still here and you would be her likely target. I'm not trying to frighten you—"

"If you were, I'd be in serious trouble then, wouldn't I?" she asked soberly. "But I do see your point. A few days. I'll accept your offer of full-time protection until Friday. If you haven't found her by then, we'll shift to my way and I'll accept escorts to and from work and limit my social activities. I don't intend to alter my schedule, or my plans for the holidays. And I won't live in fear of this woman, Agent Wharton. I have a life . . ."

And in an odd moment, she knew the danger passed. Lisa Blythe was the least of her problems. Life without Darius . . . Unconsciously, she swiveled Mason's chair, looking through the louvre blinds to catch the sparkle of white lights dancing on the hedges outside the glass. An overwhelming sadness threatened to buckle her resolve. A single day, not a lifetime.

Unconsciously, she fingered the diamond at her earlobe and just for a moment, she imagined his handsome face sitting across from her in her dining room, his dark mustache in sharp contrast to the stark white whipped cream on his twitching lips.

If they had a lifetime, it still might not be enough.

EPILOGUE

C hains clamored, amplified in the narrow black tunnel to sound like the gates of hell opening. The flashlight jittered on the powdery dust lifting, puffing from the shuffling soles. Only at a primal level, Ray Conners understood fear, not the how or why of it, just the fear. He'd been lumbering through these tunnels for years, one of the first contractors to begin mapping the ancient labyrinth, and the only survivor after one of the tunnels had caved in three years earlier. He'd lost a cohort in that collapse, or in the maze of catacombs—he never remembered which had come first, losing Jeremy Fields or racing from the crumbling debris that chased him through the blackness. They'd found Ray wandering in the darkness, dehydrated and dazed, unable to recall his own name. Blood loss, the doctor's had attributed to his mental state and amnesia, compounded by the trauma of losing his friend.

Ray couldn't recall any friendship between him and Jeremy. They'd only begun working together on this project and if his memory served, the scrawny dude hadn't been the brightest bulb. Still, they'd entered the tunnel together . . . and only one had emerged four days later.

Plodding, Ray continued toward the jangling and clattering, no longer fretting despite the primal fear vibrating from his core. In front of him, the circle of dull light skittered on the rough-hewn walls, catching on his steel-toed boots. He wasn't alone. Like other midnight strolls through the tunnels, another, slimmer body ambled, keeping pace despite her shorter stride. If not much else, Ray knew the girl's name. Wanda . . . no last name necessary. He'd invited her into his pickup truck outside a bar in Buffalo. She'd been delighted to scramble up into his heated cab, what with her mini-skirt and faux fur coat clinging to her narrow waist. Those long bare legs glowed in the shivering light; her perfume reminded him of its label, toilet water, but his brow merely furrowed, troubled rather than amused by his thought.

Ahead, the chains clattered in a familiar anticipation—or agitation.

Only vaguely, Ray recognized that sound and at a primal level, he knew as much fear as relief. He no longer needed the prodding and pricking in his skull. He understood his place in the world, his single duty to obey and appease the master. His master. Connected. Whether inches or miles separated them, they were connected, his will merged to accept the commands of his master. His natural survival instinct overrode whatever human revulsion affected him.

He'd nipped her, this Wanda with her bright red hair and ivory legs, already glowing pink from the cavern chill. Just a taste, and she was his.

Ray had never enjoyed a female voice, not the purring kind or the high pitchy tones. He still heard his aunt's screeching and shrieking, ordering him about while criticizing his awkward, teenage size. If she were still alive, he might nip her without a command and deliver her through the darkness of his own accord. His father's sister hadn't been her father's pride. By court order, she'd taken him in after his mother died of a rare blood disorder and his father had run off with her cousin. Over ten years had passed since Ray had last seen his old man and nearly four since his aunt had succumbed to her heart problems. A pity she hadn't stuck around to meet her maker. He might have enjoyed trudging her through these caves.

With his hand loosely clasped about the woman's arm, Ray felt her bulking as the master called.

Commme to meee.

"Yeah," Ray grumbled, only happy to oblige, though he hoped this one—this Wanda—wouldn't become another like the other.

He'd felt the severance when that one had ignited. Like a heated sword slicing a cord, he'd known the separation, but whether he'd suffered the loss personally or responded to the master's outrage, he wasn't of clear mind to decide or care. Gladly, he'd brought Blythe at the master's bid months, if not years ago, needing little else than the implication of a treasure trove of vintage wine to lure her into the .catacombs. Only later, only after the master laid his claim, Ray understood the woman's intention to seduce Hugh von Hendricks. An opportunist, their Lisa Blythe, and the master had only enhanced her natural volitions before sending her back into the world.

Ray hadn't nipped her. He'd merely answered the master's call to seduce her with the promise of showing her an ancient cache of wine. Through Ray's eyes, the master had learned about her visit to the winery and chosen her.

Fully conscious, the woman had barely paused at the master's chamber door, snatched the flashlight from Ray's hand, and hurried to the laden honeycomb shelves. Silent and still, not a single clink of chain intruded as the concubine had huffed, 'Sure hope the stink down here didn't seep through these old corks—' And the master shuddered his anticipation, jangling the chains and startling their visitor.

The flashlight zoomed through the dark, Lisa had barely parted her lips to scream, stumbled a single step into Ray, and by command, he'd caught her, bound her arms to her sides and lifted her off her soles. Even in the master's loose trance, she'd tried to struggle, and Ray heard her silent scream then, like now, echoing in haunting memory . . . less worrisome than the master's raging of the moment.

Brinnng her heeere to meee.

Just a little taste at times, but Ray had grasped enough of the master's nature to know Wanda wouldn't see another daylight, not that it mattered. Enough others had joined the master's cause to become legion.

Soon, very soon, the master had promised time and again. Soon he would be whole again, and strong enough to have his revenge. First the child—then its father. That glorious day was coming . . . soon. But until then, the master spent hour after hour watching the world beyond his black chamber, plotting, scheming. Waiting.

The Vampire Tales

Book Two

Turn the page for a sneak peek!

DAMNED BY DEATH

Even in daylight, the castle wore a pall of shadows, the narrow windows holding the light at bay as effectively as the winter winds which swept across the Carpathian Mountains. In darkness, the immense weathered black stone melded into the forest and purple sky; the arched slots offered little more than candle glow despite the capacity for electric within. As forbidding now as eight years earlier, Darius Brock suffered a chill inside and out, refusing to acknowledge the torrent of emotions threatening the edges of his mind. He'd lost his life, his son, his ignorance and his innocence within these black walls, and he had no more choice now than then.

Behind his cousin, Teddy Brock, who followed the Baron Amadeus von Hendricks, Darius strode up the spiral stairs to the cathedral entrance, refusing to consider the likeness to the hotel where he'd glimpsed and gasped his last clear breath of life. Wide awake, akin to the darkness as never before, he continued through the door that one of a half dozen butlers held while bowing. Old school, by no will of their own, the castle staff adhered to the subordinate status, several of them hurrying to collect the Baron's long coat, assisting Teddy and offering Darius the same courtesy. Slipping from the wool, though he might have preferred keeping it wrapped around him a tad longer, Darius handed the coat to an elder steward, who bowed smoothly and ducked away. Already, the chauffeur and two stewards hustled in their wake, delivering their bags. Before Darius could fully grasp the musty scents and familiar sights of the great hall, he spun and glimpsed the blurry image racing into the Baron's outstretched arms. As the child settled on the Baron's hip, he became clearly visible. A split second passed before the wide blue eyes, as livid as a summer sky, pivoted from the embrace and shot over the Baron's wide shoulder, lancing Darius in a quick silver shine.

If not at that instant, the lad knew a second later when landing smoothly on Darius's hip. "Darius!" Raphael heaved, but something in his handsome round face carried more wisdom than joy. His full, soft lips quivered; his brow furrowed beneath a scruff of thick black curls. "I dinnae 'spect to see you so soon!"

"Nor I you, lad," Darius admitted and despite his every effort, he breathed the child's scent, the faint musty odor that never seemed clearer, more familiar. Looking into the stark blue eyes, Darius quivered a smile, an uncertainty in his mind. The scent . . . a scent of corruption, but an odd mix. The child reminded him suddenly of the sunlight he had glimpsed in the streets of Pittsburgh, the scent reflective of the snow melting on the walks and posts . . . and meadows . . . and sea air beneath a rich blue sky as brilliant as the immense eyes. Innocence! By all that was real, the scent professed innocence . . . as if it emanated from within the musty odor, escaping through a crack of the fetid armor. How was it even possible? How could a child of so many years, a damned soul, offer such a scent as this? Far more stunned, Darius drew warmth from the small arm linked over his shoulder, the hand clasping his neck for balance. Beautiful, the boy truly was beautiful and, as if to enhance the essence of his innocence, he lifted his free hand, a delicate ivory hand, and nibbled his index fingernail under his quivering lips. A nervous habit which Darius had seen dozens of times in the past. The dark lashes dipped shyly, but the eyes held firm, speculating and calculating.

In every instant, Darius gleaned the Baron watching this exchange inside and out, and there was no point in attempting to deceive this night child. "Lad, we'll need to talk," Darius said quietly.

"No," the boy stated. In a single motion, he withdrew his hand and slid from Darius's arms, hitting the floor without a sound. Neck wrenched to lift his too perceptive, piercing eyes, Raphael decided, "I dinnae want to speak with you, Darius." Arrogantly, despite his slight size, he spun and tilted his gaze to his father. Pools of water swam over the blue eyes, the lips quivered more on the verge of tears. "You, Pappa? You've done this to him? Boot I dInnae know why. Why did you dooo sooch a thing?"

"Mind, lad," Amad said smoothly. "You'll note, he's no worse for the wear. Alive, too, I should think you'd notice."

"How loong, Pappa? How long before you take what's left of him and leave his carcass to the wolves in the hills?"

"Raphael," Darius said and reached, touching the boy's shoulder. The child danced away and spun his angry gaze skyward as Darius continued, "I don't think there was a choice, lad. There are things you don't understand. Things I couldn't explain—"

"Aye, and if ye believe that you're a damned fool, Darius," the boy said gravely. "Oh, and I see it clearly, so I do. Tis more than a bit of me father in me, you'll notice, if you're not tae blind already to notice."

"Oh, I notice, lad. Especially with your temper showing," Darius commented, if only to prove that he still held something of himself inside.

"Darius, m'friend," Raphael spoke in a descending tone, the sadness spilling across his youthful face like clouds pouring over a clear sky. "You know the loss, m'friend, but ye'll never know the lie. Oh, ye'll wrestle with it, as you are now, believing there was nae choice besides this end, but let me ask you, lad . . . are ye safe here, now? In the keep. With not a scratch to show for the hell ye've endured?"

In a heartbeat flash, Darius knew what the child meant to show him—what he'd feared to realize for himself. The Baron could have spared him the change and dealt with the madness in Pittsburgh with no help from him. In slow motion, Darius lifted his gaze and found the dark glitter in the far more menacing blue eyes. "What mistake did I make to pay this price?" he asked simply and suffered the amusement at the edges of his mind. "Why?"

"Do you expect an answer, truly, son?" Amad asked in a beguiling tone.

Raphael sidled closer to Darius then, clasping his hand and tugging. His free hand lifted again to nip his index fingernail between his teeth. "Dinnae be mad a me, Darius," he uttered. "Perhaps, I don't know — joost what my pappa wants me tae know. Tis moore the lie I fed you. C'mon then."

Darius held firm against the gentle tug, more intent on the Baron's gaze. Jenna. If nothing else at this moment, he knew he'd paid the ultimate price for loving Jenna Windrow . . . and even that was a lie. No choice and none needed. This end had hovered at the fringe of his existence for the past eight hellish years.

Whether he heard the footsteps or merely reacted to an accumulation of senses, Darius listed his gaze. The Baroness and another young cousin strode from an arch across the great hall. Dark and brooding, the entire manse composed of narrow passages and high arches, pillars and curtained walls or entries. Bronze sconces, some still sporting the original oil lamp fixtures, stood at opposing points in the room. Overhead, a gas chandelier offered an economy of light with an even mix of ruby and clear-colored crystals to disorient the natural eye. He suffered no distortion now, if he ever had. Brian still appeared as fierce and headstrong, as hot-tempered as ever, with his pale blue eyes darting and lips lined in a curve to suggest a wry sense of humor. Bookends, the Baron had called Brian and Teddy, and Darius had recognized the concept even then. Nearly the same age, born of different fathers and different mothers, the pair complimented each other more like brothers than second or third cousins.

Where Teddy wore the softness and effeminacy of his nature, Brian boasted the hardy physique and macho arrogance of his preferences.

From the onset, Darius had failed to warm to this hot-blooded cousin. The lad had struck him as a bully at the onset, a condition which set his arrogance on the rise, and nothing had changed with the years. To Brian, Darius nodded cordially.

The Baroness ignored Darius entirely, other than to glance at Raphael with a gray, undoubtedly disapproving glance. Gray, an odd crystalline gray. Her eyes evoked less life than either of the anomalies to nature in their midst, and on her heavily lined face that hadn't changed in the past eight years, the lips seemed never to move. Upon a time, she might have been regal, even beautiful, but whether time or attitude had transformed her, she evoked only a shrew's persona now.

Almost in comic tolerance, the Baron accepted her proffered, spindly hand, and bowed as he brushed a kiss on the mottled taut flesh. "My dear, so good of you to make such a trek to welcome my return."

"For you, dear, anything," she said with a twisted smile. Almost as smoothly as the Baron rose, the old woman lowered her gaze and lanced Raphael. "Have you welcomed your father properly, child?"

"Aye, and tis none of your business if I hadn't!" Raphael snapped.

Darius stifled a smile at the shrew's annoyance and, by no surprise, landed under her dead glare. "Madame Baroness," he offered and tipped his head in acknowledgment, not entirely stifling the smile until he caught the scent . . . a rotten scent. Rather like raw meat festering under a midday sun. Stifling a cough, he tilted his head further as she started toward him, and far more warily, recognized the stench emanating from her.

"Darius, I've never known you to be shy. It's good to see you, child. Come here now, let me get a good look at you—"

"Not on your life," he stated, and nearly bit his tongue with the force of the slash inside his head. Uttering a breath, he shook his head and flashed his gaze toward the Baron, who studied him with an indifferent gaze. In front of him, the Baroness stopped cold. Her glare turned granite. "I uhm . . . do apologize, madame," Darius managed.

A few paces away, Brian studied him avidly. Teddy just appeared more depressed, which had changed very little over the past twenty-four hours. If the boy's condition declined much further, he'd be dripping tears by the barrel.

Again, looking at the Baron, Darius's gaze heated. *What the hell do you expect of me here? Should I bow to this wretched hag? Or strip and bed her now in my cousin's stead? Name it! My wish is your command! I've nothing left. Why consider my moral outrage or the vulgarities of life?*

Temper, son. I've warned you once and not again, you may reap what you sow.

In a stopped instant, Darius studied the cold blue orbs and realized suddenly, he truly didn't give a damn what he reaped or sowed. Perhaps his morality had ebbed with his mortality. Of his own free will, he turned his gaze to the hag, flashed a glance at the worried child spying on him, and slipped his hand free of the soft grip. In two steps, Darius moved forward, caught the startled old shrew's bony shoulder before she recoiled, and drew her into a lover's embrace. Dropping his mouth over her parted lips, he snatched her breath in a kiss that threatened to pitch his stomach acids into his throat. Her spindly fingers ceased to struggle, crawled into his hair above his shoulders and clawed him with an unnatural strength and lust for a woman of her years. If evil possessed the power to endure, this elder crone would endure for a hundred years. Before she attempted to climb his trunk, he withdrew and stepped back, leaving her breathless and stunned with lusty light ignited in the depths of her platinum eyes. Suffering to appear only amused with the anger burning behind his eyes, Darius commented, "A proper greeting for a proper lady, Madame Baroness. Do hope I haven't offended you."

Both Teddy and Brian stared from opposite sides—bookends—lips parted in disbelief.

The Baron rumbled a low idling chuckle, drawing the old woman's startled gaze. "Apparently, m'lad's feeling his oats, Rebecca. I apologize if he's taken you by surprise."

Nothing left for him, nothing left but to endure and cling to every breath. His smile lingered in perfect contrast to his thoughts. Unwavering, he met the old woman's returned gaze. If the Baron forced him to endure this hag's carnal ministrations, it would be neither surprise nor shock. He retained only one recourse. To accept and survive whatever injustice or outrage the Baron commanded, and it didn't matter one way or another in his mind. His body, his mind, nothing remained at his disposal. Nothing left of him. To believe otherwise was as great a lie as to believe the Baron had changed him, destroyed him, enslaved him . . . to protect him.

Perhaps, though, perhaps, something remained inside of him . . . something festering and rising all too swiftly, like a coiled snake unfurling for a strike, and he was no stranger to this sensation. Hatred. In all its wicked essence. A bitterness lingering in the depths of his tarnished soul, collecting and boiling from these eight years of service, if not all the years of his life. He could bed this harpy, could tumble her in total degeneracy, and he would revel in his hatred and decadence. Humanity. Humanity bedamned! He was no more human than the little beast at his side or the monster holding his leash.

ACKNOWLEDGMENTS

I've always acknowledged my immediate family and siblings in these pages, but I'd like to thank my many other family members for their support and encouragement, beginning with John Grueber, the patriarch of the Grueber clan and all the brothers, sisters, nieces, and nephews who've contributed to my life story. Despite the miles of highway to separate us, from the Florida coast to the Alaskan wilderness and all points in between, know that you are all appreciated! I hope you continue to enjoy every adventure!

Thank you again to Anne Graff, Mary Trunick, Andrew Grueber, William Grueber, and Gail Kataro for your input, and for never critiquing the questions regardless of the content.

Thank you, Bruce Sanderson for your assistance and support in the cover designs as well as your encouragement and help in finding and tweaking the perfect photos to bring these adventures to life.

The images on my covers are generally created from photographs of genuine locations that tend to depict either a scene or theme within each novel. The cover of CURSED AT CONCEPTION: The Vampire's Henchman isn't the exception.

A special thank you to Jeannie Hemm-Shaw, a representative of The Castle Inn Bed and Breakfast, for authorizing the use of the original photograph provided by Sanderson-Decello Design. In creating The Chateau Suites Hotel pictured on the cover, we took the liberty of changing the ambiance of The Castle Inn to accommodate the forbidding fictional world within CURSED AT CONCEPTION.

In actuality, The Castle Inn Bed and Breakfast, located in downtown Circleville, Ohio, is truly a fine combination of old world elegance and modern conveniences. Whether you're looking for a Gothic venue for your wedding or a pleasant overnight stay, you'll be delighted with the Inn's accommodations.

And let me assure you . . . you won't be visited by a vampire.

Jkgrueber.com

"Thank you for reading!" J. K. Grueber

www.ingramcontent.com/pod-product-compliance
Lightning Source LLC
Chambersburg PA
CBHW030729310726
48969CB00005B/1159